THE

MERRY WIVES OF LONDON.

A ROMANCE OF METROPOLITAN LIFE.

BY THE AUTHOR OF THE "SOCIALIST GIRL," ETC., ETC.

WITH NUMEROUS ILLUSTRATIONS.

"When a woman is depraved by man, her own sex, strange to say, are her bitterest enemies."
MRS. HUTCHINSON.

LONDON:
G. VICKERS, 28 AND 29, HOLYWELL STREET, STRAND.

CONTENTS.

ILLUSTRATIONS.

THE

MERRY WIVES OF LONDON.

CHAPTER I.

CONJUGAL WHISPERINGS.

It is to the interior of a sumptuously-furnished mansion that we would introduce our readers. It stood in a spacious square at the western extremity of London, and ranked high among its distinguished neighbours. It was the abode of a titled husband and wife, and frequently the scene of festivities that were invariably minutely recorded in the chronicles of fashionable intelligence. Other dramas, though, were played within its walls, which, from their splendid exterior, no one would have imagined were of dark and fearful import. Its wealthy owner, the Lord Bloomfield, had just risen from his bed of down, wearied and jaded with the previous night's debauch; and upon inquiring for his lady the countess, he was informed that she was in her bath.

"She would make a capital water-nymph," thought he, dismissing her from his consideration, and submitting himself to the process of a vigorous shampooing at the hands of a swarthy Moor, who seemed an adept at the exercise. It was correctly reported that the countess was taking her morning bath, and the scene of that luxury was adorned with numerous specimens of classic art. Its colour was a subdued orange, fringed round the borders with purple, which stretched from the walls in curved lines until they reached the centre of the pure white ground of the ceiling, and ended in a circle which contained a beautifully painted figure of a rosy Cupid. The furniture corresponded with these rich tints; the only exception being the sofa, a spring one, which was covered with satin of a glossy blackness. The peculiar reason for this deviation from the pervading style of the apartment must be gathered from the character of

1

some of the incidents comprised in our narrative. Such sensual couches are common in the chambers of the wealthy. The paintings were few, but served to heighten the tone of this voluptuous bath-room. The figures were all nude, and in their groupings embraced the principal features in ancient Greek mythology. There was Mars embracing Venus, Juno supplicating the God of Thunder, and a warmly-characteristic one of Alcmena being deceived by Jupiter in the shape of her husband Amphitryon. Adam inflamed with love at the first sight of Eve (a delicious performance) was hung at the foot of the bath, which was of pure marble, and was fitted in silver with all the modern appliances for regulating the supply and temperature of the water. There was only one piece of sculpture in the apartment, and that was a small, but beautifully carved statue of the hunter Actæon in the attitude of surprising Diana while bathing.

The countess lay at full length in her marble bed, reading, while an attendant, arrayed in a coquettish morning costume, every now and then dipped a thermometer into the water to ascertain whether the required temperature was maintained. The bright chestnut locks of the lady lay in floating masses on the purple velvet cushion that supported her head high above the level of the bath, and as she occasionally slightly moved, a shoulder, or thigh and leg, would rise out of the water and disclose their wondrously fair and rounded proportions. The countess herself was a being of marvellous beauty. Above the average stature of her sex, her frame was developed to the minutest requirement in bodily proportions. Her feet were slender, not too short—we detest fat dumpy ones—and their insteps swelled up to ankles which an ordinary sized hand could easily span, and above them her limbs increased in volume so regularly that they might have been rather taken for the chiseled creations of genius, than the warm flesh and blood of a divinely formed woman. Her form was cast in the choicest mould, which at every undulation of the body displayed the graceful curves that make up beauty in its most captivating sense. Her bosom was full, but not too large, and the carnation tips of two dazzling white globes every now and then peered out of the warm spiced liquid like the red berries from the deep green of the holly. From these twin life-giving fountains the neck rose grandly, pure, stainless, and arched as proudly as that of the spouse of the fabled Olympian god. Then came her face, lit up by a pair of deep blue orbs that now sparkled with every variety of passion's impulses, and then melted into the sweet tenderness, the humid glances of love in all its dreamy languor. Her features were prominent, but richly delicate. A rosy hue suffused her silken cheeks, and played on her ripe full lips like a ruddy flame, and made her dimpled chin look whiter by the contrast. Her brow was ample and fairer than virgin snow; and behind, a head larger than is usually bestowed upon woman was balanced to the minutest degree of well defined anatomical proportion. Such was the magic being who revelled in her perfumed bath, as she devoured page after page of the warmly penned fiction she held in her hands. Presently she arose, and as she stepped on the soft foot-cloth ready to receive her, she looked no inapt embodiment of Eve with her golden tresses emerging from a paradisiacal fountain.

The attendant removed the pearly drops that glistened and rolled down her firm flesh, and then completed the ablution by sponging the whole body, from the nape of the neck to the soles of the feet, with eau-de-Cologne. That completed, the tedious operations of the morning's toilette commenced. First of all the countess donned a loose robe or wrapper, and then submitted her glorious hair to the operations of the nimble fingers of the damsel who mutely attended her; for, with the quickness of her class, that individual, overflowing though she was with gossip and scandal, had the sagacity to perceive that her mistress on that occasion was in no mood for conversation. Indeed the countess had never been less disposed than at that moment for indulging in any frivolities with her maid; for no sooner had she cast aside the book she had been perusing, than she fell into a painful reverie. To follow her through the meanderings of her fertile brain would be impossible, but as her meditations took their origin from a repulsive incident in the recent conduct of her husband, and her sentiments, the result of long ago matured convictions, shadow forth one of the social theories intended to be developed in the course of this narrative, an analysation of her troubled reflections will be tolerated or at least serve as a prelude to the varied transactions in which she is destined to figure as the imperious, exacting heroine.

"Married, indeed," thought she, "and expected to fall down and worship a sensuality more gross than one of the physical myths of the Hindoo! I'd rather be a bond slave to the vilest tyranny than such a minion to marital caprices. Married! sold and bought should be the terms, and to a man who thinks a woman a mere chattel for his personal accommodation, a domestic utensil, a goblet which he may fill and quaff at pleasure! Oh, my soul leaps from its sovereign seat, indignant at such an infliction upon the sacred chastity of my sex, and flies for solace to the subtle promptings of a revenge as suggestive of retaliation as the earth is beneficent and fruitful. Talk of man rather being a toad, and feeding upon the vapour of a dungeon, to keeping a thing in the corner of his heart for another's use! Why, woman's apostrophe to her wrongs would utterly extinguish this lame apology for the jealous promptings of a jealous heart. True the woman errs: the world, the snarling carping mass who *lawfully*—Heaven save us!—gratify their propensities, swears she does, when, by yielding to her provoked instincts and untrained propensities, she seeks relief from tedious, monotonous vassalage in some pleasure or excitement forbidden by 'man's' law! But let these very just men take a wife's position as it actually is; let them only fancy the slow torture endured for years—the sly blow, the foul oath, the jealous sneer, the disgusting epithet, the drunken fury, and the monkey-like, sickening pawing, as if woman's purity were only a lie, her tender clinging only a fiction, and herself made for pollution—a wretch who gives rein to the lowest appetites! Only fancy the passive resistance, the meek endurance, the unseen tear, the sob, the shame that blisters her very heart; and then, 'drest in a little brief authority,' blame her if your consciences can, should her accumulated wrongs stir up such a mutiny in her soul that she flies from the stye in which she has been immured, and takes the first revenge that offers itself. —God of heaven!" she exclaimed, starting up and hurriedly pacing the floor, "the life of a sultan's slave would be preferable to such an one! But we can have our revenges. Oh! husbands! husbands! you little dream in your gaieties and wild dissipations that your wives can have their stolen pleasures, their delicious promptings, their everything that can make up a compensating felicity for your nauseous favours, and all the while, in the green simplicity of over-rated authority, you domineer over them as if they were the very patterns of the Lucretian chastity your brutality would, for the sake of a delicious monopoly, insist upon their being."

As this last thought struck the countess, a flush spread over her lovely countenance, and she once more permitted the nimble fingers of her maid to arrange the manifold garments that composed her morning costume. Presently a somewhat vigorous tap was heard on the outside of the door. The countess knew it too well, and a deep red spot gathered on her alabaster forehead.

"The shameless wretch!" she half muttered, and added aloud—"tell him I am engaged with my toilette."

The girl obeyed, and partly added, "You can't come in."

"It's only me," whispered a voice, intended to be soft and insinuating, but which, on the contrary, was extremely hoarse and uninviting.

"Mistress is in her bath," ejaculated the abigail, secretly enjoying the scene, for she well knew the purport of my Lord Bloomfield's visit. It was to gloat over the undisguised charms of the lovely wife, whom he seldom approached but in such satyr-like fashion.

"Do admit me, Violet, darling," he entreated, applying his pale thin lips to the keyhole.

The countess struggled with her indignation for a few seconds, and then, as if actuated by a sudden impulse, threw over her person a large wrapper, which completely concealed her form, and granted the desired admission; upon which the servant, with a considerably heightened colour, retired, and, as usual, entered an ante-room, where she was within call.

"My life! my queen!" he exclaimed, as, loosely attired in a dressing-gown, he approached the countess, with the intention of embracing her—"why did you keep me so long from your adorable side?"

So saying, he made a grasp at the wrapper for the purpose of removing it from her shoulders, but she energetically resisted, and keeping it tightly clasped across her bosom with one hand, quickly disengaged the other, and with it dealt her lord a sharp, ringing, open-handed blow on the cheek.

Astounded at such a repulse to his conjugal caress, the husband rubbed his smarting cheek, and gazed rather vacantly around him.

"Zounds, madam!" he exclaimed at length, "you hit hard with that little hand of yours, upon my word you do; but what does it mean?"

"It means," said the countess, sternly, "that I will not have my privacy disturbed, nor shall you approach me out of the chamber you so rarely enter, in that disgusting garb. The law declares me to be your wife; but my heart, my mind, my instincts, my woman's pride and modesty, all inform me I am not your concubine."

The gesture that accompanied this declaration was superb. Her figure dilating beneath her robe, her flashing eyes, that seemed to throw light upon her clustering locks and dazzling white outstretched arm, formed a grand picture of a true woman avenging an insult offered to the delicacy of her sex.

"Very fine, 'pon my word!" replied the peer, rather bewildered at the novelty of the language; "but as I don't perceive your drift, I must conclude that it is only a little scene got up to vary the monotony of our caresses. Come, Violet dear," he added, as his eyes drank in the shadowed lines of the glowing form that stood at a few paces from him, "let us leave off this child's play, and, as Milton says, let us have endearing smiles, and

"Youthful dalliance, as beseems
Fair couple, linked in happy nuptial league."

"Back, sir!" almost shrieked the countess, as he drew towards her with extended arms, and an hideous leer, that sadly disfigured his otherwise handsome countenance—"I will not have my lips sullied by those that are yet damp with the kisses of a paramour. Away from my sight, my hearing, brute!"

The peer reddened at this accusation, but determined not to be baffled, sprang forward to lay violent hands upon his wife, but she stepped nimbly aside, and the head of the house of Bloomfield, in his impetuous haste, stumbled over a chair, and measured his length upon the floor. The sound of the fall brought in the maid; and my Lord Bloomfield finding himself in what he considered a rather ridiculous situation, rose, and precipitately quitted the chamber.

As the door closed upon him, a smile of triumph tinged with one of contempt, broke over the face of the countess, and throwing herself into a seat, she indulged in a loud and prolonged fit of laughter.

"Vanquished, most shameless, wicked, and imbecile seigneur!" burst from the countess, as soon as her merriment had subsided; "but I have to thank the chair for half the conquest. I will finish dressing, Alice, now," said she, turning to her attendant, who having witnessed her mistress's triumph, participated in her satisfaction.

"Did your husband treat you kindly, Alice, when you lived with him?" inquired the countess, after the lapse of a few moments.

"At first he did, my lady. Nobody could be kinder," was the reply.

"Why did you leave him?"

A burning blush suffused the young woman's countenance, and she falteringly said:

"He changed, my lady; made me do servant's work. But that I didn't care about, for I liked to make the house tidy. It was something else he did which made me go away from him, and it almost broke my heart."

A tear glistened in her eye, but she soon brushed it away.

"You loved him, then?" said the countess, involuntarily feeling a sympathy for her humble dependant.

"I did dearly, until he asked me to do that which makes me wild when I think of it!"

"What did he ask you to do?"

"Why, my lady, owing to his extravagance we got reduced in circumstances, and he one day hinted that I was pretty."

"Ah!"

"And—and—said I might carry my face to a good market!"

"The monster!"

"I did not understand him at first; I thought he was joking; but when he mentioned the name of a person who had been following me about and annoying me for some time, I understood him at once, and fainted dead away."

"What brutes men are!" said the countess, and looking Alice keenly in the face. "You left him, of course?"

"The same hour, my lady, and from that day to this very one I have neither seen nor heard of him."

"How curious!" said the countess, her eyes increasing in earnestness of gaze as she playfully laid her hand on Alice's arm, and laughingly added: "And have you been faithful to such a blackguard of a man ever since?—did your fancy never stray, as the song says, from your absent wicked one?"

The girl—for in truth she was scarcely twenty-one—hung down her head abashed, for she felt her hot blood tingling in her arms, neck, and face.

"Never mind, Alice," laughed the countess; "it would have been a sin to have remained a widow for such a rascal; besides, Eve fell; so banish the carnation from your remarkably white skin, and attend to what I shall say to you, for I have a mission for you to perform, and I feel satisfied you can do it well and expeditiously."

"Command me, my lady," said Alice, inexpressibly relieved at the turn the conversation had taken. The frail woman is the one who can least bear an allusion to her faults.

"Serve me in this," continued her ladyship, slightly blushing, "and you shall be amply, munificently rewarded. A young friend of mine, a poor timid creature, under the lash of a cruel guardian, has fallen in love with a captain in the Guards, whose fortune is not ample, and of course the match is not deemed suitable, therefore the young couple can only meet by stealth. Yesterday the poor girl came to me with tears in her eyes, and solicited my advice upon the propriety of meeting her lover after nightfall as he had requested. Well, what could I do but extend my sympathy to these unfortunate young people, and sanction their meeting? I have changed the venue though, and that is the reason why I need your services. Here is Captain Morris's address; you must see him personally, the sooner the better, and request him to name a place for a meeting to-night about eleven; the rendezvous must not be a dwelling, but at my house or on or near some public promenade. Say the lady will be under my charge for the evening, and he must convey his answer to me through you."

Alice, glad to accommodate a mistress as beautiful as in her eyes she was lenient, hastened to fulfil her errand.

The countess, left to herself, revolved scheme after scheme in her mind, and at last concluded with the consoling reflection, that pleasure must be the source of all happiness, and the merrier a married woman spends her allotted days, the more does she recompense herself for the gilded tyranny, the slavish restraint imposed upon her by a selfish and scrupulously exacting husband.

CHAPTER II.

HOW ALICE SPED ON HER ERRAND.

It was broad noon when Alice, attired in her best, emerged from Bloomfield House. The sun was playing all manner of sportive tricks among the green leaves and dark green carpets of the noble squares through which she had to pass, and everybody abroad at—for that locality—early hour, had a jaunty air about them, which seemed to say that then at least they had an opportunity of exhibiting themselves to the best advantage. Alice, we have said, was pretty, but she was more than pretty, she was piquant; there was a vivacity in her speaking features, lit up by a pair of wicked looking black eyes, which bespoke intelligence, and with the healthful glow on her cheeks

and active rolling gait, a temperament ill-adapted for the atmosphere of Dian's temple. Her dress was well adapted to develope the contour of her petit, but rounded and well filled-up figure. Her blue paletot sat closely round her shoulders, and fell smoothly down to an undulating artificial development, which might have excited envy among the gifted daughters of Southern Africa. From beneath her not over-scanty petticoats a pair of feet alternately peeped in and out, and carried her over the clean flagstones as trippingly as if she had been a fairy disguised in a blue silk-drawn bonnet, with waving streamers of the same colour to match. Altogether she was as enchanting a little creature as you would desire to meet in the gloaming or any other part of the twenty-four hours, and so thought the numbers whom she passed, especially one, a gay handsome-looking young man, who followed her, and several times attempted to engage her in conversation; but Alice was not to be caught by casual overtures, and hastened on without deigning to take the slightest notice of her impudent admirer beyond remarking that he was excessively good-looking. As she suddenly turned a corner she ran right into the arms of a man who was coming as hastily in the opposite direction.

"Hollo, my armful of beauty, hope I aint hurt you!" exclaimed the man, giving her a vigorous squeezing with his brawny arms. In the struggle to disengage herself, Alice looked up, and with a scream recognised her husband. "What Alice!" he shouted, grasping her tightly by the arm; "you don't escape me so easily this time, my precious, so come along with your own Henry Burton."

Alice detested the ruffian, and loudly cried out for assistance. The stranger who followed her had witnessed the scene, and bounded to her rescue. One, two, three heavy blows, given with the strength and skill of the practised boxer, sent the brawny, meanly clad fellow stunned and reeling into the middle of the road.

"Take my arm and fear nothing," said the stranger soothingly.

Alice was too terrified to hesitate, and with a graceful curtsey departed with him from the spot. The husband, as soon as his disordered faculties had somewhat recovered, looked around him, and perceiving the pair in the distance, stealthily slunk after them.

Alice's gallant deliverer from the violence of perhaps the only man in the world whom she could and did cordially hate—for a wife outraged in her sexual modesty rarely forgives—was tall and elegant in person, with one of those round barrel-like chests that have such amazing power, and are larger in reality than they appear to the eye. He looked slender, but an accurate observer could not have failed to have noticed the play of some large rigid muscles in the arms of his well-made military frock coat, and that his lower extremities were muscular, and gave him a firm, iron tread. His eyes were of that dark grey colour which is found in men of great force and breadth of character. His other features were of a pleasing cast, which his firmly closed mouth did not lessen, but served to impart to his whole appearance that air of manliness and decision which rapidly makes an impression on the susceptible heart of woman. There is something about a man in the fullest signification of the term, and a woman in the bloom of her loveliness, which fully explains the phenomena of first love. The one excites emotion by the perfume breathed from her beauty, the other by the spirit of authority which ever accompanies his splendid proportions; and the two feelings approaching create the intense love which brings two young people, hitherto entire strangers to each other, into an intimate though silent interchange of the warmest of all sympathies.

"Oh sir, I am so much obliged to you!" murmured Alice, as soon as she had recovered herself a little; "I cannot thank you sufficiently."

"A mere bagatelle, I assure you," replied the stranger, with marvellous ease of manner and no slight dash of assurance. "I should like a similar adventure every day, if it introduced me to such a charming creature as yourself. May I inquire whither I shall have the pleasure of conducting you?"

This remark recalled Alice's wandering faculties, and she faintly attempted to withdraw her arm; but the gentleman was too good a tactician in such affairs to permit it; so he persuasively ejaculated—"Nay, nay! Let me see you out of danger before you leave me. Low people like the one who just now insulted you are vindictive; and who knows but at this moment the fellow is following us?"

This was sufficient. Any society was preferable to Alice than that of her husband's, and she clung nervously to the vigorous arm of the stranger. He meanwhile beguiled her with such a fund of humour and gossip, that she forgot both the adventure and her errand, and insensibly wandered on, fascinated with his seductive conversation, until she found they had left the western parts of London, and were approaching towards Charing Cross. The whirl of the mighty traffic that was flowing eastward caused her to look around her, and she became sensible that she was wandering far from her destination. She paused, and hurriedly said:

"I must leave you, sir, now, indeed I must; and I have gone far out of my way already."

"'Twere a sin to part such good company," urged her companion; "and besides, I thought that after your recent alarm a sail on the river would have done you infinite good."

"No, no—I cannot think of such a thing!" exclaimed the now agitated young woman; for she was experienced enough in the stratagems of gallantry to know what the termination of such a journey would be. The stranger entreated, swore he loved her, would listen to neither expostulation nor entreaties, and at last wrung from her a consent to meet him at a place he named, at eight o'clock in the evening. With this promise, and a tender pressure of the hand, he allowed her to depart.

But Alice's interruptions were not destined to end here; she had no sooner left her importunate deliverer from a dangerous situation, than she encountered a thriving bevy of married women, who happened at one time to have been her neighbours. They were all heavily laden, some with children in the arms; others with baskets, from which the necks of flat stone bottles protruded; while others were encumbered with shawls and children's over-alls. Some of them were young, but the majority were fat, fair and forty, rather red in the face, and the majority as heavy-footed as the most uxorious husband could desire. No fox ever burst from cover under a more hearty chorus than that which greeted the unmistakably agitated Mrs. Burton, for she was still such an uncorrupted votary of Love as to believe that the attentions of a handsome young fellow were worth any thing rather than cold rejection.

"Well I never!" "Who'd a thought it!" "How do you do?" "Why it's an age since you were at our end?" "How's your husband?" "How stunning you're a looking!" Such were the exclamations that were showered upon her by the little mob that surrounded her, followed by a general and elaborate shaking of hands.

"Vy ve had a given you up for lost, Missus Burton," said a fiery visaged dame, whose nose bore testimony to a powerful vinous affection; "but as you has a turned up at last, it follows in konsikence you aint dead; so come along vith us and take pot luck."

"Do, Alice," said a blooming young wife with a babe tugging vigorously at her breast.

"Of corse she vill," echoed a plump good-humoured looking creature, "when she knows we're a having a lark unbeknown to our husbands; and won't we enjoy ourselves! We have got lots of grub, lashings of porter, and anything short anybody would like to take."

"Ve are a hactually going down to Greenwich," almost screamed another, while a more subdued voice declared they would have such a lark, and perhaps go on to Woolwich, and see the gallant handsome "fellers" that were ready at any time to shed their gore for their country.

Alice with difficulty extricated herself from the affectionate throng, and, stepping aside with Mrs. Wriggles, while the rest in solemn conclave stood aloof, held the following brief but important dialogue:

"I sawd you a talking to a swell," said Mrs. Wriggles, a "sure card," a "vinning horse," as her friends in confidence proudly termed her, but of whose extraordinary professional and other peculiarities more by-and-bye; "but you always vos a sly one. Have you seen Harry lately?"

"No," replied Alice, boldly; for she deemed such a denial merely an excusable piece of prevarication—"nor never wish to see the brute again. He never was a husband to me."

"He was a racketty cove, I must say," returned the old woman; for Mrs. Wriggles owned to fifty-two, and for her wisdom was held among her acquaintances to be a perfect Solomon in an ample black stuff gown; "but," continued she, "vot became of your child—the sweet little fellow vot I brought into the vorld and dandled as fondly as if it vos my own?"

Alice at this question looked frightened, and hesitatingly replied:

"It's out at nurse."

The old woman fixed a long and penetrating gaze on the pale face of her former neighbour and patient; but if any evil thought possessed her, she did not give it utterance. She merely said, "Perhaps that vos for the best."

"Vot are you a doing of now?" at length inquired Mrs. Wriggles.

"I am lady's maid to Lady Bloomfield," replied Alice incautiously.

"Maid!" said Mrs. Wriggles, indulging in an immense laugh; "precious few of them now, I'm thinking. Howsomdever, good bye, Alice; I'll see you some of these odd days."

"Good bye," roared the excursionists simultaneously, waving handkerchiefs, baskets, and babies, to the great delight of a critical and approving body of cabmen, with whom the more elderly of the ladies had been exchanging pungent compliments.

Alice hurried away, and after half an hour's walk arrived at her destination, the residence of Captain

PUBLISHER'S NOTE

pp.7-8 are misbound / missing.

Morris, to whom she had to deliver so interesting a message. The captain was not at home, but on her declaring her business to be imperative, a grinning footman ushered her into a neat, but not very elegantly-furnished apartment, on the first floor. It was evident, from the style of its furniture and the prevalent slovenliness, that it belonged to a bachelor. Fencing foils, boxing gloves, and books, were heaped promiscuously on a side table; the chairs were more solid than ornamental, and the pier glass was most wofully fly-speckled.

Every thing betokened the lodger destitute of the protecting influence of the habitual society of a woman, and while Alice was speculating on this and many other things which struck her, the door opened, and in walked the unknown, who, but a short time before, had rendered her such essential service. Both started, Alice from confusion, the other from surprise and rapture.

"Captain Morris, I presume," said Alice timidly, for the remembrance of her interview with the gallant soldier, and the nature of the communication she had to make, totally unnerved her.

"I have the pleasure to be that happy individual," replied the amorous captain, as he gracefully raised her hand to his lips; "I never, in all my life, felt more disposed to call myself the luckiest fellow alive, than at this moment."

"Pardon me, sir," said Alice, with more firmness, "such language to one in my situation in life ill-becomes a gentleman; and however grateful you may expect me to be for the service rendered this morning, you cannot, surely, weaken its value by taking advantage of the painful situation into which I was thrown by accident. For when I met you I was on my way to your house, as the bearer of a confidential message from Lady Bloomfield."

"The devil you were!" half muttered the surprised captain, and then aloud, "may I know, my pretty one, what her ladyship wishes with me? I was not aware that I had the honour of her acquaintance."

This was a falsehood; but the experienced captain had an object to gain in deceiving the countess's confidant.

Alice then, in some trepidation, informed Captain Morris of the countess's wish that he should name a place where he could meet the lady of his heart without suspicion or reproach to her fair fame. Morris at first was remarkably surprised at the tenor of this message; but gradually a light broke in upon his active mind, and a smile very perceptibly played round his ripe full lips. Alice, as she stole a glance at them, thought that richer ones were never kissed by woman.

"I see through it all," said he to Alice; "a military friend of mine, of higher rank than myself, is the principal in this delicate affair; and, as a trustworthy agent, I presume I had better at once pen a little note to her ladyship, who, it would appear, takes a warm and—where the happiness of a young and loving couple is concerned, I must say a commendable—interest in this affair."

Alice was not so unsophisticated as to believe all this to be implicitly true, but she felt some relief from the explanation; for the dashing, nobly-formed soldier before her was, in her opinion, just the kind of man a woman ought to adore. Already she felt an interest in him, and when he had sealed a very lover-like epistle, and requested her gaily to partake of lunch with him, her heart beat so violently that the refusal she was about to give trembled on her lips, and died gently away, and in a few seconds she was unbonneted, and seated at a table, covered with a substantial repast, with one of the greatest rakes in her Majesty's service. Generous wine warms the heart, but it makes dizzy the head. Resolution thaws under its genial influence, and as Alice was neither a prude nor very tenacious on the score of chastity, it is not extraordinary that she should, to a slight extent, have yielded to the fascinations of the dangerous individual whose acquaintanceship she had so singularly made, and permitted many freedoms incompatible with the cardinal rules of strict propriety. But when the gallant Captain Morris proceeded to liberties of a graver character, although almost delirious with the burning fever that possessed her, a sweet vision of her child stole so brightly on her excited fancy that she burst into a flood of tears, and was saved. A brave man, not wholly corrupted in his desires to gratify his propensities, cannot withstand the effect of those pearly drops that glitter in a woman's eye; and it was even so on the present occasion.

"One kiss from those luscious lips," exclaimed the captain, "and we part; and believe me, until we meet in a more propitious hour, I will remember you as the sweet girl whose overpowering beauty deprived me, for an instant, of reason and self-control. Good bye until we meet again."

And Alice, drying her eyes and composing her features, left the house with a secret determination never to enter it again. If we all adhered to our private resolutions, what singularly consistent mortals we should be! Time, and the tide of events, carry the strongest of us along with them.

CHAPTER III.

THE MERRY WIVES.

ON the evening of the day upon which our narrative opened, the mansion of Lord Bloomfield was one blaze of light, from the basement to the uppermost story. Rank and wealth were holding one of their revels within its walls, and every thing in the interior betrayed the bustle and confusion incidental to such occasions. There was an interminable hurrying to and fro, a ceaseless hum and bustle; and as the darkness deepened, they increased tenfold. Carriage after carriage arrived; and as they deposited their jewelled burdens at the door, the commentaries of the crowd assembled became more and more liberal. There was the dowager, in the full glory of her exuberant proportions; the stately matron, with an eye of fire, and a step of exulting pride; the timid maiden, who scarcely felt the ground as she alighted; and the mob of gentlemen who hover on the skirts of beauty and opulence like vultures hungry with expectation. All classes of the patrician and commercial aristocracy had been invited, and among them the feeling was general that the representatives of the third estate assembled outside were as unworthy of notice as the lowest members of the animal creation. But if several of the guests had been aware that in the crowd they so thoroughly despised there were several who nourished hatred and revenge in their bosoms, and, with the tenacious ferocity of the North American aborigines, only bided their time, they would not have entered that ample doorway with quite so confident a tread and imperiously placid countenance.

An orangery diffused its rare perfume around, and, from the association, excited the gratified loungers to indulge in those sensations which provoke warm whisperings and thrilling touches, which, as they go and come, strike such chords of melting ecstacies in the heart, that when it has once laved in the voluptuous flood of pure unsullied love, it only emerges with renewed vigour to wish to play in the same burnished waters again. O.her senses, too, were charmed in these delightful gardens; for the eye could dwell with pleasure on the brightness of the colours of the various shawls that wrapped the forms of a hundred lovely women as they flashed through the trees, and watch the receding busts, whose contour they disclosed, until the lightly tripping figures of their owners were lost in the distance. Scarcely a voice was raised to disturb the stillness of the air, but there was a hum that betokened the presence of life, and occasionally a silvery laugh would ring over that region of delicious repose, and then all would be quiet once more. There was a subdued tone in the scene, which found its way into all hearts, and proved that, however artificial we may be in our habits, nature will at times exert its sovereign sway. Whoever

gazed into the clear depths of the sky without holding solemn converse with the stars that thickly crowd that blue sea, so liquid and intensely calm, where golden rolling orbs are moving upon its waveless surface? The passion of Endymion for the moon was no fiction, for we all of us partake of the adoration when we gaze into the depths of her bright essence, and hold communion with her in a weird language. And into whatever sensualities, coldnesses, or blighting sorrows we may plunge, there are moments when silvery sounds come upon the ear,

"Sweet, short, and broken, as divided strains
Of nightingales."

The grossest at times has his world of sweet whispers; his amorous breath, unlike that of Leander's, does not all bubble away as he casts a look behind him; nor do consuming passions or dark red thoughts play so cruelly with life but that we can walk beneath the stars that flood the green grass and the sleeping flowers with glory, and in some degree become sensible of the radiance that fills space, like holy fires lit upon the altars of heaven. We are not perpetually offering vain words to Diana, nor in the delirium of unsatisfied appetites. Even love has its delicious calms, its deep musical reveries, as well as its wild transports and fiery anticipations.

The Countess Bloomfield, as, well cloaked and half disguised, she strolled leisurely through her beautiful gardens, felt some portion of this poetic glow. Memory was busy within her fertile brain, and she wandered back to the days of her pure girlhood, when, guileless as a sleeping infant, she yielded to the love that filled every cell of her virgin heart. Happy spring-time! how often do we refer to it with the fondest enthusiasm, and yet take no lesson from the remembrance of its innocence? As this idea struck the countess, she sighed, and was so profoundly engaged in the reverie that followed, that she scarcely felt the slight touch of the hand that was laid on her shoulder.

"Violet!" murmured a gentle, yet manly voice, in her ear.

She started, and upon looking up, recognised in the gentleman beside her, clad in the full dress of an officer in the Guards, the playmate of her youth, and her companion in many a happy ramble—Captain Morris. His tall figure, soldier-like bearing, and imposing costume, appeared to great advantage in the half shaded walk in which they met.

"Walter!" was all she could utter, as she extended her hand, which he carried with warmth to his lips.

Accepting his respectfully tendered arm, they walked on in silence for several minutes.

"We did not use to meet thus, Violet," said he, at length, but in rather mournful tones. "May I ask whether the past is all forgotten? Have all the tender links that formerly united us been entirely broken?"

"Not all, Walter," softly replied the countess. "I should be less than woman were it so. But as we grow older, and our destinies become more dark and troubled, the romance of our early days fades, as these leaves around us will when a few brief months shall have elapsed. We are the creatures of imperious necessity, and our inclinations should be subservient in all things to the dictates of our judgments."

"Yours is, perhaps, an extremely orthodox philosophy," said her companion; "but it happens to be a rather impracticable and inconvenient one in the present day. Had I followed it to the letter, I should probably have been some poor curate, expected to be as pious on sixty pounds a year as a holy apostle gifted with the faculty of procuring the best wheaten bread from the hardest stones, and good wine from the foulest waters. No, no, Violet; we must certainly accommodate ourselves as decently as we can to existing circumstances, but at the same time we must create circumstances for our own accommodation; that is the creed I have worshipped, and I shall continue to do so as long as I carry a sword by my side, a stout resolution at my heart, and a disposition to be as merry in this money-grubbing world as it is possible for a man to be."

The countess smiled at this bold acknowledgment of latitudinarian social principles, but did not reply; had she done so candidly, she must have admitted the existence of corresponding sentiments in her own mind.

"It is in business as it is in intrigues, whether of love or politics," continued he—"the ablest strategist wins."

"Love! Walter!"

"Certainly. Who wins beauty and wealth? Not the open hand and warm heart, but the cunning watcher for favourable opportunities—the pliant tool of a woman's caprices—the booby worshipper of her person — the crawling hucksterer, that prices and cheapens her body as he would a horse or a hound;—

these are the men who skip into our ladies' chambers and carry off the dainty morsels, for whose loss fools shed tears, and even the wise fall into the yellow melancholy of hidden grief."

"You are severe, Walter!" uttered the countess reproachfully. "You did not formerly think so meanly of my poor sex. What has changed you?"

"Disappointment," answered the soldier, bitterly. "Between the boy and the man, I had a dream, and imagined the world better than I afterwards found it. A gentle blue-eyed girl, with locks that wantoned in the breeze of the fair country side where I roamed, threw a spell over my buoyant nature, and I placed her image in the stainless temple of my devotion, and worshipped it as ardently as the poet does the myth that fires his imagination to give utterance to high thoughts in burning words. I loved; she was to me a divinity that fed me with hope, gave wings to my soul, and carried it into an atmosphere as pure as that empyrean in which fable tells us the spirits of the good float everlastingly. I awoke and discovered I had bowed my idolatrous knee to a piece of rarest sculpture. I had played the part of Pygmalion and embraced a statue—I ought to have said an icicle—that reflected a thousand rays, and yet not one fell on me."

A deep, choking sob arrested his sarcastic fluency; he paused in amazement and no slight trepidation, for he felt the hand of the countess, that had nestled on his arm, tighten into a grasp, and heard her low voice piteously entreating him to forbear.

"Violet, dear Violet," he murmured, his manner instantly changing to one of subdued tenderness. She turned her tearful eyes up to his face, and would have thrown herself into his arms, had not a rustling of leaves and a suppressed breathing from some one evidently in concealment close at hand warned her of the danger of her position.

"We are observed," whispered the captain, as cool and collected as ever; "suppress your agitation, and do not move from the spot, but inform me of what you wished to speak to me about."

The admirable self-possession of her companion assured the countess that she had no occasion to fear any indiscretion on his part, and being thus reminded of the immediate object for which she had sought an interview with him, she said in low but clear and distinct tones, "Do you remember my mother, and the old house at home?"

"Can I ever forget it?" replied the captain, with enthusiasm; "it was a sweet spot, embosomed in our native hills, and in the language of our forefathers it was called 'the dell of the roses;' and well it deserved the name, for its girls vied with its flowers in loveliness, and were known far and wide for the splendour of their eyes and hair, and the neatest ankles in all North Wales. Your mother was a peerless Welsh beauty, and as amiable as she was beautiful. Why did you ask me the question?"

"Because I can recollect, as if it were only yesterday, myself and little sister and you being with my mother in our pretty little garden. My mother was very sad as she regarded us gambolling at her feet, and calling us all to her side, told us how our father had fallen in some terrible battle in India—that we were the daughters of an officer of the king's, who loved honour before all things, and had no cause to blush for one single action of his life. 'He lived,' said she, 'in the eye of Providence, and when he died gloried in having left his children an untarnished name. In the hour of temptation think upon him, and his spirit will sustain you throughout all trials. Come hither,' continued she, addressing you. 'I know you come of a brave race; now tell me, would you fight for your chosen sisters here, if you should chance to see them injured or insulted?' Your little eyes flashed fire, Walter, and you swore—your father's oath—by your country's unpolluted valleys and glorious mountains, that you would wash the affront out in the heart's blood of him that offered it. Little Lucy was so frightened. Do you remember the occasion?"

"I do," answered the captain, firmly, "and something besides—a sort of promise that I would make you my sisters, and love you dearly as such all the days of my life."

"And nobly did you keep your word, Walter, until we were severed by our separate fortunes," said the countess with animation; "and my motive for requesting this interview was to levy another tribute on your brotherly affection."

"Command me, Violet—my sword, my unblemished name, and purse, as far as it will go, are at your service."

"My sister Lucy has been in town for some months——"

"I thought so. Bless me, what a difference twelve years make in a girl's appearance! That beautiful creature with raven hair, and full deep blue eyes, I have seen with you at the opera and in the park, is then the little Lucy for whom I used to chase the butterfly, and commit petty larceny on the birds' nests for miles round? I could have sworn I knew the face well, well——"

"You are correct in your surmise," interrupted the countess; "it was Lucy you saw; and you may imagine how unsophisticated she is, when I tell you she only left our native place scarcely half a year ago. As you must have observed, she is very beautiful—remarkably so; she was called the lily of our valley. Well, she has already attracted considerable attention; but, being portionless, her admirers entertain any thing but respect for her helpless, motherless condition."

"Ha!" exclaimed the captain, and the fiery blood flew through the frame of that usually so self-collected man, until it seemed to centre in a deep red spot on his forehead.

"It is even so, Walter," continued the countess, sadly, "and one of them has dared openly to insult her!"

"How—how?" was the impetuous demand.

"In the worst sense in which a true woman can be offended," was the low response, as a flush as well of anger as of shame crimsoned the noble features of the countess, until it vanished in the masses of hair that clung round her temples.

"Some low-bred ruffian, is he not? No gentleman would dare offer such an indignity to an unmarried gentlewoman. But tell me his name."

The distinction thus unconsciously drawn between the respect due to a virgin and a married woman pained the countess, the more so because she felt that the follies of fashionable life gave it countenance. Her cheek paled. Had her husband spoken so, the remark might have passed by unheeded; but for him unwittingly to breathe a reproach was wormwood to her proud and sensitive disposition. At length, after some hesitation, she said:

"Colonel Stanley, the same whom I have seen in your company."

Captain Morris could not avoid a slight start at this announcement, for the personage designated happened to be the commanding officer of his regiment.

"My position was an embarrassing one," continued the countess, observing the hesitation of her companion. "I knew the colonel to be on intimate terms with my husband, and in the emergency I thought I could not solicit the advice of any better or abler one than the friend of my childhood, and the sworn champion of the gentle Lucy."

"Nor shall the request be made in vain," uttered the captain, gaily. "Poor Lucy's honour shall never want either a defender or an avenger."

"For heaven's sake don't be rash!" entreated the countess, alarmed; for not until that moment had it struck her that the headlong valour of the young soldier might hurry him into the commission of some act of imprudence.

"Do not be alarmed," was the assuring reply; "I know with whom I have to deal too well to risk too much. I promise that Lucy shall have satisfaction, and yet nothing compromise me in any way. But stay—does Lucy love him?"

"She detests—hates the wretch!"

"Enough; the annoyance from this day shall cease. But, Violet, the night air is getting damp, let me conduct you inside, and as we pass along you can tell me how Bloomfield, who used to be a good fellow, and you agree together. Some rumours that reached my ears pained me exceedingly."

So saying, he adjusted her shawl, and drawing her slender fingers within his arm, led her away with a graceful manner in which kindness, perhaps a warmer feeling, was mingled.

As soon as they had gone the figure of a man emerged from the arbour near where they had been standing. It was Lord Bloomfield, who had been playing the spy on his wife. His face was deadly pale, and his eyes moist with emotion.

"Why did she not consult me?" he asked himself; "what have I done to lose her young heart? It is strange she should prefer Walter Morris to her husband; but now I think of it, I heard some tale of their having once loved each other; but she is pure, and Walter is generous. Yes, yes—Walter is generous. Besides, she jilted him for me. Pshaw! Now I look at the matter again it was silly to entertain the shadow of a doubt; and, on the whole, I am glad he has to bring the colonel to account instead of me. I detest a broil with a fashionable acquaintance. Ah! what a pair of ankles! See, the dress has caught in a bush, and shows a leg of divine proportions! The walk, too, shows a daughter of the game, or I'm confoundedly mistaken. Such an opportunity is worth half an hour's ambush, listening to a wife and a Welsh cousin."

The volatile peer hurried after the solitary unknown, who, sooth to say, did not allow her garments to brush away the dew of night, just as Captain Morris returned, after having consigned the countess to the care of Mrs. Smythe and the other ladies, who formed an animated group in one of the saloons.

"Not here!" muttered the captain; "I could have sworn some person was in the arbour, and it could have been none other than Bloomfield. Well, I hope he profited by what he heard. So now for the colonel, and heaven give him a civil tongue in his head; for in such a cause, if my Welsh blood, in this atmosphere of cold experience, had become as frosty as Saturn's, it would, at the slightest provocation, turn to the burning liquid that in ancient days won the loftiest renown for dear old Cambria. But what the devil does all that uproar mean?"

Shouts, that sounded very like the loud huzzas of a mob, the screams and laughter of women, and the roarings of some snatches of popular melodies, came upon the still night air with startling suddenness and vehemence, and to explain their cause we must conclude this and commence another chapter.

CHAPTER IV.

THE REVENGE OF THE MERRY WIVES.

WE have hinted that Alice did not return to her mistress after her interview with Captain Morris, but that the message, of which she should have been the bearer, was forwarded through apparently another person. The truth is that Alice, after her opportune escape from the amorous importunities of the captain, was in a rather bewildered state of mind. The wine and the provocation her eager temperament had received produced in her an excitement which seriously deranged her geographical knowledge of the streets of London, and instead of preferring the most public thoroughfares she deviated into the intricate windings and interminable dingy alleys which crawl behind the splendid mansions of the western division of the metropolis, like colonies of snakes in slow precession behind the luxuriant borders of the walks of a rich parterre. All her movements had been watched by the vindictive foe who hung upon her track, and she had no sooner got entangled in the labyrinth which, even had she been in a state of composure, she would have experienced some difficulty in threading, than he promptly determined on the course he should pursue. Darting down a court, he knew that by making tolerable good compasses of his legs he should be able, from his knowledge of the warren-like locality, to get considerably in advance of her; which he did, and, under a low archway, awaited her approach. Alice was carefully picking her way with gently uplifted dress, totally unconscious of danger, when all at once she felt herself violently dragged into a filthy entrance to a court composed of the most ricketty and dismal-looking dwellings imaginable. She tried to scream for help, but one glance at the man who had assaulted her made her tongue cleave to her mouth in terror and astonishment. He was that dreaded being—her husband!

"Speak a word louder than a whisper, and I'll throttle you!" said he, glaring ferociously upon her pallid countenance.

"Have mercy, Henry!"

"Silence!" was the hoarse reply, as his brawny hand grasped her like a vice by the shoulder, and he pushed her before him up the court, until he gained one of the doorways, into which he thrust her, and, with as little difficulty as if she had been a child, forced her up into a room on the second floor, which he had no sooner entered than with a brutal oath he released his hold and sent her reeling to the other extremity. He then locked and barred the door, and, folding his arms, looked down triumphantly on what he considered his lawful prize. Alice, breathless and faint, leaned helplessly against the wall; and in this position the husband and wife remained for several minutes.

The apartment was a horribly squalid one. The only furniture was a deal table, jagged like a butcher's block, a broken-backed chair, and a truckle bed with scanty coverings as brown with age and dirt as the skin of a mulatto. The window, which, like most attic ones, only gave an upward view, was small and strongly barred, and the whole place had very much the appearance of a burglar's stronghold for there was no fireplace, and the fastenings of the door were peculiarly strong and suspicious-looking. Alice felt her heart sink as she cast one despairing look around this dismal council-room of crime, for in truth it was nothing else.

"I have got you at last, have I, my dainty one?" cried the ruffian, chuckling; "and my name's not Harry Burton if I don't have all I want out of you before we part."

Alice, upon hearing this threat, sank fainting to the floor. A doom worse than death opened hideously upon her, and overstrained nature mercifully gave way, and for a brief space plunged her faculties into oblivion.

"I'm in luck's way," thought Burton, for we suppose we must give the fellow his proper name; "she won't squeal after this—women never does when they comes out of these die-aways. Let's see whether she has any tin about her."

The heartless vagabond then proceeded to search the insensible form of his wife, and upon thrusting his hand into her bosom found her tolerably well-filled purse.

"Yellow boys, as I'm alive!" he exclaimed, as he told over the contents by the dim light that entered the room. "Well, I'll just now have a little spree after a new fashion, and my name's Walker if I don't make as jolly a blowen of my wife for an hour or two as any girl that pads the hoof."

As he uttered this atrocious determination he struck a light, and held the emptied purse over it until it was entirely consumed. This must have been done from the mere force of habit, for he was too shrewd a rascal not to know that a husband may commit a robbery upon his wife with impunity. He little cared what privileges our laws conferred upon him; if he could gratify his appetites, he did not concern himself much about the means of doing so. On the present occasion, out of the spoil that had come to hand so opportunely, he first of all procured an abundant supply of brandy, and tobacco, and pipes, and then sat himself down, with all the coolness imaginable, to enjoy himself. After he had tossed a few glasses off, he deigned to bestow a glance upon his wife, and finding her still in a state of insensibility, poured a copious supply of the raw spirit down her throat, and then lifted her on to the miserable apology for a bed, and left her to recover as she best could. He afterwards arranged his table so as to face his intended victim, and in smoking and drinking waited patiently for her recovery. While he was thus employed, he was studying how he should not only gratify his libidinous propensities, which were immense, but torture his wife so as not to unfit her for his diabolical purposes on other occasions.

"I'll teach her to turn up her nose at me!" growled he, as he recognised some symptoms of revival in the poor girl, "and to go and do what I wanted her to do for me on her own account. I married her, and she's mine, and I'll do what I likes with her. By God! she shall do the w— for me now, and steal and murder if I order her! She's coming round, and my name's not Harry Burton if I don't show her the difference between a man—yes, a man and a whipper-snapper of a gentleman."

As Alice slowly regained consciousness she gazed around her for a while, utterly bewildered, but her wandering glances no sooner fell on the burly figure of her husband as it loomed in the dense smoke that filled the room, than she gave vent to a cry of stifled agony, and buried her face in the dirty bed-clothes.

"So you have waked up, my precious, have you?" said her cowardly tormentor, seating himself on the edge of the bed, and proceeding to disencumber her of her outward garments, which he laid carefully by, declaring with an offensive jest that they were just the things to take the swells in with. Alice was too weakened to resist this proceeding, but when Burton was about to take off her dress, and had exposed her bosom, she piteously entreated him to forbear.

"You let me do it once as a joke; now I'll do it in earnest, just to please myself."

Alice resisted with her utmost strength, but she was as powerless as a mouse beneath the paws of a cat. The beastly fellow subjected her to every indignity that can harrow up the feelings of a woman, and amused himself during the "peeling" process, as he termed it, with copious libations of brandy. Finding her struggles to retain her garments useless, she abandoned the attempt to husband her powers for a resolute denial of the last favour a woman can grant. Burton, seeing he had it all his own way, allowed himself a respite from his labours, for the purpose of having, as he thought, a very amusing bit of chaff. But this did not last long, for as the dazzling white skin, warm plump flesh, and beautiful limbs of his wife met his sight, his fierce carnal nature became infuriated, and, with the howl of a wild beast, he flung himself upon the bed. We must draw a veil over that fearful contest, but in the end the ruffian was baffled. Alice had sworn to resist his embraces, and nobly did she keep her oath. To his blind, drunken fury, she offered the resistance of the eel, and slipped from his grasp so repeatedly that his burly frame every two or three seconds fell heavily to the floor, and he several times ran his head in full tilt against the wall, and brought the blood gushing in streams from his mouth, nose, and ears. At last Alice took advantage of one of his staggering gyrations, and with the large stone bottle she had picked up from the floor dealt him such a blow on the temple that it broke into a hundred pieces, and he dropped down with the dull groan of a felled bullock. Alice stood for a moment panting, while her eyes drank in the outlines of her prostrate husband with savage exultation.

"I have baffled the wretch!" she gasped. "I swore he should never touch me again alive, and I have kept my oath."

The gleam of a knife came before her vision: to clutch it, kneel by the snorting monster's side, and bare his hairy bosom, was but the work of an instant. Her attitude was fearful. Her arms, bosom, and breasts were entirely naked; her hair hung in disordered masses on her snowy shoulders; and her lower garments were so torn, that they revealed her polished limbs in all their exquisite proportions. Her face, ordinarily so arch in its warm play of features, was pale with ferocity. One blow—her slender finger was on the spot where she should strike—and she would be revenged. She hesitated; her features relaxed into a cold smile, and she softly said:

"That would be murder, not revenge! For his worthless life, mine would be claimed by the gallows! No, no, Harry; that shall be thy doom. You are not the father of my child; and here, on my bare and bended knees, I swear that you shall swing like the vilest dog that ever howled."

The whole of her oath is too fearful to record; but it comprised the infliction of a punishment as common in the Celestial Empire as whipping is in England.

O woman! thou art as bitter in thy retaliations for monstrous wrongs as thou art sweet and gentle in thy love; and woe be it to the man who provokes thy unappeasable anger. He had better encounter the tiger in his jungle, or the serpent in its grassy shade, than the indomitable ferocity of thy outraged instincts.

When roused thou art capable of resentments that would appal the hearts of the most savage of men. Husbands either do not know or despise this truth; and behold how our daily records describe their slow agonies and sudden ends! But to our narrative.

Alice arrayed herself as she best could in her torn and sullied garments, tied up her hair so as to let it fall in dark braids on her pale cheeks, and putting on her crushed little bonnet, with the keys that hung on a nail in the wall let herself out of that apartment of horrors, and carefully locked the massive door after her, thus making a prisoner of the man who had, in a few hours of unholy contention, severed the last link that bound them together, not as active enemies. She could have forgiven the past, but the recent occurrence recalled in all its deformity, and the deep impression of both acting upon her excited organisation, produced a vow of vengeance as terrible as its fulfilment was destined to be sure and exactive.

As soon as she had emerged into the court, she heard the noisy sounds of female revelry, and fancied she could distinguish among the voices one or two that were familiar to her. All her doubts upon the point were set at rest by her being seized, when she entered the street, by Mrs. Wriggles and the whole of the Greenwich party, on their return home in a state of joyous excitement. The rotund Mrs. Wriggles was frantic with joy when she beheld her former *protegee*, and bore her triumphantly back into the court, followed by the whole troop of married revellers.

"This is my house," said Mrs. Wriggles, inserting a ponderous key into the dingy door of a ruinous-looking dwelling.

Mrs. Wriggles was too well known to Alice for her to wonder at the old dame having such a residence; and as she thought of her brute of a husband opposite, the suggestion stole upon her mind that the circumstance might be rendered serviceable to her projected revenge. She had taken the precaution to possess herself of the balance of the money of which Burton had deprived her; and aware of the tastes of the company into which she had been thrown, dispatched one of the body for a copious supply of gin.

"Vy, bless my heart, vot a mess you are in!" ejaculated Mrs. Wriggles, as she surveyed Alice's haggard looks and torn habiliments. The majority of those present had known her in her early and remarkably tidy wifehood, and she felt no hesitation in boldly disclosing to them the whole of the details of her husband's fiendish treatment. The women, heated with drink, indulged in the most violent threats, and a perfect Babel of a council of war was held as to what should be done to such a "wagerbond." While they were thus debating, Alice called Mrs. Wriggles aside.

"You know I can be of service to you among the best families in town."

"I does know it, Ally, and I expected you would do me a good turn some day or another. Vot is it I am to do for you."

"Help me to a little bit of my revenge," replied Alice, fiercely. "I could have killed him, mother, but I wasn't going to be hung for his sake. I want to listen to his howls—his harmless curses!"

"Hush! not so loud—any thing in reason. But vere is he?"

"In that house opposite. What I have told you about took place in a room upstairs, where I left him insensible."

The old woman opened her little eyes very wide; for, aware of the violent character of Burton, she stood in some awe of him.

"Vell I never! And me to look through the vindow

all day and never to see him!" said she; "but the people that belong to it have all gone down to a fight in Lancashire, and won't be home for two days, so we have a chance of serving him out. But vot are we to do?"

"Flog the flesh from his bones," replied Alice, resolutely, "and then ——"

Here her voice sunk to an almost unintelligible whisper; but the old woman heard her proposal, and started back, petrified with astonishment.

"Vot, take his———. But no, no; you are only a joking," said Mrs. Wriggles, rather frightened.

"I have sworn it," said Alice, with quiet resolution; "but let us begin with the mildest punishment; he is helplessly drunk, and we have nothing to fear."

Mrs. Wriggles shook her head doubtfully; but having some ulterior objects to pursue, in which Alice could be of service of her, she reluctantly assented to the proposal, and turning to the ladies who were discussing the wrongs of Alice, with startling vehemence addressed the following powerful appeal to their already excited sympathies:—

"Vives and mothers of Hengland!" commenced Mrs. Wriggles, "is a married voman a hanimal or a vife?" ('Vy a vife, what else?' 'In course she's a wife!' 'La! vot a quextion!' were the interrupting cries). Vell, if she's a vife, oughtened she to be treated as sich? ('In course she ought!') and not kicked and cuffed like any common voman? A vife gives up all she has to one hindividal, and isn't that enough for him? ('In course it is!') Is it fair or manlike for him to ramfoozle * her as if she was only dirt under his feet? ('In course it's not!' and shouts of indignation.) Them sentiments of your's is very konsoling. They show's that the married vomen of Hengland has got 'arts in their busoms, and von't stand any of their husbands' hanky-panky tricks. (Uproarious applause.) And now I vant to ask you, vether this young voman, Ally here, has a right to put up vith vot Harry has a done to her? ('No, no!') Isn't she entitled to communeration—to have it out of the wagerbond somehow or another? ('Yes, yes,' and great excitement.) That's jist vot I say; and as Harry Burton is dead drunk in the empty house over the vay, I bags to move that ve all goes in and gives him a jolly good tanning."

The motion was seconded by the entire company, and carried amid the most frantic demonstrations of applause. After each had fortified herself with a liberal drain, and Mrs. Wriggles had providently thrown some thirty yards of strong cord over her arm, Alice seized hold of a lighted candle and led the way, followed by the others, some of them also bearing candles in their hands.

They found Burton still insensible, and, by the prudent Mrs. Wriggles' advice, securely bound his arms and legs before they attempted to move him. Some half dozen of the most stalwart of them lifted him up, and bore him to another room, which Mrs. Wriggles well knew was frequently used for the most questionable purposes. There they laid him on the floor, with his face downwards, where a square was formed by four strong rings, with their bolts driven deep into the thick timbers that supported the flooring. Their next step was to bind a hand, and then a foot, to each of these rings; so that where the operation was completed he looked very like a huge frog at the full stretch of his limbs. Mrs. Wriggles, who had often witnessed the same experiment, examined the fastenings, and pronounced them perfectly safe—indeed, she averred they were strong enough to hold

* The editor presumes that the erudite Mrs. Wriggles meant bamboozle.

the largest bull in the universe. That was sufficient, and in a trice the man's clothes were cut and torn from him until he was naked from his head to his dorsal extremity. Mrs. Wriggles produced a formidable accelerator of the circulation, and all was ready for the punishment of the merry wives; for each felt that in flogging the brawny rascal before them she would be avenging many a wrong she had unjustly suffered at the hard hands of her own spouse.

"Wake him!" cried Alice, her eyes emitting flashes of fire as she saw her unrelenting foe bound and helpless at her feet; "he must see and hear, as well as feel. But had we not better gag him? He can roar like a lion."

No sooner suggested than done. A rough piece of wood was forced between the fellow's jaws, and tightly fastened with some twine round his neck.

"Now then," shouted Alice, "pinch him until he wakes."

No second bidding was required, for the whole of them, with the exception of Alice, flung themselves on the body, and began to apply their forefinger and thumb to the fleshy parts with amazing rapidity and dexterity. One of them, by way of a cooler, as she facetiously termed it, dashed a pailful of cold water on the small of his back; and the shock, added to the pain of the thumb-and-finger-nail process, brought the drunkard to a perception of the reality of his situation, as effectually as if he had had four-and-twenty hours' sleep.

"Hold!" cried Alice, seeing him staring at her with distended eyes. "Now ain't you nicely caught?" said she, stooping down and looking him full in the face. "You are a dear, ain't you, Harry? Kiss um's Ally, will it—that's a darling?"

"Do kiss um's Ally!" echoed the crowd, enjoying the scene with grinning satisfaction.

"Kiss um's Ally, that's a darling," said Alice, stooping down lower.

The stupefied man, as well as he could, mechanically held out his lips, into which Alice spat with the hissing of a cat; and springing to her feet, seized the whip, and giving the heavy lashes a swing, brought them down upon the bare back of her husband with a force that made his powerful frame quiver with agony. Again and again came the blow, cutting into the very flesh, and making the wretch writhe like an eel grasped in the middle by the hand. He tried to bellow, but the sounds died away into something like the snorting of a horse; and on went his punisher, until, from sheer exhaustion, the whip dropped from her hands. It was promptly picked up by a stalwart dame, and for upwards of an hour did that merciless punishment continue. When one was tired out, another was ready to begin. Every one seemed imbued with the recollection of the injuries they had received from their husbands, and plied the instrument of torture with a vigour that would have done no discredit to the expertest farrier in her Majesty's service. Thus the man who had so frequently laid the lash on the delicate shoulders of defenceless woman, had the same degrading scourge applied to his own, and that too by the very sex whom he had ever regarded but as the minions of his brutal pleasures. Oh, how true it is that our vices make whips for our backs! All this man's struggles to free himself only added to the pain that he was compelled to endure, and he was gradually falling into a state of insensibility when his punishers gave over; and guessing that he was too weakened to sound an alarm that might be heard out of the house, took the gag, which he had nearly bitten through, from his mouth. They were about to release him altogether, but Alice with an imperious gesture bade them desist, and prevailed upon all of them to leave the room, with the exception of the now very much blown Mrs. Wriggles.

There was a fearful expression in Alice's eye, which the old woman shuddered as she noticed.

"You cannot surely mean *that* now?" whispered the old woman.

"I do, though," was the hissing reply. "His power over woman shall cease from this night. Do not deceive me, or you will find me a bitter foe; serve me, and you will find a fast friend."

"You can't peach against me," said the old woman, in a slightly quivering voice.

Alice whispered a few words into her ear; their purport must have been electric, for she shook more violently than if she had been smitten with palsy, and without uttering another word, tottered from the room. Alice extinguished the lights, and followed. In a few moments afterwards, an old serpent-like man crawled in on his hands and knees—there was a deep hollow groan—a kind of wrestle of life with the body—the cords that bound the now utterly prostrated provoker of his terrible doom were cut—a powerful restorative forced down his throat, and he was left alone weltering in his blood.

It was a sad spectacle of passion, that young wife's face, as Mrs. Wriggles tottered into the room where she was, and, more by manner than words, conveyed an intimation that every thing had been done as she had desired.

"I am not half revenged yet," said Alice, with energy. But further colloquy was cut short by the lively demonstrations which were being made by the merry flagelators of a brutal husband.

"What a lark!" vociferated Mrs. Spratt, whose reeking visage was of alarming proportions.

"Jolly!" echoed a substantial-looking matron, the perspiration starting from her forehead.

"Well, this is a spree!" chimed in another, and added in an under tone, "I wish somebody would serve my Tom out so."

The gin bottles circulated pretty freely, and under the combined influence of that fiery compound and the recent excitement, it was moved and carried that the day's enjoyment and triumph should be completed by giving Alice an escort to her residence. But the latter, over whom a sickening sensation was rapidly creeping, strongly demurred, and some belligerent symptoms would have broken out had not Mrs. Wriggles, who had fortified her resolution with a bumper of brandy, sternly insisted upon the proposition being carried out.

"I know Bloomfield House well," said she to Alice, "and as I have served you, why you must serve me. The countess will not be angry; besides, the detail of your adventures will be greedily received by her guests."

It should be remarked that this mysterious old woman, when in earnest, spoke with remarkable fluency and correctness, and only indulged in the vulgarities of a provincial phraseology—your Cockney dialect is a rank provincialism—when jibing, driving a bargain with a customer, or engaged in conversation usual to one in her apparent position in life.

Alice, finding herself largely compromised with Mrs. Wriggles, gave a reluctant assent, and as the mention of her mistress's name had recalled the purport of her morning expedition to her memory, she, in some trepidation, felt in her bosom for the note which had been delivered to her by Captain Morris. It was gone, however, and she concluded that her husband must have taken it from her when he stripped her of her garments. He had done so,

but, contrary to her forebodings, had first read it, and then forwarded it to its destination during his visit to the neighbouring tavern.

"Now then, let's be a moving," cried Mrs. Wriggles, jumping about with an agility quite astonishing for one of her years. "It's twelve o'clock, and it 'ull take us a good half hour to get to Bloomfield House. One drain more, my merry dames, and then, as my old man—God help him in his confirmities—says, 'Hurrah for the road.' "

The parting glass was drunk in solemn silence, and bonnets and shawls being duly adjusted, out sallied the now rather inebriated wives of St. Bridget's Court, Oxford Market. First marched Mrs. Spratt, as a species of forlorn hope; then came two sworn gossips, deep in a thrilling recapitulation of each other's domestic grievances; afterwards Mrs. Wriggles and the trembling Alice. She would have been more than woman, now that the reaction in her system had taken place, had she not felt some sympathy for the man in whose arms she had lain, and whom, for his crime against the conjugal law, she had visited with such dreadful retribution.

The rear was brought up by the youngest of the party, many of them with a gait decidedly the reverse of steady and graceful. It was rather an unusual procession for that advanced hour, and attracted no small share of attention from the stragglers who infest the streets after the iron tongue of St. Paul's has boomed its duodecimal warning over the darkly stretching dwellings and solemn stillness of the metropolis of the world. There was not a very great noise in the throng, but there was a ceaseless chattering—a peal of voices that rung shrilly on the night air, and startled many a drunken staggerer home with their similarity to the tones that generally greeted his procrastinated arrival. Mrs. Wriggles repressed all attempts at getting up a convivial demonstration in favour of the break-of-day time of inserting the latch-key; but a wild snatch of a ballad would now and then break out—married women cannot forget the music that charmed them in their girlhood; and thus the procession progressed, followed by a troop of idlers, until it reached the portico of Bloomfield House, where, as it has already been stated, a mob was congregated. To salute so singular a throng with a cheer might naturally have been anticipated, but several in the crowd had recognised Mrs. Wriggles, and giving the cue to the others, commenced such an uproarious chorus that the policeman on the beat thought that nothing else than the prophesied rebellion had broken out. The comeliest of the merry wives received unexpected salutes and divers pinchings on prominent regions, and, amid the delivery of heartily-bestowed and well-aimed cuffs, suppressed screams, and a liberal distribution of the choice epithets that are the especial property of certain classes of her Majesty's female subjects, the whole body rushed headlong into the spacious hall of Bloomfield House, to the terror and dismay of some half-dozen lacqueys, who, putting shoulder to shoulder and back to back, with extreme difficulty restrained their further advance.

Alice, who had conceived a devoted attachment to her mistress, burst from the crowd, indignant at the outrage, but feeling satisfied that a conciliatory measure was the most advisable, entreated the amazed and indignant servants that the party might be allowed to retire into the kitchen. The request was reluctantly complied with, and Alice was about to proceed to her own room when she encountered Captain Morris, who had been drawn to the spot by the uproar.

"Ah! my divinity of the morning," said he; "the Fates, you see, in their reckless benevolence, will throw us together. But what is the matter with you? Why, you are as disordered as if you had scoured the streets over night. Your hair dishevelled too, and the pretty little bonnet I admired so much a few hours ago all broken and bent! Why, what in heaven's name can have happened to you?"

Alice, who until this moment had not shed a tear or betrayed any excessive feminine emotion, no sooner heard the kindly inquiries of the captain than she threw herself into his arms and sobbed like a child.

"Take me to my mistress!" she murmured.

"I am here, Alice," said the countess, her cheeks reddening at beholding the tender manner in which the soldier supported his fainting burden.

"This way, Walter," said she, as the captain bore Alice in his arms upstairs to the private apartments of the countess. "Now leave us, and let me see you by and bye."

Morris, with his habitual nonchalance, turned upon his heel, but, with all his trained placitude, wondered what the deuce the whole affair meant. As he descended, and was about to enter one of the suite of rooms thrown open to the assembled guests, his quick eye fell upon the unmistakable, and, when once seen, never-to-be-forgotten figure of Mrs. Wriggles, in earnest expostulation with a powdered official, whose saffron visage betrayed the dilemma in which he was placed.

"I'm known here, I tell you, Mister Stuckup," exclaimed she, purple with assumed indignation.

"I beg pardon, really; but not whaving seen you afore, and your card—ahem!—you must—I beg pwardon, but weally I must require your name," stuttered the perplexed flunkey.

"Hoity, toity, Mister Madeup, I'd have you to know that I'm meat for your master, and something to spare for his brothers and his cousins, and——"

Her volubility was suspended at the appearance of the captain, who advanced towards her with a cordiality that betokened an old acquaintanceship.

"Let the lady pass, Robson," cried he. "She has the *entree*, for she's a jewel of a go-between." The latter was an under-toned commentary, intended for no other ears but his own.

"Vell I never, captain!" exclaimed the extremely gratified intruder, "who'd a thought of seeing you here?"

"Only the devil and his dam—I beg pardon, how's Wriggles?"

"Weakly, captain, weakly; he's a going wisibly. Trade's bad, the cholry and fevers has cut, and he has taken it to heart. Vy he hasn't had a stunning job for this never so long."

"I'm devilish glad—a-hem—sorry to hear it; but what, in the name of the great Priapus, of whom thou art so exemplary a votary, make ye here?"

"Vy a lark, to be a sure. Do ye think I'm too rusty-fusty for a bit of a go in for fun? If you thinks so, as the pen-and-ink sketched cove in the play says, 'lay not the flattering unction to your soul.'"

"Not a touch of it, I assure you, my plucky one; there are more things in heaven and earth than I can manage in my dreams. But I doubt whether your unction would much help the growth of my whiskers. But what the devil brings you here?"

"Hush! sich a lark!"

Morris was a great favourite with the facetious Mrs. Wriggles, so she drew him into a corner, and confided to him the particulars of the adventure of Alice with her husband, and the punishment inflicted upon that unfortunate wight by the merry wives on their return from Greenwich. She did not inform him of the terrible incident of the mummy-like man stealing into the dark room, and creeping out again like one whose hands had fallen on the slimy scales of a reptile.

"Talk of prattling with twenty she-devils," muttered the captain; "why, I would rather face a regiment of Sikhs; but are all of them here, say you?"

"Vy, yes; and they're a pitching into the cold mutton."

The captain mused awhile, and as a suggestion struck him, a mocking smile played round his lips, and he slapped his thigh with a vigour which caused the confiding Mrs. Wriggles to spring on her swelled supporters as if she had received a galvanic shock.

"Come, my merry daughter of Venus!" exclaimed the captain, gallantly tendering his arm to the unbidden guest, "introduce me to these vivacious revengers of woman's wrongs, and I will, in return, inform all the frail spinsters of London that thou art the most reasonably accommodating creature alive."

What the nature of the interview was must be left to the imagination; suffice it to say that at the end of half an hour the whole of the jovial kitchen party, led in grand style by the redoubtable Mrs. Wriggles, entered the gardens of Bloomfield House by a private entrance, and created no slight degree of commotion among the aristocratic loungers, who brushed the dew-drops from the flowers that embroidered the walks.

Some demon must have prompted the invaders to deeds of mischief; for they singled out an individual in the gay assemblage for the especial object of their exuberant sport. He was an exquisite as far as correctness of costume, as regulated by the ancient Bond Street class of dictation might be concerned, and also in every other external respect that makes up the conventional gentleman.

"Vell, I'm blow'd if he isn't the thing!" "My eye, vot a leg!" "Oh, I say Poll, look at his thigh!" "Ah, but dere is de expression of his eye!" "He's a stunning cove ven he likes." "S'help my blessed goodness, I never seed a finer man in all my born days!"

The object of these flattering comments did not seem at all obliged by the bestowal of them upon him, but appeared excessively bewildered as he gazed vacantly upon the ruddy-faced visages that encircled him in one of the most secluded portions of the luxurious gardens of Bloomfield House.

"Drive him to his kennel, merry wives of London!" exclaimed a clear, stentorian voice; "that is Colonel Stanley!"

The shout that followed would have done no discredit to an Exeter Hall meeting, and for a few moments a disinterested spectator would have imagined that the witches' dance in *Macbeth* was being performed for the gratification of an unlimited admission of orders.

"Go it, my tulip!" "Poor thing! will it dance the polka now—do!" "Does your mamma know you're out?" "I'm blow'd if he isn't stumbleficated!" "Oh! vot a lark it is to run a swell into ninepen'orth of ha'pence!"

Colonel Stanley—for it was that scion of a princely blood that had to endure these plebeian inflictions—looked bewildered, and, it must be confessed, excessively silly. He was a strikingly handsome man, and

wore a heavy moustache as black as jet. His dark hair curled in thick masses over a not very lofty forehead, and his full military dress set off his figure to the best advantage. His good looks inflamed some of the women to acts of familiarity, which roughly disturbed his equanimity, and it was only by great exertion that he kept them from clinging round his person. In his attempts to break through the cordon, he had to back, and twist, and dodge about, and cut such a ridiculous figure that the visitors whom the noise had drawn from the house could not resist an irrepressible burst of laughter. Enraged, he drew his sword, and flourished it about rather threateningly; but a merry wife, no way daunted, passed swiftly behind him, and darting between his legs, nearly threw him down at his full length on the grass. In that position he was easily mastered, and no poor devil ever before received such a mauling at the hands of a score of half drunken women. He was pinched and tickled, until he screamed and roared—he was literally worried, and might have been seriously injured, had not Morris induced Mrs. Wriggles to call the pack off.

"That will do," he whispered to her. "Get them out of the house as quickly as possible, and come to the countess in the morning; she wishes to see you."

The released colonel sprang to his feet, and, with the howl of a madman, rushed from the gardens, and thence out of the house into the noble square, where he met with an adventure, the recollection of which he ever afterwards recalled with a cold shudder.

CHAPTER V.

THE COUNTESS IN THE BED-CHAMBER.

THE mistress of that noble mansion, the fascinating Countess of Bloomfield, was sitting before a superbly-enamelled escritoire which she had in her bed-chamber, with a pen in her hand, but not employed in writing. Her deeply flushed cheek rested upon a delicately white hand, gemmed with rings of rare value; and her large blue eyes were fixed in deep thought upon the rich carpet at her feet. A pale pink dress, the open sleeves of which, falling back, disclosed the exquisitely formed arms they pretended to cover, was the only covering over the garments that composed her chamber costume. A white silk cord and tassel confined the whole round her waist, and on her head she wore a small lace cap, trimmed with plain blue ribbon, that partly concealed the glossy bright tresses that were coiled in a mass at the back of her head.

What were the thoughts of that lovely creature? were they as faultless as her beauty—fair and open as her white and placid brow? Alas! no; there was a smile about the full and parted lips that told another tale; a gleam within the half-closed eye that spoke of many passions. No line upon the high, clear forehead—no contraction of the long and pencilled eye-brow revealed them; each feature of her face was quiet and serene, saving when a smile played upon her lips and a faint glow suffused her cheeks, as the ruling idea that occupied her mind broke upon it in renewed warmth of colouring.

"He loved me once, and will love me again. Yes, he will come to be the slave of her whom he too easily gave up; but I cannot blame him—I preferred false splendours to real happiness; sacrificed my dearest wishes to the subtle promptings of my ambitious spirit. Bloomfield, too, was attractive, and the old nursery rhyme, of a dark man being the natural wedding mate of a fair girl, swayed my fancy. I was told too, love would come with marriage; but oh, how bitter—bitter has been the deception! My husband's embraces are loathsome; a sickness creeps over me when he approaches me with love; and I only yield to the imperious necessity which the tyrant custom imposes upon me; and when I do, the image of Walter seems to stare at me with anger and reproach."

The countess paused in her musings, for she fancied she heard a footstep; but after listening attentively, and not hearing the sounds repeated, relapsed into her reverie:

"He must love me—he called me beautiful;" her eye glanced slowly towards a large mirror that hung before her, where her fine form and face were reflected in full dimensions; "I am so still; and he has often declared I had expression and life upon my countenance. Few, indeed, can call up such a soul-sparkling look as this." And, with her beautifully-formed head thrown a little back, her glossy curls, carelessly yet gracefully falling from the face, her brilliant eyes glancing upwards through the long silken fringes of their lids, her ruby lips parted as if about to speak, and showing the pearly teeth within them, she sat before the glass with an exquisite expression of amorous earnestness upon her features. A thought, like a flash of lightning, flitted across her brain, and she gently murmured: "Walter—dear Walter—you must be mine yet." A thrill passed through her frame, and she yielded to the delirium of that dream of love, into which the instincts plunge persons with ardent temperaments.

A gentle tapping at the door roused the countess from her state of intense agitation.

"It's only me, Violet. For heaven's sake, admit me!" uttered a female voice, which the countess at once recognised as Mrs. Smythe's.

To open the door was but the work of an instant; and in rushed that lady in her night-dress, pale and breathless.

"Oh! Violet, darling, I have had such a fright!" exclaimed she, as she nervously clung to the countess. "I had just got into bed, and was dozing off, when I heard a rustling, and, upon looking up, I saw a man standing by the bed-side."

"A man? Nonsense!"

"A man, I assure you."

"Did you notice what sort of man he was?"

"Captain Morris, or some person bearing a remarkable resemblance to him."

The countess reddened to the temples, but suddenly recollecting that the captain had taken his departure with several ladies, whom he had volunteered to escort home, laughed outright.

"You were dreaming, Caroline; Walter never slept in my house in his life."

Mrs. Smythe, who happened for that night to be a sleeping guest in Bloomfield House, looked perplexed and incredulous, and intreated that she might share the countess's bed. The latter willingly assented; and neither feeling much wearied, directed their conversation to the incidents of the previous evening.

"What a scene that was in the garden! I really thought those terrible women would have killed the poor colonel outright. How, in the name of wonder, did they obtain admittance?"

"By the contrivance of Captain Morris," replied the countess, laughing at the remembrance of the whimsical appearance of the colonel, when surrounded by the merry wives.

"What a duck of a fellow that Walter is!" said Mrs. Smythe. "I imagined it was him that invented such a game of hunting a veritable colonel."

"Walter was always fond of mischief," said the countess; and, wishing to change the topic, added, "Did you observe that stout old woman, with the red face and ferret-like eyes, that seemed to be the leader of the party?"

"I did," replied Mrs. Smythe, uneasily; "I fancy she bore some likeness to the woman who used to come prying about our school."

"It was the same," uttered the countess, slowly, as she fixed a penetrating gaze on the face of her companion.

The latter turned pale, but retained her composure.

"It could not have been the same person, Violet;" said she, "or I should have immediately recognised her."

"Perhaps not," said the countess; "people in her class of life strangely resemble each other."

From widely different motives they both permitted the subject to terminate. Each of them had a secret in which that strange old woman was mixed up, and each was desirous of retaining it inviolable.

"Does our arrangement for our river excursion hold good?" inquired Mrs. Smythe.

"Certainly; I long to see the busy world face to face. Besides, there will be a bit of romance in being *incognito* for a few hours."

"I am heartily tired of this drawing-room life, and would turn nun were there not such lively, charming fellows as Captain Morris to trifle time away with."

"Captain Morris?"

"Yes, Captain Morris, dear; I consider him the most amusing and handsome man I am acquainted with. If I were single, I am afraid I should doat upon him."

"Indeed!" ejaculated the countess, a cold shiver running through her frame at the bare possibility of Walter's becoming acquainted with the fact that he was admired by her beautiful friend.

"He is fair and I'm dark," prattled Mrs. Smythe,

unconscious of the pain she was inflicting on the countess; "and they say a dark woman likes a fair man best, and *vice versa*; but I married—worse luck—a man as swarthy as a creole."

"Do you place any reliance on the idle gossip about a difference of the complexion being necessary to create true love?" inquired the countess, anxiously.

Mrs. Smythe was one of those well-read women, and shrewd observers, who amuse themselves with little theories of their own, and dabble in suggestions with quite the placitude of the men who style themselves philosophers; so she promptly replied in the affirmative.

"Strong contrasts," said she, "are the soul of love, because they relieve the intercourse between the sexes of its monotony. Now, as a fair person and a dark one belong to opposite temperaments, it follows that the one has qualities which the other does not possess, and they perceive in each other that variety which is the food of love."

"Variety? Caroline; is not that rather a rakish sentiment."

"Not a bit of it. Your prudes may chatter as they like, but us women doat upon variety, and that is one of the reasons why a dark man and a fair woman generally live more happily together than a pair of the same complexion. Where there is a sameness of disposition there is too much equality of character, and that has a tendency, after the novelty of matrimony has worn away, to engender coldness and indifference, and other causes of marital infelicities."

"Walter is fair!" murmured the countess.

"As yourself, and that is why I like him."

A pang shot through the heart of the countess, and, to hide her confusion, she turned away her face.

"What a brave, dashing way he has with him!" continued Mrs. Smythe, a light playing in her eyes, whose character could not be mistaken; "and such a shape did you ever notice his thigh, why it's as thick as my waist; and then his eyes, so intense in their brilliant flashings. I have longed, when looking at him, for just one downright good hugging in his arms."

The countess with difficulty stifled the cry that rose to her lips, and, in some amazement, asked her companion whether it would not be treason to her wedded lord.

"Treason!" responded the ardent Mrs. Smythe; "not unless you are discovered. Why, the men have their frailties—I know my husband has; and I would undertake to say that at this moment he is in the arms of a pert hussy he has secreted somewhere near St. John's Wood. I don't interfere with the thing—I know it would be useless; and, therefore, I think that as he deprives me of a portion of his society, I ought to have some compensation for the loss."

"How can you say so, Caroline?" exclaimed the countess, her countenance crimsoning, though, at the suggestions which the remark provoked.

"Tit for tat is man's law; and why should it not be woman's also?" cried the vivacious Mrs. Smythe; "and the men, I believe, in speaking of us married women, irreverently say that, 'Slices from cut loaves are never missed;' so that they not only ill-treat us by their neglect, but actually put mischief into our heads. If the men will be merry, they teach their wives to be so also; and if that noble-looking fellow, Walter Morris, was to fall into my way when I'm in this humour, I am rather inclined to think I should be excessively good-natured."

"Why you just now ran away from his shadow."

"Oh! but I was taken by surprise. You would have done the same had you seen, or fancied you had seen, a tall man standing by your bed-side."

At this stage of the conversation these two lovely young women retired to bed, and were soon enlaced in each other's arms. The dark hair of the one mingled on the snow-white pillow with the clustering bright ringlets of the other, and formed, with their matchless faces glowing and radiant with beauty and health, a picture upon which no male eye could long have gazed with impunity. They were both falling into the slumber that brings either good or evil dreams, when Mrs. Smythe murmured:

"Violet, darling."

"Yes, Caroline."

"We may as well go to the fortune-teller's to-morrow."

"Very well."

"Good-night, and may each of us dream of the man we like best."

The image of Walter floated before the mental eye of the countess, until she fell into a light sleep, broken by murmurings and whisperings, and every now and then a firm clasp of the neck which her beautiful arm encircled.

They had not been long asleep, when a panel in the oaken wainscoating of the room was pushed aside, and the figure of a man crept from a recess behind, and stepped gently on to the yielding carpet on the floor of that sumptuously-furnished bed-chamber. The subdued light of the lamp fell on the bed, and disclosed the sleeping beauties as they lay nestled in each other's arms. Their mingled hair breathed a delicious perfume, and their breathings were like the gentle sighs of the wind through the trees on a calm summer's night.

"She here!" muttered the intruder, as he stood gazing on the bewitching occupants of the bed with inflamed eye-balls.

"Oh, Violet, Violet, if you knew the agony, the deep, unutterable anguish your coldness causes me, you would pity, perhaps forgive him, who never wilfully sought to do thee a wrong!" As he uttered this half-aloud, he leaned over the bed, and imprinted a warm kiss on the moist lips of the countess.

"Walter! my own loved Walter" whispered the sleeper, as the touch of the hot lips thrilled through her to the remotest nerve.

"Walter! dear manly Walter!" escaped also from the voluptuous lips of the lady whose dark tresses lay in glossy masses on the unspotted linen. And each, as if inspired by the same impulse, drew close to the other, and their musical murmurings mingled in broken but sweet strains.

The listener to these involuntary confessions of attachment stood for a while like one who has been smitten with the palsy; and then, heaving a groan of suppressed but fearfully acute anguish, noiselessly departed by the way he had entered, carefully closing the aperture after him.

"Lost!—lost to me for ever!" was the agonising reflection of Lord Bloomfield, as he staggered into a drawing-room, and threw himself on an ottoman.

"A pretty ridiculous figure I should make, if detected in this burglarious-looking exit!" said Captain Morris, as he dropped himself from a window of the mansion on to a soft bed in the garden. "Here have I been prowling like a thief about the house all night, and then to be foiled at last; the devil take the women! they get me into all manner of scrapes, and are so confoundedly coy in keeping their promises, that I begin to think of exchanging into some marching regiment, and trying my luck among the squaws of Canada or the Hottentot Venuses of the Cape Where the deuce could the little baggage have bestowed herself? I could have sworn I knew her character; well, well, I shall have another opportunity. And that fawn-like figure with the raven tresses, whom I disturbed—whom could she have been? not Mrs. Smythe, with her dark eyes, flashing Cupid's own fire, I trust, for she is mischievous enough to make me the butt of the whole town."

As the captain, who was rather surly from having been disappointed in his rakish views on Alice Burton, indulged in these ruminations, he scaled the garden wall with the agility of one well accustomed to such nocturnal exploits. His alighting on the other side disturbed the equanimity of a gentleman in blue, who was disposed to be somewhat uncivil; but the captain unceremoniously drove the hard hat of the policeman over his eyes, and, in the official language used to describe such misadventures, made " clean off."

CHAPTER VI.

THE MERRY WIVES VISIT A FORTUNE-TELLER'S, AND RESOLVE TO LEAD A GAY LIFE.

IN fulfilment of a long-ago formed resolution, the countess and her gay companion, Mrs. Smythe, left Bloomfield House early on the following day, to pay their intended visit to a fortune-teller who had acquired some celebrity among the ladies of the fashionable world. She was one of those shrewd adventuresses who know so well how to take advantage of the tendency to superstition which appears to be natural to every degree of civilisation, and, perhaps, will never be wholly extirpated from the human mind. Indeed, so long as the doctrine of fatalism mixes so largely in all our religious convictions, it never will; for circumstances are so perpetually altering the complexion of our lives, that we are led to attribute every change in our condition to the operations of some rigid law of destiny. And thus it is how the great human family are so anxious to pry into the future. Madame Robertina extensively advertised her ability to gratify this powerful, all-pervading feeling of curiosity, but discarded all the ancient methods of imposing on the credulity of her visitors. She professed to be a mesmerist, and always had a clairvoyant in the person of an interesting young girl, gifted with the faculty of reading the past, present, and future; of calling spirits from the vasty deep, and also of describing the occurrences taking place, while in her mysterious state of coma, at the uttermost extremities of the earth. New Zealand was as easy a flight for her prescient imagination as the newly-erected house over the way, and as for the North Pole, she had long ago ascertained the precise situation of poor Sir John Franklin and his unfortunate companions, and government, acting upon her unerring intelligence, had instructed the commanders of the several searching expeditions to steer direct to the ice-bound harbour she pointed out. And as to the thoughts of any individual, either in her presence or out of it, provided their ideas assumed the English garb of language, she could read them as easily as she could the page spread before her eyes when in a state of every-day existence.

She was a wonderful creature, that clairvoyante; and no lady ever left her presence without feeling either awed or terrified at her revelations. Then, Madame Robertina ascertained the characters of people on receiving a lock of their hair or a specimen of their handwriting, and thirteen uncut postage-stamps. Piles of the latter were continually on her table, and her numerous agents could only dispose of them by allowing a liberal discount. Altogether this Madame Robertina was a very clever person; there was nothing vulgar either about herself or her establishment; all was decorous and modestly genteel; and the porter who attended to the hall door wore a solemn expression on his countenance, which no impertinent scepticism could disturb. The apartment into which visitors were first ushered was a neatly-furnished parlour, with a round table in the centre covered with the light literature of the day. As the divinity upstairs announced herself ready to receive another feverish trembler on the brink of his or her destiny, a powdered and liveried servant conducted them in turn upstairs to the drawing-room.

It so happened that the Countess of Bloomfield and Mrs. Smythe were the only arrivals; and in all due form and courtesy were promptly introduced into the presence of Madame Robertina; that lady was seated at a large writing-desk, perusing, possessing herself of the inclosures, and answering the numerous letters of her correspondents. Her replies were only lithographed copies of the various forms she had prepared to suit each particular case, and the only labour she had was writing the addresses on the envelopes. The original letters were thrown carelessly into a waste-paper basket, and another held the countless locks of hair, of every imaginable hue, which were daily submitted to her minute inspection. This learned interpreter of the decrees of the fates was something beyond the middle age, and had a venerable, imposing aspect. Her black hair was streaked with grey, which, when the light fell on it, gave her a kind, motherly appearance. Her face was as pale as marble, death-like in colour; but a close observer might have noticed that it was an artificially-prepared one; the enamel disclosed itself when the mouth opened, which it seldom did; for, like the oracles of old, she only spoke when inspired. Her vocation was to listen, and solemnly expound. The dress which she wore was of black satin, and fitted tightly round her short, plump figure. A massive gold chain, suspended from her neck to her waist, sparkled on this rich rich ground, and completed her official costume.

She bowed gravely to her visitors as they entered, and with a gesture requested them to be seated. Regarding them with more curiosity than she usually bestowed on her votaries, she, in not an unpleasant voice, demanded their names.

" Mrs. Brown," " Mrs. Jenkins," were the replies.

These were duly entered in the visitor's book, and then, in a very business-like way, came the question as to the purport of their errand. The two ladies, who evidently had anticipated seeing an old woman of the ancient pack-of-cards and dismal-owl school, were much embarrassed at the position in which they found themselves, and for some little time were unable to speak. At length Mrs. Brown, alias Mrs. Smythe, hesitatingly said:

" Having been informed of your extraordinary powers in the art of—what the vulgar—I mean what is generally termed—fortune-telling, we desire some proofs of your ability."

" Ask and you shall receive; but, as a preliminary,

I require the payment of a guinea from each of you."

The money was speedily paid; and Mrs. Smythe, whose natural assurance was rapidly returning, then inquired:

"You say you can describe a person's character from the colour of the hair. You see what mine is; now what should you say my disposition was?"

"Hum! dark hair, dark eyes, and a rich embrowned complexion. You belong to the sanguine-bilious temperament, and, although possessed of immense control over your emotions, are naturally fiery and impetuous, ardent in your passions, and bold in seeking to gratify your inclinations."

Mrs. Smythe, with a slight sneer, objected that these were the attributes commonly assigned to persons of her temperament.

"Not always," retorted Madame Robertina, rather sharply; "they may be subdued by culture. Yours never were, from your cradle to your present blooming womanhood. You never permitted a want or a longing to remain unsatisfied. You belong to that high class of sensualists who mingle a refinement with their desires which softens their moral asperities. Your career has been a chequered one, bright and dark by turns; and so it will be to the end of your existence."

And, as if her words were as precious as the golden links by her side, she turned to the countess.

"Light hair, floating in golden masses over shoulders of dazzling brightness, eyes of deep blue, and a complexion in which the red struggles with the white of the Parian marble; you, my sweet young lady," continued she, addressing the countess in milder tones than those she had previously assumed, belong to the sanguine-nervous class, with no slight dash of the lymphatic. In disposition you are yielding and unsteady, but when influenced by one grand sentiment, can be pertinacious in your hastily-formed determinations, even to the extreme of obstinate persistance in error. Your desires are not violent, but they are impulsive. You would yield to the ardour of love, and then bitterly regret the concession. You are peculiarly susceptible of love in its sexual sense, and, when animated by the presence of an object to which you would be drawn by an invisible and imperious attraction, would bathe in the flood of ecstacy into which you would willingly plunge, until your senses reeled with the intoxication of enjoyment, and you fell into the stupor of satiety."

"Hold!" exclaimed the countess, her warm blood firing at the suggestion, and her eyes emitting flashes of light.

"Would you know something of the past and the future?" said Madame Robertina, relapsing into the formal manner in which she had first addressed them.

"Yes," resolutely exclaimed Mrs. Smythe, who thought the old woman before her no other than a mere stringer together of apt phrases; "tell me of the past, and then I shall be able to estimate your prognostications as to the future at their real value."

"Be it so." And, with this brief reply, this learned expounder of physiological attributes left the apartment.

"Caroline, dear," whispered the countess, "let us go away; I feel alarmed already. That woman has a mysterious knowledge of human nature."

"Tut, tut," was the laughing reply; "she has only told us what we both knew long ago. It needed neither witch nor ghost to tell us that we were partial to the society of the opposite sex."

"Hush! she comes!"

"Madame Robertina returned, leading by the hand an interesting-looking girl, of apparently about fourteen years of age. She was clad in a white dress, that fitted close up to the throat, and tightly round her slender, sylph-like shape. Her face was pale—painfully so; and was rendered more so by the expression of two remarkably-large black eyes, that threw their glances around with a kind of stealthy rapidity.

"Allow me, ladies, to introduce you to Miss Fanny Clarinville, the most celebrated clairvoyante of the present or any other time, since the world lost its faith in the spiritual communings of the soul;" said Madame Robertina, with some pomposity.

Both the ladies regarded the child with affectionate interest; but her conductress, contrary to her usual custom, prohibited any approach or conversation between them; and proceeded, in the usual manner of the mesmeric operators, to place the young creature in a chair, and then go through the ceremonies that are considered necessary to produce that state of repose which is supposed to liberate the mind from the restricted sphere of action inseparable from contact with the body.

The remainder of the formula having been gone through, the girl, who either feigned or was really under the influence of the mesmeric sleep, was pronounced ready for examination. The death-like features, and the rapid passes which the operator made over the head of the girl, producing occasionally spasmodic contractions, had their influence upon the already severely taxed nervous strength of the countess and Mrs. Smythe; but the latter disdained to exhibit any signs of timidity in the presence of the presuming old woman, whom she had begun instinctively to hate. Dislike, as it is with one ardent species of love, commences at first sight—it is an intuitive prejudice, which defies the strongest judgment and the most elaborate reasoning. It was precisely so in the present instance. Mrs. Smythe had never, to her knowledge, seen Madame Robertina before; but she felt a repugnance to the society of the latter rapidly stealing upon her. And, strange to say, as this sentiment grew stronger, so, in proportion, did the more amiable one of a warm concern for the pale fragile creature who sat so motionless in her seat. Little time, however, was allowed for silent speculations, for Madame Robertina's manner became impressively imperative, as as she requested that the clairvoyante might not be kept in her exhausting condition longer than was absolutely necessary.

"Let us go away," whispered the countess, frightened at the rigid expression which the face of the girl conveyed.

Mrs. Smythe returned a resolute denial to this request, and, flashing the full glance of her brilliant eyes upon the small ferret ones of the operator, emphatically demanded to be informed of the incidents in her previous life. Madame Robertina placed several of her fingers on the various organs of the girl's head. The questions addressed to her elicited the following startling revelations—startling to their object, for, in her bewilderment and terror, she never surmised the possibility of collusion between the mesmerist and the clairvoyante:

"I see a country school, with a rippling brook at the end of the pleasant old garden. There are girls of various ages romping and playing with each other. Among them is one of striking beauty—dark, tall, and slender, with eyes overflowing in their liquid radiance. She walks apart from her merry playmates, absorbed in thought. An opened letter is in her hand, which, as she reads, brings blushes to her cheek, and a brightness to her large black eyes. I see the sun go down behind a range of forest-clad hills; the twilight is deepening into the sable of night, and that fairy-looking girl is stealing through a gap in the fence of that old garden; she crosses the brook over the trunk of a prostrated tree, and, with the swiftness of the wind, flies to the shelter of a clump of trees on a gentle acclivity. A gentleman darts forward, throws his cloak over her shoulders, and then clasps her passionately in his arms."

Mrs. Smythe started as if she had been stung by a wasp; her face became deadly white; and, to sustain herself, she grasped the back of a chair with one of her slender gloved hands. This emotion was unobserved by the countess; but the small, keen eyes of the mesmerist noted it with a twinkling satisfaction. The girl went on, her low voice falling sweetly on the silence that prevailed.

"The pair indulge in the caresses of fond lovers, and walk beneath the stars that, one by one, are peeping out above, and, with his arm about her thrown, they slowly enter beneath the dense foliage that decks the mountain side. A mist hides them from my sight—all is dark and indistinguishable, save a long, unbroken sea of forest leaves. But the moon opens her silvery eye upon the night, and I see them again. They are seated on the mossy root of a huge tree—she is weeping on his bosom, and he is soothing her with the long-enduring kisses of early love. The rays of the moon, pouring through the branches of the tree above them, fall on his bare, lofty forehead, shaded with clustering chesnut hair; there is a gleam in his eye, and a glow on his cheeks, like that which mantles the face of a warrior flushed with conquest. Now she is calmer—her frame quivers with the thrill of love—and she hangs convulsively round his neck. Their eyes meet, and they yield themselves up to the rapture of a long and passionate embrace. Now they arise—the lover tenderly adjusts his cloak on her shoulders, and, with an arm encircling her waist, half carries the sinking girl to the brook-side. She is too faint to cross, and he bears her over in his stalwart arms. Another kiss—another—and another, and the girl totters up that old garden, and disappears."

A choking sob burst from the now terribly-agitated Mrs. Smythe, which so alarmed the now ashy-faced countess, that she earnestly intreated that they might leave the place at once.

"Not yet," uttered Mrs. Smythe, hoarsely; "let the dreamer proceed. I wish to know more."

"The school, and the old garden, and the forest scene vanish," resumed the pretended or real clairvoyante; "and I see a room darkened, and in it a bed, on which that same fairy-like girl tosses in unutterable agony. There is a lean old man and a stout, ruddy-faced woman, in whispering conversation. There is a bustle and confusion, a long-drawn shriek, the shrill cry of a child, and the ruddy-complexioned woman hurries from the room, with something in her arms carefully wrapped up. The sufferer falls into a state of insensibility, the room darkens, the bed, the furniture, the old man disappear; and I can see no more."

"The child! what became of the child?" gasped Mrs. Smythe.

"It lives, but——" Here the utterance of the girl died slowly away.

"She is exhausted," said Madame Robertina.

"One more question?" hurriedly asked Mrs. Smythe.

"The gentleman—him with the high clear forehead and curling chesnut locks?"

The girl appeared suddenly to revive, and with some animation revealed, as bidden by the conductor of her will:

"I see a battle field; men are marching through grass that nearly tops their shoulders; there is a flash of steel, an overhanging smoke, and rapid advances. The turbans of men approaching are seen in the distance. The combatants close upon each other—there is a waving to and fro—and men are falling like the leaves in autumn. The turbans are borne away at the bayonet's point, crushed and trampled down by the ranks of red squadrons of cavalry. At length they have all gone; the smoke rises in curling wreaths; and there are the dead and dying in their ghastly disorder. In one corner of a field, upon some hastily-collected branches, lies an officer, his life-blood oozing rapidly from a frightful wound in his chest. He kisses the portrait of a full, dark-eyed girl; his head droops—he sinks upon his face. Ah! merciful heaven! a roar, and a bound—and the next instant that once gay and manly form is borne, in the jaws of a ferocious tiger, into the dark recesses of the neighbouring jungle. I saw his face as his head trailed through the grass—it was that of the chesnut-haired lover's."

"My God!" exclaimed the countess, as she clung to the fainting form of her friend.

Madame Robertina, more collected, administered a powerful cordial, which soon had the effect of restoring her patient to a state of consciousness.

"Do you wish to put any other question to the clairvoyante?"

"No, no!" exclaimed the countess.

"Can your *protegee* read the future?" inquired Mrs. Smythe, with energy.

"I see nothing but a golden light, falling on gay forms and festive scenes; oh! now I perceive some bright red characters over the portico of what appears a temple; they are—'Eat, drink, and love; the rest's not worth a straw.'"

"Nor is it!" exclaimed Mrs. Smythe, starting up, now thoroughly recovered; "and I accept the lesson—it is worshipped by lordly man; and now that the last fond tie of my unsophisticated girlhood has been severed, so it shall be by me. It shall be a tripping without measure. Come, Violet, ask, and you shall receive. I am all anxiety to know what this young enchantress can read of your past."

The more timid nature of the countess recoiled at the proposal; but the girl, probably in obedience to some preconcerted signal from her mistress, broke out into the following strain:—

"The twin rose of the dell had a pliant heart, and, in the greenwood shade, exchanged vows of stainless love with the fair-haired playmate of her happy childhood. She wantoned in the summer breezes her luxurious temperament called round her voluptuous form, and played with the destinies as a fond lover would with her floating ringlets. She sang like a bird, all the day long, and at night dreamt of the hot breath and bubbling kisses that fell on her rosy lips during the sylvan ramble of the evening. The girl sprang into the woman, and the playmate who had respected her youth and innocence stood aloof, while another, cast in Apollo's mould, soothed her senses with honeyed words and flattering promises. The glance of his dark eye kindled in her a fire she had never felt before, and she bartered the love of the greenwood shade for that of his who had the gilded trappings of rank and wealth to bestow on the rose of the dell. Her maidenhood was unspotted—pure as the fairest lily of her native valley—because she was untempted. Her wifehood has been one of trouble, because it has been a dissatisfied one. The traditions of her youth cling in her memory; and, tossed upon a wild sea of sorrow, regret, and passion, her course, like that of her ardent friend, is towards the temple on which the Assyrian voluptuary has set his seal—'Eat, drink, and love; the rest's not worth a straw.'

"Courage, Violet, our woman's wit will carry us safely through it all!" exclaimed Mrs. Smythe; " and it is consoling to know that we are to go the primrose way to the everlasting bonfire."

The countess composed her visage, from which the roses had fled, and allowed its lineaments to relax into a smile; the manner of her more determined friend had inspired her with courage, and she saw nothing very dreadful in the prospect of breathing the incense of enjoyment and adoration. She ventured to put a question, and the reply of the girl was as prompt as, to her, it was startling.

"The fair-haired friend of your youth is even now gazing earnestly into the clear depths of the eyes of a sylph-like girl, over whose head scarce eighteen summers can have passed."

"The scene—the place—where?" uttered both the ladies simultaneously.

"Bloomfield House."

"Lucy!"—"My sister!" were their separate ejaculations, as a jealous pang made their hearts leap again.

"Let us go," said the countess, softly.

Mrs. Smythe no longer objected, and in a few seconds Madame Robertina and her apt young pupil were alone.

"Wake up, my little queen," said madame, gaily; and, "as you have acquitted yourself so well, you shall take a whole holiday."

The child's eyelids slowly drew up, but quickly fell down again, for the light proved too strong for their weakened power; and it was not until she had repeatedly opened and shut them that they distended to their natural size. At first she stared round her vacantly, and then, as she gradually recognised the familiar objects around her, in piteous accents imploringly said :

"Oh, mother, don't let me say any more lessons to-day!"

"You shan't, my queen," was the assuring reply. "You shall have all the day to yourself."

The clairvoyante clasped her pale, thin hands together, and rapturously exclaimed :

"What a good mother you are. I know, when you say that, you are going to take me into the country to see the green fields and the flowers, and the trees, and hear the pretty little birds sing, as if they were thanking God for giving them such nice homes."

"Not to-day," was the brief but not severely-spoken negative.

The child, with her well-trained docility, knew that was sufficient, and although the tears sprang into her eyes, meekly curtseyed, and left the room.

"I have them both in my toils," muttered the mesmerist; "I have breathed upon them a spell which will prepare them for any purpose. Their natural desires are already inflamed, and the old woman will yet revenge the slight of her poisoned youth. True, I fell, and disobeyed a human law, by obeying the dictates of a natural one. I dared to take my fill of love without the sanction of parson or priest, and I was scorned, reviled, and thrown helpless on the cold, hard stones of a colder and harder world. My own sex hounded me on to my destruction, avoided me as a contagion—a moral pestilence; and I went forth to seek my fortune under the doom of a bitter curse. For that wrong I swore to be revenged—to make woman's lust her punisher—and well have I kept my oath. I have made and then unmasked the secret harlot; and she has felt, as I once did, the agony of shame, remorse, and what fools call repentance."

"Repentance! pshaw! it is the loser, the puny thing who lacks courage to browbeat, tamper with, and hoax the gullible multitude, who should repent; not the woman or the man who sharpens her or his instincts by indomitable perseverance and consistency in a chosen line of conduct. But our moral teachers hash up the nonsense of traditions and precedents, and, forsooth, fancy them sufficient to restrain the appetites and propensities of races who daily and hourly have sensual provocatives before them. It is in this, as it is in everything else they attempt to deal with. They first deny the mind and the heart elbow-room, and then look grave, and frown and punish, should those expansive commodities find it for themselves. But it is only a few of the victims to the code who know anything about it, and, as I am one of those, perhaps a favoured one, it shall be my task to turn my knowledge to my own advantage; and who dare affirm it an impossibility that, in the pursuit of wealth and my revenge—that is my attendant genius—my ministering demon—but I may in time bring princes and potentates to my feet."

In about an hour after this extraordinary scene, the squat, dumpy figure of Mrs. Wriggles might have been seen emerging from that mysterious house, and standing upon the door steps for a minute or two, in the true style of old womanish hesitation. Yes, there was the veritable Mrs. Wriggles, with her inflamed visage, burning eyes, faded straw bonnet, black stuff dress, and ample snuff-coloured shawl. With all the gravity of her advanced years, she gazed round her awhile, as if pondering upon the direction in which she should go, and, after due deliberation, took that which led to Bloomfield House.

CHAPTER VII.

THE ADVENTURE OF COLONEL STANLEY.

IT was mentioned, at the close of the fourth chapter of this narrative, that Colonel Stanley, after his precipitate exit from Bloomfield House, met with an adventure of a severe character. It is therefore in this place that the particulars should be detailed, as well as those of a subsequent incident, of no slight influence in the development of this narrative. The colonel had rushed wildly into the square, and had plunged desperately through the throng there assembled, and from thence into the first street that offered itself, when his headlong course was arrested by several herculean men springing upon him, and forcibly placing him in a cab, which had evidently been in waiting some hours.

"Squeak louder than a prowling mouse," whispered a gruff voice in his ear, "and, so sure as your name's Stanley, I'll drive this chisel into your heart."

"What is the meaning of this outrage," demanded the colonel, the most terrible suggestions crossing his mind.

"Silence!"

"If it is robbery you intend, take all I have—my purse, my watch!"

"Silence, fool!"

"Would you murder me, ruffians? Help! help!"

A handkerchief was thrust into his open mouth; and the same instant he fell senseless to the bottom of the cab.

"He's safe now for some hours," muttered one of the two men in the cab; and, putting his head out of the window, added, "drive like blazes, Jem, or I'm afraid we shall be too late. The moon has turned, and they say those in consumptions go off at that time. Heaven send that she may be alive to see the scoundrel face to face, and identify him!"

The other man never spoke a word, but buried himself in a corner of the cab, as if absorbed in either thought or sorrow.

For upwards of an hour the vehicle, proceeding at a rapid pace, traversed the miles of streets that compose the territory of this gigantic metropolis, and finally stopped before a mean, solitary house, that stood at some distance from one of the most dismal roads in Bermondsey. To alight and drag their prisoner inside, was but the work of a minute.

"How is she?" asked the man who had previously spoken.

"Better—much better; she is now asleep; don't make a noise, for people in her state towards the last are very wakeful," replied a withered hag-like woman, as she held up her skinny finger to enforce her wish.

Both of the men seemed relieved by the information, and, throwing their heavily-breathing burden on a heap of straw, left him to recover as he best could, while they seated themselves on low stools by a bed rudely formed of boards, but curtained by sheets fastened to hooks in the ceiling. Daylight had long since broken, and coming through the broken window of that squalid room, disclosed the whole of its contents to the eye. Its appearance was miserable in the extreme. The floor was clogged with dirt, and the walls were of the hue of the chimney, with here and there a coarse print of a tawdry female figure suspended from them. The furniture consisted of a solitary chair, a two-legged square table, which leaned against the wall for support, and the two stools which were occupied by the men who sat so grimly silent. The old woman, with her head leaning over the fireless grate, was smoking from a short black pipe, the fumes of which she puffed up the chimney, and between every "draw" turned to cast a glance of malignant hatred on the prostrate form of the colonel, which she watched intensely with her glittering, rat-like eyes. The two men, who were in the garb of mechanics, appeared about the middle age, and were strong and thick-set in figure; but there was a peculiarity of expression in their bronzed and hairy faces, which spoke of evil passions, coarse indulgences, and familiarity with scenes of violence and mischief. One of them appeared to be labouring under excessive emotion, for his burly frame shook, and his eyes moistened, as he glanced at the ominously-still bed, and then, as he directed them to where the colonel lay, they would glare with intense ferocity.

"She is waking," whispered the old woman, whose more acute hearing had caught the sound of the rustle of the bed-clothes; "when does the tide turn?"

"At seven," lowly replied the more indifferent of the two men.

The old woman gave vent to a groan, and then retired again to the chimney corner.

"Father!" uttered a feeble female voice from the bed.

The curtains were hastily but gently put aside, and the sun, which had long before poured its beams into the room, fell upon the pallid features of a young girl, evidently in the last stage of that fell disease—consumption. She must have once been pretty, for her face was cast in a delicate mould; her nose, though now pinched and sunken, was beautifully formed, and her mouth small, and slightly pouting over a dimpled chin. Her eyes were of winning blue, and her dark auburn hair was neatly braided on her pale and sunken cheeks.

"Father!" she murmured.

"Yes dear," responded the man, whose agitation has been noticed.

"Shall I see him before I die, as you promised?"

"I swear you shall," was the hushed reply; "but keep quiet; you will soon be better, my poor child."

The sob that accompanied this assurance prevented further utterance, for, from the change that was rapidly taking place in the invalid's countenance, the agonised parent saw that all would soon be over."

"Wake him up, Bill," he hurriedly whispered to his companion; "give him water, brandy, or hell-fire, but wake him up; my child must die in peace."

Bill proceeded to do as he was bidden, and, with prudent forethought, dragged the still insensible colonel into an outhouse at the rear of the premises.

"Bill," said the father, suddenly standing in the doorway, "when he comes to, tell him all about my poor girl; you know what to say—her dying request; say nothing about the serving out—palaver him over."

"Leave it all to me, Ned; I loves the child as if she was my own," replied Bill, in the same low key, as he commenced operations by taking off the colonel's neckcloth, and propped him, in a sitting posture, against the wall.

"Father, are you sure he will come—did he promise?" inquired the dying girl, with touching confidence.

"He did, my pretty one," said the father, choking with grief. "Don't speak. Be quiet, darling, as the kind doctor wished you: do, Mary, for my—your poor father's sake!"

The girl, by a motion of her eyes and mouth, desired her father to kiss her—he did so; and as she appeared to be dozing off to sleep, that man of sin knelt down, and, for the first time since he was a boy, prayed for the salvation of his deceived and broken-hearted child. It was a blessed space in that man's life, offered up to the throne of Sovereign Goodness. And who knows, but in that glorious interval stolen from the hours of blood-red passion, but many a deed of guilt was wiped away for ever? Be that as it may, he was soon recalled from his prostrate attitude by the feeble moanings of the dying girl.

"Frederick!" she murmured.

"Is here," said Bill, softly, as he rather dragged than led the colonel to the bed-side.

"Frederick!" she again murmured, a smile like the first faint blush of morn radiating her countenance, as she recognised her seducer; "one kiss!—it will be the last poor Mary will ever give you!"

The colonel, whose hair was damp and matted, his face haggard, and eyes bloodshot, mechanically stooped down and took the proffered salute.

"Father—dear father!—do you forgive me?" gently sighed the fast sinking girl.

"I do, I do; but you need it not—you are as pure as one of God's angels," sobbed the wretched parent, as he buried his broad face in the bed-clothes.

The smile deepened into one of ineffable joy; the dove-like eyes fastened a forgiving look on her undoer, and, with a gently-drawn sigh, all was over.

"She's gone — the tide's turned," said the old woman, softly, as if afraid of disturbing the dead.

The colonel, upon whom the announcement operated like an electric shock, turned to flee; but a gripe of iron was laid upon his shoulder, and a stern visage peered menacingly into his.

"We haven't done with you yet," said Bill.

"Give me back my child!" shouted the bereaved parent, springing to his feet, and seizing the colonel savagely by the naked throat. The minutes of the latter would have been few indeed, had not the over-taxed energies of his assailant suddenly given way,

and he have fallen back on the bed insensible. Bill, with a sudden jerk, threw the colonel violently on the floor, and, kneeling on his chest, with the willingly-afforded aid of the old woman, bound his arms tightly and securely to his side. That done, the feet had similar restraint imposed on them; and the now thoroughly exhausted colonel was dragged by the heels to the outhouse, and deposited in a corner on some straw, with as much deliberation as if he had been a log of wood.

"Mercy!" he gasped. "I have wealth—a thousand pounds—two—three——"

The only reply was the bang of the door as it closed upon him, and the gruff voice of Bill, saying to the old woman:

"Give him water or brandy in abundance, but not a bit of grub—not even a dry crust. He let that poor dead girl starve to death; and now let him feel what it is to be hungry, and cold, and wet!"

The old woman chuckled forth a dry laugh, and the colonel—the rich, the fashionable Colonel Stanley, the most accomplished and successful gallant of the day—was left to his dismal meditations, with a conviction every moment freezing his heart's blood, that only a few yards' distance from him lay the inanimate remains of the once simple girl, whom, with his fine person and warm promises, he had lured from virtue and the peaceful avocations which she adorned by her neatness, taste, and honest industry.

On the following day there was a very humble funeral in the squalid churchyard close by. On the coffin was simply inscribed, "Mary." The only mourners were the father and the man designated as "Bill." Both were pale; but beyond that, neither of them betrayed any other signs of emotion. They waited until the grave had been filled up, and then slowly and sadly left the spot.

"She's gone!" said Bill, "so don't take it to heart. This is a queer world for the womenfolk. If they goes a point out of their proper course they takes it to heart, and those that does the same and is never found out begins abusing of them, and the poor things either takes to drink, or jumps into the river, or dies sweetly."

"If it warn't for serving that swell out, I'd wish to be in the coffin with her," said the father.

"Hold up Ned! Mary's better off than we are. She is in a place we shall never darken."

Upon arriving at the solitary house, which looked more dismal by day than night, the pair adjourned to the rear of the premises, and by means of a trapdoor descended into a long passage, leading to a number of vaults, which in former times had evidently been used for contraband purposes. They each carried a lighted candle to guide them, and, upon arriving at a low, massive-looking door, undid the fastenings on the outside, and admitted themselves into a recess or cell, the roof of which barely permitted them to stand upright. In a corner upon some newly-spread straw sat the colonel. A pitcher of water and a loaf of bread was by his side, together with a black bottle, evidently containing something more potent than the liquid in the other utensil. The colonel, whose appearance was wretched in the extreme, was fastened to the wall by means of a strong chain about three feet in length. He evidently considered that the hour of his final doom had arrived, and had summoned up resolution to meet it with fortitude. But to die in such a horrible place, far away from friends, home, and the multitude of affections which cling round the heart-strings of even the most dissipated, was too much for his endurance. He asked for mercy.

"What mercy did you show my child?" demanded the father. "A year ago she was a good, virtuous girl; three weeks ago I found her dying of cold and hunger—starved to death villain, and all through your base treachery! My God! I wonder what keeps me from tearing you to pieces!"

"Be cool, Ned; a promise is a promise," interposed Bill, "and it ought to be kept.'

"I will keep it, Bill" rejoined his companion; "but I must speak. What good did it do you to ruin my poor innocent child?"

The guilty can only make specious defences. The colonel little thought when he seduced the milliner's pretty apprentice, that he would ever have to be called to account for the deed.

"She voluntarily consented to avail herself of my protection, and left me of her own accord," said he, falteringly.

"Its a lie!" thundered the indignant father; "you introduced yourself to her under a false name, and left her three weeks after she went to live with you. She told me all, and how, to prevent going altogether to ruin, as she had seen other girls do, she took to

needlework—to making those d—d cheap shirts, that I wonder don't blister the backs of the men that wear them; and by sharing a garret with another victim of the cursed Jews of London—the curse of God light on the whole tribe! She managed to live on bread and tea, and p'rhaps a potatoe now and then, until one day she saw you in a fine carriage, and found out that you was not Frederick Smith, the linendrapers' assistant, who only waited for a berth to marry her; but Colonel Stanley, a name as well known among the milliners' girls at the West End, as the rankest bawd's in St. James's Street. From that moment she sickened and pined away, until she could work no longer, and then she starved, for her fellow-lodger had died of the fever. An acquaintance of mine heard of her by accident, and that's how I brought her to my place, and tended her until she went to heaven, like a blessed angel as she was."

"May God forgive me!" exclaimed the colonel, burying his face in his hands.

"Well may you ask that," resumed the father, and, unheeding the interruption, went on with what he had evidently charged himself to deliver before consummating his purpose.

"She prayed to see you, and I wrote to you, and called several times, but you took no notice; and seeing that she was fast going, and wouldn't die happy without seeing you, I put some hands on your track, and at last took you as you was coming, harum scarum out of Bloomfield House. That's all I have got to say; and now hearken to what I am going to do to you, just by way of revenge."

"Would you murder me in cold blood?" interrupted the colonel, horror-struck at the cold, malignant smile that swept over the man's face.

"Murder you!" replied the man, sneeringly; "what good would that do me? No, no, I promised *her* not to kill you, and I'll keep my word; but I'll make you howl like a mad dog before I have done with you. Just look round the nice little place you are in."

The colonel could not resist casting a glance at the fearful vault that was his prison, and shuddered convulsively as he did so.

"Well, then, my precious jewel," said the man with an unearthly chuckle, "just consider it an eligible little bit of freehold of your own!"

The colonel started up with a cry of horror.

"It's a fact," continued the man; "here you live and here you die, if it was a hundred years to come; so, as you'll have plenty of time on your hands, I hope you will make good use of it. You will never see me again, so take the curse of a man in whom all mercy died when his child died, and may the ghosts of all the girls you have murdered haunt you night and day!"

This malediction was uttered with passionate energy, and when he had concluded, he turned abruptly on his heel.

"In the matter of grub," said Bill, in a mocking tone of consolation, "you'll have lashings of bread and water, and a quartern of gin every day to keep the steam up; and as to company, you will find the rats rather lively, especially when the tide's up!"

The pair then left, and carefully locked and barred the door. The colonel, thus left in utter darkness, gave vent to a piercing cry of agony, and then fell back, utterly crushed by the hideous doom which his punishers had inflicted upon him. After the lapse of many hours, consciousness returned, to disclose to him once more the frightful horrors of his situation. It was appalling; not a sound reached his ears, save, now and then, the squeak of a rat; and the darkness was rendered more intense by the small red spots which his weakened vision threw into it. He groaned and wept, and for the first time in his life that haughty man felt humbled and subdued. He tried to pray, but the words died away in rattles in his throat, and all he could do was to weep. After a while, he became more composed; and, feeling the gnawing pangs of hunger, for he had eaten nothing for upwards of forty hours, groped about for the bread and water; which, having found, he partook of ravenously. The spirit bottle having also fallen in his way, he took a hearty draught; and then, completely tired out and exhausted, lay down, and was soon in a sound, refreshing slumber. How long he slept he had no means of ascertaining; it must have been for many hours, for when he was awakened, by the jarring of the door opening and shutting, he felt considerably refreshed. His day's allowance was placed within his reach by some person who maintained a rigid silence; and for seven days did this painfully regular visit occur. The colonel, into whose very marrow the chill and damp of his cell seemed to have penetrated, was rapidly sinking into the despair which produces madness; life had become a heavy burden to him in that dreadful darkness, and it was probable he would have dashed out his brains on the wall, had not relief come most opportunely and unexpectedly. It was on the eighth day, about the hour, as he guessed, his food usually came, when, as the door opened, a dazzling light from a lamp darted into the dungeon, and half blinded his weakened eyes. When he had become able to endure it, he observed that it was borne by a man of ghastly visage, who supported himself by leaning on a staff. Long sickness, or some other prostrating cause, had reduced a once evidently remarkably vigorous frame; and although perhaps, from the smoothness of his face, he might not have been supposed in reality to have exceeded thirty years of age, gave him the appearance of fifty. He was closely shaven, but his hair was white as snow.

The colonel at first imagined the figure to be an illusion of his disordered brain, or the ghost of some former tenant of his noisome dungeon; and it was not until the intruder had spoken, that he was assured of his being of really flesh and blood creation.

"Be not afraid!" said the spectre-looking man, in hollow tones; "I have partly heard your story, and pity you. Now I am, or rather used to be, a blunt kind of man, and all that I can say is, if I serve you will you serve me?"

"Give me liberty—let me see the blue sky once more!" cried Stanley, catching with extraordinary avidity at the prospect of release that opened thus dimly upon him, "and the moment I reach my residence, a thousand pounds shall be yours!"

The man, who seemed scarcely to have any life in his body, coldly assented to the proposal, but annexed two conditions.

"What are they?" exclaimed the colonel.

"First, that you obtain me a situation in Bloomfield House—anything, I don't care what it is, I only want to pass the rest of my days under its roof!"

"Granted—conclude it done. I know Lord Bloomfield well, and he cannot—dare not, refuse me the request."

"The second is, that you never tell anybody how you got in and out of this place."

"I cannot do the latter, for I shall surely prosecute the ruffians," objected the colonel, excitedly, forgetting that he had to accept, not make, conditions.

"Then you must stay here."

And the man turned to totter from the room.

The colonel instantly saw his mistake, and gave the required promise.

"You must swear to it."

The colonel readily complied, but was somewhat astounded and alarmed, when blood drawn from his arm was insisted upon as a ratifying accompaniment. The oath was a shockingly blasphemous one, and made the colonel shudder as it was administered to him.

Everything being agreed upon, the man said:

"We ought to be friends."

"I shall be ever grateful for such an unlooked-for and timely rescue," replied the colonel, warmly; "but, for heaven's sake, knock this cursed chain from my leg!"

The man handed him a key, and, as he did so, said:—

"Our cause is a common one. You have been the victim of ——"

"Man's hatred and revenge—the bitterest passions in existence," replied the colonel.

"More bitter in a woman," said the man, his palsied-looking body quivering again.

The colonel had now disengaged himself from the manacle, and eagerly pressed forward to make his escape.

"Hold! You must be blindfolded. You would be murdered if seen, without being so, by any one."

The colonel for some time strongly demurred.

"Well, then, I don't stir; and without me you would as soon get out of this place, as a mouse would out of a steel trap. Don't hesitate, for time is precious; and I heartily wish you may get out as soon as possible; for in obliging you I oblige myself!"

This was unanswerable; and his conductor, trembling excessively while he did it, securely bound a large handkerchief over his eyes. That done, he was taken by the hand, and led for nearly an hour along filthy passages, some of them so low that he had frequently to crawl along on his hands and knees, until he emerged into the cool, open air; and oh, how refreshing to him were the first bracing draughts! No parched traveller in the desert ever quaffed the long-sought waters of a gushing spring with more delight. But, notwithstanding his piteous entreaties to be allowed to have the bandage removed, it was obstinately refused. At last they reached the river-side, and embarked in a boat; and when it had been rowed for perhaps half an hour, the colonel was allowed the privilege of looking round him. The time, he found, was night, and he had passed under Southwark Bridge; and the tide being favourable, soon reached the pier at Blackfriars; where he, together with his liberator, was landed. A cab was procured; and the strangely-assorted pair, each indulging in warm, but totally opposite kinds of exultation, were driven to the residence of the colonel in Park Lane.

CHAPTER VIII.

YOUNG LOVE'S FIRST BLUSHES.

LUCY VILLIERS was a gentle, timid creature, of much the same style of beauty as her sister, the Countess of Bloomfield. Her hair was as bright in colour and as luxuriant in quantity; her eyes of the same deep, thrilling blue, but their soft rays were those of the virgin; and her lips, innocent of the prurient kiss, were fresh, moderately full, and most temptingly rosy. Her shape, though, was more slender—it had not the splendid properties of the ripened woman; she was the guileless girl, just on the borders of maturity, and there was a sweetness in her beautiful English face which won irresistibly upon the heart. She was little versed in the intrigues and mysteries of fashionable life; the great world to her was a frightful up-roar, from which she shrank back in bashful timidity, and her rural habit of blushing was as strong as when she was at coy fifteen. She was in truth one of those fascinating young things that hover on the skirts of society—like fawns afraid to mingle with the bois-terous herds—that spread themselves in dazzling array over the surface of life. On the morning that her sister paid a visit to the fortune-teller—or, as we ought to term that learned personage, the graphiologist, hairyologist, and mesmerist—Lucy was engaged in embroidering something, which had the appearance of a rich satin neckerchief, and looking quite enchanting in her pale blue morning dress. Her hair floated on her taper shoulders in endless layers of sweeping ringlets; and as she moved they would roll over each other, and creep about her small ears, and come coaxingly down to the plump little globes, which her close-fitting dress revealed, in such a bright and winning way, that you felt every moment tempted to take them in your hand to feel their glossiness, and, inhale their perfume. While she was thus engaged the door of the apartment was gently opened, and, upon Lucy raising her dove-like eyes, she beheld the tall and elegant form of her early friend, Captain Morris. She had not spoken to him for nearly twelve years, and only once had a slight glimpse of him on the previous evening. But she had never forgotten him—his hand-some, daring, dashing boyhood was as fresh in her memory as when she saw him, for the last time, waving his adieu as she stood in tears, with her mother and sister, on the threshold of their quiet home. From a child he had been her beau-ideal of manly perfection, and his continued correspondence with her family kept his image before her as clearly as if he had con-stantly been by her side. Then there were the reports of his exploits in India, of his rapid promotion, and improved worldly fortunes—for the Welsh youth had gone to England's richest colony as a mere ensign in a marching regiment—which all tended to embalm him in her recollection. She knew, too, of his love for Violet, and, when the latter wedded another, wept for the absent soldier, who thought he was fighting under a burning sun for the rose of the dell—the bride of his heart. Poor Lucy had not the courage or the inclina-tion to upbraid her sister; but, in her unsophisticated heart, she thought Violet ought to have preferred Morris before all the world. In nursing these senti-ments, it is not to be wondered at that the love of the child should have gone on gradually increasing in volume and tone, until it ripened into an attachment, of which the susceptible girl herself was scarcely conscious. It was only natural, then, that upon the entrance of Morris she should blush and pale alter-nately, and exhibit such unmistakeable symptoms of agitation, that the gallant captain rushed to her relief by apologising for the abrupt manner of his intro-duction.

"Do not be alarmed. You have probably forgotten me. By the way, the countess last night strangely neglected to introduce me; but, hearing you were alone, I introduced myself, after the old country fashion. Your angel of a mother detested formality. But have you forgotten me, Lucy?"

"Walter!" murmured the girl, tears of welcome and joy springing from her eyes.

"You were quite a rosy little child when I left home," said Morris, as, with the tender manner of an old friend, and the well-bred courtesy of a gentleman, he clasped her outstretched little hand within his own; "and you have grown so marvellously tall and beautiful, that I at first imagined I saw Violet, just as I left her on the day before I went away. But time

works wonders, and I ought to have known that, at the end of twelve years, we are very different beings to what we were at the commencement."

Lucy's excessive embarrassment soon subsided, under the influence of a long gossip about the "old house at home," their former rambles, absent friends, and those thousand fond inquiries which are interest-ing to parties who have been long absent from each other.

"Do you remember all the sunny places we used to visit in our long rambles?" inquired the captain, gaily; "our races up the hill-sides, and the nut-gatherings, and the tree-climbings?"

"And the swing in the old garden, on which you used to hold me?" interrupted Lucy, with almost childish glee.

"Bless my heart, yes!" exclaimed the captain, as a hundred reminiscences of his uncorrupted youth flashed across his memory.

"And your dear mother used to scold you for tearing your clothes in climbing the trees!"

"And me, thoughtless fellow, never thinking she could ill afford to buy me fresh ones!"

And in this kind of prattle they whiled away the hours, until Morris felt a large portion of his youth-ful feeling returning, and the glow of purity warming his heart to sensations to which he had long been a stranger. The most dissipated, nay, even the lowly depraved, have their communings with the spirits that labour so industriously in the promotion of the goods that hang, round the world's neck, richer than a "jewel in an Ethiop's ear."

Morris was not naturally bad, but, like most men who have been disappointed in their early fondness for women, he entertained a sordid opinion of the whole sex, and never scrupled or hesitated to avail himself of any favours they could bestow. But on the present occasion his sensations were of that refined character which gives such a zest to female society. No ignoble yearnings sullied the complexion of his thoughts. He saw before him a girl whose purity was mirrored in her soft, unruffled brow and angelic eyes; and he esteemed her as a devoted brother would a sister. His heart had been seared by too many intrigues for him to fall desperately in love at first sight, or even to entertain any warmer partiality than that which arises out of respect for innocence, and admiration for beauty. It was very different, though, with Lucy. The object of one of her most cherished memories was before her, in all the pride and grace of manly per-fection; and as she stole timid glances at his noble proportions, and noticed the pleasing vivacity of his handsome features, she felt that she had never seen a nobler-looking being. The countess little imagined, when she introduced the subject of her sister's being insulted to Morris, that there would be any danger in their meeting. The truth was, that Violet made it a pretext for once more seeing and conversing with Morris; for, despite many struggles with her convic-tion that her duty to her husband demanded an alienation from the only man she had ever really loved, she could not successfully combat the temp-tation to have him near her in the confidential capacity of adviser. Her coldness and disgust towards her husband also largely operated to bring about this disposition of mind; and when it is considered how susceptible she was to all the ardent impulses of love, it may be conceived how dangerous was the position in which she was placing herself. But sexual passion is ever reckless of consequences, and, in the end, will have its own wilful way.

"Have you known Colonel Stanley for long?"

inquired Morris, abruptly interrupting the previous conversation.

"Only since I came to town," was the low reply, as Lucy's face crimsoned at the recollection of that person's familiar behaviour.

Morris observed the change in her complexion, and candidly confessed, that in all his wanderings he had never before met with so entirely beautiful a creature. He was not the description of man to gaze unmoved upon a lovely, blushing countenance; but, to relieve Lucy from her evident embarrassment, turned the conversation to the memorable incident of the previous evening in the gardens.

The merry wives of St. Bridget's Court had not made a very favourable impression on the sensitive Lucy, and she naively inquired who they were. Morris equivocatingly replied, that they were probably some of the friends of the divinities of the kitchen, who, wishing to revenge an affront one of the party had received, had selected Colonel Stanley for their victim.

"Dismiss so trivial a circumstance from your memory," said the captain, gaily; "and let us, as in the olden time, wander, for a while, where nature holds her silent revels. Your secluded, but delicious gardens, will afford us a promenade that will at least remind us of some of the happy rambles and wild rompings we used to have in the old one at home."

Lucy readily assented, and in a few minutes afterwards they were slowly pacing the smooth walks behind Bloomfield House, engaged in animated prattle about the days that had flown, and old friends whom fate had snatched away, or allowed to remain to be the sport and playthings of their inexorable destiny. Nothing more effectually thaws the icy barrier raised by a long separation, than the reminiscences of a period of unreserved communication. The heart trained to be ruled in its yearnings by codes and creeds of conduct, relaxes in its rigour before the warmth of impulses long cherished, and which have grown out of recollections treasured with the care of a miser for his gold. The gentle girl, whose timidity takes the alarm in the presence of a stranger, no sooner hears him talk of the scenes in which he has mingled, or listens to his rapturous praises of associations with which she has been identified than he ceases to be unfamiliar to her perceptions—he is no longer a new or casual acquaintance, but one between her and whom there is a strong link connecting them together in thought and feeling. So it was with Lucy, as the past rose up before her in all its bold revealments; the rosiest pictures possible were presented to her imagination, and, under their potent influence, her virgin reserve opened, like the petals of a flower to the morning sun. Morris partook of the genial sentiment, his cultivated sensuality was hushed in the presence of such purity, and he experienced a return of those unsophisticated sensations which are natural to uncorrupted youth, when woman, in the joyous burst of her early spring time, first dazzles his ardent mind. The pair had thrown off all restraint in their manner, and Morris, led away probably by the novelty of his situation, had Lucy's hand quietly clasped in his own; and thus they sauntered along, conscious of little else save the presence of each other.

"That witch of a mesmerist was right!" uttered Mrs. Smythe, with savage slowness, as her glittering eyes fell on the forms of the youthful pair, as they turned an angle in advance of her.

The countess, as she regarded them, trembled excessively; a cold perspiration bathed her forehead, and, perhaps, for the first time in her life, she felt the bitter pangs of jealousy—the more bitter because she had hitherto indulged in the dream that Walter's affections were entirely her own. How many women who, through a mere whim, a caprice, the desire for a more distinguished social position, or any of the other causes of ill-assorted marriages, indulge in the same delusive hope! as if the love of the man for the maiden could endure in its intensity after she had bestowed her person on another! Violet, without an acute and impartial criticism, was one of this kind of young women, and she had yet to learn the lesson, that the jewel we neglect in our youth, loses its lustre as we grow older.

Mrs. Smythe was not of this avaricious disposition: her feelings were more seared, for she, perhaps, had never really loved, and in her devotion to a present grand passion she could forget every previous one. Besides, she was more calculating in her wishes, and knew mankind better than to expect that a partially extinguished love could ever be revived in any of its former strength. Disappointment, too, in her tender yearnings had rendered her somewhat sceptical as to the existence of real, unselfish affection. "The men only love us for what they can obtain from us," was her motto, and she determind that, in its application as regarded herself, it should not be exclusively monopolised by its authors. Still, with all the cold worldliness with which she clothed the attributes that constitute the harmonious union of the sexes, none could give the rein of imagination to warmer or even more wanton impulses. She was fiery and resolute in the pursuit of every gratification, but sheltered herself beneath the cold exterior of a conventional prudence, to which, for better protection, she added the pungency of a cultivated sarcasm.

Walter and Lucy, totally unconscious of being attentively watched, walked leisurely on until they had gone the round of the garden, and then came abruptly upon the countess and Mrs. Smythe. The former darted at him a look of keen reproach, while the latter indulged in a shrill laugh, which so confused the timid Lucy, that she drew her hand from the captain's, and fled hastily away.

"Captain Morris, I see, is a proficient in more characters than one," said Mrs. Smythe, bestowing on him a look full of significance.

"He can champion the cause of a friendless girl, and yet take good advantage of her sister's absence," was the spiteful reflection of the countess.

There is no position in which a man looks more silly than when detected in any familiarity, however slight, with a young woman. Walter felt the blood mount to his face, and would speedily have beaten a retreat, had not the insinuation of the countess wounded him deeply.

"By heaven! Violet, you do me great injustice!" said he, with animation; "Lucy and I were talking about all the old places we knew, and——"

"To refresh her recollection, nursed her pretty little hand."

"Such abuse of confidence is shameful."

And the two ladies sailed indignantly away, leaving the astonished Walter to indulge in any species of meditation he might think proper.

"Phew! sits the wind in that corner?" exclaimed he to himself, as he caught the parting glance of Mrs. Smythe's brilliant eyes; "I am not the one to refuse even the ghost of an invitation from a pretty woman; but as for Violet, I must save her, in despite of herself. And Lucy—what a sweet girl! upon my word I do begin to think there are more unculled flowers in the world than we gay fellows imagine. And how beautiful Violet looked in her superb anger! I must save her—reconcile her with Bloomfield, who, as a man of fashion, is not remarkably vitiated at heart. Yes, I must—*I will* save her!"

How far this virtuous determination was indebted to the impression which Lucy had made upon the volatile captain, is open to consideration; but that he was serious, could not be questioned.

"He shall be mine!" was the silent resolve of Mrs. Smythe; "he is fair, and I am dark, and it will go hard with me if I don't triumph over such innocents as Lucy and Violet. What a noble figure he has in his undress! and such eyes! And as the wind turned aside his coat, what a thigh he had!"

"Lucy shall march into the country this very day. Walter is decidedly too gay an acquaintance for a mere girl," thought the countess; and each, lady, busied with her own schemes, retired to her respective chamber. Their plots and counterplots, as will be seen, provoked some mirthful, as well as secretly grave, incidents.

As for Walter Morris, he withdrew; and as the hour was still early, he resolved to call upon his colonel, and see what plight he was in after his rough usage by the merry wives.

"Not at home," was the reply of his confidential servant; "and I feel rather alarmed about him, for he never before went out of the way without letting me know where to find him."

"Don't be alarmed, Simpson; Colonel Stanley is too good a soldier to get into any dangerous scrape."

"I am not so sure of that. Two or three queer-looking fellows have been lurking about the house lately. Do you remember that little Mary the colonel had about a year ago?"

"Perfectly. A sweet-tempered creature, was she not?"

"Master said so; but in a month or so I suppose he found a sweeter one, and left her. Well, her father was one of the men I have seen skulking about this neighbourhood."

"The d——l! And now I remember, the girl was was not a common one. Fathers, too, are vindictive. If the colonel does not turn up in the course of the day, let me know."

"I shall do so, captain, and be grateful for your kindness."

"I begin to think we men, and especially her Majesty's Guards, are most consummate rascals," thought Morris. "I have a distinct recollection of that poor girl; she was pretty, but unpolished, and I know she loved Stanley with her whole heart and soul. I must say he behaved as a confounded scoundrel in the matter, for he cut and run after he had got all he wanted. And now I dare say she is dead, and all's found out. Well, well, if Stanley does get a knock in the head it will give me a devilish good chance for a majority, so 'it's an ill wind that blows good to nobody.' As I live, there is that bewitching little creature of Violet's, who held a drum-head court-martial on her brute of a husband! She *is* fair game, or I am most deucedly deceived in that saucy wagging gait of hers."

It was indeed Alice, with a pale, severe expression of countenance. In her hand she carried a little carpet bag, and was otherwise equipped for a short journey. With her was a stout dame, having much the appearance of one high in authority in the culinary department of Bloomfield House. The captain's moralising vein gave place to one of a giddier kind, as he gaily saluted the femme de chambre of the enamoured countess.

"Whither away, my pretty little dickey-bird? Not flying from the dove-cot of Bloomfield, I trust?"

"I am going to Richmond for a few days. The countess has kindly given me leave, and Mrs. Smith is with me to—to—" stammered the young woman, blushing deeply as she encountered the ardent gaze of the now thoroughly amorous captain. How speedily our virtuous resolves disappear in the presence of temptations, and how soon do we become slaves to the vilest impulses when our instincts rebel against the convictions of our calmer moments? Captain Morris was an excellent illustration of these acknowledged maxims.

"To be your guardian angel, I presume?" said the captain; "and a capital one she will make, no doubt, for her charming face is the very picture of good-nature."

A chuck under the chin gratified the portly cicerone, and she made not the slightest demur to Morris's proposal to accompany them on their journey. Alice did, but very faintly, for in less than five minutes afterwards they were all seated in a cab, and progressing merrily towards the Nine Elms Station of the South-Western Railway.

Before four o'clock they had dined at Richmond, and were strolling through its noble park. Alice, leaning upon Morris's arm, walked first; Mrs. Smith, whom the porter and hot gin and water had rather blown, brought up the rear. Alice at first objected to their rapid pace, from the fear of losing sight of her aged protector; but Morris made love to her so desperately that he soon coaxed her out of her reluctance, and he hastened her on, heedless of the entreaties of the fatigued matron to accommodate their pace to her own. At last she was fairly tired out, and the pair had disappeared, when, making a desperate rush, she caught sight of them again, but in such an attitude, as she afterwards declared, it made the blood boil in her veins. Morris had his arms wound round the form of Alice, and the latter was passively receiving his burning kisses. The vision of the astounded Mrs. Smith grew faint— she staggered —and when she looked again, the loving couple had vanished beneath the branches of the tall trees that sheltered the velvet sward around them.

"Well, I never!" exclaimed the agitated Mrs. Smith, as, overcome with emotion and her recent panting exertions, she sat herself down at the foot of a venerable beech tree; "the hawful hiniquity of this world is dreadful—horrid; I never seed a more howdacious thing done in all my born days. For to bring me here, and then hop away, without saying how d'ye do, or good bye, or anything—it really is scandalacious, and I'm blowed if I stand it—no, that I won't!"

With this severe determination, Mrs. Smith pulled a pretty good-sized flat stone bottle from her pocket, and, extracting the cork, applied its neck to her lips, and took such a long pull, that her face assumed a deep purple dye.

"As good Old Tom has any I've tasted this many a long day. But oh!" sighed the coughing and gasping dame, "the hawful hiniquity of the young people now-a-days! They thinks on nothing but jigging and gallivanting, and having sweethearts —and the married wimen's the worst; they knows a slice from a cut quartern isn't missed, so they comes it uncommon strong when they can, and that's not seldom, for where there's a will there's a hopportunity. (Another pull at the flat bottle.) It's all very well, perhaps, while it lasts. I have gone the whole hog myself afore now, for a bit of fun; but there's a time when it aint convenient; and when a friend's in the way it's the height of impe rence to do it afore her very eyes, as if she hadn't any feelings of her own. Would I a done sich a thing? I should think not. I'd a said, 'Go snacks, and then there 'll be no snitching.' But ways alter—what was the thing five-and-twenty years agone, is called vulgar now. But, thank heaven, there's a Providence that watches over us old creatures, and throws a chance in our way now and then!"

With this consoling reflection the hopeful cook took another inspiration from the bottle, and then relapsed into some wild theory of parturition, which a friend had broached to her in confidence only a few days before. Another draught carried her into the region of song, in which she trilled until balmy slumber locked up her senses, and left her, with a pair of substantial legs, clad in white stockings and black cloth boots, stretched temptingly on the grass. Her last articulations referred to some clandestine proceedings of one Dinah,—

"Somebody's in the house with Dinah,
Playing on the old banjo."

These were her last words; for sleep sealed up her utterance, until the stars had twinkled above her head for many hours.

CHAPTER IX.

THE MYSTERIOUS ADDITION TO BLOOMFIELD HOUSE.

At the end of the stipulated week's leave of absence, Alice and her chaperone, the sleeping beauty of Richmond Park, returned to town under the protection of Morris; who, singular to relate, had every day found time to pay them a visit, and every evening, after dinner, so bewildered and led astray the astute Mrs. Smith, that she either "dropped dead asleep," as she termed it, or found herself most strangely whisked off early in the morning to Hampton Court, or some sylvan retreat on the banks of the silvery Thames, in company with one of the most impudent rogues that ever donned livery, or dived into the kitchen, on evil thoughts intent. In shady bowers, and under cover of hedges and clumps of trees, he dared to whisper certain cabalistic words into her chaste matronly ears, at which she would frown, then think darkly of her gouty old Adam at Bloomfield House; and finally, after a world of titterings and blushes, and numerous drops of comfort from the never-failing flat stone bottle, consent to wander deeper into the recesses of a charming woodland scene with that nice young man. Both parties having thus so far committed themselves to one of the extraordinary indulgences of a country excursion, were bound to each other by a mutual vow of secrecy; and, as the captain could not consistently escort them home in the style one of them ardently desired, that duty devolved on the accomplished Mr. Thomas Jackson, the smartest tiger that ever stood at the beck and call of an adventurous master.

"A jew!" cried Mrs. Smith; "I shall never—not never—forget you!"

"Nor I you!" drily responded Tom, bestowing a wink upon the now very blooming Alice.

The latter understood it perfectly well, and, reddening at the familiarity, hastened into the hall, where she encountered a person whose appearance riveted every faculty she possessed. He was a man with hair and whiskers white as snow, and such a peculiar expression of countenance, that, once noticed, it could never be forgotten. In age, he was apparently still in early manhood, for not a line wrinkled his smooth, cadaverous features. His lips, it is true, were of parchment hue, and slightly puckered, but there was not the rigidity of advanced years about them; their compression seemed more owing to smothered emotions, than the wear and tear of contending passions; and there was something in the man's whole demeanour which impressed an observer with the idea that he had become prematurely old—that a blight had fallen upon him in his prime, and reduced him to something like a ghastly wax-work automaton. In figure, there were the outlines of a burliness; but the flesh had gone, and the eye only dwelt on the sharp points and angles of an emaciated frame. His eyes, naturally of a light grey, shone with preternatural lustre, and contrasted painfully with the death-like colour of his complexion. The livery, too, bedaubed with lace, added to the frightful *ensemble*; and altogether he was such an one as might have been supposed to have had an untimely resurrection.

"What a wretch!" ejaculated Mrs. Smith, sighing over her separation from the merry companion of her last week's trip.

Alice regarded the man with a vague terror—a cold shuddering crept through her as she looked at him; and she stood gazing at the white-haired porter with an uneasiness of manner as palpable to her companion as it was to its object. He detected the spasmodic working of her features, and saw, in the dilation of her eyes, that she was striving to recal where, and under what circumstances, she had seen that singular being before. To disabuse her of this impression, he spoke in a voice so thin and reedy, that Mrs Smith actually jumped several paces aside, and looked in every direction for the blessed baby, that she was sure had crept beneath her petticoat.

"Was it you?" at length she inquired, regarding the man suspiciously.

"It was, mem." The voice now appeared to have come from the opposite extremity of the hall, and made even the stronger-nerved Alice look around her in some dismay.

"How long have you been in my lord's service?" at length she inquired.

"I entered it this morning," was the answer, in the same wonderfully small voice, that might have been supposed to have come down from the ceiling, or up from the floor, as far as direction of sound was concerned.

"Well, I never heard such a thing in all my born days!" cried Mrs. Smith; "a man for to speak out of his big toe or the hair of his head!" and, pressing closer to Alice, she whispered, "p'rhaps his voice is in his posterities, and the blue plush won't let it come out natural-like!"

"Nonsense!" said Alice, more assured, and laughing at the whimsical surmise; "he is some poor creature upon whom affliction has pressed with killing severity."

"Half-starved!" responded Mrs. Smith, in the same low key; "look at his bones sticking out like naked ribs of beef! we girls must fatten him up, for the sake of the character of the house."

"Do you belong to this mansion?" demanded the man, in a shrill voice, that sounded immediately behind the astounded cook.

"The devil himself!" roared the latter, now thoroughly frightened; and, clapping her hands behind her, flew to the kitchen, where she fell souse on the floor, and commenced kicking vigorously, and muttering her suspicions about the arch-fiend having made a mouth-piece of a certain region of her portly person.

"To come to my years and then to be bewitched

by a white-headed Bob of a walking skeleton! Oh! that ever I should have lived to hear words come out of my posterity! Oh my precious soul! Richmond Park! I knows the grass is soft and dry!—hands off, Mister Impudence! Oh!" and with this the persecuted Mrs. Smith, overcome with rum, love, and her dread of the mysterious hall-porter, fell into a state of insensibility, and was tenderly borne to bed.

Alice, more collected, stood her ground; and, having gratified the man's curiosity, with the privilege of a fellow-servant of higher rank, proceeded to put several questions to him—among them, one as to his age.

"Thirty-two last birthday."

"So young and yet so old! Excuse me, but pray is that the natural colour of your hair?"

"No, miss; it once was raven black."

"Incredible! yet I have read of such things. What caused such a sudden and dreadful change?"

"Trouble, miss. My hair turned to the colour you see it now in one night; and in three days my flesh dropped off my bones."

"Dreadful! and at your age, too! What was the cause of such misery?"

"Grief!" and as the man said this, he relapsed into a moody silence. To every other query he returned a brief, monosyllabic reply, and baffled all Alice's ingenuity to extract more from him. She was about to leave him, when she suddenly asked him his name.

"Jasper Sampson."

"Jasper Sampson!" murmured she, as she proceeded up stairs to her chamber, oppressed by a vague feeling of disquietude. A dim foreboding of impending evil weighed upon her spirits, and effectually banished all traces of her recent bloom from her cheeks. There was something in the man's physiognomy which made her heart-strings quiver with instinctive terror. She had not seen him before, she felt assured; yet faint glimmerings of something familiar to her smote upon her memory, and, in puzzling herself to impart to them shape and identity, they faded entirely away.

The eyes of the man, as he watched her receding form, emitted intense flashes of fire, and, as he clenched his hand menacingly, he muttered to himself the most repulsive word that can be applied to a woman. His thoughts, as he sat, like a bedizened mummy, in his chair, wove themselves into sentences of gloomy and hostile import.

"My calamity has sharpened my intellect, and brought back, with a hundred-fold increase, the knowlege of my youth. I can see and read now with a thousand eyes, and woe be it to those upon whom the hand of my vengeance shall fall! It shall not be one or two, or even scores, that I shall consume in the fire of a retribution kindled by the most remorseless hatred. I am not now the drunkard or the pugilist, but the tiger, with the cunning of the fox, and the perseverance of the vulture. Drink, hot as the hell that burns ceaselessly in my heart, harms me as little as a kettle full of boiling water would the sand of the sea-shore. I am adamant, and, were it not for one all-devouring passion, would have no impulses but those burning ones which spur me on to my revenge. But the sight of a woman maddens me; her feet tripping before my eyes inflames me to desperation; her form floating before me in its soft voluptuousness, possesses me with a fury; and when I think of her hair—oh, how beautiful is woman's hair—her neck—her bosom so soft, so warm, so fair and delicate, my scanty flesh creeps on my bones, and if I did not cry out, I should fall down dead! Yes, dead—dead!'

When this awful-looking man arrived at this climax,

he uttered a short, sharp cry, which much resembled the barking of a dog, and the perspiration started in huge drops on his pallid forehead. He then put his hands before his eyes, as if to shut out some horrible vision, and, after one or two convulsive heavings of his chest, became calmer.

"I want more schooling," thought he. "I must train myself to look upon a woman as a eunuch should—a eunuch! aha! but it must be done—I must see, and feel calm and unmoved; I have money, and it shall purchase me the lessons. I will feast my sight on the charms of a hundred glowing forms—press their limbs until the blood comes in rosy spots, and spreads and deepens like the blush upon a maiden's cheek. Oh, I am on fire with the frenzy of desire! but I must school myself. Money will do anything in London, and if I could but shut out that horror—subdue that raving lust, I should be as cold and impassable as the man who would torture woman should be. The harlot who threw down the strong man must perish first, but slowly; the iron must not be heated too quickly; death is only the happy oblivion into which we must all fall; and that with her must be postponed, until my fertile brain has exhausted its tortures on her delicate frame. Her boy, aha! that shall be my first stroke; but where to find him? I I must watch—play the cat; and then for the pleasure of seeing her writhe with that thorn in her side. Old Wriggles knows all about it; I must wring the secret out of him; he has others too—and then—aha!"

His brows grew black as midnight, and his bony structure almost rattled as it shook with the intensity of some dreadful purpose, which the recollection of a revolting reminiscence strengthened into an iron, unyielding resolution.

Thus did this extraordinary being ruminate in vengeful silence, until he was summoned to dinner below stairs. There his presence created no slight commotion; for he had no sooner taken his place at a side table, than the eyes of the whole company were fixed upon him, amid a dismal silence. The majority were the under servants, with a sprinkling of the higher ones to enforce authority. Alice was not among them, for, in her capacity of personal attendant upon the countess, she was privileged to dine either in her own room or at the housekeeper's table.

We should have mentioned that the new hall-porter had been the theme of conversation all the morning; and not a servant but had several times crept up the landing to take a view of him as he sat in the occupation of his lamented predecessor's chair. Various had been the speculations about him, but they all tended to establish the general belief that he was something awfully ugly and inscrutable.

In accordance with the ancient regulation, that the new comer should be served first, the senior footman, who presided, timorously inquired:

"What will you take, Mr. Sampson — beef or mutton? The mutton's excellent."

"Beef—and lots of it."

The answer appeared to have come from the recesses of Mr. Tompkins's ample legs; and as that worthy had a high notion of his dignity, and the decorum that should be observed on such occasions, he crimsoned at the supposition that some one was hiding under the table, and looked under it, deeply indignant; but, finding no one there, he turned resentfully to his right-hand neighbour, and severely inquired:

"Did you indulge in them observations?"

"Me, sir?" replied the astounded flunkey. "I knows my place better."

Mr. Tompkins made a savage thrust with his fork into the joint before him, and said:

"Beef, Mr. Sampson, did you say?"

"In course he did."

The response this time seemed to have issued from the lips of the pretty housemaid, who faced Mr. Tompkins.

"*Very* well."

And forthwith a plate was piled with the required commodity.

"Greens and potatoes, Mr. Sampson, of course—here you are. (Mr. Tompkins was getting vexed.) Now, then, ladies—beef or mutton? What is it, Miss Price?"

"A leetle bit of your nice beef."

The answer this time came from the inmost depths of Mr. Tompkins's unmentionables; at which he turned slightly pale, and sat down; but had no sooner done so, than the shrill cry of a child escaped from the very place where he was seated. At this he started up again, as if he had been shot, and turned whiter than the table-cloth before him."

"I believe I heard—a—a—cat!" stammered the bewildered Mr. Tompkins.

"Wery extrawadinay!" "How dwedful!" "The likes of it vos never heerd on afore!" were the remarks that circulated among the affrighted guests.

"Pooh! pooh! A cat—must have been a cat," said Tompkins, attempting to look composed. "I think you said beef, Miss Price? Anybody else take beef? Come—be lively!"

"I never said beef—I always prefer mutton!" cried the indignant Miss Price.

Mr. Tompkins stood, with his knife and fork poised in the air, actually confounded; and while in that interesting attitude, some peculiarly loud and significant notes were heard to proceed from the locality of Mr. Tompkins's chair. The whole company stared at each other in blank amazement at such a flagrant breach of propriety, and rained indignant glances upon the now terrified caterer. The ladies would have left the room, had not astonishment and wounded delicacy glued them to their chairs. As for Tompkins, he was the very picture of ghastliness; and as the unearthly noises from his remote regions continued at short intervals, and with increased vehemence, he faithfully realised the idea conveyed in the painting of the alarmed Dutch burgomaster.

The whole company were preparing to make a precipitate rush to the door, when suddenly the Tompkinsonian eructacity ceased, and the plaintive wail of a child was heard to proceed from precisely the same region. Horror now sat on every countenance—dismay upon every heart; and the whole of them, rising simultaneously from the table, dashed through the doorway in wild disorder, and raised, throughout the house, the startling alarm that Tompkins—the sedate, middle-aged Tompkins, was in labour. The tumult might have been dangerous to life and limb, had not Alice and the butler succeeded in restoring some degree of calmness. None of them would, however, return to the table; and the now tottering Tompkins was led to his room, and an accoucheur sent for instantly. The new hall-porter all this time preserved a rigid silence, and ate his dinner with an appetite rendered keener by his relish of the commotion he had created.

"I must husband my power of conveying and imitating sounds," thought he, chuckling, "or I shall be discovered. It is a wonderful faculty, and will help to amuse me when I see others happier than myself. In addition, it will aid me in my cherished projects."

As this thought flashed through his mind, he seized the decanter full of brandy from the table, and poured the whole of its contents down his throat. After putting the empty decanter down again, his glistening eyes fell upon Alice, and assumed an unearthly brightness, as he saw her advancing timidly to where he sat.

"Can you explain the cause of this unseemly uproar?" demanded she, with some show of resolution.

The mummy-like porter "grinned horribly a ghastly smile;" but, perceiving an elderly, slender woman in sober black, with a pinched shrewish visage, standing behind Alice, he quietly composed the lineaments of his repulsive countenance, and assumed the dull, vacant look of stupid terror.

"Gracious heaven! what a deplorable object!" ejaculated the housekeeper; for the lady in black was that important personage; "where can my lord have picked up the creature?"

A scowl, like a faint shadow flitting over a white ground, crossed that terrible visage. Alice detected it and shuddered, but ventured to repeat her question.

"I cannot tell; the gentleman, Mr. Tompkins I think they call him, was taken ill, and the rest took fright and cut away," was the reply delivered, in the same piping key which had so startled her some few hours previously.

"Can he be a man?" whispered the housekeeper to Alice.

"Come away!" said the latter hurriedly; "he is frightful, and the sight of him makes me feel giddy!"

There needed no second request of the kind, for the housekeeper turned quickly on her heels and flew up stairs, but not before the noise of a dog, barking up her petticoats, tended wonderfully to accelerate her flight.

Jasper grinned as he caught a glimpse of the woman's thin legs; but when Alice's tempting ones, clad in flesh-coloured silk stockings, met his view, his whole countenance changed to an expression of lust fearful to behold. At this moment the trembling valet of Lord Bloomfield entered the kitchen, and summoned him to his master's presence. This message dispelled his excitement, and he hastened after the precipitate valet.

Lord Bloomfield had just risen. An ample Turkish dressing-gown enveloped his well-proportioned body; but its glaring colours rendered his haggard features and yellow skin more conspicuous by the contrast. As it has already been stated, when freed from the corroding lines of dissipation, he was a handsome man. His hair clustered in thick raven masses round his polished temples; his eyes were of that brown which is to be found in men of great genius, allied to an excessive preponderance of the lower instincts, and his mouth and nose were finely-formed, but strongly characteristic of the tendency of his organisation. His lips were full, and, being invariably closed, displayed a plumpness ever to be found in men of immense physical desires. His short upper lip, garnished with a thick, glossy moustache, and an aquiline nose, completed a face upon which a woman might have dwelt with pleasure; but a man, according to the bias of his nature, with either envy or dislike. He had not seen Jasper Sampson before, and rose from his seat in some perturbation as that individual was somewhat abruptly introduced into his presence.

"Whence, and what art thou, execrable shape,
　That darest, though grim and terrible, advance
　Thy miscreated front athwart my way?"

he unceremoniously inquired, as his glance wandered over the shrunken and emaciated figure before him.

"The hall-porter, whom your lordship desired to see," answered the valet, accustomed to his master's morning aberrations, and looking at Jasper as if he thought it was not very safe to leave his lordship in such company.

"The most hell-begotten looking mortal I ever beheld!" muttered his lordship, when left alone with Jasper; and then added aloud, "the strong recommendation of my old friend Colonel Stanley, induced me to take you into my service, and give you the situation you desired; but I must confess, your appearance is not exactly of the description I anticipated. But as Stanley was urgent, and I made a promise, I suppose I must keep it. How the deuce, though, did you come by that shape?—

"If shape it might be called, that shape had none
　Distinguishable in member, joint, or limb."

"Few days have passed away since the men called me sturdy, and the women praised my herculean limbs, and bold manly face," was Jasper's rather mournful reply.

"Indeed!" said his lordship, incredulously; "and how came this sudden metamorphosis about?"

Jasper, whose powerful natural cunning and sagacity had received a tremendous impetus, with the rapidity of lightning reviewed his position and designs, and saw how much he had to gain and how little to lose, by a partial explanation to a man of his lordship's position in life.

"My lord!" said he, firmly, "I provoked a woman's vengeance, and she maimed me for life. In one short hour I was scourged like a wild beast—a sea of blood swam before my eyes, and I became insensible. When, after the lapse of three days, I recovered, I found myself in the condition of one of those miserable creatures who are prized by Eastern despots for their neutrality."

Lord Bloomfield comprehended it all instantly, and a feeling of pity for the miserable object before him found room in his bosom.

"Did you not seek for redress? Why not apprehend the woman?"

"She fled, my lord; besides, I saw no benefit to be gained from making all the world aware of my calamity."

"Perhaps you were right; but I fancy in such a predicament I should have been horridly resentful."

"So am I," said Jasper, with energy, his sternness slightly deepening the tones of his weak voice. "I hate women so intensely that I do not know a wrong too great to be inflicted on them. But what can I do? my impotence crushes me for the moment, and, if I were to yield to blind fury, the most I could do would be to murder, and then there would be the mockery of a trial, and a winding-up with the farce of the devil's dance in the Old Bailey. No, my lord, revenge is very sweet, but it ought to be obtained as cheaply and easily as possible. I hate women as I hate hell-fire! but I can wait."

"Your prudence is commendable, and I should advise you to retain the secret in your own breast; if you do not, the sooner you leave London the better, for if it should once get generally known, you would be jeered and hooted to death. With me it is safe, that is, so long as you are faithful to my interests. Should you betray me I would not hesitate to make it known wherever you might go."

Jasper slightly coloured; but he had been too unreserved in his communications either to retract or be supplicatingly submissive; so he merely asserted his capability to be faithful in all that his lordship might require him to undertake. Lord Bloomfield mused for a few minutes, and then said:

"I perceive, from your address, that you are not wholly uneducated; indeed, unless I am much deceived, your shrewdness and penetration are far beyond mediocrity. Now this is what I want you to do. From your situation, and by your natural tact, which your necessary isolation from the rest of the household must greatly foster, you will have favourable and numerous opportunities of forming observations and conclusions upon the conduct of the members of my family, and the parties who visit them. All these I desire you faithfully to record, and hand to me, when you have observed anything that demands my immediate attention. You understand me—I wish you to take notice of everything that transpires in this house, and forthwith make me acquainted with it."

Jasper readily understood him; but, as if desirous of knowing that there was at least one man in the world who approximated to him in misery, bluntly said:

"Do your orders extend to my lady the countess?"

"I fancied you comprehended me, without the necessity of my answering such a question," replied Lord Bloomfield, colouring. "Would I employ you in this espionage if I had not doubts in *that* quarter. Watch her," continued he, sternly; "watch everybody that comes in and goes out of the house. Watch *her* friends and visitors of both sexes, especially, and let me know all, and above all be prompt and faithful; and although one enjoyment is debarred you, shall have the means of procuring a thousand others."

Jasper, secretly delighted with the commission, for it materially furthered his own views, bowed, and was about to retire when something suddenly struck his lordship, and he commanded him to remain.

"Are you well acquainted with town?" inquired he, after a little consideration.

"There is not a nook or corner in all London, but what I have been acquainted with since my boyhood."

"Do you know the —— Road?"

"Well."

"There is a tobacconist's shop on the left hand side, near the middle."

"I know it—it is kept by the wife of a class leader among the methodists—a young woman about five and twenty; fair, full-bosomed, and above the average stature of her sex. Her eyes are beautifully blue, and with their demure, but liquid glances, make the heart send the hot blood bubbling to the brain."

"You know her then," exclaimed his lordship.

"I never spoke to her in my life," he replied, perceiving the error he had committed; "but I have frequently seen her, and when I could feel the softer emotions, I thought she was the loveliest, softest morsel that ever a man pressed to his panting side."

"The tradition of the satyrs is no fable," thought his lordship; as he looked at the flashing eyes of his emasculated confidant; "but as I have nothing to fear from his prowess, I will even make his ardour subservient to my purpose."

"Will you?" said he, aloud, "undertake to ascertain her sentiments? I entertain no doubt that she is approachable; but will you endeavour to find out how she is circumstanced, such as her pecuniary condition, whether she loves her husband, or has any children; you know what I mean."

"Perfectly; and I pledge myself that she shall be yours."

"How? You are remarkably confident!"

"I say, my lord, she shall be yours! I know womankind well."

"But your appearance—I forgot that? Why, you would scare her out of her senses!"

"I can disguise myself—a black hair dye will effect a wonderful difference!"

"So it will; and I think you are clever enough to deceive the devil. Set about it as soon as possible, and if successful, depend upon a liberal reward. But to-night the countess holds what she is pleased to call a conversazione, and I want you to keep every faculty of your mind on the *qui vive*. You understand me?"

"Quite, my lord."

And so saying, that singularly deformed man with a low bow left the room.

"He is not a Cupid's messenger!" laughed his lordship, as the door closed; "but as he cannot love a woman, he detests the whole sex. Stanley hinted as much, and I have ascertained his surmise to be well founded. His sharpened instincts will fit him admirably for the office of spy, and woe be it to Violet, much as I love her, if I detect her tripping! A husband is privileged both by nature and custom, a wife is not; and if she does but transgress the bounds of prudence but a hair's breadth, I will sacrifice her though the effort tore my heart-strings asunder!" And with this selfish and consoling determination, my Lord Bloomfield coolly addressed himself to his toilet.

Some few hours afterwards, Jasper was seated in the hall, indulging, as was his custom, in the most vindictive reflections.

"The work goes bravely on," thought he; "I am promoted to be pimp to a nobleman; and with Bardolph, I may say, ''tis a life I have desired,' for it will help me to my revenge. Every woman that falls will be honey to my blighted faculties. Yes, honey! for her damnation will be sweeter to me than her chastity. For one hideous and gigantic wrong, I will revenge myself on the whole sex, by industriously urging them on to perdition! A knock! Now for the mysteries of Bloomfield House!"

The first comer was Mrs. Smythe.

"Ah! a dark-eyed elastic daughter of the game.

Heavenly father! what a tapering waist; and what a bosom—full, heaving, and as soft as down!"

The guests arrived in quick succession; and as the man feasted his eyes on the beauty of the ladies, desire gnawed at his heart, and made his whole frame quiver with a burning wish to hug the whole of them in his fleshless arms. Among the gentlemen was Colonel Stanley, whom Lord Bloomfield had pacified by an assurance that the attack of the merry wives was a mere drunken freak of some frolicsome women, who had unaccountably obtained admission into the gardens. The colonel affected to receive this explanation as an apology, but had taken effectual steps to discover the promoter of the outrage.

"Have you ascertained what I wished to learn?" inquired he, from Jasper.

"I have," quickly answered the latter; "the contriver and abetter of the attack, was one Captain Morris!"

"As I suspected," muttered the colonel; "the hair-brained fool shall pay dearly for his lark! Have you seen or heard anything about the ladies of the house?"

"The countess and my lord are still two folks; and the young lady, Miss Lucy, is to start for the country—some place in Wales—to-morrow morning."

"Confusion!" ejaculated the colonel; "am I doomed to be thwarted at every corner? but this night shall settle the matter. Did you procure the philter?"

"I did," was the prompt answer of Jasper, as he produced a small paper package; "three grains of this dropped into a glass of wine, will inflame the coldest virgin, and make her yield at the first solicitation!"

"Give it to me!" exclaimed the colonel, with brutal earnestness; "at all hazards I will try its efficacy."

Jasper handed the paper to him, and then hastened to the door to admit another visitor—it was Captain Morris.

"The lady-killer," sneered Jasper, as he greedily perused the manly outlines of Walter's figure; "a good looking sort of fellow, with a fist, I'll be bound, as hard as iron. He walks as if the ground beneath him was dirt. A bold open countenance, too, one that women doat upon; he must be watched—he is dangerous. But surely I have seen him before! Ah! I remember."

Some painful recollection must have struck him, for he gasped for breath and smote his breast with fearful energy. A scowl dark as that of a cloud blotting out the stars, passed over his face, and gave an appalling cast to his death-like features.

"He dies, had he a hundred lives!" was the exclamation that escaped from his attenuated lips, in a demoniac whisper.

Walter had evidently been drinking, for he was inclined to be facetious. Jasper's scarcely human physiognomy furnished him with a subject on which to exercise his powers.

"You don't seem well, my friend," said he; "I trust the cholera and you have not hashed up an acquaintance?"

"I am well," said Jasper sturdily, yet striving to subdue his rage, for he had every reason to believe that the man before him had deeply and irretrievably injured him.

"Well, what in the name of all that is wonderful would you call ill? why you look more like an animated remnant of the age before the Mosaic deluge, than a thorough-bred cockney. Talk of a goose-look, why yours is the very perfection of high-dried ourang outangism!"

Jasper made a furious gesture.

"Never mind, my friend, I am only joking; some damned phlebotomist, or another—a very Sangrado of a rascal—has been testing the endurance of the human frame, and you survive as a living witness that bones can with impunity disdain allegiance to the flesh. Take my advice, Tom, Dick, or Harry, or what the devil your name is, and get married; matrimony soon brings a man into condition. You are as hairy as Nebuchadnezzar, and therefore have the germs of good substantial fat about you. Get married, my meagre friend, and show the girls that a straight, lean-backed fellow can go through his paces in half the time a porpoise-built one would take.

Jasper's face became even more livid than it naturally was with rage, and he shook his fist after the reckless captain as the latter made his way, laughingly, towards the drawing-room. More arrivals served to divert his mind a little from the subject, but he found opportunity to register a vow of implacable enmity.

"You are a gay, dashing blade. The women doat upon you; and you play havoc among the too-willing wives of London. I wonder whether they would like you so well if you were like me? Ah! I must hug that idea. If practicable in my case, why may it not be so in yours? Let me only catch you asleep, my bold captain of the dandy guards—that's all!"

He ground his teeth together, as he contemplated the commission of the very crime which, in his own case, had wrought such terrible effects.

And now all the fashionable characters of this narrative are once more assembled under the roof of that stately mansion, to indulge in the countless plots and intrigues which fill up the measure of the lives of the dissipated to the brim. There were some score of the most fashionable and beautiful women of London—the wives, with their magnificent forms, in all the stately pride and warmth of their glowing charms, contrasting pleasingly with the more sylph-like figures of the virgins, whose ripening bosoms were more carefully concealed from the prying gaze of the men who hung around them, gloating over their perfections. Mrs. Smythe, arrayed in a sumptuous robe of blue figured satin, had her fine person set off to the best possible advantage; her dark braided hair fell on her plump cheeks in thick braids; her eyes sparkled with intense lustre; and in all her movements she betrayed the languor, the subdued ardour of the woman of fiery temperament, fully armed for admiration and conquest. Beside her was the countess, whose appearance was most ravishing; her brilliant complexion shone in the light of that gorgeous room, and her light hair, disdaining the trammels of silken cord or comb, fell loosely, but not disorderly, on her radiant shoulders; her full figure and swelling bosom were displayed in all their glorious proportions; and, as the soft light from her piercing blue eyes fell on the noble-looking throng of men before her, she seemed no inapt representative of the Paphian Queen, on her throne of power. Lucy was by her side, but there was a sadness on her exquisite face, which imparted to it a pensive cast. The cause of this depression was, that the countess had imperatively insisted upon her immediately returning into the country, to escape the snares and temptations that beset a young unmarried girl in the dissipated metropolis. The truth was, the countess saw in her sister a dangerous rival; and as Mrs. Smythe shared in this conviction as regarded herself, poor Lucy, just as she had begun to feel that love was really the divine rapture of the human heart, was forthwith to be dispatched out of the way. Only Stanley was acquainted with this arrangement, and he most inhumanly resolved to make the information serviceable to his base views. Keeping as close to Lucy as possible, he endeavoured, by every stratagem, to ingratiate himself in her good esteem. Lord Bloomfield had promised to favour his honourable suit; for, with all the peer's vices, he would have scouted with indignation even the supposition of having in any manner been accessory to the debauchery of his wife's sister. In fact, he rather liked the gentle girl, and would have been glad to have seen her happily married. As for Morris, he was wandering about, and making himself as much at home as if he were in his own apartments, with only a gay fellow like himself for a companion. Amid the prevailing bustle and hum of conversation, he had leisure to take note of many things that transpired, and only waited for a favourable opportunity of gratifying his indomitable propensity for mischief. But the transactions of this eventful night in Bloomfield House demand particular attention; and it is preferable that the mysterious Jasper Sampson should be followed in some peregrinations he undertook. As the clock struck ten, he left Bloomfield House, dressed in a suit of rusty black, and he had so arranged his garments, that, with his white hair and whiskers, he had much the appearance of one of those unfortunate men who wear their lives out in hopeless toil at the smoothly-worn desk of a griping attorney.

"This death's head of mine secures me from detection," thought he; "if my own wife failed to recognise me, I fancy nobody else will."

And, placing his faded hat firmly on his brows, he bent his steps towards St. Bridget's Court. The streets through which he passed were unusually crowded with females of all degrees of character and beauty, and of every age; and as he had to wind his way through the throng, and every now and then came into contact with the persons of some of the prettiest and most gaudily dressed, a burning thrill shot through his frame, and it was with difficulty he could refrain from seizing upon one of them, and hugging her in the savage frenzy of his impotent but excruciatingly tormenting embrace. His tongue clave to the roof of his mouth, and to relieve himself he plunged into a dram shop, and drank off at a single draught half a pint of raw brandy. This stimulant appeared to relieve him, and to avoid being again subjected to a similar attack, he took to the dirty bye-streets and squalid passages in the rear of the gorgeously lighted-up panaroma of western London by night.

While he is collecting his scattered thoughts, and maturing his mode of procedure during his intended visit, it may be as well to anticipate his arrival at the dwelling of Mr. and Mrs. Wriggles, by some description of that remarkable tenement. As previously intimated, it was situate in that remarkably bright specimen of metropolitan architecture called St. Bridget's Court, and consisted of one large house, whose exterior was in a state of such dilapidation, that the interior scarcely promised lodgings to the rats that daringly prowled about the neighbourhood after nightfall. The building itself was evidently the remains of one of those substantial brick edifices which belonged to the time of Queen Anne, and, as regards bulk, was the most imposing of the whole range. Dirty paper-patched windows, and a certain dinginess of the whole outside, added exceedingly to its ambiguity as to moral character. The locality itself was rank and fetid; there was everywhere to be seen not the squalor of poverty, but the filth and abominations that invariably congregate in the places where the votaries of crime hide themselves from the prying curiosity of the guardians of the public safety. In this mansion Mr. and Mrs. Wriggles had resided for upwards of five and twenty years. The latter ostensibly pursued the lucrative calling of midwife, the former collected herbs, and ministered in a variety of ways to the ailments common to both sexes. This enterprising couple occupied the ground floor, the rest of the premises being sublet to as motley a crew of tenants as were ever assembled under the roof of a lodging-house. Mrs. Wriggles was a very popular personage in the court, for she not only attended her lady neighbours on certain annual occasions gratis, but frequently, when the parties had not the means, provided even a little beer or wine, besides the common necessaries.

Being thus the favourite of the women, the men were all ranged on her side, and pledged by the most solemn conjugal refreshers to protect her to the utmost of their power.

As to Mr. Wriggles himself, he was so seldom seen that with numbers he was a species of myth; but that was a prejudice, for there was such a personage, and on that night when Jasper Sampson purposed calling upon him, was at home and alone. He was a lean and withered old man, with a long and thin, but very shrewd face. A rim of iron grey hair rendered his bald pate, if possible, more glossy and shiny, and his small eyes, twinkling brightly through his spectacles, deepened the impression that he was one of those men who had made their natural cunning the object of their careful study, and cultivated it to the most frightful perfection. The room in which he was seated was a spacious one, and furnished in a very old-fashioned and irregular manner. The chairs were high-backed, and the few drawings that hung on the walls were of Hogarth's school. Some few of them were extremely broad and coarse, and referred chiefly to the low amorous adventures of the early days of George IV. Although it was summer, a large fire sent its flame roaring up the chimney, and disclosed the figure of the old man bending over a crucible, in which he was compounding something that required a high degree of heat. Behind him, on a large table, was a little army of phials and jars, together with heaps of dried and newly-gathered herbs, some mineral substances, and several human skulls. In one of the recesses an entire human skeleton was suspended, and on the side tables there were skulls and casts of heads in some profusion.

But the great feature of the room was Wriggles, or, as he insisted upon being styled, Dr. Wriggles. He was short in stature, dry as one of the stuffed reptiles around him, and as brown in complexion as an Egyptian mummy. In age he must have been far advanced beyond seventy; indeed he had quite a centenary look about him; but when he moved or turned, or bent his body, he had the quickness and agility of the lean, long-backed man of fifty. Altogether he was an extraordinary-looking personage, and quite as extraordinary in reality as in appearance.

A low knock sounded on the well-secured door, but the doctor heeded it not, although several times repeated, until he had completed the experiment upon which he had been so intently engaged. Then drawing a slide in a lamp, he produced an intensely brilliant light, which he so managed that its rays penetrated through an aperture which he opened in the door, and fell on the unearthly face of Jasper Sampson.

The doctor had long been familiar with hideous deformities of countenance, but one so utterly and incomprehensibly ghastly he had never seen before His iron nerves and wonderful experience in the world had long ago disabused his mind of any superstitious weaknesses, but he could not avoid slightly starting when he saw that marvellous face, with its burning eyes, burst upon his vision like a spectre of the night.

"What and who are you?" at length he asked, in a voice in which there was not the slightest shrillness or harshness; on the contrary, it was rather soft and pleasing.

"One who solicits your assistance, and is not disposed to cool his heels at any door," replied Jasper, irritated at the delay.

"Few but the sons and daughters of misfortune come to me. Tell your story, and be brief."

"Open the door, and I will. You surely don't expect me to talk to you through the keyhole?"

"That has been my custom with strangers for upwards of forty years."

"But I am not a stranger, man! You know me as well as I know myself," cried Jasper, petulantly; but immediately added, as if some new thought had struck him, "that is you ought to know me, for I consulted you about five years ago."

"Your name?" demanded the doctor, incredulously.

"Jasper Sampson."

He turned the leaves of a large book that lay on a table, and under the initial letter found the name indicated. While he was thus employed, Jasper chuckled over what he deemed his ingenuity:

"I remember the name of the man that came here about five years ago, as well as if it was only yesterday. He was trapped by the boys, and never seen or heard of again; but old Wriggles didn't know anything about it, and the name will suit me better than any other for the present."

"Such a person did call upon me once, but I don't think you are the man, for I never forget a face I have once seen. You really must speak what you have to say where you are," said Wriggles, hesitatingly, and striving to recall the horrible lineaments before him to his recollection.

"I have the pass-word. You know none have it but those you can trust."

"Ha! that is quite a different thing! Give me the word that was never yet divulged to strange ears but by myself, and I will think twice of your request."

"Leoline," uttered Jasper, in a soft whisper.

"Good!" said the doctor, in the same key, and then to himself, as he walked to the other extremity of the room, "you are not the man; I never forget a face, but with my *usual* precaution I will venture;" upon this he thrust a long rod of iron into his immense fire, and, proceeding to a corner of the room, unfastened what appeared to be an iron grating, and in a low voice addressed some words of affection to some animal inside. Jasper was then admitted, and the doctor so seated him that the occupant of the cage could watch his every movement.

After a vain endeavour to recal to his memory something concerning his singular visitor, the doctor, who, all the while had eyed him curiously, said to Jasper:

"I remember the name, but either you are not the man, or have become so wonderfully changed that I cannot recognise you!"

"I am changed!" replied Jasper, doggedly, an implacable hatred tugging at his heart; "and I wish for revenge—deep, bitter, and lasting! a revenge as swift and sure as appalling! But first of all I wish to have the power to disguise myself when I choose. Look at this face, is it not dreadful to behold!"

"It would become a vampyre amazingly!" cried Wriggles, feasting his eyes on the novel "subject" before him.

"You mean a blood-sucker!" said Jasper, with a gloomy scowl; "and —— me if you are not right—I will be a blood-sucker! But I don't wish always to like one!"

"How came your metamorphosis about?"

Jasper felt inclined to spring upon that, as he imagined, rather leering old man, and tear him to pieces, but he restrained himself. The wretched man could control every passion but one. Even his ferocious longings became fiercer by subjection, but for the exception he could forge no chains strong enough to bind its impetuous fury.

"I—I—I went abroad," stammered he — "to Turkey—I mean to the Indies—no, it was to China—and having been detected with a great officer's favourite wife, I was punished according to the laws of the country. In the evening I was as strong as a bull; in the morning I became what you see me."

"Indeed!" exclaimed the doctor, placing his hand before his eyes, so as to allow him to inspect the upper and lower divisions of Jasper's face separately. As he did so, a countenance, which had long been familiar to him, became once more revealed to his perception; and as the recognition became fixed in his mind as instantaneously as if the portrait had become fixed by some mental photographic process, he felt his remotest nerve tingling with apprehension. A glance at the open grating, however, reassured him, and in a few seconds he was as cool and collected as ever.

"I understand you perfectly," said he. "It was a cruel—a barbarous punishment; but a more terrible and effectual one than death. If murderers were served so in this country, the mere spectacle of them afterwards, crawling like useless vermin between heaven and earth, would lessen the tendency to commit the offence. However, such a speculation as that can only be distressing to you. In what respect do you wish me to serve you?"

"In the first place, I want to hide these grey, or, I should say, these snow-white hairs, and this ghostly face."

"Soon done, that, Mr. Sampson—soon done. Only attend to my instructions, and you shall be an Adonis, or even Apollo, if you please; although I fancy the former, in your case, would be the most practicable embodiment."

With this half-born sneer on his lips, Dr. Wriggles produced several small phials, one of which he handed to Jasper, with a request that he would apply it as a wash to his hair. By varying the applications several different colours were given to the hair, in the course of, perhaps, a quarter of an hour; and Jasper was so pleased with his transformations, that he immediately concluded a bargain with the erudite Dr. Wriggles, for the purchase of the various preparations.

"How long will any of these dyes last, though?" inquired Jasper.

"Four-and-twenty hours."

Jasper was apparently well satisfied, and then obtained a variety of washes and cosmetics for the complexion.

"In what character do you wish to make your first public reappearance?" inquired the doctor, regarding his customer intently, as he observed Jasper's eyes intently fixed on an escritoire, that contained his most valued papers.

"In that of a methodist—not a parson—but one of those class-leading humbugs."

"Shave off those whiskers, pencil your brows, and

you will be as smooth-faced a piece of iniquity as any that infests London."

"I desire no more at present; and now answer me truly — can you restore to me my former strength?"

"In that respect my power over you is infinitely less than it is over that grim remnant of a once-powerful man."

And the doctor pointed to the skeleton, to which allusion has been made. Jasper, in whom super-stition was a powerful element, instantly averted his eyes, and, after a pause, said:

"Can you not give me some stuff to cool me, or make me insensible, when I'm on fire at the sight of a woman? Ugh!"

Doctor Wriggles had some humanity in him, and thus reasoned within himself:

"Bah! what a miserable! The loss of what is the cause and motive power of one half the misery that curses the world is to him unendurable. He is fiercer now in his imbecility, than he was in the prime of his manhood. What stings we carry about us to remind us of our poor dependent lot—that we are the mere creatures of our passions and propen-sities! Ah, well! it ever was and ever will be so, and I must allow this poor devil some temporary relief. Ah, Mr. Jasper!" said he, aloud; "you tax my knowledge pretty severely; but I will do all I can to aid you. When attacked, take two drops from this phial in a wine-glass full of water—mind only two drops, or you drop down dead."

Jasper clutched at the bottle with nervous eager-ness, and then hastily demanded to be supplied with some of those stimulating compounds, popularly known as love-philters.

"For yourself, eh?" grinned the doctor, elevating his heavy grey eyebrows.

"No!" said Jasper, savagely; "they are for those who need them."

"The names of those parties must be given me?" said the doctor, resolutely.

"I cannot give them—I am employed confiden-tially."

"Then I cannot accommodate either you or them."

"As I intend to do for him it won't much matter," thought Jasper; and then, as if with desperate reluc-tance, said, "Colonel Stanley and Lord Bloomfield."

"Very good!" replied Wriggles, handing over the drugs with as much coolness as if he had been vend-ing common magnesia. "Anything else?"

"No; what do you charge?"

"Altogether twenty pounds—should be thirty; but you may appropriate the difference."

Jasper fumbled in his pockets as if searching for money, when, suddenly drawing a short dagger from his breast, he sprang upon the little old man, and seized him by the throat.

"I have you now, and you shall go to hell without one prayer for your murderous soul! You know me—I could see it in your eyes and your mocking lips. You cannot deny it, and thus I revenge myself, and gain all the secrets you have hoarded up in that damned cupboard of yours!"

He raised his arm to strike, but almost before the weapon was well poised for the blow, he found him-self pinioned and dashed violently to the floor, where he was rolled over and over in an embrace which made his fleshless bones crack again.

"Ah! ah! ah!" laughed the little doctor, drawing his feet up to his seat, and adjusting his spectacles.

Jasper tried to scream, but the sounds dried away in rattles in his throat, and he felt himself rapidly sinking under the pressure of that iron gripe.

"Don't kill him, Leoline; we won't be quite so desperate as he was; we shall want the darling; he will be useful to us by-and-bye."

The application of the red-hot iron to the flank of Jasper's opponent, induced compliance with this re-quest; and, upon being permitted to breathe more freely, he looked up and beheld the nose of a great bear within a few inches of his own face.

"Mercy! stab or poison me, but don't let me be worried to death!"

"Remember the poor dogs you sacrificed to gratify your love of such sport!"

"Mercy! I am not a dog; call him off!"

"Fine sport, bear-baiting, eh, Mr. Sampson? I re-member the time when it was patronised by the Prince of Wales and all our proud British nobles. Our country dames were even wont to grace the scene with their presence."

"Mercy!"

The doctor kept the wretch for upwards of an hour in this torturing suspense, now urging the bear to lick his face, or give him a tighter hugging, and then jibing at him in the most merciless manner.

"Listen to me, Jasper Sampson, or whatever your name is," said he at length; "you say I know you—I do; and could send you to the gallows whenever I chose to set the officers of justice on your track. From a boy I have watched your progress, and saw from the first that you were destined to a life of vio-lence, lust, and rapine. Up to a certain period, you indulged all your propensities with the headlong fury of your brutal instincts. You gave no thought to the morrow, and forgot all your yesterdays. A change has come over you; and, instead of the coarse courage of the bull-dog, you have the cunning and ferocity of the tiger. Go on and prosper, for I love mankind too well to deprive it of so useful an ornament; but re-member this—never take life if you can avoid it! murder is a foolish expenditure of the means of grati-fying an inextinguishable resentment. Torture and maim, but do not slay. Now then, away! you know me, and I know you. Instead of being enemies, we can be useful to each other. I will help you to your revenge! study and invent new ones for your comfort, but you must serve me—be my lacquey, my spy, my everything docile and faithful. Consent to this, and you shall go free! refuse, and, for the little time you have to live, you shall be the plaything of Leoline, and you know how she amuses herself in her leisure hours. The polished remnants would bring me in a ten pound note from any young surgeon."

"I consent; I will do everything if you will only release me," gasped Jasper, terrified into submis-sion.

"Wait a little," said the doctor composedly, as he produced a lancet; "the men of your fraternity have an oath which they never break. It is a relic of the Odin worship of the sprightly sea-kings of the north; and for fifteen hundred years has been the only bond of communion between the robbers of Europe."

Jasper consented, and took the frightful oath he had administered to Colonel Stanley in the dungeon. The doctor then drove the bear back into the den, and, having secured the grating, approached Jasper fearlessly.

"We are as one now!" said the doctor with some solemnity.

"We are," responded Jasper, regarding that old man with awe and trepidation.

"Tell me then what has occurred to you since your misfortune?"

The now thoroughly subdued Jasper related the whole of his adventures without the slightest reservation, up to the moment of his seeking the interview with Dr. Wriggles.

"You have a splendid opportunity before you!" said the latter, "and must profit by it. Follow the instructions of both your master and Colonel Stanley, and let me either see you or hear from you daily. Watch the women closely!"

"Their presence maddens me!" interrupted Jasper.

"Take what I have given you. Mind, two drops of the fluid in the red phial, and in a month you will be able to look upon a woman as ravishing in her nudeness as the Paphian Queen herself, without the slightest emotion. In the meantime take no step without consulting me."

"But the woman—the harlot—the author of my tremendous misfortune—am I not to torture her?"

"No," said the doctor, coldly, but emphatically, "she is one of us!"

"D—n!" shouted Jasper, trembling with grief and rage at the announcement.

"You shall be revenged, though!" said the wily doctor, knowing how useful to the energies the basest hope is when encouraged with even the most distant prospect of realisation.

"I am satisfied. I know you never break your word," replied Jasper, reassured.

"I never do; and your revenge, if you serve me faithfully, shall be one that shall make even the fiends shudder!"

"I am satisfied," said Jasper, boldly; "only make me cold—frosty—a piece of ice before a woman, and I shall more willingly obey you; indeed I shall not be able to serve you without!"

"You shall be all you wish, and more. Are we not brothers?"

"So we are. I shall never forget that!"

Jasper then arranged, as he best could, his torn and disordered garments, and, pocketing his various purchases, prepared to depart.

"What, commit an act of pecuniary fratricide in your noviciate?" exclaimed the doctor, extending his hand.

Jasper readily took the hint, and told over all the money he had in his pockets. It was not sufficient.

"It does not matter," said the doctor, placing his brown, skinny hand on the golden coins; "next time will do; besides, are we not *brothers!*"

The stress laid on the last word was peculiarly strong, and slightly smacked of the pungent sarcasm which the aged can so well distribute when patting the inexperience of youth. With this assurance the pair separated, Jasper to return to Bloomfield House. As soon as he had gone the doctor counted over the sovereigns he had received, and, holding them in his open palm, said, with a dry chuckle, "Dear gold! how much more precious thou art to the mind than the eye! For ages thou hast been the cause of war, and bloodshed, and strife, in all its infinite variety! Yet I can win thee without stirring from my chamber, or exercising any more potent sway than that of my experience over the lazy and superstitious multitude! But my power is here!" He laid his hand on a skull. "I know each pulsation of this living globe, and can tell to a hair's breadth the boundaries of each organ, and measure its capacity as accurately as if balanced in the hand of pure justice! So much for knowledge; but where would be its authority, if there were no ignorance in the world? Knowledge houses itself in the thick branches of ignorance, like a bird in the stateliest oak, which, when it lists, can soar and sing hymns at heaven's gate."

Dr. Wriggles then sat down and chronicled the the circumstances that had occurred during the even-

ing in the huge book he had opened to search for the name of Jasper Sampson.

Years afterwards, when all traces of the doctor had vanished, that book survived, but its contents were in a character that could not be deciphered. They were simple enough in appearance, but, with many of the remains of the languages of antiquity, the key to the hieroglyphics had vanished.

While the doctor was thus employed a side door in his apartment opened, and gave ingress to the stout figure of Mrs. Wriggles, clad as usual in her old black bonnet, dingy shawl, and black stuff dress.

"At work as usual, my pet!" she exclaimed, laying down her bonnet and shawl, and approaching him with affectionate familiarity.

"Ah, Jackina! is that you?" said he, putting aside his pen.

"Yes, darling, and I have a delicate little bit of business for you too."

"Very well, Jackina. But guess who's been here?"

"Somebody from Bloomfield House, I'll be bound; I have heard there are rare goings on there."

"Why certainly he came from Bloomfield House, but only in the capacity of hall-porter on his own account."

"Oh, is that all?"

"All! he is a strange fellow, I can tell you, and one you know well!"

"Me? if it's the person you mean, he is a stupid-looking old man, in a perpetual state of beer."

"It's not him," said the old man, chuckling; "he was superannuated yesterday. The one I mean was the man who calls himself Jasper Sampson, but he is no other than ——" here he put his mouth to her ear and whispered something.

"No?" she exclaimed, opening her eyes to their fullest extent.

"Fact!" Colonel Stanley picked him up, or rather he picked Colonel Stanley up, in the caves of the coves over the water, and they scraped an acquaintance which led to his obtaining the appointment he sought."

"His motive must be revenge. We must warn Alice of her danger."

"There will be no necessity for that. I have him bound to us hand and foot. He took the oath, and as he knows we can hang him, he will not venture upon any proceeding without consulting me; so you see he is perfectly safe."

"So he is! so he is! and now I reflect he will be a useful agent in our little business at Bloomfield House."

"I cannot conceive how it is you take such an interest in that family! we never made any money out of it, and, from what I have heard, they are not the parties to recommend us to any connections of any value to us."

The doctor said this with great gravity; Mrs. Wriggles listened as gravely, and, after a pause, said·

"Neither of us has much reason to entertain sentiments favourable to any human being; but we cannot resist the invasion of partialities for particular individuals."

"We cannot—the most seared heart is vulnerable under peculiar circumstances."

"Just so," replied Mrs. Wriggles; "and I cannot divest myself of a prejudice in favour of the countess, her sister, and that wild, harum-scarum young soldier, Captain Morris. The tale is not a long one, and I will relate it:—You are acquainted with what the world termed my early misfortune; how, with my living burden in my arms, I was driven forth to the

mercy of the elements. Well, it happened that I came from the county where the mothers of these young people resided, and they, in common with the people for miles round, knew of my bruited-about shame. But they did not join in the savage cry that hunted me from my native place; they supplied me with money, and with tears implored me to reside in obscurity in a neighbouring town, and offered to supply me with the necessary means. I gratefully accepted of their kindnesses; but my child died, and, after many fruitless appeals to my friends, I fell into the wildness of despair, and embraced the life of a courtezan. At the end of about ten years I was seized with a longing to once more see my native village, and journeyed thither secretly; but I was spurned by all who recognised me with curses, and even blows. The mothers of these children were the only exceptions. Mrs. Morris sheltered me from the fury of the mob. Her income was scanty; but she gave me twenty pounds to help me on my journey to London. Little Walter, her son, then about five years old—this occurred more than five and twenty years ago—a fine little fellow he was, insisted upon breaking open his money-box, and pouring the contents in my lap. He also gave me his Bible."

The old woman's voice slightly quivered as she said this; but it quickly recovered its usual tone.

"Do you know," continued she, "I never recal that little incident to my recollection, but quite a novel kind of sensation possesses me. However, I left ——, and for ever; and with a letter of introduction in my pocket obtained a situation, which afforded me opportunities of studying human nature; and gradually I followed the pursuits which, twenty years ago, led to my acquaintanceship with you. From what I have told you it is not difficult to imagine that I take some interest in the welfare of this Captain Morris, and as often as I could have thrown myself in his way. He little dreams that for one step in his promotion he was indebted to the outcast his mother and himself befriended in his infancy. But so it was—a little job done for a titled lady procured me any favour while she lived."

"I can understand it all!" said the doctor, musingly; "and to be candid, rather like this Walter, for he is neither a fool nor a knave, but just a cool, ready-witted man of the world. Although brave as steel, he never heedlessly runs his head into danger. He would make a capital general; for, unless I am deceived in his head, his talent is large and well cultivated. But the women, Jackina—I don't understand that portion of your sympathy. I thought you had sworn eternal hatred to the whole sex?"

"So I have," replied Mrs. Wriggles; "and well I have kept my word; but some how or another, I cannot forget their fair-haired mother as she handed me her purse, and, with tears in her eyes, gave me her blessing."

"But are they not like the rest of their sex, unkind and unmerciful to the frail?"

"One, for the sake of appearances, would be rigid and repelling in her demeanour to an unfortunate girl; the other would leap to her assistance."

"Well, well, do as you will; but how can we serve them?"

"Listen. The countess loves Walter; so does her sister. Now, as the latter is more worthy of him than the former, to save him from the intrigue, we must save the countess."

"Admirable, Jackina! from necessity you assist the countess; from affection, the captain and so wipe out the debt of gratitude to the parents of both.

"Just so! And the danger of Walter falling into the meshes the propensities of the countess are spreading for him, is greater from the circumstance of her having a rival in the person of one Mrs. Smythe, a superb Juno kind of woman."

"Would you save her too?"

"By the great God, no!" exclaimed Mrs. Wriggles. "She is the daughter of a race I hate, and is herself as cold and cruel as the most worthless of them. She must fall. Walter cannot love her; but he may be made the means of lowering her from her haughty position."

"Would not the connexion contaminate him, and so defeat your views?"

"Not at all," replied Mrs. Wriggles, laughing; "he is a perfect Don Juan with women, but not so wholly corrupted as to be insensible to a pure passion. The gentle Lucy has already made an impression upon him which time will mature into a confirmed and devoted love. Besides, he never takes an unfair advantage. His tastes have lain among the merry wives of London; and let him take his fill of enjoyment out of all that throw themselves in his way."

"Jackina, thou reasonest well! and this gay fellow unconsciously ministers to thy revenge!"

"He does; and heaven speed him in all his amours, save one!"

"Ah! by the way," said the doctor, suddenly, as his eye ran over the pages of the book before him; "I thought I had something about that, Mrs. Smythe —here it is:—'Caroline Fitzherbert, delivered by me of a female child, December 10, 18——.' Three years afterwards she married Mr. Smythe, the then junior partner in the banking-house of Messrs. ——. Why we have that woman completely in our power. The child is ——"

"Our little Fanny," interrupted Mrs. Wriggles.

The doctor chuckled in his usual dry way, and said:

"I see a little amusement before me in all this mass of intrigue. It will be delightful to sit here among all these old-fashioned and grim relics, and dictate terms to so many people flaunting it bravely in the light of the garish sun. Delightful, won't it, Jackina?"

The reply of the old woman was interrupted by a knocking at the door. It was a messenger with a letter to Mrs. Wriggles, which ran as follows:—

"Bloomfield House. Midnight.

'The countess and Mrs. Smythe have arranged to go to Greenwich to-morrow, disguised. The countess

is to give Mrs. S. the slip, and meet Captain Morris at some place to be appointed before the party breaks up.

"ALICE."

"They must not meet," exclaimed Mrs. Wriggles' excitedly, "or all my schemes will crumble into dust!"

"Cannot you manage that Mrs. Smythe should meet him instead?" insinuated the doctor.

"Capital! I know Alice is jealous of Walter, for she seems to have set her heart upon his taking her into keeping; so we shall be able to manage it through her."

A bell at this moment sounded, and Mrs. Wriggles, starting up, exclaimed:

"That is your patient!"

"Another married woman?" inquired the doctor.

"Yes, her husband holds a high post in India," was the reply; "and her situation is such that concealment is every day becoming more difficult. She is supposed to have gone to Brighton for the benefit of her health, and can only remain here for a week."

So saying, Mrs. Wriggles hurried away to receive her well-muffled and half-fainting visitor.

The doctor opened a secret drawer, and drew out, with much care, a case of steel instruments, several of which he took out in his hand, and polished on his coat-sleeve with much care. As he did so, he muttered:

"Not a farthing under a hundred pounds. I can't afford to receive less. The peccadilloes of the rich ought always to pay for professional services to the poor."

CHAPTER X.

THE LOVE POTION.

BLOOMFIELD HOUSE, as midnight approached, was the scene of much light-hearted revelry. The music of merry voices floated from room to room; and, as the beautiful forms of the loveliest of women, luxuriously attired, swept through the gorgeously-furnished apartments, and mingled at intervals with the dark, manly figures of the more stalwart promenaders, the effect, in the glare of countless lights, was brilliant in the extreme. But behind this fair exterior there was much that was false and hollow,—envy, jealousy, hatred, and lust, were tugging at many hearts, and lending a false glow to cheeks that seemed as stainless as the unclouded sky. Eyes emitted the unholy light of the various passions that influenced their possessors; and even the haughtiest dames, who would have had the world believe they owned no other allegiance than that demanded by their conjugal vows, deigned to cast furtive glances of envy at those to whom the most distinguished and handsome of the men paid homage. The fire in the eye mocked the smile on the lip, and the heaving bosom told of the pang, or the keen desire, that lurked beneath. The admiration that was not voluntarily bestowed, was sought to be obtained by the most finished coquetry, and looks that flashed anything but the purity that should beam from the unspotted windows of womanly chastity. Yet all was not gross. With many, the appetite for applause was a mere mannerism—the result of habit; with others, an amusement, to which they had become accustomed; and with several, a wish for a delicious lulling of the senses. The latter wished to breathe the incense of love, just as a poet dreamily drinks in the sound of distant bells, or the murmurings of flowing waters on a hot summer's day.

It was a refined sensualism, a voluptuous repose, which they desired, and, in doing so, they never imagined that temptation, coming in the hour of ardent impulses, could make the feeling subordinate to indulgences of a lower grade. The countess had a perpetual craving after this sensation; but to women of Mrs. Smythe's temperament and training, the "wish was father to the thought." Her eyes spoke the language of her heart, when she turned them in all their radiance upon the man for whose society she manifested an inclination. She had striven during the whole evening to keep Walter Morris by her side; and, sooth to say, he was nothing loth; for her dark glances, proud, flushed face, and full, voluptuous figure, had charmed and excited his already sufficiently heated imagination. But the countess, with the watchfulness of jealousy, effectually defeated the manœuvre by also keeping by his side. Lucy, in her timid modesty, held aloof, and thus fell a prey to the companionship of an insipid lord, who had descended to pronounce her the most passable girl in the company. She was the only virgin present; the rest of the ladies had all of them worn the orange blossoms for their brief hours of promises of felicity; and her position was rather an embarrassing one. The freedom displayed in the deportment of several of those of her own sex, was to her puzzling and distressing; the more so, as she perceived that Walter, the cherished object of her warm girlish attachment, met it more than midway, and appeared to encourage it by his bold, unruffled assurance. Poor Lucy! she was as much a novice in love as in the deceits and frauds of the world, and had yet to feel the thrill that accompanies the enjoyment of nature's unsullied attributes, or plunges the soul into the wild delirium of unrestrained passion.

As for the gentlemen assembled beneath the hospitable roof of Bloomfield House, they were occupied, as is usually the case in such assemblages, in exhibiting their good looks and fair proportions to the best advantage, quizzing the ladies with that disgusting impertinence which marks the man of fashion and dissipation; and indulging in all the nonsense and frivolities that distinguish whispered courtships and undisguised flirting in high life. In one corner were assembled Lord Bloomfield, as usual, half inebriated, for his appetites had become so depraved, that he had resorted to that noxious stimulant, brandy; Colonel Stanley, rather pale, but looking excessively handsome in his full military dress, and Mr. Smythe, a low-built, swarthy, Jew-looking personage, with the keen, shifting black eyes of the men you only see in the gambling-rooms of the West End, or the pestilential one of that abomination of the City, Capel Court. Both his fashionable acquaintances kept accounts at his bank, and that circumstance, added to his being allied by marriage to some of the aristocratic families of Britain, doubtless originated and kept alive the friendship that subsisted between them. Mr. Smythe, however, was a gay man; it was notorious that he maintained a couple of actresses as his mistresses, and in his leisure hours devoted his valuable person to the society of any pretty woman who would accept of his devotion. Three such choice spirits could not reasonably have been expected to have applied their cultivated powers of conversation to any less important topic than that of the folly of woman, and hence the highly seasoned character of their remarks, two of the party, for the nonce, wholly forgetting that in one essential moral respect they were not conjugally impregnable.

"I entirely dissent from the old adage that ' beauty is only skin deep,'" observed Lord Bloomfield, in reply to a remark of Mr. Smythe's, whose ideas of beauty were somewhat oriental; "figure, colour, and delicacy of feature combined, attract more than the mere plumpness of a leg or lazy rotundity of body. Look at my sister-in-law yonder, talking to that puppy of a De Vere; see how gracefully her head sits upon her alabaster shoulders, and what grace there is in the play of her swanly-arched neck! Her form, too, tapering so finely and imperceptibly to her tiny waist, and then enlarging and seeming to fall downward in waving curves, that float before the eye like the drapery of a sylph borne on the invisible air!"

"She is, indeed, divine!" exclaimed Colonel Stanley, gazing at the girl rudely through his glass; and then, as if desirous of diverting the conversation into another channel, added, "but to some tastes our friend Smythe is correct in his analysis. Observe how magnificently that Lady Tyrone queens it with her splendid contour!"

Lord Bloomfield turned lazily in the direction indicated; but Mr. Smythe rapturously ejaculated:

"A remarkably fine woman! By Jove, what a bust she has! A waist, too, where is something soft and warm to fondle! I'll bet anything she has the best ankle and leg in the room! Is she married?"

"Yes, to an Irish peer, as bankrupt in purse as person, for he has only some imaginary estates in Ireland, an hereditary pension, and a gout that keeps him constantly on cratches."

"Indeed!" said Mr. Smythe, abstractedly. "Will you introduce me?"

"Oh, certainly!" laughed the colonel; "but I would warn you to be cautious, for she has some fiery Irish brothers and cousins, who prowl about as much as anybody else in search of cash and beauty, but are excessively tenacious of the honour of *their* family."

"Such cattle are to be purchased in herds," thought Mr. Smythe, as he accompanied the colonel to be presented to the lady, who was certainly one of the most substantial present, and had a wicked expression in her large stag-like eyes.

Upon the return of Colonel Stanley to the spot where Lord Bloomfield stood, for the purpose of ungraciously criticising his own guests, the latter said:

"Will our millionaire succeed, think you?"

"I rather suspect his difficulty will not lie with the lady, but with those brothers and cousins I referred to," replied the colonel. "They follow in her train like attendant demons!"

"You were singed in that quarter, were you not?"

"The affair cost me a cool thousand, and a couple of meetings on Wimbledon Common; and I do believe if I had not shown a bold front I should have been shot at by the whole tribe, and fleeced into the bargain!"

"Why, at that rate she must be quite a bait for the family. But she is amorous, is she not?"

"As a cat, and quite as scratchy if you once let yourself get within reach of her talons," said the colonel; and then, in a more serious vein, continued, "What does the countess say to my proposal?"

The face of his lordship slightly clouded, as he said:

"I am afraid your hopes in that quarter will not be realised. All my advances and arguments have been repulsed quite as severely by the countess as Lucy."

"Did you not enlarge on my fortune, my connections, and my devotion?" demanded the colonel, with a dissatisfied air.

"I did all that, my boy, and everything else that could be expected from one friend to another; but it was useless. There seemed to be some stubborn objection in the way, and, to tell you the truth, matters are not the same with me at home as they used to be. But there is Lucy alone; go and make your peace with her. I will carry off De Vere, so you will have a clear field."

This arrangement was speedily effected, and Lucy was left to be exposed to the attentions of a man from whose presence she instinctively recoiled. Bloomfield soon managed to get rid of De Vere, and was proceeding to join his wife, when he was carried off by a voluble patrician dame, whose immense literary tastes were the terror of the whole company. The countess, to whose kindness her husband was indebted for the seizure, rejoiced over the capture, and strove with still greater zeal to detach Walter from the volatile and fascinating Mrs. Smythe, a task of no little difficulty, for he respected *her*—Mrs. Smythe he did not. Walter, as before intimated, had been slightly worshipping at the shrine of Bacchus, and was therefore more than usually merry.

"Love!" he sneered, glancing at the countess, "is a holiday enjoyment dished up for youth before it meets the world face to face, and afterwards thrown aside with as little remorse as a bride does the wreath that bound her brows when she stood entranced at the altar.

"How can you say so?" stammered the countess, with a look of reproach.

"He is certainly severe!" chimed in Mrs. Smythe "but if we all related our individual experiences, perhaps not unjustly so. What is termed love by boys and girls, in most cases is merely a delicate partiality, which may deepen into habit, and then, of course, become a confirmed affection; but with the majority of these tender juvenile affairs, the heart changes soon after the object that engaged its attention is removed."

"I cannot subscribe to that creed," objected the countess, warmly; "if I did I should think I was outraging the most sacred sympathies of my sex. In young persons, love is unquestionably a more flighty feeling than it is in older ones; but who ever heard the full-grown woman refer but with pleasure to the first admirer of her charms. Is not the recollection of him ranked among the most cherished of her earliest reminiscences? and when in a gossiping mood, does she not invariably allude to him as a kind man, or a handsome man, or as possessing some attraction which found favour. I contend that, however the girl may change, either through choice or compulsory circumstances, she never wholly forgets the object of her first attachment."

"Well argued, Violet!" said Mrs. Smythe; "but what you say goes far to substantiate what I contend for, and proves, if anything, that first love is no love at all; and that what is recognised as love, is the passion we acquire when our faculties are matured, and we have had opportunities of making the selection most agreeable to our fully developed wishes."

"There is a good deal of truth in that observation," thought Morris; but he prudently reserved the conviction for his own edification.

The countess stoutly demurred to the doctrine, and appealed to Walter to promote her views. He would willingly have done so, for a memory still clung to him, but was dashed with the remembrance that, however dearly he had prized it, the boon he once sought had been conferred upon another. Your disappointed lover is slow to forgive.

"Admitting that you are both correct in your philosophy," said he, "what does it all amount to. The boy and the girl love—so do the full-grown man and woman; and the only difference between them in my opinion is, that more insurmountable obstacles lie in the way of the realisation of one affection than the other."

"Then we must infer from your remark," said Mrs. Smythe, "that the older *penchant* is a more practicable one than the younger?"

"Not so!" exclaimed the countess, catching the extremely unequivocal glance which Mrs. Smythe had bestowed on the gallant soldier; but before she could proceed any further, she was interrupted by a summons to the supper table. A royal duke, celebrated for his dining-out propensity, at this moment approached, and etiquette demanded that she should accept of his escort. Mrs. Smythe thus fell, as it were purposely, to the share of Walter; and in a few minutes afterwards they were seated together at the midnight banquet. Lucy, rather compelled than led, accompanied Colonel Stanley, while a little lower down sat Mr. Smythe and the Hibernian beauty, to whom he had clung during the whole evening. Lord Bloomfield was inextricably entangled in the literary meshes of the titled authoress, and compensated himself liberally out of the bottle before him for the infliction.

The supper, which was intended as a finale to the so-called conversazione, was, as such things generally are, exceedingly vapid; but the bye-play was admirable, especially in the vicinity of the redoubtable Captain Morris. He was making silent but fierce love to Mrs. Smythe, against whose warm knees he was pressing his own rather familiarly, while a little lower down the lady's husband was performing the same little drama with the fat Irish peeress. Stanley was exerting himself to the utmost to please the timorous Lucy; and by the time that the wine had begun to circulate more freely, the conversation became general and unrestrained. Morris, although intent upon the conquest of the banker's wife, was not quite so absorbed in his devotions as to be insensible to what was transpiring in his immediate neighbourhood. He once or twice caught the imploring glances of Lucy, and this induced him to observe the colonel more attentively, and as he did so, he fancied he saw an uneasiness and restlessness in his manner which betokened mischief. It was not long before his suspicions were confirmed, for he distinctly observed him dexterously throw something into the untasted glass of wine which he had poured out for Lucy, and which he was pressingly inducing her to partake.

"A philter, as I am alive!" thought he. "Now what shall I do? pull his nose or knock him down? No! by Venus and all her jolly nymphs, I have it!"

All this passed quick as lightning; and as Lucy was in the act of putting forth her reluctant hand to reach the glass, the chair of the colonel slid from under him, and he toppled to the floor; and during the confusion the untasted glass was exchanged for one that stood before a frosty, vinegar-faced spinster of forty.

"Falls are lucky, it is said!" laughed Mrs. Smythe; "so I presume the colonel will prosper in his suit."

"I have had no tumble to-day, and yet I venture to hope," said the captain, gaily, as he noticed the spinster draining the drugged glass to the bottom, while Lucy merely sipped at the one before her. "Am I too presumptuous?"

"No!" whispered Mrs. Smythe, her face, despite her natural self-control, reddening to the temples.

"Where shall I meet you to morrow?"

"I will send you word."

"It shall go hard with me if it is not to-night," was the captain's reflection, as he thought of the certainty of his companion complying with the countess's request to stay all night, and his own intimate knowledge of every nook and corner of the house, to say nothing of the efficacy of a bribe to the servants to wink at his delinquency, if detected. Mr. Smythe had been so assiduous to the stout peeress that he escorted her home, having first, for decency's sake, ascertained that his wife had determined to remain all night at Bloomfield House. Walter, after bidding the countess an affectionate "Good night," also departed, to gossip with the servants on the landing, from whom he soon learned where lay the chamber that Mrs. Smythe was to occupy—it adjoined that of the countess's. After the customary bustle of departure had subsided, the only persons remaining in those fine rooms were Lord Bloomfield and Colonel Stanley; the latter challenged the former to play, which they did; but at the end of half an hour Lord Bloomfield fell asleep in his chair, completely prostrated with drink; and the colonel rose exultingly, for the purpose of putting his fell design into execution; for Jasper had taken care to inform him of the exact position of Lucy's chamber. And now commenced the nocturnal mysteries of Bloomfield House.

The spinster, who had partaken of the favour intended for Lucy, retired to rest, labouring under the most unaccountable sensations. Her pale grey eyes were unusually inflamed, and her bony features crimsoned so violently, that a stranger might have imagined she was attacked by erysipelas. She felt hot and restless, and wandered up and down her chamber like a lost spirit.

"What can be the matter with me?" thought she, seized with a nervous trembling. "I feel as if I was going to melt; for something warm is trickling through me from my head to my feet. I never felt so but once in my life before, and that was when I was two-and-twenty, and was squeezed by young Mellon, who, poor fellow, did with me as he liked. What can it be?" A bright idea seemed to strike her, for she stopped short in her limited promenade and ejaculated, "No! it cannot be that. In the absence of any object the thing is ridiculous—absurd. If possible, though, it would be delightful!"

As she uttered this, her eyes emitted a most un-spinster-like light, and she playfully threw her arms round one of the bed-posts, and returned some imaginary kisses, with an ardour that showed that there was some vigour left in her cold and withered frame.

"Dear Fred!" she murmured, with difficulty maintaining her equilibrium.

Her attendant, a sage unmarried damsel, who had long arrived at maturity, was inexpressibly shocked at this display of a powerful amorous tendency, and with horror remarked that her mistress must have become intoxicated, and the best thing that could be done with her was to induce her to go to bed. But this was not so easily affected, for the spinster hugged her so tightly round the neck, that she ran great risk of strangulation, and in the efforts she made to free herself, received sundry scratches and bruises. At last the excited lady was denuded of her clothes, and robed for the night. Her scanty hair was concealed in a cap of elaborate dimensions, and from out of the interstices of the lace border of her dress a glimpse could be had of a very brown and wrinkled bosom. With difficulty she was placed in bed, into which she had no sooner got, than she commenced hugging the pillow, as she murmured something expressive of satisfaction at once more having her dear Fred in her arms.

The attendant, nervously susceptible of alarm on the score of fire, cautiously removed the light, and the spinster was left to roll and toss in her bed, a prey to the most distractingly warm emotions. She had not been left alone for more, perhaps, than half an hour, when the door of her chamber was cautiously opened, and the figure of a man stole into it and softly approached her bed-side.

"Come closer, Fred!" murmured the spinster, frantically embracing the pillow.

"Better than I anticipated," thought the colonel, who, by the way, was half drunk, for he had primed himself for the adventure. "The potion, as a cockney would say, 'has made her as right as ninepence.' And now for a banquet fit for high Jove himself!" He then divested himself of his garments, and, like another Tarquin, crept into the bed, and nestled by the side of the faded, but still warm and yielding beauty.

While this little bit of iniquity was being perpetrated, the countess, Mrs. Smythe, and Lucy, were each in their chambers, indulging in very different kinds of reveries. Lucy was crying bitterly over the recollection of the inflictions of the evening, and the fancied indifference which Walter had displayed for her.

"He does not, cannot love me!" she sobbed, "or he would never have behaved so very strangely with that Mrs. Smythe; and sister, too—she prevented his speaking to me, and for what I really cannot form the slightest idea." It was to have been her last night in London, and at the thought of the peremptory arrangement she felt heart-sick and oppressed, and, not having any inclination for sleep, opened her window, and looked out into the garden. The night was a very fine one, and the light from the stars lent a silvery tint to every object around. It was such a night as that on which Dido, with her willow wand, "waved her love again to Carthage;" and as Lucy, who was peculiarly sensitive to the beauties and poetry of nature, gazed into the mysterious depths of the sky, that hung in unbroken grandeur above her head, she thought of her mountain home, its wild scenery, and quaint melodies, that in the stillness of the evening would break on the ear in such gushes of mellowed music. With this cherished idea came the image of Walter, as he appeared when a boy, as fleet and nimble as the goats that browsed on his native hill-side. Then in her fancy she followed him through all the stages of his career as a soldier, and then dwelt with rapture on his appearance in the bloom of his manhood.

"Dear Walter!" she unconsciously exclaimed aloud, "if you only knew how dearly I love you, you would not slight me for the unlawful and false smiles of others!"

"The devil!" almost escaped from the lips of the individual himself who had been honoured with this avowal of a preference, as he paused at the foot of a ladder he had reared against the window. "What a lucky discovery! Listeners, they say, never hear any good of themselves; but, by St. George! I shall be able ever after this to give the proverb the lie. Poor Lucy! I'd rather have lost my commission, than given you reason to suspect that I entertained even the ghost of a sentiment hostile to your purity. But what a lucky fellow I am among the ladies! I am afraid my success will be the means of my degenerating into a miserable puppy—something so vain and conceited that, like Cruikshank's little dog, my tail will curl so tightly that I shall be lifted off my hind legs. Come what will, though, Lucy shall be the guardian angel of my nobler hours of existence; and it shall be my study to keep her ignorant of the errors and vices that blacken and deform this otherwise goodly world of ours. So for the nonce, let me lie perdue, and console myself with the reflection that if we men do take advantage of woman's weakness, her frailty, in nine cases out of ten, first gives us the preliminary wink of encouragement to proceed in our designs. This dark-eyed banker's wife is a treasure—a merry wife of the right sort; long in the waist, dark, and quite as juicy-looking as a peach; wanton as an Indian dancing girl, with an eye and foot that, as Ulysses says, speak an invitation to kiss at every moment. But what the devil's that noise all about. Hide me, ye friendly shrubs!"

The uproar was occasioned by an occurrence that deserves narration.

Jasper Sampson, the spy hall-porter, was prowling about the house in his stockings, listening at every bed-room door, and carefully noting even the breathings of the occupants, so as to detect the presence of one or two individuals. After listening at the countess's door, and applying his eyes as well as ears to the keyhole, he passed on to Lucy's, where he performed the same manoeuvres, and, feeling disappointed at not hearing anything, was proceeding to the chamber occupied by Mrs. Smythe, when he heard a door violently thrown open, and some one running hastily towards him. Before he had time to get out of the way, he was knocked down by some one evidently familiar with the science of pugilism, and the next moment he found himself locked tightly in the arms of a woman, who almost smothered him in kisses, and addressed to him every endearing phrase with which gratified love fills up its leisure time. The warm breath of the woman, together with the contact of his hands with her naked body, almost maddened the unsubdued sensuality of Jasper, and he actually shrieked, so intense was the agony he endured. The uproar alarmed the whole house; and in a very few minutes every person in it came rushing into the passage, where Jasper and his arms-full of bliss were struggling. The female was the ancient spinster, in such a state of disorder as regarded apparel, that the ladies dispersed immediately; and several of the female servants, at the bidding of the chaste and indignant housekeeper, precipitated themselves on the frantic lady, and by main force bore her back to her chamber, shrieking and clamouring for her "beloved Fred," the myth lover of her hallucination. Jasper's explanation, that he was perambulating the house in obedience to commands from his master, coupled with the insinuation of the unfortunate lady's maid about the vinous affection, was held to be a sufficient explanation, and all parties again retired to their rooms, shaking their heads rather gravely over the conclusion that chastity must neither be measured by age nor ugliness; for the hitherto unspotted virgin relative of the ancient house of Bloomfield had been so far above suspicion, that the marble statue on the first landing would as soon have been suspected of a *faux pas*.

"Who the deuce could the first one have been?" thought Jasper, as he resumed his office of spy. "Ah, I hear a footstep! By heaven, 'tis the colonel! and he has mistaken the room, and given that parchment bit of flesh the benefit of his company, instead of the tender young thing with the blue eyes and chesnut hair. How funny! Hist, colonel! colonel! This way—follow me to my room."

"I shall be made the butt of the whole town," said the colonel, encasing his lower extremities, "if I do not recover the whole of my garments. Help me, my good fellow!"

"What a mistake you made!" grinned Jasper.

"Mistake!" said the colonel, savagely; "you told me No. 15."

"So I did; but the lady you was with sleeps in No. 18."

"Curses on it! To risk so much, and then to be baffled after all—it is unendurable! But I will have another venture; cannot you see if Lucy's chamber is to be entered; and also, for God's sake, get my clothes; they are on the floor at the foot of the bed in a heap."

Jasper went on his errand, and speedily returned.

"The old woman," said he, "is fast asleep—quite done over, so is her maid; and I'd only to open the door—which I suppose they had forgotten to fasten—and creep in and get the things. Here they are; but it's all up with Miss Lucy—her door is locked and bolted."

"The window—she will not have looked to that, will she?"

"'Tis not likely; and if you like to venture it, you will find a ladder in the garden."

"Venture it!" cried the colonel, whose disappointment had rendered him furious and reckless; "having gone so far, I'd sooner go to hell than be baffled! Show me the way."

Jasper did so with alacrity, for he loved mischief and outrage, whether perpetrated by man or woman.

As soon as the colonel had gained the garden, Jasper left him to attend to his own interests himself, for he had a strong impression that he should make some wonderful discovery before the night elapsed. The colonel, after cautiously looking about him for a while, espied the ladder, which Walter, who still lay concealed, had prudently thrown down, when the first sound of the disturbance had reached him.

"This will do admirably!" muttered the colonel, as he proceeded to rear and place the means of ascension under Lucy's window.

As he put his foot on the first step of the ladder, he said, half aloud and exultingly:

"Now for my satisfaction for having wasted an hour on a withered witch. Lucy, by this time, must be half dead with expectation, or the philter was a weak one."

"Oho!" chuckled Walter, in his concealment; "the colonel, who I see is rather drunk, has visited Miss Skin-and-Bones!—I should like to have witnessed the encounter!—and now, furious at having expended his powder on a barren conquest, would complete his rascality by an assault on the only sinless inmate of this, I must say, rather extraordinarily conducted household. Well, well! the Scripture says 'out of evil cometh good,' and I do begin to believe it; for here am I, on an evil errand, and yet so circumstanced that I am happily enabled to frustrate the horrible purpose of a downright villain. Not that there is any harm in kissing a woman with her consent; but against her will—faugh! it is abominable—atrocious! why the blood of old Saturn himself would warm into resentment of such cowardice!"

Stanley had now ascended more than half way up the ladder, when Walter crept on his hands and knees to its foot, and, with the former, while still in a recumbent posture, seized it, and, lifting it from the ground, with a powerful swing sent the colonel flying into the very bosom of a tree that formed one of the principal attractions of the gardens. Not being prepared for so sudden an excursion in the air, Stanley dropped through the branches like a stone, and fell heavily to the ground. Before he could recover himself, he was dragged to the other end of the garden, of the back door of which Walter had a key, and thrust, stunned and helpless, into the narrow street behind, where he did not long remain; for when the policeman on the beat discovered him, he had him conveyed, as one drunk and incapable, to the nearest station-house; and so, for that night, ended the amours of the adventurous Colonel Stanley. It is to be desired that the same virtuous conclusion might be related of those of the equally desperate, though not a tithe so vitiated, Captain Morris. The chronicle of his deeds is obliged to confess that, after having thus summarily disposed of the colonel, he adhered to his original resolution; and, with the hardihood of the leader of a forlorn hope party, raised the prostrate ladder, and erected it right against the bedchamber window of, as he imagined, the seductive Mrs. Smythe. The casement, as he had anticipated, was open—the morning air is so balmy that ladies frequently require it to fan their flushed cheeks. He leaped into the room without hesitation, and at the first glance was rather surprised at the sumptuous character of the furniture. The subdued light from a lamp suspended from the ceiling fell upon the richest and most massive drapery, while the other senses were regaled with exquisite perfumes, and that peculiar aroma which invariably pervades the chamber of a lady who industriously studies her physical health.

It is particularly desired, in deference to the better qualities of Walter Morris, that it should be borne in mind that he had sacrificed pretty freely during the previous evening to the god whose inspirations are injurious even to the well-balanced temperament, and that with his lax morals, it is not to be wondered at that he should have become dangerously excited under the influence of such a highly flavoured temptation as that which fell before his dazzled and bewildered eyes. Entirely destitute of the brutality that operated so powerfully with Colonel Stanley, he did not proceed to take advantage of the opportunity offered him without due deliberation. Indeed there was a refinement in his nature which revolted at the too greedy seizure of any object, however ardently coveted. Some allowance must therefore be made for his indiscretion in lending himself at

all to this nocturnal adventure, the more especially when it is considered that in no single respect did any anchorite tendencies mingle in his disposition. With this extremely superficial apology for his moral delinquencies, it is left to the reader's imagination to guess the frame of mind he was in when he approached the most bewitching bed that ever coaxed a frail mortal out of his last scruples of conscience. Fancy a couch, soft and warm as the down that the gentle summer wind collects in its favourite corners, curtains falling around in countless waving folds, and ending in a sweep that had no termination that the eye could detect—a silent mass of rich drapery that concealed the form of the loveliest of sleepers! Fancy all this, and much more that cannot be conveyed in language, and then feel surprised, if you can, that the intruder should have put aside the screen nervously, and then have gazed on the discovered treasure with intense trepidation.

"Confound this giddiness!" muttered Walter. "I tremble like a child who sees a Christmas present, and is afraid to grasp it. Perhaps a peep will assure me!"

He did peep, but drew back as quickly as if he had seen a boa-constrictor. The sleeper was the countess, and he had mistaken the chamber.

"Violet!" he exclaimed, as he rapturously bent over the insensible form of the only woman he had ever truly loved; "how beautiful, how divine thou art in thy surpassing loveliness! Oh God, do not let me go mad, and forget myself in this unlooked-for and thrilling dream!"

He shook, as if with an ague, and stood regarding the countess in speechless admiration; and well he might, for her beauty was powerful enough to enthral every sense. She lay upon a pillow whiter than snow, with her long tresses, which had escaped from the delicate net-like cap that had vainly sought to confine them, floating around her glorious head, under which an arm, covered to the wrist by the purest lawn, nestled as cosily as a child's does round its mother's neck. Her face was as radiant as the first blush of morn; and from the long lashes of her eyebrows the most delicate shadows were thrown upon her enamelled complexion, and contrasted so pleasingly with its rosy hues, that you might have thought you were gazing at the closed eyes of a sleeping bird. Her lips were slightly parted; and her breathings were as regular as the sighings of the wind through the trees, when the undimmed stars look down from their lofty abode on an unruffled evening. The outlines of her form, as, spread before the enamoured gauze it lay in all its matchless undulations ravished and took by storm every faculty that pays allegiance to woman's enchanting proportions; and as Walter drank in the whole of the voluptuous scene, in every variety of its provoking display, he began to totter in the respect, which, in the temple of his chivalry, he would, in calm moments, have cheerfully accorded to that resplendent embodiment of feminine perfection.

"Violet! dearest Violet!" he involuntarily murmured; "why were you not mine? The love I bore you was the frankest and sincerest that ever man entertained for woman, and yet in an hour when your better nature must have slumbered, you fell off from me, and remembered not the time when your hand grasped mine, and the homage of my lip was received with a yielding and graceful courtesy. Oh Violet, Violet! the remembrance of your inconsistency at times unmans me! and now, when I have not only your person but reputation within my power, a subtle demon prompts me to take the satisfaction which a gourmand would exact from a liberal feast! but the past rises up in judgment against my treasonable will, and compels my disorderly propensities to have mercy on your helplessness. One kiss—the first ever so received—and it may be the last!"

He pressed his warm lips to hers, and, as he did so, distinctly caught the sound of her breathings, moulded into one electric sentence—"Walter! dear Walter!"

Alarmed for the safety of his resolution, he tore himself away, and plunged recklessly through the window. A walk for about seven or eight minutes through the garden cooled him down, and had the effect of restoring to him a great portion of his habitual self-possession.

"How disgraceful to be thus prowling about another man's premises!" were his thoughts, as he stalked recklessly over the gravelled walks; "and for what—for the mere excitement of clasping a woman once more in the embrace whose pleasure ends with the relaxation of the hold? Pshaw! I should be more a man than such a slave to my appetites! And by heaven I will! But then, to throw away such a jewel—to be laughed at and scorned by her for my lukewarmness; my broken word, too! D—n! my virtuous determinations are like wax in the presence of the sun! Place a woman in all her glittering radiance before my prostituted sensuality, and I am no longer the Walter Morris whose slender purse was ever open to the distressed, or allowed wrong to be perpetrated in my presence with impunity—but some brute whose instincts overpower his reason, and who cowardly submits to the promptings of the most inglorious impulses!"

Thus chafed, he strode along for several minutes, and then broke out into a sneering laugh.

"Well, well! we must all of us obey our destiny, and I presume mine is to be the slave of woman; so heigho for one more attempt to reach you, my dark-eyed Caroline!"

Once more was the ladder raised, and this time with success. He easily gained admission into the chamber to which he had originally intended to pay a visit, and found it not quite so luxuriously furnished a one as that occupied by the countess. Its occupant, too, lay on the outside of the bed just as she had left the supper-room. She had evidently fallen asleep, completely tired out with waiting for her dilatory lover; and, anticipating his arrival, had not removed her garments. Her appearance in her golden slumber would have thawed even the icicles that hang on Diana's temple, and Walter could not forbear imprinting on her lips a multitude of impassioned kisses. But they did not arouse her. Once or twice he fancied she was on the point of waking; but no—she had gone far into the land of dreams, and only acknowledged the salutes on her cherry lips by broken murmurs and indistinct articulations. The image of Violet floated before the mental eye of Walter, and, despite his weakened control over his self-command, he refrained from profiting by his successful accomplishment of the assignation. Observing some writing materials in the room, he hastily penned a note, which he deposited by the sleeper's side, and then withdrew, taking care, as he descended, and before he left the garden, to remove every trace of his visit. He thought to have

escaped unobserved; but in that respect he was disappointed; for Jasper, who had been lurking about, anxious for the reappearance of Colonel Stanley, to whom he had promised to give egress, detected and recognised him in the act of crossing the garden and liberating himself by means of the door that afforded a back entrance into Bloomfield House.

"He here!" hissed Jasper through his teeth. "Curses on him, and the whole of his tribe! I wish I had caught him! But perhaps it is better as it is. I shall have a tale to tell to my lord. Yes, yes; the Life-Guardsman must account for his appearance. The countess—ah, may it be so! God grant it may have been so! for I begin to hate womankind as I do the horror that gnaws into my very marrow!"

This deplorably wretched being, after indulging in this diabolical sentiment, leisurely proceeded to the room where Lord Bloomfield sat snoring, and having aroused him, communicated the particulars of the clandestine visit of Captain Morris. His lordship, quite stupefied by his half slept-off inebriety, listened to the narrative with a vacant stare of astonishment and incredulity; and then, as if reluctant to hear more, laid down his head again on the table, and resumed his broken and disturbed drunken slumbers.

"The fool!" said Jasper, regarding his master with an air of contempt; "the privileges his wife denies to him she is willing to confer on another' and yet he has not the spirit to resent the misappropriation. If I were as powerful as he is, I would rend her to pieces. But I ought not to say so—I have been gulled myself, and by the same man, too. I am cursed with a calamity, but I have not ceased to feel all the stings that dart their venomous points into the flesh, and make it creep with a wild and savage longing for retribution. That man—that brave and gallant soldier—that adored of the women and envied of the men—shall yet feel how dangerous it is to play with the sharp edge of a husband's honour. All is quiet now; and as I cannot learn any more than I have for my idiot of a master, I will once again, before that freezing medicine Wriggles gave me turns my blood to water, look upon her whom I hate above all living things!"

His features, as he indulged in this latter deadly prejudice, assumed so terrific a hue that he himself started as he caught a glimpse of them in the mirror that he happened to glance at in turning.

"No matter!" he hoarsely said, "the uglier the better for my purpose! I should like to frighten her into a fit, and when she came out of it have her believe it was all a dream!"

Creeping up stairs like a felon, he opened the door of a bed-chamber of more humble pretensions than those which have been before referred to, and, passing through a secret door that opened from a closet, gained admittance to a prettily-furnished dormitory, through the partially blinded window of which the rising sun poured its first faint beams, and revealed the forms of two female sleepers. One was a stout woman, whose head was enveloped in endless layers of cotton and woollen, the other a pretty creature, with raven locks, that bestrewed the spotless pillow, and a face flushed with the fever of disturbed slumbers.

"Alice," whispered Jasper in her ear, as he gave her a shaking.

She opened her large bright eyes, as if the sound of the voice had been familiar to her; and upon looking up, beheld the hideous countenance of the hall-porter leering upon her's, and protruding his lips, and putting forth his tongue, as if he would

blow kisses to her mouth. As he performed this disgusting pantomime, he slowly backed himself out of the room, and, indulging in a loud smacking of his lips, vanished by the way he had entered. A cold tremor stole through the body of the half-aroused girl, and with a wild shriek of terror she flung herself on the substantial person of her sleeping companion. A suppressed grumbling was all the action, violent as it was, elicited from her corpulent bed companion, and the girl, with a shiver buried herself beneath the clothes, to shut out that horrid vision.

CHAPTER XI.

THE MERRY WIFE OF THE PIOUS TOBACCONIST.

THE day succeeding the incidents that distinguished Bloomfield House on the memorable evening of the conversazione, was destined to be an important one to the majority of the personages comprised in this narrative; but before what befel the more aristocratic of them is related, it is necessary to follow Jasper Sampson in the adventure he undertook with the young wife of the Methodist class-leader, herself being also a shining ornament of the congregation among which her husband was one of the most dazzling of tabernacle luminaries. The residence of this charming and gifted lady was situate in one of the business streets of the great West End, and had standing at one side of its door a remarkably fine specimen of a pipe-clay highlander, and at the other a grinning negro, performing a grand masticulating feat on a surprising roll of pig-tail tobacco. The shop from these tokens was adjudged to be one where the "weed" was vended, and a glance at the old-fashioned bay-window confirmed the surmise, and informed the gazer through its panes that none but pious snuff-tobacco boxes were there sold; no girls pirouetting on one leg and extending the other in the air, or woman in a state of questionable scantiness of apparel, was displayed in glistening rows for the edification of the "gent" tribe; all the figures on the various articles were chaste, staid, and suggestive of divers moral siderations. The bills in the window, too, did nearly relate to the profanities of the theatre or the concert room, but to holy teachings of men, who moderate he stated at the foot of their bills that to defray expenses collections would be made at the conclusion of the service. Inside, everything betokened a propriety of the most rigidly exacting order; and when a customer happened to be standing at the counter, his eye was magnetically attracted to the radiant young proprietress, poising the scales in her long, slender fingers, and either adding to or subtracting from the quantity in the balance, with that delicate nibbling exactness which only a woman can display. Arrayed in a brown silk dress, that fitted close up to a throat of dazzling whiteness, she was certainly the most pungent-looking commodity in the shop. Her face was beautifully regular, and delicately fair. The cheeks were soft and plump, and under her small and slightly-dimpled chin was a miniature copy of it, that coaxed the pressure of the amorous finger. Her blue eyes were full of light, and, by their arch expression, contradicted the Quaker-like composure she evidently strove to impart to her countenance. Report, that mother of exaggerations, had said that she could wink when she chose, and was the most provoking and tempting-looking of all the enchanting creatures that are perpetually struggling with the natural playfulness of their dispositions. Even in her devotional exercises her eyes had a peculiar lustre, which, it was gravely alleged, tempted many souls to wander in dangerous proximity to the jaws of the beast that goes about seeking whom he may devour. Be that as it may, she was an immense favourite among the elect, and commanded the patronage of all the tobacco and snuff consumers of three exemplary congregations. In short, she was a noted character among the self-elected, and attended chapel, prayer, and class-meetings, with a punctuality that gathered round her lovely head all the odours of professional sanctity. Her husband was a gentleman of remarkable attainments. For the first ten years of his manhood, he sinned grievously at a lawyer's desk, for the paltry pittance of five-and-twenty shillings per week; when, having in a blessed hour most miraculously been brought to see the light, he betook himself to the more congenial office of saving souls, and levying contributions on the purses of those whom he had brought within the pale of salvation. He commenced his labours of love in the bye-lanes and alleys of wickedness, and preached with such fervour and unction at street corners, and on wild and sterile commons, that he gradually rose to the dignity of class-reader and preacher extraordinary in the chapel of the Reverend Jabez Smashevil, a worthy divine, who had grown fat in his snug ministry. It was while in the latter capacity that he had met with the lovely Susan Hopgood, the daughter of a prelatical costermonger, and, of course, a man for whom there could possibly be no manner of hope. William Bond—or, while he was in bondage to Satan—Billy Bond no sooner saw this fair daughter perilously sporting on the borders of the everlasting bonfire, than he was smitten with a desire to save her. He felt that, like Ruth, she was in tears and tribulation amid alien corn, and if, through his instrumentality, she could be introduced into the fold of assignezzian faith, so signal a victory over the evil one would be an astounding triumph for him among the zealous and successful brethren.

The first step he took was to assail the obdurate mortal costermonger, but that worthy repulsed all efforts with disdain; and finally ejected him from the house with sundry blasphemous expressions, and

numerous assaults on certain sensitive regions of his body. The agency of a female devotee was then invoked, and Susan Hopgood's eyes were opened to the error of her ways. Despite the injunctions of her father, she attended class-meeting with unswerving regularity; and listened to the exhortations of her deliverer with such attention, that in a short time she became as thoroughly inoculated with the Smashevil doctrine of redemption as the most gifted member of the community. When this gracious work had been completed, the "Reverend" William Bond, to render it permanent and enduring, offered the security of his immaculate person, which, after due prayer and solitary communings, assisted by some holy embraces and kisses in the spirit, was accepted. The pair were married amid a perfect tempest of rejoicings in the tabernacle they attended, and as Susan brought her husband a legacy of some four hundred pounds, left her by a deceased maternal uncle, it was mutually agreed that it would be sinful to let it lie idle in the strong box of a bank, and therefore they cast their eyes about for some suitable investment.

"Thy father's business abounded in profit, did it not, beloved one?"

"It did; but I am fearful the days of its prosperity have passed away."

"What thinkest thou, then, of vending some carnal commodities, such as bacon, eggs, and fish?"

"The profit is small, for I have an uncle in the trade, and he is as poor now as when he started."

"Ah! my blessed lamb, I have it! but peradventure you would object?"

"Not to anything from you, beloved William!"

"The light and the grace ever be with you, my adored one!"

"Amen!"

"Then, as thou dost not object, I will tell thee of a scheme I have thought of. The sisters and brothers with whom we are acquainted number six hundred. Now I have calculated, and know from personal observation, that out of that goodly, and—glory be to Him—godly number, one hundred and ninety-one do smoke the weed called tobacco; two hundred do take snuff, to stimulate their nasal powers; and the remaining two hundred and nineteen do smoke and snuff too. Dost thou comprehend me?"

"Partly, my beloved. But proceed."

"Those six hundred right-minded individuals would prefer buying their soothing and titillating compounds from one of themselves, would they not?"

"It would be sinful if they refused."

"I rejoice amazingly that thou agreest with me so far; and, without further circumlocution, would suggest to thy better wisdom that we should, certain of such godly patronage, commence as dealers in pipes, cigars, snuff, tobacco, both in shag and returns, and every variety of articles sold at what is called a tobacconist's."

"Our money would be safe in such a business, I am certain; but do not the sons of Belial frequent such places to feast their eyes on the gaudy young creatures that serve in them?"

"They do—they—" groaned the Reverend William Bond, as he piously added, "Let us pray, Susan!"

Down they both fell on their knees; and, after much wrestling with some invisible demon, brought their fast-moving lips into such close contact, that their arms fell round each other's necks; and when, after due pausing for recovery from their emotions, they arose, it was with the understanding that a suitable place of business should be forthwith taken, and Susan installed in it as sole manageress; the public duties of the conscientious "Reverend" William Bond precluding his taking any active share in the undertaking. In due time this arrangement was carried out; and while the husband was fulfilling his mission among the godly and wicked, the wife, arrayed in a dress which combined goodness of quality with a charming simplicity of style, was meekly dealing out snuff and tobacco to the upright six hundred, and any of the profane that tendered sterling coins of the realm for what they desired.

It was to this shop that Jasper Sampson hied, as hath already been intimated. He was arrayed in a goodly suit of black cloth, of the accepted cut of the "elect," and wore the ample and spotless white neckerchief of the order. His hat was craped to the crown; and, with his raven hair falling in orthodox straightness about his ears, presented a very good picture of the man who is supposed to have no other vocation than to weep over the sins of the multitude. His pale, attenuated features served him admirably—they would have carried him safely through any religious imposture. As soon as he had entered the shop, he sat himself down on one of the stools placed outside the counter for the accommodation of those customers desirous of having a gossip with the exemplary Mrs. Bond; and, having abstracted a massive silver snuff-box from his pocket, with a smile presented it to that suavious lady.

"What shall I serve you with?" said she, in the sweetest voice imaginable, at the same time disclosing such rows of perfect teeth, that their pure white actually deepened the richness of her full, ripened lips.

"Brown rappee — plain brown rappee, my dear lady!"

"How much?"

"One ounce—just one ounce, my dear lady!"

Mrs. Bond bowed gracefully, and, taking the handsome box in her lily hands, was about to open it, when the inscription on the lid caught her eye. It was,—

"Presented to

THE REVEREND JASPER SAMPSON,

Of Salem Chapel, Troy, Cincinnati, U.S.,

As a

Mark of Love and Respect, by his Affectionate Congregation."

This announcement threw the pious Mrs. Bond into a fit of trembling. And no wonder; she had before her a live clergyman of the true faith from the Far West, beyond the wild waters of the Atlantic; and his appearance considerably prejudiced him in her favour. Jasper saw that the bait had taken, and with secret delight watched the tremor of her hands, and the slight flush that spread over her excessively handsome face.

"The medicine I find works," thought he; "for I can gaze upon her unmoved; but I must be cautious, for she's a rare piece of womanhood. What moist, cherry lips, and what a skin—smooth, warm, and soft as velvet—and such a bust—stout, but not fat—just that full one made to warm and infuse vigour into the lean one of a man! Ugh! but I must be cautious, these prudes are apt to fly at the first shot!"

"Excuse me, my dear lady," said he to her at length, as he saw her either purposely, or could not in her agitation avoid, delay, in serving him; "but,

being a stranger in your great metropolis—indeed in England—and having taken up my residence in this neighbourhood, I am desirous of knowing something about the places of worship hereabouts?"

"The Lord surely must have thrown this heavenly light in my way!" thought Mrs. Bond, as she greedily drank in every word of the strange divine's nasal address. "I shall be but too glad to assist you in your inquiries," she said to him in reply; "and I am fortunately in a condition to do so, for my husband is an unworthy teacher of the truth."

"How fortunate, indeed!" exclaimed the seeming divine. "May I ask to what persuasion he has lent his talents and services?"

"We are a branch, sir," answered Mrs. Bond, a little proudly, of the Primitive Methodists; we worship from our hearts and from direct inspiration."

"Heaven has been kind, to introduce me once more to my kith and kin in the spirit!" responded Jasper, elevating his eye-brows in a transport of gratitude; "and I pray that I may deserve the favour. In my far-off home, thousands of miles in the interior of the vast continent of America, I have a little flock who maintain the same belief with me, and disavow the Pope and all his errors, and defy the devil and all his iniquities."

"The holy man!" thought Mrs. Bond, glowing with rapture; "may heaven and all the good angels wait upon him!"

"Yes, madam, in that little kingdom of ——, we abjure all the errors of popery and prelacy, and stick to the one true and indivisible doctrine of the early church. We despise tedious formalities, and preach from the very bottom of our hearts. But pray, madam," continued he, taking a pinch of snuff, "do you hold the doctrine of invincible necessity?"

"Certainly!"

"And that no soul can be saved but by special grace?"

"Such is our humble belief."

"My worthy young lady!" said Jasper, strongly affected; "allow me to grasp your sisterly hand, for I do perceive that in coming to this distant region of the world I have not vainly cast my bread on the waters!"

Mrs. Bond stretched forth her hand without reluctance, and Jasper, holding it in both his own, appeared to be overcome with emotion; and so indeed he was, for the touch of the warm, soft hand of the fully-developed woman before him thrilled through him to the core. His eyes lighted up, as Mrs. Bond imagined, with enthusiasm; and he pressed her hand with such fervour, that she burned with the desire to have him visit the Ebenezer Tabernacle.

"Beautiful!" murmured Jasper, increasing the pressure on the hand.

"Beautiful, indeed!" echoed the lovely tobacconist; "to be all brought into one fold, and——"

"Expire in one embrace!" interrupted Jasper, rising to compose himself, for he felt a whirling giddiness stealing upon him, and a strong inclination to leap over the counter and clasp that voluptuous form to his burning and panting breast.

"A glass of water?" he gaspingly asked for, at the same time abstracting the phial that contained the sedative from his pocket; "I sometimes feel faint."

It was supplied to him instantly; and, as he carefully let fall into it two drops of blood-red fluid from the phial, and drank the whole off at a draught, the compassionate Mrs. Bond consoled herself with the reflection that his ministerial labours must have preyed on his constitution, and that he was on the high road to a glorious martyrdom.

"I am better now," said Jasper, from whose countenance every trace of his late agitation had vanished. "I am subject to slight temporary attacks, but they are not dangerous; and I confidently hope to live until I have accomplished my mission!"

Mrs. Bond lifted up her fine eyes to heaven, as if in silent echo of the wish; and then tremulously proceeded to the subject that at the moment lay nearest to her heart.

"Our chapel, sir, is close at hand, and this evening we hold our monthly love-feast," said she, hesitatingly.

"You keenly interest me!" exclaimed Jasper; "for nothing would give me more pleasure than to once more hold loving intercourse with a wo—— I mean the pious of my own faith. If you will direct me I will attend, and perhaps the exhortations of a stranger may not be unacceptable."

"Oh, indeed, no!" said the delighted Mrs. Bond; "you will be received not only gladly but with a loving welcome!"

"Here's a chance for my master!" thought Jasper; "he would like to have a bit of fun among the Methodist girls, I'll be bound! Ahem! what shall I say to her, so as to bring him with me without suspicion? I have it! Such a visit will be like balm to my troubled soul!" said he, turning to her with an air of affectionate concern; "and I have a young friend whose eyes it has pleased Providence to open, whom it would equally please to have such consolation."

"We shall be delighted!" said Mrs. Bond, pricking up her ears.

"My friend," said Jasper, "is young, rich, and noble; but, tired of the gaieties of the sinful world, he now seeks to employ his time in bringing back lost sheep to the fold."

"You interest me much!" exclaimed Mrs. Bond; and her manner did not contradict the assertion.

"Yes, my dear lady," said Jasper, tenderly and modestly; "he has long acknowledged the power of our church, and, during his wanderings in the back settlements of America, stumbled over my little congregation, and remained with it until I was called to this great country, whither he voluntarily accompanied me. He is Hungarian by birth, and was driven from his native land by the cruelties of a barbarous government."

"Is he very young?" inquired Mrs. Bond, striving in vain to appear collected and unconcerned.

"About thirty-one or two, tall, dark, and strikingly handsome; with a countenance cast in a truly Grecian mould. Although amiable and pious, he has one partiality—I can scarcely say fault—of which I cannot break him."

"What is it?" nervously asked Mrs. Bond.

"He will persist in conforming to one of the customs of his country—he wears mustachios and an imperial."

"Is that all?" suddenly exclaimed Mrs. Bond, relieved by the explanation; but, correcting her vivacity, she added, "in a little time he may be induced to abandon the fashion."

"I have no doubt he will!" said Jasper, with a paternal smile; "and perhaps the influence of the society into which he will thus be thrown, as it were, by the design of Providence, may cause a speedy change of his habit in this respect."

The entrance of some customers gave Jasper an opportunity of beating a retreat, which he did, after an exchange of address cards and some parting unctuous benedictions.

The fresh comers were a couple of Ebenezers, and to them the joyful news was communicated that their chapel in the evening would be honoured with the presence of a converted Hungarian nobleman and a celebrated preacher from the United States of America.

The pair prayerfully turned up the whites of their goggle eyes to the bright chandeliers above their heads, and each, with a couple of fingers applied to his nose, hurried in opposite directions, to spread the glad tidings among the community.

As for Mrs. Bond, she was in a perpetual twitter all the day. The vision of a dark, handsome foreign nobleman, with glossy appendages on his lips, praying by her side, was perpetually before her mind; and when Mr. Bond returned home in the afternoon, smelling rather strongly of cigars and a certain potent transparent liquid, he was almost overwhelmed with his wife's frantic statement of the new triumph over Satan.

"Love-feast!" roared Lord Bloomfield, as soon as Jasper had informed him of his brilliant success with the fair tobacconist; "what the devil's that? not one of the old-fashioned cock and hen clubs, is it?"

"Not exactly," grinned Jasper; "but I don't think the difference with some of them is very great. It's a sort of prayer-meeting, with cakes and wine, and then those that are moved by the spirit, as they call it, get upon their legs and tell all the lies, thefts, fornications, and adulteries they have committed; and then the whole company falls down and prays, with a hundred-horse power, for the soul of the repentant sinner."

"D—n it!" ejaculated his polite lordship; "it's nothing less than a species of popish confessional, without its secresy and decency. But I will go; let me see, I am to be count—eh? what?"

"Bumbinski, my lord."

"Yes, Count Bumbinski, a Hungarian refugee, converted from the errors of a thousand centuries of ancestors, to the truths of the evangelical interpretation of the Protestant faith. A pretty sort of masquerade for an English nobleman—but there is something exciting about it; and as I am cut—divorced *a mensa et thoro* from my wife—it will be a little bit of diverting excitement, besides giving me an admirable opportunity of carrying off that adorable demure creature of a tobacconist. How did she look, my most clever of Cupid's ambassadors?"

"Bewitchingly, my lord! I feel satisfied the germs of dissatisfaction with her husband have taken deep root in her heart."

"How so? What did you observe to have enabled you so speedily to form that conclusion?"

"Her manner, my lord, is restless, her eyes are bright and wandering, and her bosom heaves and pants, as if she wanted something, and yet did not. Besides, I have heard that her husband is exceedingly attentive to more than one of the girls who frequent the chapel!"

"She must be jealous, then?"

"Yes she is, but does not know it. Her husband gammons her to believe that all he does is for the love of the Lord; but in my opinion, it's only her religious madness that keeps up her spirits."

"An easy conquest!" said his lordship, rubbing his hands; "give me a jealous wife, and a neglectful husband, and I will gallant it as bravely as Paris did with the Greek Helen. But where is the written daily report I ordered you to prepare? Oh! that's it, is it? well, that will do. At six o'clock I will be ready to attend you."

Jasper bowed and retired to his own room, while his lordship perused the document which had been handed to him. As he did so, his handsome brow darkened, and his frame became convulsed with some powerful emotion.

"Prowling about my house by night, and yet having the assurance to meet me calmly face to face; but let me be patient! I am not fool enough to expose myself to the certain bullet of the practised duellist, or sufficiently an ass to publish my dishonour to the world, without the certainty of proving it beyond the power of contradiction. The bloodhound on their track will scent them out to the scene of their amours; so, in the mean time, let me cool my revenge in the rolling waters of dissipation. If I am to be a cuckold, scores shall keep me company in my disgrace; and who can distinguish one horned beast from another?"

With this philosophic determination to do evil unto others, because others had done it unto him, he characteristically addressed himself to the decanter of brandy before him, and, propped up on a sofa with a cigar in his mouth, was soon profoundly interested in the licentious pages of the French romance he held in his hand.

The Ebenezer Tabernacle was a snug little brick edifice, situate in one of the streets on the borders of the great metropolitan artery, Oxford Street. The interior was fitted up in the form of an amphitheatre, so that all the members of the congregation might be upon an equality as far as sitting accommodation was concerned, and have the same advantageous view of their pastor, who, at the end before the door, "rolled his moral thunders o'er the subject soul," and occasionally frightened the more timid of his flock out of the little common sense they had left. Indeed, Smashevil was so noted for his successful combats with the powers of darkness, that his great rival, Jedediah Hornum, was frequently plunged into such fits of envy, that he had the audacity to dispute the soundness of that great luminary's doctrines, and to cavil and sneer at him in class-meetings; and on one memorable occasion ventured to insinuate, in print, that snakes and other slimy reptiles sometimes crept up the trousers and petticoats of the true Israel. This hostility of course provoked the ire of Smashevil—the most devout cannot bear their fardels lightly—and when Hornum honoured the Tabernacle with a visit, the former put forth his utmost strength, and had been known to pray that whole legions of devils and imps would assail him, so that he might have the pleasure of slaying them with that tremendous weapon which Balaam swung so lustily about him in the olden time. On the evening destined to be so remarkable in the Ebenezzian annals, the chapel was unusually thronged; and it was gratifying to behold the affectionate manner in which the various members of the flock recognised and saluted each other during the process of entrance and taking their seats. The demure, and, by the way, exceedingly well-dressed matrons and spinsters, indulged in a vast amount of kissing; and those chosen leaders of the other sex who were entitled to that ecstatic privilege, availed themselves of it without stint or measure; and it was especially to have been observed that their lips lingered longest on the soft cheeks of the

youngest. Mr. Hornum embraced and kissed those of his followers who where present with great unction. The class-leaders, among whom the great Bond shone conspicuous, were also assiduous in their attentions; and it was remarked that they also gave the preference to the most delicate and blooming of the congregation. As the appointed hour approached, the mass by degrees settled down comfortably into their places; but there was a hum and an agitation which denoted the expectation of some unusual occurrence; and this surmise was strengthened by the fact, that Mr. Bond and his coadjutors were assembled near the door, holding a whispering, but apparently animated conversation. Presently there was a bustle, the mass opened, and the eyes of the elect were gratified with the appearance of the Reverend Jasper Sampson and the Reverend Count Bumbinski, standing together arm-in-arm on the threshold; who, after a calm, unruffled survey of the sea of heads before them, returned the fervid salutation of the feverish throng around them.

"This way!" chorused the leaders, as they escorted the distinguished visitors to the seats which had been provided for them by and near the pious Mrs. Bond, to whom the count was introduced, and condescended to seat himself close beside her. The Reverend Jasper Sampson placed himself between her and the exemplary Mr. Bond; and the whole four forthwith indulged in a few low and edifying scriptural remarks. And now the eyes of the whole congregation were fixed on the two illustrious strangers. Both were dressed in the newest black cloth, and of the approved saintly cut. Their white cravats became them admirably; but, of the two, Jasper, in the estimation of the majority of the males, best realised the idea of a Christian pastor. His long, thin, and pale face, rendered paler by contrast with his dark coat and white neck-tie, declared him to be a chosen vessel, and one from whom even the blood and marrow had been drained in his laborious attempts to soften the hearts of the wicked multitude. With the ladies the count was an immense favourite, and, sooth to say, they did not err in their selection, for the disguised nobleman looked remarkably handsome. His raven locks, clustering in glossy masses over his fine, clear forehead; his full, dark eyes, splendid features, and blooming complexion, which his sombre costume considerably heightened; together with his fine figure and aristocratic bearing, rendered him the very beau-ideal of manly perfection. Mrs. Bond entertained this conviction, and as the count pressed his knees closely against hers, felt a strange and unaccountable twittering in the region of her heart, and looked down blushingly before the gaze of the divine eyes bent rather unclerically upon her beautiful placid face. But the mighty Smashevil had now ascended to the pulpit, and, as if in obedience to the wand of an enchantress, every head was bent down in silent devotion. When they arose, every face turned towards the preacher bore the well-trained simper of self-satisfaction. Smashevil evidently felt himself in condition for a tremendous onslaught, for he selected a text of appalling significance. Perhaps the presence of his antagonist Hornum, and that of the two apostles from the Far West inspired him; but, whatever the moving cause was, never, within the memory of the eldest of his followers, had he fulminated so powerfully against the evils that afflict the world, and especially against false doctrines and false preachers, who, like wolves, go about seeking whom they may devour. Hornum bristled with indignation and wrath, and when, at the conclusion of the sermon, he was called upon, according to complimentary usage, to deliver himself of a prayer, he most Jesuitically retorted upon his formidable rival, and words of fire, not peace, fell from his lips. The audience, accustomed to such displays, if they deplored them at all, did it in secret; but Jasper, prompted, no doubt, by the arch-fiend himself, resolved to turn the incident to advantage, by the exercise of his ventriloquial powers.

"Smashevil! who's Smashevil?" burst from the excited Hornum.

The congregation started up aghast at this indecorum, and the object of the query actually crimsoned in his pulpit.

"A wolf in sheep's clothing!" was the startling exclamation that seemed to escape from the prostrate Hornum. Horror now blanched every countenance!

"Yes!" apparently said the inflamed Hornum; "a fellow grown fat on the purses of the husbands of frail wives—the seducer of innocence—the ——"

The remainder of the sentence was drowned in a storm of groans and shrieks.

During the confusion, Bloomfield whispered to Jasper:

"That was you—I know it was, because I received lessons from Love, the cleverest vocal deceiver of the day. Go on. Give it to the lean rascal! he looks as astounded as if the devil was clawing his back!"

The assumed count turned to sustain and comfort the agitated Mrs. Bond, and his arm somehow or another stole round her waist.

Smashevil, who had been studying his part, lifted up his tearful eyes to the ceiling; but, before he could utter a single word, he was petrified by the following tirade, that appeared to roll volubly from his own meek lips:

"Who's Smashevil? He is the chosen of the Lord! the sworn champion of the Ebenezers, and the defyer of Satan and all his imps! But who's Hornum? Doth not his name declare his abominations? Hath he not sinned in the vestry? Yea, in the temple itself! Hath he not lain with the ungodly, and contaminated the righteous? Hath he not been defiled by harlots?"

Such a torrent of screams and unearthly noises surely never inundated the lowest theatre in the east end of London, as followed this startling recrimination from the hitherto invincibly mild and gentle Smashevil. Both the reverend gentlemen stared at each other as if smitten by some pestilence, and, for the first time in their lives, believed in the existence of a potent invisible spirit of evil. The congregation swayed to and fro, like poor deck passengers in a gale of wind; the women shrieked and fainted, the men raved and tore their hair; and the scene was becoming so dangerously frantic, that Bloomfield entreated Jasper to allay the storm. He arose, and no sooner did his tall form and unearthly face appear in the throng, towering like some black pillar with a whitewashed pinnacle, than order was instantly restored; but the ladies, young and old, married and single, had each a stalwart arm pressing their trembling forms. Jasper's shrill voice rang through the building as he shouted:

"Down on your knees! humble yourselves, ye sinners, for the evil one is among ye! Pray, fast, and ye will be delivered!"

And Jasper, with the reckless daring of his character, committed himself to an extemporaneous adjuration, which, for insane violence and blasphemy, had never been paralleled even in the tabernacle of the Ebenezers.

When he had concluded, the silence was so profound, that even the wagging of a cat's tail might have been heard; and Smashevil, availing himself of the calm, returned thanks for their deliverance, and extended the hand of renewed friendship to the terrified and bewildered Hornum. A hymn was then given out, which the Reverend Count Bumbinski, by special invitation, was requested to lead off. It fortunately happened to be one he had often sung in his infancy, and, having a fine voice, he acquitted himself admirably; and so ended the public service. About fifty remained to partake of the feast of the heart, but speculations as to the cause of the recent disturbance for a time monopolised their attention. Hornum and Smashevil retired into a corner to deliberate on the untoward event, when, after divers learned surmises, the latter all at once called to mind that he had forgotten to announce the fact of the collection and to send round the plates, in consequence of which the paying portion of the congregation had, in vulgar terms, departed scot free. Both the divines groaned—the omission touched them both deeply; but Smashevil more, as being the intended recipient. Tears actually rolled down his cheeks, and he gnashed his teeth in the agony of his disappointment. Hornum did all he could to console him in his tribulation, and after a little soothing they jointly attributed the catastrophe to the direct agency of the person upon whose Atlantian shoulders all the sins of the world are heaped; and Smashevil contented himself with the conviction that the circumstance afforded scope for such pathetic expiation, that on an early occasion the purses of the faithful would contribute treble the amount lost.

"My brethren," said he, when he had revived, "let us proceed to that communion of spirit which is given unto the faithful!"

"The love-feast?" whispered the imaginary count to his new very agitated companion; for the latter, having seized an opportunity, had visited her lips with a warm, brotherly salute.

"Yes!" said Mrs. Bond, flutteringly; for, being the last in the kind of procession that was formed, the count had thrown his brotherly arms around her plump, compact body.

The whole company then adjourned to an underground, dimly-lighted apartment, *alias* a cellar, around which benches were dispersed; and now commenced one of those scenes, in which the disgusting and ridiculous are so blended, that they almost beggar description. Of those present, as regards sexes, there was a pretty equal division, and the ages ranged from sixteen up to forty. The women were all of them good-looking, not a few were handsome; and the men-folk were passable, but their faces had that sleek, greasy complexion, which bespeaks the hypocrite and the Jesuit, both in mind and heart. After some wine and cake had been handed round, the more spiritual portion of the ceremony began with an extemporaneous piece of extravagance from the "Reverend" William Bond. Then, at the invitation of the now thoroughly composed Smashevil, all sinners present were invited to make an open and voluntary confession of their wickednesses. A pause ensued, which was at length broken by a slim, sickly-looking young man rising, and unblushingly declaring that, within the week past, he had been guilty of the crime of incontinence. The females, at this announcement, held down their heads; the males groaned, and were so overpowered by the enormity of the offence, that they let their tingling hands fall into the laps of the delicate creatures beside them.

Mr. Hornum, after a preliminary howl, in a most sepulchral voice said:

"Bid defiance, young man, to Satan! beat him off with the staff of faith! Plunge the dagger of love into his heart, and triumph in thy redemption! But how did the evil one ensnare thee? Tell the manner of thy falling off, so that thou mayest again be received into the fold, and be armed against another visitation?"

The repentant, but unabashed sinner then whiningly said:

"The flesh rebelled strongly against the spirit, and, being in propinquitous allegiance to the person of the comeliest damsel that mine eyes had seen—I mean that the devil had placed before me. I did even give her an Adamite embrace, and was beguiled again and again by this flesh-pot of Egypt!"

Now, whether it was the allusion to the carnal vessel of the land of bondage, or the irreverent association of the damsel with his infernal majesty, or some outraged feeling of womanly delicacy that prompted her; but certain it was, that this sleek-faced hypocrite had no sooner fallen on his knees, with the true whack of humility, than up sprung a slender spinster, with wrath on her lips and fire in her eye:

"He was the beguiler—the betrayer—the deceiver!" she frantically exclaimed; "I am the lamb that he sacrificed to his concupiscence, and now the ungrateful Judas would slander me with his abominations."

The prostrate sinner groaned like one distraught; and the partaker of his iniquity would have fallen upon him, tooth and nail, had she not been restrained by some conciliating matrons who held out the cup of peace, sweetened with the honeyed words of religious consolation.

"A brother and a sister have fallen!" burst in Smashevil, as excited as a young medical student, with a case of broken collar-bone and concussion of the brain in hand; "but, being truly penitent, there is hope and forgiveness! Let us pray!"

A veil must now be drawn over a portion of the proceedings, and they must be resumed at that point when, after a due categorical examination and sage reproof, the erring brother and sister fell into each other's arms, and exchanged the pure kiss of reconciliation amid the warmest promises of better conduct for the future. Public confessions of a similar character were made, and it required the united praying power of Smashevil, Hornum, Jasper, Bambinaki, and Bond and Co., to prevent the self-accused from being annihilated and consumed on the spot. The shrieks, groans, and yells of the maddened devotees created a deafening noise; and what with tearings of the hair, rendings of bonnets, stamping, wrestling, tusseling, and struggling, the place resembled a minature pandemonium, in which a select company of doomed men and women emulated some of the Satanic revels so grandly described by the immortal English epic poet.

"Nice company!" whispered Bloomfield.

"Hush!" said Jasper, in the same key. "The quiet fun is beginning now! Excuse me, my lord, but how do you get on? Shall I get up a scene?"

"Not yet! She's mine!"

"Lecherous—eh?"

"Silence, scoundrel!"

The "fag" of these cellar orgies now retired to the upper end of the place, and, turning his face to the wall, began to pray most lustily for the human race, the present company being especially included. Upon this the whole company paired off, each male kneeled by the side of a female devotee, and both were soon apparently engaged in a species of mutual exhortation to turn out of the broad way that was tempting each of them to journey to everlasting destruction. Mrs. Bond, of course, fell to the share of Bloomfield; but that lady was so agitated, that the words she could so glibly use on other occasions, died still-born on her lips, and she felt herself glowing with some new and mysterious sensation, as her eyes fell on the glorious countenance of that foreign divine, and felt his warm breath fall on her cheek, and his poetical murmurings sounding in her ears, like the memories of long past experiences. Smashevil was sustaining the faltering zeal of the spouse of a corn-dealer and baker, who had been heard to declare that, for a hundred or so, that shining light should not want a more commodious chapel to radiate in; while Hornum was laying close siege to the spiritual weakness of the young wife of a retired publican. Bond was battling with the fiend on behalf of a meek-faced girl of seventeen, whose face slightly flushed—nature will have its royal sway—when he pushed his sleek, satyr-like face into her bonnet, and, under cover of that attitude, pinched her elbow, or tickled her knee. The rest of the company were all similarly engaged, with the exception of Jasper, who sat apart in a supposed state of prayerful meditation. The spectacle before him would have influenced him powerfully, but a timely application to his phial calmed him down into a state of cold, malignant satisfaction, at beholding the number of small sensual dramas played on every side of him.

"The devil, if there is any such fellow, can really cite scripture for his purpose!" thought he; "and all these people only adopt religion as a cloak, to hide their love of money, and give scope to the loosest desires! My master here is a professed rake—so will the pious Mrs. Bond be, by and bye; so I cannot blame either him or her. Her beast of a husband deserves serving out. See how he is pawing that girl about! She is a virgin; and if I didn't hate, detest, loathe the whole race of she-devils, I'd save her from his clutches! But let her go the primrose way, as they call it; hell cannot be too full of such cattle! Look at that greasy Hornum—how nicely he is slavering over that merry little devil of a landlady! I remember the time when she could be as smutty behind the bar as any drunken drab before it; but now the rooks have got hold of her, she is as sly as a cat watching a pantry; but she wont beat Hornum. He'll tickle her purse to her heart's content, and, as I know her bloated old man is horridly jealous, I will have a bit of fun. She refused to trust me a quartern of gin once, and now I'll serve her out. It shan't be my fault if she doesn't walk the streets yet! Bravo, Smashevil! lick the fat chaps of the Scotch baker's wife—she cheats the poor! Take the alum and short weight out of her pocket! Hurrah! this is fun! but, as I should like to try my hand on my own account, here goes to frighten the whole kit of them!" and, suiting the action to the word, he threw his voice over to where the indefatigable Bond was pushing his thick lips towards those of the girl whom, to use a phrase of his own, he was rapidly mesmerising:

"Don't Mr. Bond—oh, Mr. Bond! take your hand away!"

The effect was electric; both started and looked

around them in undisguised amazement. Bond caught the indignant glance of his wife, and, fearful of a scene, plunged into a perfect paroxysm of religious zeal. Smashevil looked daggers at the delinquent, and Hornum inwardly chuckled over the imprudence of the young class-leader; for every abstraction from the Ebenezer fold was added to his.

"Take your hand out of my bosom, Mr. Hornum!"

The exclamation came from the publican's wife, and Hornum stammered forth a protestation of innocence. The landlady felt half inclined to faint.

"Innocent?" said a voice at the further extremity of the room; "vot vos you a doing with Miss Juliet Hanson, in the baker's pew, arter chapel last Sunday night? Innocent, indeed!"

Hornum was too terrified to reply, and the eyes of the whole of the kneelers were bent upon him. The "fag" ceased his howlings, and for a minute or two there was a dead silence.

"Smashevil!" cried a voice from the opposite extremity; "didn't you, ten years ago, dance three months on the treadmill at Brixton, for an infamous indecency in St. James's Park?"

"The Lord have mercy on us!" burst simultaneously from the two afflicted divines; "for of a verity the Great Enemy is here!"

"Verily he is!" Ha! ha! ha! ha! Oh! oh! oh! oh!" And such a rapid utterance of yells, squeaks, and all manner of diabolical noises, sounded through the apartment, that the audience rushed pell-mell to the ricketty staircase. Bloomfield supported the fainting Mrs. Bond, and prudently remained behind; with Jasper in the rear, industriously making the "confusion worse confounded."

The struggle at the door was dreadful, for the men struck out right and left, in their frantic efforts to escape; the women shrieked, and there was such swearing in that holy throng, that Jasper burst out into a wild and unearthly fit of laughter. At the same moment he espied the gas-meter, and, giving it a tremendous kick, the place was enveloped in total darkness. The struggle now became absolutely furious, and some lives might have been lost, had not the stairs fortunately broke, and brought the whole mass tumbling head and heels over each other.

Bloomfield, who pitied the ladies, strove to release them, and sternly insisted upon Jasper assisting him. As they were at the tail of the frantic mob, this, with some little difficulty, was speedily effected, and they were induced to remain on the spot, where the voice of the supposed handsome count, reassured and soothed them.

"Do not be alarmed, ladies!" he cried; "this uproar must soon bring assistance; meanwhile, let those selfish fools tear each other to pieces!"

Mrs. Bond clung to the count, who embraced and kissed her with such warmth that she soon ceased sobbing, and passively allowed him to entwine her arms round his neck.

The Ebenezers still continued their fierce struggle, and, from the noise they made, seemed as if they were tearing each other to pieces, to the wild roar of a chorus of profane swearing. The alarm, as Bloomfield had predicted, was soon raised, and some two or three policemen, with their bull's-eyes, and still more effective truncheons, speedily restored order.

"Let us out!" they clamoured; but Bloomfield stepped forward, and said:

"The ladies first. Quick, men, and earn a ten-pound note!"

This was enough. The ladies were all extricated in the course of a few minutes; and then, at Bloomfield's request, the saints were left to scramble out as they best could, Jasper all the while throwing the most appalling sounds into their subterranean prison. As they one by one emerged into the now-lighted and rather densely-thronged chapel, they presented a sorry sight. Their coats were all torn—some even had their skirts hanging about them in festoons; while not a few disclosed the fact that their under garments were rather scanty. The mob were inclined to be facetious; but a timely arrival of police reinforcements preserved the peace; and the whole party, although torn and battered, and suffering from innumerable contusions, at the suggestion of the venerable and sedate-looking Jasper, were marched off to the nearest station and locked up, charged with riotous and disorderly conduct. Bloomfield took the agitated, terrified, and most curiously-confused Mrs. Bond under his care; and early next morning prevailed on her to strip the house of everything portable, and accompany him on a mission to Brighton, to save the souls of the wicked at that fashionable and ungodly watering place. She was never seen or heard of again by any of the Ebenezers; and when they had fully recovered from their terrible calamity, and found that both the Reverend Jasper Sampson and the Reverend Count Bumbinski had disappeared, without leaving a trace of their presence behind, it was at once concluded that Ebenezer Chapel had been honoured by the presence of Messrs. Satan and Beelzebub; and that for some undivulged enormity they had been allowed to carry off the seemingly immaculate Mrs. Bond. The husband was at first inconsolable, for her pretty face drew custom to his shop; but, after due prayer and wrestling with the spirit, he felt commanded to replace her by the meek-faced girl, who had already experienced the full effect of his wonderful spiritual training powers.

CHAPTER XII.

THE ABDUCTION OF LUCY.

THE mysteries and intrigues of Bloomfield House were rapidly deepening in interest and darkening in purport; and the occurrences that succeeded the literary *soiree* demand separate notices. They were so numerous that they must be taken in some degree of order; and, as the prettiest flowers first attract the eye, on this occasion let one of the fairest and purest of her sex—the gentle Lucy—have precedence over the rest of the personages comprised in this veracious chronicle. She had arisen, as was her custom, much earlier than the countess, and, until lately, had sprung from her couch with a heart as light as her foot; but on this morning she felt unusually depressed, and for some time sat on the edge of the bed in her night costume, which, by the way concealed everything but her face—from which the roses of her slumbers had not all vanished—and a pair of delicately-small white feet. It was to be her last day in London, and a distressing sadness crept over her as she dwelt on the fact.

"Cruel Violet!" she murmured, "to drive me away from the only joy my young heart ever knew since my merry childhood. To banish me from the presence of *him* whose memory I have cherished so fondly for many, many long years; and at a time, too, when I find him more, oh! far more, than I ever dreamed of in my wildest fancies! Dear Walter, if you only knew how I loved you, the false smiles of the imprudent would not win you from the side of one whose loyalty to your real worth and kindly heart is as firm as one of our own native hills!"

As she indulged in this kind of depressing, yet soothing reflections, she drew a miniature portrait from her bosom, and gazed upon it in tearful rapture.

While she was thus engaged, the door of her chamber was noiselessly opened, and Mrs. Wriggles entered. Lucy had not seen her before, and, as she caught the sound of her footsteps and looked up, she started, and could not avoid a shriek, as she beheld the not over-fascinating old woman before her.

"Don't be alarmed, my pretty young lady!" said Mrs. Wriggles, in her most persuasive accents; "I am come to do you a service!"

Lucy's modesty was extremely sensitive, for even in the presence of one of her own sex, she drew up her feet under her night-clothes, and folded her arms across her bosom.

"I am the friend of yourself and Captain Morris," continued Mrs. Wriggles, "whose portrait I perceive in your hands. Let me look upon it, Miss Lucy, for I knew him at the age when it was drawn." Lucy mechanically held it out in her hand. "Just the features! the same bold eye and high forehead, crowned with clustering chesnut hair! Ah, Miss Lucy, he was a fine boy for his years, and although in his manhood he has become stained with some of the vices of the world, his heart is still as warm as ever!"

"Who are you?" tremulously asked Lucy, venturing to regard the intruder more steadily.

"One whom your mother did not think beneath her regard," replied Mrs. Wriggles. "Do you remember the flowers that grew on a grave in the churchyard of the village where you lived?"

"I do well," said Lucy, surprised. "My mother when living tended and kept them alive, and they are cared for to this day."

"By whom?" inquired the old woman, eagerly.

Lucy hesitated, and blushed.

"I see it!" said Mrs. Wriggles, with animation. "You have been the kind guardian of that humble grave, and bless you for the good deed! But did you ever hear the story of the little being who sleeps there so quietly?"

"My mother never mentioned to me the name of the little child's mother, but she often told me, when I inquired, that the poor woman had been used unkindly, and that as her name was almost forgotten, it would be uncharitable to revive it."

Some powerful emotion seized upon Mrs. Wriggles as she heard this; she breathed thick and shortly, became pale, and only by a strong nervous effort prevented tears from springing to her eyes.

"Your mother was a good, amiable creature—an angel!" said she, at length; "and out of love for her memory I am here to warn you of danger!"

"Danger?" exclaimed the surprised girl.

"Yes, danger, sweet innocent! for you are pursued by a man who only seeks your ruin. He pretends love, but it is only a cloak, under which he may take advantage of your weakness. Avoid him!"

Lucy trembled, and, forgetting all hesitation and reserve in the interest the warning created, listened with breathless attention.

"Yes, Lucy—lovely image your sainted mother! you are menaced by a villain!" continued Mrs. Wriggles; "and the sooner you avoid him the more secured will you be. Colonel Stanley is a ruffian amongst women!"

"Colonel Stanley?" almost screamed Lucy, as the remembrance of that personage's rude and offensive conduct flashed across her memory.

"The same," said Mrs. Wriggles, slowly, as she eyed Lucy intently.

"I detest him!" cried Lucy; "and my sister has frequently requested me not to associate with him, but he will persist in annoying me; and when I complain, Lord Bloomfield laughs, and says I am too fastidious, and that the colonel means no harm."

"Trust nobody," says Mrs. Wriggles. "Lord Bloomfield is no modest girl's friend. Your sister is too much occupied with her fashionable follies to be watchful enough. So fly—go to your own peaceful country side, and wait the issue of events. In a year or two you will be a happy, honoured wife, and bless the old woman who advised you to fly from the vile dissipations of London."

"A wife?" uttered Lucy, crimsoning up to far beyond the richly-laced borders of her night-cap.

"Yes, and a good one too. Don't blush so, for I know your secret! You love my favourite, Walter Morris, and he loves you!"

Lucy, at this announcement, started to her feet, and advanced several paces towards where Mrs. Wriggles stood, and stared at the latter in troubled amazement.

"I am as certain that Walter loves you as I stand here!" said Mrs. Wriggles; "for you are the very image of your sister at your age; and did he not love her?"

"And may do so still?" suggested Lucy.

"No!" replied Mrs. Wriggles, rather sarcastically; "a trust once broken is like a cracked tea-cup—it may be pieced, but never restored to its original perfection. Walter *did* love Violet—he doated upon her—but she deceived him, and his romantic devotion vanished in anger and spleen."

A smile, like light, broke over the features of the now hopeful girl, and in the undulations of her bosom, and the parting soft lips, the experienced old woman read the signs of a partial emancipation from a state of painful suspense.

"He loves me?" she murmured to herself.

"He does, and as a man should love a woman—warmly, honourably, and respectfully," said Mrs. Wriggles; "but his affection requires maturing, and he must be purified from many an error before he should approach your unstained purity. Every reason, therefore, urges you to retire from town for a season or two."

"I am to start for my native place—the home of my mother—this very day," said Lucy, but not without a sadness of manner; for, apart from other considerations, the young, after mingling in bustling

scenes, hesitate to return to the subdued ones of strict retirement.

"So much the better," said Mrs. Wriggles, delightedly; "for then there will be no fear that the colonel and Morris will have the opportunity of quarrelling about you."

"Quarrel?" echoed Lucy, a new feature of the affair bursting upon her.

"Yes," replied Mrs. Wriggles; "were Walter made aware that Colonel Stanley had insulted you, he would shoot him with as little remorse as he would a hare!"

"A duel?" cried Lucy; "oh, let that tragedy be avoided! I will now go, not only without reluctance, but gladly!"

"Bless you for the wise determination!" said Mrs. Wriggles; "and take with you the good wishes of one who, through life, has had little cause to wish well to any one. And when you get down to ——, do not forget the grave! Plant a rose-tree on it with your virgin hands, for one, who in life was as pure as yourself, rests beneath the flowers for which the old woman blesses you—farewell!"

And before Lucy could address another word to her, she had left the room as quickly as she had entered.

In the hall, Mrs. Wriggles found Alice waiting, and accompanied her to her room.

"Will she go?" inquired Alice, hurriedly.

"She has not only promised," said Mrs. Wriggles, "but goes willingly and cheerfully."

Alice heaved a sigh of satisfaction; and then, turning a pale and haggard face to Mrs. Wriggles, said:

"I had a fearful dream last night: I thought *he*—Burton—came to my bed-side, and laughed and jeered at me; and, like a devil, kissed me into madness!'

"Pshaw!" was the assuring reply; "you cannot avoid your old habit of lying on your back, and so had your circulation impeded; and that produced what in men is called the nightmare."

"What became of *him*?" inquired Alice.

"'Pon my word I don't know!" said Mrs. Wriggles, boldly; "he was never seen in our neighbourhood after the precious colting he had from the merry wives; and I shouldn't wonder if he hadn't gone to America, or some other outlandish place. But never mind talking about him, he can't harm you! let us talk about something else. Do the countess and Mrs. Smythe still intend to go down to Greenwich?"

"They do; and the countess intends giving Mrs. Smythe the slip, to meet Walter at some place in the park."

"Don't look so spitefully!" said Mrs. Wriggles, laughingly; "if you will assist me, they shall never meet at all. The countess and Mrs. Smythe are almost certain to go, and as they wish to see something of real life, they shall be amply satisfied; so let me have pen, ink, and paper."

These were readily procured, and Mrs. Wriggles, who, to her varied accomplishments, added that of imitating any style of handwriting, sat down and penned a note, purporting to be from the countess to Captain Morris, requesting the latter to be in Kensington Gardens at a particular hour.

"Don't you see, my dear," said Mrs. Wriggles, coaxingly; "the ladies will go to Greenwich long before the time named; and Morris, not doubting the authenticity of this little favour, will be all that while, and for some couple of hours afterwards, cooling his heels in Kensington Gardens!"

"Admirable!" said Alice, suddenly struck with an idea which pleased her exceedingly.

The countess's bell at this moment sounded, and as Mrs. Wriggles undertook the delivery of the treacherous note, Alice hastened to her mistress, whom she found *en deshabille*, but fondly caressing her sister Lucy, with whose compliance with her request to return into the country she was inexpressibly delighted.

"I will accompany you to the railway station, my darling Lucy," said the countess; "and, with your maid and Robert for company, you can coach it from Hereford."

This arrangement was agreed upon, and in about two hours afterwards, Lucy, the countess, and the two servants were at the London and North Western Railway station. After a tearful adieu, the sisters separated. And now for a journey by rail with the gentle Lucy.

She occupied a seat in a first-class carriage, and *vis-a-vis* with a fashionably-dressed lady, with some pretensions to beauty and fascination of manner. Lady travellers do not maintain the sullen reserve towards each other that male ones do; and therefore it is not surprising that Lucy and her railway companion should have soon been engaged in that species of conversation known as gossiping, which has such charms for women of all ages and ranks in society. The fashions, the theatre, music, and the trifles that men neither understand nor appreciate, occupied their time very agreeably until the train reached its destination; and Lucy had become so charmed with her casual acquaintance, that she regretted they were soon to part. Ladies are as proverbial for their inquisitiveness as their freedom of communication to each other; therefore, it is not surprising that the pair thus casually met, should have made each other acquainted with the localities of their mutual destinations; or that, as it happened that the strange lady travelled more than half way to where Lucy lived, the latter should have offered her a seat in her post-chaise, and arranged with the servants that they should follow in the stage coach. All this was easy and natural; the more especially, when it was observed that the strange lady mentioned the names of a score of Lucy's neighbours in the country, and professed to be on familiar terms with several of the families who visited at Bloomfield House. The confidence of the young is easily obtained, and Lucy resumed her journey with a light heart, and prattled and laughed with her agreeable friend, heedless of the progress of time or the change of horses, until the coach came to a halt, in what proved to be an exceedingly dark road.

"My house stands at some little distance from the high road," said her companion; "and as you must be fatigued, you will oblige me by alighting, and partaking of some slight refreshment before you proceed any farther."

Lucy, although of a timid disposition, never suspected that there was the least impropriety in the step, and cheerfully accepted the invitation. The really innocent are the last to question the motives of others.

The short distance proved to be a walk of about a mile; but, as the night was fine and the moon shone pleasantly, was rather agreeable than otherwise to a traveller who had been confined all day in a close carriage.

"This is my dwelling," said the lady, as they approached a handsome structure at the end of a long avenue, bordered by stately beech trees. "The carriage will wait for you at the gates."

Lucy entered without hesitation; and in a few minutes found herself seated at a profusely-covered table with her hostess, who, having put off a portion of her travelling accoutrements, displayed the fine proportions and splendid bust of a woman of some thirty-three or four years of age. The only peculiarity which struck Lucy was the presence of a footman of colossal proportions, who waited at table. He could not have been less than six feet in height, and was stout in proportion. Nevertheless, his physiognomy was agreeable; and Lucy, as she stole a glance at his burly frame, did not feel the slightest repugnance or alarm. Her entertainer charmed her with her affectionate and cheerful solicitude about her welfare, and amused her with a fund of sprightly anecdote. Lucy, contrary to her usual habit at meals, partook of a couple of glasses of wine; and, as the conversation progressed, felt her heart warm towards that kind and fascinating lady. But she had no sooner partaken of the second glass of wine, than a drowsiness crept over her memory, and self-control vanished; and, while listening to an amusing narrative of a frolicsome foible in high life, fell fast asleep in her chair.

The hostess no sooner observed this, than she summoned an aged female domestic, and by their united assistance Lucy was borne to a sumptuously-furnished chamber, and put to bed.

"Another?" said the footman, who, seated at the table, familiarly saluted the hostess upon her return to the supper-room.

"Pretty, is she not?" uttered the hostess, as she drew her chair close beside that of the industriously-feeding giant.

"Very. Who is she?" replied he, tearing the flesh from the leg of a fowl with his teeth.

"Miss Lucy Villiers, of ——."

"The devil! That colonel of ours is a bold fellow; he'll be shot one of these odd days."

"I suspect this affair will finish him off. Have you the plate all ready packed for a start?"

"All right, duckey!"

And the brawny fellow, laying aside the bone he was picking, placed the fascinating travelling-companion of poor Lucy in his lap, and commenced a series of amorous toyings, which he diversified and enlivened by pouring glass after glass of the generous wine before him down his capacious throat.

CHAPTER XIII.

THE MERRY WIVES GO TO GREENWICH.

WHEN the sun shines high and brightly in the stainless sky that London at intervals is favoured with, Greenwich and its park are especial objects of attraction to the high-dried and pent-up denizens of Cockney-land; and the ancient highway, the Thames, except to those who love the dull rumbling of the rail, is the chosen route; and with good taste; for how pleasant it is to glide smoothly over the bosom of the queen of rivers, and behold on each side of you the evidence of a greatness which neither Babylon nor Alcario, in all their magnificence, equalled; to be, as it were, borne along the mighty artery of a nation's wealth and glory, and instead of the sounds of armourers "closing rivets up," to hear the ceaseless voice of industry, the animated cheer, the distant song, and that indescribable roar, which seems more like muttered thunder than anything else. And then the wondrous bridges, the miles upon miles of edifices, with towers and steeples rising amid them, like giants overtopping dwarfs; the forests of masts, with their countless flaunting flags; the ever-moving steamers; the puny boat, with its white sail glistening in the sun; and the dense smoke that overhangs certain localities, like funeral-palls, make up a scene of intense interest and high excitement. But re-flections of this type animate but few of the voyagers to Greenwich—there is always something of more immediate import to engage; and so, heigho! for a voyage to Greenwich by water, starting, of course, from that most glorious of suspensions in the air, Hungerford Bridge. The time shall be noon or thereabouts—just that witching hour when the late riser likes to fill the lungs with fresh air, and give life and elasticity to the limbs that all the night long have been tossed about in feverish restlessness. The bridge is swarming with idlers, and among them may be discerned those interesting specimens of metropolitan Aspasias, who, in neat morning costume and a pretty market reticule, and the never-failing latch-key in their hands, take the air and adroitly display their admirably-formed ankles for the gratification of old gentlemen, who come there to regale their watery eyes with such spectacles. The pier is crowded with the miscellaneous multitude of river passengers, ladies, and children constituting the majority. The groupings of the former are exceedingly characteristic of life on the river. There is the servant of eighteen arrayed in her flaunting holiday attire, who is going down to Woolwich to see a cousin and have a sly peep at the soldiers on the common. The odds are sadly against her returning as innocent as she went. Nay, if anything, she is rather anxious to know more of human nature than she does; for, as that impudent young fellow with an elaborate neck-cloth casts the most wicked glances at her, she actually smiles and seems to invite a nearer approach. He takes the hint, and gallantly volunteers to pay her fare. "She is booked!" is his mental calculation, and, having formed an engagement for the day—in such affairs the whole four-and-twenty hours is meant—he strives to render himself as agreeable as possible, and from her blushing it must be presumed he has succeeded.

Next to this casually-introduced pair, is a bold-eyed matron of about thirty-five. She is plump and good-looking, and has evidently a design on that staid-looking, substantial man in sober black, who every now and then steals a glance at her, and then hurriedly looks another away, as if afraid of being observed. When the boat has got under weigh, he will contrive to obtain a seat by her side; and at the end of the journey, she, nothing loth, will consent to dine with him at the Ship or the Trafalgar. They are both married persons, and are evidently out on what is called the "secret" spree. A little further on, half a dozen mechanics' wives, with faces as red as their shawls, are talking loudly, and indulging in coarse satire on each other, and those who fall under their notice. Near them stands a gentleman evidently enjoying their merry observations, for he is laughing heartily, and ogling the prettiest of the lot.

"We shall have some fun," thinks he, "for they are evidently on our trail; and as that she-devil, Mrs. Wriggles, is amongst them, the day will prove a more interesting one than I anticipated. Ah! yonder 's Violet and my Juno-eyed banker's wife! By heavens, she is superb in that delicious walking costume! Oh, for a quiet hour in some leafy retreat, with a nice mossy couch—but fortune favours the brave!"

And with this consoling reflection, Captain Morris, for it was that renowned personage who thus stood communing with himself, hastened to meet the captivating wives of Belgravia.

The countess looked adorable in her disguise, and Mrs. Smythe, with her ardent looks, would have fired old Saturn himself. They attracted universal atten-tion, and not a few admired the good fortune enjoyed by Walter of being their "beau," as several merry dames on board the steamer called him, as they glanced at his noble figure. Mrs. Wriggles and her party went forward and studiously kept aloof, but maintained a rattling, and not over-delicate, conversation with the men who surrounded them.

And, now the steamer is fairly on her voyage, the opportunity may be seized to explain how it was that so many of the characters of this narrative were on board of her.

The countess and Mrs. Smythe, wearied of the pleasures and gaieties of their exalted position, were desirous of borrowing a little excitement from other sources, and, under the protection of Walter Morris, had long ago agreed upon this excursion; but both had private reasons for undertaking it on this occasion. The countess, now thoroughly enamoured of her early lover, wished to enjoy his society unfettered by the conventionalisms of rank, and had secretly arranged to meet him at a place previously named; and to accomplish that purpose had to elude the vigilance of Mrs. Smythe, of whom she began to be acutely jealous. More timid than the latter, she could not wholly surrender herself to the intoxicating thrill of her absorbing passion, and therefore submitted to the presence of Mrs. Smythe, as a kind of safeguard. Nevertheless—so inconsistent are people who involve themselves in the meshes of wrong—she wished to get rid of her; and during the whole of the progress below bridge, as it is termed, was studying how she could manage, in vulgar parlance, to give her the slip. Mrs. Smythe had divined what was passing in her mind, and was influenced by the very same desire. Being of a bolder, though perhaps not more amorous temperament, she panted for the opportunity of surrendering her person to the tender mercies of one of the finest-looking men in the British army; and, in her reckless ardour, never speculated on the consequences of the amour. As for Walter, his respect for the sex had become so depreciated, that he never neglected a chance of succeeding with any one of them for whom he had taken a fancy; and it mattered little to him whether the woman was maid, wife, or widow, provided she was young, passable, and willing. The strength of his newly-born passion for the beautiful Lucy had, unknown to himself, considerably weakened his fondness for the countess; but, as he was not a very close reasoner in love, he thought himself bound to keep the assignation he had made with her. His physical preference was for the less refined and more openly inviting Mrs. Smythe, and he trusted that some lucky incident would occur to throw her directly in his way. However, the journey was to Greenwich, where he little doubted the problem would be solved; and he, with his usual light-hearted recklessness, relieved the trip of its tediousness by pointing out the distinctive features of the splendid public buildings of the metropolis, which are seen to such advantage from the river. In the Pool, the flags of all nations give their colours to the breeze; and at its mouth anchors a magnificent sight—the Dreadnought Hospital Ship, formerly part and parcel of the "wooden walls of Old England." She was in the thickest of the fight at Trafalgar, and captured the San Juan, a Spanish three-decker. The ladies, after landing, expressed a wish to visit her; and, upon being rowed to her, did not forget, when leaving, that she was there moored to administer relief to the sick destitute mariners of every country.

"God loveth a cheerful giver," thought Walter, as he saw the golden mites of benevolence fall into the box; "and, come what will, this will not altogether be a day of iniquity with us!"

But on landing the incident was soon forgotten in the multitude of sights that surrounded them in the far-famed town and park of Greenwich. Everything around was novel to ladies, who all their lives had been accustomed only to the amusements of the drawing-room, the theatre, or the fashionable promenade; and, as they enjoyed the beauty of the scenery and inhaled the delightful breeze, under the boughs of the wide-spreading beech and oak, they felt all the pleasure and excitement of children who had purloined a holiday to roam over a fair country side.

They had gained the ancient oak in the park, which is perhaps now the oldest in the southern counties, when they were arrested by one of those wandering females, who prowl about such places in the guise of gipsies. She was an elderly dame, with keen, dark eyes; and, despite the cloak and shawl she wore, and the deep artificial brown of her features, Walter had no difficulty in recognising Mrs. Wriggles.

"Shall I tell you your fortune, young gentleman?" said she to Walter, as she returned his wink of recognition.

"Certainly," replied he, promptly, as he perceived that she desired a private conference. "But is it to be public or private—are these ladies to hear the thrilling details?"

"By no means; Jael the Wanderer is silent when a third person stands by!"

The countess and Mrs. Smythe, taking the hint, retired to a convenient distance; and Mrs. Wriggles, taking Walter's hand, and pretending to examine it, said to him:

"You are here to-day on an evil errand?"

"Out, witch! is kissing a pretty woman a sin?"

"No; but debauching the child of your mother's friend—the playmate of your youth is," rejoined the old woman, solemnly.

Walter started; and, after an exclamation more adapted to the region of a camp than a court, said:

"Why, you beat Hecate herself in witchcraft, Mother Wriggles!" How came you to know all this?"

"Because I remember all I hear, can see further than the length of my nose, and when I choose can purchase information. Now, listen to me, Walter Morris: you are here to-day on an evil errand—don't interrupt me, you are—you are at this moment meditating how you may take advantage of the countess's infatuation—her simplicity—for it is nothing else; and I am here to thwart you!"

"You?" exclaimed Morris, superciliously.

"Yes, me!" retorted the old woman, energetically. "And if I cannot do it by an appeal to your sense of honour, I can accomplish it by force. Let me but give one signal, and in five minutes you and your party would be surrounded by a hundred sturdy vagabonds; but I am sure that will not be necessary. Listen calmly to me, Walter Morris. For the first time I address you in the polished language of every-day life—the old woman with you has forgotten her slang—and for what? Because I knew your mother and Violet's too!"

"Where—when?" said Walter, whom that magical name thoroughly aroused to attention.

"In ——, five-and-twenty years ago; you were then a fine little boy of five years old. Some day I will tell you all, but not now. Be satisfied that I knew the parents of both you and that lovely young wife, and that they were pure, gentle, kind——"

"They were angels!" interrupted Walter.

"So they were; and perhaps you now learn, for the first time, that it was their joint moneys that purchased you your commission."

This was news indeed to Walter, and, as he weighed it over, he began to entertain some compunctious visitations of conscience for the eagerness with which he had caught at the idea of unlawfully embracing the countess.

"The means of both were straitened; but, imbued with a noble zeal for your welfare, and a desire that your father's repeatedly-expressed wish should be realised, they placed you in the British army as a gentleman; and your mother deprived herself of many comforts, and even necessaries, to maintain you as one."

"Bless her!" murmured Walter.

"Violet's mother, aware of these sacrifices, frequently insisted upon sharing them; and the only difference they ever had, was when your mother proudly rejected her assistance."

This narrative profoundly affected Walter; and it was only by great efforts that he prevented his emotion being observed.

"Both those sainted women had your interest at heart—the one as a doting parent, the other with the wish and arrangement that she should become another one."

"My poverty lost me the heart of the only girl I ever loved!" said Walter, bitterly.

"Not so. Violet never loved you as a girl should love a man she intends making her husband."

Walter, at this announcement, opened his eyes very widely; and was about to give utterance to an indignant denial, when the old woman laid her hand on his arm, and proceeded:

"I know my own sex well; I know their virtues as well as their foibles; and I can safely pronounce that Violet Villiers never loved you. She admired you, Walter, and that was all. Had she loved you, she would have waited for you until she had grown grey in her virginity, and died with the hope of wedding you, singing sweet tunes in her ears."

"If that be true, how can you account for her too-evident partiality for me now?" inquired Walter, struggling against his convictions.

"Easily," rejoined Mrs. Wriggles. "Her husband, whom, in her heart, she still loves, has disappointed the romantic expectations she formed when she married him; and as he has treated her with the same beastly familiarity as he would a common harlot, disgust has succeeded to love; and that, together with indignation at his flagrant infidelities, has laid the foundation of an alienation, of which almost any practised seducer might take advantage. So that you see, the only pleasure you would derive from her fall, would be the mere gratification of your sensual desires."

"The countess is safe with me," said Walter, firmly. "What you have told me of her mother, and the memory of some transactions when a boy, have recalled me to a sense of duty."

"Spoken like the Walter Morris, into whose gallant father's cheek the blush of shame was never called; and as a reward for such virtue, you shall yet realise the wish of your mother, and marry the child of her most loved friend."

Walter, at this, blushed—the expression of pleasure cannot be so well suppressed as that of pain—and actually turned aside his head to hide his confusion.

"The blush at thirty," said the old woman, "proves the heart is still uncontaminated; so hope, Walter, for pure days of love with Lucy Villiers; and when they come, you will find how different the joys of wedded love are to casual embraces with the mere-tricious. Now, then, listen to me. You must complete the good work I have so auspiciously begun, and leave the countess to me — I will escort her home."

"You?" exclaimed Walter, stepping back a pace or two; "I cannot consent to that arrangement. The countess would never forgive me the insult. Besides, to leave her in this rude place alone and unprotected—impossible!"

"Not so," coolly replied Mrs. Wriggles; "for unless you accede to my request, you will inflict an irreparable injury on the countess. A spy, more subtle than the serpent, is on your track. You have been watched from Bloomfield House; and it only requir s one act of imprudence to fix the stain of adultery on the child of the friend of your mother."

"What pledge have I that she will arrive home in safety?" demanded the bewildered Walter.

"This!" said Mrs. Wriggles, drawing a miniature portrait of a beautiful woman from her bosom.

"My mother!" exclaimed Walter, pressing it to his lips. "Such a guarantee is more than sufficient. But how is it to be accomplished? Shall I explain the necessity ——?"

"Leave all to me, and don't say a word to her about it. This Mrs. Smythe has set her heart upon having you for a sweetheart; so go and meet her at the 'Sun in the Sands,' on the road to Charlton. While I am talking to the countess, do you slip away. I will take care the dark-eyed lady follows you."

What!" said Walter, staring incredulously; "would you advise me to do that in one case, which you would not in another?"

"Indeed I would," coolly replied the old woman; "for if you don't take this Mrs. Smythe to your arms, somebody else will; for she is as amorous as the great Catherine of Russia. And as to yourself, why you know you cannot do without some fair creature. So, away with you, and profit by your advantage, for she is a remarkably fine woman!"

Walter at this moment caught the fiery glance of the subject of these free remarks; and as the arrangement was just the one he wanted, he agreed to it with alacrity; and while the two ladies were disputing as to which should have her fortune told first, he adroitly disappeared below a declivity, and made for the park gates as fast as his legs could carry him.

"The dark lady has won the preference," said the seeming fortune-teller, as the countess turned away from the interview with some show of chagrin, but with secret satisfaction, for she anticipated an agreeable tete-a-tete with Walter. How great was her disappointment, when she found that he was nowhere to be seen!

"Your hand is small, lady!" said Mrs. Wriggles, as she slightly touched the long, slender fingers, whiter than the glove she wore, which Mrs. Smythe laughingly extended to her; "but I read in its palm that your heart is large. You love a fair-haired man?"

The banker's wife slightly crimsoned, but merely replied:

"So, they say, does every dark woman."

"But your husband is not a dark man?"

Mrs. Smythe started, but retained her composure.

"Your husband loves a fair woman—a titled one, too, and is now fast entangled in her web."

"A coincidence, certainly," thought Mrs. Smythe, as the image of the Irish peeress flashed across her mind.

"You have the same description of partiality for a fair complexion; and at this moment your dearest wish is to be clasped in the stalwart arms of the gallant soldier for whom I have just read such a good fortune. He doats upon you—he called you his Caroline."

This announcement, coming from such a quarter, and so unexpectedly, almost stupefied the licentious Mrs. Smythe; and the indignant reply that rose to her lips dropped from them in an inarticulate manner.

"He doats upon you!" continued Mrs. Wriggles, with imperturbable composure; "and is now hastening to meet you at a road-side tavern on the Charlton Road. He bade me communicate the intelligence. So hasten to him, lady, and gladden his heart."

Mrs. Smythe looked around her, and finding Walter had disappeared, yielded to the delirious suggestion that was thrilling through her from head to foot.

"But the countess—I mean my friend?" said she confusedly.

"Will be cared for!" replied Mrs. Wriggles with emphasis; "the soldier has already provided for her safe return to town. A crowd will presently assemble on this spot, from which I will insensibly draw the lady; and cannot you afterwards plead that in the confusion you lost sight of her?"

The opportunity, impudent as it was, tempted the enamoured Mrs. Smythe out of her last scruples of reluctance; and the experienced Mrs. Wriggles saw that she would hasten to the place of meeting at any sacrifice.

"While I am engaged with your fair friend, a little confusion will arise," resumed Mrs. Wriggles; "and one of our tribe will accost you and lead you to the rendezvous."

So saying, the seeming gipsy left the glowing and sadly confused banker's wife to her warm meditations. As the former had stated, while engaged with the countess, a crowd of noisy women began to gather on the spot; and, as the countess receded from her view, was pressed upon by them rather rudely.

"This way, lady," said a plaintive voice at her elbow; and, upon Mrs. Smythe turning suddenly, she beheld by her side a delicate girl of about fourteen years of age. The face, lit up by two splendid black eyes, was of a deep brown colour, and remarkable for its expression and intellectual type. The costume of her race scarcely concealed the outlines of her slender frame, and when she repeated her salutation, the sound of her silvery voice struck upon Mrs. Smythe's sense of hearing like the echoes of something she had heard in days long gone by.

"This way, lady," said the girl again; and Mrs. Smythe, still keeping her gaze of intense interest fixed on the speaking features of her guide, suffered herself to be led away.

"Who are you?" at length she inquired.

"Jael the Wanderer," was the simple reply.

"Whither are you conducting me?" asked Mrs. Smythe, as they emerged from the park, and took a footpath over some common land, where numbers of people, of all ages and sexes, were diverting themselves in swing-boats, on horses, donkeys, and the other species of amusement usually to be found at fairs.

"To the Sun in the Sands," was the girl's brief reply, as, slightly in advance, she tripped lightly onwards.

Mrs. Smythe felt a strange yearning for the fragile-looking girl, and endeavoured to draw from her answers to the most minute inquiries; but all she could obtain from her was a simple monosyllable answer.

When they had walked about a mile, the girl pointed to a sign-post which could be discerned in the distance, and after briefly saying, "Yonder is the Sun in the Sands, lady," turned to retrace her steps.

Mrs. Smythe, at this point, was seized with a fit of trembling, and sought to detain her by an offer of money; but the girl merely curtseyed her thanks, and fled swiftly away. Mrs. Smythe gazed after her until she had long disappeared from view, and then, with a deep sigh, mechanically bent her steps in the direction the girl had intimated.

And well might that imperfectly trained woman, with her wild passions, feel agitated as she parted from the gipsy girl, for the latter *was her own child*—the offspring of her first ardent error—the poor innocent, born in shame and privacy, whom, until that day, she had only seen once since its birth. And how horrible was the studied revenge of that mysterious compound of good and evil—Mrs. Wriggles. *The daughter conducted the mother to infamy*—showed her the way to a still deeper pit than that into which she had fallen in her youth. A woman's vengeance is like night—it comes slowly but surely.

But sequence in this narrative necessitates a return to the countess and Mrs. Wriggles.

The former, during the conference between the latter and Mrs. Smythe, felt dreadfully annoyed at the absence of Walter; and was busied forming a thousand conjectures as to its cause, when the seeming fortune-teller approached her with the customary proffers of service by the tribe of gipsy women.

"Sweet lady!" said Mrs. Wriggles, throwing a plaintive sweetness into her voice; "shall I make you as happy as your friends?"

The countess, who felt in no humour for trifling, turned away with a haughty gesture, and was crossing over to where Mrs. Smythe abstractedly stood, but Mrs. Wriggles firmly blocked up the way.

"Hear me, lady, for I have that to say which concerns both your present and future welfare. You are on the edge of a precipice, and one false step will involve you in dreadful and irretrievable ruin!"

The countess paused; and, as Mrs. Wriggles observed the blood leave her cheeks, she followed up the advantage.

"Yes, lady, you are pursued by malignant demons, who would drive you into the pit from which there is no redemption! Your enemies are legion, and they compass your total and entire destruction!"

"Who are they?" demanded the countess, yielding before the solemnity of the old gipsy's manner.

"Your own passions and wayward impulses!" was the cool and startling reply.

The countess reddened with indignation, and would have spiritedly resented the insult, as she deemed it, had not Mrs. Wriggles impetuously proceeded.

"Yes, sweet lady, your own passions are your enemies; I read it in your restless, deep blue eyes, your alternately blushing and paling cheeks, your heaving bosom, and nervous gait! If you will let me quietly read your lily hand, I will unfold to you the story of your life, and teach you how to avoid the snares that beset your path like quicksands on the level sea-shore! Do, lady, dear? Your beauty was never intended for the pollution of the spoiler, or the rapid decay of premature age! Believe me, life has more charms, more delights, more ecstacies than those we dream of in our volatile youth, or fancy in the matured desires of our riper years!"

The countess was amazed, as well she might be, at so extraordinary an address from a person of such questionable appearance; and, having no slight modicum of the superstitious in her character, was seized with a wish to test the value of pretensions to superior knowledge so warmly urged.

"There is my hand," said she, timidly ungloving; "and if you can do what you say, you will be the most wonderful woman I ever heard or read of!"

"Trust me, lady," was the quiet reply; "our tribe are the descendants of the children of the sun, and do not speak but of what they know, or is matured and sanctioned by their judgment!"

Mrs. Wriggles then commenced a careful perusal of the beautiful hand she held in one of her own brown skinny ones, and while doing so indulged in a sort of running commentary on the conclusions at which she had arrived.

"A merry childhood, and a happy girlhood. Like the first friend of your youth, you were fatherless, but were blessed with the love of a noble mother. At sixteen you fell in love, or fancied that you did so—nay, do not tremble—I can read all that I say, very plainly depicted on this warm, open palm—but it was only a fancy; your young heart, like the early rose, had not then opened itself fully to the rays of the sun of true love; and you were possessed by a melting enthusiasm, which inclined you to regard with tender confidence the objects that mostly attracted and best soothed your sympathies!"

The countess felt rather bewildered by this philosophical explanation of her early sensations, and innocently asked:

"How came you to know all this?"

"By studying human nature, drinking at the well of knowledge, and treasuring up each fact, circumstance, and analogy, that fell in my way; until, when their like came before me again, I was able to recognise every distinctive feature, and guess at truths from the similarity of appearances in each new case with those of previous ones."

The countess, whose mind, like that of all those of her class of temperament, was of too material a cast to either understand or comprehend such obscure definitions of a mystical mental process, merely smiled at what she considered the earnestness of the old gipsy; and the latter continued:

"Under the influence of this fancy or predilection, you became engaged to the young man who first made love to you, and when circumstances compelled him to leave you to go and seek his fortune in a foreign land, you remembered him until you met with another, who, despite your wish to remain faithful to the absent one, irresistibly enlisted your warmest emotions. The new lover was a dark, handsome man, rich in purse, and chivalrous in sentiment."

The countess, as she heard this, looked thoroughly frightened, and would have run away had not her curiosity been too powerful for her fears.

"Fear nothing, sweet lady," resumed Mrs. Wriggles, whose powers of perception were singularly acute; "the words of the gipsy cannot harm you. This dark man had wealth and rank to offer you, his person pleased you, and after some little hesitation you married him."

"Married him?" echoed the astounded countess. "How do you know that I am a married woman!"

Mrs. Wriggles slightly chuckled in her *natural dry* way, and replied:

"My dear lady, our acquaintance with the world is so extensive, that all classes of people come within range of our observation; and we know at a glance what position in society a person we see holds."

"But how can you distinguish a married woman from a maid?" somewhat petulantly demanded the countess.

"We can tell a maid very quickly!" replied Mrs. Wriggles, with a slight sardonic laugh; "and as it is the etiquette to give all those who are not maids the credit of being married, out of politeness we give them the benefit of the term. A maid, my sweet lady, differs from a married woman in deportment, dress, facial expression, and that peculiar mannerism which a close observer can almost instinctively recognise. The maid has a more timid gait, a milder eye, more rosy lips, and a less rolling, sailor-like fashion of walking. She is thinner in the waist, and straighter in the back, squarer in the shoulders, and more prominent in the bosom."

"Having children alters the shape," chimed in the countess; "but where there are none there surely cannot be any difference?"

"That makes little difference," said Mrs. Wriggles; "the woman who has surrendered herself up to the sovereign law of nature, can as surely be known as a new coin is from an old one. The manner—everything about her is changed, and any person of tolerable powers of observation, accustomed to mix much in society, can detect the difference; and that, in my opinion, in some measure accounts for the freedoms which men will take with women upon a very slight acquaintance, and for the great number of people called old maids, who burden society. But let us pass this by, and resume where I left off. You married the dark man, and for many months lived happily with him?"

"I was, indeed, *very* happy!" interrupted the countess, dreamily.

"I know it!" said Mrs. Wriggles, decisively; "and would have remained so until this day, had your husband been of a less plastic disposition, and sown his wild oats ere he had married you!"

The countess sighed over the recollection of her past nuptial joys, but did not interrupt the weird woman in her recapitulation of experiences, that smote keenly upon the former's recollection.

"Your delicate organisation revolted at the indelicacies to which his vitiated taste subjected you; and when you discovered that he had other sources from whence he derived the enjoyment that is supposed to be the peculiar attribute of marriage, you became resentful—waspish, and the honeyed cup of your existence became dashed with gall. You both changed—you held aloof from him, daily became colder and colder—and he, in his morbid restlessness, giving his propensities the rein, soon created in you a disgust which merely required encouragement to become a vitiated and depraved sentiment of estrangement. I speak plainly, because I reason advisedly, but beg of you not to be offended at my boldness."

The familiarity of this style of address did not strike the countess so much, as its vivid truthfulness of detail reminded her of the indignities that had sown the seeds of alienation between her and her husband.

"Proceed—proceed!" said she, impatiently.

"In this frame of mind, you met your first lover again; and his bold, manly style of feature and demeanour, insensibly impressed him in your favour. His reckless, off-hand manner both surprised, piqued, and pleased you. Had he fallen at your feet and whined for a favour, you would have spurned him with indignation. He adopted quite a different line of conduct, because he could not help it; he felt as indifferent as he appeared."

"Liar! and slanderer!" screamed the countess. "I will hear no more!"

And with this passionate exclamation she turned away from the gipsy, expecting to find the captain and Mrs. Smythe in waiting; but great was her terror at seeing neither of them, and finding herself in a different part of the park.

"Where are my friends?" she demanded.

"Gone, lady! at my request, to save you; and Mrs. Smythe to save herself also; they have returned to town by separate ways."

"A most base and unmanly desertion!" cried the countess, all her courage evaporating now that she saw herself, for the first time during her residence in London, so far away from home and alone.

"Not so, lady!" said Mrs. Wriggles, warmly; "Walter Morris is incapable of a cowardly or mean action. He knew that you had been watched hither from Bloomfield House, by one of my Lord Bloomfield's spies; and, to put him off the scent, he has left you to my care, well knowing that I have the power and will to afford you protection."

"Walter! Bloomfield!" exclaimed the countess, excessively agitated; "why then you know all of us?"

"I do; and avail myself of the chance fortune has given me, to warn you, lady of Bloomfield, of the dreadful peril in which you stand!"

"Warn me of peril?"

"Yes, countess, of peril that menaces you in the most tender point in which a woman can be injured—reputation!"

"Who are you, in the name of heaven, that dare hold this language to me?"

"One who knew your mother, whose image you are, and who would blush to see a stain on the hitherto unspotted escutcheon of the Villiers of —— !"

The countess, as these revelations broke in upon her, staggered; and, to prevent herself from falling, took a seat at the foot of a venerable beech tree.

"I am not what I seem, lady! this is a disguise I have assumed to enable me to prevent your carrying out this attempt to have a clandestine interview with Captain Morris. Hear me; your husband, whom you have banished from your bed, suspects you, and has surrounded you with spies. Every day he receives a written report from one of them; now, what will he think when he is informed that you were seen in Greenwich Park with that rakish fellow, Captain Morris—that you were traced to the shelter of a copse, or some secluded nook devoted to the mysteries of love. Why you would be driven ignominiously from your home, paraded in the newspapers, become—like many ladies you yourself have known in high life—a nine-days' wonder; afford gossip and plunder to the lawyers, and then be forgotten—buried in the oblivion to which erring woman is driven by those whose tact in concealing their infirmities of passion is their only virtue!"

The countess shuddered at the picture thus forcibly presented to her imagination, and would have given worlds to have once more been under the shelter of Bloomfield House; but Mrs. Wriggles, determined to pursue her advantage, continued:

"Let me tell you a story—a true one in every particular. I will call it

"THE HARLOT WIFE.

"Not many years before you were married, there resided, in the very square where you now live, as handsome a woman as ever the sun shone upon. She was the idol of the circle in which she moved, adored by her husband, and beloved by all who either came within reach of her fascination, or participated in the liberality of her benevolence. The only alloy to her

happiness was that she was childless; and that, after the lapse of some four years, became to her a serious consideration; for, in every respect, she was a healthy, well-formed woman. Dissatisfaction at her barrenness at length operated so powerfully on her mind, that she privately consulted the most celebrated physicians as to the cause; and they all, with a wonderful unanimity, attributed the fault to the husband. Some early excesses, they said, must have prostrated his powers, and thus have rendered him unfit for one of the highest purposes of marriage. The poison thus sown in her mind, soon worked its way into her system; and she became querulous and restless, kept her chamber, sometimes barred the door against the husband, and at last so offended him by her conduct, that he relapsed into all the wild extravagancies that characterised him before marriage, and again became a sot and a rake. In this condition, it is not extraordinary that he seldom sought his wife's society; and that, being thus left to herself and neglected, for no fault of her own, as she imagined, she should, with her naturally amorous temperament—the more amorous because she was childless—have experienced those acute physical wants which prey so powerfully on women, and which they conceal with such art and tact. A burning fever consumed her; and, while thus inflamed, she fell in the way of one of these Lotharios who are to be found in every rank of society. He pleased her eye, and, after some slight struggle with her educated modesty, submitted to his embraces. This amour lasted a few months; and, when her lover abandoned her for a new conquest, she had become too vitiated to retrace her steps, and, with shameless alacrity, replaced him by another. He, too, left her to enjoy the favours of another; and this kind of system she pursued for two years without being discovered. Although her family were blind to her faults, and her husband had become too soddened to care whether she had them or not, her frailties were blown about town. Your rakes, as regards loose women, are true freemasons; and, when her last patrician lover left her, none other approached. She had become so bold, that many who had the will to enjoy so fine a woman were deterred by the fear of detection; and thus did this unfortunate woman find herself slighted by that portion of the other sex for whom she had risked so much, and by whom she had been so polluted and degraded. Driven to extremities by this desertion, and burning with the disease which had eaten into her soul, she descended to the depravity of an illicit intercourse with her groom; and when the fellow, grown impudent by the control he had over her, became insolent, made serious inroads on her purse, and threatened exposure in case of refusal, she concocted a charge of felony against him. The evidence was strong—for some of her valuable jewels were found secreted in his box—and he was transported, amid a torrent of indignation at the infamous accusation he preferred against his mistress. Warned by this indiscretion, but not reformed, she took to prowling about the parks morning and evening, and actually purchased the attentions of several of her Majesty's common soldiers in the Guards. In addition to this vice, she had gradually contracted that of drinking, and frequently went home intoxicated. This drew upon her the attention of the whole household; and she was watched, and, one evening in the dusk, followed to a bagnio, where she was surprised in the arms of a brawny soldier. This catastrophe led to the employment of the detective police; and such a career of profligacy was laid bare, that the fashionable world stood aghast; and the victim of her own ungoverned propensities was driven forth to still deeper ignominy and shame. She became an avowed courtezan, and, having money—the remainder of her jointure—led a life of such horrible profligacy that all her money speedily became dissipated, and she sank down to the common, repulsive, gin-drinking drab. After prowling about the lowest neighbourhoods for a year or two, she died, raving mad and actually rotten, in one of our metropolitan hospitals. That miserable creature was the late Lady D——."

The countess almost shrieked as she heard the name, and piteously entreated to be saved from such a contamination as that which paved the way to the downfal of the fashionable woman whose horrible history she had just heard.

"There is a way," said Mrs. Wriggles; "win back your husband."

"How?" cried the astounded countess.

"I repeat it—by regaining the affections of your husband; he loves you still; and you, in time, will love him again. Your temperament and disposition require male society; and what could be more agreeable to a woman's mind, person, and reputation, than that of her husband's — the man with whom, by human and divine law, she is authorised to cohabit?"

"It would be a consummation most devoutly to be wished!" murmured the countess, tearfully.

"Be guided by me," said Mrs. Wriggles, consolingly. "I know of a hundred schemes; and you may be assured that if his lordship did not love you, he would not be jealous of you."

The countess saw too much probability in this surmise to give it the slightest contradiction; and as the terrible picture of the harlot wife impressed her conscience with a sense of the indiscretions to which her passions had been hurrying her, the idea of losing Walter rather soothed than distressed her. Mrs. Wriggles cautiously refrained from making the slightest allusion to the attachment which subsisted between Walter and Lucy; for she well knew that any allusion to a rival with a woman would weaken the best intentions in the world.

"But who are you who possess such a familiar knowledge of my affairs, and indulge in a womanly wisdom which sounds strangely in my inexperienced ears?" inquired the countess, after a pause, as she regarded her singular companion with curious interest.

Mrs. Wriggles hesitated a moment—it was only a moment; for, with her extraordinary sagacity, she could dart swiftly to conclusions; and, from her knowledge of the character of the beautiful and ingenuous being before her, correctly reasoned that a plain, candid statement of facts, would best win the confidence she sought to obtain. She then related the principal events in her early career, as given to her companion, the erudite Dr. Wriggles; with such additional particulars, and that softening down of the harsh points, which she knew would mostly engage the attention of her listener, and, at the same time, not violently offend the countess's modesty. When she had concluded, she almost triumphantly asked whether every feminine motive and feeling of gratitude and interest did not prompt her to prevent the countess from plunging into irretrievable ruin.

"They do—they do! and you will not find me ungrateful!" said the countess with emotion.

"Tush, my sweet child, never fear! 'tis a long lane that has no end, and you shall be happy yet. Your husband, ere long, will be a penitent at your feet, and in the chase after him you will have plenty of fun, amusement, and excitement!"

"Fun and excitement?"

"Why not? we will follow him to all sorts of places, involve him in every species of intrigue, and so surround him with grave and ridiculous difficulties, that he will be glad to surrender at discretion, a better man than ever he was in his life before. In addition, the adventures we shall undertake will give you an insight into the habits and affairs of the world; and you will be enabled to detect the hollow heart beneath the glittering exterior, the spurious chastity lurking behind the modest veil of the prude, the lasciviousness which matronly pride can scarcely conceal, and the utter depravity of thought and sentiment that pervades society throughout all its ramifications. Ample opportunities will be obtained for the study of man, and you will find, to your regret, disgust, and horror, that the great plague-spot, the pestilence of the community, is the audacious and revoltingly low estimate at which he rates woman. I promised you, in my anger, a sensual life; but you shall find, before we part, that your true epicure is the most spiritual of mortals. All our rambles promise this, and much more, both for yourself and husband."

A light here broke in upon the countess, and she suddenly said:

"What, are you and Madame Robertina one and the same person?"

"Ah! you have penetrated that secret, have you?" laughingly replied Mrs. Wriggles; "so much the better, for it will confirm your confidence in my ability to serve you in what we purpose undertaking. I need scarcely, though, enjoin you to preserve it in your own breast; and now, my dear, after this long gossip, let me bid my allies in the park good bye, and then the sooner you get to Londer the better."

In less than two hours after this memorable interview the countess was at home, vainly inquiring what had become of her absent attendant—the frail but pretty Alice Burton. Her disappearance, in one respect, will be satisfactorily accounted for during the detail of the incidents of the perilous adventure which the amorous Mrs. Smythe undertook. The young girl, from whom she had so reluctantly been separated, had saddened her, and recollections of the past came thronging on her memory. She thought of herself when her warm heart was tremblingly alive to love and joy, and with enraptured ear she drank in the sounds of the enchanting serenade, and to each soft note returned as soft a sigh. Ah! then she had—

"—— What no wealth can buy, no power create—
A little world of clear and cloudless day,
Nor wrecked by storms, nor mouldered by decay—
A world with memory's ceaseless sunshine blest—
The home of happiness, an honest breast."

But the seraphic visions of the spring-time of her virginity were as wayward as her wilful passions—

"Remembrance, sweetly-soothing power,"

only rendered the contrast between what she was and had been more glaring, and she shrank back upon her present self with the wild despair of the reckless mariner, who would go down in his surging grave to the harsh notes of a dissonant bacchanal song. In her youth she had trembled, and thrilled, and wept, as each thought and passion inspired; but she had never been taught the lesson of prudence.

"Oh, in thy truth secure, thy virtue bold,
Beware the poison in the cup of gold—
The asp among the flowers! Thy heart beats high,
As bright and brighter breaks the distant sky;
But every step is an enchanted ground!"

She had never learnt how to control the impulses of her ardent sex, and in her youth lent too willing an attention to him, who

"With sweet discourse would win a lady's ear,
Lie at her feet, and on her slipper swear
That none were half so faultless, half so fair."

Sometimes she would think of the child she had borne and *sold* to the mercy of a world less pitiless than herself; and, as she did so, the poetry of her nature would conjure up before her mental eye a married life, where

"Pure transports, such as each to each endear,
nd laughing eyes, and laughing voices fill
Their home with gladness!"

"No matter," thought she, with her large dark eyes flashing haughty defiance; "our destiny is woven for, not by us; and as the ship flies before the gale, so must all the thoughts and passions that stir us into life, yield obedience to inexorable circumstances! It has been my lot to feed my will with costly indulgences, and the rarest and rosiest is the kiss—the melting, dying enthusiasm of love. The poet tells us:

"The soul of music slumbers in the shell,
Till waked and kindled by the master's spell;
And feeling hearts—touch them but rightly—pour
A thousand melodies unheard before."

"The poet was right, but the master hand with me is that of a lover—a chosen cherished one—who will hang on my lips as the bee does on a flower; and when he withdraws his hot touch, come again reeling and staggering with joy!"

At this moment Walter darted from behind an angle in the road, and, heedless of observation, she, with a cry of delight, threw herself into his arms; and while their lips were glued together, their eyes met in one long burning gaze of fierce passion, and they surrendered themselves wholly to the spell that was upon them.

＊   ＊   ＊   ＊

＊   ＊   ＊   ＊

The pretty tea-gardens that environ London on every side, were surely invented for the accommodation of people's sins. They are so snug and cozy, so buried in the leaves of well-trained branches, that they contrive to be made into the most convenient Paphian bowers imaginable. They absolutely tempt prudery out of its last scruples, and coax the amorous youth into a display of the boldest gallantry. The waiters move about as noiselessly as eunuchs in an eastern seraglio; and the place altogether, with its trailed vines, clustering jessamines, blushing roses, and rustic seats, with perhaps a fountain in the centre, sending up its sparkling jets of water, and sometimes music mellowed by distance, seems more like a temple dedicated to Venus, than a mere vulgar house of entertainment. However, in the present state of society, it is imprudent to give things their proper names; and, with this axiom in view, it only remains to be stated, that into one of these love-retreats Walter and Mrs. Smythe retired, after having partaken of a substantial repast, well spiced with the wines that tempt the palate and enliven the senses.

"Will you love me then as now?" softly whispered the flashing-eyed lady, as she felt the arm of her companion pressing tightly on her glowing waist.

The passions do not recognise the offence of perjury in love; so Walter replied with enthusiasm:

"Love you, Caroline? why, how could I do otherwise? Besides, such love as ours is like the kissing of two fires, that make one fierce, mounting flame that never dies out. For is there not an immortality in everything that once had life?"

"Yes; such is the doctrine of the material school of thinkers," replied Mrs. Smythe, placing her burning hand on the one that pressed rigidly on her stomach; "and, as I am an elected disciple, I must not belie my faith by entertaining a doubt. But, as a matter of conscience, don't you think we are a very naughty pair?"

"Devil a bit! I beg pardon—not at all!"

"But I am a married woman?"

"So much the better for you; for the law fathers everything on the husband."

"Oh, fie! Vows and promises are nothing, then?"

"Oh yes, they are; but when the husband is the first to break them, the engagement is weakened, and, by the law of nature and common sense, should be terminated."

"But expediency demands their continuance?"

"And so holds out a premium to what are called irregularities — in fact, sanctions them," laughed Walter, as he played with the jet locks of the impetuous woman by his side.

"It may be so—indeed, I have found it so, for after I detected Smythe in an intrigue with my maid-servant, I lost all regard for him; and it was not long before I shuddered when he approached me. He used to come to bed drunk, too; and his breath was so offensive that it made me sick and faint."

With this kind of post-nuptial revelations, sugared over with a thousand varying caresses, the pair beguiled time of some portion of its treasures; and, while they are most satisfactorily convincing themselves that there was nothing wrong in giving a vigorous support to the axiom, that "stolen fruit is the sweetest," let it be the duty of the moralist to advert to one of the many causes that provoke the fall of a married woman from her high and irreproachable sovereignty.

DRUNKENNESS ONE OF THE CAUSES OF CRIM.-CON.

It is not intended to offer an apology for her offence against the most sacred of institutions, but an explanation of the species of provocation she receives to rebel against the authority which imposes upon her marital chastity. Excess in all pleasures produces disorganisation; but in none more so than in the enjoyments that result from the matrimonial

union; and it will be found, could every case of infelicity be investigated, that in the majority the responsibility lay with the husband. When in the first
blush of his new existence he forgets that gluttony
produces satiety, and that if, like a horse, he fetches
mad bounds, he must stumble over the broken
ground, and run the risk of breaking his neck over
the precipices that lie in his way. In treasuring up
his yesterdays, and worshipping the ardent present,
he disdains to think of the morrows in the calendar
of his destiny. The husband who thus prostrates
himself, in time—and short time, too—finds a feeling
of restlessness, a desire of something not within his
reach, creep over him. In his newly-born uneasiness,
the result of his exhaustion, his mind darkens,
and he begins to imagine his lot to be a dull,
monotonous one. The world of sweet whispers
into which he had recklessly plunged, becomes
darkened; his eager temperament, thirsting after
novelty, inflames his temper and poisons the atmosphere of his home. He becomes a reveller, and
looks upon his wife as no better than a legalised concubine; and thus he plays with his propensities until
they sting him into madness. What a dreadful fall
is this! The remarks of Mrs. Smythe suggest a picture of the decline and fall of married force. The parties are young, and the husband, with a joyous and
bounding heart, revels in the felicity afforded him by
the society of his sweet wife; he gazes upon her
countenance, on which smiles seem to struggle with
the lingering blush of maiden modesty; and, as he
presses her warm and yielding lips to his, and looks
into the sparkling deep of the eyes that beam only
for him, he feels a thrill of exquisite delight pervading his frame—a rapid dancing of the blood through
his veins—and he gives no heed to the thought, that
although time weaves coronals for us all, it rouses the
passion-winds that can tear them from our brows,
and scatter the leaves over the howling waste of
human misery. He is in the throes of an ecstacy
which unsettles calm reason, and renders him peculiarly susceptible to the emotions which are born out
of the qualifications of the instincts and animal propensities. In this disordered condition, and before
he can adapt himself to his newly-acquired social
and domestic relations, he is peculiarly liable to be
led astray by those grosser temptations which hang
on his skirts, like vultures in the rear of an army
marching to battle to the inspiriting strains of music,
that inspire even cowards with resolution and confidence. His heart is as open as a summer's day,
and his whole disposition is so plastic and unresisting, that it will take its form from the impulse of
the moment. Reflection is drowned in a tumultuous
sensation of unrestrained joy. This intoxication of
the senses—this moral and mental aberration—commences in the innocent hours of pure enjoyment, and,
when unwatched and unchecked, lays the foundation
of other excesses. Drink, the demon that seduces
men from the paths of pleasure and propriety, and
pours its burning liquid down the channels of life,
coaxes the tickled and excited appetite for sensual
enjoyments into a craving after novelties; and, when
the brain swims and the eye flashes with desire, it is
then that the man abandons himself to the delirium
of gratification, and sacrifices his delicacy, his hallowed supremacy over the animal in his nature, at
the degraded shrine to which Belial at first, with
silken strings, draws his victim, and afterwards binds
him there in adamantine chains. The homage which
men pay to this same Belial is immense; but, were
they prepared with protectives in the hour of danger,
it would be less. The young married man, starting,

as he does, upon a journey teeming with incident and
adventure, and exposed, as he naturally is, during its
progress, to many trials and temptations, cannot be—it
is impossible for him to be—too cautious, or to exercise too much prudence and moderation in the early
stages of an undertaking charged with so much
solemn responsibility. His honeymoon is a sanctified
dissipation of time; but if it leads to that abstraction
of mind and volatility of disposition which tend to
produce riot and confusion in the moral organisation,
its transports must be moderated, and its wild, dreamy
excitement subdued; otherwise he will fall into dis-
repute with himself, and be prepared to regard the
courses of Belial with that forgiving and extenuatory
eye, which winks at those irregularities, of which
the worst and most dangerous is the liability to
contract the depraved habit of drinking to excess.
To a sensible man it would be totally unnecessary
to detail any of the effects of drunkenness in a husband; but when the offence has been found to be one
of the provoking causes of a wife's infidelity, it cannot
either be too frequently or severely commented upon.
A corruption of morals and manners in the husband
contaminates the wife. A breath tainted with the
poison of the dram-shop, clothes reeking with the
stenches generated in an ill-ventilated public-house
parlour, a watery eye, sunken features, cartridge-
paper kind of complexion, and shaking hand, are
of themselves quite sufficient to shock a wife's delicacy, and lessen her respect for the man whom she
has chosen, in loving confidence, to be the partner and
promoter of her joys. If a candid disclosure of the
secrets of married life could be made, it would be
found that the estranged feeling, the incipient disgust,
which wives entertain for their husbands, might be
traced to a breach, on the part of the latter, of the
rules of etiquette and decorum. There is never anything very pleasing in the look of the nightcap worn
by men: its ugliness is indisputable; but how much
more ugly does it look when there is a head inside of
it, snoring and snorting as if its owner were in the
last throes of suffocation! The wife with a drunken
husband by her side must feel insulted, wounded in
her sensitiveness, and degraded in her honour; and
cannot resist the invasion of a sensation of loathing—
of an aversion which tempts her to creep away from
the sot, whose belching fumes pollute the atmosphere
of the chamber, and give to the very bed-clothes a
rank and sickly odour. To this very cause alone many
wives may attribute the abatement they feel in their
love for their husbands, and the unhappy consequences
arising therefrom. Woman has a more powerful vital
organisation than man: and it follows that her senses
are more acute, and her tastes and pursuits more
refined and delicate; so that she is more easily annoyed and offended, and more prone to revolt against
practices that offend and shock, and are opposed to
what, among civilised people, is recognised as the
standard of conduct. No social offence disgusts a pure
woman more than the habit of drunkenness: for, independent of its inevitable weakening of the physical
powers, she intuitively knows that it is the parent of
a host of abominations and vices. The inebriated
husband paws his wife as he would a favourite cat or
dog, and becomes grossly offensive in his libidinous
effrontery. He is maudlin in his silly endearments,
and looks more like a satyr than a human being.
This the wife feels acutely: she is disappointed,
wounded in her self-respect and innate modesty; the
charm that bound her to the Hyperion of her young
dreams and waking reveries is dissolved, and she sees
before her a man who contrasts strangely with those
who can be cheerful and merry, without submitting

to the brutalising ordeal of a debauch. In these moments of bitterness, of crushed and mangled delicacy, conjugal alienation commences; the mutual caress becomes colder, the kiss is more reluctantly given and received, the eye grows harder, and the whole manner declines into a repelling reserve. The result is reproaches, disgust, total alienation, and flight from home, honour, and the reputation that the exacting and hypocritical world sets such store by. A bad husband makes a bad wife, and before he can justly complain of her misconduct, he ought to go into quarantine himself. So, heigho! for the illicit loves of Walter Morris, the rake, who would take advantage of every pliant woman, and Mrs. Smythe, the rake upon principle—for, to her credit let it be placed, that she only fell in obedience to the dictates of the fieriest impulses that ever thawed woman out of the icy sea of artificial propriety.

* * * * *

"My subscription to that doctrine absolves me from all blame!" cried the excited Mrs. Smythe, raising the wine-glass to her lips.

"It does, my adored Caroline!" exclaimed Walter, upon whom the wine had made some impression; "and, while love rules the heart, the soul cannot be very angry with the body. So let us to our devotions."

The position occupied by the enamoured pair was at this moment exceedingly picturesque. The long hair of the lady was streaming in thick masses over her shoulders, which, although she wore a travelling dress, were partially uncovered, as was also her bosom. Her bonnet and shawl were thrown carelessly on the table before her, and the ends of the one and the ribbons of the other lay dabbling in the spilled wine. She herself was seated in Walter's lap, with one arm round his neck; her face was flushed, her eyes absolutely emitted sparks of fire, and her whole demeanour was such as to impress a beholder with the conviction that she had abandoned herself to the wild delirium of unsatisfied passion. As for her paramour, he was in the highest possible spirits, and kissed and laughed with such vivacity, that she would have sworn a merrier man could not have been met with. Time to them in that mood was no object, for Walter had made arrangements for passing the night at the inn; and Mrs. Smythe had become so reckless, that she would have risked anything rather than that the adventure should have partially failed. While, as one of the Simon Pure school would have said, they were in the extremely warm attitude just described, the branches that concealed them from the observation of the occupant of the adjoining bower were gently pushed aside, and in the aperture thus formed, appeared the never-to-be-forgotten lineaments of Jasper Sampson. A demoniac smile lit up his cadaverous features, and, as he quaffed off the brandy before him, he played the spy with marvellous patience.

"I have you fast, my pretty birds!" thought he. "Yet it's a great pity that all such fine kissing—and I _do_ call _theirs_ kissing—should end in discovery, and perhaps blood; 'twould be a farce, though, without the latter. Tremble, thou potent game-cock! thou valorous Guardsman! thou pet of the merry wives of London! for, unless I am a fool, this night one injured husband shall revenge the wrongs of many! It will only cost me a smart ride to town, and a still smarter one back. But, what's that she says? 'Tell me a love tale?' Oh, yes, something spicy, I'll warrant! I may as well stay, for listeners hear more than they bargained for sometimes!"

"A love tale?" cried Walter, in reply to his companion's request and unmistakeably warm kiss; "I will do my best, but my budget is rather a monotonous one."

"Pray don't trouble yourself to relate a lackadaisical story," said Mrs. Smythe, playfully patting him on the cheek; "let it be something not like anything told before—either horribly bad or most outrageously good!"

"Suppose we make it a compound of both," replied Walter, slyly; and, without further prelude, he dashed into the following

"NIGHT'S ADVENTURE.

"I had been dining with the officers of the gallant 33rd, and, as they are proverbial for late hours, it is not at all surprising that it was midnight when the party broke up, or that the majority of us, in military phrase, should have been a little fresh. I felt as jovial as any mortal need wish to be, and, not entertaining any very great predilection for my bachelor couch, threw my coat over my shoulders, and, with a cigar in my mouth, sallied out in search of adventures. The night was remarkably fine, and by the time I had reached Charing Cross, my sentimentalism had grown so large, that positively I pronounced the stars to be very fine, and the moon a perfect paragon of beauty. When I had perambulated Trafalgar Square perhaps half a dozen times, I sat down on the margin of one of the silent fountains, and, lighting another cigar, prepared myself for another hour's meditation. But in that I was doomed to be disappointed; for I had scarcely drawn up my legs for a comfortable _tete-a-tete_ with myself, when I was accosted by one of those wandering daughters of the night, who beguile men of their purses and bodily health. I had never much fancied the poor wretches, so did not much heed her solicitations. You asked me to give you a veritable story, so you must excuse the fidelity, and, probably, coarseness of the picture I am drawing. However, happening to bestow more than a casual glance on her features, I perceived, to my surprise, that she was not only pretty, but beautiful. Her eyes were blue, but her eye-lashes and eye-brows as raven as her deep, glossy black hair. Her features were splendidly regular; and her figure was tall, full, and graceful, and corresponded admirably with the wonderful dial she turned to my astonished gaze. I was struck—fascinated; and it is not at all extraordinary, to a man of my temperament, that I should, meanly clad as she was, have consented to accompany her to her lodgings. She appeared a well-educated girl, for she conversed freely and correctly, and on topics that were not likely to be at all familiar to a lowly brought-up person. In this way the long distance we had to traverse was relieved of its tedium, and I was not at all glad when we arrived at our destination, which was a gloomy alley of the most filthy-looking and ricketty houses I ever beheld. I was not to be deterred from prosecuting the adventure by my personal fears, and boldly stepped through the mud and filth after my casual _chere amie_. When we arrived at the end of the passage, she took me by the hand and led me along the hall of an open house, and up several flights of stairs, that creaked and groaned abominably under my heavy tread, until we gained a dilapidated chamber or attic, which, on a light being struck, looked horribly squalid and dismal. There was a low truckle-bed in one corner, a broken-backed chair, and a deal table in another; and those, with a few pieces of cracked delf, completed the furniture. The very air of the place was shivery, and the odour intolerably offensive. The girl must have noticed my look of disgust and dismay, for she sat herself down on the edge of the bed, and began to cry. I detest tears as fervently as I hate and detest the crocodile-men who drop them as readily as a woman does her words of wrath; and the girl's emotion induced me indignantly to exclaim:

"'What villain was it that reduced you to this misery?'

"She looked up, and, I presume from my looks, judged I was in earnest.

"'Fortune and myself are the only persons I have to blame for my degradation,' said she, with touching sadness, as she divested herself of her scanty apparel.

"She was speedily disrobed, and the sight of her unadorned charms soon turned my austerity into a lascivious channel. In paddling with her titties, pressing her velvet flesh until the blood went and came, and running my hand over her smoothly-polished limbs, I was so absorbed that I did not perceive that tears were rolling rapidly down her cheeks. As I have observed, I have a horror of tears, and the sight of them recalled to my memory the desponding reply of the girl to my remark; and I endeavoured to comfort and reassure her with some consolatory reflection, which all only meant, that if every one had their deserts who would escape whipping, &c.; and concluded a rather long tirade, by lamenting, that in cases of seduction the woman should be the only sufferer.

"'I never was seduced,' said the girl, turning her brilliant eyes full upon me.

"I was staggered.

"'As I have told you,' continued she, with increasing energy, 'fortune and myself are alone to blame.'

"'What, did you voluntarily embrace this odious profession?' I inquired, thunderstruck at her remarkable coolness.

"'Yes,' replied she; 'but, if you will listen to my story, you may perhaps find some excuse for my fall, and be disabused of the vulgar prejudice, that the men are the sole cause of our streets being thronged with prostitutes.'

"I kindled another cigar; for my nostrils did not much like the effluvia of the place, and prepared to listen.

"'Of my origin,' commenced she, 'I can relate little that would interest anyone. Both my parents, who belonged to the middle class of life, died when I was very young. I was thus left to the care of an aunt, who also died soon after them; and I was transferred from relative to relative until I attained the age of sixteen, when I was apprenticed to a milliner in London, with whom I remained only a year—for she, too, died; but within that time I had gained a good deal of knowledge of what is called the world. The girls with whom I was obliged to associate in my employment, initiated me into all the mysteries of town, and those sexual ones, of which before I had but a vague idea. They say a little knowledge is a dangerous thing, and so it proved to me, for I was seized with an indescribable longing to know more about the relation between the sexes; and some familiarities I had to endure from the young men in the establishment inflamed me to a violent degree. However, after my mistress's death I was turned adrift, and, in my struggle to earn a living by my needle, partly forgot the sensations I had entertained. But stitching is a bad business, and before the end of another twelve months I found myself reduced to the most deplorable shifts. Hunger and cold are ready casuists, and one night—the old fit had come upon me—I took to the highway, and, in the fever of desire, expectation, and the gnawing pangs of an empty stomach, I impatiently waited until some man, whether young or old, would accost me. A young one at length did, and it did not require much persuasion to induce me to accompany him to a tavern. In the morning I awoke in my humble lodgings, with a sovereign in my pocket, a dreadful headache, and oh, such—such a heartache! I thought I should have gone mad! But hunger menaced me, and after a little reflection I laughed sardonically, and philosophically endeavoured to console myself for the loss of my virginity. I lived on that sovereign for a fortnight, and then sinned again for half a one. Work became distasteful to me, and I fell into the wild frenzy of a horrible delirium. Six months passed rapidly away, and I awoke to a sense of my degradation; but habit was powerful with me, and, although friendless, I had not the courage to die. With my blasted character I could not obtain work, and thus there were no means of redemption left open to me. Hunger drove me into the streets, and there I have remained—the sport and pastime of every ruffian; and there I suppose I must remain, until I can summon up sufficient resolution to pay a visit to old Father Thames.'

"As she finished, she buried her face between her knees, and sobbed bitterly. You may suppose all this operated on me pretty much like a shower-bath, and that, instead of passing the night with her, I made her a present of my purse, and, in vulgar parlance, bolted."

"Did you ever see her again?" inquired Mrs Smythe.

"Never; but she reformed, and I procured her some employment; but her constitution had been undermined, and she soon sickened, so I had her altogether on my hands, for I had not the heart to let her go to an hospital. I sent her down to Croydon, where she died a very good Christian, and was buried under a little mound, on which nothing grows but a few unpretending daisies. So, having told my story, let us go inside, for the night air in the neighbourhood of these marshes is unhealthy."

Mrs. Smythe adjusted her bonnet and shawl, and, taking Walter's arm, they adjourned to the house, where, as already stated, they had ordered accommodation for the night.

"So, so!" muttered Jasper, as he crept from his concealment; "the dainty creature must needs have her appetite whetted by an amorous story; but I'll spoil her entertainment, as well as that of the gallant captain's! I'll have the husband down here in a crack, and, if he does not cut this game-cock's comb in a brace of shakes, I'm deucedly mistaken. A good blow—only one—dealt according to law—for a husband may kill both wife and paramour, if taken in the act of adultery—and farewell to the lady-killer, Captain Morris!"

Having discharged his reckoning, he walked rapidly away, but not unobserved by any person who knew him; for a muffled female recognised him as he emerged from the house. It was Alice, who, burning with jealousy, had, through the agency of Mrs. Wriggles, been enabled to track the pair to their place of assignation.

"He here?" she muttered; "then there'll be murder before morning! for he is sure to bring Smythe down; and as money can effect anything, the pair will be surprised, and Walter will be stabbed; for I am sure that Smythe would use a knife as soon as look at anybody. How the sight, though, of that man Jasper, terrifies me! my blood curdles when I look upon him! And although Mrs. Wriggles says I have nothing to fear from him, I have an impression that I have. I feel, too, that I detest, hate him; and should like to spite and thwart him! And how nice it would be if I could but cheat both him and that brazen hussey, Mrs. Smythe!"

While Alice was puzzling herself how she could best carry out the plan she had matured, one of the females of the inn came to the door; and Alice, assuming the pert airs of an abigail, soon became familiar with her. To learn the position of the chamber which had been prepared for the couple, and to be conducted towards it, was the work of but a few minutes. Mrs. Smythe was alone, and partially unrobed. She sat before a mirror, absorbed in speechless ecstacy.

"Fly, lady—you are discovered!" exclaimed Alice, in breathless agitation. "You were followed here from Bloomfield House, and the spy has returned to town to bring down your husband!"

"My husband?" said the bewildered lady, with a countenance of ashy paleness.

"Your husband, ma'am, and none other; and perhaps he will bring a score of men with him. Oh, fly, before there is bloodshed!"

Mrs. Smythe, having recognised the attendant of the countess, started to her feet, and hastily demanded some explanation of the grounds for the alarm.

"I saw you, my lady, leave Bloomfield House; and, as you were going out, I perceived the hall-porter on the watch; and you had no sooner turned the corner of the square, than he followed you. Knowing him to be a spy, set on the countess by my lord, I apprehended mischief, and followed also. He took the same boat; I did so also, and kept by him while he dodged you, step by step, through the park. Having missed the countess, who had received a timely warning and escaped, he pursued you and the gentleman; and, being concealed in an adjoining arbour, overheard the whole of your conversation: and when you adjourned to the house, he came out and ran towards the railway station, as fast as his long legs could carry him. Depend upon it, he has gone to your husband, who will certainly come down with a cloud of witnesses, and ruin you for ever. There will be bloodshed, too, for he is vindictive—all husbands are; and Walter—I mean the gentleman with you— is violent!"

This reasoning was unanswerable with a woman who, however warm and irregular were her desires, had as strong a wish that the world should believe her to be pure and immaculate.

"How can I escape from this fearful dilemma?" she tremblingly inquired.

"By hastening, as fast as four steeds can carry you, to Bloomfield House. Don't take the rail, for the London Bridge station will be watched! We can have a cab to Greenwich, and, once there, we can soon procure a chaise."

"But Walter—the gentleman?"

"Must be left behind; when he finds you have flown, he is too good a soldier not to hasten after you. Besides, I can return, after seeing you in the chaise, and apprise him."

Mrs. Smythe promptly agreed to this. With Alice's assistance, she dressed herself; and, under the pretence of taking a short walk to drive away a slight headache, left the inn. A passing fly was soon engaged, and in not more than half an hour afterwards, Mrs. Smythe was in a post-chaise travelling to London as fast as four horses, and a gratuity of ten

pounds each to the post-boys, could carry her. Alice, having seen her safely off, returned in a cab to the roadside inn; and, having regained the chamber, prepared with alacrity to avail herself of the opportunity thus filched, as it were, by circumstances and her own cunning, from the now acutely disappointed and rather terrified Mrs. Smythe.

Night soon spread its sable mantle over that old inn, and everything was hushed into a profound repose, when a gentle knocking was heard at the door, and voices demanding accommodation for travellers. An ostler had sat up carousing with a complying damsel of the genus kitchen, and, fearful of being detected, stole out the back way, and confronted those who were beginning to be clamorous for admission.

"Who be ye?" he asked, reassured when he saw only two men at the door.

"Travellers, who wish to rest here for the night!"

"The house is full, and ye had better go on to Greenwich—it lies straight before you, and you'll get a bed there from sixpence to a guinea."

The fellow at this turned surlily away, when one of the seeming travellers arrested his footsteps by exclaiming:

"Would you like to earn a ten-pound note?"

The man opened his eyes very wide at the proposal, but muttered something about being in no humour to be chaffed.

"I'll be candid with you my good man," said Jasper Sampson, for the speaker was no other than that worthy; "this gentleman here is in search of his wife, who has bolted with another man, and he wants to pounce upon them in bed, and give the fellow a jolly good tanning!"

"Is that all? I am your man!" replied the fellow. "Where is the crim.-cons.?"

"In your house. Did you see a dark lady and tall gentleman here this afternoon?"

"I did; and I thinks they have been abed this never so long!"

"The jezebel!" muttered the hitherto silent Mr. Smythe.

"In what room do they sleep?" inquired Jasper.

"Wait a bit, I'll soon know from Peggy, in the kitchen."

"Have you the knife ready? See that the spring is all right!" whispered Jasper.

"I am perfectly prepared!" replied Smythe; shivering though, at the idea of taking human life.

"It's all right!" said the ostler, returning. "They sleeps in the best bed-room, on the first landing. Ten pounds, did you say?"

"Of course we did; but we want the door opened first."

"It's not locked; the key's lost."

"It may be bolted?"

"Peggy says there's only a latch, which may be shoved up with a knife."

"Lead the way!" cried Jasper.

"The ten-pun note first, and no snitching. I knows nothing about it?"

"Nothing at all. Here's the tin, and don't say another word."

The man at this led them through the stable-yard into the kitchen, where a blousy young woman sat in her short chemise, warming her splay feet at a lively fire; and, after inducing them to take off their boots, they went up stairs, until they came to the chamber door.

"Here's the room. If you can't undo the latch, a good shove will send the door in. My eyes, wot a lark!" and the fellow hurried to his bed in the stable-loft, his *chere amie* pertinaciously insisting upon accompanying him.

The door was speedily and noiselessly opened, and the pair, on murderous thoughts intent, entered the chamber on tip-toe. It was now about two in the morning, and the brilliant moon poured such a flood of light through the unblinded window, that every object in the room could plainly be discerned. The curtains of the bed were drawn, and the forms of the sleepers could be plainly recognised. Walter lay on the outside, and, from the masses of black hair that were strewed over his bosom and neck, it was too evident that a woman's head was pillowed on his breast.

"It is *her!*" whispered Smythe, agitatedly; for at heart he was an arrant coward.

"Strike!" whispered Jasper, lifting the other's right hand, in which gleamed the long blade of a knife or dagger.

Twice was the hand raised to plunge the weapon into Walter's heart, and twice did it fall down as if palsied.

"It's murder—I shall be hung!" whispered Smythe, cold drops of perspiration standing on his brow.

"Hush! it's revenge! You will be applauded for the deed!" said Jasper, in the same key. "See how she clings round his neck! Look how their naked legs are interlaced, and his hand—see how it is paddling in the soft flesh of her waist! Strike!"

Thus incited, the jealous man became thoroughly maddened, and made a desperate thrust at the sleeper; but the blow fell short, and the blade buried itself in the bedding. In the plunge the intended assassin stumbled, and fell right across his contemplated victim, who, startled out of his slumbers by the assault, sprang from the bed, and grappled with his assailant. The struggle was short but severe, for your jealous husband, when in anger, is tolerably strong. Walter, however, was immensely his superior in physical strength; and, recovering from his surprise at the suddenness of the attack, with a movement of his hip and thigh, threw his antagonist heavily to the floor, and planted his knees firmly on the fallen wrestler's chest.

"Lie still, dog!" he shouted; "or I'll drive every rib you have into your heart!"

The piercing shrieks of Walter's companion alarmed the whole household; and in a few minutes a dozen lights, in the hands of people in their night-dresses, came dancing into the room.

Jasper, who had run behind the door to conceal himself, no sooner glanced at the prostrate figure of the woman on the floor, than he uttered a cry, which resembled more the suppressed cry of a dog than anything else. Walter's bed-fellow—the adulteress—was Alice! The male portion of the candle-bearers, conceiving the cry came from the man whom Walter had pinned to the floor, hastened to his rescue; and, after a desperate struggle, in which every shirt suffered damage, succeeded in placing the discomfited Smythe on his legs, and placing his opponent under restraint. Jasper, profiting by the confusion, emerged from his concealment, and, plunging recklessly down the stairs, upset the ostler and his casual spouse, as they were hastening to the scene of the uproar. Quickly regaining his legs, he fled into the highway, foaming with rage, and muttering the most diabolical curses.

Meanwhile, the disturbed inmates of the inn very naturally inquired into the cause of such an unusual disturbance in their hitherto decently-conducted house.

"I want my wife, whom that villain has seduced from me!" gasped Smythe, panting and quivering in the seat in which he had been placed.

The females, at this announcement, uttered such a chorus of groans, that Walter became dreadfully excited, struck out right and left, and, with the bound of a lion, precipitated himself on the already well-pommelled banker. The confusion was now dreadful, and both the combatants might have been severely injured by the parties present, had not Alice screamed out:

"It's all a mistake—he is not my husband! Oh, for heaven's sake, separate them!"

This was easier said than effected; but numbers ultimately prevailed, and Walter was torn from off his well-bruised opponent.

"Is this your wife?" said the innkeeper, pointing to Alice, who, in her short chemise, disclosing her legs and bared shoulders, arms, and bosom, stood by the bed-side, wringing her hands.

"Turn him out—turn him out!" she frantically exclaimed. "He's not my husband—I don't know him!"

It would be difficult to say which of the two, Walter or Smythe, was the more astonished, as they stared at the all-but nude figure of the certainly lovely Alice.

"Is this your wife?" demanded the innkeeper, impatiently.

"No!" stammered forth the bewildered banker.

The tide was now suddenly turned against him, and, amid a shower of intensely-indignant glances, he was asked to account for his burglarious visit to the premises. Alice crept up to Walter's side, and in a soft whisper said to him:

"Don't betray any surprise—acknowledge me to be your wife; and when they are all gone I will explain everything!"

Walter saw instantly that, by some mysterious complication of circumstances, he had to some extent been duped; but, as he had no reason to be much dissatisfied with the exchange, he, like a sagacious soldier, resolved to reap all the advantage he could from his novel, and, taking everything into account, not so very unpleasant position. At his suggestion Alice crept into bed again, and he slipping on his nether garments, boldly confronted his new thoroughly abashed antagonist.

"It's a mistake—a dreadful mistake!" ejaculated Smythe; silently vowing vengeance against the, as he esteemed him, treacherous Jasper.

"A mistake?" sneered Walter; "is this a mistake?" he picked up the formidable knife which lay on the floor; "to break into a man's chamber and attempt to stab him while asleep?"

"Horrible!" "Shame!" "The scoundrel!" exclaimed the mob of half-naked people assembled menacingly round the discomfited banker.

"Send for a constable!" shouted the indignant landlord; who, standing in the middle of the room in his shredded shirt, disclosed something more than a remarkable rotundity of abdomen. His cry was taken up by the females, and one, whose small grey eyes flashed over the forms of the shockingly shirted menfolk, seized hold of a certain useful utensil, and dashed the whole of its voluminous contents into the face of the pale and disordered banker. She completed this exhibition of her wrath by breaking the vessel over his head, and was preparing to make a

vigorous use of her talons, when she was prudently thrust from the room amid a torrent of applause.

"Let him go!" interposed Walter—a fellow-feeling in some matters makes us wondrous kind;—"whoever he may be, it is evident he has made a mistake. Let him make our worthy landlord compensation for the damage done, and pay ten pounds for a frolic for the servants to-morrow."

"Yes, yes; I'll do anything—quite a mistake, I assure you!" exclaimed Smythe, rejoiced at such a prospect of escape.

"Hooray!" shouted the mob.

"Away with you all, into some other room," said Walter; "your Adam and Eve costume must be very annoying to every one of you!"

The landlady, at this hint, glanced at her bare nether extremities, and hurried away, followed by her tittering bevy of still more slightly-clad domestics. The men also profited by the example, but left one of their number outside the door to prevent the escape of the contrite intruder.

"What, in the devil's name, brought you here?" demanded Walter, as soon as the room had been cleared of all but himself, Alice, and the banker. Alice had discreetly drawn the curtains of the bed, so could not be seen.

"The devil himself!" groaned Smythe; "I was told my wife was here with you, and I felt as every husband would, d—ly annoyed. You would have done the same yourself!"

"Who was your informant?"

"The fellow they call Jasper, the hall-porter—the man, mummy, or old Nick himself, for ought I know, at Bloomfield House!"

"I'll wring the fellow's neck, when I see him!" cried Walter. "But be off with you to town; for of course you cannot give me satisfaction for this affront to-night. To-morrow you shall though, by G—d!"

"What?" cried the dripping banker; satisfaction, when it's only a mistake?"

"To-morrow I shall do myself the honour to shoot you as dead as a herring!" said Walter, coolly.

"Now then, come along there, will you?" said the landlord, popping in his head; "we're all a waiting!"

Smythe, with a very lugubrious physiognomy, obeyed the invitation; and, being led into the parlour below, had presented to him a bill for 24*l*. 19*s*. 6d., for broken furniture, glass, &c., which he discharged, together with the promise of ten pounds to the servants. After this he was politely conducted to the front door, and pushed into the road, to the encouraging accompaniment of three stentorian cheers. While he stood irresolute as to the way he should take, the grey-eyed fury darted from the stable-yard, and, constituting herself the avenger of calumniated female honour, pounced upon him with the fury of a tigress. Defence against such eagle-claws was an utter impossibility; so Smythe ingloriously took to his heels, his foe hanging on to them as closely as did the naughty "cuttie-sark" wench on those of the flying Tam o'Shanter. A ditch, over which he easily leaped, saved him; for his vengeful pursuer, in her headlong haste to overtake him, did not perceive it, and souse she fell into it, to be, as Smythe fervently hoped, suffocated in its mud. He had not all the fun of this nocturnal chase to himself, though; for, just as as he had congratulated himself on his escape, he encountered the spectre-looking figure of Jasper Sampson.

"Scoundrel! get out of my way!" shouted Smythe, whose excitement turned into a very strong channel of resentment against the man who had led him into such a ridiculous and expensive blunder.

"Why didn't you strike, and it would have been all right?" said Jasper, mockingly.

"Strike, fool? would you have me hanged for murder?"

"Murder? Oh, you ninny!" said Jasper, mockingly. "Why your wife was with the soldier all day, both in the house and in a nice *crim.-con.* sort of arbour in the garden. They were alone—mark that; and the last time I saw them together, she was sitting on his lap, with her dress up, showing her splendid legs; her neck and bosom bare, her hair dishevelled, her eyes as fiery as a dragon's, and her hand playing with his whiskers!"

"Liar!" shouted Smythe, as, with the rapidity of lightning, he dealt Jasper a heavy blow on the chest, which made him stagger back more than a dozen paces.

"Oh, that's your game, is it?" cried Jasper; "come on, I'm your man!"

So saying, he threw himself into what would have been considered a fine pugilistic attitude. Smythe, who had studied under Alec Keen, nothing loth, accepted the combat, and to it they fell, in the most approved and scientific manner of milling. Smythe had the advantage in strength and weight, but Jasper was more agile, longer in the reach, and evidently more experienced in such affairs; for, while Smythe planted his blows on the body, Jasper levelled them at the face; and, in the course of one short half hour, a fair moonlight stand-up fight was brought to a conclusion, by Smythe's being dead beaten, with both eyes bunged up, and copious streams of blood running from his mouth, nose, and ears.

"Done! I give up!" he murmured, as he lay on the grass.

"Everything was fair, wasn't it?" said Jasper, indulging in a thrill produced by the recollection of many similar exploits.

"Quite; but how the devil am I to get home? I can't see the length of my nose?" complained Smythe.

The chivalry of the boxer animated Jasper, and he carefully conducted the blinded and bleeding banker to the merry town of Greenwich; where a well concocted tale of assault and battery by highwaymen, and the card of the leading banking firm in the city, soon procured them a conveyance; and about sunrise the well-pommelled Mr. Smythe found himself in bed in his own house, with a dozen leeches tugging at his swollen eye-lids and cheeks.

"Is your mistress at home?" he inquired of his valet.

"She is, sir."

"Has she been out at all to-day?"

"I believe not, sir; the carriage was not ordered, and her maid informed me she dined by herself."

"What a fool I have made of myself!" groaned Smythe.

The medical attendant enjoined quietness. He was left to his troubled meditations, not the least of which was the threatened and dreaded duel with that crack shot, Captain Morris, a man whose fire was not to be bought off at any price.

Jasper returned to Bloomfield House, but bruised and aching as he was—for Smythe's visitations on his ribs had been severe—he resolved to wait in the hall, and see whether Alice would return before the domestics were roused up.

"No, no," thought he, as he ensconced himself in his official chair; "I won't expose her—it would do me no good that—for, if she was to leave here, that cursed captain would take her into keeping, and then she would be out of my clutches altogether. She has baffled me this time, I know; but how the devil that w—e, Mrs. Smythe, got out of the way I don't know! Next time she won't, though. She thinks herself pretty! Aha, so she was once, and I must say is now! as I dare say that fiend of a captain would acknowledge; but oh, I'll have such a revenge!"

In such kind of sullen and gloomy thoughts did this extraordinary man indulge himself, until at length sleep weighed down his wearied eye-lids, and he fell into a deep slumber. While in that state, Alice, who had gained admission into the house by means of a key to the door at the back of the premises, crept softly up the kitchen stairs; and, seeing her daily and nightly terror fast asleep, paused to look at him. As she did so, something in the lineaments of his countenance smote upon her memory—her face became paler than virgin snow, her limbs tottered, and stealing upstairs on her hands and knees, she gave vent to one low, heart-rending moan of pain and anguish.

CHAPTER XIV.

THE RAKE AND THE VIRGIN.

On the third day after the adventure of the Countess of Bloomfield in Greenwich Park, she was dreadfully alarmed when the two servants, whom she had deputed to escort Lucy to her destination, presented themselves at Bloomfield House, and with tears related the fact of her non-arrival at her beloved country home, and the fruitlessness of their search after her. All the petty piques and unsisterly jealousy of the countess vanished at this alarming announcement; and, as well as her nervous excitement would allow her, she questioned the domestics, to ascertain from them all the particulars of the distressing occurrence. That Lucy had been inveigled away the countess did not doubt; as she wrung her hands in mute despair, the helplessness of her condition smote her keenly, and, when she found utterance amid her hysteric sobbings, gave vent to the bitterest exclamations against her erratic husband, whom she had not seen since the eventful evening of the soiree.

"The sot! the idiot!" she almost hissed through her marvellously white teeth, "to leave me thus uncared-for, unloved, and unprotected, to do just as I liked! Who could blame a woman, situated as I am, if she did overstep the bounds of prudence. To be left to the mercy of the world—it is abominable—worse than cruel—unmanly—cowardly! And at a juncture, too, when I have the most need of assistance, leaving me to the resource of applying to those who might take advantage of my humiliation! But my sister—my darling Lucy—must be cared for at all hazards; and to whose generosity could I more safely appeal than that of his whom my mother loved!"

And the countess, much as she desired, in obedience to her lately-formed resolution, to avoid Captain Morris, carried away by her solicitude for her sister, addressed to him a hurriedly-penned note.

That dissipated, reckless individual was at his lodgings, indulging in a substantial repast, after the fatigues of the morning parade. His imposing Guards' helmet, and other dazzling and ponderous military accoutrements were heaped confusedly together on a side table; while he had thrown himself rather carelessly across three or four chairs, and, propped up against the back of one of them, was dexterously using his knife and fork. His reflections partook rather of a personally reprehensive character. A review of his conduct for the past few weeks far from satisfied him as to its morality.

"I have been a sad boy latterly!" thought he, as he washed some viands down his throat with a glass of rich old port. "What between the married women and the spinsters, my conscience will be drained as dry as a rascally attorney's! I must mend, and, as Falstaff says, 'purge sack, and live cleanly as a nobleman!' But the deuce of it is, all my saintly resolutions vanish at the sight of a pair of pretty ankles! and, as to a lovely face, the contemplation of it warms me into a perfect fever, which ultimately exacts for its owner a willingly paid homage! What a remarkable affair that at Greenwich was! I had two of the finest women in the world with me, and had actually made it all right with one, when in pops some meddling demon, and substitutes for her the most amorous little devil that ever walked on two of the daintiest legs that ever supported a woman! Well, well, I suppose the upshot of it all will be that I shall have the baggage altogether on my hands. She hinted something about a cottage at Brompton. If I had the cash I would not mind. Overrunning the constable's no joke, when you have not an indulgent father, or rich old uncle to fly to. Orphans should never be rakes; but what the devil can they do when nature has made them as rampant as goats, and they don't happen to live in an age of self-denial? Why, there is nothing left for them to do but go the pace, and trust fortune with your neck! But, oh, this money, this money! it breaks the back of the boldest spirit, and drives him to expedients he so detests, that he feels inclined to rather hang himself than resort to them! I am afraid I must take Smythe at his word, and get him to give me that thousand pounds or do a bill for me."

The reference to the banker brought the adventure at Greenwich again to his recollection, and he could not help laughing heartily at its droll termination. He had threatened to call Smythe out for his un-warrantable intrusion, and the first object upon which the eyes of the latter fell, when he awoke about noon on the following day, was the figure of a grey-whiskered, hard-visaged military gentleman, standing by his bedside.

"I must apologise for my abrupt visit," said the intruder, in a cool, off-hand manner; "but in affairs of honour it is not usual to stand upon niceties."

Smythe rubbed his half-closed eyes, and tremblingly asked what he wanted.

"My friend, Captain Morris, has placed his affair with you in my hands, and if you will refer me to a gentleman I will not trouble you with my presence."

"Captain Morris—friend!" stuttered Smythe; "why—why—do you want me to fight a duel?"

"Something of the kind," was the dry response. "There's my card, and if it's not convenient to name a friend now, perhaps you will do so by-and-bye. The sooner the better, for these things get d—d rusty when they are kept over a day or two!"

"Lieutenant Grey, Grenadier Guards," read Smythe, perspiring at every pore, and, despite his excruciating head-ache, recalling to his memory a vivid recollection of the events of the previous night. "It was all a mistake, I assure you," said he, lugubriously.

"I cannot discuss the matter with you," said the lieutenant, sternly. "You must appoint a gentleman to act for you, and then, the affair being in his and my hands, we can see what can be done with it; but I don't think Captain Morris will be satisfied unless you meet him."

"But I can refuse. I'll swear articles of the peace against him!"

"Then he will flog you from Hyde Park Corner to Whitechapel Gate."

"What!" exclaimed Smythe, roused by this remark, "do you mean to insult me?"

"I will make so dreadful an attempt!" slightly sneered Lieutenant Grey; "so good morning, Mr. Smythe. I shall be at home all day, and shall be glad to arrange everything with your friend."

"D—d cur!" muttered the soldier, as he strode heavily down the broad staircase.

"The devil take the women!" ejaculated Smythe, with difficulty raising himself up in bed, for his bones ached, and his whole frame was stiffened after his severe pugilistic encounter; "they are the root of all evil, and if they were at the bottom of the Thames it would be no bad job! First of all to go on a wild-goose chase, then to be beaten black and blue, and now to be shot at by a fellow who, I dare say, can split a bullet on a penknife—and all through a jade of a wife. If she had been there I would not have minded it so much, for I want to get rid of her; but being innocent, or precious cunning, I'm done brown! A friend! a pretty friend he will be to stand by and see me riddled like a partridge! I must send for Stanley, and see whether I cannot get out of the confounded mess!"

Colonel Stanley was at home, but in no condition for taking upon himself the office of peace-maker, for he had that morning been fined forty shillings at Bow Street for being drunk and disorderly.

"Fight him? of course you will, and shoot him too, if you will only follow my advice," said he, abruptly cutting short all Smythe's appeals for a pacific settlement. "Lieutenant Grey, say you? a sharp fellow, that; I'll take a cab and settle the business at once." And before the astounded banker could reply, the colonel, glad to have an opportunity of placing Walter's life in danger, hastened away, and in less than ten minutes afterwards, had arranged all the preliminaries with the fiery lieutenant of the Grenadier Guards.

"You seem very ill?" said the attorney, who at midnight was preparing Smythe's will.

"I shall be worse in the morning!" groaned Smythe.

"Nonsense, my dear sir! a passing weakness, nothing more. After you have signed this family document, you will be much better; and, for your consolation, I must inform you that people who make their wills early, are the longest lived; their minds are easier—remarkably easier, I can assure you, and that promotes longevity. 'I give and bequeath'—yes, yes; who next—'to my beloved wife——'"

"Not a d—d farthing!" roared Smythe.

The attorney bowed, and calmly proceeded. The verbiage was scarcely completed, when Colonel Stanley entered, and, with a burst of hilarious confidence—for he had been spending the night in drinking—bore off the affrighted banker to the field of victory or death. When they arrived upon the ground, they found Captain Morris and Lieutenant Grey already there, quietly engaged in smoking cigars, to destroy the pernicious effects of the fog, that was lazily creeping up the low land that skirts the base of the region of Highgate. Smythe, whose appearance was wretched in the extreme—for his face was shockingly disfigured by the contusions he had received in his combat with Jasper—eyed the very methodical proceedings of the "friends," in such blank dismay, that he felt inclined to take to his heels and give the belligerent trio the benefit of a matin steeple-chase; but shame, the coward's inspiration, glued his feet in the yielding clay.

"Stand here!" whispered the colonel, pushing him some few yards in advance; "now be steady, and fire low, and you'll be sure to hit him. I have won the toss, and have to give the word, so, when you hear me say, one—two—three, gently raise your arm, and go bang at him!"

"Y—e—s!" faltered the trembling duellist, stealing a side-look at his antagonist, who, at twelve paces distance, stood firm as a rock, and buttoned up to the throat.

"One—two—" but before the astounded colonel could conclude the signal, the banker, smitten with one of those bright ideas which only adversity or perilous positions can extract from the human brain, threw down his pistol, and, rushing up to where his imperturbable opponent stood, shouted:

"I'll buy your shot! name your price, and if it's a thousand pounds I'll pay it!"

The uproarious burst of laughter that greeted this proposal was so vehement and continuous, that it was heard by a mounted police officer, who galloped to the spot, and opposed an effectual obstacle to the fulfilment of the sanguinary engagement.

"A thousand pounds!" cried Smythe again.

"Done!" said Lieutenant Grey, seeing, that with such a spiritless opponent, the affair must end without a shot.

A gratuity soon quieted the policeman, and the whole four returned to town in the same carriage; and, as might have been expected after such an adventure, in high glee. Smythe was so rejoiced at his escape, that his buoyancy of spirits mastered his prudence, and he convulsed the party with a naïvely-told narrative of his Greenwich exploits. After a hearty breakfast, the quartett separated with solemnly-exchanged pledges of secrecy on their lips.

While Walter was indulging himself over this reminiscence and the dainties spread before him, his servant entered, and handed him the following note:

"DEAR WALTER,—For the love of heaven hasten to me! Lucy has disappeared, and I apprehend something dreadful has happened. I am distracted!

"VIOLET."

Never, in this merry England before, did a man bound to his feet with greater agility, or upset a well-furnished tray with less regret for the crash or the damage. A galvanic shock could not have done the trick more effectually. The tiger—albeit, once in his life-time, a dashing light dragoon—was actually cowed by his master's impetuosity; and, as an electric telegraph conductor would say, brought the cab to the door "in no time." And certainly no well-blooded horse ever raced at a greater pace through the western streets of London, than did the one driven by Captain Morris. The very sight of the vehicle, dashing at full speed round a corner, suggested a compound collar-bone fracture case; and as for the spectacle of the tiger dangling in the air by the attenuated straps behind the cab, it could only have been excelled by a daring performance of the kind, minus the risk, in Astley's far-famed circle.

"I'm blowed if the captain isn't high-flying it, and no mistake, to-day!" muttered the breathless tiger, as his master, pulling up at Bloomfield House, leaped from the cab, and threw the reins to the wind.

"Violet! dear Violet!" almost shouted Morris, as he burst into the apartment where the countess was seated; "What is the matter? what can have befallen Lucy—our Lucy?"

The countess rose as he entered the room, and he would have clasped her in his arms, but for the presence of a third party—the incomprehensible Mrs. Wriggles.

[We must, even at this distressing juncture, pause to relate that the captain, even in his saddest moments, liked an embrace to flavour his emotions. Oh! woman! woman! your overpowering beauty intoxicates us all! and when we sin, we conveniently put the blame on the broad shoulders of the devil! and "what's the odds so we are happy?"—As many as could be put under a lady's thimble. But the staid Mrs. Wriggles—the petticoat Mephistophiles—that would alike bend vice and virtue to her immaculate doctrine of expediency, is present;—so on with the dance, and let chastity jig it to the tune it likes best.]

"Disappeared in the company of a lady traveller?" ejaculated Walter, his hair almost crisping at the agonising thought of the horrible temptations to which she might possibly be subjected. "What kind of person was she?" demanded he, bestowing on the unfortunate male servant so furious a glance, that he quailed and retreated into a further corner of the room. "Speak, scoundrel!" cried Walter, advancing towards him, "or I'll throw you through the window!"

"She was a flashy kind of lady, sir," stammered he; "and hired a po-chaise at the inn."

"Some procuress, no doubt!" groaned Walter.

"God of heaven!" screamed the countess. "Can nothing be done to save her?"

"Certainly there can," broke in Mrs. Wriggles. "If Captain Morris will but follow my advice, Miss Lucy will be rescued before the dawn of to-morrow. Her abductor and intended cold-blooded ravisher is Colonel Stanley."

"Colonel Stanley?" said Walter, amazed.

"Even he," replied Mrs. Wriggles; "and he left town, from the Euston station, at six o'clock this morning, for some shooting-box of a place he has down in Herefordshire. You must follow him, and take with you a Bow Street runner, who knows something about the colonel's haunts and habits. Here, take this card, and be off at once to the Red Lion in the Strand, where you will find your man. Ask for Mr. Johnson, and follow his instructions. These stupid servants will meet you in an hour at the station."

"Not a moment shall be lost! Adieu! Violet; and, believe your old schoolfellow, Lucy shall be preserved or avenged!"

So saying Walter hurried away, and in a few minutes afterwards alighted at the door of the tavern to which he had been directed; there he found Mr. Johnson, a lean, but muscular fellow, with an eye as furtive as the ape's, and as keen as the hawk's.

"All right!" said the detective, plunging into a great coat, with large pockets, containing handcuffs, pistols, loaded and primed, and other etceteras of his agreeable profession. "Don't talk here—plenty of time on the road," said he," gulping down his glass of brandy-and-water. "I know all about it. Special engine, of course?"

"Certainly!" replied Walter, delighted with his new companion's cool, prompt manner.

In little more than an hour—a period, though, of cruel suspense to the impatient Walter—he was dashing on towards Birmingham at the rate of forty miles an hour.

And now to return to poor Lucy.

When she awoke, on the morning succeeding the supper with her seductive travelling-companion—who, by the way, had declared herself to be the Honourable Mrs. Douglas, and that her husband had been a cabinet minister—Lucy found herself in a splendidly-furnished bed-room, with her faculties in a state of remarkable obtuseness. Her first thought, as she took a survey, was that she was in her old room at home, and that her sister had altered its character, for the pleasing satisfaction of giving her a delightful surprise; but it seemed infinitely larger, and the window, too, was of quite a different form. Alarmed at the sudden transformation, she sprang from the bed, and hastened to the window. But, instead of beholding the beautiful valley and distant hills of her sweet native place, she saw a rich woodland scene, such as are presented in the parks of England. Under other circumstances it would have commanded her admiration; but at present her terrors subdued every other emotion. She fancied she must be dreaming; and it was not until she had rubbed her eyes repeatedly, that she became convinced that she was really wide awake. At last the whole of the incidents of the previous day flashed across her memory; and, although labouring under severe nervous agitation, she formed the conclusion that, being oppressed by fatigue, she had been kindly provided with accommodation for the night.

"How imprudent and improper!" she blushingly exclaimed, as she resolved to array herself, without calling for assistance; but her clothes where nowhere to be found. Startled at this untoward circumstance, she instituted a careful search throughout the whole room; but not a single article of apparel, not even the night-dress she wore, could she recognise as belonging to herself; but, instead of her own, she saw the most costly garments, including a snow-white morning dress, placed within her reach, and evidently designed for the occupant of the chamber, whomsoever she might be. She looked for the bell-rope, but the room did not contain one; and, to complete her dismay, she found the door locked on the outside. Thoroughly frightened at these ominous appearances, she sat down on the bed-side and began to cry. Thoughts of home, her sister, and Walter, crowded upon her mind, and she would have given worlds to have known that one of them was within call; but so pure was her nature, that the slightest idea of evil oppressed her. She was frightened, puzzled, absorbed in a confused mass of conjectures; and, while she was torturing her little head to account for her for her situation, the door opened, and a young female entered with a vessel of warm water, and the other appliances for the morning ablution.

"Where am I?" exclaimed Lucy, starting up, and clutching at the girl so eagerly, that the water was spilled over both of them. "Oh, do tell me what house is this, and bring me my clothes? Or perhaps this is an inn, and Violet, my sister, or Lord Bloomfield or Walter is here. Do tell me what all this means?"

The girl, who might have numbered two years more than Lucy, and had the dark complexion and luxuriant hair of the Creole, turned her deep-black eyes upon Lucy suddenly, and with such a vacant look, that she released her hold, and gazed at the girl in troubled astonishment.

"Me no understand," said she, at length, in such sweet tones, that they thrilled to the listener's heart.

Lucy's courage revived at the sound of the voice, and she again piteously entreated to be informed how she had found her way into that apartment.

"Me no understand," repeated the girl, as she arranged the toilet-table with much readiness.

Lucy became more urgent in her demand, and, to call the girl's attention more decidedly to her request, gave her by no means a gentle shaking. The girl, at this, drew herself up indignantly, and her large, lustrous eyes actually glowed in her head.

"What place—whose house is this?" cried Lucy, assuming a peremptory air, which was very foreign to her gentle disposition.

The girl looked at her from head to foot; and as she saw how fair and beautiful the questioner was, a smile, of something very like hatred and jealousy, curled her thin red lips, and she swept out of the chamber.

Lucy, upon finding herself so cavalierly deserted, gave way to her terrors, and uttered the most piercing shrieks. They evidently had attracted attention, for the sounds of feet, hurrying to and fro, were heard; and presently the Creole returned, with a more placid expression of countenance.

"Me wait upon—dress you," said she, curtseying.

"Oh, tell me where I am, or return me my clothes, and let me leave this place? I cannot, will not stay here any longer!" ejaculated Lucy, the big tears running rapidly down her pale cheeks.

The girl was evidently softened, but pertinaciously refused to enter into any conversation. She gracefully urged upon Lucy to dress herself, and the latter, after many ineffectual attempts to obtain an explanation of the mystery, resigned herself into the hands of the Creole, who speedily performed her office, even to the skilful arrangement of poor Lucy's long silken tresses. After the operations of the toilette had been completed, and Lucy was fully equipped in a bewitching morning costume, the Creole conducted her down stairs to an apartment which proved to be a breakfast-room, and, with a silent obeisance, left her alone. Lucy, more and more bewildered, could only gaze around her in blank dismay, and offer up a prayer for her safety. As her glances wandered about the room, they fell upon the pictures that embellished the walls; but she quickly withdrew her gaze, and bent it in shame and disgust upon the floor, for the subjects of the paintings were abominably licentious. They were all, or pretended to be all, of the beastly school of Greek mythology.

There was the derider of Bacchus, rendered so intoxicated by that god, that he was actually pursuing his own daughter; and, as a companion picture, there was a miserable caricature of a painting, depicting Bolina's successful resistance of the amorous Apollo. Venuses in every variety of attitude were plentifully distributed about, and, to complete the disgusting *ensemble*, there was a horrible scene borrowed from the mysteries of the Hindoo worship. Lucy's modesty was so shocked by even the slight glimpse she had, that she did not dare to look up, and, half fainting, slid almost mechanically into a chair.

"God help me!" she murmured.

"Good morning, love!" said a rather husky voice; and, upon Lucy looking up, she beheld a face which she immediately recognised as that of her travelling companion's of the day before.

Lucy could not speak, and all she could do was to fling herself sobbing on the bosom of her decoyer.

"Why, in heaven's name, what is the matter?" exclaimed the *pseudo* Mrs. Douglas, pretending the utmost astonishment.

"I want to go home," sobbed Lucy.

"Home? why, love, this is to be your home for a few weeks! Surely you are not tired of Douglas House ere you have well entered it?"

"Douglas House?" said Lucy, lifting up her eyes in amazement.

"Yes, darling; have you forgotten that you are to be my guest, for, *I* hope, a long while?"

"Guest? Long while?" stammered Lucy, utterly confounded by the other's audacious assurance.

"Certainly; unless you should take it into your pretty little head to fancy we are too dull for you. So banish your tears, and let us have a comfortable *tete-a-tete* over our breakfast?"

"But I must go home!" reiterated Lucy; "some unaccountable mistake has been committed. I am not the person whom you mean!"

Mrs. Douglas gave way to a merry burst of laughter, and, patting Lucy's cheek, said, coaxingly:

"Ah, you sly puss! you want to slip through my fingers, and leave me to amuse myself as I best can; but I cannot permit it. I'll play the tyrant, and retain your dear society even against your will. Why, you must have been dreaming, to have forgotten that your sister, the countess, agreed that you should stay with me for a week or two!"

"What, did Violet—did my sister consent to my coming here?" cried Lucy, more and more amazed.

"She did; and, hoping to have an agreeable surprise in reserve for you, did not admit you into her confidence. But I will show you her letter."

And here the artful woman drew a letter from her bosom, which she handed to Lucy. The latter, insensible even to the bare suggestion of the possibility of there being any deception practised, greedily perused the well-known characters; and, with a sinking heart, admitted that it appeared to be her sister's wish that she should remain at Douglas House for a short period.

"But why not acquaint me with her intentions?" urged Lucy; "my sister's will has ever been dear to me."

"She had no desire to see you altogether buried in the country, my dear; and, like the majority of our sex, she likes a little mystery being mingled with an engagement. Come, darling, breakfast waits, and after that we will have a nice ramble."

Lucy had no feasible objection to offer; and, in most lamb-like simplicity, took a seat at the obnoxious breakfast-table.

The room was grossly offensive to her delicate organisation—not that familiarity had made her acquainted with the gross features of the paintings; but her repugnance was a spontaneous and involuntary sensation. Yet she could not complain—her undiluted modesty would not permit her the privilege of resenting such an affront; and, in a state of painful trepidation, she allowed her seductive hostess to charm her out of so much of her reserve as enabled her to appease the slight cravings of her appetite. Yet Lucy, in one respect, was a brave girl; for many young persons situated like herself would have fallen into the meshes of such delicate blandishments, and been wholly carried away by the novelty of their position.

Not so with Lucy. Her sensitiveness and high-toned confidence had been injured; and after that all the temptation and cajolery in the world would not have won upon her noble capacity to candidly appreciate those whom she instinctively felt deserving of a trusting preference.

The hostess, whose imposing charms were set off to the best advantage, had the conversation all to herself, and when the meal was concluded Lucy felt thankful; for it was a positive relief to her to leave that odious room. When she regained what the attentive Mrs. Douglas was pleased to term her own suite of apartments, Lucy, left to herself, began to ponder over her strange situation. That her sister should have sent her down to such a place and in such a manner, she could scarcely credit; yet there was the note in Violet's own handwriting, and Lucy was obliged to be convinced against her will. While engaged in adjusting a bonnet for a morning promenade, she happened to glance through the window, and observing a groom cantering a horse; she was induced to look at him attentively, and, as she did so, to her horror she identified him as one she had frequently seen accompany Colonel Stanley to Bloomfield House. The faintest surmises will soon deepen into the most terrible conjectures, and Lucy, shivering with the apprehension that she had fallen into some snare, emerged into the passage, and seeing a young girl advancing, accosted her with a cheerfulness that was very badly assumed. The girl was a raw, unsophisticated one, and evidently a dangerous personage to permit to roam over a suspicious house.

"Why this house be the colonel's, miss," said she, regarding Lucy's lovely face with a stare of rustic admiration.

"Stanley—Douglas, I should say, is that the name?" inquired Lucy.

"Sometimes one and sometimes t'other," answered the girl. "When the Lunnon chaps come here a shooting, its Colonel Stanley; but when everything is as quiet as an empty church, its Colonel Douglas."

"Then Colonel Stanley and Colonel Douglas are one and the same person?" uttered Lucy, tremblingly.

"The identical same!" laughed the girl; "it's always Colonel Douglas when a pretty girl like yourself comes on a visit—but don't look so pale; the colonel, they say, bean't a bad chap, only a little wild like among the girls; but if you would just take a fool's advice, you would cut and run. The visitor girls, who, like you, come here by themselves, sometimes cry and tear their hair, and one poor thing went mad. A nod's as good as a wink to a blind horse, so good bye."

And before Lucy could extract another word from the girl, she had flown. All the poor girl's suspicions were now confirmed, and, as the warning of Mrs. Wriggles broke in upon her recollection, she shuddered at the prospect that opened upon her imagination. Flight was her first impulse; and, hastening down the corridor, she fell plump into the outstretched arms of the Honourable Mrs. Douglas.

"Let me go!" screamed Lucy; "I will not stay in this house another minute. I have been deceived and insulted, and insist upon departing at once!"

Mrs. Douglas dragged rather than led her into a room, the door of which stood open; and then, in seeming amazement, inquired what was the matter.

"The matter?" echoed Lucy, indignantly; "do you affect ignorance of having beguiled me into a strange house, and that house, too, belonging to Colonel Stanley, a man whom I detest?"

"Colonel Stanley?" said Mrs. Douglas, her face slightly crimsoning; "a gentleman of that name does certainly come here in the shooting season, but this mansion belongs to Colonel Douglas, my husband."

Lucy had but a very imperfect idea of those unlawful connections which subsist between the depraved of the sexes, and therefore could only regard the daring personage before her with a troubled countenance. But, convinced that any prolonged stay under such a roof would be indecorous, she determined, at all risks, to leave the house, and find her way, even on foot, if necessary. She sprang towards the door, but, to her dismay, found it fastened.

"Release me, woman!" she frantically cried, her warm Welsh blood mantling her temples. "I will not remain in such a place!"

Mrs. Douglas stood regarding her with a cold sneer; and this so inflamed the agitated Lucy, that she rushed to the window, threw up the lower sash, and in a second was scrambling through; and would inevitably have leaped, high as it was, had not Mrs. Douglas by main force dragged her back into the room.

"Would you murder yourself, silly girl?" said she, angrily.

"Let me go, any way? I would rather die than remain here!" supplicated Lucy.

Mrs. Douglas was puzzled. Had her victim been of the lower ranks of society, she would not have hesitated to have coerced her into obedience; but belonging, as she did, to one of the noblest families in England, was a rather awkward circumstance to contend against, and unquestionably saved Lucy from the indignities that would have been inflicted upon a poor girl, with no aristocratic connections to avenge her wrongs. But this bad woman had been accustomed to such displays from those whom she had entrapped in her den; and, being no ordinary adept in the art of persuasion, tried the effect of her powers upon Lucy. Her endeavours, however, were all fruitless, for Lucy persisted in her energetic desire to leave the place. Such obstinacy, as she termed it, exasperated Mrs. Douglas, and she lost her temper.

"Without my permission you cannot go out of this room, even!" said she, savagely; "and that, in your present humour, you cannot have, for I cannot afford it."

"Would you detain me a prisoner?" demanded Lucy.

"Consider yourself one!" replied the woman, haughtily; "and, to end this scene, let me tell you that your coming here was a planned thing long before you left Bloomfield House. You are to marry Colonel Stanley—certain family reasons render the marriage indispensable, and also that it should be performed in secret and this evening; so leave off whimpering, and be prepared for the happy, the glorious ceremony. Why, if I were in your place, I should be half crazy with delight at such a prospect of happiness! The colonel is rich, handsome, and loves you

to distraction, and what more need any girl want in a husband?"

"Lost—lost!" sobbed Lucy, as she sank helplessly to the floor.

"Lost?" cried Mrs. Douglas; "why you have not been found yet! To-night, love, on a bed of down, and in the arms of the man who adores you, you will awake to a new existence—a new world will open upon you—new joys will thrill you to the heart—and in the morning you will only be sorry that the night did not last much longer!" Cheer up, for, as sure as you sit there, this will be your bridal day!"

"Bridal day?" said Lucy; "I'll die first—we mountain girls are taught to prefer death to dishonour!"

"Death! fiddle-de-dee! Wait until to-night, and you will find that the best death is a swoon of burning joy! The colonel will clasp your naked form to his, and, while giving you a thousand burning kisses, will teach you how a man loves a woman! Die—yes, you will die, and have a resurrection—and then wish to die again!"

Lucy's blood curdled in her veins, as she listened to her licentious betrayer. Ruder natures might have been susceptible of giving birth to kindred ideas, and so have yielded to the lascivious temptation; but Lucy was shocked, disgusted—her virginity recoiled from contact with such impurity; and the poor girl was fast yielding to the despair that was creeping upon her, when, actuated by a sudden impulse, she threw herself at the woman's feet, and appealed to her womanly pity:

"I was the delight of my mother, the pride of my sister, and the delight of all who knew me!" said she, the hot tears blinding her vision; "it was the wish of them all that I should grow up to womanhood, unstained by any vice, or uninjured by the follies that mar the glorious work of His hands; and oh! let me depart, ere the wickedness I have been taught to avoid comes upon me, and makes me what I scarcely know, and dare not name! I implore you, as a woman—by the love you bore your mother, and him that was dearer than all—to let me go hence before dishonour blights my young days, breaks my sister's heart, and brings down, as it surely will, the vengeance of heaven!"

That sinful woman stood abashed in the presence of that angelic girl. She remembered the time when she could have pleaded with as pure a heart and firm a purpose. But then came the dreadful reminiscence of her fault, and hatred—black, intense hatred—crushed every feeling of pity. Envy, too, smote her, as with a burning brand—that girl at her feet was her superior—she knew it, and, like the arch-fiend gazing upon our parents in Paradise, she felt, that to ruin her would help her to her revenge—minister to her hatred, and assuage the fire of the deep hell of her guilt. She had plans to complete, schemes to carry out; and, if she were to thwart the colonel, she knew she would be driven penniless on the world. Expediency—the fiend that breathes his spells upon all human calculations—thus armed her with another power; and, had she been less black-hearted than Satan, she would have felt compelled to exclaim, with that fallen spirit, that necessity compelled her—

———"Now
To do what else, though damned, I should abhor."

Smothering her emotions, she raised Lucy gently from the ground, and calmly said to her:

"I have heard your request, my love, and with no little surprise: for I cannot conceive why you should be so unjust in your wish to leave the shelter of my house, and go away unprotected. Why, you are at least fifty miles from what you yesterday thought your destination. But if you will persist in going, defer it till the morning, when I shall have everything arranged for your journey?"

"To-day—it must be to-day, lady!" cried Lucy, impetuously.

"It cannot," was the cold reply.

"It shall! Who shall dare prevent my egress?" said Lucy, proudly.

"I will; and what is more, my pet, can. So, be quiet ——"

"Traitress!" shouted Lucy. "Beware how you stir up the ancient blood in my veins; or you may find that a Welshwoman may not be insulted with impunity. Stand aside, and let me pass through yonder door!"

"Had you all the blood of your kinsfolk and countrymen in your veins, you should not leave this residence. So tame yourself down, Miss Lucy Villiers, and prepare yourself to accompany me."

This was uttered with chilling coldness; and, after ringing a bell, the Creole appeared on the threshold of a door which Lucy had not before perceived.

"This lady will occupy the Chamber of Roses tonight. Is all in readiness to receive her?"

The Creole bowed in the affirmative.

"Is the altar prepared, and are the candles ready for lighting?"

Another bow; and Mrs. Douglas, indicating by a gesture Lucy, said to the Creole:

"Conduct this young lady to her bridal apartments."

Lucy became so indignant at this supercilious disposal of her person, that she was almost choking with passion; and, as well as she could, exclaimed:"

"Are you determined I shall be a prisoner?"

Mrs. Douglas turned away from her with an imperious sway of her bulky body.

There were several knives and daggers, mingled with other ornamental articles, on a table close by where Lucy stood; and, quick as thought, she possessed herself of one of the latter; and, advancing upon Mrs. Douglas, said, excitedly:

"An ancestress of mine was once tempted by a bad woman to do wrong. The story is told in our family to this day; but she repulsed the fiend with scorn; and when persecuted, and there was no help near, did ——"

"What?" inquired Mrs. Douglas, curling her lips disdainfully.

"This—and the praises of the dead are still sung in hall and hamlet!"

And swift as lightning Lucy raised the dagger, and made a violent thrust at the naked bosom of her tormentor. The latter caught the gleam of the brightly-polished steel, and, with a shriek, raised her arm. The action saved her life; for the sharp point of the weapon glanced off from her arm at the elbow, and the only injury it inflicted was a flesh-wound, of about a couple of inches in length. More terrified than hurt, the woman made the house ring again with her appalling clamours; and in a short time the servants poured in from every quarter of the mansion.

"What is the matter?" inquired the gigantic footman, who, it will be remembered, had waited at the supper-table the evening before.

"That wasp has stabbed me!" screamed his dreadfully-frightened paramour; for, like all creatures of abandoned principles, she was afraid to die.

Lucy being thus pointed out, felt that every eye was upon her, but she saw nothing but the blood—

the crimson beads that dripped to the floor; and, with an hysteric laugh, sank down into a swoon.

"Carry her to the Chamber of Roses, and do you, Agnes, attend to her—the wasp!" growled the ashy Mrs. Douglas, as, with much satisfaction, she saw the insensible form of Lucy borne from the room, followed by the Creole, whose eyes spoke of her admiration of the deed, and promised some consolation for Lucy, when she should have recovered the use of her faculties.

"It's only a scratch," said the footman, whom it may be as well to designate as Charley Wilson.

"Scratch?" exclaimed Mrs. Douglas. "I'll tear the little Welsh devil's eyes out for it! Would to God the colonel were here, to give her a taming-lesson or two! By heaven, if he does not do it, you shall, Charley!"

"No, thankee!" replied Charley; "that's a sort of business I never tried my hand at; and, d——e, if I wouldn't sooner fight six men than have a tuzzle with an unwilling girl! You are the only darling of my heart; and I think the best thing we can do is to bolt from this accursed place at once. I had a queer dream last night!"

"Pooh! Do you think I would allow that minx to triumph over me?" said his *chere amie*, who, by the way, was a cast-off of the colonel's. "No—I'd rather be cut to pieces first!"

"Leave her to the colonel, Kitty. Don't burn your fingers if you can help it.—Here comes the postman!"

The letter was from Colonel Stanley; and it informed his precious housekeeper that he could not possibly be down before noon on the following day.

"Curses on his dilatoriness!" exclaimed Mrs. Douglas, tearing the letter into a thousand fragments. "Treat her kindly! oh, yes, I will treat her kindly; and here goes to give her a taste of it!"

And she was hurrying away, when her brawny paramour caught her in his arms, and, despite her desperate struggles, bore her good-humouredly away. After she had cooled down a little, she assented to the wisdom of Charley's advice, and left poor Lucy, unmolested, in the hands of the Creole, whom she addressed as Agnes.

"Agnes hates her!" said this precious specimen of womanhood; "so it's some comfort to know that she won't have a very quiet time of it until to-morrow!"

"Them dark girls love pluck," thought Charley to himself; "and I'm blowed if I don't think you will be mistaken there, my precious. Come Kitty, my pet," said he, aloud; "let's have a little drop of brandy together and be sociable—to-morrow will soon be here."

Kitty, nothing loth, readily agreed to the proposal; and, after a few drams and some maudlin caresses from her gigantic lover, become somewhat pacified, and more disposed to wait patiently until the downfal of Lucy had been accomplished. The monotony of their conversation was relieved by some instructive comments on the question, whether it was more sinful to seduce a maid than a married woman. Kitty Douglas, *alias* Kitty Bell, sided with the *femmes couvertes*; Charley elected himself champion of the spinsters.

"A slice from a cut loaf is never missed," grinned Charley, chucking her under the chin.

"Get out, you blackguard! hasn't a married woman got feelings as well as another? and then look at the discord it introduces into families!"

"Isn't it the same thing with a young woman. A daughter gets in the family-way; well, what's

the consequence? she's kicked out of doors to help herself, and then what does she do? Why, perhaps goes to some old ——, and gets the child's goose cooked, or lets it be born and then shoves it down a petty, and sometimes goes arter it herself. Married women now, whether the children be their husband's or not, stick to 'em like bricks—so there's no murder done with them."

"It's all very well to talk in that way, Charley; but, if you had the chance, I know which you would like best. You men are all alike—you go mad after the maids."

"It's all owing to their scarcity, that," replied Charley, drily; "but I stick to it, that of the two it's less sinful to go with a married woman than a single one: for the married one's are more sly, and know how to conceal it—and, as they have been tapped, they like it better. But what's the odd's? any woman can keep off a man if she likes, and I never hears of a downright case of seduction or *crim.-con.* but I believes one side is as bad as the other. The women will show themselves off and throw eyes at the men; and, as that leads to a precious lot of

kissing and hugging, the natural consequence is, that the deed is done before either of them knows much about it."

"You blackguard—give us a kiss?"

And in this delectable manner the pair beguiled time of its tedium, and then discussed their plans for the future.

The day and night wore slowly on for poor Lucy, for, although the Creole scarcely ever left her, she fancied that every sound she heard was but the herald of the approach of her dreaded persecutor. The only favours she could win from the Creole were the use of pen, ink, and paper, and a solemn promise to post the letters she wrote. This the girl faithfully kept, and thus the only relief Lucy had, during that terrible day and night, was the assurance that the moment her friends heard of her situation, they would hasten instantly to her rescue.

Towards morning, being completely wearied out, she fell asleep; and, as the sun-beams fell upon her placid face, so chaste and beautiful in its heavenly repose, a jealous pang smote upon the heart of the frail Creole girl.

"He will love her better than me!" she murmured.

And, as she gazed, her vengeful temperament became dangerously excited. A knife, with a long, keen, well-polished blade, met her eye. To grasp it, poise it in her hand, and bare the snow-white bosom of Lucy, was but the work of an instant.

At that moment Lucy smiled, and a rosy hue, like the faint blush of early morning, stole over her angelic features.

The knife dropped from her hand, and, with the soft exclamation, "My mother looked so when asleep!" knelt down and prayed for poor Lucy's safety.

The morrow came in all its bright significance, as if there was neither sin nor sorrow in the world, and with it Colonel Stanley, who, without hesitation, presented himself before his captive.

"Retire!" said he, angrily, to the Creole, who lingered near the door.

She reluctantly obeyed, and Lucy was left alone with the man whom she dreaded and cordially disliked.

His manner was tender, but respectful, and he urged his suit with all the vehemence of which he was capable.

"I love you, Lucy!" he passionately exclaimed; "your beauty has fired me beyond the control of reason! Day and night it haunts me! and for one kiss, or one hour's play with those bright locks, I would resign half my life! My fortune, my liberty, my whole possessions shall be thine, if you will but consent to be my wife! I belong to an ancient, a princely family—one that has given kings to England!"

"Your ancestors would blush to find one of their descendants insulting a defenceless girl! *They were men!*" said Lucy.

The insinuation did not call up the hue of shame to the colonel's face; it merely exasperated his craven spirit.

"Your friends approve of the match," urged he. "You are poor, I am rich!"

"Liar!" exclaimed Lucy, glancing at him in supreme disdain; "my friends are too noble to palter with a maiden's honour; and, as for your riches, they are as nothing compared to mine! I possess an unsullied name—you have one that is so defiled that I have heard the very gamesters at Bloomfield House mock at it, and say that it had been trailed through the kennel! Riches! talk not of them, for they have neither earned for you fame nor honour—but infamy, deep and lasting infamy! And for this outrage on a maiden thou art a scoundrel, and a coward, and darest as soon stand before Captain Morris as at a loaded cannon's mouth!"

"Then you refuse to marry me?" uttered the colonel, trembling with suppressed passion, for the words of the spirited girl had galled him to the quick.

"Marry you?" shrieked Lucy, her countenance expressing the utmost disgust. "I would sooner dash my brains out against the altar!"

"Then, mark me, proud beggar—I give you until dusk, and if you then refuse to be my wife, by the living God I'll make you my ——" and the colonel rushed from the room.

Lucy's excitement soon abated, and she experienced that sinking of the heart, which only those in the lowest depths of despair can describe. Suddenly her eyes fell on the knife which the Creole had dropped, and a ray of hope illuminated her countenance.

"With this," said she, "I can both preserve my honour, and avenge myself. Spirit of my mother, look down upon me! In my native vale they do say the spirits of the dead watch over the good; and if it be true, oh, mother, mother! look down upon your child this night!"

While the colonel was enacting and concocting this little bit of villany, Mr. Charles Wilson, in another part of the mansion, was regaling himself with an old crony — one Jemmy, from town. The colonel was closeted with the quondam Mrs. Douglas.

"We've had many a lark together, Jemmy," said Charley, sententiously; "and I doesn't see why we shouldn't have another."

"Nor I," answered Jemmy; "but it's a heavy venture, Charley. How much plate?"

"About a thousand pounds' worth!"

"Any tin?"

"Kitty has some, but she's precious close—and, between you and me, I rather think she intends to do me!"

"No?"

"Fact! The last time the governor was here, I overheard him promise to send her to France, if she'd only assist him in getting over a Welsh girl."

"Ah, Charley, them colonels are sad fellows among the girls! But if that's the fly, oughtn't you to be wide awake, and cut at once?"

"Hush! the girl's in the house, so is the colonel, and I don't half like what's going on. The girl won't have him at any price; but d—e if I don't think they're a-going to ravish her!"

"Keep clear of them sort of things, Charley, for you can't make any tin out of 'em nohow. But, I say, wouldn't it just be the sort o' night for your little job?"

"I was thinking so myself. How can we manage it?"

"Where's the swag?"

"In Kitty's room."

"Good. She'll be on the watch for the colonel and the Welsh girl. Where's them to be?"

"Last room on the second landing. They calls it the chamber of roses, 'cos I suppose it has proved thorny to many a girl."

"Good—the thing can be done; but as the swag's heavy, I must bring a pal with me. Where's the colonel?"

"Gone out a-riding."

"Good. Leave this window open for me, Charley, and leave all the rest to me."

With this assurance the pair separated.

"It's to be done at last," said Charley to himself, as he puffed out immense volumes of smoke from his pipe, "and I'm not sorry. That Kitty would wear Goligolia himself out, and as I can't afford to spend all my manhood on a colonel's cast-off trull, the sooner I'm off the better. And the best of the joke is that if they suspect me, they darn't follow it up, for I know too much about their goings on."

At dusk Jemmy and his pal, a tall, strapping fellow, in a smock-frock, faithfully kept their appointment, and were cautiously introduced up stairs by the now half-drunken Charley himself.

"First-floor, second room, pals," whispered he; but they paid no heed to him, and continued ascending as noiselessly as before.

A slight scream now broke on the ear, upon which the tallest of the two burglars burst away along the second-floor passage, overturning in his way a woman, crouching down in an attitude of listening, and soon arrived before the door from which the sound, increased in intensity, proceeded. To apply his shoulder, and force it from its hinges, was but the work of a minute, and into the apartment he rushed, closely followed by his companion, Jemmy. The scene that presented itself explained the nature of the drama which had been playing. In one corner, the furthest removed from the bed, stood Lucy, holding a knife menacingly in her hand, and before her stood Colonel Stanley, with one of his cheeks slashed from the temple to the base of the jaw.

"Walter!" shouted Lucy, and the next instant she fell insensible on the breast of her deliverer.

The colonel stood aghast at the interruption, and turned to fly, but Jemmy tripped him up, and in a trice handcuffed him. The woman who had been on the watch uttered a howl, and took to her heels. As for Charley, he guessed that there had been a successful rescue, and followed her closely. He found her hurriedly secreting several small bags about her person, but as he fancied he had a greater right to them than herself, he gave her a tap on the head, which sent her into a comfortable state of oblivion, and then made off with every farthing which his paramour had saved out of her wages of iniquity.

"It's only a fainting fit," said Jemmy.

"That's all. Where's the landlady and the chaise?"

"At the hall-door."

"I'll carry her down, and have her conveyed to the inn: do you wait here until my return."

The captain speedily returned, and turning to Jemmy, said, "bring him along with you."

Jemmy unceremoniously and ingloriously dragged the captive colonel after him, until they reached an open glade, in front of the house.

"Stand by, and see fair play," said Walter producing two sabres, one of which he offered to the colonel, whose hands had been liberated.

"Would you murder me?" he ejaculated.

Walter's only reply was a ringing back-handed slap in the face; and the colonel, maddened by the assault, the only one of the kind he had ever received, seized the proffered weapon, and fiercely attacked his opponent. The combat was vigorous, but short: Walter in his fury, the stronger and more dangerous for being cooled by a fierce determination to shed blood, could have slain a dozen such colonels, and in less than a minute the baffled ravisher lay, to all appearance, a corpse, on the greensward. He did not die though—his hour had not then come—and when his senses returned, he saw by the light of the moon that the only person beside him was the Creole, and she was stanching his wounds. Her love in the hour of trial proved stronger than her hatred.

CHAPTER XV.

THE MERRY WIVES GO TO BRIGHTON.

CAN any apology be offered for Lord Bloomfield having robbed the pious tobacconist—the immaculate class-leader of the Ebenezers—of his spouse, and carrying her off to that dissipated watering-place, Brighton? Can any mitigating circumstances be pleaded in palliation of the offence? It is to be feared that the canons of morality are too rigidly exacting for anything of the kind reasonably to be expected from them; and thus, in such extreme cases, the chronicler of human eccentricities is confined to the simple duty of recording facts as they occur in their pure, unembellished simplicity. Well, be it so; and as the handsome peer, in the guise of a converted Hungarian refugee noble, did induce the lovely Mrs. Bond to accompany him on a soul-saving errand, it may be as well that the amorous couple should be followed.

The first few days of their pilgrimage were spent in a state of blissful preparation, or rather of holy preliminary training for the fatigues of their pious undertaking. The peer had not thrown off his disguise, and on the morning after their first night by the sea-side, they were seated together at the most elegant breakfast-table the most aristocratic hotel of the town could furnish. The lady was attired in one of her prim morning dresses, for, like a provident purveyor for the eternal welfare of the sinful multitude, she had taken the precaution of carrying away with her the whole of her personal effects. The robe fastened close up to her white throat, and at its extremities, barely permitted the points of her tiny slippers to be seen. In complexion, she had been considerably improved by her journey, for her satin cheeks wore a permanent bright, rosy hue; and her eyes—thrilling in their deep-blue intensity—actually swam in the pearly light that glittered from them. Her lips were red and moist, and her whole appearance betokened a sense of boundless internal satisfaction. Bloomfield, habited in a sweeping morning gown, confined to his waist by a crimson-tasselled sash, looked excessively handsome—he had retired to bed sober the previous night—and as Mrs. Bond gazed bewitchingly upon his noble countenance, her lips would softly part, and she would fling herself upon his capacious breast, and fasten them, with a fond exclamation, on his finely-chiselled mouth.

"My own Bumbinski!" she murmured.

"Bum—devils!" thought Bloomfield; "such a name would d—n a Napoleon or Wellington. I must get rid of it, for it sticks in my throat like Macbeth's Amen. A pretty laughing-stock I should be made, if it travelled to the West End."

"My own one!" said the plastic beauty, throwing her arms round his neck.

Now it is well-known that men, at certain seasons, appear to ungratefully refuse the warm caresses of the ladies who have surrendered to their passionate and unremitting ardour; therefore, on this occasion, it is not at all surprising that Bloomfield should have gently extricated himself from the suffocating embrace of the fallen class-leader, and hinted that cold eggs and toast were not the most reviving viands in the world. The lady had a somewhat sharpened appetite, and speedily took the hint; but kept up a contact with her lover, by placing her feet on the insteps of his; and when warm looks were exchanged, pressed upon them tightly.

"Do try another egg, my dear Bumbinski!" said the lady, in her sweetest manner.

"Bum—devil! I beg pardon, I thought I heard a cat in the room. I detest cats. But don't call me by my odious paternal name: say Fred—Fred Jackson—your own Fred."

"I like Fred, its so short and sweet," said Mrs. Bond, as, with the most engaging smiles, she went through the fascinating pantomime of preparing and handing over a cup of coffee.

"And, by the way, darling," said his lordship, wafting kisses across the table, "we may as well sink, drop, annihilate, smash the Bumbinski altogether. Plain Fred Jackson sounds much better."

This suggestion did not altogether agree with Mrs. Bond's notion of gentility: she had been wooed by the Count Bambinski, and to be, as the count had faithfully promised she should, the Countess Bambinski, was too dazzling a vision of greatness to be dispelled without a struggle. She strongly, and, as his lordship thought, unreasonably, objected to the change.

"It is customary with people of rank to travel incognito, darling," urged his lordship.

"Incognovit?" almost shouted Mrs. Bond; "why, I have heard that was an awful thing. My husb—, the person I have left, said it was a sort of sudden death—a kind of seize and be-something dreadful!"

The pretended count laughed at the blunder, and, having satisfactorily explained it away, induced her to accede to his proposal, by making it appear to be a personal favour bestowed on himself.

"But when you preach?"

"It shall be as the most noble and right reverend Count Bumbinski," replied his lordship, with a species of casuistry worthy of the school in which he had taken his rakish degrees.

Mrs Bond brightened at the concession, and then, with the humility of a lamb, begged to know how they might best improve the little time allotted to mortals on earth.

"Ahem," replied his lordship; "I think—but of course you are the best judge—that we could not do better than proceed as we have begun."

Mrs. Bond lifted up her fine eyes to the ceiling in speechless gratitude, and dwelt with unction on the fag-end of a well-known dinner-invocation.

"The lark, though, darling, is now the bird of the ascendant; and while he sings, we mortals should gather strength for the mysteries which the nightingale invigorates with his delicious harmony. So what do you say to a walk or a drive, love?"

"Let us walk into the ungodly!" ejaculated Mrs. Bond, overcome with a gush of Ebenezzian fervour. Her nerves, poor thing! were just in a delightful twitter for an onslaught upon the carnal-minded. "Let us arise and go into the bye-lanes and alleys, and teach the wicked wisdom!" continued she.

"What the deuce has come over her?" thought Bloomfield, regarding her with some astonishment; he did not know that persons addicted, like herself, to religious enthusiasm, invariably have their hours of inspiration, when satiated with grosser excitements. It is only your strong, fierce-appetited being, who can plunge at once into the frenzy of mystic or poetical hallucinations. The plague of St. Anthony is upon them; and to scourge their bodies, they lend their morbid minds to the excesses of devotion. Frantic appeals, and an enormous tendency to promise largely are among the distinguishing features of their fits; and it is worthy to be observed, that during the paroxysm they only are gifted with the praying power of saving the whole human race from perdition.

"Let us pray!" exclaimed Mrs. Bond, throwing herself wildly on her knees, and, with a keen relish of the twang that at street-corners disturbs the peace of the working-man's holiday, pouring forth such a flood of expletives, that his lordship began to entertain serious doubts of her sanity.

"Here's a situation for a peer of the realm!" thought he, as he paced the floor, and began to speculate on the propriety of making, what he termed, "a bolt of it!"

A glance, however, at the plump form prostrated before him, banished the truant thought, and he wisely determined to allow her to exhaust herself.

"It is a species of hysterical affection," reasoned he, "and will have its way. D——d provoking, though, to see a pretty woman give herself such pain and trouble. I must teach her better manners, incense her with the errors of her ways, as my old nurse used to say. Let me see: dancing is recommended as a certain cure for the hipped—I'll try it, and see whether excitement will eradicate the effect of an old one; for this confounded canting is evidently a part of the machinery by which those Ebenezer rascals raise the wind."

In a few minutes the devotee's voice lowered, and then sank to a whisper. Just at that moment some itinerant players outside struck up a lively waltz, and his lordship, seizing the opportunity, raised her to her feet, and whirled her rapidly round the breakfast-table. The motion, together with the rigid embrace of her partner, soothed her, and she shortly began to foot it, and keep time as exactly as he did it.

"The same again!" cried Bloomfield, throwing some silver through the window.

"How ecstatic!" murmured the now thoroughly-changed Mrs. Bond, as she clung to her lover, and glided in graceful circles round the room. She looked up into his dark, handsome face, glowing with the flush of his novel morning exercise; and, could she have reached it, would have given him twenty kisses. Presently the music ceased, and the panting pair, locked in each other's arms, sank down upon a sofa.

"My own one!" gently uttered Mrs. Bond, as she wound her arms nervously round his lordship's shoulders. He, not at all averse to a continuance in their extremely close position, showered kisses on her lips, and, between whiles, whispered:

"Cannot our feet pray as well as our mouths?"

"They can, they can! Bless you, for learning me that divine movement of the body!"

And up she sprang for a renewal of the dance, but Bloomfield restrained her; and, after inducing her to partake of a couple of glasses of port wine, so soothed her down, that she willingly acquiesced in his desire that she should retire and dress herself for a morning promenade.

"Very agreeable occupation, this, for a peer of the realm!" laughed his lordship, as he wiped the perspiration from his forehead. "If I persevere, I have no doubt I shall dance myself into the good graces of Venus herself, and be made her Lord Chancellor. Well, well—anything for a change in this dull world; and a dance with a girl, with a soft, plump figure and pretty face, after breakfast-time, has novelty, at all events, to recommend it!"

His volatile lordship then coolly proceeded to light a cigar, and place himself in an attitude of repose by the open window. The mob of idlers who flock to Brighton in the summer season, had begun to flow in streams towards the sea-side; and, by the variety of their appearance and demeanour, afforded his lordship some room for comment. And here a few words about the moral salubrity of this lively watering-place may opportunely be introduced. It is well known to be one of the resorts of those of the mighty multitude of London who can afford either an annual or more frequent pleasure-trip, as well as of those whom bodily infirmities and debilitated constitutions drive to the sea-side. The gay and the thoughtless mingle with the tide; and perhaps in no single place in the neighbourhood of the metropolis do so many of its features present themselves to the eye of the observer as in Brighton. A few walks along the noble parade, and one or two trips to the Chain Pier, would soon afford a pretty good glimpse of the moral condition of several classes of the inhabitants of Cockaigne. First of all there is the fashionable man who has run down with his girl for an airing, and to see whether a prettier, or rather fresher one, might not be picked up. His insolent assurance renders him remarkably conspicuous on the pier, and with his audacious stare he frequently calls the blush to cheeks that had almost forgotten the practice. His gaudily-attired and flippant mistress ogles the male promenaders as impudently as if she were in the saloon of a theatre; and, as she trips along, she industriously discloses a neatly-turned ankle, and as much of a well-formed calf as will provoke a desire to see a little more of her perfection of limb. Behind her, in an agony of admiration, struts a "gent," in all the radiance of a Moses fit-out, and, as he stares at her undulating, bold, inviting form, and roguish eyes, he unconsciously dives his hand into his cash pocket, and asks himself the question, whether he might venture to have a lark with such a divine, dashing creature. While thus buried in pecuniary and amorous speculation, the keeper of the girl approaches, and, in a very careless manner, carries her off, in order that he may return to fulfil an engagement with a syren of sixteen, who had promised to meet him on that identical pier precisely at noon. The "gent" is roused to a state of desperate inflammation at the sight of the prize thus disappearing before him, and, with a suppressed oath, vows "He'll have a gal and no mistake."

At this critical moment he is accosted by a simpering damsel of blooming appearance, and, after one or two very unnecessary compliments to her charms, they take a turn or two, and then, at the "gent's" passionate suggestion, he is carried off to his charmer's lodgings, where he passes the remainder of the day and following night; and next morning, having only just sufficient money left to pay his fare, returns to town; and, in a few days afterwards finds out that visits to Brighton are frequently attended with consequences more warm than agreeable.

The next class of persons who attract attention are the professional gamblers and pickpockets who prowl about in twos or threes. Each of them has one, sometimes two, women at his command, whose duty it is to pick up the multitudinous tribe of "swells," who are desperately striving to create what they term a sensation. This, they are aware, cannot conveniently be effected without the company of a woman, and their ambition is excited to possess themselves of the finest and most showy-looking. They thus step on to the trap-door which conducts them to the brothel-gambling *hotel*; and, when well fleeced, are liberated. Some of these dashing-looking personages have the good sense to avoid the "decoy-ducks," who pass and repass them with a gait that requires no words to explain its meaning, and apply themselves to the conquests of those merry dames who come to spend their month or six weeks at Brighton, while their husbands, always saving and excepting the Saturday night and Sunday, are toiling in their offices, warehouses, and shops at home.

These merry wives form the great bulk of the female promenaders on a week-day, and in their classification present some amusing features. The whole body are bent upon obtaining the greatest amount of pleasure during their stay, but soon get rid of trips to Worthing, Shoreham, the Devil's Dyke, &c.; and, at the end of a fortnight, feel rather languid after their morning immersion. They then saunter about, and occupy every imaginable kind of seat to be found on the parade, the pier, and the sea-shore. The natural affinity that attracts mothers to each other, leads to the formation of numerous gossipping connections; and, in descanting upon the merits of their respective children, for a while manage to deprive time of some portion of its tedium. But a profusion of maternal sweets soon cloy upon the appetite, and the poor things, overpowered with *ennui*, take to sewing, reading novels, and solitary rambles. During the latter, each one of passable appearance is sure to meet a gentleman on the same spot for one or two mornings or afternoons. On the third day the gentleman ventures to salute; as the lady finds him passable she ventures to return it, and thus, by a remarkably easy process, an introduction takes place, and they enter into conversation. On the following day the lady, by way of precaution, is accompanied by her children, and as their appearance affords a theme on which the heart can dilate and expand, the icy reserve of the lady's manner immediately thaws, and the gentleman takes the opportunity to lard his praises of the offspring with a few well-timed compliments to the mother. These she blushingly receives; and, of course, dreaming no wrong, confesses that she has long entertained a partiality for moonlight walks.

"They are so charming by the sea-side!" exclaims the gentleman; "to sit and hear the music of the waters rolling on the beach—to see the distant vessel moving gracefully in the tender light of the queen of heaven—and watch the long lines of foam that embroider the pebbled shore—is very delightful occupation, I assure you."

"Very," murmurs the lady; and, without at all expecting to meet the gentleman who had thrown out the hint, she returns to the shore after sunset; and, as she inhales the gentle breeze of the placid ocean, thinks of corsairs and the other romantic beings embalmed in poetry and legend. Suddenly the gentleman appears by her side: she starts, but it is not with anger; and, after a little hesitation, accepts his proffered arm to assist her footsteps over the yielding sand. At the end of perhaps half an hour the gentleman earnestly declares that she must be fatigued, and insists upon her resting herself on a soft, dry hillock of sand, which his keen eye had long ago marked out as an appropriate couch. Then he throws himself carelessly by her side, volunteers a song or a story, or recites some thrilling stanzas on the sea; during this occupation he insinuates his arm round her waist, creeps closer towards her, presses her to his side, and, as their glances happen to meet—accidentally of course—their lips come into contact, they have such a vigorous embrace that the hillock crumbles beneath them, and they roll on to the dry beach. The lady returns home with a brighter eye, but not so light a heart, as she had when she went forth;—and thus it is that many of those connections are formed which bring discord and disgrace into families. In the majority of instances the acquaintance is only a butterfly one—forgotten as soon as formed—and numerous ones only a species of flirtation, during which the merry wife teazes her admirer until she nearly drives him to the frantic necessity of employing force, and then flies from him as easily as a bird does from a boy who has been lying *perdue* to catch it by putting salt on its tail. These wives rarely fall into the captivating nets of Brighton idleness; but with the great majority it is quite different. They are literally picked up, and when the fellow is good-looking and the lady warm, the result is an illicit amour. They think it very wrong, and promise not to sin again; but next year's trip to Brighton, brings about the same *ennui*—the same temptation; and with a married woman, accustomed all the year round to sleep with her husband, the latter, in too many cases, is irresistible. They have the admirable tact, however, to conceal their delinquencies; and at the conclusion of the stipulated sojourn, return to London with the plumpest of forms, the rosiest of countenances, and the most elastic of gaits. There may be something very ungallant in these disclosures—certain facts are always disagreeable—but if husbands will foolishly persist in thrusting their wives into a sort of stony desert, with nothing to divert either their minds or bodies, they must expect that the poor things in in their solitude will scrape an acquaintance with some living thing or another. Prisoners cultivate the friendship of rats and mice, and why should expatriated wives be abused for exercising the same kind of privilege? The more especially when those selfsame partially-deceived husbands are guilty of similar practices, for the truant spouses—the men who absent themselves from their wives under the false and easily invented pretext of a country journey—form no inconsiderable item in the total of the summer and autumn *habitues* of Brighton. That they are among the shrewdest and gayest of the gay is unquestionable, for they run down when they know a friend's wife is there by herself, or by a preconcerted arrangement with a girl to whom they may have taken a fancy. Married men are sad sly rogues, and may be seen, in all their naked audacity, any fine day, at merry, wicked Brighton.

After the rakish Benedicts come the runaway couples; and if a sentimental, deeply-enamoured couple be observed, sauntering along the beach with a slim, sallow young fellow dodging after them, you may be certain that the latter is a vulture of the law, on the look-out for evidence to establish and complete a splendid case of *crim.-con.* for the next sittings in Westminster Hall.

The girls in search of husbands rank numerically after the elopements, and a sprightly lot they are! Poor merry, bright-eyed little devils, they catch more sharps than flats on and under those chalky cliffs! and seldom return home without grievous rents in the cambric that they once fluttered so gaily in the breeze. Many never return at all, but are borne off by old, well-dressed hags, who yearly recruit their dilapidated forces from the ranks of the water-nymphs of Brighton. Apropos of these fiends in petticoats, it may be observed, that they come down with a string of invalids, who, for a couple of months, inhale the invigorating sea breezes, and refresh their exhausted frames for winter campaigns in the provinces: for after a poor girl, as the atrocious phrase goes, " gets stale in London," she is draughted off into the country, to minister to the sensual appetites of those who are unacquainted with her previous horrible career. The groups of these miserable victims of licentiousness to be met with on the Brighton beach are the most melancholy objects imaginable. Pale, withered, and shrunken, with diseased eyes, and teeth blackened by the frequent use of mercury, with nothing to buoy up their spirits but gin, they are frightful proofs of the criminal and beastly character of the debauchery of the age. *The bodies of some of them are tormented with running sores and ulcers, and yet the bathing-dresses of these rapidly festering victims are merely rinsed after they have been used by them, and perhaps before they are quite dry, are presented to delicate maidens or unblemished matrons,* who, unconscious of the appalling danger, plunge into the clear blue water; and, after some half hour's joyous play, emerge with the blue woollen clinging closely to their bodies. This is one of the horrors of Brighton, and a glance at some of the men, does not by any means mitigate the evil. Worn-out rakes, tottering on crutches, or being wheeled about in chairs, offend the sight from " morn till dewy eve;" and if to these be added, those male and female victims of excesses and vicious habits, who crawl about in the last stages of consumption, it must be confessed that the coarser features of Brighton during the season are shockingly offensive. But what care the hale and vigorous for calamities that have not yet overtaken them? Not a whit, so, as the Lord of Bloomfield and the excitable Mrs. Bond are going to a fancy dress ball, let every healthful devotee of the united shrines of Bacchus

and Venus exclaim, in the language of England's most sensual poet:

> " On with the dance! let joy be unconfined;
> No sleep till morn, when Youth and Pleasure meet
> To chase the flying hours with glowing feet."

His lordship had duly paraded his new conquest in the fashionable quarter of the town, and been complimented by those who recognised him on the freshness and charming style of her beauty. During the excursion he had purchased tickets for a grand ball at the —— hotel on the next evening but one, together with a most bewitching ball-dress.

"Will it not be sinful—a manifest backsliding again the Lord?" timidly objected Mrs. Bond, as she wistfully eyed the ball costume temptingly displayed before her.

"Backsliding be d—d!" exclaimed his lordship; "no, it will be a frontsliding, and very pleasant sliding too."

"Will the company be decorous and godly?" inquired she, demurely.

"Oh, yes, certainly," he replied, and then added to himself, "all the iniquity, like yours, will be done behind the scenes. But what a little hypocrite it is! here she has been my willing bed-fellow for half a week, and yet she will prattle after that cursed tabernacle fashion. I must give her a lesson or two. My dear," said he, after a suitable pause, to give fitting solemnity to his address, " are you aware that now we are living at a gay watering-place, where we are obliged to mix with all sorts of people, that we must accommodate ourselves to the tastes and habits of those around us, and not appear at all singular in our habits and demeanour. In fact, we must abandon our mission for a time?"

"What!" said the petrified Ebenezzian; "give up preaching? forget the holy errand on which we came?"

"Of course!" answered his lordship, peevishly, for her stupid pertinacity annoyed him; " our holy errand, on the whole, has been fairly accomplished. But am I not the Alpha and Omega of thy thoughts, the darling of thy heart, and the fructifier of thy wishes? Answer me, my celestial dove."

"Thou art—thou art, my chosen one! and when in thy arms I feel as I never felt before."

"Follow my advice, and thou wilt be plunged into such burning transports, that what has passed between us will be but ice to what is to come."

"My own one!" she murmured, placing her hands on his bosom, and looking up into his face in a perfect fever of joy.

"Thou must obey me, though, in all things," continued his lordship, "and in this matter of the preaching and soul-saving humbug, especially. The most self-denying saints had their hours of enjoyment, so it is only proper that two such buxom young people as we should have the same. Besides, day pleasures are but heralds to the night's enchantment. We will dance ourselves into such a glorious state, that when we return home thou wilt fling thyself into my arms, and give me ten thousand—a million burning kisses."

"Oh, don't!" exclaimed Mrs. Bond, her face crimsoning to the roots of her wavy hair.

"You will indeed, and I will devour your snowy bosom, and hang on your lips until I go crazy with love."

"Oh, heavens!"

And with this ejaculation, the pious lady, perfectly subdued, began to indulge in such strong demonstrations of affection, that his lordship grew somewhat alarmed for the safety of his person, and it was with some difficulty that he persuaded her to retire, and take an afternoon siesta to prepare her for the fatigues of the ball.

"You will lie down, too, won't you, Fred dear? it will do you good!" she said, pausing at the door.

"By-and-bye, dove—by-and-bye," hurriedly replied his lordship; and, as soon as the door was shut, irreverently added, "d—d if I do, though: I am neither Hercules nor Sampson, and as I saw an old pal on the pier to-day, who once went at that pace pretty tidily, in a rather declining way, for I fancy that I might safely risk a wager that I would eat all the flesh on his bones in five minutes—and must take warning by his example, and not come it too strong, even with such a dainty morsel as you, my pretty little darling of a saint in petticoats."

A knock sounded on the door, and, in obedience to the usual summons it opened, and in walked Jasper Sampson, clad in the identical clerical suit which had made such havoc in the breast of the merry * wife of the pious tobacconist.

"Ah, you rascal! where have you been all this while?" cried Bloomfield, not displeased, though, to see his clever love-agent again.

"Peace and good-will to all who dwell here," said Jasper, lifting up his eyes, and reverently clasping his hands.

"Silence, you profane scoundrel!" thundered Bloomfield, of whom it must be admitted that he had no relish for any irreverent mockeries.

"What!" said Jasper, removing his hat, "are we no longer reverends? Have you dropped the Bumbinski?"

"Yes, and take care I hear no more about the matter."

"But, please my lord," requested Jasper, boldly, "may I not be the Reverend Jasper Sampson for a little longer?"

"You may be the devil, if you like—which I believe you are—for ought I care!" replied his lordship. "But treat me here as Mr. Jackson—Frederick Jackson. Mind you don't make a mistake; if you do, I'll crop those long ears of yours! Sit down and tell me all that has happened in town—the countess?'

"Is well, and at Bloomfield House, but in a sad way about something!" said Jasper, with an expression which plainly said, "I'll tell you all if you will only be patient."

"Is she ill?" exclaimed Bloomfield, hurriedly.

"Not exactly; but had I not better begin at the beginning?"

"Go on—be quick! Don't teaze me, or I'll break your head!"

"Well, then, my lord, I watched my lady, as you ordered me; and, on the very morning you came down here, she and Mrs. Smythe went out together on foot. I followed them to Hungerford Bridge, and then they were joined by Captain Morris."

"D——n!" muttered his lordship.

"They all three got on board of a Woolwich boat, and of course I did the same, and a jolly trip we had of it to Greenwich, where the ladies and the captain took to the park, and had some sport with the gipsies, and a nice bit of romping on the grass! Glorious fun they had, I can tell you!"

"I shall have to shoot that Walter yet!" groaned his lordship.

---

* The intelligent reader can scarcely have failed to observe that the word "merry" is here, and has been, frequently throughout this narrative, used in the sense in which it was employed by the renowned Othello.

"Wait awhile, my lord, and save yourself the trouble, for his goose is cooked already!" continued Jasper. "Well, the ladies fell to palavering with an old gipsy woman, and got terribly scared, and while she was gammoning my lady, the countess, the captain and Mrs. Smythe slipped away, and left the countess to find her way back herself."

"Indeed?" exclaimed his lordship; and, starting up delighted, "then Violet—I mean the countess, and Walter—the captain, were never left alone together?"

"Not a second; and as soon as my lady found she was cut, she got into a grand passion, started off to the railway-station, and got to Bloomfield House, I afterwards found, in less than half an hour."

My Lord Bloomfield at this announcement rubbed his hands, and looked the pleasure he felt.

"Well," said he, "and what became of the other two turtles?"

"I dodged them into a tea-garden place on the road to Woolwich, and when they got into a snug little box, I got into the next to it, and saw ——"

"What?"

"The captain doing what he liked with the lady, and she kissing him like fury."

"No?"

"Fact! and I overheard them plan to sleep together there that night, and upon that hint I cut back to town, and told the husband all about it."

"The devil you did?" exclaimed his lordship. "But that was not quite fair."

"Supposing it had been my lady instead of Mrs. Smythe, would you ——"

His lordship raised his hand to strike Jasper, and his brow grew black as midnight.

"I only meant to put a case," said Jasper, deferentially; "and, as it wasn't the countess, I didn't mean to offend."

"Proceed?" said his lordship, haughtily.

"Well, I found Mr. Smythe, and told him about it; but he didn't look half as vexed as I should have done. He swore a good deal, and said he'd have a divorce, and it was as much as I could do to persuade him to go down to Charlton and catch them in the fact. Well, he did go, and I went with him; and we got into the bed-room; and just as Mr. Smythe was going to stab the adulterer to the heart, Walter awoke, and there was a row; lights came; and the woman in bed wasn't Mrs. Smythe at all."

"How the deuce was that?"

"I can't tell," replied Jasper, studiously; for covert purposes of his own, concealing the circumstance of Alice having been the substitute.

"Smythe must have looked confoundedly stupid at the discovery?" laughed his lordship

"That he did, and had to pay a good round sum to the landlord before they'd let him off. That made him savage, and when we met outside, he pitched into me, and we had a regular fair set-to by moonlight."

"Indeed? How did the battle go? I have heard that Smythe is a famous boxer."

"Why, my lord," replied Jasper, with some modesty, "he was a hard hitter; but when a man's peepers are shut up, what can he do?"

"Then you won the battle?"

"He was dead beat, and his eyes are still as black as my hat."

Bloomfield gave way to a hearty fit of laughter, and termed Jasper a hero—a second Scroggins—a Tom Spring.

"But what of the countess?" suddenly asked Bloomfield, as he recollected the remark about her indisposition.

"Oh, she's in a way about Miss Lucy, who was inveigled to a house in Herefordshire."

"Good God!" exclaimed Bloomfield, who entertained a warm respect for the timid and retiring sister of his beautiful wife.

"It's all in this evening's paper," said Jasper.

Bloomfield hurriedly rang the bell; and, having obtained the *Sun* newspaper, after a nervous search found, and greedily devoured, the following paragraph:—

"DUEL IN HIGH LIFE.

"The fashionable world was startled this morning by a telegraphic report that a most sanguinary duel had been fought in Douglas Park, between Colonel Stanley and Captain Morris, both of the Life Guards. The weapons were swords; and the contest, which only lasted a few minutes, was terminated by Colonel Stanley receiving a mortal wound in the breast. He expired on the ground.

"FURTHER PARTICULARS.

"The duel occurred at about ten o'clock last night, and was perhaps the most fierce and deadly one it was ever our sad lot to record. Both the combatants fought like demons; but the well-known skill and bodily strength of Captain Morris gave him such an advantage over his opponent, that the latter never had a chance; and the gallant Colonel Stanley, instead of dying at the head of his regiment at some future Waterloo, fell ingloriously in the vicinity of Douglas House, an obscure country-seat, of which we never heard before this sad occurrence. It is rumoured that there was a lady in the case. A sad gloom prevails all over the West End; and the blinds of all the houses of the deceased's noble relatives and friends have been down during the day. Colonel Stanley was one of the most dashing officers in Her Majesty's service, and was a great favourite with the officers and men of his regiment. His untimely end is generally deplored.

"LATEST PARTICULARS.

As soon as the intelligence of the untoward event reached Field Marshal the Duke of Wellington, he hastened to the Horse Guards, and gave orders that Captain Morris should at once be suspended from his command. His grace's well known determination to suppress duelling in the army, precludes the possibility of any hope being entertained that, whatever may be the result of the judicial inquiry that will be instituted, the too gallant captain will have his commission restored to him. It is rumoured that he has absconded, and that the abduction of a young lady, nearly related to one of the most aristocratic families of the country, was the cause of the duel. We may add, that in all quarters the most lively sympathy has been excited for Captain Morris. In addition to his commanding figure, true soldier-like qualities, and gentlemanly manners, he was the only officer in the regiment that had ever been in real service. His achievements under Sale, Nott, and Gough in India, earned for him a martial renown which rendered him quite a pet with the men. The army will have to deplore the loss of one of its most promising officers."

"Is all this true?" inquired Bloomfield, with an ashy countenance.

"Quite, my lord," replied Jasper; "Miss Lucy was carried off by a woman of the colonel's, and when the news came to town, the captain took a Bow Street runner with him, and soon beat up their track. He rescued Miss Lucy, and then cut down the colonel as easily as I would a cabbage!"

"Leave me," said his lordship, waving his hand.

And Jasper, with a low obeisance, left the room.

The information had evidently powerfully affected his lordship, for he paced the room for several minutes, and frequently smote his forehead, as if accusing himself of some neglect of duty.

"He will be a champion—a hero now," muttered he; "and Violet, with her warm imagination, will be ready to worship him. She always liked him, but now she will doat upon him. Poor Lucy! I'm glad she is safe; and Walter, too, of course he will get off from a jury—but then he will lose his commission. D—d bad job; if he'd only marry Lucy, I'd soon make it up for him, though. Who knows but this adventure may be the means of making up the match? More unlikely things have happened. Well, well, time and tide wear out the longest day, so I must wait for the current of events to set in; and then, heigho, for a favourable wind for my bark! The colonel—hum! ah! rather sudden, I must admit. He owed me a bet, too, but let it go with many others. He was a rough wooer, and won't be much of a loss to society."

With this consoling reflection he rang the bell, and ordered some hot brandy-and-water; and having summoned Jasper, told that worthy, to his delight, that he was to prepare himself for the fancy dress ball in the evening.

"Your dress will do admirably," said his lordship, "for the character of Doctor Syntax; but hark'ye, don't let me have any of your hanky-panky ventriloquial tricks too early in the evening?"

"No, my lord," replied Jasper obsequiously, and, as soon as he was out of hearing, adding, "here goes for a jolly lark, and no mistake!"

The ball was what a whiskered *Morning Post* penny-a-liner would have termed, "a splendid affair." It was held in the large room of one of the principal hotels in Brighton; and the admission, as well accorded with the freedom of a watering-place, was easy to obtain. In fact, it was unrestricted to all who could afford a guinea for the privilege. The decorations were on a scale of magnificence commensurate with that sum, and the company as decorous as a crowd of Turks, Greeks, Hungarians, Russians, and Highlanders, could have been expected to be, under the exciting influence of something more potent than the sherry-cobbler handed round the room. But for a while the decorum observed at such places was strictly maintained, and all went merry as a marriage bell.

Mr. and Mrs. Jackson, as Bloomfield and his *chere amie* had styled themselves, arrived early; and their appearance created no slight sensation. Bloomfield looked imposing in his richly-laced Hungarian costume; and Mrs. Bond's fine figure was displayed to great advantage in a blue satin dress, embroidered with silver roses and lilies. Her dazzling neck and bosom were exposed, and her pretty auburn hair, arranged *a la* Victoria, with a single white rose, set coquettishly over the left ear, excited the envy of at least half the women in the room. The men, both infidel and Christian, pronounced her admirable. Both wore a half-mask, which completely prevented their being recognised; and as they threaded the glittering throng, and heard the praises that were lavished upon them, the heart of the pious Mrs. Bond heaved with a rapture hitherto a stranger to her. Jasper Sampson, habited as a full-blown divine of the evangelical school, was decidedly the best character in the room. He carried his head high and his body erect, as became an appointed apostle of the truth; and, as he passed along, dropped maxims which pointedly alluded to one of the kingdoms he represented. He had also a

most orthodox and catholic fondness for brandy " cold without," and before the ball had well begun, had drunk as much as would have put a dozen stalwart troopers *hors de combat*. From this it may be imagined that he was in high glee, and ready for any mischief. His introduction to Mrs. Bond was a rich bit of devilry. That lady, upon being informed that the great western luminary, the Reverend Jasper Sampson, stood before her, was thrown into a state of intense fluttering. She felt that her terpsichorean irregularity was sanctioned by one of the mighty elect, and, in a fit of enthusiasm, carried his broad, coarse hand to her lips.

"Am I in godly company?" she whispered to him.

"The sons and daughters of Satan do abound here; but presently we will slay them with the sword of Gideon!" replied Jasper, giving her hand a palpable squeeze.

"Is it sinful to dance?"

"No; or else it were sinful to lie with a man."

"Fie! that is natural."

"Quite; and proper, too, when the parties are agreeable. The world must be populated, madam."

"Verily it must; it was the law given to Abraham."

"The wages of continence are death."

"I feel it to be so. Would that we could pray!"

"On your back, madam—very proper wish; but not allowed here."

At this moment the band struck up a waltz; and Mrs. Bond, whisked away by Bloomfield, was soon in the giddy whirl of the most lascivious of dances. Jasper, thus deserted, wandered among the nondancers, and sadly belied his clerical assumption by the peculiarly loose style of the remarks he scattered profusely around him. But to the dance: the flying forms of some thirty couple kept gyrating within a given space; and it was curious to observe the difference in manner that prevailed. The youngest of both sexes, consequently, as may be presumed, the least corrupted, kept more widely apart. The gentleman's fingers certainly lay on the lady's waist; but the touch was light, and her delicate hands merely brushed his garments like feathers. The motion, too, was gentle, and their eyes were more frequently bent on the floor than each other's faces. It was very different, though, with others. In the slow movements they maintained a respectful distance, but when the quick ones came their forms advanced, and there was a mutual pressure of the bosoms. With others, again, the arms were tightly interlaced, and every now and then the 'gentleman' bobbed the front part of his person against his partner, and the action was reciprocated. Some were locked in such a rigid embrace, that their backs described curves, and each inhaled the hot breath of the other. As the dance proceeded the excitement became less restrained, and, amid the fury of the waltz, the most lascivious postures were assumed. Waltzing may be a very agreeable pastime when decorously conducted; but when a brute of a fellow protrudes his stomach against a young girl, it is scarcely probable that she will not feel warm, and have impure ideas flitting through her mind. The eyes, too, are the prime organs of sensualism, and flashing when the bodies are in close contact, it is impossible but that there should be a mutual intoxication of the senses, which pantingly coins the desire to have them gratified. Waltzing is immoral—shockingly so; and as the ladies will persist in patronising it, on their fair, naked shoulders be the blame and responsibility of the thousand and one peccadilloes that follow upon the heels of this courtezan employment of the limbs and body.

Jasper regarded the proceedings for some time unmoved; but when his gaze wandered along the array of dazzling white shoulders that everywhere met his view, and thence travelled to the exposed legs of the lady-dancers, his blood began to tingle in his veins, and his eyes to sparkle so brightly through the holes in his mask, that many women whom he approached shrank from him in terror; and, retiring to a corner, he thus communed within himself. With Satan, he exclaimed:

"O hell! what do mine eyes with grief behold?
Sight hateful, sight tormenting; thus these two
Imparadised in one another's arms,
The happier Eden, shall enjoy their fill
Of bliss on bliss; while I to hell am thrust,
Where neither joy nor love, but fierce desire—
Among our other torments not the least—
Still unfulfilled, with pain of longing fire."

"I feel," writhed he, "as if I had been dipped in molten lead, or passed through a furnace. Every nerve of my body tingles; and the little resolution I have reels like a foundering ship. Oh woman, woman! my appetite makes me gloat over your glorious forms, that yield to man's touch like clay to the potter's hand. But my wrongs—one damnable and unutterable wrong, makes me wish to gripe ye all by the throat; and, while drinking in your groans, yell in your sly, bawdy ears, that I did it—I, Jasper, the impotent—Jasper, whose love for woman is so burning, that he could ravish the whole sex, and then triumph if every matron and daughter, both young and old, bowed the knee to a filthy, rank prostitution. Curse ye all! and doubly curse ye! and may ye all be debauched before the morning! But oh, God! how I burn! I shall go mad, I think! Perhaps a spin round the room will cool me."

And so saying, he sprang upon a rather robust Dutch broom-girl, and, clutching her nervously round the waist, darted into an opening, and was soon spinning round the room at the rate of twelve miles an hour.

His excited demeanour attracted the attention of two ladies who had assumed the characters of gipsies. One of them was considerably stouter, and much shorter than the other, and was evidently many years

her elder. The younger one had a splendid figure, and tripped about with a grace which none of her sex present could assume. The pair had arrived late, and were so closely masked, that no portion of their features could be discerned.

"Do you observe that figure in black, who is playing such pranks with his partner?"

"Yes. How wild his eyes glare! What is the cause?"

"Lust—raging lust. In him behold one of its lowest features. See how rudely he grasps the fat waist of his partner, who, by-the-bye, does not seem to dislike it, for she is pressing her hip against his."

"How disgusting! I never dreamed that such a scene as this was possible!"

"Worse cannot follow, for here the preliminaries of a vile prostitution of the functions of nature are arranged. Look at that commanding Hungarian—do you see him?"

"I do. As he passed I noted that his dark eyes flashed, as if they would consume his partner."

"That is lust of another type—he can gratify his inclinations, the other cannot."

"What do you mean?"

The elder gipsy requested the younger to incline her ear, and she would explain. The information was evidently strange; for the younger one started back, and exclaimed:

"Who was the mutilator?"

"His wife."

"His wife? what a diabolical wretch!"

"It was a revenge worthy of the devil himself; but he deserved it. He was, in his strength, a huge mountain of a coward; and now he is as cunning and fierce as a tiger. You will see that presently he will break out into some dreadful extravagance. I should not like to be in that young woman's place for something!"

"That Hungarian interests me much. I cannot see his face; yet I fancy there is a strong resemblance to ——."

"Hush!—it is Lord Bloomfield!"

The younger gipsy, at this announcement, trembled, seemingly, with suppressed passion; for she ground her beautiful teeth together, and muttered, "The wretch!"

"Be calm. Violence never yet reclaimed an erring mortal. Leave him to me."

"Who is his companion?"

"Either a hypocrite or a lunatic. Her husband kept a tobacconist's shop in —— Street, and Bloomfield carried her off in the —— disguise of a foreign minister, assisted by that imp of darkness, Jasper Sampson, the hall-porter at Bloomfield House, whom you see before you, performing beastly antics, in the black coat of a clergyman."

"You astonish me! is that monster the singular-looking being I have noticed in the hall at home?"

"It is the same; and he is now promoted to the office of pander to his master, and spy on your ladyship."

"Me?"

"Even so; it was he who watched you to Greenwich Park."

"Such conduct is scandalous—a spy upon me!"

"Be calm, and excuse me when I remind you, that if his lordship's suspicions were groundless, your penchant was at least dangerous to yourself."

The blood mantled to the young masquerader's ears and artificially-embrowned neck, and there was a pause before she replied:

"You are correct, but severe," said she, at length;

" and perhaps I am justly punished in my husband's infidelity."

"Not justly, Violet: he fell first from his allegiance, and had you fallen too, there would have been ample excuse for you. But you were not fated to fall. Your husband will be restored to you wiser and better than ever he was, and you will have children to bless and sanctify your union."

"Children?"

"Yes, children, Violet: both you and he will assimilate more in constitution; he will take better care of his health, and, being wholly yours, will cling to you as fondly as man can to woman. Unity of thought, agreement in mind and physical tendencies, are essential to conception."

"God grant that what you say may happen, for I am certain that where there are no children there is no happiness between married people."

"None; they are the golden links that bind them together, by investing their conjugal love with variety."

"It has often struck me that man and wife, when too much together, are apt to get dull and tired of each other."

"So they do, and husbands are much to blame for it. They will hang on to their wives' apron-strings at first, and then the poor things get so accustomed to the mollying attention, that when it is withdrawn they consider themselves very much ill-used. As I said before, it is variety that constitutes the great charm of wedlock: too many sweets surfeit, and no wife likes to be mauled as if she were a harlot for a year or two, and then be treated only as a domestic convenience. What an uproar that beastly fellow is creating."

And truly it was an uproar: for Jasper had become so excited during his gyratic pilgrimages round the room, that he absolutely yelled, and so frightened his partner, that she screamed; and, as it stopped the music and the dance, many ladies joined in the chorus. But Jasper heeded it not: on, on, round, round, he spun his partner, and, despite the frantic entreaties of her friends, persevered in his wild evolutions until the girl fell into his arms in a swoon, and was torn rather than taken from his grasp. A cry was raised that he was drunk, and Jasper, having just sufficient discernment left to take the hint, staggered from the room, sadly pitied by Mrs. Bond, who, glowing with the warmth of the exercise, and feeling unusually giddy, attributed the "reverend" gentleman's emotion to his being unaccustomed to such preparatory amatory exercise.

"Poor man," she thought; "he never was married, and of course knows nothing about it. A little prayer would bring him round; I wonder where he is? Our reverend friend is unwell, love," said she to Bloomfield, who had just tossed off half a pint of wine; "shall we not go and console him?"

"Console be——I mean you may go if you choose; the soothings of a woman are better than the rough expostulations of a man. He entered that room; this way, love, and see what you can do for him."

Mrs. Bond went on her errand of mercy willingly, and, as she glided from his presence, Bloomfield drily chuckled:

"I can trust any woman with him. What a poor, miserable devil he must be; why don't he shoot himself at once? I would if I had his raging torments. Aroint thee, witch, when wert thou belched from his serene highness's dominions?"

This was addressed to the elder gipsy, who had plucked him by the sleeve, and requested to be allowed to tell his fortune.

"With all my heart," he replied, directing a glance of admiration at the beautiful figure and nobly-proportioned bust of the younger masquerader; "but, with all due deference to your concealed charms, may I not prefer this forest damsel for my questioner?"

"She is fitter for the dance than for the mystic art of our race; retire, Linda, to yonder ottoman, while I unriddle strange things to this gentleman."

Violet, whom the presence of her husband and the sound of his voice had powerfully affected, was glad of the temporary release, and seated herself at some little distance from them.

"You are noble," said the gipsy, running her finger over his white palm.

"So are all men who are honest."

"That is a democratic interpretation of the term, which is not true in any sense in your case."

"How—would you insinuate——"

"That you are noble by birth, but not honest."

"D—n the hag, what does she mean?" muttered Bloomfield, disliking the tone of the category.

"I repeat, you are noble, but a slave to your appetites and passions. Your devotion to abandoned women is excessive."

"I give a flat denial to the latter accusation, for I am well known to be decidedly refined in my tastes."

"What refinement is there in stealing like a thief from a beautiful, accomplished wife—nay, wait until I have concluded, and then speak—and in a felon manner and hypocritical garb, inducing a silly young woman to desert her home and husband, to be your plaything for a few days? Refinement, indeed! rather of an Old Bailey kind, I fancy."

A violent expletive rose to Bloomfield's lips, but, repressing it, he sarcastically inquired whether she had more agreeable things to say.

"Many. You have asked me to tell your fortune. I will do so. Persevere in your present mode of living, and you will die a bankrupt in fortune, and of as horrible a disease as the Marquis of ——"

"What the devil did he die of?"

She whispered one word into his ear, which made him turn rather pale, but his natural recklessness of disposition soon enabled him to laugh away the depression; and, the band striking up a spirited waltz, he approached Violet, and solicited her for a partner.

"You may dance with this gentleman, my dear," said the old lady, condescendingly; "but do not over-exert yourself. You will, of course, know how to behave to the daughter of the gipsy queen."

"Very well indeed," thought Bloomfield. "If the mother is so knowing, the daughter cannot be very green, and, as I have received my cue, it will go hard if I don't see what sort of a piece she is. Her figure is unexceptionable, and she has the most perfect foot and ankle that ever I saw under a woman. Should her face correspond—curse that gipsy hood! but I'll have it off before the waltz is over."

Violet's heart beat violently as her husband, for the first time for many months, placed his hand on her waist. Memory stirred up a thousand fond recollections, and tears, not of despair, for a moment glittered like pearl drops in her eyes. Jullien's music may be flashy, but for dances it is exhilarating. If it displeases the listener, it has a wonderfully quickening power on the motion of the feet and circulation of the blood; and this the countess discovered ere she had twice traversed the room, and at once committed herself to the impulses of the waltz.

Mrs. Bond, leaning on the arm of the new composed Jasper—for he had taken one of the draughts prescribed for him by Dr. Wriggles—regarded her paramour, with his arms wound round the form of another, with anything but composure, and petulantly demanded from Jasper whether he did not deem such a proceeding a wanton and unjustifiable falling off from the faithful.

"A daughter of Belial, no doubt," said Jasper; "but let you and I, who have abjured the worship of the flesh, set these amorous children a lesson of staid propriety. Even things sinful may be made holy by example. Your hand, sister, and let us sanctify this dance of the ungodly by our chaste movements."

Mrs. Bond, nothing loth, surrendered to the "divine's" embrace, and followed in the wake of the waltzers. Quicker sped the music, and faster went the figures on the floor, and as Jasper encircled the plump body of his partner, he felt her heart beat against his, saw the moisture gathering on her lips, and could detect the tremulous workings of her nerves, as every now and then he touched her knees with his, or pressed more closely against her panting form. A devilish thought seized him as he perceived his master wholly wrapt up in the gipsy girl, and he resolved to have what he termed a bit of fun with the pious Mrs. Bond. He saw that she was in an intense state of nervousness, and was ripe for any extravagance.

"My lord," thought he, "is quite taken with that hussy of a gipsy, and I shall do him a service if I keep this hot wench from his side."

The waltz raged more furiously than ever, and so many sighs and spasmodic exclamations of pleasure were heard above the din of the music, that the place more resembled a secret chamber of the Hindoo mysteries than an English ball-room. Mrs. Bond was so overcome that she actually gasped for breath, and Jasper, seizing the opportunity, drew her away, and conducted her down stairs into the gardens of the hotel, where many an inviting alcove afforded accomodation to the sentimental.

Meanwhile Bloomfield got quite fascinated with his new partner, and, when she complained of fatigue, gallantly led her to a seat in the cooler atmosphere of one of the retiring rooms.

He evidently fancied her to be, as the saying is, "no better than she ought to be," and treated her accordingly. Indeed his freedoms became so rude, that the countess had some difficulty in preventing him tearing the mask from her face.

"Desist, sir, or I will alarm the place?" she cried.

"One kiss from those ruby lips, and your will shall be law?"

"Shall it indeed? But that is only a man's promise. Give me some assurance that you will keep your word?"

"My honour!"

"Is not in your possession to bestow. I must have a more substantial token. Give me that ring on your finger?"

"Here it is, and a thousand besides, if necessary."

The countess held up her lips, which Bloomfield rapturously kissed at least half a dozen times, and was slily proceeding to unfasten her mask, when a terrible uproar in the ball-room caused her to start from her seat alarmed, and dart to the door. His lordship followed, but, in the confusion, she escaped from him; and, being joined by her elder companion, hurriedly left the hotel. After an ineffectual search, his lordship, with some chagrin, confessed that he had been "done brown;" and then,

with a ruffled temper, turned to ascertain the cause of the disturbance.

"To his horror he saw Mrs. Bond elevated on a chair, and holding forth, supported by Jasper, who, every now and then, howled in dismal chorus. The audience, imagining the scene to have been got up for their especial delectation, applauded vociferously. Mrs. Bond, though, had never been more in earnest in her life. During the interview with Jasper in the garden, the scoundrel had so tickled and mauled her, that she was half crased; at his suggestion, she rushed into the ball-room, and, mounting a chair, began to denounce the whole company as fornicators and adulterers, for whom a tolerably hot blue fire had been prepared, unless they repented in time, and plunged themselves into the cooling waters of continence and decorum. Bloomfield was so exasperated at the display, that he dealt Jasper a swinging box on the ear; and in return received one from a grinning bystander, who felt indignant at the fun being interrupted. Jasper, smarting under the disgrace of the blow, knocked down an applauding Turk, and then the battle became general; and finally extended to the women. Mrs. Bond pounced upon a short-petticoated Greek girl; and the din, and breakage of furniture became so alarming, that the landlord called in the assistance of the police, who, with the assistance of his posse of waiters, expelled the whole company into the street. Bloomfield carried off the insensible form of Mrs. Bond; and Jasper, whose dress was not very remarkable, departed in search of adventures.

Brighton, at midnight, in the month of August, is the reverse of dull, for the town appears in one blaze of light, from the railway station to the seashore. The signs and sounds of gaiety are everywhere to be met with, and perhaps in no place in her Majesty's dominions, not even excepting the locality which the great Regent Street intersects, do so many outcasts annoy the pedestrian with their abominable solicitations. Jasper threaded through them with marvellous ease, for he was in that cold-blooded humour, which scarcely ever shows that it takes anything amiss.

"Go it my tulips! There's a regiment of hungry Cockney snobs not far off! Lots of tin—easy taken in! Go it my cripples!

"'I once know'd a voman
Vot studied the stars;
She talked like a rum 'un
Of Wenus and Mars.'

Hooray! a short life and a merry one—

"'For it's a riddle,
Without a diddle'

now and then—we can't all be honest! so never say die! There's life in a muscle yet."

With these low sentences, addressed to the girls he encountered, some of whom he facetiously termed "stunning mots," he arrived before a low archway over a long dark passage, from which the sounds of rough revelry issued.

"This is the crib," muttered he, "or I'm deucedly mistaken. All right!"

Down the passage he plunged, until he came to a house where some bacchanals were evidently worshipping. After knocking loudly, he roared lustily through the key-hole:

"May the wings of friendship never lose a feather!"

The door was opened, and he stood before mine host, a pot-bellied rascal, with a villaneously-low forehead, and a countenance that would have convicted him of any crime of which he might have been accused.

"The pass-word?" said the publican, surlily.

"Drain a flat dry!"

"You have it right; but I don't like your looks. Who told it you?"

"Harry Burton!"

"What! slashing Harry? It's all right, then; he'd never do a pal an ill turn. What's he a-doing of now?"

"I'm bless'd if I know. He's dead."

"My eye! he vos a game chap! What did he die on?"

"Lush and women!"

"Ah, me! the best on 'em goes that way. If they'd only stick to honest drink, vith maybe a spree now and then, it vould be all wery vell; but they vill go the pace vith the gals, and then they sinks into natomies, and goes off like that ——" and, suiting the action to the word, he snapped his fingers, and emptied his glass.

Jasper took the hint, and "stood treat," and was then allowed to go up stairs and mingle with the noisy audience of a veritable "cock-and-hen club." They were common all over the country thirty years ago; but, through the establishment of more stringent police regulations, they have nearly all been suppressed; and many of those that are held in such holes as this Brighton one are winked at by the authorities, because they serve as traps in which to catch offenders, for whom, were there not such, and equally opprobrious places, Mrs. Justice might vainly look out.

The room was a long one, and at the upper end, on raised seats, sat the president and members. Before them, but considerably lower down, was a table, on which sat, at opposite ends, a young man and woman in a state of semi-nudity. The one was presumed to represent Bacchus, the other Venus. As far as scantiness of attire was concerned, the latter ably sustained the character, for her only garments were a flesh-coloured pair of tights, that fitted up to her waist, and a bit of transparent muslin thrown over her shoulders. Her bosom was entirely exposed. The creatures evidently belonged to the tavern-vocalist tribe; for at intervals they sang solos and duets, all of them of a brutally-licentious cast; but they suited the audience, which seemed to be composed of some of the holiday refuse of the metropolis. Jasper recognised many of them, with a grinning satisfaction that his disguise, or rather transformation, was so complete that even his own parents could not have recognised him.

"Lots of gallows-birds here," thought he; "and, my eye, what rum-uns the blowens are! There's old Poll, of the Strand—now, I'd wager anything she's been on the turf these twenty years or more. But, halloo! who do I see yonder? Yes—no—why it really is Bill Jones, that married Alice's sister Jane. Here's a discovery, and no mistake!"

Without much difficulty he managed to obtain a seat near the person of Bill Jones, and soon entered into conversation with that inebriated worthy.

"So Harry Burton's dead, is he? I'm d—d sorry for it, for when he had money, he spent it like a brick!"

"What's become of his wife and child?"

"Oh, Alice—saucy Alice, as we called her—is lady's-maid up in London, and we've got her kid—my missus is as fond of it as her own."

Jasper almost jumped from his seat at this intelligence, and very suddenly took such a particular fancy —indeed manifested such an affectionate anxiety—for Mr. Bill Jones, that he quite won that gentlema'ns heart; and he was invited to take a "bit of sommat" for supper at his crib, which, he kindly assured Jasper, did not happen to be remotely situated.

The offer was accepted with alacrity, and, arm-in-arm, the now newly-made friends—but in reality very old acquaintances—sallied from that den of iniquity. Mr. Bill Jones was in the last stage of beastly intoxication, and swore that if his old woman had dared to go to bed and let the fire out, he would kick up such a jolly row—yes, that he would—the fine, brave fellow!

For months he had staggered home in the same state, and left his poor, suffering wife to the howling solitude of an uncomplaining poverty; for she still loved him, and, poor, fond, credulous thing, fancied he would change.

But let his midnight return to the home he had blighted be anticipated by a few hours. The sun had long gone down, and the stars were shining pleasantly in the sky, but the meek wife sat patiently waiting the coming of her husband. She must have once been beautiful, for there were traces of a loveliness which even sorrow could not deface. Her deep-blue eyes and dark auburn hair still retained their original brightness. Her other features were pinched and lined, and her whole appearance denoted wasting care, hunger, and sad thoughts. She was sewing, by the light of a wretched candle, for bread—yes, bread for herself, children, and *him*—for she loved the monster with the tenacity of wedded affection. By-and-bye the needle was plied less swiftly, the eye-lids grew heavy, and, after several desperate but vain efforts to keep awake, the half made-up garment rolled from her lap to the floor, her head fell back, and she slept and dreamed. Pleasant dreams are the poetry of misery, and a right pleasant one had this poor, tortured wife. She thought she was once more a

"Laughing child, and gaily dwelt
Where murmuring brooks and dark-blue rivers rolled."

and that her fond parents were smiling over her gambols and sportive innocence. Then she gathered sweet wild flowers in the bright-green fields, while the birds sang merrily around her. The sheep spotted the distant hill-side, and upon the quiet air came the cheerful song of the rustic. Her heart was gay, for she was far away from biting misery; and her imagination borrowed inspiration from the beauties she saw around her; and memory, throwing over them a brightness and perfume, rendered the scene more enchanting than if a fairy had conjured it up before her awakened senses. Then her budding womanhood came before her in all its sunny array, and home and its dear associations came thronging upon her mind like angel visions. She was once more in the merry dance, with the gay young party; and when evening had darkened into night, she sat at her parents' feet, and read them the page they loved best. Then came love and its sweet delirium, and her young heart, in its devotion, clung to him she had chosen, as the tender vine clings to the sturdy things of earth. She loved, and loved, too, with a purity undarkened by a grosser thought. The love she felt lit up her young existence, and made her feel more kind and gentle. Another delicious and distinct idea had entered her soul, and lifted it far above the natural selfishness of every-day life. Yes, she loved, and that warm first love, mellowed and ripened by time, shines yet brightly in her heart; and hunger, neglect, misery, and cruelty have been unable to drive it away. In the midst of toil, privation, and struggles, which too often deaden and destroy human feeling, she can, in her lowliness, still feel and admit that

"No love can match the early one which young affection nursed."

Then came the wedding-day, with its smiles, tears, and trembling delight; and then her new home, hallowed by the presence of her young, affectionate, and industrious husband. The merry fire sparkled in the grate, and sent its bright light sparkling around the comfortable sitting-room. Her husband was by her side, unpolluted in heart and mind; and they talked of the future, and built airy but pleasant castles; and planned, and sketched, and anticipated, until their young eyes would run over with tears of joy; and they would fall into each other's arms, and have a long and loving embrace. Old faces, old places, and old times came back to her memory; and she smiled in her dream, and so, sleeping and painless, was borne away on the wings of eternity.

"I fancy, friend Jones, this is a decided case of bilk," said Jasper, after the other had been engaged for some minutes in a fruitless knocking at the door.

"Never!" shrieked the drunkard, and, throwing his whole weight against the door, he broke it in; "we'll see who's master!"

And so saying, he staggered into the house, followed by Jasper.

"She's sulky; but never mind, never say die!"

And the fellow, after many plunges and tumbles, managed to strike a light.

"Jane! Jane, I say!" he cried, as he placed the candle on a crazy-looking table against the wall; "come down and let's have no more of this —— nonsense."

"What's this?" asked Jasper, touching a blackened and charred substance, which lay on the floor, with the toe of his boot.

"I'm blessed if I know!" exclaimed the drunkard, taking the candle in his hand, and stooping to examine what Jasper unceremoniously rolled over with his foot.

The action disclosed a human face—that of the drunkard's wife; her body was crisped to a cinder She had been burnt to death while sitting up for her sot of a husband. A spark from the fire had ignited the garment upon which she had been working for a wretched pittance, the flame caught her clothes, and in an instant, in the midst of her dream of early wedded happiness, she was hurried from the earth The miserable husband gazed at Jasper with a wild look of horror, and then, with a deep groan, fell senseless on the floor.

"Here's a pretty go!" ejaculated Jasper, who, despite his assurance, was somewhat alarmed at the horrible scene before him; "if the police were to come they'd swear somebody had a hand in it, so ' bolt's ' the word."

He turned to depart, but the thought that the child of the woman towards whom he bore such a mortal hatred was in that house of death, flashed across his brain and rooted him to the spot. After a moment's irresolution, he suddenly snatched the candle from the table, and mounted to the upper part of the house. In one of the two rooms was a bed, cleanly, but scantily furnished, and in it lay the sleeping forms of four children. A rosy smile lit up each of their features, and as that man of sin gazed upon their beautiful faces, and listened to their gentle respirations, it struck even his hardened nature, that to disturb such innocent slumbers would be profanation. He left the room, and descended the stairs

as softly as a mother would have done. His passing emotion, though, was diluted by the reflection, that as he was unable to identify the child he wished to carry away, it would be prudent to affect to commiserate with the bereaved husband and unfortunate children, and so quietly obtain the information he desired. Having an instinctive dislike to any familiarity with the police, he hastened back to the tavern he had just left, and solicited the interference of the landlord; but it was coarsely refused, and Jasper, driven to his wits' end, accosted the policeman on the beat, and together they entered that now effectually ruined and desolate house. Death had completed the hideous doom provoked by the drunkard.

"Poor woman!" said the officer; "she was a good wife and a good mother, and the neighbours used to cry shame on the good-for-nothing fellow of a husband."

"Had we not better get him to bed?" suggested Jasper.

The proposal was acted upon, and Jasper, after leaving his address, departed with a promise to call again in an hour or two. Not feeling disposed for sleep, he wandered down to the beach, and, seating himself on the gunwale of a stranded boat, busied himself in weaving another web of schemes in his dark and tortuous mind. At about eight o'clock in the morning he returned to the house of death he had so lately left, and found his quondam acquaintance, Mr. Bill Jones, shedding bitter, but unavailing tears of remorse, over the little that remained of the body of his once-idolised wife. The children were clamouring for food, for they were too young to comprehend the frightful nature of the loss they had sustained.

Groups of filthy-looking women, surrounded by clusters of wan and thin children, gathered round the door. As Jasper glanced at this repulsive throng, some exceedingly Malthusian and unpopular ideas broke in upon his mind.

"Those roaring vagabonds who talk so much about the rights of the people and the liberties of the country," thought he "ought to see these women, dried up with gin, and their children, more like skeletons than anything else, before they spout such gammon about marriage and morality; for I'm d——d if getting married and bringing a wife down every day, and bringing children into the world to starve or thieve, is the sort of thing at all. The young fellow who goes a-raking, or the girl who pads the hoof, are not half so bad: they hurt nobody but themselves, and have no children to curse them. But poor people are precious obstinate, and the old ones tell the young ones, that if Providence lets children come into the world, Providence will be sure to do something for them; they goes on getting children until they are eaten out of house and home, and then the father takes to drink, and there is an alarming knocking of each other about, until a fever comes and walks away with the kids, or the father amputates his chalks, and then there is the workhouse or a scatteration altogether. I'll write a book some of these odd days, to prove to a hair's breadth that —— is a precious sight less sinful than marrying, and getting half a score of beggars to be starved to death, or driven to the streets to learn to be as cunning as weasels."

The cry of the children for food interrupted the progress of his meditations; and, yielding to one of those impulses of humanity which do sometimes visit the most cruel natures, he forthwith bad the house stocked with a plentiful supply of provisions, actually fed the children all round with his own hands, and, as he did so, inquired their names.

"My nam'th Harry," said a sturdy little fellow, about three years of age, who, together with the others, was ragged, but remarkably clean.

"Harry what?"

"Burton."

Jasper gazed long and earnestly into the boy's clear, candid face; and, as he did so, he read an expression in it which brought a smile—a steady, bright smile—to his pale, unearthly-looking features. He took the boy up in his arms and kissed him, and as he did so, the smile deepened into a flush, which seemed to fill up his wasted cheeks, and soften the intense glare that was being constantly emitted from his fiery, deep-set eyes. Some virgin fountain in his heart must also have been touched, for a solitary tear glittered in each of his strange orbs, and, falling among the child's hair, were lost for ever. After this almost parental scene was over, he turned his attention to the now more composed Mr. Bill Jones; and, after some slight persuasion, succeeded in inducing him to part with the child of his wife's sister Alice.

"Here is twenty pounds," said Jasper, "to bury the poor thing that lies dead there—she was the best of the family; and a curse will fall on you if you neglect the children. Leave off drink, Bill, and stick to your trade."

"I will—I will," sobbed the repentant drunkard; and, springing to his feet, he removed the sheet, which a benevolent neighbour had spread over the body of his wife, from her face, and, passionately kissing it, swore that from that day forth no drink of an intoxicating kind should pass through his lips.

"Stick to that, Bill," cried Jasper, squeezing his hand, "and you will be a man yet. It's only fools and devils that get drunk."

"I shall emigrate," said Bill. "I know I shall never be happy in England after this. I think I shall do well in America; so I had better go at once."

Jasper eagerly promised some assistance towards the outfit and passage to New York; and, after a solemn assurance that little Henry should be conveyed safely to his mother, the pair separated, never to meet again; for, in about a fortnight afterwards, Mr. Bill Jones and his three motherless children perished in an emigrant vessel that was wrecked in the English Channel.

Jasper's first care, after obtaining possession of the boy, was to take him to a clothier's, and have him sprucely dressed; and the next, to consign him to the custody of a servant in the hotel, with strict injunctions, supported by a handsome gratuity, not to let him wander out of the establishment, but to have him forthcoming at any time he might be demanded. It now approached noon, his master's hour of rising; and, shaking off the transient emotion the presence of the boy had conjured up, he was as grim and sardonic as if nothing had occurred to interrupt his tendency to dabble in mischief and evil. While the servant had been thus engaged, my Lord Bloomfield had passed a sorry night with the fair wife of the pious tobacconist. Instead of the transports of love, he had been regaled with the frenzy of religious delusions; and the repose of the inmates of the hotel had been so disturbed, that when he arose in the morning, the proprietor plainly intimated that he could not permit the propriety of his establishment to be invaded by such nocturnal disturbances.

"Send my servant here," said his lordship, imperiously.

The host bent his pliant body, and vanished.

Jasper, upon entering the room, immediately perceived that his employer was in no humour to be trifled with, so he assumed as demure an air as possible, and stood patiently awaiting his lordship's pleasure.

"You scoundrel!" growled his lordship. "What do you mean by such conduct?"

"I don't understand your lordship."

"What insufferable assurance! Did you not get up that scene last night?"

"No, my lord; the lady had danced too much, or perhaps taken too much wine; and her sort, when excited, get obstropolous. Those like her dives into exhortation; others are smutty. Why, my lord, I've seen a girl, touched up like her, ax a whole company of ladies and gents to kiss her latter end; but when their monkey's up they can't help it—it's natural to them."

"Did you observe those gipsy women?" inquired his lordship, abruptly.

"Oho! sits the wind in that quarter?" thought Jasper. "I did, my lord," replied he, "and fancied the young one had the most graceful-looking figure I ever beheld. Such a foot and ankle!"

"Superb!" said his lordship; "the instep rose grandly, and the foot tapered off to the toes so finely and tenderly, that when she stepped out she scarcely touched the floor."

"Light as a feather!" interposed Jasper.

"And then her ankle," continued his lordship; "small and cleanly cut as a full-blooded racer's! By heaven I never saw a limb like it, but on canvas, and that was by Haydon! He did know how to draw!"

"Her motion was springy too, my lord, and when she bent to the step, anybody could see that there was no gammon about her bustle."

"Her shape was exquisite, and her waist and shoulders as warm to the touch as the feathers of a bird."

"Her eyes were bright, soft ones—like doves', my lord."

"Were they?"

"Indeed they were. How precious close her mother watched her."

"You must find them out, Jasper," said his lordship, after a little reverie.

"I'll try and do it. But what about Mrs Bond?"

His lordship's brow darkened, for the lady referred to was the most enigmatical he had ever encountered.

"Don't you think a good cooler in the sea this morning would do her good?" suggested Jasper.

"We can try it, and, as I fancy a swim would do me no harm, go down to the beach and engage the vans."

"Do you want two?" inquired Jasper, curiously.

"You know that," said his lordship, reddening.

"Regulations are strict," grinned Jasper, "but the thing can be managed. Quite common for the woman to go dressed as a man, and two to go into the same van."

"Begone, and do as I ordered you," said his lordship, waving him off.

"Well, as you won't have a spree, I will," muttered Jasper, as he strode down stairs to proceed to execute his master's bidding.

And now, as the opportunity serves, and the too beautiful and, alas! frail Mrs. Bond, is not quite prepared for her excursion to the beach, a little gossip about sea-bathing, and its characteristic irregularities, may serve as a tolerable preface to the adventures about to be recorded.

The beach is one of the finest in the kingdom for the purpose— too flat for mariners, for they invariably give it a wide berth—and of this peculiar advantage cunning architects and builders have not been slow to take advantage, for the houses have been so constructed that they command a noble view of the sea, and a fine man's-eye view of the bathers. Handsomely-mounted telescopes protrude through the windows of these accommodating habitations, and behind them, in the height of the season, when the scorching heat tempts hundreds to have a refreshing dip in the waters, may be discerned a variety of human heads—from that of the bald old fellow of sixty, down to the luxuriant one of sweet sixteen. Each of these lovers of marine views is intently observing the animated spectacle on the beach. The old men are greedily devouring the forms of the women, as they are to be seen paddling merrily in the waters. Sometimes they take a sweeping glance at the males, with their ivory shoulders flashing in the dark green of old father Neptune; but the animated, ducking figures, in loose blue dresses, grouped on the reserved part of the beach, are the great objects of attraction, and when, in the excitement of a good romp or frolic, an accident happens to the exceedingly fragile covering, many a dashing London lady has disclosed more to the eyes of these peering old rascals than ever she did to her husband. Old ladies have great fondness for anatomical studies, and they level their glasses at the brawny forms of the males, as they float on their backs, or make arches of them as they dive, after the most approved methods. Married ladies indulge in this pastime, and when two or three are gathered together, their comments are more lively than modest. "What brutes men look when they are naked!" "Oh, shocking!" "They have no shame in them!" "Really they ought to wear drawers!" "The authorities insist upon it at Boulogne!" With such kind of exclamations they express their dislike of the spectacle, but will persist in looking at it, aye and laughing heartily, too, when one of the number makes a remark that tickles the fancy. The younger feminine gazers enjoy the pastime by stealth, and, from the second or third floor of a Brighton lodging-house, receive the first serious impression of the real character of one of the, to them, hitherto profound mysteries of nature. In the attic stories the domestics, refreshed by the lively touches of wit that are peculiar to the region of flunkeyana, are more hilarious over their criticisms; and, as a "drop of something short" relieves and flavours the most pungent emotions, the gin or brandy bottle is kept in a state of active requisition. Thus the houses that encircle the Brighton shore, like so many boxes in a flourishing theatre, with a spacious gallery over them, are constantly filled with an approving and admiring audience, who, strange as it may appear, find something to gloat over in the most harmless and invigorating of all the summer recreations the pent-up denizens of towns can possibly enjoy. Nor is this all: boating parties of both sexes are formed, for the express purpose of rowing close to and having a near view of the bathers; and it is not unusual to see a stout swimmer clinging to the side of a boat, and returning the "chaff" of its male and female occupants. Sometimes two larkish young "men?" will pull their boat right through the women's bathing-ground, and scatter them right and left, like so many frightened water-fowl. But what is considered the raciest bit of fun is, to row out to a respectable distance, and, through a powerful glass, view the ladies, as, unconscious of observation, they strip themselves with the doors of their bathing-machines wide open. There are no means of checking these practices; and as they are more indigenous than offensive to the moral habits of a not inconsiderable section of the temporary inhabitants of a popular watering-place, all the dull preaching in the world will not eradicate them. So to relate what befel the too merry Mrs. Bond, while laving her polished limbs at the upper end of the ladies' bathing-ground.

The day was remarkably hot, and, as she felt excessively languid after her previous night's exertions, she undressed herself completely, and, throwing open the door of her bathing-machine, sat herself down to allow the refreshing sea-breeze to fan her splendidly-shaped and remarkably fair body.

While so seated, she busied herself in confining her beautiful hair in a cap, and looking vacantly upon the placid water that splashed gently around her.

"A sea-nymph attiring, by Jove!" exclaimed Jasper, who, having hired a boat, was lying-to right opposite, and could see her distinctly. "Oh, that I could hold her in my arms as a man should! Why, a mere look at her makes my head spin round as if I was drunk. I had better make a bolt of it, or I shall go mad outright. Oh, heavens! what a woman!"

And Jasper, unable to gaze any longer, sat down, with his sight dimmed by the rush of blood to his head. This was caused by Mrs. Bond having risen, and leisurely donned her bathing-dress.

"Balmy air—delicious coolness!" ejaculated she, as she waded up to her waist, holding fast, though, by the stake rope. Oh, that Fred, my own one, were here! surely those who commune in the spirit, may take lawful pleasure in the body. It would not be sinful for him to clasp me in his arms, and bear me away on the bosom of that clear, tranquil sea."

And thus wishing, she went on until the whole of her body was immersed, and she had some difficulty in retaining her footing. A swimmer, who cleft the waters as a bird on the wing does the air, approached her noiselessly, and whispered in her ear:

"Come with me into the deep-blue waters, and float like a mermaid warming herself in the sun?"

The rising scream of the lady was drowned in the swell that washed her off her feet; and the next instant, her head was pillowed on Jasper's bosom, and she was borne rapidly away from the shore.

"Oh, let this be a blessed baptism!" she murmured, as Jasper—for her aquatic abductor was no other than that identical personage—allowed himself and his burden to float, and be borne, like a brace of corks, back gently to the shore. To her, he was a divine of the unadulterated evangelical school; and, as she listened to his suppressed murmurings, and almost counted the violent throbbings of his heart, she fancied he was engaged in some great and glorious work of regeneration through faith. And when Jasper, every now and then, uttered a shriek, or a howl, as if of pain, she sympathetically responded, and would have turned to embrace him, but every time she made the effort, their buoyancy was destroyed, and both plunged down into the water like two pieces of lead. When Jasper, clutching his burden, rose for the last time, he heard shouts from the shore, and, upon rising himself, looking round, he perceived several boats approaching, for, as he correctly judged, the laudable purpose of rescuing the lady and her brave preserver from a watery grave. For one all-powerful reason, he did not wish to be dragged into a boat, like a captured fish; so, making a prodigious endeavour to calm his frenzied senses, he

assured the parties who lifted the half-insensible Mrs. Bond into their boat, that he was not at all exhausted, but quite able, as the lady was now in safety, to swim to his own boat, which he pointed out to them, as it lay moored close to some jutting rocks. And, to verify his assurance, he slipped from their grasp, and struck out with the energy and skill of a man bent upon accomplishing a feat he had undertaken.

"A brave fellow, I'll warrant," said one of the men; "and doesn't look like a man who'd step forrard and say he did such a thing as this; so, I say, Bob, we'll go snacks in the reward."

"All right!" was the response; "and God bless the wimen, for if it warn't for them, we boaties would make but a poor job of it in this ruinated place!"

Mrs. Bond, after some not over tender manipulation on the part of three or four she-water-dragons, to whose custody she was committed, revived sufficiently to disclose her place of residence; and thither was borne, and immediately placed in bed between half a dozen blankets. As for Jasper, he managed to arrive at his boat in safety, and dress himself, but not unobserved by two boys, who, having noticed his scarecrow

appearance, jeered at him unmercifully. Jasper took not the slightest notice of them, but, having dressed himself, and assumed the venerable appearance of a *bona fide* parson, mildly rebuked them for their impertinence; and, taking a couple of shillings from his purse, presented them, with a request that they would be better boys for the future. The bait took, and Jasper no sooner got them within his reach, than he seized each by the collar, and, after a preliminary kicking, soused them over head in the water, all the while bestowing on them the most parental admonitions imaginable. Leaving them prone on the beach, more frightened than hurt, he walked leisurely away.

"May I be rammed, jammed, and d—d, if ever I do a good action again!" he growled. "There's nothing good in human nature—even boys are but devils in disguise; and as for women, they are walking lumps of brimstone. But they are beautiful—delicious! I felt as if I could have died happy when that warm, plump piece lay on my stomach; but it wasn't to be; and I hate everybody, and the women—especially the pretty ones, for they torture me—make me hissing mad. They are all serpents, every one of them; but the worst of it is, it's only the rotten ones can sting a fellow to death. It's clear I can't be put out of my misery that way, so I must make everybody I come near as miserable as I can. Hillo! here's a row. Just the thing for me, for I hate a quiet life!"

He had by this time approached the Chain Pier; and, observing an unusual commotion upon it, paid his twopence admission fee, and mingled in the throng, to ascertain the cause. Let, as it happened, his opportune arrival be forestalled by a few particulars.

Bloomfield, glad to be rid of his rather too fond companion for a short time, had a comfortable bathe, and then strolled on to the pier for a quiet walk by himself. The first person that he encountered, whom he knew, was Mr. Smythe, the banker, attired very smartly, but still bearing traces in his countenance of his recent pugilistic encounter.

"Ah, Bloomfield, my boy, how dye do? haven't seen you for an age."

Bloomfield shook him more warmly by the hand than ever he had done before, for he felt that there was between them a common cause of grievance. The jealousy the peer successfully instilled into the bosoms of others when it touched his own, warmed him towards a man as criminal as himself, and for whom he had always, until that chord had been struck, entertained an instinctive aversion. After an interchange of mutual greetings, his lordship inquired, with apparent carelessness, after Mrs. Smythe.

The banker winced, and, thrusting his arm through Bloomfield's, replied, in a tone intended to be confidential:

"Between you and me, I don't half like matters at home. My wife has not been the same to me for some time past as she used to be. There's something rotten in the state of Smythemark; but what it is I cannot make out. A cock-and-bull story about her and Captain Morris, a friend of your wife's, reached my ears, and led me into a ridiculous mistake. I presume your servant told you all about it?"

"I heard some nonsense from him, but did not pay much attention to it. What was it all about?"

"Nothing very agreeable, I can assure you. I was informed by him that my wife was with Captain Morris at Charlton, and, went down, intending to take the villain's life. The captain was there, certainly; but the woman was a young girl I had never seen before, and I got into a precious scrape, and had to pay through the nose to get out of it. Instead of obtaining redress for a grievous injury, I had to promise to pay the captain a thousand pounds, for not sending a bullet through my head for interrupting his pleasures, and traducing his character. Husbands, after all, are poor devils, and have to put up with every sort of annoyance. If their wives are ill-tempered, they must bear it; and, if they happen to be pretty, why the poor devils mustn't grumble when a fellow admires them, or their whole time would be occupied in breaking heads, or having their own broken."

"Have you heard anything about Captain Morris?" inquired his lordship.

"Of course you know all about his duel?"

"I saw the account in the papers."

"Well, he has since been cashiered, and is now on the hide-and-seek, for the officers are after him."

"Is Stanley dead?"

"No; but it's touch-and-go with him."

"Has the cause of the affair oozed out?"

"There are a hundred whispers afloat, but his relations are doing all they can to stifle them. It seems he had a shooting-box down in Herefordshire where this happened, and that he carried a girl down there who turned out to be a virtuous, plucky one, but who she was, nobody can tell but Morris, and he's in Paris, I should think, long before this."

"I hope so," said Bloomfield; "but here are those confounded bogtrotters—the O'Blazes; let us avoid them."

Smythe turned pale at the mention of the name, and wheeled round with alacrity; but the gentlemen with the fiery appellative were not to be done so easily, and disconcerted the manœuvre by a rapid flank movement.

"The top of the marning to you, my lord! Illigant weather! Sweet place Brighton, at this time of the year!" were the phrases showered in profusion upon Bloomfield.

Those addressed to Smythe amounted to an invitation to retire to some "convaynient" place, and settle a little matter, either peaceably or otherwise.

Smythe manifested the most decided reluctance to this proposal; and Bloomfield, with a polite "Good morning" on his lips, was about to lead him away, when the two brothers laid violent hands on his collar, and effectually arrested his progress.

"Where's my sister, ye spalpeen?" thundered the eldest of the two, a brawny fellow, evidently more acquainted with the shillelagh than the sword.

"Troth, an I'll shake the white liver out of yez, if yez don't spake the truth immadiately!"

"What do you mean?" stammered Smythe.

"Mane?" shouted the eldest; "come, none o' your blarney over me. I mane my Lady Tyrone, whom you two days ago invaigled from her illigant home, her husband, and darlints of brothers."

Smythe quaked for fear, and Bloomfield, observing his discomposure, hastened to his relief.

"Cannot you postpone such a question until a more desirable opportunity—at all events until we are not so much exposed?" said his lordship.

"Anything in rayson," responded the O'Blazes, bowing obsequiously; "but the divil's in it if a man can't kick up a row for his own sister, the more to the main when she's been abused and decaived."

"Allow me a moment's conversation with my friend?" requested his lordship.

"Sartainly; a hundred if you desire it."

"Have you had anything to do with Lady Tyrone?" inquired Bloomfield from Smythe, as soon as he had drawn him aside.

"Yes," groaned Smythe.

"Where is she?"

"At the Steyne."

"You are in a mess!"

"I know it; only assist me to get away from those cursed Tipperary rascals, and I'll be your debtor for ever."

"Gentlemen," said his lordship, approaching the wrathful brothers; "such grave charges as those you have preferred, are better discussed through the agency of third parties. My friend will give you the name of his solicitor."

"Solicitor be d—d!" roared the O'Blazes; "that will do after the bating."

And both, suiting the action to the word, laid violent hands upon the banker.

"The lady, you spalpeen!" cried an O'Blaze, giving Smythe a hearty shake.

Now Smythe, in fisticuff matters, was no coward, and resented this roughness by planting a good straightly-delivered blow on the Irishman's nose. The elder brother, seeing this, fiercely attacked the banker; and in both their clutches he would have fared very ill, had not succour arrived, in the person of Jasper, who dashed into the *melee*, crying:

"Two to one, ye Irish blackguards, and on a gentleman, too! Take that—and that!"

And he rained such a torrent of blows on the faces of the two O'Blazes, that they were dead beat in a trice, and took to their heels, to the lively accompaniment of a derisive cheer from the assembled crowd. Bloomfield and Smythe also retired from the pier followed by the triumphant Jasper.

"You have got into a scrape," said Bloomfield to the banker, who sat by his brandy-and-water, the very picture of despair; "but I can't blame you, for Lady Tyrone is a fine woman!"

"There is plenty of her, Bloomfield, and she's a merry bed-fellow; but, confound it, am I to be hunted to death by her infernal highwaymen of brothers?"

"My dear fellow," said his lordship, "you had better compound the affair with them. It's not the first of the kind in which they have engaged."

"Not the first?" exclaimed Smythe, opening his eyes very wide.

"No," replied Bloomfield, laughing; "charge your glass again, and I will tell you the story. You remember Lord Midriff?"

Perfectly—he was a light-haired, rather soft-looking young fellow."

"Well, he is somewhere up the Mediterranean now, whither the occurrence I am about to relate drove him. He happened to meet Lady Tyrone at Bloomfield House, one night, and I could see that the youth was at once fascinated with the solid proportions of her ladyship. She, having ascertained that he was a clear twenty thousand a year man, ogled him into such a fever, that I thought the poor devil would have exploded in the room. She saw his agitation, and led him into a retiring room, where I suppose she pawed him into the desperate resolution of proposing an elopement. Her ladyship, who has a *penchant* for young bachelors—she was once accused of having debauched a youth of sixteen—must have readily consented, for early the next morning the pair set off for Paris, where they remained a whole fortnight before her ladyship disclosed their whereabouts; and when she did, those bullies, her brothers, pounced upon the pair at breakfast one morning. There was a dreadful row, you may imagine, and Midriff was so frightened that he gave them a check for ten thousand, and posted to England, where he packed up, bought a yacht, and felt inclined to go anywhere but round Cape Horn."

"Ten thousand pounds!" ejaculated Smythe; "why, I got ten of the finest women in the world for that sum—it was monstrous!"

A servant at this moment entered, bearing a card.

"It's from Lieutenant O'Blaze," said Bloomfield; "shall we see him, and hear what he has to say?"

"As you like."

Lieutenant O'Blaze had by this time assumed the air of a deeply-injured person; and when he had entered upon the purport of his errand, began to talk affectingly of the deep and lasting stain which had been cast on the hitherto unsullied escutcheons of the Tyrones and O'Blazes.

"Cannot the thing be hushed up?" suggested Bloomfield. "Tut, tut, her ladyship often goes to Ireland for a few weeks, to look after her tenantry."

The lieutenant elevated his eyebrows, and began to think his lordship too knowing a card to be either bilked or trifled with.

"Come," said Bloomfield, "it is always preferable to arrange these mishaps quietly—what do you say? My friend is ready to make gentlemanly and reasonable compensation."

"In that case," said O'Blaze, his eyes brightening, "there 'ul be no occasion to go to law at all, at all. A check would settle the matter?"

"Certainly it would; but, as you are perfectly aware, it would be indecorous for my friend to make an offer—that would be buying the lady; why, the proposal must come from you."

The proud O'Blaze, who boasted of a direct descent from some Tipperary prince, whom the Saxons had hanged for cattle-stealing, scratched his shaggy head for a few minutes, and then, without the slightest discomposure of feature, said:

"A jury, sure, would give a dacent sum—my Lord Tyrone belongs to the oldest family in Ireland."

"But his lordship is bed-ridden, and of not the slightest use to a wife."

"Faith, and I'm thinking that would aggravate the damages: to stale away a wife from a sick and helpless husband, would be sure to exasperate twelve honest men."

"Well, well, take that for granted: if I were on such a jury, I know what I should do. Our present business is with your proposal to settle this unpleasant business."

"Well, I'm thinking, a trifle like ten thousand would satisfy his lordship."

"Ten thousand?" roared Smythe; "I wouldn't give ten farthings for such a w——e!"

And, snapping his fingers in the face of the O'Blaze, he defied him to do his worst.

Now, the O'Blaze was a very valorous man, and his Milesian blood boiled at the coarse appellative applied to his sister; but in matters that required legal interposition, he was a prudent and remarkably self-collected individual. He drew himself up to his full military height, and, looking down upon the banker with a violent attempt at ineffable scorn, turned to Bloomfield, and said:

"The thing must go into coort, now, but I appale to your lordship, whether I am not entitled to satisfaction for the affront put upon me by this low-bred scoundrel? It's base ingratitude to seduce a woman and then call her a 'w——e.' Faugh!" and, by a rapid movement of his hand, the indignant O'Blaze seized the banker by the nose, and gave it such a vigorous pull, that his eyes seemed to be starting from his head.

Smythe, furious at such an outrage, seized the decanter on the table, and flung it at the head of his antagonist. But the lieutenant dexterously avoided the missile, which went clean through a mirror, worth at least twenty pounds.

The O'Blaze marched dignifiedly out of the room, leaving Bloomfield half suffocated with laughter.

"You are in for it now, and no mistake," said his lordship, to the extremely-flushed banker.

"I won't pay a farthing!" roared Smythe.

"Perhaps not," said his lordship, drily; "but the lieutenant is sure to call you out. I'll wager anything he's gone to the barracks to ask some old crony to be his second. Irishmen, generally, are rather prompt in such engagements."

Smythe turned pale at this new phase in the affair, and, wishing his lordship a hurried good-morning, left him.

"Beg pardon, sir," said the waiter to him on the landing, "decanter and mirror broken—five-and-twenty pounds, please."

"Curse all women! and Irish women in particular!" he growled, as he handed over the amount, and forthwith betook himself to the railway station, and jumped into a train that was just on the point of starting for town.

Bloomfield, relieved from his presence, turned his attention to his own affairs, and, after a hasty review of them, arrived at the conclusion that the sooner he quitted Brighton the better. But what to do with Mrs. Bond puzzled him.

"If she would only buckle to her fate," thought he, "and remain contented as my mistress, I would put her in a nice cottage at Brixton or Barnes; but she is such a crazy creature, that I am afraid I must part with her. How, though? is the question. I wonder whether that mysterious iniquity, Jasper, could help me out of the hobble?"

Jasper, when summoned, guessed that something important was about to happen, for his master, for the first time since their introduction, requested him to be seated, and to help himself to the brandy on the table.

"What's all this I hear about Mrs.—Mrs.—You know who I mean?"

"Oh, nothing. She went out of her depth, and was picked up by some boatmen."

"Is that all? Ahem! do you think she is exactly sane?"

"Why, as to that, my lord, I sometimes fancy she's not all right in her upper works."

"Just my impression. Ahem! do you think her husband would take her back again?"

Jasper grinned, and suggested, that to hint such a thing to her would drive her completely out of her senses.

"What the devil am I to do?" inquired his satiated lordship.

Upon that hint Jasper spoke right boldly.

"Give me a hundred a year while she lives, and I'll take her off your hands."

"You?" exclaimed his lordship, pushing back his chair, and staring at Jasper in unmingled astonishment.

"Yes, my lord," replied Jasper, composedly; "and I'll wager anything she goes with me contentedly."

"What, in the name of Cupid and all his devilries, could you do with a woman?"

"Women are fit for more things than what your lordship means, and, as she believes me to be a new-cut minister, I'd gammon her to do anything."

"I must be satisfied that she will be well treated before I part with her."

"I could do her no harm, your lordship."

"True;" and his lordship, after musing awhile, added, "could she not be placed in some way of business—the cigar or coffee-house line?"

"If your lordship will leave all that to me, I'll see that your wishes are carried out. But she wants taming down; her nerves are too twittery at present for anything."

Bloomfield, after giving the proposition, as he thought, the maturest consideration, became convinced that, under the circumstances, it was the best that could be suggested."

"I do not," reasoned he, "abandon her to misery and prostitution, but hand her over to a man incapable of doing her an injury, and, moreover, under my own eye, and where I have the opportunity of detecting, and immediately redressing, anything wrong. It shall be done, and, as I would rather not see her again, I'll be off to town. Jasper," said he, aloud, "not a syllable about my identity."

"Oh, trust me, my lord, I am not so green as that!"

The settling with the hotel-keeper was soon dispatched, and his lordship, after providing Jasper with ample funds, departed, giving that Mephistopheles of a gentleman a week's leave of absence to perfect arrangements.

"Tol lol lol, ri tu loo la ra!" screamed Jasper, pirouetting round the room; "won't I have a lark with the handsome, satin-skinned love of a gay wife!" A glass of brandy went gurgling down his throat. "Well, I am a gentleman at last, for I have got a woman, and a hundred a year to keep her! I'll have a bit of fun with her, and then—then—yes, by God, I'll sell her to some swell! I'll be bound I'll get a couple of hundred for her!"

And with this very moral consolation, this prince of accommodating rascals tossed off another glassful of brandy, and hied him to the chamber of his newly-acquired purchase; for, to all intents and purposes, my Lord Bloomfield had sold her to his servant, the only difference from an ordinary bargain and sale, being that the latter, instead of the former, was the payee.

But, previous to chronicling the systematic iniquities of Jasper, it may be as well to follow my Lord Bloomfield in an adventure which he termed a merry leave-taking of dissipated Brighton. Being convinced that Smythe had flown to town, to escape the vengeance of the Hibernian defenders of their sister's honour, the solitary condition of that jovial lady touched his sense of gallantry, and he thought it would only be an entertaining piece of etiquette to call upon her, and tender his condolence. He found her, but in no alarming state of disconsolation; for she was seated at a substantial luncheon, wondering what had become of her chevalier, the banker. She started on Bloomfield being announced, and when he introduced himself into her presence, the blood mounted so quickly to her face, that the rouge on her cheeks lost considerably, by the contrast, in colour. Her native assurance, however, soon came to her aid, and she invited Bloomfield to take a seat at the table. His volatile demeanour soon placed her at her ease, and she ate and drank and chatted, with as much freedom as if nothing had occurred to disturb her matronly serenity. In appearance she was, what the men who prefer imposing styles of beauty would term, a fine woman. A little above the average stature of her sex, she possessed a bust of capacious volume. It looked firm, though, and the neck, throat, and part of the bosom that was exposed, were totally destitute of that flabbiness which, in stout women in their prime, is so glaringly prominent. The neck was unwrinkled, and shone dazzlingly above the two large globes that swelled out above the region where a substantial waist commenced, and tapered to hips that gave a sensual rotundity to a region, which, of all others, to the eye, tells of the well or ill-made woman. The limbs fell, from this inviting prominence, in a graceful sweep down to well-shaped—remarkably, so but not over small—feet. As for her face, shaded by thick braids of wavy black hair, it was a marvellously-wicked one to look upon. The eyes were large, black, and swimming ones, and when they looked at you, the whole soul of the woman flashed burning passion into yours. In fact, she was a species of Catherine of Russia, in her amours, but had hitherto managed to maintain a decent position in certain circles. She was not received at court, but that did not trouble her much, for, as she good-naturedly observed, she would rather be the recipient of respect and devotion, than the contributor; and preferred pleasure and frolic to all the pomp and ceremony in the world. Her career, from sixteen up to her present age—thirty-five or six—proved her to be the possessor of no mean abilities. Born of humble parents, in the obscurity of a remote Irish village, she threw herself into the arms of a captain that one day marched past her father's door at the head of his company, and, after a two years' polishing at the hands of her gallant lover, fascinated the colonel, who bought her from his sub, and kept her in dashing style, until he broke his neck while hunting; and then, thrown upon her own resources, she betook herself to the stage, and created quite a sensation in a range of light characters, in which donning male attire is frequently an essential. In this capacity, her charms and mental qualifications ripened, and she became the mistress of the Lord Lieutenant of Ireland. Her next conquest was that of her husband, the whisky-loving Lord Tyrone, who fell in love with her ample legs; and, as he offered her a peerage, which, if only an Irish one, still conferred a title, she consented to be made as honest a woman as nature would allow her. My Lord Tyrone, after a brief season, proved as decent a husband as any the soil ever produced; and, as even genuine poteen or Islay malt will in time sap the foundations of the goodliest human temples, he fell a martyr to the gout, and, in vain endeavours to drink it away, he did not much concern himself about his wife. The brothers of this accomplished lady abandoned their native bogs when her star rose in the ascendant, and had been her faithful satellites, throughout every phase of her career. The ancient blood of the O'Blazes was in them worthily represented; for, as long as they could be maintained in idleness, they cared little, if the means were abundant, from what source they were obtained. It should be mentioned, that her ladyship, through her private influence with the highest government functionaries, pursued a lucrative business in the sale of official situations. When a certain nobleman occupied one of the highest situations in the country, scarcely any request preferred by my lady Tyrone was refused; and, as a consequence, many of her mornings were agreeably passed in opening letters that contained souvenirs in the shape of pretty pieces of paper, embellished by the signature of the old lady of Threadneedle Street. Such was Lady Tyrone, the warmest and most daring Aspasia in high life, but one whom Lord Bloomfield had hitherto avoided. Indeed, to her ladyship's credit, it must be admitted that she had no great liking for intrigues with married acquaintances. Wives are apt to be waspish, and not over solicitous to keep a husband's secrets, when they happen to trespass upon her connubial rights and enjoyments. Frailty is the last thing a woman forgives in a woman. So my Lady Tyrone preferred the society of buxom bachelors with large rent-rolls. Bloomfield she had always considered a good, tall, proper man, but never formed the faintest conception of adding him to her list of captives. However, when she learnt the news of the defection of Smythe, and that her brothers, like bloodhounds, were on his trail, she first laughed heartily, and then, catching the ardent glance of the peer fixed upon her own, the thought struck her that he would make an extremely agreeable escort back to town. His lordship had an equally roving taste for variety, and so strove to render himself as acceptable as possible. The deluded Mrs. Bond was soon forgotten in the presence of the imposing charms of the dashing Irish beauty; and, before an hour had elapsed, the pair managed to establish between them a very cozy familiarity. Her ladyship's large, lustrous eyes, devoured the fine person of his lordship; and he was not slow to retaliate upon her ladyship's

magnificent bust. The hands have a strange propensity to indulge in those freedoms which the eye first suggests; and Bloomfield was not long before he had his busily employed about the form of her ladyship.

"Be quiet, Bloomfield, will you?" she exclaimed, starting up, and, as she did so, purposely so entangling her dress in the chair that the whole of her fine leg, with its glowing calf, so large, that it seemed bursting from the silk stocking, was fully exposed to his view. The sight enthralled him instantly; and, throwing himself on his knees, he gave the majestic limb a hearty hugging. These toyings speedily deepened in intensity; and, as her ladyship was accustomed to yield to a handsome man without exhibiting much coyness, the pair surrendered themselves up to the advantages of their position, and in the evening left Brighton for a week's sojourn in the delightful town of Hastings. At the end of that period both returned to London, extremely well pleased with each other, and parted with a promise to meet as often as circumstances would permit. And thus, in a manner more expeditious than moral, did Lord Bloomfield add another merry wife to his list of lovely frail ones.

But to return to Mrs. Bond. As may have been surmised from the details of her conduct given in this narrative, her sensualism was as strong as her religious fanaticism; and the former, in its gratification, became so mingled with the types of the latter, that it would not have been uncharitable to have affirmed that they were identical. Her passions had never been properly cultivated; and, having been stimulated in the Ebenezzian school of morals, they required but few stimulants to excite them to the commission of any species of extravagance. The handsome Bloomfield had endeavoured to soothe the senses he had inflamed, when, finding the task impossible, he coolly handed her over to the tender mercies of his menial. Had she continued to vend tobacco and snuff, she might in time have acquired the dissimulation necessary to have enabled her slily to have had a few of the indulgences which her temperament craved; she might probably have become as artful as any lady that ever walked, with downcast looks, to the handsomest confessor she could select; but it was her fate that it should not be so: her burning passions were destined to exhaust themselves in a probation as horrible as any that can befal a poor woman who has not been trained to exercise a severe control over impulses, which, when properly directed, are the most glorious implanted in her sex. May her fate be a warning to all who feel inclined to bask too frequently in the hot sun of desires, which, when abused, only death can quench!

Jasper found her in bed, asleep, while an old woman, seated on a chair, with her legs stretched across one another, was dozing, in a state of profound gin-and-water-ishness. Jasper quietly took a seat by the bedside, and, as a preliminary, took a survey of the apartment. The nurse seemed a fitting subject upon which to play a prank. After carefully filling her glass, he dropped into it one of the love-powders he had procured from Dr. Wriggles, and, stealing on tiptoe behind her, breathed gently into her ear. The old woman awoke, looked at her patient, and, perceiving that she still slumbered, applied herself to her glass, and then dozed off again. Jasper nerved himself for the coming scene by partaking of the cooling draught, or rather counter-stimulant, with which the erudite doctor had supplied him. He then sat himself down again, and began to hold, as he termed it, a cogitation with himself.

"Now what on earth am I to do with this young

woman? I shan't be any good to her as a husband, but I suppose I must make myself a sort of dummy one. My eye, though, won't she kick up a row when she finds it all gammon! If she'd only stick to the spiritual, it might be managed well enough; but, confound it all! these religious sort of people are as rampagious as old Nick himself; I don't wonder at it, for they work themselves into such stunning frenzies, that they want something in the shape of a cooler now and then. If I could sell her to some frisky old gent, I might put some tin in my pocket, and do her a service, too; for an old chap, when he takes a fancy to a girl, soon gets precious nutty upon her, and lets her do just as she likes with him. That's the best thing I could do, only it would be too venturesome, and the thing might get blown about. I see I must take her in hand myself, and risk the consequences. I don't see, again, why I shouldn't have a bit of fun with her. She's a woman, too; and as I hate her whole tribe, root, stump, trunk, and branch, I may practise a few original experiments on her soft, plump, luscious body. Halloo! for a lark with old snuffy, now!"

The sage dame so designated opened her little bloodshot eyes to their fullest extent, and fixed them in a sort of trance upon the extraordinary countenance of Jasper, who regarded her with the rigidity of marble. An immoral request sounded softly in her ear; and, as the potion had now taken effect, she turned her head suddenly, and felt rather surprised when she did not see an insinuating young fellow bending over her.

"How doth the afflicted lamb?" inquired Jasper, in a low whisper.

"A good deal easier, sir; but, bless me, how queer I feel!"

The old woman's eyes began to wink at a rapid rate, and such a deep flush came over her saffron visage, that Jasper fancied she would thaw and dissolve on the spot.

"What is the matter, my good woman, that you wriggle so on your seat?"

"I itches—I burns—scalding water is running down my back!"

"Have you the fear of the Lord before your eyes?"

"I hope so; I was well eddicated."

"Then what makes you itch and burn?"

"The devil himself—or—or ——"

"That Satanic compound called gin. Sinner, repent; throw gin to the dogs! Arise, and go into the air of heaven."

The poor old woman, who felt convinced that the commotion that was raging within her was to be attributed to the gin, rose, and plunged through the chamber door. Not being familiar with the house she obeyed the tendency of her spirits, and ascended to the topmost story, where, seeing a bed-room door open, she staggered through it, and, puffing and panting like a steam-boiler, threw herself on the bed. As fate would have it, one of the men-servants of the hotel, in an inflammatory state of beer, was proceeding to the same chamber, to sleep off the fumes of his morning's debauch; and, as the votaries of Bacchus are not gifted with a keen vision, he rolled on to the bed without observing that it had previously been occupied. Jasper had become aware of the proceeding, and, after fastening the door on the pair thus promiscuously thrown together, listened at the key-hole, until he heard something that sounded very like the spluttering and savage mewing of a couple of cats, mingled with the grunting of a hog; and then he descended, heartily wishing that the couple would

clapper-claw each other until not a particle of their visages remained.

Having regained the room where Mrs. Bond lay, he proceeded to put into practice a piece of most fiendish cruelty. Baring the feet of his victim, he took a quill pen, and, with the waving, feathered end, tickled her soles. She was evidently still under the influence of a powerful narcotic; for she did not awake, but writhed and uttered prolonged hysterical laughs, while undergoing the torture. This he persisted in for perhaps half an hour, grinning and, chuckling over each contortion or prolonged wail of the sleeper. When he left off, her frame quivered as if it had been galvanised, and, with a single dissonant cry, she seemed to fall into a state of insensibility.

"The bare sight of a woman," said he, with suppressed ferocity, "tickles me into madness; and why should I not retaliate when Providence gives me the opportunity? Providence—aha! The only Providence is fate—firm, immoveable fate; and, as it is mine to be wicked, I'll not be slow to do my utmost to fulfil my destiny. And this is good practice—capital! But oh! what would I not give to have *her* here instead!"

The veins on his forehead swelled at this thought, and he clenched his hands in the agony of his passion.

"But the day will come," resumed he; "and, until then, the devil aid me in my hatred to every woman who falls into my clutches, up stairs and down;—aha! my bonny things, the wretch you in your wantonness despise, can revenge himself on you; and yet none of you know it!"

This latter remark was elicited by the sounds of an uproar, which he did not doubt proceeded from the chamber in which he had confined the nurse and the drunken man-servant. On proceeding to the scene of the confusion, he found a mob of servants, male and female, assembled outside the door, wondering what could be the meaning of the mysterious noises that proceeded from the room.

"Where's the key?" "Break open the door!" "It's Bill!" and, amid a variety of suggestions, the door was forced open, and a scene disclosed which elicited a simultaneous roar of laughter. The old nurse, stripped to her short chemise, with her attenuated brown shanks and bald bullet head, was frantically endeavouring to induce her drunken companion to return her embraces; but he, sturdily resisting, had rolled off the bed on to the floor, where he lay snorting and puffing, and vainly striving to release his mouth from the withered lips that had fastened upon it. When the pair were separated, the old woman was carried off by half a dozen of her own sex, and the now half-sobered fellow being called upon for an explanation, told a most dolorous tale.

"I feeled a clawing, and pawing, and licking of my chaps, but, Lord bless you, I thought it wor Towzer, and I bid un be off. Bymby I feels a mighty scratching, and when I opened my heyes, and sees a head as bald as my hand, and a face as red as a pothecary's bottle, I got mighty frightened, and cried out, and then there wor a tuzzle, and that's all I knows about it. Who was 'un?"

"A voman, as old and scraggy as the cock vot crowed ven Moses vos born."

The fellow's hair stood on end, and he mentally vowed never to defile himself again with any one of the sex. He retired, amid the jeers and scoffs of the hilarious crowd. Jasper, as much pleased as any of them, returned to Mrs. Bond's chamber, and seated himself, in expectation of her soon waking.

Her slumbers were, however, prolonged until near

midnight, and when she awoke, the thirst of a burning fever was upon her. This Jasper assuaged with copious draughts of lemonade, and when her confused senses had settled down into some degree of composure, he was prepared with the most artful replies to her queries.

"Where is Bumbinski," she faintly asked.

"Absquatulated," was the word on Jasper's tongue, but he refrained from giving it utterance, and, lifting up his eyes to the ceiling, said, "the Lord hath called him hence, but after a brief space he will return, and once again gladden thine heart."

"Oh, he was as lovely and sweet-smelling as a rose!" murmured Mrs. Bond, as with a thrill she recalled to her memory many of the reminiscences of the past few days.

"Verily he was," chimed in Jasper, with a true professional tone; "and it grieves me sorely that the light of his presence should be withdrawn from us; but until his return I will be thy friend, thy protector, and thy spouse. Let us pray."

A screen must be drawn before that blasphemous scene. When it had been brought to a conclusion, Jasper, whose arm encircled the neck of the recumbent Mrs. Bond, said to her, in a half-whisper:

"Shall I not be thy spouse in the spirit?"

Her reply was faintly delivered, but the listener promptly interpreted its meaning.

"Blessed are they who believe, for they shall not be deceived," ejaculated Jasper, as he handed the too credulous woman a glass containing a powerful narcotic, which he himself had prepared.

She drank it, and in a few minutes fell fast asleep.

In the morning she arose with a deadly-pale countenance, but the intense light that gleamed in her eyes bespoke a raging fire within. Jasper breakfasted with her, and throughout the day strove to amuse her with his edifying conversation. Towards evening his remarks became lax and irregular, and he even ventured to play with her hair, pat her cheeks, and once or twice he thrust his hand into her bosom. She smiled, and gently reproved his frolicsome mood, and another night passed, in the same manner as the preceding one, over her doomed head. On the following evening Jasper proceeded to still greater liberties, and so wrought upon the heated imagination of his victim, that she consented that her spiritual spouse should share her bed. The horrors of that night were realised in the morning. She rose paler than usual, and apparently more collected than on the two preceding days; but the fire in her eyes burned more steadily and deeply, and every now and then a bright-red spot gathered on her white brow. Her attire and hair were more neatly arranged than usual, and Jasper, who was disposed to be merry and pleasant, warmly complimented her on the improvement in her appearance. Her replies were only in monosyllables, and he observed, not without surprise, that she breakfasted with a ravenous appetite.

"Eat heartily, my precious dove; for the fat of the land is the heritage of the saints!"

The words had scarcely issued from his mouth, when the hitherto statue-like Mrs. Bond sprang from her seat, and, with a wild, howl-like cry, threw herself on Jasper, and with her hands tore furiously at his face.

"Mad, by G—d!" shouted Jasper, upsetting the table in his efforts to escape; for, after a severe struggle, finding it impossible to restrain her, his sole desire was to get out of her reach. She chased him round the room, and then, snatching up a knife, like a winged fury sprang over the *debris*, and levelled a blow at his breast. He caught it upon his uplifted arm, and the knife, coming into contact with the bone, snapped in two, leaving a fragment two inches in length sticking in his flesh. Jasper, roused now to a state of ungovernable rage, felled her to the floor, and hastened to a surgeon's, to have his wound dressed. Upon his return he found the victim of lust bound down in a chair, and laughing and weeping in a state of confirmed lunacy.

"I expected this," exclaimed Jasper, regarding the poor idiot with a look of compassion; "and all my watching, and care, and hourly exhortations, have come to nought. My child! my child."

And the hideous hypocrite wept so bitterly, that he excited the profound compassion of all the spectators.

"Where has her husband gone to?" inquired the landlord.

Jasper meaningly touched his forehead, and the landlord said:

"I thought so. Why they used to waltz before breakfast, and turned my house topsy-turvy since they have been it."

"We must have assistance," cried Jasper, appearing as if endeavouring to rouse himself out of a condition of stupor. "Is there no establishment at hand for unfortunate cases like these?"

"Oh, yes," answered the landlord, "plenty; but I should recommend Dr. Jenkinson."

"I have heard of him," responded Jasper eagerly. "I have faith in his great skill. Call a cab, and we will convey her to him instantly."

In less than half an hour the once blooming wife and fascinating mistress was an inmate of one of those disgraces to the English law, a private lunatic asylum, shorn of her graceful, redundant hair, and subjected to the restraint of that horrible instrument of torture, a strait waistcoat. Jasper, after depositing fifty pounds with the proprietor of this frightful gaol, hastened to town, taking care to carry with him the little boy he had procured from the infatuated and ill-fated Bill Jones. He easily induced Lord Broomfield, when he next saw him, to believe that the misguided woman, who had been inveigled from her home and so scandalously treated, had consented to receive his annuity, and to live in decent retirement. Other engagements multiplied upon his hands, and he soon forgot her; and when he recalled her to his mind, it was with a smile at what he termed her eccentricity and very convenient hypocrisy.

The termination of the tragedy in which this "merry" wife had played so conspicuous a character, may be briefly told. Under judicious treatment—for the liberal pay of the seeming father had stimulated the doctor to exercise his utmost skill on his patient—the violent symptoms gradually abated, and she became, except at fitful intervals, that most difficult of all lunatics to cure—a religious monomaniac. The occasions when she relapsed were when a handsome, dark-complexioned man was introduced into her presence; and then she would make the utmost efforts to approach and lavish caresses upon him. When winter set in her health declined, and she took to her bed. Her constitution had evidently been radically undermined; and Jasper, with whom the principal had maintained a correspondence, was duly apprised of the approaching event. But that "gentleman" was too glad of the incognito he had so cleverly preserved to take any notice of the information, beyond, for prudence sake, furnishing the stipulated pecuniary supplies. He, accustomed to mystery and secrecy in his profession, was not at all surprised, and attended to her wants as punctually as he did to those of his other patients. Within a few weeks of the final catastrophe, the mental condition of Mrs. Bond wonderfully improved. It has been observed, in the majority of cases, and especially in those where lunacy has been a chronic affliction, that, as death approaches, the mind recovers a more healthful vitality and vigorous tone. As if to confirm the belief, that decay of the body is but the prelude to a glorious enfranchisement of the soul, the brain on the threshold of extinction—

"Springs upward, like a pyramid of fire,
Into the wild expanse"

of the chaos into which it is entering, and would burn the brighter, because for the last time—

"Or expire"

like a star hurled from its sphere, and quenched, in all its glittering beauty, in an instant.

She had forgotten the whole of the frightful demoralisation she had received at the impious hands of the impious Jasper; but distinctly remembered the particulars of her intrigue with the handsome Bloomfield. It broke upon her without a single regret, for her heart told her he was the only man she had ever loved. She resolved, though, to carry the secret with her to the grave. As to her husband, she thought of him and his connections with disgust, and wondered she could have been so infatuated as to have fallen into their snare. Buoyed up—let it not be said deceived—by the only real sexual attachment she had ever formed, she did not—she had not the moral capacity to discern—that she had afterwards, as far as mere consequences were concerned, fallen into one of a worse and more fatal description. But it is one of the blessed prerogatives of ignorance not to see too far, or weigh things too nicely, and so let the poor victim of the passing fancy of one of the real gods of nine-tenths of society—a man of rank and wealth—pass to her account, without the conviction in her mind that *she* had sinned by submitting to the casual alliance. It was a memory that mingled a little honey with the gall in her bitter cup of death.

As her debility increased, she was seized with a longing to see her father, her only surviving parent; but a nervous timidity prevented her preferring the request until she was informed that her days were numbered. Then a shivering dread of meeting him crept over her, and she would hide her face in the bed-clothes, and weep in secret. The clergyman who visited her fortunately happened to be one of those mild, gentle-hearted creatures, who addressed his Maker in the modest language of pious sincerity; and his meekness and unadorned simplicity so won upon her confidence, that she made him acquainted with the wish. A letter was instantly dispatched to her father, and, by noon on the following day, she beheld, for the first time since her ill-starred marriage, his portly figure, standing, in silent sorrow, by her bed-side. The good minister retired, and the old costermonger, who had previously been informed that there was not the slightest hope of her recovery, took the wan hand of his sadly-wasted child in his own brawny one, and sat looking at her pale, pinched features, until the scalding tears prevented him seeing anything but a shadowy outline of a poorly-furnished bed.

"Susan!" at length uttered the afflicted sire.

"Father!" was the response.

The old man bent his grey head down to his daughter's face, and imprinted a kiss on her thin lips, which assured her of full and implicit forgiveness.

"How do you feel, Susan, dear?"

"Happy! oh, so happy, dear, kind father! I have not felt like this for many a long day!"

A pause ensued, which the father, although he longed to ask many questions, did not dare to break.

"Bury me in some country churchyard, where there are plenty of pretty flowers, will you, father, dear?"

"I will—I will; but it won't be yet. You must bury your old father first."

"Don't cry, father! I'm going to a good place, and when you go there, a long, long time after me, we shall be so happy! And mother will be there, and she will sing 'My pretty Jane,' again for us; and perhaps that funny old song, that used to make us all so merry."

The old man groaned, and in his heart bitterly cursed the canting crew who had wiled his child from her cheerful home. He laid all the blame on the shoulders of the Ebenezer congregation of hypocrites. He felt convinced they had driven his child mad with their insane demonstrations of piety, and then left her to die, without friend or acquaintance near her, to close her eyes. His daughter, however, did not, could not possibly know what his sentiments were: for he had too much kindness in him to distress her by an utterance of them; and her mind was too much occupied with other sensations for even the suggestion to cross it, that she ought to tell him everything.

"Don't tell anybody about me, will you, father, dear? I wouldn't like to be talked badly about when I'm dead. Will you promise me, father, dear?"

"Certainly. I shan't be long after you, so it shall be forget and forgive with me."

"Bless you, father! Kiss me—don't leave me?" The old man clasped her hand, and she murmured: "what a good, dear father you are!"

Then she gently dozed off to sleep, and the old man, fearful of disturbing her, retained his seat on the bed, until he was interrupted by the entrance of the clergyman, who informed him that his child was gone to "another and a better world!"

CHAPTER XVI.

IS RETROSPECTIVE AND DIMLY EXPLANATORY.

ALL things, says the babbling dame—tradition—have a beginning, a middle, and an end; now, as this most veracious narrative of some of the transactions of metropolitan married life has arrived at the second and most critical stage of its transitory career, it behoves the learned compiler to pause, and, like a skilful wielder of the pen, collect and reorganise the forces, scattered, in pleasant confusion, over some two hundred columns of the smallest type that ever levied contributions on the flying quill of an author, before new scenes are ventured into, or old friends are tempted into the bewildering mazes of more marvellous adventures.

The gallant Captain Morris—having constituted himself the approved champion of virgin innocence, and thereby incurred the pains and penalties of not only a temporary exile from the sphere where bright eyes and rosy mouths are the constellations that attract to them the bravest hearts, but actually the loss of a flattering social distinction, with its pecuniary advantages—is surely entitled to precedence in this explanative category, for it is intended to be nothing else. After his midnight duel with that rather rough wooer, Colonel Stanley, he did himself the honour to escort the gentle and uninjured, but excessively

frightened Lucy, to her destination, in the bosom of the rugged but picturesque—and when measured by the value of the term applied to towns—honest mountains of old Cambria. What occurred between them, when, on the following morning, they stood under the old tree by the brook, the music of whose running water had rippled through their brains when they were gleeful children, it would be unbecoming to disclose. All that it is needful to relate is, that Lucy, who had studiously been kept in profound ignorance of the startling termination to the incident of her shameless abduction, parted from her deliverer with a blush on her fair cheeks, and a language in her dove-like eyes, which made the remotest pulse of the warrior thrill more keenly than ever did the trumpet-blast of battle.

"She loves me," thought he, as his eye drank in all the beauties of his native valley; and then unrepiningly saw them tossed carelessly at the feet of one all-absorbing, effulgent idea. "She loves me!" And down the mountain-path he strode, like one distraught. What recked he of precipices or unfenced mine-shafts? A maiden, as pure as the first sun-beam that burst through the mists of his native hill-tops, had deigned to think him the foremost man of all the earth; and he walked, as only does the man who, after a weary search, has found the diamond he sought. To his imagination her charms were so matchless, beside the recollection of those he had impurely enjoyed, that a new and more delicious prospect opened upon him, and he felt amazed within himself that he had ever yielded to any one of the exotic pleasures that delude men into the paths over which, in their hours of correction and contrition, they fancy they ought to have trodden with reluctance. But who would live and thrive if he did not do periodical penance for his transgressions? There is an up-hill and a down-hill in all sublunary transactions; and it is only the fools who imagine they remain on the top of the ascent. It is a sign of honesty when the self-esteem of a man now and then feels a twinge of regret or compunction, or in any manner submits itself to the chastisement of that arrogant doctrinarian, conscience. We all of us have our idols; and if we can at any time knock down the worst, there are hopes of amendment in us. Walter was rapidly whipping himself into a virtuous fever, which might have led him into a labyrinth of promises, when he was pulled from the stilts he had mounted, by the brandy-and-water sounding voice of his *vis-a-vis* from town, and sole witness of his duel—the detective, who owned to the *soubriquet* of "Jemmy from Town."

"I say, captain, these hills aint 'zactly the place to skulk in, and as the colonel's as dead as a herring, the sooner we get to town the better for both of us. Of course you're for the continent, and as that aint in my l'ne, the sooner you and me parts company, the better for both of us. It's my duty to arrest you, but as I'm only one, and there isn't a bumpkin of a constable about, of course you mizzled, and I couldn't help it!"

Walter handed the complaisant and broadly-hinting detective all the money he could spare, and, knowing every inch of the country well, he acceded to the prudence of the advice, that they should at once separate. Jemmy, without looking either to the right or left—Justice and her minions are always blind—trudged away; the moment he had disappeared from view, Walter followed his example, and, taking what country people term a "near cut," speedily arrived at a posting-house, and had himself whisked to the nearest railway station, from whence, on the same day, he reached town; and, after visiting his lodgings, and providing himself with all the cash he could command, went forth to play at that exciting, but rather troublesome game, hiding from the officers of justice. The first place he visited was Bloomfield House, where he was promptly ushered into the presence of its lovely and conjugally deserted mistress, the countess. Anxiety for her beloved sister of a verity was the paramount sensation that prompted her to rush to the valiant soldier, and almost throw herself into his arms. But Walter was now adamant against any such approach from that quarter, and, after greeting his old playmate kindly, he respectfully relieved her tender solicitude by an assurance of Lucy's unquestioned safety. He related the particulars of his sanguinary duel with the attempted violator of the house of his mother's best regarded friend. Violet trembled in every limb as she listened to the recital, and, with pathetic earnestness, entreated Walter to depart immediately for the continent. He warmly thanked her, and having, by his protestations, convinced her that he stood in no danger from the authorities at present, he kissed her fair hand—had not the new feeling for Lucy sprung up in his bosom, it would have been her lips—and hurried away. At the hall-door, a note was slipped into his hand; it was from Mrs. Smythe, and tenderly invited him to her house. To take a cab and obey the summons was but natural, it will be said; but it must also be confessed that Walter had a secret desire to bring his intrigue with the gay and beautiful wife of the banker to a more successful, or, at all events, more satisfactory termination. She, on the other hand, ardently desired to elope with Walter—for, since the summer-house affair, she had fallen madly in love with him, and felt convinced that, with his high sense of honour, he would marry her immediately after Smythe had divorced her. She was spared the pain of knowing how deeply and enthusiastically Walter loved the innocent Lucy. He was of too amorous a temperament to refrain from the society of the beautiful—would they could be said to have been good—and, to his shame be it declared, had set his heart upon completing the conquest of the dark-eyed Caroline.

"She is evidently as willing as I am, and it would be doing an injustice to both of us to disappoint her expectations." But Walter had not the slightest idea of an elopement: he hated the scandal and gossip such an affair provokes, and thought people who entertained a mutual partiality should gratify it without letting all the world into the secret. "The slier a love intrigue is, the sweeter it is," was his maxim.

Well, he met Mrs. Smythe, and their encounter was as warm as that impatient lady desired it should be. She felt rather glad than otherwise at the difficulty in which Walter's duel had placed him, for she felicitated herself on having him more completely in her power. She had no sooner been made acquainted with the whole of the details, than she resolved she should be the companion of his flight. She was so impetuous, and cast such bewitching glances on the susceptible Walter, while he told his plain, unvarnished story, that he, too, in the event of a journey being necessary, began to think she would be a cosy addition to his baggage. However, he had many arrangements to make before he left town, and reluctantly tore himself from her passionate embraces, after making an assignation to meet on the following day.

"Now," said Mrs. Smythe, while her beautiful bosom heaved, and her face actually beamed with exultation, "I shall get rid of my brute of a husband for ever, and in his stead have one of the finest and noblest hearted men in England. His kisses linger on my lips like the bloom on a peach, and I feel as if the light from his ardent eyes was shooting right through my heart. I must—I will have him, if I risk my present and eternal salvation by the deed. Oh, heavens! how hot I feel."

And, overpowered by her varying emotions, she sank upon a sofa, and surrendered herself up to the most intoxicating of love reveries.

Walter Morris, after leaving her, sought out Mrs. Wriggles, and from her learned the gratifying intelligence that Stanley's wounds had not proved mortal, and there were some faint hopes held out of his ultimate recovery. She offered him an asylum until the storm had blown over, which he gratefully accepted; and the same day he was put in possession of a small suite of apartments in her mysterious house, which had never been profaned by either the glance or footsteps of an officer of the law.

Mrs. Wriggles' object was to keep the captain out of the way of Mrs. Smythe, and Walter very obligingly promised to assist her, and at the same time maintain his agreeable correspondence with the latter.

As for Mr. Smythe himself, he was being driven half crazy by the persecution of the O'Blazes, who, on behalf of Lord Tyrone, had not only instituted legal proceedings against him, but lay in wait for him with the alternative of a hostile meeting with pistols, or a sound horsewhipping in a public thoroughfare. In such a situation it is not to be wondered at that he chose rather to console himself in obscurity with one of his mistresses, than run the risk of such an—in every way formidable—encounter. His wife, therefore, had all the field to herself, and she was not the woman to neglect such a favourable opportunity for improving her interests and gratifying her inclinations. Her friend, the countess, was busied—countenanced by her—in schemes to recover back her husband, and win again his love. Thus, while one lady sought to lose her spouse, the other was nervously endeavouring to regain hers.

Bloomfield, after his liason with the peeress, felt dreadfully fatigued; and, to relieve the monotony of his existence, devoted himself to some parliamentary duties, and actually, for the novelty of the thing, accepted several invitations to attend public meetings. His wife he rarely saw, for she had resolved not to permit him to approach her as a husband until he became entirely reformed, and thoroughly repentant. Thus the two merry wives of this chronicle were engaged in a series of plottings which, clashing with those of their husbands, and powerfully contrasting and occasionally mingling with those of the fiend Jasper, the pretty, but frail Alice, and the enigmatical Dr. and Mrs. Wriggles, produced a series of rather astounding incidents and marvellous occurrences.

CHAPTER XVII.

DR. WRIGGLES AT HOME.

Dr. WRIGGLES was one of those mysterious men who wear generations out, and yet retain possession of a wonderful bodily and mental vigour. He was one of those natural curiosities who are connecting-links between the past and present, and whose lives seem to be spun out like a thread of cotton, attenuated to a surprising fineness and extraordinary length. Thin, wiry, and bronzed, they appear more like Egyptian mummies than animated beings. Yet what a brightness is in their eyes! what an unyielding firmness in the play of their features! And how, when after sitting in as solemn a repose as grey-haired Saturn, turned to stone, they will start up as if moved by invisible wires, or re-animated by a touch of the life-giving power of the world—electricity. Like a frog, released from the knotted oak in which it has been entombed for centuries, they will frisk in the sunlight, and wonder that people should be surprised at their active vitality. Whole families and races fall before their eyes, and are swept away like the leaves that strew the ground in October; yet they betray no surprise, and, when their own immediate connections have disappeared, little sympathy. They have scarcely any affinity beyond that of kind to the living; and their sapless hearts only cling to their personal necessities and enjoyments. Their perception of the weaknesses of others is almost intuitive; and when they perceive the vanities, littlenesses, and selfishness that sway men and women in all things, they retire deeper into the recesses of their own well-stored existence, and become cold, harsh, and crabbed. They repel, instead of inviting approach. But all the warmer human passions do not die in them: there is one which lives, and breathes mellow tones, until the last string of the instrument breaks—it is love of children. A man may be as withered as a hoary tree, and as frozen in manner as the ancient god, but at the sight of a child, "fresh, with all its youthful pulses playing," the long-closed chamber of his soul will open to receive it, and he will caress it as tenderly as its mother would; his eyes will beam upon it with a fond expression; and, as he plays with its silken hair, and dreamily listens to its prattling, sweet visions of his own young days will steal upon his memory, and open up a gushing fount of the undying and inexhaustible love that mingles with and cherishes all human existence. With extreme age, petulance, doubt, and suspicion vanish, in the presence of a lovely child; and, in the reciprocity of the affection, how beautifully is it acknowledged that the child is the father of the man!

Dr. Wriggles was one of those cold, arbitrary old men, who, having apparently outlived all the uses for whose service the truest and noblest impulses were created, seem to look upon them with dry scorn and contempt; but he, like all his mummy prototypes, had a warm corner in his slowly-beating heart, and it was occupied by a devotion for the dark-eyed girl who crept to his knees in the darkness and the light, and sang for him snatches of old ballads, or talked with childhood's rapture of the green fields, bubbling brooks, and bright flowers that gem the earth as brilliantly as do the hues of health a virgin's cheek. This young girl, or rather child—for she had not yet attained fourteen years of age—was the clairvoyante Fanny, mentioned in previous chapters; and a more intelligent and docile creature never lived. Her shrewdness and vivid imagination were of great service to her protectors, or, as she had been taught to believe, parents, in their systematic and cleverly-managed mesmeric and other deceptions on the gullible public. Her strong, retentive memory, and a cultivated, poetical mode of expression, enabled her to go through the prescribed routine of her revelations with remarkable fluency and accuracy. All her senses, especially those of touch and hearing, were so acute, that she understood the slightest signal which her conductress gave her. Mrs. Wriggles, or, as she was known in the fashionable world, Madame Robertina, was her tutoress; and, owing to that personage's very prolific sources of information, and her intimate knowledge of the secret doings of high life, she was enabled, through Fanny, to make many a proud beauty tremble and quiver at her revelations. The doctor, who had loved Fanny from her birth, took delight in instructing her in all that forms the intellectual education of a woman. The rest he left to his co-partner; but Fanny did not thrive under the instruction. Her accomplishments, beyond a natural and assiduously-cultivated love of music, were extremely limited; for, when emancipated from control, and allowed to rove over the house, she was as giddy and wild as a kitten. And no wonder, for her only playmates were the doctor and Leoline, the bear. She loved both of them dearly, neither was ugly to her—the law of kindness robbed them of all their repulsiveness; and as for the doctor, he always felt amused and happy when alone with her, or sat watching her gambols with the grisly Leoline. It is proper, though, that this singular trio should be formally introduced to the reader.

The apartment was the same as that in which Jasper Sampson received so severe a chastisement. There was the same display of the ghastly remnants of mortality, the same chemical apparatus, and the same quaint, old furniture, and licentious pictures and engravings. The doctor was seated in his high-backed arm-chair, with his hands folded on his knees, and his glittering, serpent-like eyes bent, with a merry expression, on Fanny, who was playing with the bear on the hearth-rug, and making her perform a variety of antics. The group of the bear and the girl was an interesting one, and so thought the doctor, for as he gazed upon them, his meditations, clothed in language, took the following shape:—

"Beauty and strength, the twin pillars of nature! How glorious the colours shines of the one, and how rugged the exterior of the other! It is the same throughout all existence. The duality extends even to the smallest grain of sand or the minutest ray of light. How happy might the world be if it only knew its power; but the tiger-feeling, self, spoils all. The lion may lie down with the lamb—which means that beauty may ally itself to strength and yet not be disfigured; but both man and beast mar their natures, and set at nought the sovereign law of the universe—

kindness. See how this child, who has twined herself round my heart-strings, fondles upon that brute? And see how gently the dumb savage lets her heavy paws fall upon her fragile form, and with what care she enfolds the child of her mute adoption in her brawny embrace. Me she would devour, because she fears me; Fanny she would protect, because the child has been kind to her, and grown up in confidence under her eye. It is the same with man as with the lower animals—instinct and habit rules them all. Mind is but a higher grade of instinct, and who can set limits to its boundless extent?"

The doctor fell into one of his reveries, which lasted for some time, and, when he awoke from it, he found Fanny seated on a hassock at his feet, and the bear crouched close beside her. The doctor bestowed an earnest gaze upon the classic features and splendidly-dark eyes of the child as they looked up into his, and, patting her head playfully, inquired what she was thinking about.

"I was wondering whether Leoline had got a soul like me," was the response.

Now, before the doctor's answer is given, it should be premised that he was a philosopher, and, consequently, as a Catholic priest would say, a very great infidel.

"How do you know that you have a soul?" he inquired.

"I don't know, but when I go off into those mock trances that mamma makes me do, I sometimes go to sleep in real earnest—that is, I don't sleep, for I see mamma and the people in the room—but feel something like myself, and yet not myself. I feel cut into two pieces, and have such pleasant thoughts, and sometimes see strange things. It is that which makes me think I have got a soul."

"And so you have, my dear," said he, and then added to himself, "but it is in your mind, and that can be educated to any degree of perfection. Soul, indeed! what a vulgar idea of a solid, enduring materiality; but the world is fond of myths, and this is about as pretty a one as it could have. And the best of the joke is, that people fancy this mesmerism is a practical exemplification of the theory, quite forgetting that it spoils it altogether, by demonstrating that the powers of the mind are derived from the body, and that when the latter dies both are annihilated. Diseased brains give birth to incoherencies, and those, applied to current events or past relations, frequently startle by the correctness of their application; but it is mere coincidence. Revelation and prophecy are but coinages of the brain; but, being adopted as ideas, as expectancies, the mind can command their realisation. By dwelling on them, they become interwoven with the texture of the mental power of communities; and so circumstances are actually created—made purposely for the accommodation of what originally were fictions; and thus it is that prophecies are fulfilled, and pretended revelations corroborated."

"Many things I have seen and thought of, when that way, have come true, father," said Fanny, interrupting the thread of his sceptical reasoning.

"Name one thing that has been verified?"

"Oh, I could mention twenty; but one was very strange—at least I thought it so. Long, long ago I dreamt that I saw a handsome, dark lady; she looked into my face, and, in a voice soft as a lute said, 'My child!' I looked up and said, 'mother!' Then she kissed me, and as she did so, I felt hot tears fall on my face, and she vanished. Long, long after that, a dark lady came to mamma's to have her fortune told, and I saw that she was the same that I had seen in my dreams. I saw her again in Greenwich Park, and she looked at me just the same way as she did when I was in my waking sleep. Wasn't that strange, father?"

"It was," replied the doctor, his thoughts wandering back some fourteen years, and then travelling to a speculation about the future.

"I should like to see that dark lady again. Oh, she was so handsome!"

The doctor mused a moment, and then, putting his lips to the child's ear, whispered:

"Your wish shall be gratified. You shall see that dark lady, and lie on her bosom, if you like."

"Oh, shall I?" exclaimed Fanny, clapping her hands, and giving way to all the exuberant mirth of childhood.

"But not a word of this to mamma?" cautioned the doctor.

"No, father; and now I remember, mamma said I was never to speak to that beautiful lady, only as she told me."

"Hush!" said the doctor, kissing her; "keep the secret, and I will keep my promise."

Fanny threw herself into his arms, and the old man folded her very tenderly on his bosom.

A knock at this moment sounded on the door, and the doctor, who always prudently reconnoitred before he admitted a visitor, upon opening the slide, to his amazement discovered a lady, closely veiled.

"Can I speak with Dr. Wriggles?" she inquired, in sweet but rather tremulous tones.

The doctor promptly answered in the affirmative, and, closing the slide, dismissed Fanny with a kiss, and sent Leoline to her den with a kick.

Upon admitting the lady, she proved to be tall, graceful, and commanding in figure, with an easy, graceful carriage of the body; but so closely veiled, that the whole of her features, with the exception of two flashing eyes, were completely concealed.

"Another slip," thought the doctor, as he handed her a seat; as she took it, he noticed that she trembled excessively. A rather awkward pause ensued, which was broken by the doctor's suavely inquiring how he might be of service to her.

"How long have you occupied these premises?" asked the lady, her agitation increasing as she glanced round the room, and apparently recognised many of its features.

"More years, madam, than you have numbered," replied the doctor, not at all surprised at the question, for he was frequently revisited by old patients; "for forty years this room has been my study, my chamber of consultation, and my closet of ease and retirement from a world I never loved."

The tones of his well-remembered voice—who that had once heard its cold, steel-like intonations could ever forget them?—thrilled through the lady; and her emotion became so violent that the doctor handed to her a restorative mixture, which he always had ready prepared for such emergencies. She took it, but without removing her veil, and, after becoming more composed, she tremblingly began with her queries:

"Fourteen years ago, a young lady, late one winter's evening, came to this house—she was very young and ——"

"Very pretty," said the doctor, seeing that she hesitated; "and that, I presume, was the cause of her coming to me."

"Do you remember the circumstance?" inquired the lady, eagerly.

The doctor shook his head, and drily remarked, that, at the particular distance of time referred to by his visitor, he was honoured by the confidence of so many young and beautiful ladies, that, without the precise date and some supporting details, he could not tax his memory with any particular instances in which he had rendered professional services.

"The night was a dark December one, and a storm swept over the metropolis. The lady—or rather girl, for she had not attained seventeen—was brought hither by a—a——"

"A midwife?"

"Yes."

"The case was a difficult one, then? Proceed, and I will endeavour to recollect it."

"The girl, as well as her pain would allow her, implored for secrecy—a large sum of money was paid—can you not remember it from that fact?"

"No, indeed I cannot. You give too meagre an outline. Describe the case itself—was it a simple delivery or an extinction?"

The lady's whole frame shook, as, yielding to an uncontrollable impulse, she replied:

"It was her desire, expressed through the medium of her attendant, to be relieved from the burthen of a shame incurred in moments of burning levity and youthful indiscretion."

"The day of the month, if you can recollect it?" asked the doctor, with professional brevity.

"The tenth of December, 18—."

The doctor quietly turned over the leaves of the huge book to which allusion has been before made, and, having arrived at the page for which he had been seeking, read the following pithy paragraph:—

"Caroline Fitzherbert, delivered by me of a female child, December 10, 18—."

The lady bounded up from her seat as if plucked from it by some strong invisible hand, and the action, throwing aside her veil, revealed a countenance whose lineaments the doctor well remembered.

"My God!" exclaimed she, clasping her hands together; "you know all?"

"I do, my dear madam; but pray be composed—there is not the slightest necessity for this intense agitation."

"Do you recognise me?"

"Most certainly. I never forget the faces I have once seen. Your charms have ripened into those of the luxuriant woman, but there are the same brilliant black eyes, the same splendid features and raven tresses, and the same sylph-like, but, perhaps, more fully-developed figure."

"What more do you know?"

The doctor returned to his book, and read:

"Three years afterwards she married Mr. Smythe, the then junior, but now principal partner, in the banking-house of Messrs. ——."

Mrs. Smythe sank back into her seat, her countenance flushing and paling under the pressure of a multitude of emotions.

"The child—what became of it?" at length she gasped forth.

The doctor paused a moment, and, as if desirous either of testing her strength of nerve or affection, said:

"It was, if I remember correctly, your repeatedly and vehemently expressed desire, that it should not be born alive?"

Mrs. Smythe groaned, and then, in piteous accents, implored to be told the truth.

"Your instructions, lady, were imperative," said the doctor, severely.

"They were; but do not taunt me now with the unnatural crime. I was mad then, and wished to bury my infatuation in endless oblivion. Now a most unaccountable yearning possesses me. I pant to see and embrace my child, if living, and, if dead, to be assured of the fact, and then strive to forget her, as I have forgotten her father. I implore—I beg—I pray of you—do not keep me in suspense—tell me the truth?"

"The child was born alive," said the doctor, after a pause.

"Did it live?" inquired the mother, bending forward to catch the reply.

"It did—but was a fragile, delicate thing. To conceal your situation you laced so tightly that it is a wonder a living child was born at all."

As Mrs. Smythe remembered all the shifts and expedients to which she had had recourse to conceal her pregnancy, and the half-suppressed accusation and ironical remarks her appearance excited, a burning blush suffused her face, but soon gave place to a deadly pallor, as she inquired what became of her offspring. The doctor, with the promise he had given to Fanny so fresh in his mind, felt an inclination stealing over him to introduce the mother to her child; but the reflection that he should have to part with his favourite, and provoke the enmity of his co-partner, Mrs. Wriggles, restrained him, and he resolved to delay a candid explanation until after his interview with her. The agony, though, depicted in the beautiful countenance of Mrs. Smythe, touched him sensibly. Old as he was, he was not adamant to a woman's appeal—his peculiar notions of the value of human nature did not comprise a recognition of the torture which only a woman can inflict upon a woman, so he determined to allow a ray or two of light to penetrate the darkness that surrounded the guilty, but still not wholly vitiated mother.

"As soon as the child was born it was carried away by the person who officiated as nurse. You, believing it dead, were impatient to get away, and at the end of the third day departed, with the conviction that the affair would thenceforth remain a profound secret. On the same day I again saw the child, and was amazed at beholding it alive, and likely to thrive. I paid it all the attention which my skill could suggest, and at the end of a month was gratified at seeing that it promised to be as likely a child as any I had ever seen brought up by hand."

"But what became of it? You torture me!" ejaculated Mrs. Smythe.

"It was sent out—together with two other children—to be nursed in the country."

"Did you ever see it afterwards?"

"Frequently. It throve amazingly, and is alive now, for ought I know to the contrary."

"Merciful powers! Where—oh, tell me where?"

"I can ascertain," said the doctor, evasively.

"Will you promise me to do so, and soon? Oh, let it be soon! To-day—to-morrow!"

"It shall be as soon as I can; but I cannot say whether to-day or to-morrow—indeed, or this week; but be satisfied that I shall keep my word. I have hitherto done so, and am too old now to begin the experiment of a new course of life."

Mrs. Smythe frantically entreated that more expedition should be used in the inquiry, but the doctor was obdurate, but exerted himself so effectually to pacify her, that she at length placed implicit reliance on his solemn assurance, the more especially as it rested on a solemn foundation—the hope and certainty of receiving a promised five hundred pounds in case of success.

"After the lapse of fourteen years, without one word of inquiry about your child, it appears strange—you will excuse me when I say so—strange that you should be so suddenly and vehemently anxious about its welfare!" said the doctor, eyeing her intently.

"I am about going abroad," she replied; "perhaps for ever, and wished to know its fate before I departed."

"But have you not all along laboured under the conviction that it was no more?"

"I certainly did until very recently," she replied, and then explained to the doctor the particulars of the revelation scene at Madame Robertina's, the mesmerist, where she was informed that the child lived, and her subsequent encounter with the gipsy girl in Greenwich Park. The doctor, of course, knew all this before, and in answer to her inquiry as to whether any human being had the faculty of reading the past, and foretelling the future, in any individual's conduct, gravely replied in the affirmative.

"The soul," said he, "can be disengaged from the body, and, untrammelled, exercise its illimitable power of prescience. It can read the past and future as plainly as we can the occurrences of the present."

"I am inclined to believe so," said Mrs. Smythe, "for the little girl whom I saw at the mesmerist's, told me of things of which I thought—indeed felt positive—that no human being had the slightest knowledge."

"It is even so. As one of our greatest writers has declared, 'There are more things in heaven and earth than are dreamt of in the philosophy of any of us!' The souls of the living and the dead are the same; but in the living they are so trammelled by the body, that their power is only exhibited in their momentary emancipations from its slavery. Mesmerism effects this liberation, and astonishes us with the mysteries of quite another world."

This species of philosophical explanation was not clear to the material mind of Mrs. Smythe; and perhaps that may account for her having fallen into a reverie, which lasted several minutes. At last she said:

"I am aware that you learned men hold the mysteries of the Catholic church in contempt; and you will doubtless smile at my asking you to favour me as you did before."

A smile, cold as that which mocks the marble lips of a statue, played round the doctor's mouth, as he comprehended the whole of the moral scheme of the lady before him.

"Have you not been to confession since I last saw you?" said he.

"Not since my marriage," she replied. "My husband was an infidel, and prohibited it altogether, and I—I ——"

"Being too much engaged with other duties, did not think proper to disobey his commands," said the doctor.

"Habit is powerful, learned sir; and, having fallen into other companies, I acquired their manners and and tone of thinking. But all my ancestors belonged to the Catholic church; and this insatiable longing to do justice to my child, has awakened a desire to once more receive religious consolation from a minister of my own creed. Will you oblige me now as you formerly did?"

"I will with pleasure. Come to me about this hour to-morrow, and you may unburden yourself to one of your own clergy—a pious, holy man."

Mrs. Smythe murmured her thanks; and, after placing a substantial sum in the doctor's hands, departed.

"A true daughter of a corrupt church," chuckled the doctor, as soon as she had gone; "she would confess her past iniquities, do penance, and then com-

mence again as jovially as ever. She shall pay handsomely for the accommodation, though; and I don't see why I should not play the priest myself. I have done it before; but, bah! I am now only fit to listen to the prattle of children. The twaddle that should comfort sinful manhood and womanhood must fall from more buxom lips than mine. I'll be bound Father Brown is blowing a cloud, as they call it, at the Magpie and Stump; and he is a clever fellow, and can do the thing well for a five-pound note. Three daughters for the church already secured, and with them rich inheritances, of which large slices will fall to me. I must be cautious, though, or all will be discovered."

A door in one of the panels opened, and in walked Mrs. Wriggles, rubbing her hands and smiling, as if highly delighted with herself.

"Guess who's coming?" said she.

"Don't know; guess who's been here?"

"Can't tell; guess first?"

"Can't."

"Captain Morris."

"Whew!" blew the doctor; "but a cashiered officer, and a harum scarum devil to boot, is no great catch. He is on the hide-and-seek, after his duel, I suppose. How is Stanley?"

"Queer! his life hangs by a thread. You will like Walter when you see him. He is one of those brave, dashing fellows who take the world as they find it."

"He is welcome, Jackina, and shall be protected. But how fare all your schemes with the Bloomfield family?"

"Never more promising. I have both husband and wife under my thumb, and could crush one or both at any moment."

"What would that avail you?"

"Nothing; and, therefore, instead of revenging any of my wrongs upon them, I intend to do them all the good I can. You said you had had somebody here—who was it?"

"A friend of yours, I believe; one Mrs. Symthe, formerly Caroline Fitzherbert."

Mrs. Wriggles stared, as if struck with astonishment at this announcement."

"What did she want?"

"Her child."

"Indeed! Then the hints I threw out to her like baits have taken? What did you say?"

"Admitted the fact of the child's being born alive, and still living."

"Did she wish to see it?" inquired Mrs. Wriggles, eagerly.

"She was half frantic in her desire; and I half promised she should have the child."

"That she never shall!" exclaimed Mrs. Wriggles, vehemently. "Sooner than let her have the sweet consolation of a mother, I'd bury a knife in the child's heart, and rip it out before her face—the faggot!"

"The hatred you bear that woman is singularly intense," said the doctor, setting himself down in his easy chair, and regarding Mrs. Wriggles with an air of curiosity. "I don't love my fellow-creatures—indeed, for sixty years I have waged war upon them—but I don't remember ever hating any one in particular for any length of time. I rather suspect, Jackina, that in your violent dislike of the whole of your sex, you single out individuals, and wreak upon them the whole of your revenge?"

A malignant expression crossed the features of the old woman, as she bitterly replied:

"Indiscriminate hatred is like indiscriminate love

—false and hollow—a mere morbid affection, which is perpetually pursuing a shadow. Real hatred can only be sustained by the presence of objects on which to pour out its wrath. Now I have those objects—they are before my eyes—and that woman is one of them."

"But hatred, like love, must be based on a motive?" interposed the doctor.

"I am perfectly aware of that; and my hatred of that woman, superbly beautiful as she is, is so intense, that there is no hell of torment deep enough for me to plunge her into."

"But the cause—the cause, Jackina?" inquired the doctor, exhibiting signs of impatience.

"Is this: when I had fallen, as the world, with its mocking hypocrisy, terms it, from the high estate of woman, and carried the fruit of my obedience to a natural law in my arms, the parents of that woman spurned me from their door as a harlot and strumpet, and threatened to let loose their dogs upon me if I did not fly. I turned and cursed them and all their race; and well have I kept my oath. I was but a beggar then; but I have lived to see them all but two buried as beggars, and rated lower in the world's opinion than the poor girl they kicked from their doors, with her starving bastard in her arms. She and a childless uncle are all that survive of the accursed brood."

"She, I presume, will be his heiress?" said the doctor, carelessly.

"She entertains the hope," replied Mrs. Wriggles; "but it will never be realised: for the obstinate old fool loves chastity so dearly, that he would cast his own child upon the pitiless world if she committed a *faux pas*. This child of Caroline's, therefore, will be damning evidence against her. Besides, she has cuckolded her husband, and I have ample proofs of her guilt. In addition, she is now preparing for flight, and it can only be with a man; for her appetites are so great, that, rather than leave them ungratified, she would prostitute herself to her own footman."

"The reasons you give for your animosity are strong ones," said the doctor, oilily, "and I think perfectly justified by the provocation; but don't you think you might manage better, through this child, than inducing the old uncle to disinherit your enemy. People of Mrs. Smythe's temperament, and especially females, are apt to be superstitious; now, could we not so work upon her imagination, as to induce her to make Fanny her sole heiress?"

"Pshaw! her husband stands in the way of any such arrangement."

"He could be got rid of. He is already tired of her, and would divorce her instantly, if he had the power. Is she not fond of your protegé, Captain Morris? Ah, have I touched the right vein?"

"No," exclaimed Mrs. Wriggles, fiercely; "he may divorce her if he likes. I am sure he will, but she shall never possess a farthing of her uncle's property. She shall be a beggar — the common strumpet that she was—and then I shall be satisfied! I want revenge, not money! Indeed I would not receive a fraction of the stiff-necked papist's money."

"Then I will," thought Wriggles; "and, to obtain my own purposes, must thwart yours; and I will begin with the priest and the confessional. Well, well, Jackina," said he, aloud, "have your own way. I would not for the world attempt to thwart the pretty project you have formed. Let us talk of something else. When will your friend Walter arrive? I should like to see this non-pareil of a man!"

"I expect him every moment, and shall leave you to entertain him, for I have an engagement to fulfil with the countess."

"With all my heart. But how do you progress with that affair of the countess's."

"Through my management her love for her husband is rapidly returning, but he is so immersed in dissipation that he never bestows a thought upon her. They meet in private like strangers, and in public like the most well-bred couple in the world. But he loves her, and she shall be happy yet."

"What queer bodies you women are!" laughingly said the doctor. "Here we have the countess, as warm a personage as Venus herself, wishing to regain her husband, and yet obstinately persisting in a refusal of conjugal rights until he shall have changed—become reformed, as it is termed. It's a funny chase, and if she don't slip by the way, I'll make Leoline make a supper of my withered bones. On the other hand, we have Mrs. Smythe running away from her husband; and, then again, as if to complete this precious trio of merry wives, we have the Lady Tyrone, whose husband would absolutely starve if it were not for her matchless impudence. She has hooked Bloomfield, I hear too. Now how the deuce will all these parties find their way out of this labyrinth of intrigues?"

"As they best can," sneered Mrs. Wriggles; "but as to my Lady Tyrone, I should think her hash was settled! Her husband, or her brothers, rather, have brought an action of *crim. con.* against Smythe, and, as the proofs are clear, they will get a verdict, of course."

"The case will never come into court," said the doctor. The husband and brothers are too needy to be satisfied with a five hundred pound verdict. Besides, Smythe, wanting to get rid of his own wife, must go into court with clean hands, and so he will submit to be fleeced of a swinging sum, and the matter will be squashed."

Mrs. Wriggles assented to the truth of these deductions, and expressed a hope that they might faithfully be reduced to practice, for Lady Tyrone was just that kind of daring intriguante whom she could tolerate, if not exactly admire.

"What has become of that little wasp, Alice?" inquired the doctor.

"She was dying of love for Walter a few days ago, but now a new calamity has overtaken her. The child she had by Burton has disappeared from Brighton, where it was at nurse, and the loss of it has laid her up. The countess seems attached to her, for she is unremitting in her kindness. I suspect that fiend, Jasper, is at the bottom of it all!"

"Very likely. What a supreme rascal that fellow is! The pranks he has played lately are the most extraordinary that ever fell under my notice!"

The doctor smiled, so did Mrs. Wriggles, and both their smiles expanded until their lips opened wide enough to allow a hard, dry, cackling laugh to escape from them. Their merriment was interrupted by a knocking at the door, so unusually loud, that Leoline growled, and, shaking herself, made the door of her den creak upon its hinges.

"That's Walter," cried Mrs. Wriggles, starting up; "he musn't see me, or I shall be kept gossiping all night." And so saying, she vanished by the way she had entered.

"Now for this paragon of a man," thought Wriggles; "I have a good mind to let Leoline loose and try his courage—it will be a bit of fun, won't it Leo.?"

He unfastened the bar of the den, and out crawled the bear. Wriggles then, as usual, reconnoitred through the slide in the door, and, having satisfied himself of the quality of his visitor, admitted him. It was Walter, looking very stately in his long blue military cloak.

"Your place, my friend, is as well barred and bolted as Newgate!" said he; but the words had no sooner escaped from him, than his quick glance at once detected the stealthy approach of Leoline. Now, although Walter had in his time hunted tigers, boa constrictors, and wild elephants, he did not feel at all comfortable in the presence of such a beast; and, quickly throwing aside his cloak, placed himself in a scientific and approved posture of self-defence. Wriggles mounted his chair to enjoy the spectacle, and, as he did so, muttered:

"Not a muscle of his body quivers! his cheeks pale a little, but see how his eyes brighten. Don't be too rash, Leoline, or you may get a compliment or two you won't like."

Leoline approached with much caution, and as soon as she had come within range, raised herself on her hind-legs, and prepared to bestow upon her antagonist her favourite hug; but, just as she was about doing so, she received such a tremendous blow under the ear, that she fell right over on her back, and howled dismally. This disgrace so enraged her that she became furious, and made a savage attack on her opponent. But Walter, not a whit daunted, planted his blows so skilfully, and dodged about so nimbly, that he kept her at bay, and punished her into the bargain. Weight and strength were against poor Leoline so long as she was kept at arms' length; but, finding her old mode of attack fruitless, she cunningly changed her tactics, and advanced against Walter on all fours. This the doctor perceived, and called her off; but she was not driven into her den before her sides had been well scored by the bar of iron which the doctor always kept red-hot for such a disciplinal purpose.

"A curious reception, this," growled the panting Walter; "you may thank your stars, friend, that I came without my sabre. If I had brought it, your menagerie would have had a tenant the less!"

"And I should have been deprived of the pleasure of witnessing as pretty a pugilistic encounter as a man might desire to see," said the doctor, merrily; "be seated, Captain Morris, and forgive poor Leoline: it's not often she sees such a tall fellow as yourself, and she only wished to try your mettle."

"Dr. Wriggles, I presume?" said Walter, speedily recovering his habitual good humour.

"The same," replied the doctor, regarding the bold, open, and handsome countenance of the soldier with admiration.

"I am sorry to trouble you," said Walter, "but an old lady—ahem, not exactly an acquaintance, but a deuced good friend in need—in fact—how stupid I am—in fact, Mrs. Wriggles herself, assured me of a hearty welcome under your roof."

"She did right," said the doctor, moving about with an alacrity quite surprising for one of his years, and producing bottles of brandy, wines, tobacco, pipes of half a dozen varieties, and cigars in abundance. "What an honest looking face," thought he, as he busied himself with furnishing the table; "a long chat with him will be quite a treat. I wonder whether he is hungry."

Walter confessed that he was, and in a trice a tray was brought in, loaded with a tempting luncheon, to which the fugitive did ample justice. After the repast, Walter betook himself to brandy-and-water and a richly-mounted, tempting looking meerschaum; the doctor did the same, and, more fuel having been heaped on the fire, the pair stretched out their legs, and prepared themselves to enter into a conversation upon any topic that first suggested itself. The doctor had taken a fancy to Walter, and the latter to the brandy and pipes placed at his disposal; so the pair managed to jog on pretty well. Walter's frankness and joviality at length so affected the doctor, that he ventured a rough sketch of his life.

"Where I was born I don't know, nor did anybody ever take the trouble to tell me, so the question of my parentage must remain in its comfortable state of oblivion. All that I can recollect of my childhood was receiving more kicks than pence, and more prayers to learn to chaunt than bread to eat. It was much the same, though, as that of every poor thing who is abandoned by its parents—hunger blows and dirt were my portion of human existence; but somehow or another I managed to creep up to manhood, and to be appointed parish priest in a little village near the obscure country town where I was whelped—this was in France, a long, long time ago. Well, I managed to get on pretty well for some time; but mixing with my parishioners introduced me to their wives and daughters, and they created such a ferment in my blood, that I took to hugging my pillow, and giving the rein to the most lascivious longings. A buxom wife—a pleasing, merry dame of about forty—one morning came to confession, and, as I was then in a burning fever, and as giddy as a goose, I was rather incoherent in my examination; and this, no doubt, attracted her attention, for she began tenderly to inquire after my health, and asked me where I felt the pain. She felt my pulse—was it there? no; my head? no; my bosom? no; my stomach? r ; she felt lower—'Yes, by God!' shouted I, 'it is there, and I do believe I shall go mad!' The merry wife pulled me into the vestry, and there I took my first lesson in love. My *chere amie* liked it so well, that she came every morning for a couple, and this system of tuition lasted for nearly two months, when I began to tire of the employment, and to wish for a more juvenile tutoress. I was getting very artful then, and had cast my eyes upon a lovely creature of sixteen, who came to me for ministerial consolation. She was as innocent as a dove, and I was puzzled how to manage. But the confessional gives us great power over females. I began with a number of questions on the subject of chastity, to which she returned the most *naive* replies, for she did not understand what I meant. I knew she had a cousin, a strapping fellow of nineteen, so I asked whether he had ever taken any liberties with her? No; what did I mean? Did he ever kiss you? Yes; many a time. Did he ever put his hand in your bosom or up your clothes? No; what should he do that for? I was puzzled, and desperately launched into the most critical questions you can address to a woman. But she did not understand me, and, as example should always follow precept, I shewed her what her cousin might do to her, and asked again whether he had? Oh, no! show it me again.

The little devil after this interview grew so amorous, that, as ill-luck would have it, she fell into the family-way. I thought of asking her to swear the brat upon her cousin; but then the fellow might want to have the privileges as well as the honour of a father, and that idea I could not bear, for I had become attached to the girl, so I persuaded her to walk off with five hundred louis d'ors, laid up in a bag for her wedding-day, and to accompany me to Paris. She did so, and I bade a lasting farewell to the village and the old church. In Paris we were imprudent, for we lived so gay a life that all our money was nearly expended; and in the midst of our troubles poor Clementine was delivered of a dead child. She rallied, however, speedily; and, both having fine voices, we procured an engagement at one of the theatres, where, alas! I lost my Clementine. A certain young nobleman had taken a fancy to her; and, as most women are accessible to flattery, I trembled. I had cause. One evening Clementine would not sing, so I went to the theatre by myself. It was closed; so I had to return to our lodgings alone, and rather sulky, you may guess. I always had a soft tread—all priests have; for it is one of the first lessons taught them. Well, I approached my chamber gently, and, having a duplicate key, admitted myself—very gently, I presume; for I was not heard by two persons who lay on my bed. They were Clementine and the nobleman, of whom I had already got furiously jealous. Tired of their amorous conflict, they must have fallen asleep; so, as I got tremendously exasperated at such perfidy, I waited behind the curtain until they awoke. When they did, of course they had another love encounter; and, in the midst of it—even while his lips were on his paramour's, I stabbed him to the heart. Clementine begged for mercy; but I refused, and cut her head off. I then rifled the place—the count's body yielded a good sum in money and jewel—and made the best of my way to Calais, thence to Dover, and on to London, where I have remained ever since. At first I tried the stage, but my Italian was too bad; and then, by the advice of a cunning countryman of mine, I turned doctor—quack doctor, if you like — for I have no diploma, and soon had a goodly army of patients. I have been in practice in this one spot for upwards of sixty years, and have had all classes visiting me, from the heir apparent down to the servant girl, whose waist she had allowed her master's son unlawfully to expand. My experience has been tremendous, Captain Morris."

"I should think it had," replied Walter, regarding his new companion with interest; "but you have omitted one of your reminiscences, that of your marriage with your remarkably accomplished lady."

The doctor laughed in his usual dry manner, and, under cover of immense volumes of smoke, made the following candid confession:

"When I came to this country first, my tutor in the medical profession told me to call myself Wriggles, and when I first met Mrs. Wriggles I told her to do the same, and so we went together. But ah! that was near thirty years ago, and she was a fine woman then, and I was as vigorous and supple as an eel. She was rather exacting in her conjugal levies, and, at the end of some five or six years, I found if I did not divorce her from my bed I should soon disappear; so she assented to the reasonableness of the proposition, and I devoted myself to my studies and professional avocations, while she did as she liked. She had many lovers, I remember; but that did not annoy me, for my philosophy taught me not to envy others the meal for which I had no appetite."

"A very sensible determination," said Walter; "but I'm afraid such placitude would not suit me."

"I don't know that: wait until you attain sixty or seventy, and you will think quite differently from what you now do at thirty."

"Perhaps so, doctor," replied Walter, refilling his pipe; "but tell me, from your long and interesting experiences of society, do you think it has improved within the last half century?"

"In one sense, it has, most unquestionably. The majority of people in the present day are more intelligent and better informed than they were even five-and-twenty years ago; but, as regards morality, I don't recognise the slightest improvement."

"What, not in the absence of that coarseness which was so prevalent in the days of George the Third?"

"The progress-mongers point to that fact as triumphant evidence of our having taken a long march ahead of the customs of the last century, but it is all illusion. It is true that now-a-days more decency is preserved, but there is less candour. The offences that were complained of in our forefathers survive in us; the appetites are as greedy and selfish as ever they were, but they are gratified slily. There is as much hypocrisy in morals as religion, and I, from actual observation, know that lust is the all-devouring and ruling propensity, and all classes bow the knee to its fiery, avaricious impulses."

"You are severe!" laughed Walter; "but to what do you attribute such an immoral pestilence?"

"To the want of an efficient system of moral and physical training. The tendencies of human nature ought properly to be educated. The mind monopolises too much of our attention. Look at a school of boys. They are vaguely told that such and such things are very wrong, but are never instructed to properly recognise what is right. They mingle together, and acquire vicious practices which can never afterwards be wholly eradicated. Young females are worse than boys, and if there be a place where a girl would more likely be corrupted than another, it is a boarding-school. The habits acquired there are very polluting. Why, I have had girls under my care not fourteen years of age, who have rendered themselves totally unfitted for marriage."

"Horrible!" ejaculated Walter.

"It is too true," continued the doctor; "and when the body is thus early defiled, what can we expect the future mind to be? No, if physical training were a part of our educational systems, all such enormities would be avoided."

"What do you mean by physical training?"

"Why, simply this: I would cultivate the muscles of the mind as well as the body. I would examine the head of every boy and girl, and notice the predominant features of the organisation. Where amativeness, for instance, was large, I would counteract its tendency by bestowing a sound culture upon some other organs, and so destroy its excess. If such a branch of education were wisely developed, there would be a remarkable diminution in the number of adulteries and fornications; as it is, the functions of the body are allowed to grow up just as the inclination or circumstances permit, and the result is, that the natural propensity, lust, has degenerated into a frightful exaggeration."

"I am afraid, if I were to judge by myself, that you are too correct," said Walter; "but surely, under so decent an exterior as that presented by the everyday world in the aggregate, there must be a larger amount of virtue than vice?"

"You are wrong," replied the doctor; "there is more deceit. The mask you see is a pretty one, but the features are sadly distorted."

"But, doctor, as the subject on the *tapis* is love, do you seriously think there is more immorality now than formerly?"

"Most positively. Take ninety-nine out of a hundred young men—you may select them from any class in society—and you would find that every one of them had lost their chastity before attaining twenty-one years of age!"

"I believe that," answered Walter; "for I was but seventeen when a strapping wench taught me how to love her nicely, as she called it."

"Just so; and it is the same with large numbers of our women, especially of the lower orders. Their propensities never having been trained, they become fierce; and, instead of resisting temptation, they rather solicit and hasten its approach."

"Then, the supposition that all women who are not vestals are the victims of men's perfidy, is erroneous?"

"Like many other things that the gullible multitude swallow as facts: it is a popular error—a delusion; for the majority of our prostitutes have voluntarily embraced that mode of existence, and were as eager to enjoy the men they first submitted to, as the men were themselves."

"It often struck me that where the girl was perfectly agreeable, it was hard that the man should, when the peccadillo was discovered, be termed a villain, and all sorts of opprobrious epithets. But what do you think of our married women?"

"In high life, their passions are hot, and many of them have secret indulgences; but, taking them, and the majority of the wives in the middle and lower classes, infidelity is rather the exception, than the rule!"

"What are the leading causes of infidelity?"

"Intemperance. A drunken husband disgusts his wife, and, failing in the performance of every duty, she naturally flies for gratification, in some instances relief, to the first man that pleases her fancy. Beastly practices by the husband are another cause. He treats his wife as a harlot; and she, in return, with blunted sentiments and perverted instincts, becomes so amorous, that he is unable to satisfy her desires, and she flies to some one who can. Incompatibility of temper is another cause, and, perhaps, the leading one; for it is not until a pair have been married, that they discover they never were intended for each other. Then alienation commences, which soon leads to mutual disgust and mutual infidelity. The leading cause, though, is the mutual lust of the parties. Young men marry to have a home, and the monopoly of a woman, and also to avoid the consequences of promiscuous intercourse. It is purely a selfish feeling that animates them. Young women, also, marry to have a home, and the society of a man; and thus do a pair of fools, red-hot with concupiscence, rush into matrimony; and, after satiating themselves with enjoyment, find themselves rather in a prison than a paradise."

"Most philosophically argued," broke in Walter; "but all our speculations won't make the world either better or wiser; so here's to worry wives, and plenty of them."

The doctor cordially joined in the toast, and added:

"Husbands generally make their own beds, so let them lie on them, in blissful ignorance that their wives take a sweet revenge for every indignity and brutality they inflict upon them."

"Hurrah, doctor! may cuckolds flourish."

"They cannot but do so, while such Apollos of fellows as you Life Guardsmen embellish human nature. You belong to a sadly immoral corps, captain."

"Tut! they are no worse than the line; for, when I was a marching sub, I had sweethearts galore at every station. The women everywhere like a red coat."

"Because it covers a lusty body," drily added the doctor. And, after a world of such edifying conversation, Walter was shown to his chamber, and went to bed, and dreamed the dark-eyed banker's wife was locked in his arms.

"A true son of the earth," said the doctor to himself, after the captain's departure; "in the prime of manhood, he forgets there are many dark morrows in the calendar of his destiny. He will find it out time enough, so let his recklessness have its way. What a splendid priest he would make; why he would proselyte a whole town, with that noble figure and handsome face of his; the women would go frantic after him, and he might be as opulent in concubines as the Grand Turk himself. By the way—and not a bad idea, either"—and here the old man smote his thigh smartly—"I'll tutor him, and he shall confess Mrs. Smythe. It will be a bit of fun. I'll see first, though, whether Brown's fit to be talked to."

The doctor, after securely barring the door, and, as an additional precaution, letting Leoline loose, left the room by the door which Mrs. Wriggles had used, and, investing his spare body in a capacious over-coat, quietly left the house, and proceeded to a tavern which stood some distance from his residence. Its appearance was questionable, and its customers much more so. However, it was the abode of Father Brown, a Jesuit, whose mission and tastes lay among the lower classes. He was a propagandist, who loved the bottle. He was seated in an upper room, administering spiritual consolation to a brace of damsels who were in a state of semi-nudity. The doctor merely looked in upon the worthy—a glance was sufficient to discern that he was in one of the last stages of intoxication.

"It is perfectly useless talking to him," growled the doctor, hastily descending the stairs; "the drunken fit is on him, and it will be sure to last a month. I must make a confidant of the captain, and,

as the woman's pretty, he will not object. Who knows, too, but that I may gain an adherent. The church is as charming to a gay fellow as the army, and if I could but win him over, what mighty things could be achieved among the merry dames of high life! The experiment is worth all the risk."

The next morning he entered Walter's chamber, and unceremoniously introduced the subject. As he had anticipated, the young soldier gladly accepted the office, and promised to exert himself to save the soul of the pretty sinner.

MRS. SMYTHE CONFESSES HER SINS.

MRS. SMYTHE was one of those ardent creatures whose natural soil appears to be Italy. When she seriously examined the state of her morals, she admitted they might, and, indeed, ought to be a good deal better; but then sin, and especially of one kind, was so very pleasant—it thrilled through her warm heart and throbbing veins, until she fell asleep, from very excess of joy; and when she awoke, and found herself alone, like Eloise, she lived on the memory of what had occurred—that her repentance was but momentary. Nurtured under the auspices of a faith which had infused into her mind a material idea of everything around her, to the spiritual conception of depravity she was a total stranger. Sin was only sin under peculiar circumstances, and, despite her strong will, and somewhat infidel tendencies, she clung to the habit—for in an educated person it can be termed nothing else—of believing in the efficacy of prayers to certain deceased personages, and the interposition of the clergy of the church to which she had been a pecuniary, if not in her own person a very zealous, friend. In her chamber she had a crucifix concealed, and a little waxen image of one Saint Fitzherbert, one of her remote ancestors. Her family, from time immemorial, had paid their devotions at his shrine, and he was regarded by them all as a sort of hereditary protective genius. In his life-time he had been something like St. Cuthbert—a very gay fellow—committing fearful havoc among virgins and matrons, and not over particular in money matters; for he had been known to have been guilty of pillaging and slaying divers persons on the king's highway. "It is never too late to mend," says the old proverb; and the roystering Fitz, all at once betook himself to a very staid and decorous mode of living. How this came about was owing to a peculiar circumstance in his career which deserves noticing. Being but slender in purse, he went out one day, and lay in wait for unsuspecting travellers. Presently one arrived who was so uncivil as to refuse the modestly-urged request to patiently stand and deliver. "By my faith, such is not the fashion of our country," urged the stranger; and Fitz., seeing him so perverse, lugged out his sword, and threatened to spit him as easily as he would a barn-yard fowl. The stranger, indignant at such discourtesy, accepted the challenge, and to it they went like two famous knights, all of the olden time. The contest was long and severe, but ended in Fitz. biting the dust, sorely smitten in a certain abdominal region, which he treasured above the rest of his body besides. The wound happily was not mortal to his burly frame—it had only incapacitated him for further exploits among merry wives and rosy maidens, and so, becoming disgusted with everybody but himself, he built a hut in a woody recess, and passed the remainder of his lengthened days in an approved state of hermitage. His fame spread; and when he died, in all the odours of sanctity, his bones were canonised, and worked miracles for ages. Great, though, as was their power over others, they had none over themselves; for they were one fine day, in the reign of the iniquitous Eighth Harry, cast into a muddy stream, and borne away for ever. Tradition, however, preserved his memory among all good Catholics, and among the number was Mrs. Smythe. Her waxen copy of her saintly ancestor was never out of her possession; and if she seldom invoked the aid of the original, when she did do so, it was with fervour.

On the evening on which she was prepared to unbosom herself to a representative of the creed of her forefathers, she experienced a mental composure which nerved her for the coming task. The conviction possessed her, that after a candid exposure of all her derelictions, it would be admitted by her ghostly father that she had been more "sinned against than sinning." There was one alloy, however, in this golden state of mind. She was perpetually thinking of the gallant soldier who was to bear her off, like another Helen. Her eyes flashed unchastely, and her bosom heaved, as certain delirious thoughts fired her brain. In fact, she was madly in love with Walter; and, in her hot haste, would have travelled as far as her of Sheba, to have tasted of his manly bounty. However, as the time for confession drew near, she endeavoured to compose herself, and succeeded so well, that she dressed herself without the assistance of her maid, and left the house without the privity of that accommodating person. The confessor, towards whom she was hastening, was awaiting her arrival in a room fitted up with all the appliances necessary to constitute a private chapel, in a very unfatherly and unghostly frame of mind. Little light entered the room, but that little served to disclose the outlines of a majestic-figured man, striding across the floor as hurriedly as a lover waiting for his over-due mistress.

"A transformation with a vengeance!" thought he; "from wielding the sword of her Majesty, to flourishing holy texts and sage precepts. I doubt much, if she be young and pretty, whether I shall be able to go through the category, which, by the way, is very long and damnably nasty."

And, taking up the manual of devotion, he improved his memory by another perusal, and was about beginning a second time to go over it, when the door opened, and in walked a lady, tall and graceful in figure, gently treading and gliding in gait, and closely veiled. The confessor, on her appearing, hastily took a seat with his back to the little window, from which the faint beams of a candle entered, and, throwing as much sweetness into his tones as possible, bade the penitent approach and unburthen herself of her transgressions.

She did so confidently, like one accustomed to tread such boards; and, with a grace which he thought bewitching, placed herself on her knees, at his feet.

"The devil!" almost ejaculated he, as she touched his knees; "I shall never be able to do it. Never mind, here goes—never venture, never win."

And, with a violent effort to banish carnal suggestions, he addressed himself to his holy task.

"Father!" said the penitent, meekly, "I fear much that I have been a grievous sinner."

"So have all of us," was the bland, mellow-toned reply of the mock priest; "but the power of the church is great, it can drive despair from the most hideous bosoms, and plant there a living hope of salvation. When did you last humble yourself at the feet of the one true apostolical and indivisible church? Confound the jargon!" added Walter, to himself; "I am afraid that, without the manual, I shall make a sad mess of it."

"Not since upwards of fourteen years ago," replied Mrs. Smythe.

"A sad omission," said Walter, gravely; "but it is given to the church to receive amends for such neglect; so be comforted, my daughter, and pour into my ears the story of your errors."

Mrs. Smythe paused a moment, and then, falling into the old habit of indulging in the connected narrative necessary on such occasions, thus began her confession:—

"Up to sixteen years of age, I was guiltless of many of the practices that are so familiar to us in after life. I may truly say I was as innocent as most children are."

"The frolics of childhood are as blameless as the laughter of angels."

"At sixteen I was a boarder at a fashionable seminary, and there more license, perhaps, was allowed me than was consistent with my religious duties or worldly welfare. I was as flighty and giddy as a bird, and my companions were no better—indeed, the majority were more evil-disposed than myself—and when we were alone we used to converse—and—and ——"

"Speculate about things forbidden—or rather—I—I should say, attempted—by the laws of our holy church?"

"Just so, reverend sir; and those freedoms created in me such a fever, that I yielded to an ardent, indescribable impulse, and, in the society of a gay young soldier, was unable to resist the spell of a youthful passion. I fell, father; but do not blame me, I was so very young."

"What were the consequences of—I presume—your clandestine meetings with this emissary of Satan?"

"A child—a little girl, I believe—for I never saw it."

"What? abandon your offspring? incredible!"

"I was so young, and my indiscretion made me mad, and insensible to every consideration and feeling, save the dread of exposure."

The confessor shuddered, as he listened to this candid avowal of the absence of the maternal sympathies in a mere girl; but, conquering his repugnance, mildly urged her to proceed:

"With whom was the child placed?" he inquired.

"I was wandering in the vicinity of the school one evening, half frantic with the idea that my condition could not much longer be concealed, when I encountered a woman who evidently belonged to some tribe of gipsies. She accosted me in the usual manner; but, after steadfastly eyeing me for several seconds, suddenly changed her tone, and abruptly taxed me with what I knew too well was the truth. In my agitation I confessed all, and implored her assistance. That she readily promised me, and instructed me how to dress so as to hide my shame. From that moment I surrendered myself wholly to her direction, and by her advice left school, and took up my residence with my guardian. As the period I so much dreaded approached, I procured an invitation to spend a few weeks in town to be sent to me from a distant relative; and, as my importunities were excessive, I was allowed to depart in the stage-coach by which it had been agreed, between me and my adviser, that she should be a passenger. On our arrival in the metropolis, she conducted me to her residence; and, on the same evening, owing to the fatigue and alarm my journey occasioned me, I was taken ill, and—and ——"

"Gave birth to the child you abandoned. Daughter, daughter, that was a heavy offence—a much heavier one than that which led to its commission."

Mrs. Smythe, at this, looked up rather surprised; but the face of her confessor was shrouded in such gloom that she only caught a faint glimpse of its outlines.

"Proceed," said he.

"On the third day I proceeded to my destination, and relieved my friends of all anxiety on my account, by a plausibly-concocted story of my having been taken ill on the road. The woman who had rendered me such assistance personated a lady traveller who pretended to corroborate my statement; and, as it was believed, and my health did not improve, in a few weeks I returned to the country, and concluded that the affair would never be discovered. I rewarded the woman out of the proceeds of the sale of some jewellery, and never, to my knowledge, saw her afterwards."

"A strange narrative. But tell me, at the time all this occurred, were you in communion with the church?"

"I was, and did penance at the shrine of the patron saint of our family—Saint Fitzherbert."

"And the hope of pardon was held out to you?"

"It was, and, as I prospered, and the secret remained undivulged, I believed that I was forgiven."

"There is always pardon for those who believe and have faith. Proceed."

"Three years passed swiftly away, and I grew up to be a woman, and all who knew me said I was handsome."

"They did right—at least, I mean they committed a spiritual error: praises of the person but provoke the lusts of the flesh. Continue your revelations. I shall make a mull of it yet, I'm afraid," thought Walter, as he felt his self-possession shaken by the warm, sweet breath of the penitent at his feet.

"During those three years," continued Mrs. Smythe, "I do not remember any very serious offence that I committed. My girlish fault had frightened me, and I led a very secluded life."

"Did you ever, during the period of which you speak, repeat the offence that led to your journey to London?"

"Never."

"Had you the inclination?"

"Sometimes."

"Did the temptation ever fall in your way?"

"Never. My guardian's friends and connections were mostly old people, and, in addition, we lived in a remote part of the country."

"Did your eyes ever carnally dwell on some good-looking menial?"

"Never."

"You conducted yourself, then, at all times, whether sleeping or awake, both in thought and deed, as became a chaste person?"

"Yes."

"Well, you attained ripened womanhood. What then occurred in your career?"

"I was married."

"The devil you were!"

Such an irreverent exclamation startled the lady so much, that Walter perceived it was necessary he should repair the mistake.

"Daughter," said he, "I am amazed at your intrepidity. Did you make your husband acquainted with the first terrible incident in your life?"

"I did not—was it necessary that I should have done so?"

"Certainly—that is, you should have done so as a matter of duty to your conscience; but, as a—a—a matter of taste and convenience, the necessity and prudence of the concealment deprived it of its most repulsive features. Where ignorance to your husband

was bliss, it would have been folly to have made him wise. Such a moral delinquency may be tolerated. In what character did you marry—as a maid or widow?"

"I was married in my maiden name—I had none other."

"No more you had: I had forgotten that circumstance. What occurred after your marriage?"

"My husband the next morning upbraided me with the deception I had practised."

"Indeed! in what particular did he say you had wronged him?"

"In my not having brought my virgin treasure to his bed."

"How did you defend yourself?"

"By tears and expostulations; but he would not be pacified unless I submitted to an examination by his own medical attendant."

"Did you permit the degradation?"

"I did, and the report satisfied my husband; he begged my pardon, and pretended to love me better than ever."

"How—how—you certainly do amaze me—how—how did you manage to deceive the doctor?"

"By telling him the truth, and imploring his forgiveness."

The pious confessor had the greatest difficulty in the world in preventing himself from bursting out into an uproarious fit of laughter; as it was, the effort made him cough and go nearly black in the face.

"Give me a woman for invention!" thought he, as he continued his examination. "Was he a young or an old man, that accommodating doctor?"

"Middle-aged."

"What reply did he make to your request."

Mrs. Smythe at this trembled so excessively, that her ghostly father had to sustain her to prevent her from falling to the floor.

"He had me in his power," said she, feebly; "and I could not resist. On my second wedded day I was false to my marriage bed.."

"The scoundrel!" muttered Walter. "And so," added he, aloud, "you purchased his certificate at the price of your honour?"

"I did. Was it a deadly sin?"

"Not on your part; on his it was—an abominable and atrocious one. What was his name?"

Mrs. Smythe without reluctance disclosed it; but, as it was given under the seal of confession, it cannot be repeated here. Walter never forgot it though, and, when his own affairs had been comfortably arranged, punished the scoundrel by frightening him out of the profession he disgraced.

"What kind of wedded life did you lead?"

"A comfortable one for the first twelve months; but, since that time, a miserable and often a hideous one!"

"Be frank and minute in your recital. In what respect did your husband offend you or you him?"

"He was unfaithful."

"And you ——"

"Was so also, but not until he had driven me to it by his coldness and flagrant neglect."

"In what manner did your alienation commence?"

"He commenced our quarrel by seldom visiting my bed."

"Then you still hankered after the lusts of the flesh?"

"I was human—and—and—married."

"A proper answer,—I mean one that will excuse you. You upbraided him, and acted as a jealous wife?"

"I did!"

"And made the chasm between you still wider?"

"From coldness and neglect it proceeded to opprobrious epithets and blows."

"The usual result in these affairs. By this time had all conjugal connection between you ceased?"

Completely. He first of all took an actress into keeping, and then another, and another."

"A perfect Don Juan, I declare! Well! and, as usual in such unhappy alliances, his evil example infected you?"

"It did, reverend, sir. His conduct exasperated me, and I swore to be revenged."

"Had your own inclination nothing to do with so rash a vow?"

"To my shame and sorrow it had; for a fiery devil seemed to have entered into me, and sent his liquid fire into my very bones and marrow!"

"Under what circumstances did you first give way to your propensities?"

"A gentleman of rank had for some time previously paid me attentions, and, while on a visit in the country, we met; and I yielded to his pressing solicitations.

"What was the duration of that *liaison?*"

"One day; from that hour we never met again. He soon after went to India, I believe."

"With whom did you next fall?"

"Some months afterwards I became acquainted with a literary gentleman, an author of great repute. I praised his books, and he praised me; and so we loved each other, until I got tired of him. He was a drunkard, and that disgusted me."

"Who was the next?" was the methodically-put question, the voice of the interrogator becoming rather severe. Indeed, it must be confessed that Walter, at this stage, was becoming rather disgusted with his conquest; for the sagacious reader must long ago have guessed that the ready-witted soldier had recognised the beautiful sinner who spoke so unreservedly of her transgressions.

"My next error was of a less venial character. I fell in love with a soldier."

"Indeed!" ejaculated the seeming confessor.

"With a soldier—a gallant, brave, handsome, noble fellow, upon whom I doated, and do to this hour!"

"Did he return your love?"

"He professed to do so; but I knew that he was so great a favourite with my sex that I could only have control over him by having him all to myself."

"What arts did you practise to attain that end?"

"Few beyond those in the power of every woman. He seemed enamoured of my charms; and I determined to yield at the first opportunity. Only one served, and that was at Greenwich; but we were interrupted, and I had to fly to town without bidding him adieu."

"Have you seen him since?"

"Yes."

"And your evil inclinations are still in existence?"

Mrs. Smythe held down her head so low that her brow touched the knees of the holy man; and her silence was more expressive than words.

"Here's a pretty kettle of fish!" thought Walter; "I am appropriated—sold—taken by storm; and yet am expected to give the pretty sinner absolution before I have half got through the questions in the manual of a true Catholic. I must be severe, or I shall make quite a St. Anthony business of it. I already feel rather queer; but, as it is, I am glad I have learnt so much. It's rather consoling when you know that you have not seduced an immaculate woman."

"Father," said the penitent, looking up, "is there any hope for me?"

"Plenty; but answer me one question. Is your love for this soldier of so strong a nature that you cannot resist its impulses?"

"It is a madness—an infatuation!" replied Mrs. Smythe, convulsively clutching the knees of her spiritual guide and monitor; "when absent from him, I am on fire to meet him again; and, when we do meet, the separation is an intolerable agony. Oh, father! had he and I but met years ago, I should never have fallen, for I feel that he is the man who would have loved me as I wished to be loved, and as I once was, for a brief—oh! sadly brief—but ecstatic period."

"Calm this raging tempest of your passions," said Walter, soothingly; for he wished the interview speedily to terminate. His power of self-control was ebbing fast.

"I cannot," sobbed the erring woman, as she yielded to the delirium which the multitude of emotions called up by her confession had excited. "It is death without Walter—life, glorious and eternal life, with him!"

The object of this passionate avowal felt powerfully inclined to throw off his disguise and clasp the beautiful woman at his feet in his ample embrace; but by one of those stern efforts of the will which seem so mysterious, so cruelly unnatural, when examined by the ordinary tests of resolution, he resisted the temptation. Perhaps an embryo-instinct drew him from the edge of the precipice on which he stood, and devoted all his energies to the task of quelling the tumult which he had largely contributed to provoke. By perseverance he partly succeeded, and Mrs. Smythe left his presence with a not over strong desire ever to come into it again. She had not accomplished the object of her visit. She wished for absolution for the past, and that the pretended confessor could not give her; or perhaps forgot it, as well as all recollection of the prescribed formula; and so construed his silence into a refusal, and departed, very much dissatisfied, but quite strong in her determination to fulfil her engagement on the morrow with Walter, and, if possible at all, prevail upon him to escape to the continent in her company.

"What a consummate scoundrel a Popish priest might be if he chose!" thought Walter. "Here have I only just dipped into the process of the confession, and yet did not put a single critical question. It being a woman, I should have put a hundred questions on the subject of private practices and unnatural offences, but I forgot the whole of them, and I am very glad I did. Faugh! I now find it to be true, that it is not the act itself that pollutes, but the mode; and the pollution may grow out of the suggestion. Only fancy asking a boy of eighteen, or a girl of sixteen, whether they had privately abused themselves. The poor things, who had previously been totally ignorant of such beastialities would go home perfectly instructed in them; and we know that, when ideas are firmly implanted in the human mind, actions are not slow to follow. Then the wife goes to one of these rascally liquory priests, and he asks her whether her husband plays any tricks with her in bed; and she learns for the first time the secret of many of the practices of the lustful Greeks and rascally Egyptians. Why, this system brings the iniquities of Sodom and Gomorrah to the door of every Christian house, and into the bosom of every Christian family. It is damnable, and, as Sir Peter Laurie would say, must be put down.

I wish Wriggles would come and release me from this horrible pantomime."

Thoroughly disgusted with the part he had played, he paced the little oratory with hasty strides, and, to relieve himself, began to whistle a multitude of lively airs.

Mrs. Smythe, meanwhile, had gained the doctor's own apartment, had paid him his fee, and was turning to depart, when a door opened, and Fanny glided in with a letter in her hand, which she delivered to the doctor, and was about to retire, when Mrs. Smythe darted forward, and clutched her by the arm.

"Holy Virgin!" she exclaimed; "it is the same face, the same form that I have seen twice before; it is a copy, too, of a form I once used to view with girlish delight in the glass. Tell me, sir, if you be human, who is this child?"

"My wife's, by her first marriage," said the doctor, coldly.

Fanny stood regarding Mrs. Smythe, with a countenance that blushed and paled alternately. The dark lady, the beautiful vision of her dreams, stood before her; and, although ordered to retire, her feet refused their office, and she stood intently regarding her painfully-agitated, but unknown parent.

"Your wife's, by her first marriage?" repeated Mrs. Smythe, keeping her gaze riveted on the young girl's face and figure.

"I believe so. She was about two years old when I married her mother," said the doctor decisively; and, at the same moment, giving Fanny a signal to retire, which she did not dare to disobey. She cast one lingering, mournful look at the beautiful lady, into whose arms she longed to fly, and then, with a graceful curtsey, quietly disappeared.

Mrs. Smythe gazed after her with strained eye-balls, and, as she did so, strange tears slowly filled her eyes. The fountain of a mother's love was opened for the first time.

"My child!" she murmured; "Oh, that I could clasp you to my throbbing breast!"

"Madam," said the doctor, "I have promised you that you shall see your child, and I will keep my word—I always do—so do not indulge in such useless sorrow. Some time must necessarily elapse before I shall be able to gratify your inclination; but, depend upon it, you will not be deceived."

"The sight of that girl has painfully affected me, and something whispers to me that in her I have seen my child. I beg—I pray of you, do not deceive me!" passionately urged Mrs. Smythe, turning her tearful eyes full upon the doctor.

"Tut, tut!" replied he; "you must not give way to such an idle fancy. I have seen hundreds of faces that startled me by their resemblance to those I had seen before. You shall see your child, rely upon it."

"When? 'hope deferred maketh the heart sick.'"

"When I have completed my arrangements and insured your safety."

"Mine? how can I be affected by the restoration of my child?"

"Your husband ——"

"I hate him; and, besides, am independent of him."

The doctor turned over the leaves of his book, and read:—

"Caroline Fitzherbert, presumptive heiress of Sir Felix Fitzherbert, Bart. The baronet is susceptible on the score of chastity; and, it is rumoured, would not hesitate to disinherit his niece, although his only surviving relative, should her reputation have received the slightest taint. Now, madam, if this be true,

this child, if acknowledged by you, would utterly ruin you in the estimation of your uncle?"

"Not at all," replied Mrs. Smythe, coolly; and here it may be stated, that when relieved from the trammels of her passions, she was a remarkably shrewd woman of the world; "the property is mine, should I survive my uncle—he has only a life estate in it."

"But there is your husband—he would have an estate for your life. You have had no child by him—no; well, then, it would only be for your life. Should he divorce you, you would, although nominally rich, be reduced to great pecuniary distress."

"All that has been provided for by a marriage settlement. The property is absolutely mine. No soul on earth can touch it but myself."

The doctor could scarcely conceal the satisfaction he experienced at this announcement. His eyes actually glittered, and a cold smile wreathed his thin lips. Mrs. Wriggles then, with all her astuteness, did not know all. His interest now was clearly to keep Mrs Smythe in subjection to him as long as he could, so that to disclose the secret of Fanny's birth would be clearly to release her from all further control. The doctor's avarice and devotion to the papal church overcame every scruple of conscience, and he determined, through the agency of the child, to exercise an iron authority over the frail girl, and the faithless wife who had placed herself in his power.

"Madam," said he, suavely, "every effort shall be made to recover your child. In the meantime rely upon my diligence, and don't fret your beauty away, but enjoy yourself while you have health and the means."

"You don't think it sinful, then, to enjoy the gifts of nature?" inquired Mrs. Smythe, with a smile.

"Not at all: it is the abuse of them that constitutes the sin."

And, with a solemn assurance that he would employ the utmost diligence in the inquiry he had promised to institute, the pair separated; Mrs. Smythe vaguely intimating that she anticipated the possibility of having to be recalled from Paris.

"From Paris!" chuckled the doctor. "So much the better. I would rather you would elope with a man of honour than a cool, calculating rascal of the world. I see it all: she knows Walter is in trouble, and would persuade him to take a journey with her to the continent. I would not baulk so pretty a scheme for the world. The step will enable her to get rid of her husband, and also keep her out of mischief for awhile. Ah! here comes our newly-fledged father confessor."

Walter, having been initiated into some of the geographical mysteries of the establishment, entered without ceremony, and with a not ever-pleasing expression on his countenance.

"I tell you what, doctor," said he, morosely, "this confession business of your church is a cursed piece of villany!"

"How so, gallant sir?"

"Why, in the first place it gives too much power to the priesthood, and in the second, its practices seem all to have been borrowed from the stews and bawdy houses of our large towns. I am not much used to blushing, but upon my honour I could not refrain from doing so as I read the filthy catechism in the 'Manual of Devotion' you gave me."

"Ah! Ah!" laughed the doctor, "it seems you have still to learn that out of the sins of the multitude come the wages of the few. If we were all good, there would be no occasion for any order of priesthood. As it is, that one thrives best which knows the most, so don't be too hard on the priests of Rome. Except with a few enthusiasts, religion in the present day is a speculation with everybody. Look at your English Church! what is it but a grand imposture—a mighty delusion—supported by enormous wealth? Why, one half of your ministers are secretly in communion with Rome, and a great portion of the other moiety lean that way, while the rest don't care a fig about anything but their stipends and lustful indulgences. Now, if our Christian churches have much to brag of on the score of morality, and when all are more or less tainted, I don't see why one should be more pecked at than the rest. But what say you to an adventure, just to show you that we abused Popish priests do not monopolise the pruriencies of the age."

"Have with you, with all my heart," said Walter, who could not refuse his assent to some of the doctor's conclusions, and therefore soon regained his habitual good humour. "I perceive that it is rather a pot and kettle affair with the generality of religious bodies; but, d—n it, doctor, it's too bad of you shaven celebratists to corrupt our women with your cursed confessional discipline. The sex are inventive enough without their having all sorts of filthy suggestions put into their heads. Geve up the confession, and ——"

"Lose all our power!" interrupted Wriggles; "become like your crazy, bloated Church of England—a mere thing of political sufferance—a scheme that an act of parliament could destroy in a day. Why, what in the name of the greatest potentate on earth—the devil—would your church be worth, if the people chose to deprive it of the wealth it so scandalously misuses—not that!" here the doctor snapped his fingers in a very derisive and significant manner. "No, no, Captain Morris, the foundations of real power are in the mind; build yourself a firm house there, and all the kings and parliaments in the world cannot eject you. But if any religious or even political body is credulous enough to trust to public professions and services for public favour and affection, it will find that when the novelty of the thing has worn away, and the necessity arises, it will be swept away with as little remorse, as a boy would toss a soap-bubble into the air. The only men who succeed and retain their authority, are those who treat the multitude as asses, and those who endeavour to keep and make them so."

"Which latter, I take it, is the ruling policy of you Roman gentlemen, when you forbid purely secular education?"

"Not quite so bad as that: there are some among us who think secular education holds out a premium to infidelity, and so disfavour it for the sin of the thing."

The doctor, as he uttered this, looked at Walter keenly from under his bushy eye-brows; as he observed that gentleman smile, he did so, too; and by-and bye they both laughed outright; but the dry, cackling laugh of the doctor sounded harshly in the full hearty volume of sound that escaped from the mouth of the soldier.

After a few preliminaries, in the shape of changes of costume, so as to disguise Walter's appearance as much as possible, the doctor announced himself ready to depart.

"Whither are we bound?" inquired Captain Morris; "no danger of falling into the hands of the Mohawks and Hawkabites, as we say in the army?"

"Not the slightest: the colonel, as you are aware, is out of danger; and the Horse Guards don't choose to give themselves much trouble in these matters. Are the colonel's relatives vindictive, think you?"

"In such a matter I would not trust them far out of my sight. It does not much matter, though—if I am to be taken, I must, and that's all about it."

"Never fear, you are safe in my company. The police have an impression that I would rather surrender a criminal than hide him; so, while we pass along, I will describe the character and constitution of the society to which I am about to introduce you."

THE EPISODE OF THE KNIGHTS OF THE ROUND TABLE.

THE gentlemen who constituted the society distinguished by the ancient and chivalric title of the "Knights of the Round Table," were a singular set of beings; for, although as loyal as Britons are expected to be, they would persist in throwing the mantle of secresy around all their proceedings. They feared not the light, but preferred that the business of their incorporation should be conducted in private. Having this characteristic, it will not excite much surprise that their meetings were held amid many precautionary ceremonies, and accompanied by several almost masonic solemnities. The locality selected was the classic one of Covent Garden Market, where, as if by common consent, the last faint lines of West End decency terminate, and those of eastern squalor and filth commence. The street was a respectable one, and the public-house in it the largest in the whole region of Bedfordiana. Imagine the hour to be nine o'clock in the evening, and that a couple of apparently gentlemanly-looking men are emerging from the snug bar-parlour, and, preceded by a hoary-headed confidential waiter, ascend a long flight of stairs, until they arrive at the third floor, where they pause, and then, by means of a house-key, open a substantial iron-bound door, which, moving inwards, noiselessly discloses a neatly-furnished ante-room, in which the two gentlemen, after ordering brandy-and-water, seat themselves. Presently others, garbed as if belonging to the well-to-do classes, arrive, and, after many whisperings and exchanges of passwords, are allowed to pass through another iron-bound door, which admitted them into the brilliantly-lighted hall of the Knights of the Round Table. This room was a circular one, painted in gold and black; but surely the artist must have had large amatory organs; for on the panels was every species of display of the perfections of woman, and the modes in which man can render them serviceable to his devouring propensities. At one end of the room was a beautiful scroll, which contained the following sentence, in raised golden letters :—

"Eat, drink, and love—the rest's not worth a straw."

Underneath this, resting on a pedestal on the floor, was a statue of the Venus de Medici, and at the other end of the room was a gigantic one of Bacchus. At intervals round were several busts, chiefly of men distinguished in literature and for latitudinarianism in morals. Among them was George IV., Charles James Fox, Sheridan, Mirabeau, Duncombe, Handsome Jack (a notorious *protege* of a distinguished actress), Edmund Kean, *cum multis aliis*. In the centre of the room was a large oval table, around which were armed and well-cushioned chairs, bearing on their backs numbers ranging from one to fifty. As the members entered, each took possession of one of these seats, and at ten o'clock they were all filled, except one, from the piece of black crape bound round the arms of which, it might have been inferred that its former occupant had departed to the unknown

realm, where the good and the bad have to render a true and just account of themselves. Dr. Wriggles—who, by the way, had left Walter in the ante-room—presided; and, after taking a preliminary glance round the table, struck it two or three sharp blows with the hammer which lay before him. At this intimation every voice was hushed, and the members adjusted themselves in their seats, so as to face the chair.

"No. 45," said the president, "read the minutes."

No. 45, a hawk-eyed, wiry little man, of about forty years of age, opened a large book before him, and read as follows:—

"Since our last meeting I regret to have to announce the loss of No. 49, the oldest member of the order, with the exception of your venerable self. He died full of years, and in the firm persuasion that, as he had never violated a single law of nature, he had nothing to fear, either for his memory or that future which is such a bugbear to the imaginations of the vulgar. On this point it may be interesting to record his last observations. 'The immortality of the soul,' said he, 'is one of those consoling beliefs which it

would be impolitic to destroy. It is the highest and last hope of man, and must exercise a beneficial influence over his mental faculties, restraining some and encouraging and developing others. The idea of an individual immortality is absurd, but that of a general one is correct; but to support the latter the former is indispensable, for few among us have the courage to recognise only the general immutable principles of nature. We make others to meet our individual wants and aspirations. The only immortality worth anything to man is the Egyptian one of the resuscitation of the body, afterwards adopted by the early Christians, under the fanciful conception of the complete resurrection of the body after its total annihilation, and the mingling of its elements with the common original ones from which they sprang.' These were his last words," continued No. 45, "and soon after he died as placidly as a child falling to sleep."

The president tapped in approval of so dignified a termination to a life of gaiety; each member, with the same object in view, gently inclined his head, and No. 45 proceeded:

"The affairs of the order continue in the same

prosperous condition, but I regret to have to report several grave cases, which call for immediate attention. The first is that of No. 7, who has been charged by one of his late servants with having caused her present pregnancy. No. 7 does not object to afford the girl pecuniary assistance as a matter of charity, for none of us can be too liberal to women in that respect; but he does object to being made the victim of extortion. He asks the advice and counsel of the order."

"No. 7," said the president, "in what private relation did this girl stand to you?"

No. 7, a bald-headed, unwieldy, plethoric man of seventy, rose, and gravely replied:

"She was my servant, and sometimes lay with me to keep my extremities warm; but I declare, on the honour of a knight of this table, that I never was carnally acquainted with her. I regret to say the capability has disappeared. My valet, I suspect, is the author of the woman's condition, but I will do as you advise in the matter."

"Then I would propose," said the president, "that No. 45 be instructed to give the girl a ten-pound note, and settle the affair. Your incapacity did not extend to manipulations of the girl's body, and your valet only completed what you began. Gentlemen, do you approve of my proposal?" None spoke. "Carried," and down went the president's hammer.

"The next case," resumed No. 45, "is that of No. 30. He has had an action brought against him by a peer of the realm, for criminal conversation with his wife, the Lady Tyrone, formerly known as Peggy Johnson, the most lascivious actress on the Irish stage. He admits the fact, but submits that, as the lady has notoriously been guilty of amours with other men since her marriage, he would be justified in defending the action, with the view of either obtaining a verdict, or reducing the damages to a nominal amount. He confesses that the case perplexes him, for, should the judgment be adverse, it would prejudice him in the proceedings he is about to institute with respect to his wife, whom he strongly suspects."

"What say you, No. 30?" inquired the president.

No. 30, who was the reader's old acquaintance, Mr. Smythe, the banker, rose, and said he had nothing to add to the statement of the secretary; all he wished to know was, whether resistance or a compromise would be preferable.

"I know something of the facts of this case," said the president; "both the lady and her husband, it is true, are adventurers: he lives upon her want of chastity, and would starve if he divorced her; but then No. 30, who has a charge against his wife—from statements already made, I fear a true one—should go into court with clean hands. I strongly advise a compromise, and will gladly lend my assistance. I know the lady's brothers — the O'Blazes — and a whisper from me into one of their ears would be sufficient. I undertake to settle the affair for a thousand pounds."

No. 30 gladly accepted the offer.

"This being a compromise, the money will have to come entirely out of your own pocket," said the president.

No. 30 bowed his acquiescence, and No. 45 continued:

"The next case is that of No. 48, who has been sued for loss of services, by the father of the girl who accuses him of having been her seducer."

"No. 48," said the president, "answer upon your honour: did the girl willingly and cheerfully submit to your embraces?"

"She did," replied No. 48, standing up and presenting the commanding appearance of a dark, handsome man of about thirty.

"Did you make any promise of marriage?"

"I did not."

"Then she was as willing as yourself?"

"Quite. The occasion was inviting. I placed her gently on her back, and she lay as quiet as a lamb."

"Has the connection been repeated?"

"Innumerable times."

"And pregnancy has ensued?"

"It has."

"A clear case," said the president. "I move that No. 45 be instructed to either compromise or defend the case. Any amendment? No: then it is carried."

No. 45 proceeded:

"The next case is that of No. 5. He has been accused of being the father of a male child, to which his servant, a girl of seventeen, lately gave birth. He admits the fact of connection, but denies that of paternity."

No. 5, a spare old man, with a profusion of white hair, here nodded his acquiescence, and the president rather briskly said:

"The admission damns the denial. He must pay; besides, it is well known that a man is never too old to get a woman with child. Many instances are on record of men being fathers at 120, and even 140 years of age. I move that No. 45 be instructed to compromise the affair, and be allowed for that purpose five pounds out of the funds."

Several members here suggested that the amount should be ten pounds, which was ultimately agreed to; No. 5 being advised to keep a complying male servant, on whom for the future he could safely throw the onus of all such responsibilities.

"The last case," said No. 45, "is the gravest of the whole. It refers to No. 29, who has been accused of a criminal assault upon the person of a married woman. He has been prosecuted, and is now out on bail."

"Stand up 29," said the president, severely.

No. 29 did so. He was a hale, stalwart, middle-aged man, with a jovial, pleasant countenance.

"Are you guilty or not guilty?" demanded the president.

"Not guilty of the assault, most decidedly," replied No. 29, with a laugh; "if there is any charge at all against me it is that of rape."

"Explain yourself."

"Being a bachelor I have no establishment of my own, but live in apartments in Park Lane. My landlady, a merry, pleasant creature, of about thirty, plump and pretty, with a large roguish eye, that follows you wherever you go, deigned for several weeks to listen to my idle nonsense, and at last suffered me to embrace her warm waist, and kiss her most lips. I saw immediately that she would, and she would not. Her husband I found out was a jealous Turk, and she was afraid of him. A few evenings ago she came into my sitting-room to make some inquiry, when I invited her to take a glass of wine with me. She did so, and I began to pull her about. At first she was angry, but soon cooled down, and went off into another kind of heat, which, I perceiving, became more ardent in my advances, and after a good deal of struggling—for at the critical moment she got horridly afraid of venturing—I had my way. She then began to cry, and who should then walk in but the monster, her husband, to whom she complained that I had assaulted her, with intent, &c. She was obliged to say something, for her clothes and hair were in great disorder, and so she put the most charitable construction on the affair, and assured her husband that, villain as I was, she had resisted so stoutly, that she was still his pure, true, and lawful wife. I was dragged to the station-house, and next morning committed, but liberated on bail."

"A narrow escape for you, 29," said the president; "but you could not have displeased the woman, or you would at this moment have been in Newgate. Will any member make a proposition?"

It was promptly moved, seconded, and carried, that No. 29 should be defended at the expense of the order, and that the president should admonish him upon his indiscretions, this being the third of the kind of which he had been guilty within the last three years.

"No. 29," said the president, with great gravity, "for a man of your years, being now ——"

"Forty-five last birthday," said the secretary.

"Being now forty-five years old," continued the president, "this amour of yours is positively an offence; and you must be cautious for the future, or you may meet with a spiteful woman, who will not hesitate to prefer the graver charge of violation. But your conduct amazes me. Until this moment I had always believed that every Knight of the Round Table was too much a man of the world to risk his liberty for the sake of possessing an unwilling woman, when, by a little diligence, scores might be found who would not make the slightest objection. The man who uses violence to a woman is a recreant knight (hear, hear) and dangerous companion. Love, like honey, must be gathered with caution. Even in plucking the rose it is necessary to avoid the thorn by its side; and how much more necessary it is, in gathering the fairest flowers of the earth, that we should use circumspection, and that gentleness which protects the tender plants from injury either by accident or design. Unless we mingle refinement with our pleasures they soon pall upon the senses; and if we pursue them further, it is only in the degenerated form of mere animals. To a knight of your experience, and established reputation for kindness of disposition and purpose, I need say no more. Be warned in time, and refrain from setting our younger members so vicious an example."

No. 29 returned thanks for the consideration shown towards him, and promised to be more discreet in his future commerce with the fair sex.

The secretary, No. 45, then read the remainder of the minutes.

"All the children of the order are in good health. Two of them—boys—with the consent and approbation of their parents, have been apprenticed to good trades. Three girls, having completed their education, have been received into most respectable families as governesses. Those approaching the age when they should mingle with the busy world, have been sedulously attended to, and the governess of the institution reports very favourably of their progress. It is perhaps scarcely necessary to repeat, that all the children are being most carefully trained under the rules of the system of education of which our venerated president is the author; and that when they leave school, they do so with a thorough knowledge of their duties, responsibilities, and passions, as men and women. It is not left to them to acquire knowledge through the channels of vice or sad experience, but are taught everything that it is proper a human being should know, and which, when unwisely withheld from them, they are sure inevitably to obtain surreptitiously." (Hear, hear.)

No. 45 closed his books, and sat down. The president then tapped three times very significantly, and every member simultaneously began writing something on a slip of paper, which he passed to those seated near the centre of the table, who deposited it in a beautiful urn standing before them. Presently the president said:

"No. 25, ring the bell."

The member so requested pulled a bell-handle, which rested in a groove in the table, and in a moment the part of the table whereon the urn stood opened, and when it closed again the urn had disappeared.

The members then indulged in a general and unrestrained conversation, which continued until the compartment in the table again opened, and closed again, but this time bearing upon its surface not only the urn, but a little army of well-filled decanters, jugs of hot water, wine-glasses, goblets, tumblers, lemons, cigars, tobacco, pipes, and all the etceteras indispensable in convivial hours. As soon as each member had filled his glass, and selected his pipe or cigar, the president again tapped, and there was again the most profound silence.

"I declare the Good and Welfare opened!" cried the president—and up sprang every man to his feet—"and give you the loyal and constitutional toast of our order — 'MERRY GIRLS, MERRY WIVES, AND PLENTY OF THEM.'"

This sentiment was received with uproarious applause, and then each member in the drinking department did as he liked. Harmony, in the shape of song, jest, and anecdote, then commenced, and at the end of an hour the hammer again sounded, and, as before, there was a dead silence.

"Gentlemen," said the president, before whom stood a steaming tumbler of brandy-and-water, "we will once more proceed to business, if you please. The only address I have to make to you, is one of congratulation. We are in a prosperous condition, and every one of us as moral as the state of society and our own peculiar organisations will allow us. But I must, nevertheless, recommend to you moderation in all your enjoyments. The true end of life is to live as long as possible, and at the same time be as happy as possible. This cannot be attained without temperance—no true epicurist is intemperate. Therefore I warn you, in the language of the poet, to—

"'Beware the poison in the cup of gold,
The asp among the flowers.'

In the shape of information I have only to communicate that a royal commission has been appointed to inquire into our marriage laws, and, from the elevated rank which many of you hold, I have no doubt you will be called upon to give evidence as to their operation among the higher grades of society. I entertain not the slightest doubt that you will denounce their stringency as oppressive and vicious, and show that, as far as morality is concerned, they are wholly inoperative. Adultery should not be the sole ground of divorce, as some of you, perhaps, to your sorrow, can too well advance. But this is delicate ground, and each member must, if called upon, act as a true knight and a man of experience and common sense. The bill legalising marriages with a deceased wife's sister, will be again introduced, and it will be for the interest and welfare of legitimate children that those among you who are legislators should give it your earnest and undivided support. On general grounds it is entitled to—it demands—our cordial support and sympathy, for, not trenching upon the objection as to affinity of blood, it does not tend to promote any deterioration of race, to guard against which is one of the true ends of marriage; if it were not so, the necessity for the enactment of laws at all would be obviated, and, like the lower animals, we ought only to obey the impulses of instinct. As to the moral features, nothing novel is introduced: sexual connection between husbands and their wives' sisters has been practised from the earliest ages, and the opinion of the multitude does not condemn the union as repulsive. Legalise such marriages, and you at once put an end to the majority of illicit connections between husbands and their deceased wives' sisters, for few women, unless intoxicated by desire, will voluntarily throw an obstacle in the way of marriage with the man with whom she is pleased; and, as you all know, surrender of person without the sanction of the body is rarely followed by the man performing either his given or implied promise. But this also is a question for your own private judgments, and to that tribunal I confidently commit it. It now becomes my duty to receive the propositions members may make."

No one spoke; indeed, there rather seemed to be a prevailing disposition to be more hilarious than methodical; but the president arose, and announced that he had a new member to propose in the room of their lately deceased one. This aroused the attention of every one, and the president commenced:

"Gentlemen, my new member, or rather candidate, is a gentleman and a soldier. Like us all, he worships more at the shrine of Venus and Bacchus than those more sacred ones which we are pledged to respect. He is in every respect a man of honour, and one in whom we may place the utmost reliance. He graduated at Cambridge, where perhaps he won more hearts than academic laurels; but, as a soldier, he acquired imperishable renown in those hard-fought battles on the north-west frontier of India, which perhaps, more than any other modern ones, have served to consolidate the power of Britain in that interesting and remarkable portion of the globe. His valour was so distinguished that, unsolicited, it obtained for him a captain's commission in her Majesty's Guards; and in that celebrated corps he established, or, I should say, confirmed, his reputation as an officer and a gentleman. Among the ladies he is an universal favourite; and, from an intimate knowledge of his career and conduct, I can confidently say that I do not know of an instance in which he has behaved with the slightest heartlessness, or been guilty of the least want of principle. He is a gay man, but a chivalric one; and a recent exhibition of his spirit on behalf of a persecuted maiden, enables me to announce his name—Captain Morris. He is now, as you are aware, owing to his duel, in a kind of abeyance, or prudent retirement; but, wishing to have him amongst us, and aware that I could safely trust both you and him, I have brought him with me to-night. I now, therefore, beg to propose him as a member of our order."

A dozen rose to second the nomination, and the election by ballot was ordered to be proceeded with. While it was going on Wriggles drew Smythe into a corner, and, after a brief, but emphatic conversation, extracted from him a promise not to oppose the election by throwing in his black ball. When the box was examined it was found that Walter had been unanimously elected, and the result was received with loud applause. Order having been restored, the pre-

sident tapped, and a slip of paper being transmitted to the regions below, through the medium of the urn, the gas-lights in the room were suddenly lowered, so as to veil it in comparative darkness.

"Tilers, admit the applicant at the door," cried the president. And Walter in a few seconds was conducted to where his proposer stood ready to receive him.

"Captain Morris," said the president, "I have the honour to announce to you that you have been unanimously elected a member of this order; but to complete your success it is necessary that you should answer a few questions, and enter into an engagement, as a man of honour, to preserve our secrets inviolable. We do not ask for oaths, because we are convinced of their inefficacy, compared with the plighted word of a gentleman, and more especially one who has carried arms in the service of his country. As a preliminary, I must request you to listen to the general rules, which our secretary will recite to you. No. 45, inform Captain Morris of the nature of our general laws."

No. 45 then recited the following, as glibly as a well-conned lesson:—

"Our motto is, the greatest amount of pleasure with the least amount of pain; and the objects of our association are, mutual assistance in cases of distress, and the promotion of enjoyment in all its phases. To carry out these views, we have acknowledged, and do abide by, the following maxims and rules, namely, that—

"Love is the keenest, noblest, and most glorious of all earthly pleasures: it is the spring from whence bubbles the pure waters of hope, and the sunbeam that gives them light and beauty. All nature acknowledges its sovereign sway; therefore, it is one of the lords of the universe. Difficulties, however, attend the gratification of its impulses, and to overcome them men often subject themselves to the gravest accusations, and plunge into dilemmas from which they can only be extricated by the charity and forbearance of their fellow-men. To afford this assistance, and, at the same time, to refine the passions of mankind, is the primary regulation of this society. And to develope the intention in its full integrity, we have adopted eight cardinal sentiments, upon which we base our laws:

"1. Love is a physical pleasure, out of which—from association and mutual agreement of organisation—proceed the spiritualities that endear a man to a woman, and a woman to a man, independent of the sexual connection.

"2. The sensual estimate of woman is the natural one, but with civilised races it is refined by marriage and other conventional necessities; therefore, it is proper to respect all the moral and social laws which have been enacted for the control and subjection of the appetites to salutary restraint.

"3. Mere coition is not love, but, being necessary to the health of the body, is, when enjoyed in moderation, a fundamental necessity.

"4. Man, having the life-giving power, polygamy does not outrage any natural law or sentiment of the human mind; but in the densely-populated countries the institution, for political purposes, is disallowed; and hence are formed illicit connections, which no human laws can repress; and the responsibilities attached to them being thrown upon the parties concerned, it follows that too much discretion, prudence, and generosity, cannot be associated with these indulgences.

"5. The union of the sexes being indispensable to

the propagation of the species, regulations placing obstacles in its way are illegal and repugnant to nature.

"6. Promiscuous intercourse is a brutish and abominable outrage upon health and decency, therefore a woman should only enjoy the society of the man to whom she is engaged, either for life or a limited term. But as extraordinary emergencies will arise, such as physical incapacity in the man, or such a bankruptcy of conduct that he is no longer worthy of her favours: then the woman, whether married by law or promise, is at liberty to choose another mate.

"7. As society, as at present constituted, is imperfect, and human beings are not all formed alike, all errors should be viewed as mildly and extenuatingly as possible; and those of woman, owing to her inefficient training, more so than those of the stronger animal, man.

"8. Drunkenness, gluttony, and excesses in love are positive crimes.

"With these views, and believing them to be correct, we have formed ourselves into a society for the promotion of the gratification of all our propensities and faculties, and their confinement within the bounds of reason, propriety, and social convenience. To develope our objects, we have pledged ourselves to be bound by the following regulations:—

"1. To meet once a fortnight. 2. To contribute rateably to the pecuniary necessities of the order; but the amount subscribed within one year not to exceed 100*l*. 3. To keep the secrets of the order. 4 To abstain from the discussion of theological or political subjects. 5. Each member in turn to deliver a lecture on the philosophy of the Epicureans. 6. To defend each other from the slanders of the world. 7. To promote the education of the illegitimate children of the members of the order. 8. To contribute by general vote towards the damages and costs which any member may have sustained in his commerce with women. 9. To obey the mandate of the chair."

No. 45 ceased, and the president then said:

"Captain Morris, you have heard the rules of our order—are you willing to subscribe to them?"

"I am."

"Will you promise, on your honour as a gentleman, not to divulge any of its secrets?"

"I do."

"Will you, at all times and at all hazards, protect women, whether young or old, from outrage or injury?"

"I will."

"Then, Captain Morris, I have to announce your complete election to our vacant number, by which you will only henceforth be recognised here; and long and worthily may you enjoy it. After you have passed your noviciate, you will be still further initiated into the mysteries of our order; but before that time shall have elapsed, you will have discovered that we are no anchorites, but that our motto is the right royal one: 'Eat, drink, and love; the rest's not worth a straw.' A health, gentlemen, to the new Knight of the Round Table."

The lights shot up and blazed brilliantly, and Walter, amid uproarious cheers, was conducted to his seat, from the arms of which, at the same time, the sign of mourning for its late occupant was removed. Merriment then became the order of the evening, and, amid flashes of wit and floods of eloquence from lips, the names of whose owners are treasured by the multitude, Walter yielded to the charm of the excitement, and soon became one of the gayest of the gay. At midnight the member whose

turn it was to deliver a lecture, read a paper on the worship by the ancients of idols, symbolising the creed of the obscene god Priapus; and at its conclusion there was held an animated but lascivious conversation, interspersed and enlivened by songs and jests. At four in the morning the president rose, and, as a hint to break up, gave the standing toast of the order—"Merry girls, merry wives, and plenty of them."

CHAPTER XVIII.
THIS WORLD'S A QUEER PLACE.

MR. SMYTHE, after leaving the peculiarly remarkable club to which he belonged, did not feel in any very agreeable frame of mind. He had voted for the admission of a man whom he cordially detested for his good looks and eminent success with the ladies, on the assurance that the captain would attempt nothing against the honour of his wife. Now that was the very thing he in his heart desired, for it had now become a kind of mania with him to get rid of her, and it struck him that the newly-acquired membership of Walter placed an insurmountable barrier between him and Mrs. Smythe. He reasoned on the principle of there being honour even among thieves, and retired to rest extremely dissatisfied with himself. When he arose at noon his mood had deepened into a surly dissatisfaction, and after swallowing a hasty breakfast, he sought his wife in her apartments. Such a proceeding was so novel to that lady, that her looks betrayed her surprise. Had Smythe, with his immense sensuality, not been in such an infamous humour, he could scarcely have failed to have been charmed by her interesting appearance. She was seated at breakfast, and had on a loose robe, or wrapper, confined to her waist, but open across her bosom, disclosing its voluptuous proportions, and the exquisite glow that played on her dazzling white skin. Her raven hair, sleek and glossy, disengaged from the net that had confined it during the night, was spread in confused curling masses over her shoulders, while her face, partly shaded by truant locks, beamed with the hues of hardy health, and the deep flush that lights up a lovely woman's countenance when newly risen. The eyes had the subdued tone which slumber invariably imparts to those glorious organs, and altogether she looked in her dishabille like a bride on the morning after her wedding night, pondering over its delirious events. The entrance of her husband, though, disturbed her reveries, and, hastily adjusting her wrapper, she looked at him with an air of inquiry. He unceremoniously threw himself into a chair, and regarded her with a scowling aspect. This roused her indomitable spirit, and she inquired, with a perceptible sneer:

"To what may I attribute the honour of this unusual visit?"

"I came here to tell you that I hate you!" was the savage reply.

"The intrusion was unnecessary, for I knew it long ago," replied the lady, smartly, as she took a sip at her coffee.

"Perhaps the feeling is reciprocated."

"Perhaps it is."

There was a pause; the husband darted looks of hatred upon his wife, while she returned them with glances of ineffable scorn.

"You sent to me yesterday for a thousand pounds,"

said Smythe. "What has become of the large sums I have given you lately? Do you think I shall put up with this extravagance? If you do you are d——ly mistaken, I can tell you, my fine lady!"

"Am I to account to *you* for the money I spend?" sneered the lady. "Why, if accounts were balanced, I don't think I receive in the course of the year half of what was secured to me."

"It's a lie!" roared Smythe.

"Be good enough to carry your vulgarity to another apartment," replied his wife; "here at least I ought to be free from the annoyance of a man as insensible to the delicacy of a woman as he is to honour. Take your wife's advice, Smythe, and meddle with nothing else but your Stock Exchange swindling, your gambling, and your women. The company of harlots suits you better than that of modest women. But I don't care, not I; only don't come near me with your filth, and you may carry on as long as you like, or at all events until you get into the *Gazette*."

"You are a nice one, aint you, deai?" sneered the husband.

"I was until I knew you."

"Indeed?"

"Wretch!"

"Now listen to me, Mrs. Smythe, I have only one thing to tell you, and that is—you are a d——n w——e!"

"Liar!" screamed Mrs. Smythe.

"I can prove it, you b——; and I have half a mind to give you a b——d good hiding. Give you money? I'll see you burning in hell first!"

And Smythe, now thoroughly infuriated, sprang to his feet.

"Touch me if you dare!" she exclaimed, her eyes flashing fire.

"Touch you! it shall be with a pitchfork first, you common trull!"

"Villain! how dare you say so? And if I were one, who would have made me one but you, you filthy monster? Take care, or I'll expose you, and have you hunted with execrations from London. I'll expose all your beastly practices upon me. By heavens! I'll have you indicted at the Old Bailey, you nasty wretch! Faugh! the sight of you makes me sick!"

Smythe at heart was a rank coward, and these reproaches rendered his cheeks as bloodless as marble, but failed to subdue his raging passion.

"Madam," he hissed, "I have abundant proof of your being a w——!"

"Liar, and fool!"

"Why, you were not a maid when I married you!"

"Poor driveller! why you were never able to ascertain the fact! I am as much a maid now as ever I was, for all you have done to me!"

"D——n!" gasped Smythe, choked with rage.

"Why have I had no children by you? Was it my fault? *Me!* I am a well-formed, handsome, healthy woman; and you—ah! ah! ah!—a bloated lump of impotence! I say, Smythe, that's a dear, give me the check for a thousand pounds, and I'll sleep with you to-night. I don't like being ill-natured to such a duck of a husband."

Smythe sprang towards her, but, quick as lightning, she placed the table between herself and him; and, possessing herself of a long dagger, she pouted her rosy lips, and provokingly invited him to come and kiss her.

The sight of the weapon cowed the banker, and, with a horrible exclamation on his lips, he ran out of the room, his wife shrilly calling after him not to forget the check, and the cuddle she had promised him for it.

"What a cur!" muttered she, as soon as he had gone; "I'd rather lay down by the side of a crossing sweeper, than such a cowardly brute. I am glad I galled the wretch. Why, he rushed away like a crazy gelding. Oh! Walter, Walter! would to God you would free me from this intolerable bondage!"

After uttering this passionate remark, she paced the floor for a few minutes, and then, as if hurried away by an uncontrollable impulse, rang the bell for writing materials, and addressed the following note to the object of her adjuration:

"Eaton Square, noon.

"Come to me, Walter, for I am half mad. The wretch who claims a legal ownership over me has this morning exceeded all his former brutalities, and I will no longer suffer his cruelties.   "CAROLINE.

"P. S.—At the usual hour and place, whether it hails, rains, thunders, or shines."

Now Walter Morris had risen from his feverish couch about the hour the note arrived, with rather an oblivious recollection of the transactions of the preceding night. His head ached, and the whole economy of his digestive system was deranged. He was not, certainly, in a humour to reason correctly on points of morality; besides, he had begun to dislike his confined quarters in Dr. Wriggles' house, and longed for a change. Mrs. Smythe's note, therefore, afforded him a prospect of relief, of which it was with no reluctance that he prepared to avail himself; but, as a matter of etiquette, he thought it but proper to consult his singular host. He found him as usual in his mysterious study, looking as cool and collected as he generally did, and without the slightest sign about him of not having gone home till morning.

Walter calmly handed the note over to him, and then as calmly waited for his comments.

"Go, by all means," said the doctor; "it will be a change for you, and, besides, place you out of danger; for Stanley yet hovers between life and death. How are you off for money?"

"Only so-so, for such a journey."

"Well, then, suppose I advance you a hundred pounds; and when you arrive at Paris, or where Providence shall take you, you can draw upon me for what you require."

Walter readily agreed to this very accommodating proposal, and at the time mutually arranged between him and Mrs. Smythe for their clandestine interview was punctual in his appointment to the minute. The locality was Kensington Gardens, and the hour six in the evening. The secluded nooks in that delightful fashionable resort must surely have been constructed to shelter amorous couples from the too-prying eyes of the multitude; for no better Cupid's bowers could have been devised. Walter sauntered along one of the retired alleys, casting eagle glances all round him, when he heard a soft, musical voice, utter his name.

"Walter—dear Walter!" murmured Mrs. Smythe, her fine countenance crimsoning with delight, as she placed her long, slender hand, on Walter's proferred arm.

"Caroline!" he gently said, as his face also flushed, after the sensual thrill that shot through his frame. Certain virtuous resolves which he had before entertained, all vanished in the presence of the almost Paphian-looking queen before him, and he was ready to fly with her to the uttermost end of the earth.

"My luggage is all prepared," said she, after the first burst of their transports had subsided. "Will you take charge of my jewel-box? I thought it would be safer with me than with the other things."

As she spoke, she handed to Walter a rather weighty casket, which until then he had not perceived she had carried under her arm.

"With all my heart," said he; "and as for my own luggage, I have arranged to have it sent after me; so, heigho! for love and ——"

"Dear, delightful Paris! do let us go to Paris, my love!" said Mrs. Smythe, winningly.

Walter was in too amorous a mood to refuse her any request; and together they emerged from the gardens, and, taking a cab, were driven to the London Bridge station. Now, a railway station is a very grand and noble place; but, as far as secresy is concerned, it is not exactly adapted for such an affair as an elopement. This Walter and Mrs. Smythe discovered; for, just as the latter was stepping into a first-class carriage, the apparition of her husband rose upon her view, and caused her to indulge in a by no means suppressed scream.

"Smythe! Here will be a row, with a vengeance!" growled Walter, as he supported Mrs. Smythe, to prevent her falling.

Now the banker, who, after the scene of the morning, had anticipated some such step as this on the part of his wife, had watched her movements all the day, and followed her step by step, until he arrived at the platform, and confronted her when en route to Paris. He did not do this for the purpose of intercepting her, but for the mean revenge of gloating over her ruin. So convinced was he that if he divorced her all her resources would be destroyed, that he would not have hesitated to have purchased for her a paramour to complete his dishonour. And there he stood, making no effort to arrest the fugitive fair one, but showing his malicious satisfaction at her conduct by grinning, and indulging in divers other manifestations of delight.

"The die is cast, Walter!" said the lady, faintly, "I cannot return—on—on!" and she sprang like a bird into the carriage.

Walter, although a remarkably bold man, felt it was rather an awkward predicament to be placed in, to be running away with a wife under the husband's very nose. He hesitated; but, observing the malignant expression in the banker's face, a rising feeling of disgust removed the impression, and he coolly took his seat, and deliberately closed the door after him. He had no sooner done so, than Smythe appeared at the window of the carriage, and, putting his thumb to his nose, extended his hand towards the certainly very pale couple, and laughed outright. This so exasperated Walter, that he turned, or, as a sailor would say, slewed himself round in his seat, and dealt the banker such a blow, that the bones of his hand were smashed, and, with blood gushing from his mouth and nostrils, Smythe reeled backwards along the platform, until he fell heavily at his full length. The train at that moment started, and the porters who assisted him to rise increased the pain he was suffering by accusing him of foolish negligence, in standing so near a train after the last bell had rung.

"It's a wonder your head was not smashed altogether," said they, as they bore him to a cab; "as it is, it's only a case of a little claret being lost."

Walter and the impetuous Mrs. Smythe meanwhile were flying along at the rate of forty miles an hour. Having engaged a coupe, they had the privilege—an ecstatic one to lovers—of being alone; and, having

prudently drawn the curtains, commenced a series of toyings, such these as it would be presumed a newly-married pair, on their way to the nuptial couch, would indulge in, to soothe or irritate their senses and pass away time. Walter first of all disengaged the splendid tresses of his conquest from the trammels of bonnet and bands, then spread them over her shoulders, opened the bosom of her dress, and, pulling her on his lap, placed the back part of her head against his breast, and leaning over, kissed her lips, eyes, and forehead vehemently, and played with the ruby tip of the globe upon which his hand pressed, until Mrs. Smythe seemed ready to expire in his arms.

"Don't Walter!" she murmured, her liquid glances, though, eloquently contradicting the request.

Walter's reply was a more vigorous hugging, and a passionately-expressed wish for the termination of the journey.

"We will sleep at Dover, darling," said he.

"Let us go to Paris first," she faintly sighed.

"I cannot afford to wait, love. Dover must be the place where we will consummate our loves."

Mrs. Smythe, lulled by the motion of the carriage, and perhaps fatigued by the excitement she had undergone, soon fell asleep, with her face turned up towards Walter's.

"How the rich blood courses under her clear, satin-like skin!" he murmured; "and what glorious features! Jove himself might banquet upon her looks. Her bust, too, is as full, soft, and warm, as that of Venus herself. And her shape—gods of pleasure, how voluptuous! Her foot and leg, too, are divine, I'll be bound."

Here it must be recorded to the gallant but dissipated soldier's shame, that he lifted the lady's dress, nd feasted his eyes upon as splendid a limb as ever supported a lovely, well-made woman. It was not a fat leg, but a straight, tapering one, with a middle-sized, beautifully swelling calf. The ankle a lady might have spanned, and, as for the foot, it looked almost too slender for a woman of Mrs. Smythe's proportions.

Walter's eyes sparkled very intensely as he devoured the beauties and symmetry of his chere amie's tempting figure, and, to prevent his having recourse to any vulgar attempts to gratify his passion, carefully covered up the portions of her person which he had disclosed, and strove to imitate her example by falling asleep. Do what he could, though, he was unable to succeed, and, by the time the train had arrived at its destination, he thought a plunge into the sea would have done him a world of good.

"I'm as hot as hell. Talk of Falstaff making the water hiss again, I fancy I could make it boil! I am sure if I were pushed into the furnace of a Dover steamer it would want no other fuel to get up the steam to take us across the Straits. Ah me! I see my region is heat, and, to carry out the simile, like the great home of fire, I'm paved all over with good intentions; but place a woman in my way, and I'm mad until I hug her half to death."

Mrs. Smythe, not without exhibiting some confusion, readjusted her dress and hair before the train stopped; and the pair afterwards proceeded to the Railway Hotel, where they ordered private apartments and refreshments. The latter were soon dispatched, and then Walter impatiently urged that it was time to go to bed. Mrs. Smythe, nothing lothe, consented, but insisted that he should not enter the sleeping apartment until she rang the bell to intimate that she was ready to receive him. "Pshaw!" cried Walter; and, taking the glowing lady in his stalwart arms, he carried her to the chamber, and with trembling hands took upon himself the office of her *femme de chambre*. As garment after garment fell from her body, and disclosed its amazing perfections—its dazzling whiteness and rosy plumpness—Walter grew giddy, and became so excited that Mrs. Smythe, only half disrobed, flew from his arms, and buried herself beneath the bed-clothes. Walter then dashed off his own apparel, and, as he threw them violently from him, a miniature portrait, which he had suspended round his neck, fell on the bed, and caught the attention of Mrs. Smythe, who, with her hair strewed on the pillow, eagerly waited for his coming. Suspecting it to be a tender memorial of some favoured lady, her natural jealousy became inflamed, and she drew it hastily towards her.

"God of heaven!" she exclaimed, starting up, and, heedless of her semi-nudity, springing to the floor; "where did you get this—who is it?"

Walter, surprised at her emotion—for her features were pale and convulsed—promptly answered:

"That is the only relic left me of a brave brother, who is now dead."

"God of heaven! there is a strange resemblance! But the name differs."

At this surmise a ray of hope darted into her mind, and she looked up and blushed at the agitation she had displayed.

"I cannot surmise why you inquire, darling; but this is a portrait of my brother, Theodore Melbourne. I took my mother's name, together with some little property left me by a maternal uncle."

Mrs. Smythe gazed long and earnestly at the glazed likeness, and then fainted. It seemed an age to Walter before she recovered, and when she did, and observed the tender expression in his countenance, she shuddered, and pushed him away from her.

"Don't touch me!" she cried; "your brother was the father of my child!"

The details of her confession then flashed across Walter's brain, and his breast heaved with an undefined sensation of relief, when he reflected that he had not carried the intrigue to its utmost limit.

"What an escape!" ejaculated Mrs. Smythe.

"D—— provoking!" grumbled Walter, as he picked up his clothes, and retired to an ante-room to dress himself.

The same evening the pair, who now stood in a new and more confidential relation to each other—for Mrs. Smythe before leaving the hotel had, to use a vulgar phrase, made a clean breast of it—returned to town by an express train; and Walter, having conducted Mrs. Smythe to her own house, sought out her husband, whom he found, as usual, at the gambling table. To induce him to take back his wife, he communicated the fact of her being entitled, at the death of her uncle, then upwards of fourscore years old, to a munificent fortune. The banker's eyes sparkled at the information, and Walter, having pledged his honour that it was correct, the former said:

"Will you swear that you have never touched her?"

"So help me God, I have not!" exclaimed Walter; "and would rather die than do so!"

"I am satisfied," cried the banker; "will you play?"

Walter consented; and before he left the room was a winner of a couple of thousand pounds.

———

CHAPTER XIX.
MERRY WIVES AND MERRY HUSBANDS.

THE charming Countess of Bloomfield had in a few months undergone a complete metamorphosis. She still retained her juvenile freshness, but her beauties both of face and figure seemed to have ripened under the genial influence of the experiences to which of late she had been subjected by the sagacious Mrs. Wriggles. The roses of youth still shed their bloom over her smooth cheeks, and her eyes—so deeply and intensely blue—retained all their original brightness; but the whole expression of her lovely countenance had been changed. She was no longer the petulant girl-wife, but the fully-matured woman, with the delicate softness and "sweet attractive grace" of the Eve who charmed Adam,

"Under a tuft of shade that on a green
Stood whispering soft, by a fresh fountain side."

There was more breadth and fulness in the character of her voluptuous charms, and this, united to greater dignity and increased confidence in her manner, rendered her the beau-ideal of a graceful high-born wife. Her mouth, that speaking index to character and temperament, although as ripely tempting as in the prime of her virginity, closed firmer, and around its corners those smiles played, which can only be detected in an individual whose natural shrewdness has been cultivated, and who has acquired habits of study and self-control. The latter quality had lately been developed in the countess. Her sensual instincts and desires were perhaps warmer and more acute than before; but reflection had taught her the necessity of subjecting them to a prudent restraint; and the conviction was gradually being formed in her mind that the more refinement there was mingled with an enjoyment, the more valuable was the pleasure, and the less danger of its palling upon and satiating the senses. In truth, her propensities, owing to their imperfect training, had previously, like a neglected vine, thrown out many shoots that were absolutely useless; but now that she had applied the pruning-knife to a number of them, she was enabled to curb the wildness of her natural physical qualities, and check the exuberance of her acquired ones. At the suggestion of her artful tutoress she had mingled more in society, and not confined herself to the circles in which her rank privileged her to move. She sought out acquaintances among the middle classes, and endeavoured to glean as much information as she could of the condition of the lower ones. While pursuing her inquiries respecting her husband, and following him in all manner of disguises to his haunts, she had been enabled to acquire a world of correction and instruction upon the moral state of the sexes, and to cultivate a disgust at the shameless profligacy of both. She had detected a mighty hypocrisy on each side. Her sex, position, and early training had prevented her from becoming acquainted with the grosser features of the intercourse between the sexes, but she had learned sufficient to enable her to pronounce an opinion upon the infelicity of marriages in general, and to be aware that both husbands and wives indulge in an enormous amount of cant.

A few words on "Husband-Cant and Wife-Cant," may not be out of place in a work embracing the private peculiarities of married life. Take the case of the husband first. Englishmen are prone to boast of being enemies to cant and humbug, yet who err

in those respects more frequently, or oftener exhibit a miserable want of candour, the more especially with respect to women, and their wives in particular. Among all the relations of life that of husband and wife is the most endearing and important, as being the key-stone in the arch of human happiness, and nothing, not even a jest, should be tolerated that has any tendency to disturb its security. But husbands are most strangely given to whine about faults and imperfections in their wives, which, in the majority of cases, are found upon examination to exist only in the imagination of the complainers, and coined for the purpose of indulging in a senseless kind of wit, in which married men delight when assembled together. The subject of temper is stock-gossip, both with husband and wife. He has offended her, come home drunk, perhaps, or ill-used her, or behaved to her indecently, and she, of course, remonstrates, and warmly too. He has neither the honesty nor manliness to apologise, compensate, or retract, but, like a coward, from that moment sets his wife down a bad-tempered woman. He knows very well that she is not, but he concocts that plea to palliate a

number of offences for which he cannot otherwise form an excuse. Thus he lays the foundation of a habit which, in the course of a few years, becomes confirmed. His wife's tongue, his wife's peevishness, his wife's everything that is disagreeable, form the chief topics of his conversation when in the least degree irritated, chagrined, or vexed with himself or anybody else. He raves about this until he becomes quite disgusting, and goes about twaddling his cant to people who do not care a rush what kind of temper his wife has. And all the time he is thus whining he is patiently enduring the riot, confusion, struggles, and noise of business, or very likely nearly every evening the uproar of a mob of tipplers in a bar parlour. This unmanly criticism is justly punished by provoking the very fault that is so much dreaded. A wife may be bad-tempered—too many, unfortunately are—but does the husband properly attempt to eradicate the defect by giving way to childish complaints to strangers, or exhibiting a peevish, growling petulance at home. Why, that is the very way to encourage and confirm the disorder, for a provoked wife will naturally retaliate with the most potent weapon of offence she is provided with. A woman must be persuaded; she cannot be driven, and the man who attempts it in civilised society is a fool for his pains. There is a medium between the husband being a tyrant and the wife a slave, and that medium creates domestic happiness. A supply of the means of subsistence is not enough, the wife must be a great deal more than a peculating, discontented housekeeper, or there will be no peace in the house. But most husbands on the subject of temper are "hipped" and incurable, and it will be as well to pass on to two other varieties of the disease. The one is that cant which is prevalent among middle-aged husbands, who lead a cat and dog sort of life at home, but abroad appear as amiable as if they had never exchanged a cross word with their wives since their wedding-day. He applies to her every endearing epithet, and seems by his manner to wish to consult her wishes before venturing upon the slightest step himself. It is "love," "dear" "ducky," and "chucky" with him, when addressing her, mingled with flimsy allusions to doves, pigeons, stars, angels, and heaven knows how many goddesses. This sickening cant is a sure mark of insincerity, and may invariably be accepted as good evidence that all is not right at home; for the husband who treats his wife well there has no occasion to lavish fondness upon her abroad, and that, too, accompanied by diluted twaddle, that would disgrace a highway pedlar descanting on his wares.

The other variety is the cant-gruff, and it forms a singular contrast to the cant-tender. It is generally observed in men who are passionately attached to their wives, but are afraid of confessing the fact from a dread of being thought henpecked. These weak men are ashamed—actually ashamed—of confessing to their predilection for a being they love and prize above everything else. They tremble at the bare idea of the influence of their wives over them being suspected, much less known, and assume towards them, in the presence of others, a gruff, growling demeanour, which impresses a superficial observer with the idea that they are perfect bears in their domestic economy.

There is, however, one species of cant in which husbands do not indulge. They never make a parade of their suspicions of their wives' fidelity: those, even when well grounded, they studiously conceal; it is very different, though, with the other conjugal moiety; for that is the leading feature of wife-cant. Go wherever you will, from the palace down to the humblest cottage, and you will find that where the wife complains of her husband to third parties, she invariably impeaches his fidelity to the marriage bed. The cant of wives about jealousy is abominable, and so is their nauseous stuff about the lowness or highness of their or their husbands' families; the marvellous superiority of their children, and their own unheard-of-before and superhuman endurance of trials and afflictions, sufficient in number and severity to break the backs and hearts of the British army, and the navy to boot, let alone a poor weak woman. But it won't do to be too hard upon the sex—it is their lot to bear great things as well as small; and when their usefulness and virtues are so conspicuous, their faults may be allowed charitable extenuation in the presence of the graver ones of the other sex.

The Countess of Bloomfield had arrived at many other conclusions besides these, during her rambles in search of her truant husband; and as she had a vast deal more to learn, it will be as well not to forestal them by any didactic digressions. Among the other changes which had occurred in her habits, she

had acquired a taste for a better class of reading; but perhaps dipped too much into the works that might be said to belong to the school of ethics which Ninon L'Enclos created. This tendency might, however, have been attributed to her connection with Mrs. Wriggles, who, like all elderly women, able to talk well, was very fond of generalising upon morals, and jumping to fine conclusions. In humble life, these conversations are larded with what is called "smut;" in better educated circles, and especially among ladies, they are more social and philosophical in tone, and have their offensive points dressed up in fine words, or disguised in Latin or innuendoes. The pruriency, though, will peep out, and that is probably the reason why, of late years, the pastime has become so popular among faded beauties and would-be philosophers in silks and satins.

These remarks will not strictly apply to the countess, for she was not a voluntary recruit in the service, but led into it at the instigation of her Mentress, Mrs. Wriggles. That lady had a motive for her conduct—perhaps a good one, who knows—but certain it is, that when she and the countess met for a quiet talk, the conversation was sure gradually to flow into the channel down which male peccadilloes and female delinquencies float so rapidly.

The countess, plainly but neatly dressed, was seated in that *sanctum sanctorum*, her boudoir, which was strewed round with books, papers, and many things not usually seen in these elegant sensual retreats. She had been engaged in writing, but had laid aside the occupation upon the announcement of Mrs. Wriggles, who now constantly visited her, but not in the costume by which she was popularly recognised. On these occasions she was habited in a brown silk dress, plain bonnet, covered with the same material, and shawl of sober colour, to match. She had a quakeress-like appearance; and throughout the household had acquired the nick-name of Mrs. Fry. The conversation had waxed interesting to the pair, for both appeared animated, and Mrs. Wriggles, more frequently than usual with her, paid court to the port wine on the table.

"I should have thought love could have existed in the female heart without any support from the sexual feeling," said the countess, with a slight blush.

"If that were true, the purposes of nature would be thwarted," replied Mrs. Wriggles. "For what is love, but a desire on the part of the man and woman for a more intimate knowledge of each other? Why do they hug and kiss each other before marriage, and approach one another with the inflamed looks of lust, moderated, on the man's part, by respect, and on the woman's by her natural timidity?"

"It may be as you say," said the countess; "but I once loved, and had no feeling of the kind. It is true, we used to kiss, and indulge in many other innocent familiarities; but I had no desire of the kind you refer to—never felt as I did a little before my marriage with Bloomfield."

"Because, in the first instance, your love was only friendship—an ardent one, I admit—but still only friendship. It was a love of the mind. Now the sexual union desires a love both of the body and mind; and it is the attachment of the instincts and propensities that constitutes the sexual union. Mere respect is not sufficient; the grosser portions of our sensuality must be called into existence."

"Then the reveries of our poets go for nothing?"

"Oh yes, they do; for the praises of the poet, and his glowing descriptions, soften and excite the feeling of love. It is an animalism, it is true; but poetry invests it with the attributes and sentiments which nature had omitted, or, probably, had no mission to bestow upon it."

"Would not what you contend for be liable to reduce woman to the condition of a mere brute?"

"Take education away from her, and what else is she? The sexual feeling is the same throughout the whole range of animated nature, and we human beings have not much to boast of in regard to superiority in that respect."

The countess, in her heart, strongly dissented from this conclusion; but not being prepared with a reply, allowed the assertion to pass over without comment on its truth.

"Then if we take your premises for granted," said she, after a pause, "the depravity exhibited by our sex is no phenomenon, nor ought they to be blamed for what they could not avoid?"

"Nor should they?" exclaimed Mrs. Wriggles, fiercely, for the remark gave her an opportunity of mounting *her* hobby; "if the blame rests with anybody it is the man—he is the prime agent in the affair."

"So he is," laughed the countess, as a few reminiscences diffused a gentle glow over the whole of her body.

"But men, having a greater number of opportunities of gratifying their desires, are more generous than women. We never hear of them, as a rule, refusing to consort with one another on the score of dissipation; nor, when their own manors are not poached upon, are they so bitter against the woman upon whom the finger of reproach—what an abused, canting term!—rests. Now, with our sex, the case is very different. They know perfectly well that men are more frail than themselves, yet who ever heard of a woman objecting to the society of a man? who had been detected in an intrigue? the discovery is rather a recommendation in his favour, as proving him to be a man of spirit and physical capacity to embrace a woman—two things a woman never turns up her nose at. With a woman it is strangely different; for, when a woman is exposed, who is her most malignant and bitterest enemy but a woman? who hunts her from society but a woman? who prevents her redeeming herself but a woman? who plunges her into prostitution but a woman? who heaps immeasurable scorn and obloquy upon her head but a woman?—one of her own sex, with kindred passions, kindred faults, and kindred opportunities of gratifying the natural lasciviousness of her disposition. Women whine to men about their defenceless position and weakness, but who does more to still further weaken it than themselves, by the cruel war they wage upon those whom they are pleased to term unfortunates and outcasts? What sickening hypocrisy! What, in the eye of nature, or of God, if you will, can be the moral difference between a woman who submits to conjugal embraces on the bare promise of a man, and her who does the same, but has taken the precaution to have the promise given in an open and binding manner? The motive and the desire in the two cases are identical; the effect the same—the wish to have the pleasure repeated. Where can the difference then lie, but in what the mawkish sentimentality—the hypocrisy—of woman chooses to create? The truth is, that the one stews herself in the bed of matrimony until she becomes as flabby as an old sow, and the other revels on the sofa of illicit gratification, until, like Sin, in "Paradise Lost," her womb conceives 'a growing burthen.' The world, and most of her own carping sex, cry out upon her, and all the time fondle upon and caress the other, and speculate with pleasure and lively gossiping upon the issue of her lawful obedience to the conjugal union. Lawful! Heaven save the mark! Law should prevent lewdness: now who are more lewd and obscene among themselves than married women. And in public who scan the figures of men with greater avidity, and can more readily ascertain whether they dress to the left or right? Faugh! the hypocrisy of my own sex sickens me!"

As Mrs. Wriggles concluded, with great emphasis, she applied herself to the decanter; and the countess, tired of the conversation, took advantage of the lull, and inquired whether it had been ascertained where Lord Bloomfield intended to spend the evening.

"At a Socialist institution, over the water," was the reply.

"Socialist institution!" echoed her ladyship; "what is that?"

"A place where male and female regenerators of the world congregate, to hear lectures, talk, dance, sing, make love, and ——"

"What?"

"Do as the rest of the benighted world does—make assignations, and keep them."

"What can have tempted Bloomfield to such a place?"

"A girl with a pretty face and neat ankle."

"Is she a maid or a wife?"

"Neither."

"What is she, then—a prostitute?"

"Not exactly: she is a young person who likes a lover, but would not submit to the tyranny of a husband. She has wisely reserved to herself the option of changing when the humour takes her. At present she seems attached to a slim young fellow, who is one of the apostles of Socialism,—at all events he is a mighty talker."

"I will go," said the countess, resolutely. "Will you accompany me, as usual?"

"With all my heart; and I promise you some glorious fun. But you must be cautious, and not fall into the jealous rage you were in at the last masked ball."

"Trust me, I will be as discreet as a witch, and as sly as a nun. What disguise shall I wear?"

"We will dress you like a milliner's assistant or tradesman's daughter, and dye your hair and darken your complexion."

"Anything you like; but, for mercy's sake, don't ruin my complexion!"

"The dyes are simple vegetable ones, and only last a few hours. Will you come to me at five or halfpast—we must be there by seven, if you wish to see the whole of the proceedings?'

The countess promised to be punctual and early, and Mrs. Wriggles took her leave.

After her departure the former fell into a musing, listless attitude, and after a while dropped off into a light, refreshing slumber. While she slept, several gentle taps were given on the door, and no reply to them being heard by the applicant for admission, the door opened, and in walked Alice, attired as sprucely as usual, but looking paler and more thoughtful.

"Asleep!" murmured she; "then there will be time to keep my appointment."

She closed the door softly after her, and tripped lightly into the garden to the back door, which she opened, and let in a tall, handsome stripling of a fellow, who could not possibly have numbered more than twenty years.

"Dearest Alice!" he ejaculated, as he almost smothered her with kisses, "when will you make me happy? Fly with me now; I have money in abundance; and love—oh! love for you like liquid fire!"

"I cannot yet, Henry; the affair I spoke to you of has not been arranged: I have not discovered my—my—friends; and until I have done so, you must wait."

"That may never be; I shall go mad—I can't wait so long—it's impossible!" exclaimed the young man, impetuously.

"You must," said Alice, firmly.

"I cannot! You don't love me, or you would consent. Come Alice—dear Alice! let us retire to one of yonder nice arbours: we shall not be interrupted; and if we are, I know the gardeners, and a sovereign or two would seal their mouths for ever."

Alice, who was afraid of losing her boyish lover, reluctantly assented; and the amorous youth, throwing his arms passionately round her waist, almost dragged her in the direction he had indicated.

"Yield, Alice, and all the treasures of my purse and person shall be yours for life."

"I will, through the church."

"The church?"

"Yes," replied Alice; "marry me, either in this country or abroad, and I will be your slave for life."

"Cruel Alice!" replied the youth, gazing rapturously into her naturally arch and expressively-beautiful features; "why now talk to me of an alternative that will bring down upon me the displeasure, nay, the enmity of my friends, and perhaps ruin my prospects for life."

Alice, knowing very well that, being already a wife, she could not legally marry again, only adopted this plea as a pretext for delay, in order to further her designs, aiming at a permanent settlement. She had so often been taught the lesson that the moment a man obtains from a woman what he wants, he cares little for her afterwards, to surrender too easily, when she saw a chance of obtaining what she ardently desired—a protector. She was heartily tired of living alone, and enjoying only casual and extremely rare intercourse with a sex she liked as well as the most ardent woman alive. But having learned some discretion in the school of her experience, she placed a curb upon her passions, and determined to avail herself of the first suitable opportunity that offered itself. One came in the person of the young soldier, who held her in his arms; and although she was as eager to yield as he was to partake, she had hitherto resisted the temptation.

"What can it avail you, to take advantage of a poor girl's simplicity?" urged she. "Besides, how do I know you will keep your word, after you have got what you wanted?"

The reply was a series of impassioned asseverations and oaths, such as lovers have used to damsels from time immemorial; and the inflamed soldier, becoming warmer by opposition, proceeded to such extremities, that Alice would soon have had either to cry out or submit, had not an interruption startled both of them. It came from Jasper, who all the while had been intently watching their manoeuvres from the opposite side of the garden, and who had become so infuriated by the freedoms Alice permitted, and the greater one she appeared likely to grant, that he could not avoid giving vent to such a cry of anguish, that it sounded very like the howl of a dog.

"Run!" cried Alice, in a terrified whisper. "Come here to-night at ten o'clock, and you shall have all you wish for."

The young gentleman, chagrined at being baffled, but appeased by such an unequivocal promise, beat a precipitate retreat, an example which Alice, without

daring to look to the right or left, speedily followed. Jasper darted forth from his hiding-place, and would have seized her, but a powerful motive arrested his intention. His features were horridly convulsed, and he jumped about, stamped the ground, and gave vent to such furious maledictions, that he seemed more like a fiend than a human being. It was a dance of curses.

"I could tear her to pieces!" said he, as he savagely ground his teeth together; "I could take her by each leg and split her to the bosom! A man once rent an oak asunder for mere sport, and what could not I do, who have been so monstrously wronged—so cut off in my prime from all connection with beings whom I adore more madly now than ever I did—made so hideously deformed, that even boys and girls, if they knew of it, would hoot at me in the streets? Why, my just revenge ought to make me a hundred times stronger than the oak splitter, or even that Scripture fellow that carried off the heavy gates of some humbugging place or another mentioned in the Bible. But I must be cautious, I must be cool—oh! yes, very cool; and yet I saw him paddling in her bosom and fingering. Oh, hell! if I saw it again I should get mad and kill her, and then farewell to revenge; but she must live—live with her pretty face until it becomes as great a curse to her as my calamity—live until her flesh drops in rotten pieces from her marrowless bones; and she, a living skeleton, be more afraid of death than I shall be of life, when I know that she will surely be eaten up by a slower and keener fire than that of the deep hell that rages in my bosom. Oh, for brandy—brandy!—fire to fire; but it cools me—ah! ah! and then to serve this stupid, sottish master of mine!"

Jasper, muttering as he went along, gained the house with a staggering gait, but, having partaken of a few cordials, he hastened to the countess's apartments, to ask, as had been customary with him of late, whether she had any commands for Lord Bloomfield; but in reality to learn all he could respecting her manner, habits, and visitors. It was only on these occasions that he saw Alice; for ever since that fearful night when she found him sleeping in the hall, and recognised in his hideous lineaments a strange resemblance to those of the man upon whom she had poured such a tremendous retribution, she had studiously avoided him; and when she did encounter him, it was with a shudder, which lent an ashy paleness to her otherwise, or at least when pleased or animated, saucy and piquant countenance.

Jasper knocked at the door of the room which led to the apartment where he generally found her ladyship; but receiving no answer, unceremoniously entered. She was still asleep, and Jasper, stealing on tiptoe, hastened to avail himself of the advantage by searching the escritoire before which the countess sat. He found nothing, however, to reward him for his pains. The letters and memoranda were all of a domestic and friendly character, interspersed with some that bore reference to the recently-adopted pursuits of the countess.

"I can find nothing worth a curse," thought he, as he carefully put aside the papers he had perused; "they all seem to be about some new fangled philosophy or another; what it is the Lord only knows. She doesn't look like a woman, though, that wouldn't care a pin for the handsomest man that ever stepped. There's something glorious—stunning—about her shape and physiognomy."

As Jasper indulged in this remark, he looked with a gloating aspect upon the recumbent figure of the sleeper. She was in truth a lovely creature—one of the beautiful woman-flowers which only the hand of the noble and generous should gather. The sensual and the intellectual were so sweetly combined in her noble features, that only the impure could detect where the one began and the other ended. Her neck, arched and haughty as the swan's, glowed with the hues of health; while in the regular pulsations of the filled-out, and tapering, and oh! deliciously-rounded bust beneath, there could have been detected the vigour and freshness of an organisation just commencing to feel that the glories of maturity, compared with those of puberty, are as the beams of the burning summer sun to those of the moon. The ardour of the girl had ripened into the mellowed but ardent passions of the woman, and the change, as the body developed itself, lent to the expression and character of her face and figure a voluptuousness so intoxicating, and yet so refined, that, while it invited the instincts of a beholder to indulge in those thrills which send the blood bubbling in hot streams through every artery and vein, at the same time check and repel brutal approaches. Even Jasper experienced some portion of this sensation as he gazed on her enchanting form, and noiselessly withdrew from the apartment.

In the hall he encountered Alice, and the scene that ensued between them was graphic in the extreme. Neither spoke, but both stood some few feet apart, gazing at each other, as if their eyes would start out of their heads.

"Miss Alice!" gasped Jasper, a cold perspiration stealing over his body, as he remembered the amorous interview in the garden.

"Mr. Sampson!" said Alice, faintly, but keeping her eyes fixed on his as if they had the power to charm her into obedience.

"We have met before!" said he.

"Have we?" replied she.

"Yes; and shall again!" said Jasper, by a prodigious effort controlling his savage hatred; "until then, remember me!"

"Remember you, Mr. Sampson?" cried Alice, starting out of her trance-like state by the chilling menace conveyed by his words; "what do you mean?"

"That we shall meet again, when I will tell you a story—such a nice one. Perhaps by some cosy fireside. Oh, yes, let it be by some cosy fire-side, where we can sit like a pair of lovers!"

"A pair of lovers!" echoed Alice, once more lifting up her eyes to those terrible ones.

"Why not? more unlikely things come to pass!" sneered Jasper, almost licking his lips with satisfaction, as he observed the hues of a death-like pallor steal over her face.

Alice could not reply—she was struck dumb by the spell which that terrible man appeared to have thrown over her. At that moment the countess's bell rang, and Alice, with a sigh that threatened to burst her prettily-formed chest, walked slowly on to obey the summons. She had to pass Jasper, and he, not moving, felt her garments brush against him, and could even inhale the lavender with which her ample, prettily-braided hair was perfumed. She passed from him, and, when she had disappeared, such a terrible groan shook his tall frame, that for several seconds his sides heaved and shook like those of a panting ox.

"Let me be calm—let me be calm!" muttered he, as he walked slowly away, with his hands clenched in the last excess of rage; or I shall spoil my revenge by some precipitation. The time will come—it must—shall—and then—and then—oh, yes, we will sit by

a cosy fire-side, like a pair of lovers! La! it will be a courting—sweet—delicious! She-devil!" And, stamping his feet on the floor of his room, he was about to yield to a paroxysm of fury, when his eyes fell upon the full-length portrait of a beautiful boy, which was suspended at the foot of his bed. The sight turned the current of his thoughts into a less rocky channel; and, mixing for himself a large tumbler full of brandy and sugar—no water—he lighted his pipe and sat down, and, while he smoked and drank, he kept his gaze firmly riveted on the portrait. His eyes all the while were tearless—he had shed the last one he had left in him when he obtained possession of the original of that likeness at Brighton.

"What on earth is the matter with you, Alice?" exclaimed the countess, as she noticed the agitation of her attendant.

"Nothing, my lady—that is—oh, dear! I'm so frightened!" said Alice, turning paler and paler as a suggestion of—to her—frightful import stole into her mind.

"What has frightened you?"

"That Mr. Sampson—that Jasper, as my lord calls him."

The countess laughed, and said she was not surprised at any pretty woman being alarmed at the sight of such an ugly, spiteful-looking wretch.

"But never mind him, Alice; if he annoys you, let me know, and I will soon have him turned out of the house. And now set about dressing me and yourself also, for you must go with me on an adventure to-night."

"To-night!" ejaculated Alice, who, recollecting her appointment, was disturbed by the announcement.

"To-night, girl; and why that start? had you some engagement with a lover? I am afraid, Alice, you are a sly girl, and have no objection to the society of a spruce young fellow. Nay, never blush so; like myself, you have tasted the sweet fruits of love, and the recollection of the feast quickens the wish to have it renewed. To-night, however, you must let him cool his heels and his courage, by vainly hoping that you will come to him. So prepare yourself to go out with me at five o'clock."

A servant at this moment entered, and announced Mrs. Smythe.

"At home," said the countess. "What the deuce brings Caroline here to-day? Go and dress yourself, Alice; it will save time. By-the-bye, make yourself smart; for we are going to a ball, and I am to be your sister; your name will do. We will be the two Misses Burton; and my coronet to your cap, we make a great sensation, and get all the beaux in the room."

This information consoled Alice for the deprivation of the society of Theodore; indeed, upon reflection she felt rejoiced that she would not have to meet him; for, much as she wished to delay granting his suit, he was so handsome and importunate, that to trust herself in the dark with him, would be tantamount to an unconditional surrender, and that would defeat the plans she had formed respecting him."

"My dear Caroline!" "Violet!" were the separate exclamations of the ladies, as they rushed into each other's arms and kissed each other affectionately.

Mrs. Smythe looked paler than usual, but her lustrous eyes retained their brilliancy, and flashed forth sparks of the fire that imparted such energy and volume to this handsome woman's ardent temperament.

"Where have you been this age?" inquired the countess, seating her friend by her side, and retaining the hand she held within her own.

"Quarrelling, as usual, with my brute of a husband, and sighing, like yourself, for a kiss from some handsome fellow!" was the saucy answer.

"Oh, don't say so, Caroline!" replied the countess, blushing; "you have surely forgotten all about that now?"

"Have I? Why I was never less inclined to be a nun than I am now; and, if I may judge from the roses on your cheeks, the sentiment would be reciprocated by my old schoolmate, Violet."

"It is so long since I tasted of the happiness of married life," sighed the countess, "that I do believe I have grown out of the habit of expecting it. Bloomfield is as bad as ever."

"Why, you have only to hold up your little finger, and he would leap to your arms," laughed Mrs. Smythe.

"And he would come to me reeking from a harlot's bed!" replied the countess severely. "No, no, Caroline, were he twenty times my husband, and a handsomer man than he is, which I think impossible, I would never, in his present state, admit him to my bed."

"Practice, they say, makes perfect," said Mrs. Smythe.

"Then let him practise at home!", laughed the countess; and the two ladies indulged in a burst of merriment.

"But, seriously, Caroline, what do you intend to do with Smythe?" inquired the countess. "Your case is different from mine. Bloomfield does not treat me either with cruelty or indifference — your husband does."

"I intend to get rid of the wretch!" replied the banker's wife, with imperturbable coolness. "The other day he was offensively personal. but since, for some reason or other— no good one I am sure—he has turned excessively civil, and last night had the impudence to creep into bed and begin to maul me, but I soon bundled him out of the room, for, as good-luck would have it, he was drunk, and my maid and myself easily managed him. He was so helpless that he lay outside the door all night in his shirt."

"Bloomfield," said the countess, "indulged in the same kind of conduct a few nights ago, but he was not very drunk, and as strong as a lion, so I had a hard task to resist him. I did so, and I do believe any woman might do the same if she liked. He swore like a trooper, so I ran away from him, and went to bed with Mrs Burton, who, by the way, is a warm little devil, for she kept hugging me all night, and calling me alternately Henry, Walter, and Theodore."

"We are all alike," sighed Mrs. Smythe; "your attendant cuddles you, but I cuddle mine. The other morning she awoke me by screaming out that I was smothering her. We are both fools for not having something more substantial in our arms. Much as I value discretion, I cannot afford to wait much longer."

"Nor I," said the countess, her fine features crimsoning as much from excitement as modesty. "When did you see Walter last?" inquired the countess.

"A few days ago he called upon me," replied Mrs Smythe, the blood rushing to her temples.

"He never comes here now," said the countess "I presume he is afraid of my imagining that he comes for thanks for the service he rendered poor Lucy.

"What of the colonel?" asked Mrs. Smythe, wishing to divert the conversation into another channel.

"He is out of danger, but maimed for life!" replied the countess.

"How."

"Walter's sword has incapacitated him for further service under General Cupid."

"What a pity!" compassionately answered Mrs. Smythe.

"It is true; and the report goes that he has done Walter all the injury he can. The Commander-in-Chief positively refuses to restore Captain Morris his commission."

"Then we must teach the Commander-in-Chief his duty," rejoined Mrs. Smythe. "Let you and I, Violet, set our wits to work, and put the poor fellow on his legs again."

"With all my heart. But what steps can we women take?"

"A hundred, if we like. Promise the old Duke, or the Prime Minister, or the Secretary for Foreign Affairs a kiss, and if they insist upon the pledge being redeemed, why do it. They are too old and sapless to do us any harm. Why I would undertake to buy the whole ministry in a twelvemonth."

"Fie, Caroline! how can you talk so?"

"I am only joking, you prude. What else have you and I left to do? Seriously, though, we must make an effort for Walter, and let us say no more about it, but do it. What are you going to do with yourself this evening?"

"Going to a ball."

"Where?"

"At some low place over the water. Bloomfield is going there, and I—I am going to watch him, and also see life of another kind."

"Take me with you?" eagerly requested Mrs. Smythe.

The countess made no objection, and communicated to her the particulars of the mode in which she had of late been following Lord Bloomfield from place to place.

"There will be excitement in it!" exclaimed Mrs. Smythe; "but who is the artiste that gets up your disguise?"

"One of the mysteries of London—a Mrs. Wriggles; the same old woman who, under the name of Madame Robertina, once told us our fortunes"

"Mrs. Wriggles?" said Mrs. Smythe, paling at the mention of the name.

"Yes; do you know her?"

"Slightly."

"She is a friend to ladies in difficulty," said the countess, regarding her friend with a penetrating glance.

Mrs Smythe did not observe it, for the reference to the old woman recalled the memory of her child, and brought vividly before her mind's eye the young girl in whom she had taken such a deep and passionate interest.

"This Mrs. Wriggles, then, attires you at her own house?" inquired she, musingly.

"She does; and, by the way, my watch tells me it is high time I was off. I will just throw on a dress, and be with you directly."

In a few minutes afterwards the countess, Mrs. Smythe, and Alice entered the carriage which Mrs. Wriggles had provided for such adventures, and the married trio were rapidly driven to the house known ll over London as the residence of the celebrated Madame Robertina.

Mrs. Wriggles experienced as much surprise as gratification at once more beholding the woman she so cordially detested. Surprise, because she had imagined her to be in Paris, revelling in the enjoyment of the sturdy society of Captain Morris; gratification, that she once more had the opportunity of throwing around her intended victim the most sinister influences she could create or promote. Although curious to be informed how Mrs. Smythe had become so soon separated from Walter, she had too much tact to betray her knowledge of the affair by making any inquiries. Her sources of information were too secure for her to alarm any of the parties in whose affairs she interfered, by any unnecessary disclosures of a knowledge of their conduct. Like a skilful diplomatist, she preferred the under current to the upper ones, and knew that tortuous means were the best conductors to tortuous ends. Having Mrs. Smythe in her power, and aware of the warmth of her temperament, she resolved to make her a partner in the adventures of the countess in search of Lord Bloomfield, and so win her confidence and lead her into the commission of every species of extravagance. Mrs. Smythe, she knew, was aware of her connection with Dr. Wriggles, but entirely ignorant, she was assured, of her identity with the woman who had rendered the service in the affair of the concealed pregnancy. The doctor, she felt convinced, would not make the disclosure; and so, armed with this confidence and her own indomitable audacity, she resolved to make the good she was rendering the countess one of the means of working out her diabolical plan of effecting the social and moral destruction of the last daughter of the race against whom she had sworn eternal enmity. The preparations for the Socialist ball were soon completed. Mrs. Smythe's dark hair was changed into a beautiful light auburn, and a tint was given to her complexion to correspond. The countess was metamorphosed into a brunette, and the pair were attired in garments corresponding in quality with those worn by Alice. Thus attired, with Mrs. Wriggles in a becoming black satin dress and formidable cap, the party left Middlesex in a cab, for the more plebeian shores of Surrey.

While the ladies were thus employed, my Lord Bloomfield was not idle. With the assistance of his valet, he had just completed his unexceptionable costume of a gentleman, when he summoned his satellite, Jasper, to his presence.

That worthy was sprucely dressed, and evidently bent on a conquest of some kind.

"Well," said his lordship, sharply, for, like all debauchees, his temper was bad, until he had again mingled in the scenes that invariably bring on the distemper popularly called the "blues."

"My lord," replied Jasper, who, having an equally ruffled equanimity, did not care to be badgered by anybody.

"Have you anything to communicate?"

"Nothing."

"Idiot!"

"My lord, I can invent stories, if you like, about her ladyship, but I'm d——d if I can make her a w——e."

"Insolent scoundrel!" cried his lordship, about to hurl something at Jasper's head; but the double meaning conveyed by the latter's remark smote so keenly upon his risible faculties, that he gave way to a burst of laughter, and soon became more good-humoured.

"Have you nothing at all to tell me?"

"Oh yes," replied Jasper; "her ladyship often goes out with an old woman they call Mrs. Wriggles; and I have watched them, but they only went to poor places, where her ladyship gave money away."

"Indeed!" responded his lordship, rather amazed that a woman of fashion should so spend her time.

"And sometimes," continued Jasper, "they go to charitable institutions—her ladyship is a trustee, or committee-woman, in many of them. Yesterday she went to the Magdalen Asylum."

"The devil she did! I thought women never subscribed to such institutions."

"Her ladyship is one of the managers, and does all she can to induce unfortunate girls to enter it."

"Does she seek the creatures out herself?" said his lordship, disquieted by the bare reflection that his wife should breathe the same atmosphere as those ill-used beings.

"No; Mrs. Wriggles does that, or gets it done. Here is a paper one of them dropped, containing a history of one of the girls."

His lordship, with some compunction, read the following memorandum:—

"Ellen Ramsay, age eighteen, born at Clapham, where her parents now reside in comfortable circumstances. She is a pretty, light-haired girl; has walked the streets—the Strand, chiefly—for two years. At sixteen she fell in love with a young fellow who daily passed her father's house, and who ultimately prevailed on her to walk out with him in the evening. The common was their chief promenade; and one balmy evening they lay down to talk nonsense about the stars and the moon. He began to pull her about, and tickle her, until she became so excited that she did not know what he was about before she felt him hurting her severely, and she fainted, or lost all recollection. When she recovered, she was clasped in his arms on a bank, and no longer a maid. She cried very much, but did not know she had been doing very great wrong. Had never been told it was wrong for a young man to take liberties with her. Had seen her father and mother in bed, kissing each other just before father got up. Often went to the common after that, and at last fell in the family way. Her mother beat her, and her father turned her out of doors. Her lover took a lodging for her and paid the expenses of her confinement. The child died. Her lover kept her until he died of the cholera. After that she was destitute, and her landlady turned her out of doors. She wandered about all day until she found herself in the Strand, looking in the shop windows. Many gentlemen accosted her, but she was frightened, and ran away from them. At length a decently-dressed old woman asked her to go home with her. She did go, and found many girls there. She told the old woman her story, and that night, after a good deal of persuasion, went to bed with an old gentleman, who came to the house to look for a companion. She was sick in the morning, owing to the old man's pulling her about so. Every night after that, for a month, she had a fresh bedfellow, and fell ill through it. She was taken to the hospital, and when she came out the old woman lent her clothes, and she walked the streets every night as a dress lodger. Should say that I brought a companion home with me every night for two years. I was young and pretty, and the rakes of the theatres called me 'Ellen, the Pride of the Strand.' I am now very ill, and thankful that I have found friends to take me from such a dreadful course of life. From what I have seen and heard, none of us girls like the life they lead. They do it for money. When several are together they talk of having a chap of their own to keep them. They can't do without a man. Few girls who have walked the streets can They have a fever always about them."

"*Note by the Taker of the Deposition.*—It would seem, from this poor girl's confession, that during two years, she had been embraced by upwards of seven hundred different men! Only imagine, seven hundred brawny, stalwart, big-boned, and strong thewed men (?) tearing at and grinding away the body of a slender girl, scarce eight stones in weight! Yet those seven hundred men (?) walk upright and unabashed along the streets of life, while their puny plaything dwindles away in a corner. After this appalling statement, it is no wonder that the average duration of life among our prostitutes is only three years!* And what a three years! Oh! ye tall and lithesome seven hundred! ye men who go upon the tiles, like cats! think of all this, and then cease to wonder that, when ye marry, your children are pale, ricketty, blotched, and stunted! 'The sins of the fathers are truly visited on the children!'"

"Only three years!" exclaimed Bloomfield; "I can scarcely credit it."

"Some of the tough ones live a good deal longer," replied Jasper; but the young ones generally go off in a year or two. They get ——, then take to drink, and then go off in a gallopping consumption. Will your lordship go to that place this evening?"

Lord Bloomfield had not a bad heart, and this narrative had shocked him not a little; so he did not immediately reply to the question. After a consultation between his better and evil nature, the latter triumphed, and in an hour afterwards he, too, was on his way to the Socialist ball and tea-party, about which and its concoctors, supporters, and promoters, it will be as well to say a few words.

That the age is a very degenerate one, will not be denied, seeing that we have the assertion supported by the authority of ladies and gentlemen of various moral denominations. The saying is one of those trite ones which do somehow or another fasten on the public mind, and retain their hold tenaciously. The characteristic is no great evil perhaps, for it is with communities as it is with individuals—a little self-debasement now and then is healthy, and, doubtless, the readiest way to forge a virtue is to beat out a vice. Declamation is a very useful agent in this work of humiliation and reform, and hence it is that we find oratory of all degrees enlisted on the side of all popular movements, be they vicious or useful. Some of this kind of apostles have had an extremely mysterious origin; like mushrooms, they have sprung in one night out of the soil of popular discontent; and probably no field of discussion ever gave birth to a greater number of them than that occupied by a philosophical race, who have taken unto themselves the appellation of Socialists. With the aggregate body this narrative can have nothing to do; but with the society to whose festive and intellectual reunion my Lord and Lady Bloomfield were separately wending their way, it necessarily has; therefore some account of the institution, and its leading members, will be an appropriate introduction to the amusing proceedings of the evening.

Alfred Walker, a young gentleman of five-and-twenty, who had run through his means, both moral and pecuniary, frequented a certain coffee-room in the Borough, where he encountered two other equally congenial and necessitous persons. These were a middle-aged gentleman, named Snowball—rather seedy in his externals, but well furnished inwardly with philosophical attainments—and a young aspirant to elocutionary honours, named Gibson, who, in a fit of delirium tremens, had walked off with his master's cash-box, and lived on his wits ever since. This trio, day by day, had unanimously agreed, over

* A fact. See Dr. Wardlow's Reports.

their coffee, that society was in a deplorable condition, everything was hastening to an universal bankruptcy, and unless something was done to arrest the progress of the devastation, human nature must inevitably wind up its accounts, and make a clean breast and whitewash affair of it altogether.

"Let us throw down the fields of bigotry, and tear up the torrents of oppression by the roots!" exclaimed the elocutionist.

"Let us bilk somebody!" exclaimed Alfred Walker, who, by-the-bye, was a young fellow of some ability, and withal had a handsome face and figure of his own.

"Let us first learn how to do it!" said the sagacious Snowball. "Now listen to me, lads. Society is in a ferment—men's minds are loose and unsettled, and ready to bite at any scheme, however daring; but as we have not the tin to do anything respectable, we must do something that is practicable. If we can't fly our kites high, we must fly them low. Now this Socialist movement in France is not exactly popular in London; but people are curious to know something about it, especially the women, and they flock to hear something about it. The girls and wives of London have heard a good deal about the iniquity of our marriage laws; and, as some are dissatisfied, and some very randy, there would be no doubt of our having lots of both at the meeting I propose. Once get the women, and the men are sure to follow. I propose that we start a Socialist institution, and have lectures, tea parties, dancing classes, and balls."

"Admirable!" cried Walker; "what fun there will be with the pretty girls!"

"I'll take the tin at the door," said the elocutionist.

"We'll see about that," drily responded Snowball.

And in that propitious hour was the Southwark Institution for the Regeneration of the Human Race established. The keeper of the coffee-house was called upon to be security for the rent of a large room, and to be responsible for some flaming broadsides; both of which requests he complied with, upon being allowed to receive the money at the door, and account for it afterwards.

On the second Sunday after the perfection of the arrangements, the society was inaugurated with much ceremony. Walker was master of the ceremonies, and pleased the shoals of young ladies who ascended the precipitous staircase so well, that they audibly vowed they would come again. The elocutionist, being an adept in finance, was stationed at the door to check the money-taker; and Snowball, at the hour of eight, ascended the rostrum, and delivered a furious discourse against "the marriage laws of all nations." He was loudly applauded at the conclusion of his lecture, and seized that opportune moment to announce the fact of the existence of the society, and that its future meetings would be of a lively, amusing, and humanising character—balls, tea, and copious flows of wit and humour, being the agents selected to regenerate those who would condescend to partake of the benefits offered by the society to the whole of the human race.

The thing took amazingly, and, at the end of twelve months, Messrs. Walker, Snowball, and Gibson lived decently, as became philosophers of such philanthropic pretensions. Walker had the sway with the prettiest of the girls, and, amid scores of Platonic attachments, always took care to have a dozen on hand of a more substantial character. Snowball, as the great intellectual gun of the concern, took the middle-aged married ladies under the wing of his protection; and Gibson, whose brilliant scintil-

lations of eloquence sometimes took the room by storm, succeeded admirably with the shop-girls and faded spinsters, whose virility and virginity had disappeared long ago.

The programme offered by this enterprising trio was morning, afternoon, and evening service on Sunday, concluding with a tea and coffee conversazione; dancing on Monday evening; concert on Tuesday; discussion class on Wednesday; mutual improvement classes on Thursday and Friday; and concert on Saturday. In addition, every fourth Monday there was held a grand ball, commencing with a tea-party and lecture.

Such attractions could not fail to draw together motley audiences. First of all, among the men there were mechanics who came on the Sunday to listen to the fustian of Snowball or the indecency of Walker—for he, too, held forth—and the obscure rhapsodies of the elocutionist. Then there were the clerks, who came to ogle the girls, and pick up the pretty ones; shopmen and linendrapers' assistants, on the same errand; middle-aged tradesmen, who came to look out for tender pieces; and swells, who came to romp, or purchase a companion for a night's debauch. Of the women, the majority were young

girls: they consisted chiefly of dress and bonnet makers; mechanics' daughters, loose girls, acknowledged prostitutes, married women, "out on the loose," as their husbands term dissipated fits, and a few girls of respectable, even superior accomplishments, whom their love of excitement and the warmth of their propensities had attracted thither. From such an assemblage it would be supposed that their meetings would be characterised by riot and confusion, but this was far from being the case: outwardly everything was orderly and decorous; the fun of the thing, its very soul and purpose, was transacted in secresy, or at least without any outrage against public decency.

The hour was seven, and by this time some three or four hundred people were assembled in the various rooms of the building, which had been hired, decorated, and dignified by the title of the Southwark Institution for the Regeneration of the Human Race.

"It ought to have said the procreation," remarked Jasper, on the first evening of his visit.

Some of the parties were congregated in knots, listening to the expositions of some Socialist leader, or laughing heartily at the bold witticisms of the young gentlemen in stiff cravats, who had ladies under each arm; others were walking about in pairs; some were in search of partners they had lost; and not an inconsiderable section of the masculines were premenading with elevated eye-glass, and taking deliberate surveys of the feminines, who sauntered about in all the inviting displays of ringlets, bared bosoms and arms, and occasionally, where the ankles were presentable, in short petticoats.

Bloomfield and Jasper arrived before the proceedings commenced, and as they threaded the rooms the latter whispered in his master's ear:

"They all look as randy as hell to-night!"

"Here is a good place to stand," said his lordship, taking up a position where he could scrutinise he company as they passed before him; "do you know any of these people?"

"Lot's of 'em," replied Jasper. "Do you see that girl with the remarkably fine shape, and wagging bustle—the one there that shows her titties?"

"Yes."

"Well, she's the daughter of a chandler, and had a child by the fellow in yellow kids yonder. He keeps her—that is he pays her so much a week—but she doesn't keep to him; that fussy old fellow yonder, a linen-draper in the Blackfriars Road, gives her a sovereign occasionally, and she also drives a tolerably brisk trade with a chemist near at hand."

"Faugh! she is common. Who is that pretty creature with timid, dove-like eyes and easy, graceful manner?"

"She is a tradesman's daughter, who goes out in the evening under the pretence of visiting an aunt, but comes here to meet that young fellow with long black hair, who is breaking his neck to run to her."

"She seems a maid."

"She is not, for he regularly every evening puts her on a form in the place they call a school-room."

"The devil! But petticoats can hide many rents and fissures. Who is that brazen-looking thing, who shows a bosom just like a brace of cow's dugs?"

"She! Oh, that's one of the female lecturers. Old Snowball owns her, and jolly good tannings she gives him when he isn't up to the mark."

"By heavens, but that's a pretty girl!" exclaimed his lordship, as a tall, dashing-looking bloade, with the gait of a queen, swept past them.

"That is Miss Amelia Jones—an adventuress, but a particular one. She likes a man well enough, but a gentleman. She lived a month with Colonel R—, and got him to give her a thousand pounds, and then she set up house for herself. The colonel married, and she refused to have anything more to do with him. All or none is her motto.

"Is she very frail?"

"Oh, no, she likes to plague the men; the other night she took an old fellow home with her, and, after driving him to the extremity of sensual madness. coolly turned him into the street to cool himself It is said that she has cast her eyes upon a modest young fellow that comes here."

"Slip my *private* card into her hand as she passes."

Jasper obeyed the request, and, as he did so, with a motion of his eyes intimated that it was from his friend. Amelia glanced at the lofty patrician figure of his lordship, and, making an almost imperceptible gesture of acknowledgment, smiled, and passed on.

"She will be at home," said Jasper.

"If the other fails, I will have an hour or two's chat with her by-and-bye. What does that bell ring for?"

"For the guzzle. Perhaps your lordship would like to see them all in, and then go afterwards and quiz the lot spanking into the bread and butter?"

In an incredibly short space of time the mass settled down into the seats in the large room, and commenced a vigorous attack on the tea and coffee-urns, bread-and-butter, and other articles on the tables. Bloomfield and Jasper seated themselves in the vicinity of two sprightly girls of sixteen or seventeen, and derived much amusement from their sprightly remarks and savoury moral inuendos. Jasper attached himself to the one by his side, because she was a little rosy-cheeked brunette, and reminded him, by her appearance, of Alice Burton in her young and early wedded days; and while he was striving, with diabolical earnestness, to ingratiate himself with the giddy thing, he was all the time devising how he might best carry into effect his determination to offer her up as a victim to his sworn hatred to the sex. Ugly and repulsive as he was, there was, to an uneducated girl, a fascination in his manner, and a drollery in his language and monkey-like antics, which prevented her being at all alarmed or feeling disgusted in his society. Women of all grades doat upon admiration, and, however foul the channel of its conveyance may be, they rarely deem the stream itself to be polluted.

Bloomfield paid marked attention to his companion, because it was as natural to him to edge himself close up to a pretty girl as it was to sleep; but all the while he kept glancing around the room in search after the fair creature whose attractions had drawn him thither.

The ladies and gentlemen who were assembled to do justice to the tea-party, sustained their individual share in the performance with immense credit. There was a mighty clattering of cups and saucers, terrible devastation among the bread and butter, and not a few brandy and rum bottles liberally circulated from hand to hand. The middle-aged ladies, adorned with caps, and decked with artificial flowers and ribbons of every hue, were uproarious in their demonstrations of delight. Their glances, too, spoke volumes to the hale gentlemen by their sides; and the exchanges of pokes in the ribs, ticklings on the knees, and pressure of feet, was highly amusing, or, as Dr. Johnson would have said, elaborately diverting. The younger people laughed and giggled, and looked at each other in that come-and-kiss-me manner, which reduces the tongue to silence, from the dread of spoiling a well understood engagement.

Before the time allotted for the consumption of the viands had been half-disposed of, a great bustle at the door announced the arrival of some one whose presence was highly popular in the community. The new comer was a neatly-clad and beautiful young woman. She was tall for her sex, but fleshy, not bony, in proportion. Her dark auburn hair fell in a profusion of long thick tresses on each side of her rather prominent brow, down to her partially-concealed shoulders, and at every toss of her head rolled over and over each other in bewitching disorder. The face, the cheeks of which were suffused by a rich carnation, was delicately fair—not snowy white, but fleshy fair—and the features were of classic mould. The eyes were of deep cerulean colour—neither grey nor blue, but of the intermediate tinge so frequently to be met with in persons of sensual temperaments and vigorous mental attainments. Not being either too large or too small, their light flashed upon you like rays from a concave reflector, and imparted to an aquiline nose, short upper lip, and full but firmly-closed and extremely fresh, rosy mouth, an expression, partly amative and party intellectual. When looking at the transparently-veiled bosom, with the tips of a pair of small, firm globes peering above the edge of the dress, the former impression prevailed; but the eyes, throwing a brilliant light over face and bust, banished the warmer suggestion, and replaced it by one which recognised in the warm living being who moved so gracefully amid loud applause, a woman with all her youthful pulses playing, but having her native promptings checked and held in control by some of those touches of mind which lift human nature from the mire of desire, and place it on the pedestal of thought. As she moved up one of the spaces left between the rows of tea-drinkers, her eye caught Bloomfield's, and, after acknowledging his presence by a glance that made him tingle from top to toe, she ascended a species of platform erected at the top end of the room; and, being followed by her chevalier, a tall, fair-complexioned, and good-looking young man, with large, deep-grey eyes, she sat down in the vicinity of the president's seat; but had no sooner done so, than another sensation was created by the arrival of a party of strange ladies, in the persons of Mrs. Wriggles, the countess, Mrs. Smythe, and Alice. The latter, while in the shadow of the doorway, caught a glimpse of Jasper, and turned so pale as she stood rooted to the spot, that her mistress noticed her emotion, as also did Mrs. Wriggles.

"That man—that Jasper—that Sampson!" replied Alice, in reply to the countess's hurried inquiry.

"Do you know him?" asked Mrs. Wriggles, as she regarded her searchingly.

"No, no; I sometimes think I do, and yet I don't; but I am so frightened of him," said Alice, staring at the object of her remark with a wild aspect.

"Send her home, or tell her to wait for you in the neighbourhood," whispered Mrs. Wriggles to the countess. "The spy is here, and, being certain to recognise Alice, may spoil all our little plans."

The countess turned her head in the direction indicated by Mrs. Wriggles, and, upon seeing Jasper, felt slightly discomposed, not only at the prospect of there being a risk of discovery, but at the situation in which she had found her husband. However, she smoothed her ruffled features, and, perceiving the wisdom of the old woman's advice, dismissed Alice; and the chiefs of the establishment, Messrs. Snowball, Walker, and Gibson at that moment coming forward, the party were ushered on to the platform, where they were also accommodated with seats in the vicinity of the chair. Alice needed no second intimation to depart, for she darted down the stairs, and did not pause until she had placed the distance of several streets between her and the dreaded object of her horrible fears. She crossed Waterloo Bridge with the fleetness of a fawn, and was emerging into the Strand, when she ran plump into the arms of a gentleman, who received her with no displeasure; on the contrary, he bestowed upon her a by no means gentle hug.

"I beg your pardon, sir," exclaimed Alice, disengaging herself.

"What, my merry sprite, Alice!" almost shouted Walter Morris, now, alas! only captain by etiquette!

"Walter?" rejoined the lady, as much relieved—so great was her terror of Jasper—as if she had met the dearest friend she had on earth.

"The same, darling," said that gallant woman-loving personage; "and as fate has thrown us together, let us make the most we can of the boon. What say you to an hour at the theatre, a hot supper afterwards, and then ——"

"I must go home," said Alice, taking his arm, nevertheless, without reluctance.

The Lyceum was open: Alice hesitated at the door for a moment—it was only a moment—and then entered, and the remainder of the evening and night was passed as Walter had wished it to be; Alice the next morning contriving to arrive at home and reach her chamber without being observed by any person in the house for whose criticisms she at all cared. Walter also went his way, whistling a lively tune, for Alice was naturally, in all such encounters, as merry a wife as had ever giggled between a pair of blankets.

But to return to the proceedings in the rooms of The Society for the Regeneration of the Human Race. After the festival of tea, or, as Jasper irreverently termed it, slops, there was a lecture delivered by Miss Laura Bell, the young lady whose rare beauty and recognition of Bloomfield have already been noticed. Her theme was the trite one—"The Independence of Woman." The scope and aim of her elaborate and well-embellished address was the deplorable tyranny and masculine cruelties which man heaped on poor defenceless woman. Her peroration was as a pretty specimen of feminine reasoning and womanly indignation as ever found its way into print.

"Men and women, married and single, old and young," exclaimed Laura, "let us, in the true cause for which *we* are banded together set society—the world—an example of independence, of chastity, of faith, of divine, glorious enchanting, thrilling, soul-dissolving love. Let us yield obedience to the sovereign laws of nature, and gladden our hearts with sweets culled from many flowers—with music drawn from the inspirations of the mind—with ecstacies borrowed from the thrills that lull us to sweet slumbers—with love—divine, maddening, voluptuous love. Our lives, compared with our capacities for enjoyment, are but like those of glittering insects, who are born, marry, and die in a day. Their golden wings sparkle in the sunshine; they kiss as do the moonbeams the waters; they live and die amid a laughing shower of splendour; and why should we not, in our sphere, and in our nobler and larger nature, emulate so instructive an example? Why should our lives be an uninterrupted round of toil? Is the crown of thorns always to be bound round our temples? Are we destined, made, manufactured to order, ever to be the galley-slaves of fortune? No. The soul, in its might and majesty, hurls back the insinuation with a lofty disdain, and tells kings, priests, and tyrants, of all grades of iniquity, that, however human institutions may fetter—however they may cramp—the energies of the body, those of the mind, like the stars above us, are beyond their reach; and all of us, even the mariner, high on the giddy yard in the middle of the ominously-swelling ocean—the lone prisoner in his cell—the exile pining on the distant beach, far from the fireside where all his affections are garnered up—all can tell, and proudly too, that there is a power beyond the reach of slavery, or poverty, or injustice, and that is

Love—unspeakable, ineffable, world-founding Love—the light, the life, the essence, the incarnation of all that we should hope for, either here or hereafter. This is the law; and as youth is the season of its fulness—of its glory and power—let us seek to be perpetually loving, while we are young, and so lay up, like busy bees, a store of honeyed recollections for our dry and withered old age."

That such advice was considered palatable, might have safely been inferred from the tumultuous applause that ensued; and amid it, the fair lecturer, with sparkling eyes, suffered herself to be conducted to a seat by the handsome philosopher who had escorted her into the room. As the last faint echoes of the cheers died away, the company rose, and confusedly left the room, for the purpose, as it presently appeared, of allowing some half dozen men, with their shirt-sleeves rolled up, to denude the place of the forms and tables which had accommodated the tea-party. In this interval the series of intrigues commenced which were destined, some of them, to progress far towards completion, and others to be wholly consummated during the evening. Jasper, who, by the way, had paid his respects to Mrs. Wriggles, and tried hard, but in vain, to discover whom her companions were, induced the smart little brunette by his side to cling to him, and also to accept him as a partner in several dances. Bloomfield made his way to Miss Laura Bell, and, despite one or two frantic efforts of the philosopher, bore her from him in triumph. His eyes glared rather furiously at the loss; but, happening to let them follow the exquisitely-handsome faces, and voluptuously-developed figures of the countess and Mrs. Smythe, their expression instantly changed; and when, after standing for a minute or so, in speechless admiration of their charms, he encountered the glance of Mrs. Smythe's full, dark orbs, the current of his thoughts was completely diverted. Mrs. Smythe instantly saw how matters stood, and, preferring fair, large-sized men to dark ones, permitted his approaches, and finally allowed herself to be borne away to indulge in the *tete a tete* of a promenade. The raven locks of the beautiful countess, and her noble glowing countenance had long ago fascinated no less a personage than Mr. Gibson, the elocutionist; and he strode up to her, with something like a blush on his sallow cheeks—for there was something about the style of the countess which rather daunted his audacity.

"Do in Rome as Rome does," whispered Mrs. Wriggles.

The countess, with a shrug of disgust, placed the tips of her slender fingers on the sleeves of the elocutionist's coat, and followed in the track of the crowds who thronged the ante-room and passage, until the large room was prepared for the ball.

Mrs. Wriggles, seeing her *protegees* disposed of, as she thought, for the evening, sought out Mr. Snowball, in one of the private apartments of the building; and, some more potent liquids than tea or coffee having been produced, the pair sat down to have a little confidential chit-chat.

"Where's your wife?" inquired Mrs. Wriggles.

A dark shadow swept over the lines of the Socialist's swarthy visage, as he answered:

"In hell, I hope."

"Is she dead, then, Nick?"

"As a herring."

"How did she die? Come, Nick, let there be no secrets between you and me. You know I never hurt a man, and you also know I could hang you at any moment—so tell me the truth. How did you get rid of the milky-faced drab?"

Snowball was partially intoxicated, and not at all disposed to be communicative to such a person as Mrs. Wriggles.

"I am certain *you* won't peach," said he, the shadow on his rugged brow deepening. "But some other time—I can't tell you now."

"Nothing like the present time, Nick. Come, old fellow, take another nip of the brandy, and out with it! You can have nothing to fear, for you must know I hated the minx."

And the old woman, after plying the man, over whom, by the way, she exercised a strange power, with more of the burning liquid, soon succeeded in extracting from him the following startling confession:

"You are aware how ardently I loved that woman—how I doated upon the very ground she trod?"

Mrs. Wriggles nodded her assent, but smiled ironically.

"Well, she dishonoured me. I was young and romantic, then, and forgave her."

"I know you did," interrupted Mrs. Wriggles; "and she showed her gratitude by spending your money, and cuckolding you whenever she could."

"D——n!" growled Snowball; "but never mind—I had satisfaction. Well, as I was saying, I forgave her. One night—twelve months afterwards—I had been out attending to a patient, and came home rather late, when, not wishing to make a noise, I stole into the house as softly as I could, and crept gently up stairs. I heard voices in my wife's chamber—hers and another. I listened, and detected the well known sounds of conjugal pleasure. I was stupefied—awed—at the woman's perfidy and ingratitude. Like one in a dream, I crept up stairs to the room where my child, a fine boy of five years old, lay. I struck a light, and oh! horror—horror!—he was dead. The fumes of the stove I had, with the kindest motives, the warmest parental solicitude, placed in his bed-room, had suffocated him. I kissed him; and when I had done so a strange revolution occurred in my organisation. My hand, which had before trembled, became as steady as a pillar, and instead of breathing like one choking, I respired as freely as if I had never been agitated. A cold chill, an iciness, seemed to have mingled with my blood, and made me as impassive as a statue. I made not the slightest noise, but descended the stairs, and then, making a clatter at the door, re-ascended them as if I had but just entered the house, and was in a hurry to get to bed as soon as possible. As I did so, I caught the sound of a flying footstep—it could have been none other than that of my assistant—but I heeded it not, so spell-bound was I by that awful congealment, that frostiness of body and soul, which had quenched all the warm emotions of my youthful nature—for I was not then twenty-five. I found my wife alone, with a smile on her countenance, and, as usual, she reached forth her lips for me to kiss her. I mechanically did so, and she fell back in the bed as if she had been shot. My lips, on her hot ones, felt colder than the frosty pavement outside would have been. She uttered an exclamation of surprise, of which I took no notice, and quietly retired to bed. From that night henceforth, whenever I approached her, the same almost intolerable coldness seized me, and I used to take a devilish delight in her shiverings whenever I availed myself of a husband's privilege, which I did as regularly as if nothing had occurred to mar our felicity. Twelve months again elapsed, and my wife during that period became a confirmed harlot; yet I endured her presence, because I did so like to see and hear her shiver. At length she and the assistant bolted, and my iciness vanished. I took a mistress into my house, and felt once more like a man. But she died: I had that day met my wife, and my coldness returned, and killed the woman. I took another to my arms, again saw my wife, and my frigidity returned, and she, too, died. I then resolved to take my wife back again. I sought her out, but she refused. I then had recourse to stratagem, and succeeded in conveying her to an apartment in my house, unperceived by any one. I walled up all communication, except through a secret door in my laboratory, and then prepared myself to take my revenge. I first cut her tongue out, so that she could not possibly make any alarm; I then amputated her feet, so that she could not leave the room; and then I cut off her hands, so that she could neither eat nor drink the food and rich wines I every day set before her. All that took me about twelve months to do: for before I undertook a fresh operation, I had to wait until the strength lost by the previous one had returned. She took her food as regularly as possible out of my hands, and throve in bodily health: she had an amazing constitution for so slender a woman. In another twelve months I cut off her legs, and her two arms, right out of their sockets; and in another twelve months I took off both her thighs in the thick part, and finished off by scoring her face in such a manner that not a single original feature could be discovered. I then carried her, in the bottom of my chaise, a few miles out of town, and left her by the road-side. Curiosity kept me near the spot until I saw her picked up by some travelling showman, who afterwards exhibited her living trunk through the country, as a nondescript animal imported from the island of Java. She died soon after that, and the showman, fearful of explanation, buried her as secretly as possible. And so that was the way I had my revenge. But when I think of her now my coldness returns, and, in addition, I shiver as she used to do when I touched her. Ugh! Ugh! give me some brandy!"

Mrs. Wriggles gazed at the monster in undisguised amazement, and when he repeated his request, she exclaimed:

"Well, I never heard or read of such a thing in all the annals of revenge!"

And, pouring out the brandy, she pushed the glass over to him and backed out of the room, gazing at him in a kind of speechless horror, blended with admiration. After she had gone he tried to raise the glass to his lips, but his hand refused the office—a convulsive movement seized upon his frame, and, unable to move or utter a word, he sat in his chair, shivering and shaking as if every nerve, muscle, and bone in his body were being acted upon by galvanism.

Mrs. Wriggles proceeded to the ball-room, and, mingling with the throng, soon managed to discover how the parties she knew were occupied or amusing themselves. Dancing had already commenced, and the old woman smilingly noticed that one of the quadrilles was comprised of the countess and Gibson, Mrs. Smythe and the philosopher, Miss Laura Bell and Bloomfield, and Jasper and the brunette, Martha.

"There is some difference of rank there, but none of passion or present purpose, except with that fiend Jasper, who, I can perceive, has already tickled little Martha into a fever heat. I must introduce him to Snowball—two such devils ought to be able to jog on together! Their lives have been the same—villanously bad; but Jasper's wife not only horned him, but gloriously served him out. What a monster! See how he is pawing that wicked little creature! She must penetrate the real secret of her sex tonight, or go mad! May every woman in the room but Violet experience the same tortures! However, 'on with the dance; let joy be unconfined,' until you are all made prostitutes and knaves; and now let me ascertain something about those creatures Bloomfield and that cat of a thing, Caroline, have got hold of!"

Mrs. Wriggles invited several of the stout elderly Socialist ladies who waddled about the room, to partake of some "cold without," and speedily ingratiated herself with them so far, that she soon gleaned the information she desired.

Laura Bell, *alias* Mary Ann Jones, was a Leicester girl, of respectable parents, who attained her eighteenth year without anything remarkable happening in her career; but at that age her parents died, and she found herself in possession of property that yielded her an income of 200*l.* per annum. With this she began to indulge in a number of extravagancies: one of them being to purchase a handsome ignoramus of a young fellow, and send him to school, to be educated after a system she herself had designed. This fellow she intended to marry, as soon as his training had been completed; but, being a poor miserable wretch of a thing, he took to tippling, and made himself so ridiculous by his boastings, that Mary Ann indignantly discarded him and her husband scheme both together. Her virginity, though, appeared to be an incumbrance to her, and she commenced an industrious search for the man upon whom she should bestow it. A clergyman was the first to perceive her weakness; but before they had even exchanged a simple kiss, they disputed on a point of theological doctrine, and she turned him neck and crop out of the house. A doctor next attacked her, and would have succeeded, but when he undressed to get into bed, she discovered that he had an ulcerated leg, and he was dismissed quite as unceremoniously, with the remark, that the man who could not cure himself could not cure her. A gentleman behind a profusion of hair next tried his hand, but she offended him by one day exclaiming, after he had uttered the only sensible observation he had ever made in her presence:

"Orson is endowed with reason!"

What the clergyman, the physician, and the man of fortune had failed to accomplish, a young carpenter, doing some repairs in the house, did successfully. She wished to learn something about the mysteries of his tool-basket, and put so many questions to him that he could not attend to his work.

"I tell you what, miss, said he, regarding her exposed bosom with inflamed looks; "if you shut your eyes I'll show you something worth seeing!"

She did so, and the carpenter, being a nimble young fellow, in five minutes beat parson, doctor, and Orson hollow; and, what is more, so satisfied Mary Ann that he came thrice a week with his tool-basket, and always had some repairs to do, which occupied him half the day. But the carpenter was a silly fellow, and in his cups talked so vain-gloriously of the wonderful value of his tool-basket, that certain injurious reports began to be circulated militating against the fair fame of Miss Jones; and this so exasperated her that she got the man discharged from his situation, and then precipitately left the town and went to Nottingham. There she formed a *liaison* with a prowling Chartist lecturer, and travelled the country in 1848, preaching fire and sword political economy, until the lecturer was arrested, tried, and transported. She herself narrowly escaped prosecution; but the solicitor employed by the government becoming enamoured of her charms, she purchased her redemption by a three months' residence with him as his mistress; and when all the danger was over, left him, and came to London, where, *a la* Martineau, she took to moral and political philosophy; and ultimately became a pupil of the celebrated Robert Owen. During her Socialist peregrinations she met with her last lover, Horace Singleton, who soon persuaded her to live with him in the holy bonds of Socialist matrimony, and after this she became an accepted light among the body. She has always been faithful to her lover for the time being, but maintains the orthodox Socialist doctrine, that until a woman has discovered the man who, in every respect, agrees with her temperament, and suits her physical and moral organisation, she may change him as often as she can. Her engagement with Horace has already endured three months, and they appear as loving as becomes staid Socialists, who never publicly betray their conjugal fondness by superfluous caresses, which only excite envy and longings in the beholders of them.

Mr. Horace Singleton sprang from a very humble family, who vegetated in Liverpool, and, partaking in no slight degree of the characteristic energies of that commercial capital, threw off the trammels of clerkship, and betook himself to railway speculations during the mania, by which he amassed a couple of thousand pounds; but having a horror of commerce, and all belonging to it, he hired a theatre, and delighted the town with some histrionic performances. His personations behind the scenes were, however, more effective. He took three pretty actresses into keeping, and had such a host of intrigues with the ballet girls, that at the end of a year he found himself in gaol, minus every farthing of his two thousand pounds, and five times that amount in debt. A whitewashing in the bankruptcy court liberated him, with not a penny in his pockets. The Corn-laws agitation then was at its height, and he procured an engagement as lecturer against those fiscal iniquities. That resource, thanks to Sir Robert Peel, soon failed him, and he came to London, where, in the course of his penny-a-line adventures, in search of Chartist conspiracies to, as Mr. Gibson would say, " Throw down the fields of bigotry, and tear up the torrents of oppression by the roots," he met with Miss Laura Bell, and so delighted her with his manual and philosophical qualifications, that she supplied him with the means of becoming a Socialist reformer, and her *cara sposa* for the time being.

The quadrille had been finished long before Mrs. Wriggles had gratified her curiosity, and the parties composing it had separated, but not without an exchange of angry looks between Laura and Mrs Smythe. The latter had taken a fancy to Horace: there was something bold and manly about him, dashed with such a confident assurance, which pleased her sensual instincts; and, as she had quickly discerned how displeasing his attentions to her were to Laura, she lent him winning encouragement, and so charmed his propensities, with her beauty and fascinating manner, that he exerted his utmost powers of persuasion to make a conquest of her. Laura was equally pleased with the lofty presence and dark flaming eye of the peer—or, as he called himself, Mr. Johnson—and omitted no opportunity of pleasing his fancy; indeed she had inwardly resolved to yield to his importunities, for her whole frame thrilled as he pressed her hand, or in the dance pushed his thigh against hers, and whispered amorous suggestions and inuendos. But no woman can brook a rival with a man in whose arms she has tasted the sweets and felt the pangs of gratified delirious love; and that rival, too, her equal, perhaps her superior, in beauty—for men doat on particular styles; and Laura, although with a dark man by her side, saw with a jealous anguish that the partner of Horace had eyes as dark as night. But Bloomfield, who had observed her disquietude, carried her into an ante-room, and commenced making love so fiercely to her, that for decency's sake she had to repulse his ardour, and, although perhaps as excited as himself, to assume an air of offended modesty. Horace tried the same experiment on Mrs. Smythe, and succeeded admirably; for he was too good a tactician to alarm her by any unseemly displays. The tongue and the eyes, with him, were sufficient in the garish light—caresses, he knew, were better liked in the dark. The countess, with her heart riven at the spectacle of her husband devouring the Socialist beauty with his looks and pawings, had to endure the annoyance of Mr. Gibson's company. At any other time she would have been amused with his impertinence; but to see the man whom, upon self-examination, she found she still ardently loved, unblushingly paying court to a woman little better than a courtesan, caused her such pain, that tears, half of anger, and half of reproach, for her having so frequently repulsed him, bedimmed her eyes, and she felt inclined to sob right out. Mr. Gibson, noticing her emotion, attributed it to his eloquence; and, upon that surmise, built a brain-bewildering castle of expectation.

" Will you partake of any refreshments, my darling of a girl?" inquired he.

The countess stared at him, as he led her into a little room with "Office" marked on the door, and mechanically took a seat, while he proceeded to fill a glass of wine. She partook of it, for she felt thirsty; and this condescension so emboldened Mr. Gibson, that he took a seat by her side, and, placing one arm round her waist, said to her, the perspiration, meanwhile, running in streams down his carbuncled visage:

" Do you recollect the story of the Quaker and his wife, on their wedding night?"

" No."

" The Quaker sat up in bed, and, twiddling his fingers, said to her: 'Shall we go to sleep or how?' Do you know what she said to him?"

" No."

" Why, 'we had better how first, and go to sleep afterwards.'"

" Indeed!"

" Yes, divinest congregation of mortal atoms—resplendent orb of a woman! let me move in your circle, and I will how better than any Quaker that ever danced Cupid's hornpipe on one leg!"

And so saying the red-hot orator placed the chairs in the room together, and was proceeding to lay the countess down upon them, when she sprang to her feet, and, drawing her glove, dealt him such a blow with her jewelled hand on the cheek, that she cut it to the bone, and sent him reeling against the wall of the room. Infuriated at such a repulse, he sprang upon the countess, hurled her to the floor, and precipitated himself upon her. At this critical juncture, and just as the ruffian had partly exposed the person of his intended victim, a side door opened, and in walked Mr. Snowball and Mrs. Wriggles. With the former, to seize the elocutionist by the nape of the neck and dorsal extremity, and shake him as a dog would a rat, was but the work of a moment. The countess, scarlet with shame and anger, cried:

"I will have the rascal flogged until the flesh drops from his bones!"

"So you shall!" hurriedly said Mrs. Wriggles. "Bring him along, Nick."

And, taking the countess by the hand, she led the way down a staircase which conducted them to the lower portion of the premises, which seemed to have been fitted up as a school-room.

"Have you a flogging-post for the boys?" inquired Mrs. Wriggles.

"Haven't we!" responded Snowball, who was just in the humour to torture any living thing.

The orator, with the willingly lent assistance of the countess and Mrs. Wriggles, was speedily denuded of his upper clothing, gagged, and tied by the hands to an iron bar. A long switch, something like a riding-whip, was produced; and the countess, claiming the right to inflict the first punishment, soon made the fellow's frame writhe with the agony her well-bestowed blows produced. Mrs. Wriggles took the next turn, followed by Snowball, who struck so furiously, that the blood spurted out from the flagellated orator's back. This the countess could not endure: at her entreaty, he was cast loose, and, minus his coat, waistcoat, and shirt, left extended in doleful meditation on one of the forms.

"Would you like Jemima to come and rub you up a little?" sneered Snowball. "Or perhaps Polly Hopkins would do?"

The orator groaned; and, the trio having gained the private apartment were Snowball had told his fearful story, the countess, breathless, and pale with agitation, inquired how it happened that Mrs. Wriggles had been enabled to come to her rescue so opportunely.

"I watched you and your partner into the office," replied Mrs. Wriggles; "and, as I knew him to be a beast towards women, I thought I would kill two birds with one stone. I had left our friend here in a queer condition, so I returned to him, put him all right in an instant, and then both of us stationed ourselves behind the private door, and burst in at the moment we were wanted."

"Let us go home," said the countess, who began to feel a faintness stealing over her. "I am sick of all this, and should not have nerve enough to face him now."

"Very well," responded Mrs. Wriggles. "But what you failed to accomplish, I have. Look here!"

And the old woman, putting her hand into her bosom, pulled forth a beautiful locket, which the countess instantly recognised as one by which her husband set great store, as having been the gift of his mother.

"How did you procure that?" exclaimed the countess, with sparkling eyes.

"I picked his pocket of his purse, and found this in one corner of it. The purse I returned—it had only a few sovereigns in it," was the cool reply.

"Home—home!" cried the countess. "My life on it, this souvenir of his idolised mother will bring him to my feet, humiliated and thoroughly repentant. My own hair is here, too. Home—home at once!"

A cab was procured, and the countess, leaving by the private entrance, proceeded direct to her residence, heedless of the remarks her metomorphosis and strange attire would provoke. Mrs. Wriggles returned to the ball-room, and was just in time to be a witness to a very pleasant scene between Laura Bell and Mrs. Smythe. The latter had become so pleased with her new admirer, that she accepted of his tremendously fierce love, and so enthralled his heated imagination, that he confided to her the particulars of his life.

"Just the man for me," thought Mrs. Smythe; "I will make him my slave—the footstool on which my desires shall either repose or trample. And who knows but in time I may love him? He is a scholar, a poet; and, I clearly perceive, can make himself a gentleman when he chooses. Besides, I have led a single life long enough, and been thwarted so often, that I won't throw away the chance fate has sent me. Horace—Horace!" murmured she; "a pretty name enough, and its owner a good-looking, tall, well-limbed man enough. I am decided."

Horace, who had been dwelling rapturously on her flushed and speaking countenance, took her unresisting hand within his own, and said, softly:

"Have I pleaded in vain? Will you allow me to show you that my predilection is based on something stronger than the fancy of the moment?"

"Yes," murmured the lady, gently, but palpably returning the pressure of his hand.

"To-morrow evening then—Waterloo Bridge?"

"Agreed."

My Lord Bloomfield had been playing a similar part with Laura; but his appointment was for that very night—he was so vehement that Laura was charmed, fired into acquiescence to the proposal that he should occupy the place of her Socialist savan for that occasion. She would take him on trial, she piquantly said. Bloomfield swore he would do his duty, and the two pair of amorous compounds of flesh and blood having separately made their arrangements, chanced to meet in the very centre of the ball-room. Now Laura wished to spite her rival, and also to get rid of Horace; so that the accidental meeting afforded her a good chance of effecting her purpose.

"Woman!" said she, bending on Mrs. Smythe a glance of scorn.

"Woman, indeed!" cried Mrs. Smythe, laughing; "aye, wench, and a merry one too."

"Poor paltry thing!" said Laura, getting savage, as she observed Bloomfield and Horace exchange pinches of snuff, and smile significantly.

"Do not come between the wind and my nobility, poor painted thing?" uttered Mrs. Smythe, slightly clenching her little hand.

"Painted thing!" cried Laura; "I never paint anything about me—perhaps you do?"

"Perhaps I do: I neither love carrots on my head nor anywhere else."

"Carrots!" screamed Laura, getting into a passion; for the inuendo as to the unseen hirsute appendages galled her, the more so as she observed Horace smile maliciously.

The fray might have waxed warm indeed, had not a startling interruption served to attract the attention of the whole room. This was neither more nor less than the appearance of the brunette, Martha, quite naked, and dancing as furiously as a nymph of Bacchus would. At this spectacle the men roared, the women screamed, and above the din might have been heard the shrill cock-a-doodle-doo-doo oh-do of Jasper, who stood regarding the whole proceeding with immense satisfaction. The poor girl had been subjected to his tortures the whole of the evening, and, having coaxed her into one of the closets, he completely stripped and played such awful pranks with her, at the same time plying her with drink from his brandy flask, that she lost all sense of decorum, and, at his suggestion, skipped into the throng of dancers and promenaders, laughing, shrieking, and giving the men love invitations in the vilest language. This scene led to a row and a general fight, in the midst of which Bloomfield drew Laura away, and escorted her to her residence, where he passed the remainder of the night. Horace remained by Mrs. Smythe; but Mrs. Wriggles, stealing up to her, whispered a request to her to get rid of him.

"To-morrow evening, at dusk," whispered Mrs. Smythe; and, darting away from him, Mrs. Wriggles pulled her into the office, where the countess was so grossly insulted, and, bolting the door, they were secured from pursuit. Horace, after a vain search after her, left the room, and proceeded, as customary, to Laura's house. It was, in truth, a "who's dat a knocking at de door" affair; for, upon his persisting in his peals for admission, the contents of a certain utensil were emptied on his head, and an intimation conveyed to the police, that he "didn't lodge there." Obliged to move on, he returned to the neighbourhood of the ball-room, and outside, even on the threshold of the institution for the Regeneration of the Human Race, picked up a young female devotee at the shrine of Socialism, and induced her to pass the night with him at a "Temperance" (?) coffee house.

The uproar inside the "institution" had assumed a threatening appearance. The male and female rivalries that had sprung up during the evening became furious under the influence of a disturbance, and the slightest sneer or taunt produced such a boiling over of the already heated vinegar, that gentle hands became clenched, and the pulling of caps commenced, and provoked more vigorous contests between the champions of the respective parties. In vain was it that the stewards ran about in a state of intense perspiration, entreating and swearing, and frantically interposing between braces of infuriated fair ones, tugging at each others' beautiful hair like fiends, while their quondam lovers, or husbands—the difference was slight—were squaring at each other, or butting like rams. Jasper, like a meddling demon, embroiled the fray by a strenuous and malicious exercise of his ventriloquial powers. Such awful things, said by somebody or another, he whispered into the ears of dames and spinsters, that their Socialist equanimity was completely overthrown, and, following the example of the unregenerated, they resorted to those physical efforts, which, according to their creed, sadly weaken the procreative powers of the benighted multitude. Mr. Walker flew about like one distraught, and, after prodigious exertion, succeeded in forcing the nude Martha into a private room, in which he locked her, with the full intent, after the row was quelled, to mesmerise her, until he had placed her whole frame in a state of voluptuous coma. As he emerged from the room he encountered Jasper, whom he incontinently charged with being the cause of the whole disturbance. Jasper grinned in his face.

"Leave the room!" shouted Walker.

"You be d—d!" retorted Jasper, performing some rapid gyrations with his arms; and these, coming in contact with the apex of the philosopher's nose, sent him reeling into the midst of a dozen drunken strumpets—the very refuse of Blackfriars Road, who had stolen in through the unguarded door—who immediately pounced upon him—picked his pockets—stripped him of all his clothing but his boots and stockings—and then, forming a circle, compelled him, at the points of pins, to dance a Socialist hornpipe for their especial edification. In another part of the room, a girl, under the inspiration of brandy and Socialist fervour, declaimed loudly against the use of dress at all; she, amid the encouraging applause of a knot of inebriated, well-dressed young men, stripped herself in their presence, and unfastening her long hair, let it hang down the centre of her bosom, after the fashion of the water-nymphs we sometimes see in the loose prints in the shop windows of nameless streets.

"Hoora!" shouted the mob of "swells," as they were termed, as the frantic creature darted through the circle formed round Walker, and, seizing him by the naked waist, compelled him to polka with her, to the watery delight of the assembled audience. Innumerable conflicts raged in every quarter, the most unearthly screams resounded through the building, and the affair was about assuming a dreadfully serious aspect, when the cry of "police!" was raised. At that critical juncture the lights were all extinguished, and then ensued a scene that baffles description.

The shrieks of the women in many instances were succeeded by deep, convulsive exclamations of pleasure; and the men, catching the first women they could, proceeded to such acts, that the Socialist doctrine of men and women being entirely the creatures of circumstances, was completely substantiated. Walker availed himself of the darkness to gain the room where he had secured the nude Martha, and from thence with her escaped into the upper portion of the building, where he used such arguments as prevailed upon her to be quiet until the uproar below had ceased. A couple of files of policemen cleared the rooms of such as were dressed; and those who were not, or pugnaciously inclined, were carried to the station-house; and thus ended the last last grand rout of the Society for the Regeneration of the Human Race. The thing, to use a phrase of Gibson's, was "howdaciously smashed up by the enemies of mankind;" and the enterprising trio, having the fear of the law before their eyes, betook themselves to the remote fastnesses of the extreme east, and started a penny admission Poses Plastiques Exhibition. Jasper busied himself, upon the entrance of the authorities, in pointing out the women—the pretty ones especially—as having been the most disorderly; and as he looked like the only respectable man present, his word was taken, and upwards of twenty weeping, dishevelled damsels, upon his charge were placed in durance vile. After this pretty piece of work, he retired to the Cider Cellars, and, after copious libations, departed in search of fresh adventures.

Mrs. Wriggles and Mrs. Smythe remained in the office listening to the uproar: the former with delight and the latter with apprehension—for she dreaded detection in such a place.

"It is that hell-hound Jasper who has caused all this," said she, laughing.

"What, that ugly wretch I saw with Bloomfield?" said Mrs. Smythe, with surprise.

"The same: he is Bloomfield's servant—pimp, pander, spy, or what you will."

"He is a curious-looking being, and has a strange expression in his fiery eyes."

"He is a prey to an all-consuming and devouring lust."

"Lust—in a monster like that? What woman would take him to her arms?"

"Not one, for he is a good-for-nothing—he is a eunuch."

"A what?" cried Mrs. Smythe, opening her large eyes wide, and staring at Mrs. Wriggles.

"What I have said."

"Born so, I presume?"

"Not many months ago he was a fleshy, large, and strong-limbed man, perfect in every respect."

"What has reduced him to his present plight, then?"

"A woman's vengeance."

"Great God! what wretch of a woman would so abuse God's precious gifts?"

"His wife: he had outraged her, and wished to drive her into the streets to support him."

"Oh, the monster! I would have scratched his eyes out."

"But hers was a bitter and subtle revenge. Had you been placed like her, and the same suggestion had struck you, you might have felt tempted to do the same."

"Never!" exclaimed Mrs. Smythe, with energy, as her face crimsoned beneath the dye on her skin. "I would have spurned him from me, deserted him, and, to be revenged upon him, given up my body voluntarily to the vilest menial; but never would I lend myself to such an atrocity. As we are made let

us die; and, for my own part, I love a man too well to wish him any other harm than if I hate him he will keep out of my way."

"A most commendable and womanly philosophy!" said Mrs. Wriggles, with a slightly perceptible sneer. "Ten years ago I would have said the same thing; but now I don't care a rush for all the men alive, except in the way of friendship."

At this moment the gas was turned off; the light in the room being extinguished, Mrs. Wriggles led Mrs. Smythe down the private staircase, and the pair left the building by the same way that the countess had previously done.

The night was a fine one: the stars studded the heavens in brilliant clusters, and the moon—a young one—shed such a distinct but mellowed light over mighty London, that every object within reach of the eye could be distinctly perceived. The waters of the queenly Thames were silver-tinted, and flowed on placidly through the huge repose of the mighty metropolis.

Waterloo Bridge looked magnificent in the moonlight; and Mrs. Smythe, who, like all women of vigorous organisations, had a somewhat poetical temperament, stopped in one of the recesses to gaze upon the glorious scene that was presented to her view, and fan her heated cheeks in the gentle breeze that came from the face of the flowing waters. Mrs. Wriggles, having no such tendency in her warped nature, would have gone on, but something struck her, and she paused beside her nocturnal companion to revolve the embryo scheme she had formed in her mind. While thus occupied, the flutter of a white garment on the opposite side of the bridge caught her eye, and, after a few minutes' earnest gaze, she caught the clear outlines of a woman, in a recumbent attitude.

"Look yonder," whispered she to Mrs. Smythe.

"Where?" said the latter, awaking from her reverie.

"Over the way—the fourth recess to the left hand of us. Do you see nothing?"

"Yes—a female, dressed in white. What is she doing there?"

"Contemplating suicide."

"Merciful God! don't say so."

"She is. Her heart is bursting with grief. But at this very moment memory is so busy with her that she is thinking of old associations, of old friends, old lovers, and perhaps, with a bleeding heart, of her stern old father and mother."

"Let us go over to her and reason with her—give her help, if needs be?" cried Mrs. Smythe, making a forward movement.

"Not so," said Mrs. Wriggles, laying her hand resolutely on her arm; "let her fulfil her destiny; she will be far happier in the soft bed of the river than in the arms of a ruffian."

"Is she one of those unfortunates who infest our streets?"

"Yes," answered the old woman, with suppressed emotion; for memory was busy within her too. "She is one of that class whom the world condemns to utter and irretrievable misery—to a life without hope —a curse, without the avenging flash that kills, and is merciful—an existence, in the midst of which the heart freezes, and yet sends warm blood bubbling through every vein and artery of the body. O God! let her die—better dead than alive—better dead than alive!"

And the old woman compressed her fingers so tightly upon Mrs. Smythe's arm, that she uttered a cry of pain, and strove to disengage the member.

"Don't be impatient," said Mrs. Wriggles, instantly recovering her composure, and becoming as cool and collected as usual; "let her depart in peace —our interference would only alarm her into a premature effort. See—she prays! Oh, ye proud men and women, even the harlot in her last hours can pray! And oh, ye hypocrites, with what gusto ye can say, 'it is never too late to repent,' and yet withhold the helping hand in the good work! My curse upon ye all! See how that poor victim of a world's censure and encouraged lust, lifts up her face in the pale moonlight, and implores pardon for her transgressions. Her transgressions—God of heaven! if there be one, what a fallacy—what an absurdity! But see—she knots her hair, lays down her bonnet and shawl, and, with one despairing look behind, springs over the balustrades!"

The object of these remarks had quickly mounted the parapet, stood for an instant in silent contemplation—her white figure and outstretched arms were clearly shown in the gentle light that prevailed— and with a spring, light as the giddy one of the merry dance, she disappeared, and all was over with her.

Mrs. Smythe had shut her eyes and shuddered, for in the silent depths of her heart a voice whispered that the poor abused creature whom she had seen before her trembling on the verge of eternity, would be better off in her grave than in a selfish world, where fierce passions and tremendous desires, lord it over the instincts and propensities with absolute sway.

"Requiescat in pace," murmured Mrs. Wriggles, and in silence the pair left that terrible "Bridge of Sighs." Its human history—its body and soul experiences—shall be published some fine day or another.

The shocking incident had awakened all the animosity that consumed, while it instilled hope and vigour into Mrs. Wriggles, and she returned to her half-formed purpose with renewed zeal and terrible unction. She saw that Mrs. Smythe, unnerved and agitated by a variety of conflicting emotions, would be ready to embark in any scheme that promised excitement and distraction from present thoughts, so rather brusquely said to her:

"What say you to our finishing the night as the men do, and not going 'home till morning, till daylight does appear?'"

"Anywhere but where that husband of mine is," thought Mrs. Smythe; and adding, aloud, "Where the goodness can we go to at this hour in the morning?"

"Trust to me," replied Mrs. Wriggles, significantly; I will take you to a place where there are no men but a couple of flunkeys, and only women as respectable as ourselves. It shall be in Belgravia, too."

Mrs. Smythe readily agreed; and a cab being called from the stand opposite Somerset House, they were driven to —— Street, one of those aristocratic offshoots of Belgrave Square where rank and fashion hold their revels, and slily perpetrate their iniquities. The cab was prudently dismissed at a little distance from their destination, and, after walking about a hundred yards, Mrs. Wriggles ascended the steps of a large mansion, and touched a knob in one of the panels of the door. It opened as if by magic, and a liveried and powdered servant, having well scrutinised Mrs. Wriggles, readily gave her and her companion admission. They were conducted to a splendid suite of apartments on the first floor; when Mrs. Wriggles, with much ceremony, introduced Mrs. Smythe to the lady of the house—the Honourable Mrs. Chamberlayne, widow of the son of a peer, who had killed himself by his excessive devotion to the ladies about town. The two ladies, after an explanation of Mrs. Smythe's masquerade, immediately recognised each other, and exchanged a cordial greeting. Other explanations ensued, chiefly on the part of Mrs. Wriggles, from which it appeared that Mrs. Chamberlayne maintained a fine establishment for the accommodation of high-born and middle-class ladies who wished to improve their fortunes, and at the same time indulge in the pleasure of play. The rooms were all brilliantly illuminated, and the most tempting refreshments, including costly wines and genuine cogniac, loaded the sideboards. The play-room was the principal drawing-room, the windows of which were completely closed up, so that not a ray of light could escape through the blinds. The company numbered about twenty, and they were all married women; many had titles, but the majority were the parvenus that follow at the heels of the aristocracy, and ape their airs and vices. The dice were the chief objects of attraction, and cheating and wrangling were as common as in the hells frequented by the men. When Mrs. Smythe entered the play ran high; the wife of a wealthy City merchant was playing against a wealthy peeress, and this so stimulated the others, that the example had become contagious. Mrs. Smythe was no gambler, neither had she any money, but Mrs. Chamberlayne kindly accommodated her with a thousand pounds, and she took her place at the table. When she arose from the table about six in the morning she was the winner of five thousand, besides paying back the one she had borrowed. She had played under the direction of Mrs. Wriggles, who, wishing to cultivate in her a taste for the pursuit, had shown her how to win. The wife of the City merchant rose from the maddening excitement a loser of ten thousand pounds. The perspiration had matted her hair, and as she staggered from the dice she gave vent to a moaning cry, and ejaculated, in low accents:

" Oh, my husband, you do not deserve this!"

The peeress had also been a large loser, and her temper was so ruffled, that, perceiving a man in the garb of a servant, grinning and chuckling at the distress exhibited by her and the City lady, she dealt him a ringing blow on the cheek. Mrs. Smythe turned her head in the direction of the sound, and recognised Jasper. As she did so she shuddered, but, trusting to her disguise, she felt confident that she was unknown to him. The party now broke up, and, accepting the proffer of her hostess's carriage, she and Mrs. Wriggles were driven to the residence of the latter, where she resumed her natural appearance.

" What business had Bloemfield's servant there?" she inquired.

" On play nights he is hired by Mrs. Chamberlayne," was the evasive answer.

Mrs. Smythe made no reply, but, bidding a hasty adieu to her strange companion, sprang into the carriage, and was driven home.

CHAPTER XX.

SLY LADIES AND SLY DOINGS.

THE present chapter will contain some immoral passages, but they will be borrowed from fact and nature; and as the theme will be love, and the cause and result of the adventures undertaken the same, a few serious expressions of astonishment and reproof may be read, by way of an apologetic introduction to some very naughty doings.

Strange, therefore—passing strange it is—that the relation between the sexes should not be taken into deeper consideration by our teachers and legislators. People educate and legislate as if there was no such thing in the world; but ask the priest, ask the physician: let them reveal the amount of moral and physical results from this one cause. Must love ever be treated with profaneness, as a mere illusion? or with coarseness, as a mere impulse? or with fear, as a mere disease? or with shame, as a mere weakness? or with levity, as a mere accident? whereas it is a great mystery and great necessity lying at the foundation of human existence, morality, and happiness—mysterious, universal, inevitable as death. Why, then, should love be treated less seriously than death? It is a serious thing. Death must come, and love must come; but the state in which they find us—whether blinded, astonished, frightened, and ignorant; or, like reasonable creatures, guarded, prepared, and fit to manage our own feelings,—this depends on ourselves. And for want of such self-management, and self-knowledge, look at the evils that ensue! Hasty,

improvident, and unsuitable marriages; repining, diseased, or vicious celibacy; irretrievable infamy, cureless insanity; the death that comes early, and the love that comes late—reversing the primeval laws of our nature. But until love comes to be recognised as an institution, an integral constituent of the social polity, we must have profligacy and those heartaches that frosten the brows ere the tints of youth should have been mellowed by moderate healthful enjoyments and sage experiences. Blame not, therefore, every woman who falls with the whole of the error; society should bear at least a moiety, as regards the sentiment of the affair, as it does bear far more than that proportion of the burthen in respect to the present and ulterior consequences.

If the sensual instincts of human beings receive no training at all, the mind and habits must be liable to become as rank and tangled as a neglected vineyard. Mrs. Smythe was a true type of this neglect; and it is proposed to follow her in her irregular wanderings from the strict letter of her conjugal engagement, more to show how far a naturally good disposition might be perverted, than to deal in the pruriences inevitably associated with female indiscretions. It has been shown how ardent were her passions, and how capable they were of being stimulated to encounter risks from which the majority of women would fall back shudderingly. But so keen was her detestation of her unprincipled husband, and so burning her desire to be revenged upon him in the way that would minister to her preying appetites, that, at every fresh opportunity of gratification, her courage gathered strength and energy of purpose, and she was ready to immolate herself on the altar of her unquenchable love. On the morning of the day destined to behold the fulfilment of her long-meditated purposes, she rose from her bed, calm and determined as usual, and with her resolution the stronger from having been slept upon. As she stood in her night-dress before the mirror, and released her raven hair from the net that had confined it during the night, her lips parted, and she murmured words of unmistakeable import. They were of love—of the deep, all-powerful, and consuming passion by which she was devoured.

" What if he be poor?" thought she; " his poverty will make him my dependent, and secure his fidelity. One man can only serve one woman faithfully; and if he in time does but learn to love me, why I might reward him with my hand. That *if* has doomed his pretensions, ulterior and shadowy though they be,—having escaped one bondage, it is not likely I should rush with my eyes open into another. No, no. When free, let me be free. I must not be too rash or I shall lose caste; so, for the present, I must be sly. And why not? The old adage says, 'Stolen fruit eats the sweetest,' and so it does; and to-night I will once more lay myself in the only elysium I care for—the burning, melting ecstasy of love."

As the voluptuous woman dwelt on the coming pleasure, her frame quivered again, and a glow suffused her neck and bosom. While thus thrilled, the door of the chamber opened; and when she turned, expecting to see her attendant, she beheld her husband.

" You here!" she exclaimed, more in surprise than anger; for her aroused instincts would not allow her to feel repugnance at the presence of a man, and that one a husband, privileged to visit her at all hours.

" Yes, Caroline," said he, mildly; for ever since he had discovered that his wife would be entitled to a splendid fortune in her own right, he had resolved to pay her assiduous attention, and, if possible, come to some arrangement with her.

"What do you want here?" inquired Mrs. Smythe, regarding him curiously, and observing that he was dressed with scrupulous care.

"To propose terms of friendship to you; and for that purpose I have snatched a few hours from business. Don't interrupt me, but pray be seated."

And, handing her a chair, he took a large shawl that lay on another, and threw it over her shoulders. Surprised at this act of unwonted politeness, she took the proffered seat, and calmly waited to hear what he had to say.

"My dear," he began, and, after a few preliminary hems, thus proceeded: "we have not lived together as happily as we should have done, and perhaps I was a good deal to blame—in fact, I am prepared to admit that I was to blame—seriously to blame; but who can control his temper. However, what I have to say is, let by-gones be by-gones, and let us start afresh."

"I will never live with you as your wife again," interrupted Mrs. Smythe.

"I don't wish it," replied he; "all that I want is, that we may live in peace, and not give people a handle to talk about us. Now listen to me, Caroline. Both of us are inclined to be gay—nay, nay, don't deny it—listen to me: we are both of a gay turn; now, as it's clear we can't go together and be happy, and as neither of us can do without that sort of thing, it would be far better if we could come to some arrangement."

"How? what do you mean?" exclaimed Mrs. Smythe, blushing, and feeling desperately inclined to be angry, or at all events insulted; but, with her utmost efforts, her indignation would not expand to the explosion point.

"Why, in plain terms, that we should each pursue our pleasures as we like, without interruption or annoyance from the other."

Smythe said this with great gravity, and with such an appearance of concession to his wife's whims and prejudices, that she was instantly conciliated.

"I can scarcely comprehend what you mean by the term pleasures," said she. "Some impudence, no doubt; but if you seriously propose that I should remain in your house and bear your name, and that we should be agreeable and polite to each other, I can have not the slightest objection.

"Let it be a bargain," cried Smythe.

"Be it so; but mark me you don't sleep with me," said she, looking at him intently.

"Not sometimes?" said he, regarding her with kindling eyes.

"Never!"

"Well, well," said he, as if satisfied; "I won't be the first to break the compact, although for that I would do almost anything. And now about money?"

"I want some."

"You shall have it. Your jointure is three thousand; suppose we make it four, and end the matter?"

Gratified at such liberality, Mrs. Smythe murmured her satisfaction.

"And now, Caroline," said he, rising, "that business happily concluded, I have only one more request."

"What is that?"

"Give me a kiss—the last I shall ever ask for."

"No."

"Oh, yes, let's kiss and be friends? Mind, only friends. Why, it's half a year since I touched your lips."

Mrs. Smythe hesitated, and her husband, observing her silence, approached, and deferentially touched her lips. The contact must have been exhilarating to both, for he repeated the salute, and finally became so warmed, that he seized her in his arms, and kissed her with such ardour that she was fain to cry out. A lightning-like current seemed to be running through her body. Smythe became furiously excited, and bore her to the bed, on to which he threw her, but not violently. She resisted, but the blood rushed in such torrents to her head, that her opposition was feeble, and, after a flood of murmuring ejaculations, and a little dallying, the husband had his way.

At the end of an hour the pair separated, with a mutual promise, supported by the husband's oath, that that should be their last conjugal embrace.

"I swore to know her again—I have, and I am satisfied," thought Smythe; and shouldn't think of going near her again."

"Faugh!" cried Mrs. Smythe; the reaction in her system calling forth the latent disgust she had ever entertained at the society of her husband. And, ringing the bell violently, she ordered her bath to be prepared instantly. "Let me at least wash the impurity away, if I cannot forget it. Faugh! give me a small glass of brandy, to relieve this nausea?"

Two hours after this not uncommon matrimonial scene, Mrs. Smythe proceeded to Bloomfield House, where she found the countess, whom she amused with a circumstantial narrative of the morning's proceedings.

The countess was certainly rather astonished at the statement, not so much at the circumstances—for there was little novelty in them—but at the revelation itself; and, turning to Mrs. Wriggles, who was present, inquired whether such gossip was common among married women.

"I have heard ladies, and high-born ones, too, deal largely in such morning stories. The husbands of half a dozen wives little dream of the style of their spouses' conversation when together. Why, bless your heart, I have heard the most minute details given during a morning call—such as the difference of the sensation between the conception of a boy and a girl—lascivious postures, and all the mysteries of the wedding couch."

"Enough," cried the countess; "I have been told of such things, but never believed it before. Such shameless hussies ought to be burnt!"

"They often are!" replied Mrs. Wriggles, drily.

Mrs. Smythe, who had suffered, understood the allusion, and laughed heartily.

"Don't let us be too hard on our own sex—our married sisters, especially; for if we are smutty, as the blackguard men call nastiness, we are not drunken."

"You are wrong there," exclaimed Mrs. Wriggles; "married women drink a good deal on the sly."

"I don't"—"Nor I!" were the simultaneous exclamations of the countess and Mrs. Smythe. "At all events," said the latter, "they don't make such beasts of themselves as the men. You never see a respectable woman going into a public-house, or any other low place of entertainment."

"In that respect you are correct, but the tippling is all done at home in the husbands' absence," said Mrs. Wriggles. "In high life there is no necessity for subterfuges or concealment; but as excessive indulgence is accounted a positive offence, various expedients have been resorted to to give the habit an agreeable colouring; for you must know women, as well as men, like to have a chat over their beverages. The last scheme is the haberdasher, linendraper, shawl warehouse, and hosiery one."

"The what scheme?" inquired both the ladies.

"Why," responded their informant, "you can go

into a large West End establishment, and, if a regular customer, and one they can trust with the secret, tipple as long as you like."

Both the countess and Mrs. Smythe looked their incredulity; but, upon the old woman's proposing to convince them of the fact, they suspended their judgment, until they had actually inquired into the, to them, astounding phenomenon. The carriage of Mrs. Smythe being at the door, was taken by the trio, and they were driven to the door of the imposing establishment well known in the fashionable circles of the metropolis. The shop—a brilliant one, by the way—was crowded with ladies of rank and fashion, and, it being the busiest time in the afternoon, the assistants were flying about in all directions.

"This way," said a spruce, middle-aged man, who officiated as the shop-walker, as he conducted the party to what was called the "Habit Room."

There both the countess and Mrs. Smythe made some extensive purchases, and Mrs. Wriggles, after a whispered conversation with a prim young lady who guarded one of the doors, succeeded in procuring their admission into a gorgeously-furnished room on the first floor. There Mrs. Smythe and the countess beheld, with amazement, several fashionable married ladies—no single ones were admitted into that apartment—of their acquaintance, comfortably seated, and chatting merrily over the choicest wines, and the purest French brandy. Among the number they recognised Lady Tyrone, with a face of scarlet, and a tongue of unbounded licence.

"Ah, Bloomfield!" said she, extending her hand.

The countess gave her such a look of scorn—of mingled hatred and contempt—that she felt slightly abashed, turned to Mrs. Smythe, and sneeringly inquired how "Smythe was."

Mrs. Smythe swept away from her with a scornful toss of her head, and the pair, followed by Mrs. Wriggles, took seats near a party of ladies upon whom the world's slanderous breath had not yet fallen.

"Do you believe it now?" whispered Mrs. Wriggles to the countess.

"To my shame I do," was the low reply; "my sex are more debased than I imagined them. Why, there appears to be a glass of spirits before every one here!"

"Some are drinking gin, but the majority prefer brandy. That young person yonder is drinking port. She has only lately been confined. Hark! that's her mother seated next to her. Just listen to what they say."

The countess unwillingly complied, and, to her horror, heard the mother talk with abominable freedom to her daughter. The mother had been more than slightly tippling.

"I tell you it must be a boy next time—the estates must never go to that whimpering nephew of his!"

"How can I help it? I want a boy as ardently as you do."

"Give him another put in for a boy; and then, if he can't do it, we must get a man that can."

"Oh, mother!" cried the daughter, painfully blushing, as she observed the sarcastic glances of Mrs. Smythe, and the indignant ones of the countess.

"It is abominable!" said the latter to Mrs. Wriggles. "Let us leave the place?"

Mrs. Smythe readily agreed, for, with her appointment before her, she was in no mood for gossipping. The countess and Mrs. Wriggles, who now seemed to be inseparable, were set down at Bloomfield House, and Mrs. Smythe was driven home, where she immediately set about preparing herself for her meeting with Horace Singleton.

The bridge of Waterloo is unquestionably the grandest in Britain, if not in Europe; indeed, it may be questioned whether for security, solidity, and beauty, there is anything of the kind equal to it in the whole world. In one respect it can unquestionably challenge comparison with any known piece of architecture. It is the stage whereon thousands of love intrigues are commenced, vigorously played, and finished—tragically enough, in some instances.

The night side of the picture has been glanced at, so it is only fair that the more pleasant portion should have the same honour. Waterloo Bridge, then, from "morn till noon, from noon to dewy eve," is perpetually streaming forth shoals of ladies and and gentlemen, who either have nothing else in the world to do, or have forcibly manufactured a holiday for the purpose of indulging in that mutual interchange of friendships, promises, and fiery longings, which make up that mysterious compound called love. About from nine to ten, and from eleven to twelve, tradesmen's wives and daughters pass and repass on their way to and from Covent Garden Market; and can it be wondered at, if impudent, good-looking young fellows are lounging carelessly about, and have the assurance to accost them, that the bloom caused by their morning promenade should deepen on their cheeks, and that after a little parley, and to escape observation, they should faithfully promise to be on the same spot at a cannier hour in the evening.

Later in the day professional ladies emerge from the slums of Lambeth, to exhibit themselves in the Strand, and inflame the imaginations of gentlemen fresh and hearty from the country. These nymphs are not "uncertain, coy, and hard to please," for a wink, or that expression of the eyes which plainly says, "I should like to kiss you," will draw them like a magnet to the bridge, and then the terms of the casual encounter may be adjusted at leisure. In the afternoon the shopping ladies take the bridge by storm, and then the London rake may be observed in the highest perfection of his art. He is on the look out for a fresh conquest, and eyes the passing throng with such steady composure, that it might be fancied he had studied in the slave bazaar of Constantinople. All are subjected to his severest scrutiny, and when he has selected the one that pleases him most, and whose capture he thinks practicable, it is surprising with what audacity he will follow her from place to place, from shop to shop, until he obtains an introduction. If she obstinately persists in her refusal to allow him to address or walk with her, he will slip a deliciously-scented, and, to the vain female heart, still more deliciously-written note, among her purchases, into her glove, and sometimes her bosom; but this latter feat requires some dexterity. When she arrives at home the *billet-doux* attracts her notice; she reads it, hesitates, reads it again—after that puts it carefully away—is nervous and agitated for the remainder of the day—and at the hour and place mentioned by the daring seducer, she is there—accidentally of course—and a meeting, purely by accident, takes place. He is handsome and fascinating, and she takes his arm. A second and a third appointment is kept, and the young woman, if married, loses her virtue in some bagnio in the vicinity of the Strand, or, if single, is forthwith installed in comfortable lodgings as mistress.

When the gas lamps are shining, a multitude of other characters come upon the scene, and there is a revel and a rout, upon which it is better to drop the curtain of prudence, and follow a tall, well-made, handsome young fellow, in his perambulations on that famous bridge.

From the style of his attire, and the evident care that had been bestowed on its making up, it was clear that a tender assignation must have had something to do with such a neat personal appearance. Not to weary the reader, it will be as well to announce at once that this was Mr. Horace Singleton, the *ci-devant* Socialist philosopher, and the discarded lover of Laura. A mild Havannah diffused its fragrance around his nostrils, as he strutted up and down in rather doleful expectation of the dark-eyed, Juno-like lady of the previous evening's ball keeping her appointment.

"Who can she be?" thought he; "evidently, from her manners, a very lady-like person—I should say a superior one. She seemed to take a great fancy to my thighs, which I must, without vanity, admit, would make pretty tidy buttresses in their way; her eyes were upon them the whole evening, and, as I fortunately happened to be dressed pretty tightly, she must have noticed that I am in every respect made as a grenadier of a fellow should be. Perhaps she's some actress who wants me to be her bully. No! d—n it, I wont wrong her by that suspicion; and I am no judge of woman if she is not a lady born—perhaps a wealthy one! I hope she is, for, since I am cut by Laura, my exchequer is deucedly low. By the way, I must convince that she-devil that I'm not to be thrown aside like an old shoe, or a discarded stay-lace. My stars, though, when I think of it, these women are taking the business of us men out of our hands! Laura carried off a dark, handsome fellow, who seemed to know a thing or two; and here am I, half invited to do all I can for as proud and voluptuously-made a looking woman as ever graced a drawing-room, or, where beauty is seen to more advantage, the green-room of a theatre. Well, I'm a philosopher: if my proportions please the eye, it is my business to make them also please the mind and the heart. The heart—ah! Horace, Horace! that region has troubled you but little! By heaven, what a walk—it's a queen's! Talk of Lacarno swans after this, and be d—d, for an ass!"

These exclamations were caused by the appearance of a lady, well shawled and veiled, who slowly swept past him. Her gait did, in truth, merit his eulogium—it was superb—sweetly majestic. Horace was charmed, and, as he passed her, uttered quite loudly:

"A bride of Venice, by G—d!"

The lady started; and, as he caught the flashing of her lustrous eyes through the folds of her veil, she murmured:

"Horace?"

"The same!" cried he, seizing her outstretched hand, and drawing it under his own.

"Did you doubt my coming?" inquired Mrs. Smythe, throwing back her veil.

"No, my sweet love—I would sooner have doubted the stars were fire, or that the sun moved! But, good heavens! am I dreaming? It is the same voice—the same glorious eyes and maddening figure! But—but there is a change!"

Mrs. Smythe, it will be remembered, had on the previous evening appeared with her hair dyed of a bright auburn—now it was of its own brilliant jet, and escaped from her bonnet on each side of her face in a profusion of black tresses. She laughingly explained how the metamorphosis had occurred; and then they paced the level pavement of the splendid river highway in discourse most sweet. Horace had

at last met with a woman who came up to his lustful *beau-ideal* of feminine beauty; and as he drank in the accents of her musical voice, and gazed into the shining depths of her dark eyes, he felt that he had yet to learn what even the love he best prized was. Mrs. Smythe indulged in a congenial sentiment. Horace was fair, and his face

"Open as day, and full of manly daring,"

so forcibly reminded her of the young soldier to whom she had surrendered her virginity, that she felt insensibly drawn towards him. Besides, he pleased her instincts; for, although but an acquaintance made within the preceding forty-eight hours, she did not hesitate to cling to him, and more than passively yield herself up to his rather bold blandishments.

"You affirm that you can love," said she. "Now tell me what love is?"

"Love!" cried Horace, giving her hand a warmer embrace, "is, in the language of Rogers, a thing of marvellous splendour,—

"Blazing by fits, as from excess of joy,
Each gush of light a gush of ecstacy."

Only, my love, instead of gushes of light, I would have those which make the heart leap on its throne, the mouth shower kisses, and the arms as tightly interlaced as ever Cleopatra's were round the sturdy Anthony. Love! why it is a thing that feeds on itself, and grows brighter, warmer, more pungent, and thrilling, the oftener its mysteries are repeated!"

Mrs. Smythe's amorous frame trembled from excess of emotion; and Horace—knowing rogue!—read her sensations in her faltering voice and changing colour. Nor, to be candid, was he a whit less agitated; the only difference was in his being more artful and cunning. While indulging in the most heated allusions, he gradually drew the lady from the bridge, and thence, holding her spell-bound in his amative ardour, conducted her to Charing Cross, in the neighbourhood of which stands a very imposing-looking pastry-cook establishment. It is indeed a dashing affair; but the interior contained resources of which the thousands who daily pass it would never have dreamed. Imagine a suite of apartments, fitted up with an almost oriental luxuriance. Splendid chandeliers drooped from the ceiling, and the richest drapery was profusely spread around. The apartment into which Horace conducted the flashed Mrs. Smythe, was adorned with delicate blue and white colourings; even the pictures and chair-covers partook of the same hues, as also did the curtains, that completely concealed the windows. The only exception was a spring couch, covered with black satin, the use of which Horace explained in language that sent the blood coursing like burning lava through Mrs. Smythe's veins. After carefully, and, considering the circumstances, tenderly disrobing her of her bonnet and shawl —indeed of all her outer coverings down to her closely-fitting plain silk dress—Horace slipped off his outer coat, and appeared very like a gentleman disposed to be as merry as a stout-limbed, hearty, loving young fellow ought to be. After partaking, as was the custom of the place, of the most costly refreshments, including a liberal supply of champagne—of which, by the way, both during supper, tasted rather charily—the blue liveried waiters retired, and the pair were left to themselves. Never did Paris and Helen leap to their nuptial couch with more ardour than these. Their theme was love—

"But soon nothing stirs
To break the silence. Joy like his, like hers,
Deals not in words."

Mrs. Smythe, with wanton avidity, wholly surrendered herself up to Horace. What recked it to her he was a stranger? she loved in her peculiar way; and when her transports had in some degree subsided, and with disordered hair and exposed bosom, she lay panting on his heaving chest, she gloried in the sacrifice. A thrill to which she had been a stranger for fifteen years, made her body glow and tremble like that of a bird fluttering in the warm hand of its captor; and her excitement was too great for any room to be left for either shame or regret, if, indeed, with her large propensities so signally gratified, she was at all capable of such emotions. Tired of the rites mysterious, of which hypocrites austerely talk—

"Defaming as impure what God declares
Pure, and commands to some, leaves free to all;"

the pair threw around them the silken strings of youthful dalliance, and proceeded to those revelations of personal structure, worldly fortune, and social condition, in which lovers have indulged from the beginning of time.

"Will you love me then as now?" asked Mrs. Smythe, as, leaning on his lap, stroking his plump thigh with her hand, she looked up into his face with a dazzling, man-bewildering expression in her own.

Horace drew his lips to hers, and the glances of their eyes meeting and mingling together, the verbal reply was drowned in a long and passionate embrace.

"Will you be faithful?" demanded the lady, when she had become somewhat more composed.

"Your beauty will be the bond of my fidelity, your glorious eyes the sureties, and the memory of this delirious night the seal—the oath—the everything that can bind man to woman!" replied Horace, vehemently.

"The newest faces, I have been told, are the fairest to men?"

"Not so, my darling Caroline; for I confidently assure you, from a lengthened experience, that it is not the face alone that man prizes most in woman. There is the bust, the waist, the limbs—soft, pliant, and plump, as the downy couch of her twin-pillowed bosom—her gait, her motion, her action, her carriage, both in talking, walking, and riding. Besides, in your case, gratitude would be certain to give consistency and firmness to my affection."

"Have you not loved before? I have heard it said a man never wholly forgets his early loves, and becomes furiously enamoured of their types, should he happen to meet them again in after life."

A shade passed over the fine features of Horace, as he gravely replied:

"I will not deceive you—I have loved before; but it was only once, and the passion was never consummated. You know my history. I sprang from the neglected ranks of the people; but, being possessed of energy, courage, and native talent, I early resolved to improve my condition. During my labours—for I read and studied hard—I acquired many dissipated habits—not the least of them a fondness for women of a certain class. At one time—I was then about twenty—it amounted to quite a mania; and when afterwards my mind recurred to the madness, it was with the conviction that I was then in a fair way of so exhausting my physical powers, that death would be inevitable. The majority of our young men and women who die, owe their ends to the same kind of irregularity. The fiend consumption, it is true, is the active destructive power; but the inviting agent is the abuse of our immature,

undeveloped, natural functions. Well, I was in the high road to that most dismal termination to all my ambitious dreams, when an angel saved me. She was the daughter of a distant relative, more affluent than my own family was; but, being a kind-hearted, spirited girl, that did not make the slightest difference between her and me. She encouraged my visits, and I, from day to day, watched her expanding beauties. She was dark—quite as dark as you are—and dark, fiery women had always been, and, thank heaven! still are, the objects of my worship. You smile—but it is so, and there is nothing surprising in it; for, as you perceive, I am fair, and men of my complexion invariably doat upon dark women. Well, from watching I took to loving, and it was surprising how easily my vicious habits fell from me, under the influence of that accumulated passion for my dark eyed cousin. She reciprocated my affection; and after many struggles on my part, and more, I verily believe, on hers—for she trusted life and honour in my hands—we surrendered to the temptation of being alone so frequently, and for some months I tasted the sweets of love in its complete sense. Her condition at length became so apparent, that I married her; but her friends, for all that, discarded her, and their cruelty so weakened her frame, that when the period of her trouble came, both she and the child died. I mourned her sincerely, and so well, that I never returned to the practices of which her society had cured me. Since that time I have enjoyed the favours of many hundreds of women, but never met with one that I could love, until the propitious hour which brought us two together. Nay, Caroline, don't interrupt me—you wished for candour, and I have given it you. I repeat it, I never loved again until I saw you, and, well assured that the antecedents in both our careers are not the most unexceptionable—I speak boldly because I mean honestly—I feel that I could love you as dearly, as honourably, and kindly, as ever man in this world loved a woman. Our temperaments agree. Although you are dark, you are as sanguine as I am. We have both received more than an ordinary education, possess more than average natural talent, are well-formed, young, and in every respect capable of enjoying ourselves, in the full measure of our keen desires and warm, unblunted affections."

Mrs. Smythe listened to this plain, unvarnished narrative with fixed attention; and when she discovered the strong similarity which it bore to her own early experiences, she drew nearer to the speaker, and, when he had concluded, she threw herself on his bosom, and murmured words of hope and confidence.

"I am satisfied," she said, after a pause; "and I think we have each found what we have lost—a heart that loves and is beloved. Let us, then, exchange promises of fidelity—of mutual chastity?"

"I will swear ——" interrupted Horace.

"Oaths are straws, whose locality every fresh change of circumstances shifts," said Mrs. Smythe, laughingly. "A promise on your manhood and love of me will be sufficient."

Horace, whose admiration for the beautiful woman in his arms was every moment deepening, readily acceded to her proposition: and, after arranging to meet thrice a week, clandestinely, until the obstacles that prevented their doing so openly could be removed, they pledged each other in sparkling champagne. After many kisses and fond adieus, Horace escorted her to a cab, and, at her earnest persuasion, forbore to accompany her home. This, though, was merely a *ruse* on her part to prevent him from following her to her destination.

"At last," thought she, as she sank backwards in the seat, "I have found the man who will love me as I wish to be loved—who will hug me like a man, not paw me like a boy or a monkey. My God! how the memory of his gentle yet vigorous embraces makes my heart beat! He seemed equally satisfied with me, so will love me—oh, yes, he will—I read it in his flashing grey eye and lofty forehead! He is one of Nature's children, and I will so tutor him that he shall be one of her sovereigns!"

And this daring woman, having given the cabman fresh instructions, gave way to the delicious languor of a voluptuous reverie, and was only roused from it by the cab stopping at the door of Mrs. Chamberlayne's mansion. In that lady's gambling hell she stayed all the night, and when she departed, in the broad light of the morning, was again a winner, although she had no Mrs. Wriggles by her side to instruct her. She played the same game as she had done the night before, and won, as she confidently expected she would when she sat down.

"It would have been a falling off had I lost, after such a glorious two hours with that dear Horace!" was her reflection, as she stepped into her bed, where she slept soundly, and happily unconscious that she had been watched by the unrelenting foe of her sex during the whole of the evening, with the single intermission about to be described.

As the reader may have expected, the spy on her actions was Jasper. Being unable to glean anything that would seriously militate against the reputation of the countess, he resolved to devote more of his attention to the proceedings of her friend, the dashing banker's wife, to whom he owed an additional grudge for having foiled him in his denunciation of her Greenwich intrigue.

"It will go hard with me if she beats me this time," grinned he, as he traced her from her residence to the suspicious neighbourhood of Waterloo Bridge, and witnessed her interview with Horace Singleton. "Where the deuce are they going to?" ejaculated he, as he pursued them along the Strand, until they came to the fashionable establishment of the vender of ladies' edibles. "Well, I'm blowed," was his reflection, as he saw them enter; "they're going to do it slap-up, and no mistake! Why, that's the dearest trap in all London! I wonder who's the chap she's got with her? I must find it out." And in he marched, determined to watch them, or kick up a row, by playing the part of an injured husband. While seated, discussing a pie, he overheard, from the whispers of the attendants behind the counter, sufficient to let him know that a rich repast had been ordered for the blue chamber. Upon that hint he promptly proceeded up stairs, and asked to be accommodated with that identical chamber.

"Engaged, sir," said the servant he addressed on the landing.

"Ah, never mind, I only asked for it because I had it the last time I dined here."

"We don't have dinners here, sir."

"Well, refreshments—it's all the same. Show me into the one next to it." And, slipping half-a crown into the hand of the fellow, all objections were waived, and he was shown into what was called the green room, an apartment as sumptuously furnished as the other. Jasper, having procured more drink than eatables, sat himself down to wait patiently for the exit of the parties he had dogged to this "sin made easy snuggery," as he termed it. After having consumed perhaps half-a-pint of raw brandy, he heard some sounds from the blue room, which made him start up with inflamed looks, and exclaim:

"I'm d——d if they are not making the beast with two backs, as Iago says. I'm never deceived in those sounds. I wonder whether I can find a peep-hole. I have heard that old codgers come here to gloat over the doings of those who are able for such fun. As I live, this is one of the peeping-rooms!"

A slide in the wall, as if for ventilation, had caught his attention; mounting a chair, with his tall body he easily drew it, and, upon looking through, enjoyed a complete view of the transactions in the adjoining room. As he looked, the expression of his countenance became horrible—revolting would be the proper phrase—and his agitation became so intense, that the chair under him quivered again. Speech and volition seemed suspended for a while; and when the climax had been reached, he slid down to the floor, tottered to the table, and poured out a glass of water, in doing which he shed the whole of the contents of the decanter over the rich table-cover. Having dropped into the water a portion of the liquid he carried about with him, he swallowed the whole at a draught, and then sat down. Presently he recovered, and gave indulgence to a low, sardonic laugh.

"I have her now," thought he; "and blast me, if I don't have a good tickle with her yet! But she's a grand puss of a thing — I musn't think of that —no—I'll tell Smythe, and so be revenged on her, and make him as mad as a hare. He's a strapping fellow that she's got to do her business. And didn't she like it! I never heard a woman squeak so loudly before. I think I had better not peep again —it's dangerous."

He followed this prudent counsel, and applied himself to the brandy. Having made friends with the waiter, he received an intimation when the blue-chamber parties were about to leave, and when they did, he followed close at their heels.

The manoeuvre of the cab he instantly comprehended, for he knew of the engagement with Mrs. Chamberlayne; so he resolved to make the acquaintance, if possible, of the gentleman who had passed two such agreeable hours.

Horace, after leaving Mrs. Smythe, was in such a state of excitement and inflammation, that he felt giddy, and turned into a celebrated tavern in the Strand, to refresh and collect himself. An unoccupied box tempted him to sit down, throw off his hat, overcoat, and neckcloth, and order some brandy-and-water and cigars. He was so overwhelmed with the details of his amour, that he had scarcely any sense of anything else. His animal nature had been plunged into a fiery lake, and the burning particles yet adhered to him. After he had become a little sobered, his first thoughts took the shape of admiration.

"What a magnificent woman! talk of Paradise, why I have been in half a dozen in a few hours. Her kisses hang on my lips still, and I seem to be drinking in the magic eloquence of her wonderful eyes. By heavens! a magnificent woman—one worthy of an emperor's love—an emperor? old Saturn himself would thaw by her side; and as for the lecherous harpist of the Jews, he would have stood by her side as strong as in his youth, had he had the chance. But I am so amazed—consumed with voluptuous joy —that I scarcely know whether I am a living being or an incarnation of some god—a Jupiter who has just smiled on Juno—

"'When he impregns the clouds
That shed May flowers; and pressed her matron lip
With kisses pure.'

I wish I could see a devil just now—turning aside with leer malign in jealous envy—it would relieve my overpowering sensations."

The wish was gratified as soon as indulged in, for there before him sat one who "eyed him askance."

It was Jasper—who, guessing the cause of his flushed cheeks, short breathings, and damp brows, had stared at him with immense satisfaction.

"Warm weather this, sir?" said he.

Horace looked at him for a moment vacantly; but as his perceptive faculties became more convalescent, he recognised in the person before him the visitor to the ball of the last evening. Jasper, in the same mutual look, detected the philosopher, and instantly recollected his name.

"Nice ball that, last night, Mr. Singleton!" said he.

"I remember seeing you there," replied Horace; "the uproar was disgraceful."

"Nice girl that Laura Bell!" said Jasper; "stunning speaker, too. And what a leg she has! I twigged her bolting with the handsome chap she danced with all the night."

"Who was he?" inquired Horace, completely restored to the consciousness of his every-day existence at the mention of the name of that false lady.

"A great lord!" replied Jasper, with a significant glance of intelligence; "but you served her out, for you walked off with a finer girl—the best in the room. Was that her you had on the bridge to-night? Ah, you good-looking fellows walk off with all the pretty women!"

Horace was not deceived into gratuitous communications by strangers, so took not the slightest notice of the remark. Jasper, finding he had a close customer to deal with, became vexed; and when a man's ruffled, however great his cunning may be, he is in no condition, as the phrase goes, to pump another.

"You took her into ——'s, and had the blue-room?" said he, savagely; "did you find the spring sofa answer?—black satin, too; they say that's worth all the Spanish flies in an apothecary's shop—better than the hard boards of the Society for the Procreation of the Human Race, eh? Come, you're a game fellow, I see, so let's take a glass together?"

Horace now saw that he had been watched, and, aware of the high station of his new mistress, and, let it be said, animated by his love for her, was extremely indignant and disgusted at Jasper's familiarity; distrusting his own temper, and also to avoid a scene, he put on his coat and hat, and prepared to depart.

"Don't go yet?" cried Jasper, enraged at Horace's silence.

"I must—I have business of importance to attend to."

And, so saying, Horace moved out of the box.

Jasper, at this, was unable to control himself, and said, angrily:

"It's no use your shirking me—I know who you had in that blue-room, and what the pair of you were doing there. You forgot the green-room, next door, and the slide above the picture!"

This was too much for Horace's endurance, and, with the whole force of his enormous arm, and practised skill in pugilistic displays, he struck Jasper such a blow between the eyes, that he fell down between the table and the seat, stunned and helpless. Horace then coolly walked out of the house, menacing a whole line of pot-house flunkeys with his long brawny arm. When Jasper recovered, which he shortly did, he merely wiped his bleeding nose, and exclaimed:

"Well, I'm d—d! Who'd a thought it? Well, never mind—it's number one for him. Never mind," said he, addressing the waiters; "it's only a tiff with an old friend. He hits to-day, and I hit to-morrow—and that's the way we square accounts."

And, tossing them his reckoning, and a shilling over, he left the place for the purpose of seeking Smythe, and making him acquainted with the full and circumstantial story of his horned and condign disgrace.

Wandering from club-house to club-house, in search of an erratic husband, realises, in some degree, the old adage of looking for a needle in a bottle of hay; and this Jasper experienced, which helped not a little to increase the sourness which had come over his temper, after he had given due reflection to his lamentable failure with Horace.

"Curse him—he hits hard!" said he, ruefully rubbing his swelled proboscis. "Who'd a thought a philosopher had such hard knuckles? Hold hard! I'll try the Reform Club. Reform, indeed! They ought to try a little of that on themselves, for they are a precious rum lot. I saw half a dozen of them at Polly Hopkins's crib the other night, pitching into one another like a thousand of bricks. Not here! well that is provoking! I'm afraid I'm flummoxed—done brown to-night. Never say die, though! Forward, Jasper, and show yourself a man!"

In the classic region of the Haymarket there are several little hells, where gentlemen (?) make an equitable division of their estates among sharpers and prostitutes; and into one of those Jasper dived, and found the object of his search enjoying the luxury of an extemporaneous waltz with a girl with a formidable display of legs and bust.

"What do you say?" said the banker, lending an unwilling ear to Jasper's story.

"I've caught her in the fact."

"Caught who? What does the fellow mean?"

"Why, your wife, to be sure. I followed her to ——'s, and there I saw a strapping fellow, doing as much service as would manufacture half-a-dozen twins. It made me feel queer, I can assure you."

"I don't believe it," said the banker, who, since the interview of the morning, had no desire to interfere further with his wife than he was absolutely obliged.

"Then I'm a liar?" retorted Jasper.

"You are! and I beg you won't bother me with your rigmarole tales. Come, my pigeon, I want to feel your bustle."

And away the half-drunken banker spun with the half-naked girl he had engaged as his partner, leaving Jasper almost speechless with amazement and indignation.

"Here's a husband for you!" said he, almost aloud; "why he glories in being cuckolded; why—why I—ah! but all husbands are not so accommodating, and my revenge is coming. Howsumever, as I have broke down with the husband, I'll try it with the wife, and my name's not Walker if I don't get a cool thousand out of her."

With this determination he wended his way to Mrs. Chamberlayne's, but, after the scene of the night before, the hall-porter had been instructed to refuse him admission.

"Not let me in—me? it's my opinion, my fine fellow, you'll be getting yourself into a scrape."

"No I shan't; I has got my orders, and I intends to stick to 'em. Here's a card left for you."

And, handing Jasper an address card, he banged the door in his face. Enraged at such a breach of hospitality, he was about to treat the neighbourhood to the devil's hornpipe on a knocker at midnight, when, by the light of the hall-lamp, he saw some writing on the card. He held it up, and read—

"You are suspended in this business until further orders. Let me see you early in the morning." On the reverse of the card was "Dr. Wriggles."

"Oh, very well," muttered Jasper; "I aint particular to a day; but damme if I don't make that snob of a banker's wife tip up yet. I must make up the stock to ten thousand for my little boy—my own Harry, and then I'll peach on the lot."

Jasper, not feeling up to the mark for any more devilment, walked moodily to Bloomfield House, and sulkily donned his livery, for he discovered the countess had a party, and he wished to ascertain of whom it was composed.

CHAPTER XXI.
BLOOMFIELD AND LAURA BELL.

THE pet of the Socialists was a striking illustration of the theory contended for by the learned Dr. Wriggles, that unless the instincts—and those of love especially—are carefully trained, all the knowledge crammed into the brain will not make the man or woman a strictly moral member of the community. In fact, that immorality is the result of the present system of training. And here it may appropriately be remarked, that this book aims at being one of the most moral in the language, for it seeks to tell the truth, and illustrate the vicious nature of our educational systems, by vigorous and striking examples. The incidents are all borrowed from real life, and the fidelity of the narrative required that they should not be garbled or buried beneath a mass of hypocritical phrases. Candour is only repulsive to those whose withers it wrings—it is only your "galled jade that winces." And with that positive conviction animating the pen that records the naughty doings of Laura Bell, it is deliberately asserted that she was a fine woman, spoiled in the training—or rather by the no training at all—for in everything that concerned the healthful development and wise direction of her physical instincts, she had sustained the most abominable neglect. Her body had been pampered with food to rear up a glowing, ardent woman, incapable of restraining her inclinations within the bounds which conventionalism prescribes; and yet it would be maintained that she had been discreetly reared. Monstrous absurdity! baleful hypocrisy! And should a creature like this fall into the very slough of her passions, society turns up its nose, and discards her as a monster of no human growth. Awful perversion from charity and true wisdom! But, as preaching against an evil in the present day is like a drunkard abusing a lamp-post against which he has broken his nose, it will show more discretion to pass on to Laura Bell, the type of a more numerous class than the dull fools who lecture and spout about progress and improved human condition, have the least idea. It has been stated that she was fair and handsome, and had an intellectual cast of countenance, with all the marked and expressive features of a voluptuary. There was indeed a plumpy softness, an enticing fleshiness—not vulgar fat—about her frame, which imparted to her appearance that wavy outline, those indescribable curves, which madden the senses of men, when their eyes wander over their infinite overlaying and involved, but unbroken mazes. After a night passed with such a woman-loving, and, withal, strikingly handsome man, as Bloomfield, her beauty had acquired that languor which is so pleasing to the majority of male temperaments. She looked coaxing and inviting in her morning wrapper; and, having neglected to put her hair up in paper before going to bed, Bloomfield swore she looked enchanting in her deshabille. Laura smiled her thanks for the compliment, and, while she is pouring out the tea, and pressing it upon Bloomfield, instead of the brandy and soda-water, for which he had called, it will be entertaining to inquire a little more curiously into the peculiar idiosyncracy of this same Laura Bell. She was sensual, ardently so, it must be confessed; but then, in extenuation it must be observed, that in gratifying that peculiar appetite, she mingled a species of refinement which revolted at the bare suggestion of anything approximating towards promiscuous intercourse. She would not be a harlot, even upon compulsion. Her idea of the enjoyment was that it was a bodily and mental necessity, as much so as food or knowledge; and, being possessed of a moderate independence, she would not, in the present state of our English marriage laws, risk its safety by entering into a matrimonial engagement with a man who might turn out to be a worthless vagabond. In her tastes as to the requisites that she expected in a husband, she was fastidious, and cultivated the impression, that where a couple, after a fair trial, found themselves mutually unsuitable—in fact, that their organisations disagreed—it was proper and *moral* that both should have the power to put an end to the engagement without in the slightest degree infringing upon their civil rights, or imposing upon the woman greater disabilities than those under which she laboured as a *feme sole*. Marriage she conceived to be purely a civil contract, and that the popish doctrine of its eternity had inflicted incalculable misery upon the civilised world. A breach of faith without the wedded badge was as much adultery as with it; and, however loose Laura might have been in her notions, she had always proved chaste to her lover for the time being. And when she discarded him, she never allowed him to approach her afterwards. She had, all her matured life, been in search of a man with whom she could permanently live; and if to this circumstantial explanation be added the fact that Laura had a somewhat poetical imagination, a sceptical turn of mind in matters of religion, and scrupulously clean and tidy personal and domestic habits, the reader will be able to draw a tolerably true portrait of this modern Aspasia. The character of Messalina she abhorred as brutish and unnatural.

As before stated, Laura and Bloomfield, both in a state of accommodating deshabille, were seated in close proximity at the breakfast table. Each participated in the enervating luxury that invariably succeeds the delirium of a night of passion. A languor was diffused throughout their whole frame, and they felt more disposed to converse than to indulge in those post-nuptial caresses, which may be said to be something like the soda-water taken after a carouse on burning brandy. Bloomfield, at Laura's persuasion, partook freely of tea, nor did she fail to pay her respects to the invigorating beverage.

"The majority of the people of this country are very silly in preferring coffee to tea at their breakfast," said she.

"Why?" asked Bloomfield, surprised at the gravity of the remark.

"Because tea is more healthful and nerve-bracing. Coffee is a stimulant that is indigestible—at least for a long while—and I have been told that our chemists extract some of our most powerful medicines from the plant. Good tea has none of those injurious qualities, and we women ought to take some credit for having not only first introduced its use, but rendered its consumption so general."

"You are certainly entitled to that merit, but, as a set-off to the good the custom has done, it is contended that tea has depreciated our race of men," replied Bloomfield.

"Depreciate fiddlestick," replied Laura, warmly. "It's the drinking and guzzling that does all the mischief. How can men who dry up their fluids by drinking ardent spirits to excess be expected to be strong and healthy, or beget strong and healthy children. It's the brandy and the gin that take the thews and sinews away from our men. Look at the pale, cadaverous creatures of young men that you see everywhere in London; do you not see gin written in their very countenances? I don't say they themselves drink—they can't afford it—but their fathers did."

"And mothers too."

"Not to the same excess. Woman is naturally a sober, moderate-eating animal. Her organisation does not require stimulating through the region of the stomach."

"Where then, in the name of wonder? I always thought the stomach, with its contiguous appurtenances, the holy ground into which a woman gratefully received everything that pleased her."

"I know very well what you mean, and will candidly admit that women are quite as voracious in their love as men are; but that's not the question, and I am not to be diverted from it by your by no means delicate pleasantry. It's tea, and nothing but tea that is on the tapis; and I contend that the man who drinks it in preference to ardent spirits, is stronger and more healthful than either your ale, gin, or brandy drinker."

"Is he able to please a woman better when love plunges a happy pair into forgetfulness of time and place."

Laura blushed, and her look dwelling for some seconds on Bloomfield's handsome countenance, she replied:

"Certainly; for his powers are unimpaired."

"We'll see," laughed Bloomfield; "for I mean to try the effect of tea on the human body by some present practice."

"That you will not," said Laura decisively. "The pleasures of love are not worth a curse if they are to be treated as a child would a toy, which it handles every moment, and then throws away, tired of the employment."

Bloomfield indulged in a low prolonged whistle, but Laura heeded it not, and continued:

"What you have alluded to I can answer very positively. Women like sober men, not only on account of their persons being more acceptable, but also that they are better members of society. No woman allows a drunken fellow to approach her with love on his lips without experiencing an acute nausea—a sensation of disgust—which increases the moment the fever into which her instincts have thrown her has subsided. A drunkard has a foul breath, and what woman would like a kiss from a mouth reeking with most abominable stenches. Faugh! the idea itself is repulsive!"

Bloomfield winced at this, and recalled to his recollection the fact that the first difference he had with the countess was owing to this very circumstance In bed she used, in pure self-defence, to be obliged to turn her back upon him; and nothing surely can be more annoying than that to a husband. But then they forget the provocation expelled from their parched mouths at every respiration, which, spreading itself around over pillow and sheets, makes the very atmosphere around offensive. A word on this subject to wives. It can be given while Bloomfield is vainly endeavouring to induce Laura to once more comply with his wishes. And the mode shall be a short story.

Once upon a time there lived a pretty maiden, who was the well beloved of all her friends and relations, and especially her mother, who daily gave her good advice, and, as she grew up to womanhood, faithfully initiated her into all the mysteries and secrets that appertain to her sex. But with all this good mother's wisdom, she neglected one important portion of her educational economy. She seemed to have forgotten that her daughter had a mouth, with certain gastronomical regions beyond. She duly enforced the observance of morning ablutions, which included a vigorous use of the tooth brush and some fashionable tooth powder, but wholly omitted to inquire whether both back and front teeth were well cleaned. The front ones looked white and glossy, and that was enough for this good mother. Her daughter progressed amazingly in bulk and beauty, and, in due time, had the supreme felicity of being pronounced the object of a certain young gentleman's idolatry. His passion was ardently returned, and the only thing that in the slightest degree marred their young affections, was the rather offensive breath which the young lady had occasionally. She was perfectly aware of it herself, but could not divine the cause, as she had robust health, and was remarkably temperate in her habits. A glass of wine rarely touched her

lips, and her food was plain and wholesome. Various expedients were used to remove this infirmity, but all of them only availed for the moment, and the poor girl soon began to tire of lozenges and orris root. Constantly chewing the latter fatigued her jaws, and when not expecting to see her lover, she would throw it aside. However, by these artifices, she managed to conceal the defect from her lover, and they were married. The wedding night passed over as merrily as all such nocturnal engagements should, but in the morning the husband detected a flavour in the kisses he took from his wife, by the hundred, which he did not relish. He was too happy, too enamoured of her beauteous person, too grateful for the bliss she had given him, to take any notice of such a trifle then, and he arose with the conviction that he had unquestionably spent the happiest night of his life. The honeymoon passed away, as all such glowing periods do, and the young husband and wife settled down for the housekeeping cares and pleasures of happy wedlock. The young wife sucked her lozenges, and, *a la* Jack Tar, enjoyed her quid of orris root, and all went on very well. But by-and-bye, when the novelty of their union had worn away, and the young wife did not object to the presence of her husband when she undressed at night to go to bed, and did other things (vide Rosse, who has a couplet which rhymes to kiss), which terribly alarm the minds of unsophisticated maidens, she began to neglect her wholesome precautions, and gradually to lessen her consumption of lozenges and orris root. Her mouth in consequence, in proportion, began to acquire a flavour to which her husband had the strongest possible objection. He therefore began to acquire the ungallant habit of turning his back upon her, and would only lie *vis-a-vis* at her earnest entreaty. Her breath eventually became so intolerably bad, that he complained about it; and of course there was a scene. The young wife went off into hysterics, and the whole household was alarmed. It's rather an unpleasant predicament for a man to be found in bed with a woman in that condition; and this the husband found out, for of course he was stigmatised as a wretch—a brute—a monster; and some ugly insinuations were indulged in at his expense. Vexed and annoyed, yet attached to his wife, he did all he could to pacify her, and their first difference was quietly made up, and the reconcilement ratified by extra-conjugal caresses. The wife, after this, became lulled into a false security, and soon abandoned her lozenges and her orris root altogether. The result was a sensible abatement in her husband's attentions: he would persist in lying with his face to the floor, and would growl whenever she put her arm round his neck and gently essayed to turn him round. He would also leave the bed without the usual morning salute, dress in a hurry, and hasten down stairs to the sideboard for a small glass of brandy. This conduct of course led to reprisals on the part of the wife, and their wedded life was soon turned to one of strife and discord. The work of alienation, indeed, went on until they occupied separate bedchambers; and ultimately, upon the interposition of friends, agreed to a divorce *a mensa et thoro.* This was the last dose in the young wife's cup of bitterness, and, twelve months after her marriage, she returned to her father's house wearied and broken in spirit.

"How did the quarrel begin?" inquired the fond mother.

The daughter blushed, and, looking down, replied :
"He said my breath was insufferable, and that it make him sick in the morning."

"The brute !" snarled the mother; and, after a pause, added : "it's very singular, but your breath used to be as sweet as a rose!"

"So it was," sobbed the daughter; "but if Alfred loved me, he would not have made such a fuss about a trifle like that."

"Ahem!" said the mother; "we women are particular about such things, and I must say a bad breath is not very agreeable, especially when in a warm bed."

The mother, after due deliberation, resolved to consult the family doctor, and that learned gentleman was duly called in, and rather puzzled with the features of the case—for his patient was as healthy a young woman as ever he had sounded. At last, a thought struck him, and he abruptly asked :

"Are you ever troubled with the tooth-ache ?"

"Oh dear, often! I sometimes cannot get any sleep for it for nights together."

"Open your mouth wide—wider!" And the doctor, unceremoniously seizing the young wife by the chin and upper lip, glanced into the remote regions on either side of her healthy-looking tongue, and the mystery was at hand. All the back teeth were in a state of decay; and the hollow ones being filled with putrid food, the effluvium, poisoned the air she respired, and occasioned all the mischief.

The services of an able dentist were then called into requisition, and, after due scrapings, a liberal use of gold leaf, the removal of stumps, and substitution of clean and useful artificial teeth, the young wife's mouth was thoroughly cleansed of its impurities, and her breath became as delicious as the morning breeze that has travelled over corn-fields and flower-gardens. The husband was made acquainted with the transformation, and took his wife back to his arms with even more ardour than when he received her first as a bride. The husband, after that, never refused to lie with his wife in his bosom; and perhaps to this little episode in their lives, they were, in some degree, indebted for the manly little fellow that two or three years afterwards sprawled about on the carpet at their feet.

MORAL.—"What great things from little things arise !"

After this perhaps unpardonable, but in such a work as the "Merry Wives of London," certainly characteristic digression, a return to the fair philosopher, Laura Bell, will not be undesirable.

"So you refuse me ?" said Bloomfield, somewhat angrily, after a contest in which he had been ignominiously worsted; for Laura threatened to cry out if he exerted his strength, and proceeded to extremities.

"Decidedly," responded she, pushing her disordered hair back from her heated forehead, and regarding Bloomfield with a steady composure. "If you are so unwise as to exhaust yourself, I am not."

"You are cruel, Laura!"

"It is you who are cruel, in urging an improper request; and I am surprised, upon our slight acquaintance, that you should be so pertinacious. If you play the game of love as the brutes in the field do, I don't; and so there's an end of it. Sit down, and be a reasonable man."

"Is this moderation a part of your Socialist creed ?" sneered Bloomfield, who was by no means well pleased with his discomfiture.

"It is a part of mine," said Laura, resolutely; "and don't plague me any more. Have another cup of tea, to compose you."

"I thought tea was rather strengthening than weakening on these occasions."

"Don't be a fool!" cried Laura, pleasantly.

She perceived her lover was vexed, and did not wish to irritate him by any caustic replies.

"Night is the proper time for the pastime you propose; and no true woman will ever engage in it in the day-time, unless, indeed, the curtained opportunity is denied her, and then—then—I must out with it—circumstances alter cases."

Bloomfield, not wishing to lose a mistress who had so much self-will, abandoned his pretensions, and, leave obtained, threw himself on the sofa, and committed himself to the solace of the fumes of a fragrant cigar.

"I have heard a good deal about this system of Socialism," said he; "but I must confess I know nothing about it. What do the parties aim at? what is their philosophy, their creed, their doctrine ?"

"If you will only have a little patience," said Laura, "I will inform you."

She then poured out for herself another cup of tea, and, after imitating Bloomfield's example by lighting a cigar, and indulging in a few preliminary puffs, she placed three chairs at some little distance from the sofa, and, seating herself on the one opposite Bloomfield's feet, placed her legs in repose across the others. Both of them, it will be remembered, had only a loose dress thrown over their night-gear, and therefore the picturesqueness of their attitudes may be imagined.

"Do you smoke ?" inquired Bloomfield with surprise.

"Sometimes," said Laura, pouring forth from her ruby lips the prettiest wreaths of vapour imaginable. "I find it very soothing after a night's excitement. Don't you ?"

"The custom has grown into a habit with me; and every day my cigar in the morning becomes more indispensable. I frequently enjoy one in bed—that is, of course, when I'm alone."

"Then you are quite accustomed to the society of women ?"

"It also has grown into a necessity. Is not that the case with you as regards my sex ?"

"No—how should it? I'm a woman; you are a man. Our propensities widely differ in character."

"I know that. But did you not, a short time ago, admit that women were more impulsive than men; in fact, that their love was greater—had more intensity, more volume, and voracity ?"

"I did; and would not hesitate to repeat what I said. But you wholly forget, or appear to intentionally overlook the fact, that women are periodically incapable of loving; so that nature wisely places their excess of ardour under restraint."

"You mean the ——"

"Hold your tongue, will you! There are sexual secrets, which men know nothing about, and it is not fitting they should."

"Oh, very well! But what do you mean by saying that the propensities of men and women are widely different ?"

Laura puffed forth from her mild Havannah for about a minute, and then replied:

"The law of giving and taking is very precise. Where the supply on hand will afford it, it is always more pleasurable to be ever giving than ever receiving. The rule applies to human charity. The donor is always a happier person than the recipient of alms. The latter feels degraded; the former elevated. So it is with men and women. The latter receive; the former give; and therefore, as a matter of course, the women the soonest tire of an engagement with such an unvarying characteristic. Nature, well aware of that, has prudently provided interruptions to her sensual gratifications, and thus enabled her to return to the fountain of love, and drink of the waters again with undiminished gusto. Were this not so, women would soon sink to the level of mere breeders of men, and only, like the rest of the animal creation, tolerate the society of the male at certain fixed seasons. You may stare at such language, coming from the lips of a woman; but, you may rely upon it, I am quite correct. If women did not occasionally refuse the favours of men, they would not retain the slightest affection for them. And if wives would only be a little more stubborn, as well as more decent in this respect, there would be less misery in their homes. Pauses in love are as necessary to love as winter is to summer; and Nature, for woman's good, has made several obligatory on her. Man, on the contrary, is not so limited in this particular propensity; and the wise ordination restraining him renders him more attached to woman; and thus love, a mere animal feeling, is created, and cemented, and improved, by association and education, into the refined feeling that subsists between husbands and wives. I hope my explanation of the difference between the sexual attachment of the two sexes has satisfied you?"

"Perfectly!" cried Bloomfield, amazed at the style of Laura's conversation; "and, as you have been so clear and explicit on that subject—a devilish knotty one, I must confess—perhaps you will oblige me by informing me what Socialism is?"

Laura hasteneed to comply with the request, by boldly affirming that Socialism was no modern innovation, but an established and fundamental institution, universally recognised by mankind.

"Our present system," said she, "is Socialism—for there is an unity and identity pervading all the interests that are comprised within the limits of what is called 'society.' There is a mutual chain of dependence running throughout all the ramifications of our present social condition; but the great evil of the system is, that the products of such an amazing combination of industry are unequally distributed. The rich are too rich, and the poor are too poor, and thus the most violent disorders and tremendous calamities are engendered among us. Socialism aims at the eradication of this monstrous inequality, and begins its mission by boldly attacking what are termed the rights of property, and proposing a more equitable distribution of the boundless resources placed at the disposal of man."

"Pretty sentiments these for a peer of the realm to listen to," thought Bloomfield; "but scarcely anything from such a pretty mouth as that could be treasonable or impure. You have given me a very ingenious description of the outline," said he; "but what are the salient details?"

"They are these," replied Laura:—

"Equality of person.

"Equitable distribution of property.

"A government, the offspring of the will of the majority.

"Unlimited freedom of conscience.

"Voluntary professions of religious faith.

"Abolition of all existing systems, so far as their compulsory elements are concerned.

"Enforced secular education, combining training of the body as well as mind.

"Marriage, with power of divorce by a civil magistrate, upon the just petition of either party.

"Recognition of woman as something more than a mere domestic drudge, ornament, or sensual convenience.

"And, lastly, all such prohibitory enactments as would be necessary, in the various stages of progression, to the perfection to which it is quite possible to educate the human race."

"Your ten points are sweepingly comprehensive," said Bloomfield, all the while wondering where the deuce a woman, and a young one too, could have picked up such ideas; "but, let me ask, would you throw religion overboard altogether?"

"As a system I would, and so release mankind from a slavish dependence on abstract ideas."

"Abstract ideas, Laura?"

"Yes, abstract ideas—ideas the children of the imagination. You don't surely believe in revelation—do you?"

"I do, indeed."

"You have made but a poor use of your faith, then, for you have broken every one of its commandments. Pshaw! your religionists are all of them rank hypocrites."

"Granted; but the good we have been taught is not to be blamed for our iniquities."

"No; but when the evil is greater than the good, we must suspect there is something wrong in the teaching."

Bloomfield, to use a vulgar phrase, was quite taken aback; finding he could not satisfactorily grapple with the dogmas put forth by Laura, contented himself with putting a few questions.

"Do you believe in the immortality of the soul, my beautiful philosopher?" said he.

"Not in the vulgar acceptation of the term," she promptly answered; "for I have yet to learn that we have any existence in us independent of the body; and if it is not in us now, how can we have a being hereafter connected by relation or memory with our present one. The supposition is absurd. Prove that there is such a thing as soul, and I will be satisfied. It cannot be the mind, for that is created and dies with the body, and, while living, varies in value, from the brain of a Byron or Farraday, down to that of an idiot or Bosjesman. Now the idea of soul includes the idea of equality; and mind being in its very essence unequal, it cannot be the thing or substance meant."

"The task of confuting these errors and fallacies will be pleasant occupation on our couch of love at some future period," said Bloomfield; "but, answer me another question, and I have done on that subject for to-day. What do you conceive to be the object of marriage?"

"The procreation of children, and the enforcement of mutual chastity while the engagement lasts."

"Mutual chastity, Laura?"

"Unquestionably. In Europe the sexes are equal; in Asia and Africa they are not: there the women far exceed the men; and, as a natural consequence, polygamy becomes an institution among them."

"Then you really think that marriage means nothing more than going to bed and getting children?"

"That is the primary object; but there are obligations and sentiments born out of its contraction, and indissolubly connected with it: such as friendship, respect, maintenance of offspring, love of each other's person, and the thousand things that constitute the attachment called love."

"And you would make the facilities of divorce as easy as those of marriage?"

"Certainly, marriage is a mere civil contract; and where the parties disagreed, and one had become repulsive to the other, the union ought to be as formally and effectually dissolved as it was entered into. Both ought to be at liberty to choose another mate."

"Why, Laura, your doctrine would make the whole world one huge cock-and-hen club. The ties of husband and wife, parents and children, brother and sister, would all be confounded and lost—swallowed up and drowned in a dark-red cloud of brutish sensualism. I'm a rake myself—a sad one, I'm afraid—but I'm sure I never could bring myself to subscribe to such an opinion as that. However, give me one of your own long-drawn kisses, and pitch moral philosophy to the dogs?"

Bloomfield sprang from the couch to embrace the daring Socialist girl, but Laura eluded his grasp; and, after an encounter, in which neither lost their temper, the peer was forced to desist from his importunities. He then dressed himself, and, after a running fire between them of bantering remarks, and a farewell salute, he departed, having made an engagement to see her again on the following evening.

"The most extraordinary woman ever I encountered," thought he, as he made his way to the nearest cab-stand. "I wonder where she picked up her extraordinary ideas. I should lose caste were it known that I had formed such a connection. Why, she never was married; but I have carried her off from a lover, and that's a harder task than inducing a wife to make a bolt of it. Well, she is a sweet creature, and a merry one, too. She shall teach me the philosophy of bawdiness, in the high-flown language of the fanatic school in which she has imbibed her knowledge; while I amuse her with the platoon exercise of the love-soldier, as Thomas Carlyle would term it. Halloo! hey! stop, cab!"

These exclamations were caused by his recognising Captain Morris, in the Strand. Walter's adventure with Lucy had tended, in no slight degree, to cure his lordship of his jealousy of the gallant captain.

"Why it's an age since I saw you!" he exclaimed, as he sprang from the cab, and grasped Walter by the hand, more cordially than he had done for some months. Surprised as well as gratified at such an unusual return to something like the former friendship which had subsisted between them, Walter felt rather awkward, and betrayed a reserve which did not at all accord with his bold and reckless manner.

"Nay, my dear fellow, don't be shy with me!" said his lordship. "I have not yet had an opportunity of thanking you for your gallant deliverance of poor Lucy; and no time serves better for such grateful offices than the present."

Dismissing the cab, he took Walter's arm, and conducted him, at no slow or measured rate, to the British Hotel, in Cockspur Street. In sooth, it must be told, that my Lord Bloomfield had so far contracted the habit of drinking, that he grew feverish and restless whenever he had long been without his stimulant of brandy. Walter was happily free from such a degrading propensity, as a custom; but, in his present desperate circumstances, it mattered little to him whether he attacked an able-bodied decanter,

seduced a girl, or made himself the leader of a forlorn hope. "Have with you!" in anything was his motto; and on this occasion he, if anything, outvied Bloomfield in his devotion to the scorching but exhilarating liquid.

"What luck at the Horse Guards?" inquired Bloomfield.

Walter shook his head, and silently inverted his glass.

"Ah, never mind it, my boy; we'll make it all right by-and-bye," said his lordship; "I flatter myself my influence will avail a little. It is true I have not meddled much in politics lately; but those who seldom ask a favour are seldom refused, at court. My Lord Clarendon said so, did he not, of that scapegrace Charles the Second? and as Beaumont would have said—'I wot the court wind blows from the same quarter as it did then.' So keep up your spirits, old fellow, and let's talk of something more agreeable. When did you see Lucy last?"

"Not since I left her at ——"

"Indeed! why I heard you were sweet in that quarter."

Walter, despite his self-command of feature, blushed, and, to hide his confusion, buried his nose in his tumbler of cold without.

"Who told you such a silly thing as that?" said he, putting down his emptied glass.

"Oh, I heard it," replied his lordship. "Although Violet and I are never confidential now, there is a little bird in Bloomfield House which tells me everything; and, between you and me, I should be devilish glad, I can tell you, if you had Lucy. She is a nice girl, and deserves a good husband. And, to tell you the truth, I should rather like you for a brother-in-law. I took Violet from you; and, to make amends, I will marry you to her sister, who, between you and me, is as like her as two pins are, with the trifling difference that Lucy is some ten years younger. So pluck up, my boy, and drink to the health of the sweetest girl in all this country, broad and bonny as it is. Here's to Lucy!"

Walter drained a second glass of almost raw brandy to the bottom, and, under the inspiration of its effect, shook Bloomfield so vigorously by the hand that the tears sprang into his eyes.

"Not so tight, if you please, Walter! my hand is not the hilt of your sabre!"

"It's Lucy I mean," gasped Walter, turning very red in the face. "The sweet angel has promised to wait for me, and I have given her the same sort of promise. The troth was given in our dear native land, and I am sure it will be fulfilled."

"It shall! said his lordship," energetically.

"Your encouragement infuses new life into me," cried Walter; "and I respond to the toast you gave by another—'Violet, the twin rose of the dell!'"

Bloomfield acknowledged it with an enthusiastic burst of applause; and then inquired, with half shut eyes, when Walter had last seen the countess.

"Not since the day I announced to her the safety of Lucy," replied Walter, in some confusion; "for, to tell you the truth, in my present position I hesitated to call."

"An unpardonable omission," exclaimed his lordship; "and for which Violet, depend upon it, will make you do heavy penance. But never mind home at present: I have no home myself; Violet won't allow me to go near her, and some day or another—but not before you are married—I must employ your intervention to arrange the differences subsisting betweed me and the countess. It's a sad thing, though, Walter, when a man cannot approach his own wife, for fear of giving offence."

Walter did not reply: he could not candidly, for he well knew that the whole blame of the alienation rested with Bloomfield. After some more conversation of a similar kind they separated, with an exchange of promises to meet again on the following day at Bloomfield House.

"Now that Morris is so smitten with Lucy, I have no fear of him with Violet, so I will carry him to her and make them friends again, and that will be a sop in the pan for me. Ah, me! I wish things at home did not run so crooked with me, but my own conduct has put me out of court; I am nonsuited by my frailties; pray heaven the contagion does not reach my hearthstone. If it should, why—a—a—I would make a huge brothel of the place—a sort of fanatic training establishment, *a la* one of the whims of my Lord H——. The exposure, however, would be confounded annoying, and the best thing for me to do, will be to wait and see which way the stream of events will turn. In the meantime I can amuse myself with Laura."

Such were the young nobleman's reflections as, in a state rapidly approaching inebriety, he was driven to one of the proud halls of one of the proudest and haughtiest races of the English aristocracy.

"Bloomfield has not got a bad heart," thought Walter, as he leisurely strolled back to his lodgings with Dr. Wriggles in Baker Street; "but he gets so horridly drunk, and that's a monstrously depraved habit. It has killed many a gallant heart long before the brain had become soddened, dull, and brutish. Poor Violet! I begin to fancy you made a sad mistake in preferring the *roue* peer to the marching sub. With the one you would at least have had the honourable and kindly treatment of a soldier; with the other you have had—but bah! the star of my hope is Lucy, and heaven lend me wings strong enough to carry me safely thither!"

Walter found Mrs. Wriggles at home in a state of some perturbation. Her schemes were not progressing so favourably as she could have wished, though she attributed their failure to the large portion of her time she devoted to the countess. In the latter affair she had already, to a great extent, made a confidant of Walter.

"I must give it up in despair," said she to him, "for Bloomfield gets worse and worse every day."

"I have just left him," said Walter. "He overtook me in a cab in the Strand about two hours ago; he seemed as if he had been on the loose all the night, and two or three glasses of brandy quite knocked him up."

"He spent the night, then, with that Socialist hussy!" replied Mrs. Wriggles, with some asperity.

"Bloomfield is not over particular when he takes a fancy; but I don't believe he ever descended so low as to take a drab off the streets," said Walter, yawningly, for he began to be terribly tired of having nothing to do.

Mrs. Wriggles relapsed into a reverie, which lasted several minutes, and Walter was nodding himself to sleep, when he was aroused by her sudden exclamation:

"Walter, you love Lucy, don't you?"

"Of course I do," said he, staring at her.

"Then you would serve Violet?"

"With my life."

"Then, for her sake, you must assist me in saving her husband."

"How?"

"I'll tell you. His intrigue with this Socialist girl is the only one he has on hand just now, for all his other mistresses have tired him out. Now what you must do will be to take this girl from him."

"What, seduce a friend's mistress—abuse his confidence!"

"He never gave you any. He's not such a fool as to tell you when he has got a handsome girl caged up. He, like a good many other dissipated husbands, would not mind exposing his wife to the gaze of every libertine, but of his w——e he is more careful. Now, don't be so hasty. If Violet is not reconciled to him soon, I'm afraid her hasty temper will lead her into some extravagance—perhaps imprudence."

"Has any one dared to assail her purity with even the breath of a dishonourable motive?" exclaimed Walter, starting up with fury in his glance.

"A neglected wife is exposed to the approaches of every licentious fellow."

"True. How black man's villany looks, when it comes home to the fire-side of his affections!"

"Tut, tut," laughed Mrs. Wriggles; "don't be carried away by any nonsensical sentimentalities, but actively interfere. Violet was your first love, Lucy your last and best; and you can serve both sisters by bringing Bloomfield back from the tangled paths into which he has strayed."

"To accomplish such an undertaking I would cheerfully submit to any sacrifice; but how can you reform a man who neglects the most beautiful wife in London, and, what with his brandy and loose girls, seems to be driving headlong to the devil."

"The man of violent habits of irregularity is easier cured than the sleek and cunning one. The one is as open as day, the other is as close as the night. If you will follow my plan, we can do all that is practicable in the way of reform."

"Propound it—discourse, deliver thyself—for mine ears are open."

"You must carry this girl away from him. I have her address, and the mode of procedure I will leave to your own skilful self."

"Well?"

"He will be enraged at the desertion, and, while the fit lasts, I will bring about an interview between him and Violet. She will upbraid him—in fact, do her utmost to gall and drive him frantic. He will fly from her presence to drink, and you must be his companion in a terrible orgie. Maddened by drink, lust, and the terror of losing Violet altogether—for in his heart he is ardently attached to her—he will gladly plunge into such excesses, that, in less than a week, will bring on a fit of delirium tremens, to be followed by brain fever, and complete prostration for many months."

"But he may die?"

"Suppose he does—he will only be cut off a few years earlier, and with a less tarnished name than if he were allowed to pursue his present courses unchecked. Besides, Violet's happiness, also Lucy's, and the honour of the family to which you will be allied, are worth the risk."

"I'll undertake it," said Walter, resolutely; "and I think I had better begin with the girl. What sort of creature is she?"

"Pretty and amorous, and rather spicy, too, I can assure you. She pretends to be very wise, and so far moderate in her desires, that she never accepts the society of more than one gentleman at a time."

"Is she on the town?"

"Oh dear, no; she is a private lady, in search of pleasure. She enjoys an independent income, which

she spends on herself and lovers. She is an epicure without its refinement."

"So much the better. I'm glad she is not a vulgar blowsy keep, whom you have the greatest trouble in the world to keep from falling into your arms. The wooing will amuse me in my forced retirement from active life."

Having completed this pretty sort of an arrangement, and forced upon Walter ample funds for the occasion, Mrs. Wriggles departed for Bloomfield House, to confer with the countess; while Walter, dressing himself with studious care *a la militaire* proceeded to concoct and mature his plans for laying siege to the heart of the fair and learned Laura Bell.

The latter, after the departure of Bloomfield, took his place on the sofa; and, with book in hand, and a fresh cigar in her mouth, began to read; but presently the volume grew less interesting, and she was drawn into the maze of certain speculations on that most interesting of all subjects to women, the peculiarities of a lover, and a comparison of them with those of others. While thus engaged, the door of her apartment opened, and her late Socialist husband, the discarded Horace Singleton, stood before her as radiant as a bridegroom.

"I thought I had given orders that you were not to be admitted again?" said she, glancing at him haughtily.

"So you did; but when a man's resolved, neither locks, bolts, nor bars can keep him away from a woman," replied Horace, as he coolly seated himself.

Laura was silent; the consciousness of having been rather precipitate in her last change, dulled her understanding, and bridled her tongue. Horace had not come to upraid her, or have a scene, but simply to show her that he regarded his dismissal with the true philosophic unconcern of a true disciple of the Socialist school.

"Am I decidedly to understand that you have dismissed me?" inquired Horace, as he lighted his cigar.

"Unquestionably," was the reply; "after your conduct last night, in paying such deference to another, what else could you have expected?"

"That is not a sufficient reason, in the presence of the fact of your having for some days previously taken the initiative, in receiving the marked attentions of a stranger—a handsome fellow, I must confess—but still a total stranger."

"So were you, when I knew you first."

"So I was, but a nameless affinity drew us together."

"Suppose the same species of attraction to have operated in this case."

"And I may apply the same argument to my fascination—eh?"

"You are at liberty to do just as you think proper. If you want a pound or two, I can let you have them. I never like to dismiss a friend without a penny in his pocket."

"Make yourself easy on that score, for my new friend is a lady of fortune, and she has already been liberal. Should you have any pressing engagements I can assist you with a hundred or so."

"I never enter into any but those I can discharge. And if I were pressed, which would be extremely singular indeed, my friend is a man of fortune, and title too. He is a peer of the realm."

"Our severance has been lucky for both of us," said Horace, gaily; "so let us finally part on friendly terms."

"We can be friends, cannot we, although our particular connection has ceased?" said Laura. "You are the most intellectual man I ever conversed with; and I could not afford to lose the pleasure of your mental society. In fact, your brain was too preponderant over mine; and, to be candid, the moment I discovered that fact, I knew we should not be together long."

"What! do clever women prefer stupid men?"

"They do."

"To lord it, and domineer over them, I suppose?"

"There are many reasons for the choice, and not the least of them is, that clever women like the opposite of themselves."

"I have heard," said Horace, maliciously, "that idiots, and persons of deficient mental powers, approach nearer to the perfection of the lower animals, in a certain physical respect, than do men of superior attainments."

"My personal observations have not extended far enough, to enable me to answer you on that point," replied Laura, coolly.

"In China a man is more renowned for the length and thickness of his tail than the breadth of his brow or the size of his breast; and I suppose the fashion has travelled to England."

"Your insinuation is not distinguished for much politeness or delicacy, either; and I must beg of you to bring this interview to a termination?"

Laura, after saying this, tried to look grand and gloomy; but the effort was a total failure, and she burst out into a laugh, in which Horace merrily joined. The pair then chatted very cosily for some hour or so; and Horace, without having even attempted to touch his late philosophic spouse, rose to depart.

"I shall see you at the institution, I suppose?" said Laura.

"It's smashed up; the row the other night finished it off," replied Horace.

"Well I'm not surprised at that. However, I shall see you at the council, and then you can tell me how you get on."

"Good bye, Laura!"

"Good bye, Horace!"

And the latter had half passed through the door, and was holding the handle in his hand, when the former said:

"Horace!"

"Yes."

"Should you ever want any money, don't forget to come or send to me."

"I won't; and my only thanks at present shall be a promise to bear your kindly offer in my remembrance. Good bye!"

"Good bye!"

The door closed, and the pair, who had been linked together for some months by the last fond tie that binds man to woman, separated without the slightest regret or compunction. So much for the stoical indifference engendered by the Socialist school of moral philosophy.

After this interview Laura looked at her watch, and discovered that it had gone five in the afternoon. She then saw that it was high time she dressed herself; which she speedily did, in a very becoming pale-blue silk dress, with a rather tempting open front, beneath the transparent muslin of which the glowing skin and rounded outline of her full bosom could plainly be discerned.

This operation over, she seated herself at the open window of her snug little drawing-room, and, partially concealed by the drapery, gazed upon the passers-by below.

This gazing from windows is rather a dangerous occupation for young ladies, for it is little better than an exposure of goods for sale. The tradesmen's price tickets are certainly wanting, but the smile and the merry glance of the eye are indubitably tokens of the value of the commodity.

While Laura was thus dissipating the languid hours, her attention was arrested by the appearance of the tall, commanding figure of the handsome Captain Morris passing and repassing on the opposite side of the way.

"A soldier, from his gait," mused Laura, "and evidently a gentleman. What a noble-looking fellow! I wonder what he wants?"

Morris had caught her glance fixed upon himself, and, having succeeded so far, next addressed himself to a policeman, as it appeared to Laura, with vehement anxiety.

Her curiosity was aroused, and, as she drank in the prepossessing outlines of his figure, and saw that his face was a noble one, and his eyes singularly bright and flashing, she was seized with an irresistible curiosity to know what business had brought such a distinguished individual into the York Road, Lambeth.

"A conversation with that fine-made fellow would no doubt dissipate the prejudice I have ever entertained against the army!" thought she. "I am afraid ignorance has more to do with even our most cherished convictions than we are aware of. My stars, but he's coming to this house!"

Laura, seized with an indescribable fluttering sensation, shrank tremblingly from the window, and in silence awaited the result.

Her *femme de chambre* presently entered, and handed her a card, which simply bore the inscription, "Captain Morris, —— Guards."

"A Guardsman!" murmured Laura; "what on earth does he want with me?"

"Please, ma'am, he said he solicits a brief interview, on a subject of great interest to you and many others."

"Admit him," said Laura, as she undesignedly placed herself in an attitude which best displayed the advantages of her fine figure.

Morris soon stood before her, making his most graceful bows, and bestowing on her beautiful person those glances which can so speedily call up the warm blood to the cheeks of either maid, wife, or spinster.

"Miss Bell, I believe?" said he, taking the seat to which she had gracefully pointed.

"That is my name," she replied, colouring beneath the ardour of his gaze. Walter had observed the striking character of her beauty, and was by no means displeased with the opportunity which the interview afforded him.

"My presence here I'm afraid will be an intrusion," said he apologetically; "but when I explain its object, I trust that I shall be indulged with some excuses for my apparently inexcusable conduct."

"I know so well that gentlemen never intrude themselves unwarrantably upon ladies, that I labour under no apprehension, sir, as to your visit, and beg you will not distress yourself on the subject of offence."

Laura said this so gracefully that Walter, who, by-the-bye, had been drinking, was rather charmed with it, and it gave him mighty encouragement to proceed. It's astonishing how soon a woman, if she likes, may break the icy barrier that separates her from man. The latter may hammer at the obstruction for hours, days, weeks—aye, for years—ineffectually; but at one touch from the gentle hand of the woman, it thaws as rapidly as snow does under the influence of mid-day heat, and disappears at once, and for ever. Walter, placed at his ease, felt more comfortable, and then proceeded to introduce himself and fictitious mission to the Socialist girl, whose face and figure had already strongly inflamed his not over moral imagination.

Before the particular incidents upon which the interview turned are related, it should be premised, that as Walter gazed upon the fair, sensuous being before him, he felt his virtuous determination, to be as frigid as the coolest political ambassador in the world, fast oozing through every pore of his body; so he resolved forthwith to disburthen himself of the purport of his mission.

"Madam," said he, "my errand to you may seem a strange one, when I explain it; but I assure you I am actuated by no desire either to give offence, or in the slightest degree wound your feelings."

"Your bearing, and the uniform you wear, would relieve you from any such imputation," said Laura, graciously.

Walter bowed, and, gathering courage, proceeded:

"I am not ignorant of your intellectual reputation, and therefore I am more emboldened to at once address myself to your understanding, in the hope that I shall obtain your sympathy for the wife of a valued friend of mine. To do this effectually, I shall put an hypothetical case. Suppose a man, in the prime of his youth, strength, and manly accomplishments, wedded to a girl as beautiful and amiable as an angel—a girl to whose loveliness and sweetness of character my feeble powers are unable to do justice. Suppose this pair to have enjoyed all the felicities of wedlock: that the wife remained happy, cheerful, and loving, and the husband gentle, constant, and dearly attached. I say, suppose such a happy conjugal existence as this, and then let me ask you whether anything that occurred to disturb it would not be deplorable?"

"It would, indeed," said Laura.

"I expected such a conclusion from such charming lips as yours," gallantly continued Walter; "and now let me put the dark side of the picture before you. What would you say of the husband who wilfully and systematically undermined all this happiness—who, unprovoked, contracted habits which affronted his wife's mind and wounded her delicacy—who became a drunkard, a brawling reveller, and a sot—who, in addition, plunged into excesses which I forbear to mention—what would you say of such a husband?"

"I should say," responded Laura, warmly, "that he was not only undeserving of such a wife, but merited the scorn of everybody."

"Your indignation is natural, and enables me to put my remaining question," said Walter. "What would you say to the woman who tolerated and encouraged this degraded man—this rake and drunkard—and placed a barrier in the way of his reform and reconcilement to his true-hearted, and still, despite all his faults, loving wife?"

"I should, without hesitation, say that such a woman would be no better than a shameless hussy—a disgrace and a scandal to her sex!" cried Laura, with unaffected warmth.

"There are many women who play such parts," continued Walter; "but the majority, I believe, entirely in ignorance of the real position of the men with whom they are connected. And now, my dear madam, I approach the disagreeable portion of my sermon. What I have been telling you is all actual truth. I have a friend so far fallen, that he neglects an amiable, virtuous wife, and is rapidly becoming a confirmed sot. This man you can assist me in saving from utter perdition, and at no sacrifice, but a positive gain to yourself."

"Me?" cried Laura, surprised; "I am not acquainted with any such character!"

Walter began to be sensible that he was treading on dangerous ground; but he had gone too far to recede? and, if the truth must be told, rather liked the idea of carrying off such a fine woman from Bloomfield. Therefore he had a twofold object to attain—to disgust Laura with her new lover, and yet not to offend her.

"Madam," said he, "the friend to whom I allude danced with you the whole of the evening at the Socialist ball held in this neighbourhood, and escorted you home. He is a tall, dark, handsome man."

Laura blushed, and, holding down her head, said, rather tremulously:

"Such a gentleman did pay me attention; but is—is he married?"

"He is, and to a woman as lovely as yourself," responded Walter; "and I should add, in addition to what I have said of him, that it is his practice to change his female acquaintances as often as he can. He is as inconstant as the moon."

"Is he a confirmed drunkard?" inquired Laura, looking up.

"I am afraid so," replied Walter; "but, to convince you of the fact, I will give you ocular proof of it. Are you engaged to-night?"

"No," said Laura, faintly.

"Then if you will do me the honour to take my arm, I will take you to a place where, unobserved, you can convince yourself of the truth of what I say?"

Laura, after a little hesitation, agreed to the proposal; and Walter, not choosing so soon to leave such an agreeable companion, exerted himself so effectually, that he drew her into a long and animated conversation upon a variety of topics, chiefly of a metaphysical description; and ended by inducing her to accompany him to Drury Lane Theatre, and every moment of their stay together, to receive his marked attentions with less hesitation. At midnight he took her to a night-tavern in Piccadilly, which

Bloomfield now constantly frequented; and there, seated in one of the boxes, with a coarse drab of a creature, whom he was plying with drink, was Laura's handsome aristocratic lover. He was so drunk that his tongue protruded from his mouth, and the saliva was running down his chin.

"I am satisfied," said Laura, a sickening sensation creeping over her.

Walter threw his arm round her waist, and supported her into a cab, where, throwing herself on his bosom, she burst into tears, and sobbed like a child. Walter soothed her with a multitude of endearing expressions, and squeezed her more tightly than became a strictly moral friend. When the vehicle arrived in the York Road, he assisted her up to her apartments. She had no sooner gained them than such a fit of trembling came over her, that Walter had to lay her on a sofa, and bathe her temples with vinegar.

"Leave me!" she softly said.

"Never! you need advice—support—consolation!" urged Walter; for his hand had roved so freely over her fine exposed bust, that he had become half frantic with desire. Her chamber was behind the folding doors of her drawing-room, and thither Walter carried her, then undressed and placed her in bed.

"For God's sake don't touch me!" she murmured.

Walter did not reply, but quickly undressed himself, extinguished the light, and plunged into the bed with such force, that its slender frame groaned under his weight, and the window and furniture of the room joined in the significant chorus. In the morning Laura removed to some apartments in a fine house in the vicinity of St. John's Wood; and when Bloomfield next visited the house in the York Road, the following epistle was placed in his hands:—

"LAURA BELL has only had one *liaison* of which she is ashamed—and that was with you. She blushes at the remembrance of having known a disgusting sot like yourself. Return to your wife, and reform your filthy habits. Faugh!"

CHAPTER XXII.

EXTRAORDINARY CASE OF CRIM. CON—THE EARL OF TYRONE *v.* THEOPHILUS SMYTHE, ESQ.

NOTWITHSTANDING the assurance of Dr. Wriggles, circumstances concurred to prevent the amicable repair of the breach in the honour of the O'Blazes and the immaculate Earl of Tyrone. The lady herself, rejoicing in the favour of the wealthy Earl of Bloomfield, and the smiles of a Lord of the Admiralty, from whom, for, as the lawyers say, a valuable *consideration*, she procured promotions and appointments for the sons of her lady friends, did not care a pin about the matter, except in so far as the termination of the intrigue lost her the friendship of the rich banker. That she did care about; but as for the withdrawal of his person, she consoled herself for it in the society of her more buxom male acquaintances. It was far different, though, with her brothers—those valiant natives of the ancient soil of Tipperary. They had certain views of their own to promote, and, having appointed a day for a solemn consultation upon the matter, they bolted themselves in the dining-room of the hired town mansion of the family, and, under the inspiriting influence of indigenous whiskey toddy, proceeded to deliberate upon the peculiarly perplexing condition of their temporal affairs.

"Pat," said the eldest.

"Well, my boy," said the youngest.

"What do you think of things in general?"

"Queer."

"D——ly so!"

And each, under the inspiration of this genial reflection, puffed forth immense volumes of smoke from the dudheens they had inserted in their jaws.

"I'm thinkin' we haven't any time to lose at all, at all," said Captain O'Blaze.

"Bedad, I'm the same way of thinkin' myself!" responded Lieutenant O'Blaze. "The ould gintleman's going under the turf at a great speed! Docther O'Milligan swears, by the blessed Virgin, that it's the toss up of a ha'penny if he walks through another tirm!"

"Them law tirms bother me enthirely!"

"So they does me, by Jasus!"

And here both the brothers puffed away more furiously than before, varying the performance with frequent visits to the tumblers before them.

"I'm thinkin' we should be up and doing," at length said the eldest.

"That's just exactly my own opinion enthirely!" chimed in the youngest.

"What shall it be? that blackguard Smythe won't bleed like a gintleman—bad cess to him!"

"Let's go into coort, and try it on?"

"Faith, and I see nothing else left. I won't take the dirty thousand!"

"Nor I!"

"What does Biddy say?"

"Go into coort, and take the chance."

"She's a sinsible girl!"

"So she is, by the powers!"

Denser grew the smoke and stronger the whiskey, until the spirits of the pair were so invigorated that they unanimously resolved to wait upon Smythe in person, and endeavour to effect an amicable and equiable pecuniary arrangement.

"Well?" said Smythe to them, as, about six o'clock in the evening, they unceremoniously entered his official *sanctum sanctorum*, and, with cultivated Hibernian *nonchalance*, unbidden took possession of a couple of the most inviting chairs in the room.

"Well!" echoed they, regarding him with the composure of men intent upon business.

Smythe had made up his mind as to the course he should pursue; and therefore did not feel in the least degree alarmed. He had provided for such a contingency, by having arranged that, upon a certain vigorous ringing of the bell, half a dozen stalwart porters should rush simultaneously into the room, and gather round his sovereign person.

"What may be your business with me, gentlemen?" said he.

The brothers looked at each other, slapped their thighs, and, affecting intense indignation, in the same breath ejaculated:

"That's cool, anyhow!"

"Come, come!" said Smythe, impatiently; "tell me your business—my time is precious?"

"Hear him!" cried the brothers; "only hear him!"

"My time's my money," said Smythe; "and I can't afford to dilly-dally here for half an hour; so say what you have to say at once?"

Astounded at such audacious coolness, both the O'Blazes looked as if they had been stricken dumb. Their perceptive faculties were for the moment suspended, and they sat, with opened mouths and stiffened bodies, staring at the banker as if he were an ogre, or some other extraordinary animal abortion.

The lieutenant, being the youngest, and perhaps

not so well soaked in whiskey as the other, was the first to speak.

"We have called about Tyrone v. Smythe," said he.

"Arrah, and so we have!" added the other. "Yes, by Jasus we have! and, thunder and turf, there's no mistake about it!"

"What do you intend to do?" inquired the youngest; "are we to go into coort, and have all the exposure and botheration of a thrial?"

"The affair is in the hands of my solicitor, and I can't and won't interfere," said Smythe, resolutely.

"But your solicitor—the devil saize him!—is a b——y Jew!" interpolated the elder.

"I trust he may prove so!" said Smythe, looking at his watch.

"Then you won't come to rayson?" inquired the youngest, elevating his eyebrows, and trying to look sober.

"As I have already stated, my time's my money," said Smythe; "and if you have any proposal to make about Tyrone v Smythe, you had better step over to my solicitor's office—it's close at hand—No. —, Broad Street Buildings."

The banker rang his bell, and in walked two rather formidable flunkeys.

"Make it five thousand, and we'll end it and the dishgrace together?" said the elder.

"Or maybe you wouldn't begrudge four thousand?" chimed in the youngest.

"Good morning. Show these gentlemen out, Thomas."

And before the baffled O'Blazes could reply, they were politely shouldered into the passage, and from thence into the street, the well-drilled servants bowing and scraping at every advanced step they took.

"Done!" said the eldest.

"Brown!" added the youngest; and the pair, convinced of having failed in their attempt to compromise with the defendant himself, hied themselves to the residence of Dr. Wriggles.

"A thousand, gentlemen—a cool thousand—and not a fraction more," said the latter.

"Make it five?" said the eldest.

"Or four?" added the youngest.

"Would you have me put my hand into my own pocket to pay for another man's licentiousness?" inquired the doctor.

"Not at all: don't mintion such a thing!" said the brothers; "but a word from you would do it clane and nate, and save all the dishgrace."

"Don't bother me," said the doctor, passionately. "Leoline, my lass, turn these fellows out." As the huge bear crawled into the room, the O'Blazes precipitately decamped; and, before the creature had been driven back into its den, Mr. Smythe made his appearance.

"Defend the action," advised the doctor; "the old peer is on his death-bed, and as the brothers have refused the thousand, don't give them a farthing. The lady herself is getting as common as dirt, and that is why Pat and Phil are getting so desperate. They know it's their last throw."

"They won't shoot me, will they?" asked Smythe.

"Is there not a policeman at every turning?" suggested the doctor.

The banker, aware that he punctually paid all his rates and taxes, professed a confidence in the vigour and fidelity of the laws of his country; and, forthwith waiting upon his legal adviser, instructed him to go into court, with the great crim.-con. cause of the term, should the plaintiff's proceedings render such a step absolutely necessary.

The O'Blazes were not less diligent. They first moistened the parched lips of their disappointment with a modicum of their favourite usquebaugh, and then, with a wisdom irreconcileable with the depth of their potations, departed for Brighton, to subpœna the necessary witnesses. A shrewd attorney's fag accompanied them, to transact the practical business of their journey; and, thanks to his six-and-eight-penny discretion, an extremely judicious selection was made from the multitude of hotel *employes* who volunteered their testimony. But still an important link in the evidence was wanting; and, as the brothers dived deeper into the realms of whiskey-toddy, the deficiency inflicted many qualms upon their fraternal consciences. Ill at ease, they returned to town in the agreeable society of two chambermaids, an imposing waiter, and a nondescript sort of animal, 'yclept boots. Each of those could prove acts of familiarity; but in the presence of the fact of the Lady Tyrone, during her stay at the Steyne Hotel, having had numerous male visitors, not one of the servants could swear to any one intimacy, so as to identify it with the criminal intercourse of any particular gentleman. However, the parties could materially support the declaration, and they were carefully housed in town, while the O'Blazes departed in search of the testimony they required. This proved to be a greater labour than they had imagined; and they were about giving up the affair in despair, when they encountered Jasper, in one of his eccentric peregrinations. That wofully-mutilated atom of humanity was in a state of intense intoxication—not of the faculties—for they were impervious to the assaults of the combined forces of gin brandy, and tobacco—but of the passions; for he had a few moments before seen Alice Burton in the company of the youthful soldier, whose attempts to flesh his sword in her susceptibility have been previously described. He was therefore in a condition to promise prodigies, and keep his word, if by so doing he could inflict an injury upon any woman who had the slightest pretension to beauty. The proposition of the combined O'Blazes pleased him mightily, and the trio adjourned to a tavern to discuss the preliminaries.

"What's the fake?" shouted he, as he facetiously gave a white-cravated dispenser of blue and brown ruin a poke in the ribs, which knocked him into the opposite box. "Who's the woman I'm to peach upon?"

The O'Blazes indulged in a preliminary fit of smoking, and its consequent expectoration; and the eldest, taking upon himself the responsibility of the disclosure, briefly alluded to the scene of the rencontre on the Chain Pier at Brighton.

"Oh, I remember pitching into the pair of you!" said Jasper, winking furiously at a pale lady that was endeavouring to steady herself, unassisted, along the passage. "There was an uncommon strong attack made upon that nincompoop Smythe, wasn't there?"

The O'Blazes admitted the truthfulness of the soft impeachment; and after some additional and, in its way, enlivening and entertaining beating about the bush, as the phrase goes, boldly ventured upon the topic in support of which they wished to engage the sympathies and credible testimony of my Lord Bloomfield's confidential and experienced secretary-general in love, and its concomitants, danger, and the equally-balanced fears of being defeated and detected.

"See them do it?" ejaculated Jasper; "of course I did. You don't suppose I goes through the world blindfolded, do you? I was under the bed, if you like."

The brothers were overjoyed at their unexpected good fortune in meeting with so valuable an auxiliary, and could do no less than, out of pure gratitude, get gloriously drunk in his company. The fag participated in the jollification, and ultimately became so uproarious, that a stretcher had to be procured, and he was conveyed to his domicile in the custody of four brawny fellows who had been worshipping all day at the shrine of Barclay and Perkins. The O'Blazes and Jasper, being harder headed, kept up the fun until the landlord insisted upon their ejection; and then they entered upon an eccentric career in the streets, which was suddenly brought to a termination by a posse of barbarous, unbribed policemen, who, by the liberal use of muscle and truncheon, succeeded in locking the whole party up, on the vague charge of riotous and disorderly conduct at midnight. However, such a characteristic termination to a spree only cemented the friendship of the O'Blazes and Jasper; and the former, elated by the possession of such a valuable witness, pushed on their great cause unto that interesting point where, issue having been joined and a special jury summoned, all the parties engaged in the momentous affair only waited for the clerk of the court to announce that his lordship—one of the puisne barons of the Exchequer of Pleas—was ready, like a sound and constitutional judge as he was, to deal out honest and impartial justice to all. Well, the day came when the mighty crim.-con. case of Tyrone v. Smythe was to be called on; and tremendous was the pressure and excitement in the noble hall of Westminster.

The day when a great cause is expected to come off in one of our central courts of judicature, invariably summonses all the moneyed idlers of the metropolis to the scene of attraction. No well-puffed drama is ever half so successful a draw; and the student of English life would do well to mingle with the throng on such occasions. He is certain to find material enough for the most extended observation, and to learn, perhaps for the first time in his life, that the nastier the expected particulars are assumed to be, the surer are they to coax a male and female auditory, at an unwonted hour, out of their beds of down, or other sensual sleeping and other conveniences, from that class which, screened behind the silken curtains of wealth, enjoys the reputation of being the most refined and moral in the community.

Ten o'clock is the hour at which the animated panorama begins to move; and without any prolix adversion to displays of prurient curiosity, that, in the aggregate, do not present any very unusual features, it will be sufficient to state that there was a large attendance of the various members and dependents of the families directly interested in the result of this, as it turned out, more than ordinarily racy bit of smutty litigation. First of all there were the O'Blazes, in all the gloom and despondency of brothers, whose ancestral virtues had been blighted by the pestiferous breath of a vulgar, low-bred son of commerce. Had the offender been nobly born, the deed would have sanctified the crime; but to be only a pettifogging money-grubber—horrible perversion of aristocratic beauty—so horrible, that there was damnation and utter social perdition in the thought; and the blood of the before unsullied O'Blazes boiled and bubbled for satisfaction before a Saxon tribunal of all-avenging justice. The train of these aggrieved gentlemen was a motley one, composed of various descendants of old Milesian families, who recognised the plaintiff as their hereditary chieftain. They were all more or less distinguished for the singularity of their attire, and a remarkable redness of the nose and eyes. The body

of the court contained a good sprinkling of ladies; but those of fashion crowded in the vicinity of the bench. Mrs. Smythe and Lady Bloomfield obtained the honour of seats next to the judge; and it was gratifying to behold the cordial manner in which they saluted, and recognised, by smiles and bows, the fashionable ladies of their acquaintance who had laughingly thrust themselves in among the stuff gowns of the outer bar. The ushers of the court were in ecstacies; for crowns and half-crowns had literally been thrust upon them in such abundance, that the weight of the gratuities incumbered their persons; and when his lordship had taken his seat, and they knew he would be engaged for at least an hour with certain motions, of course they gladly beat a retreat to the hospitable shelter of the Magpie and Stump. They were faded Exchequer of Pleas antiquities, but their brains were stored with the legal experience of half a century; and it was their pride to gather round them in the evening a listening crowd, and relate all the particulars of the remarkable cases that had come under their notice.

"Does this case of Tyrone v. Smythe promise well?" inquired an individual, poising a pot of beer in his hand.

"Pretty well—pretty well," replied Mr. Wand, the senior usher; "but nothing to what I have seen. The swells are strong in number, to be sure; but neither of us have taken a sovereign from one of them yet."

"It didn't use to be," said the junior; "but times are altered; and if we can't get guineas, we must take tanners."

"The defendant's a good tip," said Mr. Wand.

"What, have you had him in a crim.-con. afore?" asked a stander-by.

"No, not exactly that—but next door to it," responded Mr. Wand; and, after levying a heavy tribute on the proffered gin-and-water of the questioner, he said: "it was for seduction; and never shall I forget it; for that day Sergeant Sparkle came out uncommon strong. Well, the case was called on; and the plaintiff, an old man from the country, sat next to his 'torney, and next to him was his daughter, who should a' been the plaintiff in right, only the law, in them cases, says that nobody's hurt in a seduction but the father; so he brings the action, and pockets the swag. It's a point I never could see clearly through; but it's the law, and that, you know, must be obeyed. Well, the case came on; and, my eye, didn't the sergeant pitch into the defendant! Why, he twisted and twirled him about so, that if I had been him, I'd a' never touched a woman agin. Well, the daughter was put into the box to prove that the deed was done, and that she did, and no mistake; but, somehow or another, the case warn't a straightforward one. The services for which the father asked for damages were not so clear as they ought to have been; and the judge summed up agin him, and the jury found for the defendant. You should a' seen how the old man stood up—a fine old fellow—straight as an arrow:

"'Is this justice?' says he. 'It's the law,' said the judge. 'Am I to have no recompense for my daughter's honour? It's not the money I want—that's trash, and slaves to thousands—its justice—justice!' says he, quite excited. The judge had a kind heart, and tried to 'splain it to him, but it was no go; a couple of tears started out of the poor old fellow's eyes, and, clasping his hands together, he cried out: 'May God forgive him as I do!' and fell down slap on the floor. His daughter, with a shriek that made the whole court ring again, threw herself on him; we—that is, I and my mate—rushed to the spot, but the old man was dead—his heart had broke! The daughter was carried out of court in a fit; and, I must say, that the defendant did the thing handsomely. Both me and my mate had a ten-pun' note each."

"What become of the girl?"

"Can't say; this very Smythe as 'll be in court to-day, carried her off in a cab, and I never saw her again. She was a good-looking sort of keep, but rather a mammyish thing—she had no game at all in her, except for blanket and sheets work."

Here the old usher winked very wickedly for such an old man, and, indulging in another fourpenny-worth of gin-and-water, betook himself to the most ancient sanctuary of the laws of his country, where he arrived just in time to hear the opening speech in Tyrone v. Smythe. Mr. Tassiker, Q.C., led the van, supported by a tremendously-learned second leader in the person of Mr. Spunky; while, for the defence, there were two sergeants, and five stuff-gownsmen, all proud of the honour of next morning seeing their names given to the world as being retained in such a celebrated case. A great flutter pervaded the whole audience—ladies' dresses rustled—feathers waved—and there was that general adjustment of bodies to their seats, which is usual with people who make up their minds to sit long in one position. The judges' clerk handed up a fresh note-book and half a dozen new quill pens to his lordship; and the reporters, participating in the excitement of the opening preparations, mended their pencils, and tried to look, as they really did, as part and parcel of the court itself. The witnesses in the custody of a managing clerk, left the court, and the O'Blazes plumped themselves, with a commotion, right under the nose of Mr. Tassiker; and, before the trial was over, were half blinded by the copious supplies of snuff in which that gentleman indulged his nasal organ. The briefs in the hands of the juniors were opened and shut with industrious zeal, and then the jury were sworn. It was one specially summoned, and was wholly composed of gentlemen of fortune—of gentlemen who had wives and families and lofty connections, and who were therefore presumed to be better able to decide a delicate case of family honour, than a dozen vulgar tradesmen, selected at random, by ballot. The pleadings were then run over at railway pace by Mr. Spunky; and, after a good deal of snarling over technicalities by the juniors, and an interesting race by the ushers to the library, in pursuit of the authorities that were required to decide knotty points in pleading, the great Mr. Tassiker rose, and, folding his gown over his arms, thus began his moral onslaught on infidelity, and its attendant miseries—pain, exposure, desertion, dishonour, and expatriation from the good opinion of the monster-headed moral public:—

"My Lud and Gentlemen of the Jury,

"My client in this distressing case is descended from an ancient and honourable Irish family, and he belongs to that distinguished class of the old nobility, which may truly be said to be a living connecting link between the past and the present. In his youth and early manhood he served his country in the battle field, and added another to the innumerable proofs we have of the valour, fidelity, and loyalty of his brave countrymen. The cabinet has also experienced the benefits of his wisdom, and I may truly say, that the Right Hon. the Earl of Tyrone has deserved eminently well of his country. In his private capacity, as a nobleman and proprietor of large estates, he has contributed largely to the happiness and prosperity of the numerous circle by which he has at all times been cheerfully surrounded. This excellent nobleman, following the destiny carved out by a beneficent Providence for all of us, married an estimable and accomplished lady, only some fifteen years his junior—a disparity which every one of you gentlemen will admit to be an exceedingly trifling one—in fact, a difference of no moment—for it is an established opinion—I may say a law of marriage—that the husband should be older than the wife, so as to be her friend, her counsellor, and her guide. The marriage was solemnised under the happiest auspices, and for several years my client enjoyed the most unalloyed happiness. The smiles of his wife relieved and soothed him, after the dull cares of state; and when unbending and relaxed in the midst of his joyous family circle, he was the happiest of mortals. The peer of the realm, the cares of office, the anxieties and amiable consideration of the landlord, and all the weighty affairs that surround a man of rank, were merged, drowned, in the felicity, the immeasurable joy, afforded him by the society of his charming wife; and, in the distance, when time should have furrowed his brow, and whitened his hair, he saw pleasant visions of hours of ease and love in a calm, contented old age, sweetened by the treasured-up affection of a spouse, who had grown up in his sight like a sweetly-smelling flower, and expanded, under his care and conjugal tenderness, into the high-born matron who was to grace the courtly throng, and shine, like a radiant star, in the wide hemisphere of British beauty. But a cloud came over this bright vision, and in an instant the airy fabric melted away. His domestic peace was invaded by the spoiler—a Satan overleaped the walls of his paradise, and spread contagion and pestilence around. That Satan was the defendant—a man comely in person—largely blessed with the goods of this world, and one whom we should have looked upon rather as its instructor in good morals, than its debaser and contaminator. Gentlemen, the defendant is a well-known City banker; his wealth is unbounded, and, sheltered by the *prestige* which its possession ever throws around its possessor, he gained admission into those titled circles of this great country, where rank, talent, and beauty form one of the most glorious galaxies of which the whole civilised world can boast. He mingled in the proud and gay throng, as one in whom the utmost confidence could be reposed; and the wives and daughters of our higher classes did not scruple to admit him into the sphere of their acquaintance—and, in many instances, as in this deplorable one, to their friendship. The Earl of Tyrone, deceived by his plausible manners and insinuating address, admitted him into the most unreserved communion with his family; and I am here before you to-day, to show how that confidence has been abused—how the friendly feeling of my client has been outraged; how the defendant repaid kindness with villany, treachery, and base ingratitude. My lud, and gentlemen of the jury, my client, until a certain day in June last, had not the least suspicion that the elements of misery were brewing a sad potion for him within the precincts of his own once happy home. His guileless nature trusted in all, and believed in all—suspicion never haunts generous minds; but the sad time had arrived when his noble heart was to be undeceived by one of the grossest pieces of iniquity ever perpetrated by the hallowed fire-side of a British subject—when his dearest affections were to be torn and sundered, and the joy of his life rendered as polluted as that dark stream which flows beneath the towers of England's senate. He was at the time an invalid: severe parliamentary duties had thrown him helpless on a bed of sickness; and, while thus prostrated, the defendant, in the deep malignity and dark cunning of his profligacy, availed himself of the opportunity to pour the poison of false vows, the flatteries of hollow passion, and the wild, bad, and burning promptings of his lechery, into the ears of the wife of the bosom companion of my too credulous client. The adulterer prevailed: he had found Lady Tyrone, in an hour of weakness, perhaps excitement, consequent on the indisposition of her noble husband; and she yielded to the base proposals of the defendant, and fell into the snare which had been spread for her with such adroit and industrious villany. She fled—fled from home, friends, reputation, love, honour—all that makes life dear and sacred, and an adulterous intercourse commenced, for which the outraged husband demands satisfaction at the hands of the intelligent and upright jury before whom he has been compelled, by a cruel, a hideous necessity, to lay bare his wrongs. The pleas in the declaration will be supported by credible witnesses, and I shall be able to prove not only one act of adultery, but several; and I will not waste time by detailing what will be found to be so clear and positively demonstrative. My main duty now is to lay before you a comprehensive outline of this melancholy case — this horrible calamity—and to insist upon your particularly directing your attention to the awful nature of the offence with which you are about to deal. Adultery is not only a high crime against society, but against the Providence of the world. In ancient days it was punishable with death; but we, who live in more merciful times, only ask for such reparation as will purge the dishonour away from the name and fortune of the husband, and place him in such a position that, while the law marks its detestation of the offence, it also affords the victim the best means of redress in its power. Such a blot on a family escutcheon can only be removed by divorce, and that will be the next step to be taken, should we, as I confidently anticipate, succeed in the present momentous one. And now, my lud, and gentlemen of the jury, I will proceed to call witnesses, and to impress upon your understanding that this is no common case—no trifling with either the majesty of law or morals—but one in which the dearest interests of mankind, the fondest ties and holiest of social obligations, are involved—a case that introduces you to the husband and the adulterer: the former, full in years and honour, an adviser of his sovereign, a legislator of his country, and a friend and benefactor of his species; the latter, a man of immense fortune, accused of the blackest ingratitude, the vilest licentiousness, and the most envenomed offence in the long catalogue of human delinquencies. He stands forth confessedly an adulterer—a thief, who has crept, serpent-like, into the bosom of a family, to ruin and destroy it—to blast its fairest prospects, annihilate its most hopeful aspirations, and drag a woman—a poor, helpless, credulous woman—into the mire of his filth; and, while robbing a husband of his most valued household treasure, leave the victim of his coarse, unbridled licentiousness, to perish in the wild, dark depths of her own infinite sorrow and despair. Brand such a monster, gentlemen, with your reprobation, your honest censure, your human detestation of his iniquity—and you will render society one of those distinguished services of which your consciences will approve when in the retirement of your own pure, unsullied homes. You will look around you, and thank heaven that the wolf has not dared to enter your folds. And, to do justice to my terribly-injured client, and at the same time mark your sense of the enormity of the defendant's conduct, I call upon you to award the high damages laid in the declaration, and so hold out a significant warning to the whole of the detested brood of seducers."

Some slight applause followed this spirited harangue, but, as the newspapers report, it was instantly suppressed by the officers of the court. The judge, who, all the time of its delivery, had been writing letters and holding whispered colloquies with the ladies on each side of him, now brightened up, and dipped his pen with alacrity into his ink-stand, as soon as he heard Mr. Spunky call out the name of the first witness, which was Captain O'Blaze. That personage, who had despised the restraint attempted to be imposed on his devotion to whiskey, burst through the mass that impeded his way, and fairly took the witness-box by storm. His fraternal excitement was intense—so much so that he attempted to address the jury, and was only restrained by his lordship getting into a passion, and threatening to commit him for contempt. His examination in chief merely consisted in proving the marriage, the happiness of the wedded pair, and the friendly terms on which the defendant had visited at his sister's residence. His cross-examination tried both his probity and temper. Sergeant Dobbs took him kindly by the hand. A famous advocate was that Dobbs for the defence, in crim.-con. and seduction cases. He particularly prided himself on making the immediate relatives of the plaintiff, or the poor girl who proved her own shame, tremble in their shoes.

"Now, Captain O'Blaze, "you will perhaps tell us in what regiment you serve?" said he.

This question rather annoyed the gallant captain, and he felt disposed to be angry; but Dobbs, like a funny fellow as he was, would have a direct answer.

"I'm not attached at all at all just now," was the reluctant reply.

"But how do you call yourself a captain, then?"

"I was once among the Foigh-a-Ballagh boys."

"Oh! you were once in the 88th; what did you leave it for?"

"Faith! I was ordered to do so."

"But there must have been a cause—come, out with it. Now, had you not some dispute about cards with your brother officers?"

"Faith! there was something of the kind; but I forget it intirely."

"Were you not kicked by Lieutenant O'Gorman?"

Here the plaintiff's counsel rose, and protested against such a line of cross-examination; but the judge pronounced it perfectly fair, and the captain was fain obliged to admit the truth of the impeachment; he however added, that the rash lieutenant only survived the fundamental error he had committed for three days: on the fourth, he received his death bullet from the trusty pistol of the O'Blaze.

This confession, coupled with the truculent aspect of the witness, did not show him to the court in any very pleasing light.

"Now, Mr. O'Blaze," said Sergeant Dobbs, "what fortune did Lady Tyrone bring her husband when she married him?"

"Divil a ha'penny!"

This brusque reply of course elicited roars of laughter; upon other questions being put, reflecting seriously on the chastity of his sister, the plaintiff's counsel warmly interfered; and, after a long squabble, the judge decided that they could not be put.

This released the captain from the box, and Lieut. O'Blaze was called to take his place; but that gallant son of Mars was so drunk that he could do nothing but throw his burly body into an approved attitude of self-defence, and indulge in such hostile gesticulations that his lordship indignantly committed him for contempt, and afterwards detained him in durance vile, until he had purged it away by making a humble apology, and paying sundry five-pound notes for divers assaults on the servants of the crown.

Mr. Tassiker himself called the next witness, a smartly-dressed young woman, of some four or five-and-twenty. She acknowledged the patronymic of Anne Laycock.

"You are chambermaid at the —— Hotel, Brighton, are you not?"

"I am."

"And were so in June last?"

"I was."

"Very good; now do you remember a lady and gentleman coming there on the night of the 14th of June?"

"Many came on that night, and do on every night."

"Very likely, ladies and gentlemen must sleep, I suppose. Do you remember the names of any that came on that particular night?"

"I remember Lady Tyrone and Mr. Smythe coming."

"How did you know it was them?"

"Because I had lived in service with Lady Tyrone, and Mr. Smythe used to come to the house."

"Well—very well; take time, my dear—don't hurry yourself in the least. Did Lady Tyrone and Mr. Smythe sleep there that night?"

"They did."

"In the same bed."

"They did, for I made the bed, and, about an hour after they had gone to bed, I took each of them a glass of brandy-and-water to the bed-side."

"Oh, indeed! and pray what were they doing when you went into the room?"

"Oh, brother—brother!" interrupted the judge, moving uneasily on his seat; "remember there are ladies in court, and we should not carry these things too far?"

"I never carry anything where it should not go!" loftily replied the indignant Queen's Counsel.

A titter ran through the court, and Mrs. Smythe, whose thick veil prevented her being recognised—it would have been an interesting trial if the mob had known that the wife of the defendant was present—whispered to the countess that it would not be a hard task to take all the poor old gentleman had to give. The countess, who was also closely veiled, as indeed were all the ladies on the bench—laughed, but did not reply.

"The question is strictly legal," said the judge, with dignity; "but whether proper, I leave to yourself."

"My lud, I want to get at the fact, and put a plain, unvarnished question to the witness," urged the counsel.

"You may put such things too far," said the judge, quite innocently.

There was another titter, and more than one lady in court felt herself hardly pressed in the small of the back. The plaintiff's counsel was obdurate, and Miss Laycock had to reply to the question.

"Why, sir," said she, holding down her head, "the clothes were all in disorder, and Lady Tyrone had one leg round Mr. Smythe's neck, and he was nursing the upper part of the other leg. She was sitting on the pillow."

"Was that all you saw?"

"That was all."

"You were in Lady Tyrone's service at one time, I think you said?"

"I was, sir."

"Did you ever notice any acts of familiarity between her ladyship and Mr. Smythe then?"

"I have often seen them romping on my lady's bed; and once I saw them lying on the hearth-rug before the fire in the drawing-room."

"What were they doing?"

"Nothing."

"Nothing—what do you mean by nothing?"

"They were fast asleep."

"Were their clothes at all disordered?"

"Missus's were rucked up to her knees."

"Rucked up—what's that?"

"Rolled up, sir."

"Shoved up, you mean?"

"I saw her legs, and that's all the shoving I saw."

"Did you ever see them kiss each other?"

"Oh, law, yes! Mr. Smythe was always precious fond of kissing!"

"Confine yourself to the questions witness," said the Q. C., severely. "Did the defendant, Mr. Smythe, ever sleep at Lord Tyrone's?"

"Never. He couldn't, for there wasn't never a spare bed."

"You may go down," said the Q. C., alarmed at the loquacity of his witness.

"Not yet," interposed Sergeant Brandy-and-water, the second leader. "Now, young woman, you say that the defendant was always fond of kissing—did he ever kiss you?"

"Once or twice."

"Did he ever do anything else to you?"

"No; he tried, but I wouldn't let him."

"Oh! he did, did he? What did he try?"

"He said if I'd go with him, he'd give me a five-pound note."

"And you refused?"

"I slapped his face for him—the brute!"

The judge looked up, and smiled; so did the bar, and some violent partisans of virtue in the background clapped their hands. Miss Laycock was permitted to descend, and be received by her friends with many smiles and smirks of approval.

"We have proved the adultery," whispered the attorney to the Q. C.; "is there any necessity for calling another witness to the fact?"

"Certainly!" was the severe reply; "the defence may prove this Laycock a strumpet, and then where should we be? Call Jasper Sampson!" shouted he.

"Jasper Sampson!" promptly echoed the crier.

"Here!" exclaimed that individual, starting up from one of the remote seats at the back of the court.

At this up jumped the two sergeants and the five juniors for the defence, and vociferously bawled out, in chorus:

"I object to that witness—he's been in court all the while!"

The judge looked grave, and asked Jasper, when he had entered the box, why he had not obeyed the order to retire.

"What order?" said he, looking as stolid and vacant as possible.

"I submit," argued Mr. Tassiker, "that, as this witness's testimony is independent of the others, the omission will not be material."

"The objection has been made, and I'm bound to take a note of it," said the judge; "and, therefore if you examine the witness, you run the risk of having his evidence expunged on motion."

Mr. Tassiker smiled, and, with an air which plainly wished everybody to believe that he knew the law quite as well as his lordship, turned to Jasper.

"You are confidential servant to Lord Bloomfield, I believe?"

"I am," replied Jasper, standing as upright as a sentry, with his eyes fixed abstractedly on the ceiling.

"You were in Brighton on the 14th of June last?"

"I was."

"Did you see the plaintiff's wife and the defendant there?"

"I did. They walked out arm-in-arm together every day."

"Did you ever carry a message from your master to Mr. Smythe while staying there?"

"I did twice."

"On those occasions did you ever find Lady Tyrone and the defendant together?"

"On one of them I did, and precious close together they were."

"Describe what you saw?"

Jasper hesitated a moment, and then drawlingly replied:

"Let me tell it in my own way, and I'll do it sooner. You see the hotel rooms in Brighton are very accommodating—they are double, and have folding doors—and behind them folding doors is a bed, or a couch; so, if you have any private business to do, you mustn't forget to shut them doors. Well, on that identical 14th of June, I was sent with a message to Mr. Smythe's room. He went by the name of Jackson, though, then; and, accordingly, being told to go up stairs, of course I did go; finding knocking was no go, I tried the handle, and walked in. Them folding doors was open, and, as I looked through the chink, I saw everything that was going on behind them."

"Who were the parties in that room?"

"Lady Tyrone and Mr. Smythe."

"What were they doing?"

Jasper made an effort to look modest, and mincingly replied:

"Something very naughty—dreadful naughty, my lord!"

"Describe it?" said the Q.C., impatiently, "and don't keep the court waiting."

"Well, if I must, I must," replied Jasper; "but in the presence of them delicate ladies it's rather awful! Needs must, though, when the devil drives; and I suppose I must out with it. Well, the defendant in this ere case had his coat off, and his shirt-sleeves rolled up, and his arms were up the lady's petticoats round her waist, and her drawers were off, and her shape was quite plain, and they were waltzing like blazes!"

The judge frowned severely—the ladies turned away their heads, as if inexpressibly shocked—the bar simpered—and the audience grinned outright, at this sally.

"Well, go on, said the Q.C., making a frantic effort to compose his features; and, in his agitation, wriggling his person about, as if some unseen enemy was maliciously thrusting pins into his hinder legal regions.

"When they got tired of that fun," continued Jasper, "they stripped themselves stark naked, and danced an Irish jig before the mirror."

"Well?"

"Then they rolled over each other on the carpet, and I do declare that then I lost my eyesight, but not my hearing; for I heard a hard breathing, and a kissing, and the lady crying out, just like a cat on the tiles at night!"*

This was too much for a number of persons in court. Many cried out "Shame!" and others, including nearly the whole of the ladies, precipitately left.

Sergeant Dobbs rose, with a very red face, to cross-examine Jasper; but it was some seconds before he could utter a word.

"What are you?" said he.

"A gentleman at large for to-day, thanks to the subpoena, and the guinea I get for coming here!" replied Jasper.

"What are the services you render Lord Bloomfield?"

"I accompany him when he travels."

"Are you his valet?"

"No!"

"His what, then?"

"I do everything reasonable that he asks me."

"Perhaps you are a pimp?" cried Dobbs, losing his temper.

Plaintiff's counsel rose, and indignantly demanded protection for their witness. The bench rebuked the sergeant. He endured the reproof meekly, and, having received a whisper from his instructing party turned sharply to Jasper, and said:

"Are you a married man?"

Jasper turned deathly pale, and clutched nervously at the rail before him.

"Are you married?" repeated Dobbs.

"I am," gasped Jasper.

"Do you live with your wife?"

"No!"

"Where is she, then?"

"I hope to God she'll be in hell soon!" cried Jasper, furiously.

* See report of the trial Lennox v. Cardigan, as given in the "Times," and other daily papers.

The judge, seeing him painfully excited, came to his relief:

"You are separated from your wife, then?"

"She bolted from me, and became as big a w—e as Lady Tyrone!"

"You have been heard to say that you hated women," said Dobbs; "is that true?"

"It is: they are all w—s in their hearts!"

"Your wife inflicted a terrible injury on you before she left you, did she not?" inquired the torturing Dobbs.

The perspiration broke out in huge drops on Jasper's forehead, for the terrible suspicion had seized him that the dreaded disclosure of the horrible vengeance of a wife was about to be divulged. His brain reeled—his lips became parched—and, so sickly a hue spread over his repulsive features, that the whole court shuddered as it gazed at him. However, he made a prodigious effort, and, burying his face in his hands, as if convulsed with grief, sobbed forth, in heart-rending tones:

"She broke my heart!"

"This is cruelty!" exclaimed the judge.

And Dobbs, not very well satisfied with the impression caused by the witness's agitated demeanour, sat down.

"Another victim of conjugal infidelity!" whispered the jury one to another, as they made up their minds to award the poor, abused Lord Tyrone very handsome damages indeed. Jasper was led away, apparently overwhelmed with grief.

Mr. Dobbs then made an eloquent defence. He expatiated on the immense difference between the ages of Lord and Lady Tyrone,—on his infirmities,—his well-known dissipation,—and the entire absence of all proper protection on his part. He enlarged on her poverty,—on her low origin,—her lax manners,—the fact that she was never received at court,—and that her acquaintances chiefly lay among ladies of questionable character, and gentlemen whose very business and occupation was adultery, fornication, and seduction. Then he glanced off to the surmise that there had been a collusion between the plaintiff and defendant; that in fact the husband, a poor, beggared peer, had actually sold his wife. The adultery he would not deny; but contended that the character of the husband, and the startling antecedents in the career of the wife, would completely justify the jury in awarding for damages the smallest coin in the realm.

But all his argument and eloquence were thrown away—the jury were all married men; and after his lordship had briefly summed up, they turned round in their box, and, after a few minutes' consultation, announced that they had agreed upon their verdict.

"For the plaintiff or the defendant?" demanded the clerk.

"The plaintiff."

"What damages do you award?"

"Ten thousand pounds!"

"Ten thousand pounds!" ejaculated an elderly sprig of the aristocracy, as he hobbled to his carriage; "ten thousand pounds! My stars! but that's a large sum for getting rid of the greatest profligate of a wife in London! I wish I had a chance like it; but my young bitch of a wife is either confoundedly sly, or most egregiously virtuous; so I suppose I must let her wear me out, and then die in peace, like a courteous, kind-hearted, gentlemanly old fellow of a husband. Ten thousand pounds! My stars! What is the next I shall hear, I wonder?"

And the old man, in his amazement, mumbled bitter things to himself all the remainder of that day.

While this all important trial was pending, the noble plaintiff was engaged in farewell pastimes, that prematurely brought about a termination to a life of more than ordinary dissoluteness. The eloquent praises of his counsel were yet ringing through the court—startling, bewildering, and amusing those among the audience who knew him well—when the thread of his licentious existence was suddenly cut in twain, and the public, in a few hours, made acquainted with the astounding circumstance of a dead man achieving a splendid victory over a legal opponent. The inexorable destiny that, sooner or later, overtakes both good and bad, denied him the petty privilege of knowing that his countess—the daring and witty, but awfully profligate Peg Johnson—had brought him 10,000l. as the price of a dishonour no man was ever capable of inflicting on him through her instrumentality. But, to do his lordship justice, he had not been very zealous in the cause, and only lent it his approval from the pressing nature of his pecuniary embarrassments. The Encumbered Estates Commission had made short work with his estates, by depriving him even of the nominal proprietorship of which most Irish landowners can only really boast; and for several months past he had been reduced to the necessity of obtaining the means of gratifying the terrible indulgences to which he had been accustomed, through the liberality of his wife. _How_ she acquired funds it needed no ghost to tell; and as niggardliness formed no portion of her character, she did not scruple to supply him with all the money her limited resources would allow. True, he had a pension: a sale of a mistress to a royal duke had enrolled him among the sinecurists of his country; but that scarcely supplied him with the wines and spirits he consumed; and as the Tyrone paper had become rather unnegotiable in the market, the opportunity of making a few thousands out of a lover of buxom Peggy's was too tempting to be resisted. He would have spared her the exposure—for he had married her with his eyes wide open, and therefore did not feel at all aggrieved by her conduct—but as Peggy herself averred that the banker was "unraysonable," why there was no alternative left but to take the thing into court. And into court did his brothers-in-law, the O'Blazes, carry his conjugal wrongs. Lady Tyrone, of course, for decency's sake, did not reside under his lordship's roof, and her absence relieved him altogether of the slight restraint she sometimes felt compelled to impose on his wayward actions. The excitement and intoxication consequent upon the trial kept the O'Blazes from his side, and he had now a little more freedom than he had been allowed for some time.

With the assistance of the experienced old sinner who had been his valet and pimp for thirty years, he availed himself admirably of the relaxation; for, by dint of borrowing, disposing of remnants of family plate, and getting into debt with a few credulous tradesmen, he managed to raise sufficient to enable him to throw a kind of Satanic splendour over his last days. He fed his lust to the last moment of his polluted hours. But it would be preferable to introduce him _t home_. Let the reader, then, fancy himself in a large, richly-furnished drawing-room, with a costly bed at one end, and several voluptuous-looking couches dispersed around. The walls are garnished with mirrors, and some dozen lewd paintings. The floor, richly carpeted, is so arranged that its whole length is unobstructedly presented to the occupant of the bed, and, illuminated from two beautiful chandeliers, the light of day being carefully excluded, the whole place had very much the appearance of the orgie-room of some eastern voluptuary. On a table, placed conveniently near the head of the bed, there was an abundance of wines and spirits, together with all the appliances of punch and whisky-toddy making. A rich perfume pervaded the atmosphere, and the whole place was redolent of the sensualism of high life. Lord Tyrone, supported by pillows, occupied the bed, round which flitted the half-naked forms of several young girls: some of them professed courtesans, others of that degraded class of posturers and dancers who eke out the scanty pittances afforded by the theatres by exhibiting in private before the debauched, and submitting to the coarsest and most revolting indignities. All of these poor creatures were handsome and beautifully formed; but their gestures and habitual expression of countenance proclaimed them to be daughters of the game,—sacrifices to the lust of man and their own brutalised propensities.

They had been executing some wild dance, which the old lord had lustily applauded; and, after liberally refreshing themselves from the decanters, he called for the Graces.

"The group of the Graces, my cherubs?" he cried.

Three girls separated themselves from the throng, and, retiring into a corner, deliberately divested themselves of every particle of clothing. They then wreathed their arms about one another's snow-white busts, and advanced up the centre of the room to a distance of some half dozen feet from the bed, where they formed the classic group which, for loveliness, dignity, and modesty, has been the wonder of centuries. They stood like perfect statues—not a limb or a muscle of their bodies even quivered, so perfect had been their training in this particular figure; and there lay the wreck of a once powerfully-built man, gazing upon their exposed persons with the horrible, burning glances of brutish desire. His face, blotched and bloated, reddened at the spectacle, and the deep crimson, wandering up beyond his temples, rendered his scanty white hairs whiter by the contrast.

Other groupings succeeded the one he had called forth; and, as the girls became more heated by the drink and their lascivious occupation, the bolder they became in their attitudes, and, the infection spreading to the rest of the troupe, they stripped themselves, and commenced dancing like the bayaderes of an obscene Indian temple. It was a disgusting sight; but every fresh sally, every new indecency and revolting epithet, was vehemently applauded by Tyrone; and when at length the girls paused from absolute fatigue, he invited them to his bed-side, and induced them to clamber on to the bed, and seat themselves so as not to touch his enormously-swelled gouty limbs. One of them prepared for him a large glassful of whisky-toddy; and, seeing that each held a goblet in her hand, he gave as a toast the standing one of his order—

"Merry wives, merry girls, and plenty of them."

The nude and intoxicated creatures drank the toast with avidity; and then Lord Tyrone commenced a scene so disgusting, so horrible, so intensely hideous, that even the fair skins of the poor abused girls reddened at his touch, however slight, and the frames of many of them quivered like dead bodies when galvanised. Shame had not altogether died within them, and it was curious to observe how much more sensitive in this respect the street harlot was than the professional dancer and artists' model. How long this demoniac drama might have lasted, it would be hard to tell, for its conclusion was awfully sudden. The *debauchee* had just made a suggestion, if possible more abominable than any previous one, when the girls observed his hitherto dreadfully red face to become chalky white, his inflamed eye-balls to roll in their sockets, and his whole demeanour to become like that of one smitten to death in an instant. For a moment surprise and terror held them dumb, but another glance at those fast-stiffening lineaments drove them from the bed like a flock of disturbed birds, and they filled the apartment with their almost unearthly shrieks and cries. The noise alarmed the half-drunken valet on the landing, and he burst into the room.

"Run for a docther!" he frantically cried; but the girls, unheeding him, huddled on their clothes as fast as their stupor and fear would allow them, and fled from that accursed room. Some were shoeless and stockingless, others shawlless, others bonnetless—all in disorder, and without some portion of their attire—but winged with a mad terror—a blanched horror—to avoid that monster of a face, with its stony, staring eye-balls. They fled, some to die raving mad, others to plunge into the slimy river, and others to throw the past behind them, and remember that day with a convulsive shudder. The valet, after recovering some portion of his self-command, hastened to the residence of Dr. Wriggles, who immediately accompanied him back to that awful room.

"Dead!" said the doctor, taking in the whole of the scene, and its horrible accompaniments, in a single glance. "His raging passions induced apoplexy, and he has died, as he often blasphemously and cowardly wished, in the midst of an all-consuming tremendous lust-fit. A fit end to such a wasted life. Only twelve o'clock—he must have begun early this morning. I wonder how the trial goes on?"

The doctor returned musingly home, and later in the day discovered that the verdict was not returned before four o'clock, at which hour, of course, there was no plaintiff in existence—he had died even while his counsel was pronouncing a panegyric on his ancestral and other virtues. The court next morning was moved for an arrest of judgment, which, being granted, of course an investigation, supported by the most unimpeachable affidavits, subsequently took place; which resulted in the extraordinary case of Tyrone *v.* Smythe ending in smoke. Smythe escaped by paying his own costs; and in a few months the whole affair sank to the level of the legal traditions treasured up by the ushers of her Majesty's Court of Exchequer of Pleas.

CHAPTER XXIII.

JASPER SAMPSON AND ALICE BURTON.—THE HUSBAND'S RETALIATION.

JASPER SAMPSON has played such varied parts throughout the course of this most eventful narrative, that it is only a tribute justly merited by his conspicuous performances, that he should be exclusively introduced in the last scenes of the tragedy of his wrong, and its attendant diabolical revenge. The raging fire that for months had burned within his obdurate breast, was daily acquiring such intense energy, that, in his wild and and savage shrewdness,

he feared that the mere force and concentrated violence of its purpose would defeat its execution.

"To be cheated after all these months of misery—these months of useless lust and damning thoughts," were his reflections, "makes the hell I feel hotter than the one I am going to! But how to accomplish my fell intent, and make a woman—a she-devil—feel that it is safer to provoke a tiger, than a man consumed by a passion, hopeless of gratifying it, puzzles and perplexes me. It is true I could kill her—stab her to the heart, or dash out her accursed brains—but that is not enough! Death is only a momentary pang—a gasp like that a strangled dog gives—I would have her die a million deaths—I would have each minute a death—each hour bring its torture of mangled and infuriated lust! But how, is the question—aye, how—how—and speedily, for I feel that each day the game is slipping from my hands. She said she would go to India—all over the world—with that stripling booby whom she has fascinated. D——n! to think that the woman whose virgin knot I broke in my prime—whose body I have feasted upon a thousand times—should leap like a w——e to the arms of a boy—a wanton whose paltry manhood a child of our family would be ashamed to wear! There's madness in the idea; but let them marry! and, aye, let them be bedded; for what is marriage without its concupisence—its toyings—its paddlings in the bosom, and among the plump ridges of the pulpy thighs? Oh, God! of what am I thinking—my bowels are on fire, and my eyes see twenty rosy forms, all asking me to press their naked limbs to mine; suck their rosy lips, and then fasten, leechlike, on their warm, soft fronts! Off—off—away from me —hence into the highway—the desert—there are men there—I am a poor puny thing—a eunuch!"

And here the infuriated man broke out into such peals of sardonic laughter that the quiet lane through which he was passing rang with his cries, and the cattle, grazing quietly behind the hedges, lifted up their heads to have one look at him, and then, terrified, broke madly away. A few peasants, discussing their homely fare in a rural nook close at hand, threw down their meal, and hastened away, with the exclamation that "hell had broken loose."

This helped to soothe Jasper not a little, for he grinned and said:

"It is something to be feared: there's gloom and grandeur in the thought; and *that* deed once done, I will indeed, to all who come near me, be 'hell broke loose!'"

And again he laughed his hideous discord, and indulged in low chuckles and dry cacchinations—such as those with which it might be supposed Satan himself tickled his appetite for mischief. As he approached some cottages that stood on the western border of Epping Forest, he became more composed, and, as well as he could, adjusted his repulsive features, until they bore the lines of a remarkably sinister simper. The tenement to which his errand led him was a detached one, at some distance from the rest; and he walked up to it with singular caution, as if he wished to take the inmates by surprise. The garden that encompassed it was surrounded by a high, thick hedge; and to a gap in this, which he had made himself, for the purpose of both seeing and listening unobserved, he softly made his way. Pushing the leaves of the hawthorn aside, he looked through, but instantly started back, as if he had been bitten by a serpent. His features became as rigid as if he had been turned into a statue, and his whole demeanour betrayed the violence of the shock he had received. At length he somewhat recovered himself, and muttered a dreadful malediction.

"She here!" he said to himself; "there has been treachery, then, or my steps have been dogged here on my weekly visits. No matter; I'll escort her through the forest, and let her see that, cunning as she is, I can circumvent her. What's that they're talking about I wonder?"

And Jasper again gently moved aside the leaves, and looked in upon the pretty garden behind them. Seated on a rustic seat, with her back to the hedge, was Alice Burton, and in her lap she nursed a fine little boy—the same whom Jasper had brought with him from Brighton. It was her only child, and the latter, by his warm fondlings and endearing expressions, evidently well knew that it was his mother by whom he was so passionately caressed. Alice regarded the manly little fellow with the soft, beaming eyes of maternal love; and, as she hung over him, the tears of sorrow, regret, and love, sprang into her eyes, and many an error rose up in judgment against her. How often does the innocent prattle of a child alarm the conscience of a guilty wife, and wring her heart with the dread that the day will too surely come, when she will feel abashed and ashamed to stand in its presence.

"But we will go into a strange land," thought she, "and among strange faces, and, with the past in England, I will rear up my boy into a man; and he will never know the disgrace of his mother, or the infamy of his father. In three days the ship sails, and then I shall be a wife—a wife!"

Alice fell into strange musings, and it must be confessed that among them the image of her boy-husband did not very much please her imagination. Her propensities were large and not easily satisfied, and the bright prospect of having the society of her child was darkened by the intrusion of the blood-red mists of her unquenchable lust.

"He cannot love me as I should wish to be loved," was her reflection; "and who knows, as he grows older, but that a nearer and fresher love will win him away from me? Ah! but I can be revenged; and, if I sacrificed him, what could I not do to him? Let him be unfaithful—let him: it will be some consolation to know that I can better the example; and it will go hard if I don't before the voyage is over; for I saw several of the officer passengers—noble-looking fellows, something like Walter Morris! Ah, me! he was a man; but he only thinks of me as a merry bed-fellow, with whom he was perfectly satisfied. Well, well, I must take my chance, and if I must be constant I must; but, if I am, it shall only be for the sake of my darling pet—my dear, dear child! Bless his little heart, what a princely little nobleman of a duck he is! Kiss 'ums ma?"

The boy clung round her neck, and she covered his face with such a multitude of kisses that he gasped for breath.

"Kiss 'um's ma?" she repeated, looking fondly and proudly in the boy's face.

"Kiss 'um's da!" whispered Jasper, with an attempt at a sneer; but it was a total failure, for the thought uppermost in his mind imparted a pleasing glow to his pale face, while a more amiable expression glanced from his strangely expressive eyes.

"Will you go to sea, Harry?" said the mother.

"That I will," was the prompt response. "I like Biton better nor these ugly trees."

"You shall go to Biton, darling, with 'um's ma, and have a new father—that it shall."

"A new father! Isn't that my dadda that kisses me, and brings me cakes and toys? Oh, he brought me such a nice horsey-porsey! Come and see it, ma. I love my dadda—a good dadda!"

The opposite feelings of the parents at this declaration may be imagined. A jealous pang smote upon the mother's heart, as a spiteful look disfigured her pretty countenance. The solitary bright, warm spot in the father's nature, glowed and glowed, until he felt inclined to burst through the hedge, and strain the boy to his throbbing breast.

"You mustn't love that—that man," said Alice; "he's not your dadda!"

"Liar!" muttered Jasper, in his concealment.

"But he is," said the boy, obstinately; "and I will love him! He good dadda—and he love me!"

"And don't you love me?" burst from the mother's lips

The child clasped her round the neck, and looked so lovingly into her eyes, that the tears gathered in them, and she was subdued.

"He will forget him when in another country," she thought; "and, as time is short, I must tear myself away."

"Here's my old mamma!" cried the child, as an ugly, peasant-like woman approached them.

"When do you say you will come for the child?" inquired she.

"To-morrow morning. I shall be here early. Mr.—Mr. Sampson could not come himself; but I suppose a note from him will do?" said Alice, as she regarded the woman uneasily; for the latter had previously flatly refused to part with the child without a written authority from Jasper; and Alice's only resource was either to forge one, or bring such assistance with her as would enable her to carry off her child by force.

"All right!" chuckled Jasper, rubbing his hands, as he watched the party retiring within the house. "Old Moll is faithful, I see; and to-morrow morning—oh! oh! oh!—to-morrow morning I will be here. And now for a little bit of fun with Alice—Alice Burton; I wonder she didn't drop the name when she dropped the man; but it's the nature of women to be cross and contrary."

In about a quarter of an hour Alice emerged from the cottage. Jasper, who was completely hidden from her sight, waited until she had disappeared behind the bend in the forest road; and then he took an intersecting footpath, and sped on as swiftly as the tangled brushwood would allow him, until he came to a point where he knew another secluded path branched off to the main road, to which he correctly guessed Alice would directly make, in order to catch one of the omnibuses that went to town, past Woodford Wells. Alice, totally unsuspicious of such a dreaded encounter as one with her instinctive aversion, Jasper Sampson, tripped exultingly along. The prospect of her having her child constantly under her care, and being about to leave a country to which she was now bound by no very tender ties, cheered her spirits; and as she thought of her boy-lover—the young soldier—who panted to lead her to the altar, when he discovered she would not consent to gratify his passion in any other manner—she laughed, and began, like a little reckless thing as she was, to hum a song.

"How I should like to have a good romp among

these bushes with some handsome, gay young fellow!" she exclaimed, as she passed the spot where Jasper expectantly stood.

"I should be happy to oblige so pretty a young lady!" shouted Jasper, springing to her side, and bowing as rapidly, and with as much gesticulation as a dancing master of the old school of terpsichorean art.

Alice screamed, and would have fled—for few women can bear an abrupt surprise unmoved—but one look at Jasper rooted her to the spot. The colour fled from her cheeks, and such a cold shudder passed through her frame, that her teeth chattered as violently as if she had been suddenly thrust into a temperature several degrees below freezing point.

"How do you do, Alice?" said he, with a vulgar politeness, that to her was awful; "who'd a' thought of seeing you in Epping Forest! Out a sweethearting—oh?"

This pleasantry tended to increase Alice's shivering; which Jasper no sooner perceived than he redoubled his endeavours to please, and finally presented his arm to the agitated young woman. The offer served to recal her scattered senses, and she made an attempt to escape from him. But, turn whichever way she would, he was before her; and in making her last frantic effort she stumbled and fell. Jasper raised her instantly, and bore her in his arms deeper in the forest. There was a secluded dell he had often frequented in his youth; and thither he carried her, despite her struggles, with as much ease as if she had been a child. Safe from interruption, he placed her on a rising knoll, and very leisurely proceeded to remove her bonnet and shawl. Alice was totally helpless in his hands: she tried to scream, but not a sound issued from her parched throat; and, as she listened to his horrid jocularities, the dreadful idea struck her that her persecutor intended to murder her. Her love of life was tenacious, and she faintly ejaculated:

"Don't kill me?"

"Kill you!" sneered he; "oh dear no—you are too pretty to be killed! Your titties are too plump, your ankles too neat, and your bustle too large, for me to kill you! What an idea! Now if you had said, 'Don't kiss me?' you'd have been nearer the mark."

"Would you abuse me?" she exclaimed, for the first time giving him a direct look in the face.

"Abuse you! I suppose you mean ravish you? I wish I could, 'pon my soul I do! You may stare, but nothing would give me greater pleasure than to have Cupid's roll on the grass with such a tight little woman; but don't fidget yourself, I have other fish to fry; make yourself easy!"

Alice, stunned, completely subdued by his facetious yet horridly stern demeanour, allowed him to do with her as he pleased; but felt somewhat relieved when she saw him extract a luncheon, a flask of brandy, and a little drinking glass, from his capacious coat pockets.

"While we live let's be merry!" he said, as he spread an unspotted handkerchief on the grass, and made arrangements for the pic-nic party upon which he had evidently determined. "That's my maxim, so we'll just refresh ourselves, and then I'll endeavour to be as agreeable as I know your merry nature would wish a man to be."

Alice ate sparingly, but she did not refuse the neat brandy proffered her, for she fancied it would rearrange her scattered reflections. The brandy revived her a little, but failed to drive away that nameless fear she had always experienced in the presence of Jasper. She thought she knew him—that his face, the tones of his voice, and peculiar manners, were all familiar to her; but when she saw his white hairs, long, thin face, and hollow cheek-bones, and shudderingly caught the expression of his dark grey eyes, the impression was weakened, but could not wholly be eradicated.

"That's right!" cried Jasper, as he perceived her more eagerly swallow the second glassful of spirit; "if there's anything gives me pleasure in this born world, it is to see a young and pretty woman enjoying herself. And, next to kissing, eating and drinking's the jolliest fun I know of. But what shall we do to divert ourselves in this sweet spot?"

"I—I don't know—I should like to get home soon. My lady will be anxiously expecting me," said Alice, for the first time speaking collectedly.

"Home!" replied Jasper. "The forest-glade's our home—our palace—our everything; so let's be happy while the sun shines!"

"Such an ugly brute cannot mean love?" thought Alice; for it must be confessed that her paramount idea was that life was more to be prized than a mere womanly favour, granted in a moment of excitement or danger.

"I promised to tell you a story," said Jasper, after a pause, during which he had been intently eyeing her. "Don't you remember it—I met you one day going to the countess's apartments?"

"I don't remember what you said," replied Alice, the same indescribable fear coming more strongly over her.

"Ah! well, but I did promise you, and that's sufficient," said Jasper, rapidly; "and no time better to keep my word than the present. Now, what might you guess my age to be?"

"I canot say."

"Do you think I'm fifty?"

"You look—look —"

"Sixty you would say. Thank you. But just halve it, and you'll be about right."

"Thirty!" exclaimed Alice, amazed.

"A trifle over; nothing worth mentioning," said Jasper, jocosely; "but perhaps I don't look it, for few men at my years wear such an old-looking head on their shoulders. However, that's neither here nor there, you would say. Do you think I always looked like this?"

"I don't know—I—I hope not."

"Oh! you do, do you? Well, then, I didn't, and so you have your wish; and, if you like, I'll tell you how it all happened, shall I?"

"Won't it be too much trouble?"

"Not a bit of it—I'd do anything to please such a pretty girl as you; so here goes. From twenty to twenty-five I was as handsome, well built, and as strapping a young fellow as you would see in a day's march."

"You?"

"Yes, me, my forest pet. Before I go on I may as well tell you that you shall be my gipsy bride, and we'll sleep under the greenwood tree. Well, as I was a saying, I was a good-sized young fellow, sound in wind, limb, and —— But you know I mean them remote parts where women like to rove. My hair was coal-black, my flesh as firm as marble—water poured on it rolled off in beads; and my heart as big and tight as any man's that ever faced another in a fair game-fight. The women that I knew adored me, and those I'd never had anything to do with used to teaze me out of my life. 'What a duck of a fellow that Harry is!' they used to say."

"Harry! is your name Harry?" almost screamed Alice.

"Did I say Harry? oh yes, I did," responded Jasper; a sardonic smile creeping over his features, as he witnessed the shuddering of his companion; "they used to call me that, because there was a good many Jaspers and Raspers too, in our neighbourhood. Well, after gallivanting about among the girls for a year or two, I picked up one I thought I should a' liked, and, as she took a fancy to me, I married her—went to church, and no gammon. You'd scarcely believe it, would you, that a gay young chap like me would hescort a girl to the parson house, and give her his name?"

"It's only natural, when a man likes a girl, that he should marry her," said Alice, with difficulty.

"Just so," grinned Jasper; "you are a sensible young woman, I see. Well, I married her, and we lived together for a year or so, and then, somehow or another, we couldn't agree. I gave her lashings of love—in fact, did to her as a husband should do who could do; but all wouldn't do, and one day, she bolted, and took her child with her!"

"Her child, said you?" interrupted Alice, through her gaspings for breath.

"Aye, that she did!" replied Jasper, a ferocious expression gathering menacingly on his ugly face; "and I never clapped eyes on either of them for many a long day after. Well, one day I met my wife in the street quite promiscuous-like, and we agreed, quite pleasant-like, to have a drop together and a kiss at my place. We went there, and, after a bit of a tiff, just about nothing at all, I got precious muzzy, and there was a row, and all the devils in hell came into my room, and, as you may guess, there was a pretty how-d'ye-do. Blood—blood—nothing but blood—swam before my eyes. I was jumping, tearing mad in red—the room was red, the people red, myself was red—I saw nothing but red until I thought the floor opened, and I dropt clean into hell—a red hell—and then I forgot everything! When I came to, I found myself as you see me, only perhaps a little stouter. Now, isn't that a history for you?"

As he concluded, he took up the handkerchief from the grass, and spread it on his face, so as to conceal it, from the tip of the nose downwards.

Alice at this moment looked up, and no sooner caught the expression of the eyes and forehead, than she shrieked out:

"Harry Burton!"

"Yes!" shouted Jasper—for it may be as well to continue this more familiar term throughout the narrative; "I was Harry Burton—once your own fond Harry Burton—what am I know?'

Jasper looked so fearful as he said this, that Alice's instinctive love of life overcame all her other emotions; and, flinging herself on her knees at his feet, she exclaimed:

"Oh, Harry! don't kill me—I'm not fit to die yet?"

"What am I, now?" thundered Jasper, seizing her by the arm.

"I didn't do it!" she uttered moaningly, as she writhed in his iron grasp.

"Who did, then?"

"Dr. Wriggles."

"Who set him on?"

"Mrs. Wriggles."

"And who set her on?"

A sickness, more like that one which, in many cases, is a precursor of death, overcame Alice, and she could only feebly exclaim:

"Don't kill me Harry—I didn't do it?"

"Who set that woman-fiend on to get her devil of a husband to serve me so? Speak, you b—h of hell, or I'll squeeze your puddings out!" roared Jasper, shaking her terrifically.

"I didn't do it—I didn't do it!" was all the wretched young woman could utter.

Jasper saw that she was rapidly sinking, and, taking the little glass, he filled it, and then, sprinkling some powder on the top of the liquid, from a box he carried in his pocket, he forced the contents down her throat. In a few minutes she revived wonderfully; but, to all his threats and violence, only replied by an obstinate denial of any participation in the deed Jasper alluded to.

"You didn't do it!" sneered Jasper, releasing her arm from his grasp; "who did then, you liar—who did? and what had I done to you, to make you so spiteful?"

"Oh! Harry, you told me to go on the town!"

"Well, and what if I did? You went a w——g for your own pleasure, and I didn't see why you shouldn't do a little for mine!"

"I was not your blowen, Harry,—I was your wife; and, so help me God, until you struck me and kicked me in the stomach, I never did you harm!"

"Didn't you? What a virtuous, good girl you was, wasn't you now?" said he, mockingly. "But it's all over now, and, as you made a worse devil of me than I was, you must take the consequences."

"Don't kill me, Harry? I didn't hurt you, Harry—indeed I didn't!"

"Liar!"

"Don't kill me—oh, don't kill me—I know I deserve to die—but don't kill me?"

"Kill you! I couldn't afford it; you shall live as long as you can!"

"And see my child?" exclaimed she, eagerly catching at this ray of hope.

"Whenever you will choose to show him your face."

These words she remembered too well for many long years afterwards.

"Answer me one question—and, as you hope to be spared from dying this instant, answer me truly. Is that child mine?"

Alice clasped her hands together, and, in the most solemn manner, answered:

"He is, so help me God!"

"I believe you!" replied Jasper. "And now promise me one thing?"

"What is it?"

"Marry that snotty-nosed boy of a lieutenant, and go abroad with him?"

"And leave my child?"

"Yes!" shouted Jasper; " or die!"

"Oh, don't kill me? I promise anything—everything—but don't kill me?"

"Will you marry him to-morrow morning?"

"I will!"

"Swear to do it?"

"I do—may I be struck dead if I don't!"

As Alice uttered this profane asseveration her head drooped on her shoulders, and presently she sank down on the grass quite insensible.

"The powder has operated!" hissed Jasper between his teeth; "and now for my vengeance—my long-cherished and sure to come vengeance!"

As he continued to mutter these and other words

of dreadful import, he deliberately stretched Alice on her back on the grass, and, baring her arms, neck, and bosom, produced a lancet from his pocket, and some glasses of the kind used by vaccinators to hold the virus for inoculation.

"I knew the day would come," muttered he; "and this stuff, got from the rotten carcases in the hospitals, will make her more loathed than I am! As the flesh drops from her bones, and her face becomes scarred, ulcerous, and noseless, she'll remember giving me a hell to burn in! Ah! ah! she'll feel what it is to want a man as I want a woman! She'll burn—burn and stink—stink and burn—until she drops to pieces—and it 'll take years to do that!"

The monster, as he indulged in these atrocious reflections, dipped the lancet into the poison, and with it pricked the beautiful white, plump flesh of his victim, in at least thirty places in the region of the chest. He lifted up her clothes, and repeated the same detestable infliction in as many places on her legs and thighs; and, while doing so, chuckled like some demon playing tricks with a human soul. When he had concluded he leisurely surveyed his work of destruction, and gloated over the small spots of blood that stood on her skin. He then lighted a pipe, and smoked for about an hour, after which, with his spittle, he wiped away the blood, until he left nothing discernible but sixty little red spots.

"She said I looked sixty, and I've returned the compliment."

After he had carefully adjusted her apparel he filled another pipe, quaffed off several of the small glassfuls of brandy, and, puffing away as calmly as if nothing had occurred to disturb his serenity, patiently waited for her awakening.

The meditations of the man who had inflicted such a tremendous retribution on the destroyer of his manhood, during the awful pause between the accomplishment of the deed and the recovery of his wife from her slumber were dreadful. No tinge of remorse penetrated the deep gloom in which his faculties were shrouded. He rather looked to the future, and pictured to himself the revolting form of his victim, when the deadly poison that was creeping through her veins should have done its pestiferous work. No thought of the time when she lay nestling in his bosom, or submitted with transport to his caresses, shed a drop of oil on the turbid waters of his resentment. All was dark, fearful, and inscrutably savage; and the only change in him was the complete disappearance of his accustomed flippancy. He had fulfilled the mission for which he had marked himself out, and became sterner in consequence. His HATE—fearful passion—had grown, if possible, more deep, virulent, and intense, and would not change its character until he had seen the horror he had committed perfectly and entirely consummated. His sole wish now was to behold her shunned with more aversion than a leper; and yet, urged on by a consuming lust, vainly endeavouring to break through the barrier placed between her and the rest of her fellow-creatures. The ultimate result of this harrowing depravity and ferociously-refined resentment, in the time when the now beautiful Alice will have become an object of fear and loathing, will form the features of some future chapters in the physical and moral history of women, to be contained in a subsequent series of the MERRY WIVES OF LONDON.

For the present it must be stated that, after the lapse of a couple of hours, Alice awoke from her lethargic slumbers, and, upon looking around her the first object she saw was Jasper looking down upon her with a face as stern, pale, and cold as a marble one of an avenging demon. He spoke not a word, but with a gesture intimated his wish that she should rise; when she had done so, he pointed to the footpath, and, with a wave of his hand, which she gladly understood, signified that she was free to leave him. Hastily adjusting her bonnet and shawl, she stayed not to bid him adieu, but darted swiftly away; and, despite the brambles and thorns that tore her dress, as well as wounded her feet and limbs, she struggled on until she had gained the clear road. There she breathed more freely, but neither looked round nor slackened her speed until she had gained the shelter of a road-side inn; and then her over-taxed energies gave way, and she fainted. It was upwards of an hour before she could be restored to consciousness, and then, at her piteous entreaty and the offer of liberal remuneration, a vehicle was procured, and she was conveyed to town. Her day's liberty had proved her day's torture, and she retired to her chamber the moment she had stepped over the threshold of Bloomfield House. In the morning she observed the numerous red spots on her skin; but, instantly attributing them to the thorns through which she had scrambled, she felt no alarm at such unusual appearances on her hitherto spotless body. As she was dressing herself, a slip of paper, pushed under the door, caught her eye. She picked it up, and tremblingly read:

"Remember your promise! *He* will be there. JASPER."

Hastily packing up her apparel, and secreting her savings—some two hundred pounds—in a receptacle which she had prepared in her stays, she had a cab procured, and left Bloomfield House without bidding any of the inmates farewell. At Charing Cross she was joined by the youthful soldier—the "Henry" mentioned in a former chapter—by whom she was conducted to St. Clement's Church, in the Strand, and there married to him. The railway soon carried the pair to Greenwich, where they passed the wedding day and night; and the next morning the husband, more enamoured than ever, took her to Woolwich, where the ship lay in which he was to embark, with a portion of the regiment to which he belonged, for India. The soldier had his duties to perform, so he put Alice with his luggage on board at once, and told her to amuse herself in his absence by watching the interesting process of getting drunken troops on board, weighing anchor, and all the exciting preparations of a vessel making ready for sea. After spending some hours in this way, the ship, amid the roar of cheers, majestically got under weigh; as Alice leaned over the bulwarks, observing the vessel's progress, and perhaps thinking of those she was leaving behind, a boat, impelled by four sturdy rowers, shot from under the stern, and a man standing in the boat, looked up into her face. It was Jasper, cold and impassable as when she left him the day before. A chilling sensation came over her as she recognised him; her brain swam, her eye-sight failed her, and she fell insensible on the deck, from which she was borne to her berth by her attentive and dreadfully-alarmed boy-husband.

The gallant ship left the shores of old England far behind her; many a league of the blue seas had she ploughed before a single name had been entered on her sick list; but before six weeks had elapsed it contained many—and among them those of the youthful lieutenant and his pale—oh! dreadfully pale—wife! Ugly whispers began to be circulated about the ship, coupled with execrations, levelled against the invalid lieutenant. His wife was looked upon with pity —every kindness was extended to her; and she, to do her justice, did all she could, although suffering acutely herself, to transfer them to her tortured husband. But her attentions were fruitless: his disease assumed so malignant and disgusting a type, that the medical staff were obliged to abandon him to his fate, and he died in the most excruciating agony. His body, with hasty and begrudged funeral rites, was thrown overboard within an hour after his death; and thus perished, in the flower of his youth, a man innocent of all offence towards the real husband of Alice—in fact totally ignorant of his existence—but who was nevertheless deliberately sacrificed—savagely offered up as a victim—on the black altar of his remorseless vengeance. The disease in Alice assumed a more chronic type, and she was placed in hospital in St. Helena, where her history and dreadful affliction excited so much sympathy, that a subscription was raised on her behalf. She was, with her husband's effects—and they were considerable—sent back to England, and placed in one of the London hospitals as an incurable.

CHAPTER XXIV.

BACK-STAIRS INFLUENCE.—HOW TO GET A COMMISSION IN THE ARMY.

MRS. WRIGGLES, although in the throes and depths of a keener disappointment than ever she had experienced before—for her plans and intrigues would not work so well—indeed some of them not at all—as she wished, so managed to play off the countess against Mrs. Smythe, and *vice versa*, that they became better and more inseparable friends than ever they had been, even in their unsophisticated girlish days. Both these lovely women were of a high sanguine temperament; and, consequently, warmly voluptuous in their dispositions; but, owing to the exquisite management, the tact and perseverance of the admirable Mrs. Wriggles, the assurance of Mrs. Smythe only warned the countess of the dangers to which she would be exposed by giving her impulses too great a sway. She had preserved her honour, intact, up to the present time, and the more she reflected, the stronger became her convictions of the prudence and necessity of still pursuing the same line of self-denial conduct. In this virtuous resolution she was supported by her lingering love for her husband. Had she entertained the same conjugal sentiments as Mrs. Smythe, probably the result would have been different—but she did not; on the contrary, she revolted from such repulsive marital views, and all speculation upon the intrinsic propriety of her determination was at an end. Mrs. Smythe, being more audacious, and, let it be admitted, subject to more adverse influences, gave full liberty and licence to her passions; and, while being abstemious in the matter of diet, gave a loose rein to her other propensities. She gambled incessantly, became costly and extravagant in her attire, and maintained Horace Singleton in very sumptuous style. Her attachment to the countess was sincere; and, while attributing the chastity of the latter to a very silly timidity, did not in any way attempt to undermine it by any encouragement to pursue a different course. The world knew nothing of her private sins; and, as she was courted and admired wherever she went, undisturbed by her husband, and had little time on her hands to think seriously about anything that would tend to interfere with her habitual serenity, she felt happy, and wantonly postponed the day of reckoning until it should take it into its head to come of its own accord. The two ladies, thus well assorted for agreeable and enlivening companionship, met frequently, but invariably held their confidential conversations at Bloomfield House. On a day subsequent to the trial of the cause of Tyrone v. Smythe, they met as usual, and, as was customary with them, both were exquisitely dressed. Indeed, with each of them, fine dress had become a passion; and surely never did two lovely women better become their luxurious garments. Mrs. Smythe was perhaps a trifle too low in the neck, but that curtailment was balanced by an excess in the skirts, which completely concealed her splendid feet and ankles. The countess, being more sedate, did not display quite so much of her bust as her friend, but quite enough to display its glorious proportions, and send every unmarried man who had the privilege of gazing at it to bed, to dream rather naughtily about her surpassing and deliciously-ripened personal attractions.

By the way, the long-skirted dress fashion that prevails is an intolerable nuisance, and apparently serves no other purpose than to give countenance to the injurious insinuation that the ladies who so industriously conceal their tripping pedals, do so more from necessity than choice. Such a calumny is most reprehensible; but when women with pretty feet will conceal their perfections, the imagination is deceived—led astray—by drapery trailing in the dust of saloons, or the mire of the pavement, and so jumps at ill-natured conclusions. There was a time when no woman was ashamed to disclose the rounded proportions of her inimitably-bewitching feet, and some modest portion of the gently-swelling pillars that spring from them; but now the eye may rove freely over a feminine bosom—whether it be hard or flabby, delicately pale or of the hue of smoke-dried bacon,—but for the feet—the most beautiful members of the body—they are sealed books, except to the eye of the privileged nocturnal voluptuary; and then, whether he be husband or lover, he may gaze, feel, admire—censure, if he dare—or do what he chooses, or is permitted; and, with the circumstance that any denial then comes with such an ill grace that it is rarely attempted, it may safely be assumed that his actions are entirely unchecked.

The countess and Mrs. Smythe had been indulging in a little pleasant banter on this very subject, and, by mutual inspection, had disabused each other of any suspicion that they had any need for concealment, when the countess suddenly inquired:

"What has become of Lady Tyrone?"

"You must have been buried not to have heard all about it!" replied Mrs. Smythe. "Why, after the trial was over, those singular animals, the O'Blazes, went to a tavern, and got so dreadfully tipsy, that they were unable to move from their seats, and were put to bed. Her ladyship, hearing, I presume, of their disaster, and glad to be rid of them so easily, went to the house, called in a broker, and sold everything off—even the table on which the body lay. The old sinner, it is said, had no money; but her ladyship knew his habits better; for it seems she knocked the old valet down, broke open his boxes and trunks, and possessed herself of near a thousand pounds—pilferings, I presume, which he had laid by for a rainy day. She thus managed to realise a couple of thousand pounds; and with that she posted off to Paris with a rakish young gentleman—a starch merchant, belonging to the City, I believe. The brothers, next morning, upon being made acquainted with this dreadful news, hastened after her; with what result I cannot say, for my gossipping informant went no further with his budget."

"How disgraceful!" remarked the countess; "a noble house extinguished in the midst of imperishable infamy!"

"Tut, tut, Violet," replied Mrs. Smythe, "the whole family were not worth the trouble even of forgetting—for not a single member of it can boast of an acre of land that he can call his own. And the old lord was such a beastly fellow, that nobody will ever commit either him or herself, by admitting any personal knowledge of him. Let them go—they are forgotten already."

"What does Mr. Smythe think about the affair?" asked the countess.

"Oh," laughed Mrs. Smythe, in reply; "I believe he has sworn to have what he calls a spree; and spend the whole ten thousand, right out at the neck. I never see him now, thank God! so let's talk of something better. How is Walter—it's an age since I saw him?"

"I have never seen him since he rescued Lucy," sighed the countess; "he is poor, I suppose, and so too proud to visit people better off than himself."

"Poor!" uttered Mrs. Smythe, quickly; "we must not suffer that: both of us are well off, and what do you say to making him a handsome present?"

"He would never accept anything but his commission," said the countess, sadly; "and that, I hear, will never be restored to him."

"Never! what a word for you, Violet!" rejoined her more sanguine friend; "let you and I set our wits to work, and it can be done in a couple of days. Do you know how Mrs. Power got her nephew a government appointment?"

"No."

"Why, she waited on Lord ——, and, being a young and dashing woman, she teazed his lordship out of it. She saw that he was an amorous old bird, and pawed and tickled him until, as she told me, she saw the funds rising, and then she popped her question. Refusal then was impossible; and she walked away with the letter of appointment in her pocket."

"But we cannot so degrade ourselves, Caroline, even to serve Walter!"

"Degrade! what nonsense! These old men like to chat with young women; and what harm is there in it? Besides, we should be proof against anything going too far; and I should like the adventure, just for the fun of it. What say you—this is about the hour for seeing such people, before they go to their dull dinner parties? If we cannot succeed with one, we may with another; and I'll carry my suit to head-quarters—even the Queen herself—before I would be beaten!"

The countess, after a pause, agreed to the proposal; and, the necessary preparations being made and the carriage ordered, the pair were driven to the residence of one of the most influential supporters of the ministry.

The personage to whom the two ladies proceeded was at home. It was just his hour for receiving visitors; and it was remarked, by a government omnibus traffic taker, stationed close at hand, that on all these occasions the majority were of the feminine gender, and, of course, carriage people. What humble pedestrian or hackney-coach *parvenu* dare seek an interview during the visiting time of day prescribed by fashionable usage, with so great a man, unless he were one of his electors, or, male or female, one of his agents in the political espionage he so actively conducted. No—those who came to be seen must come in a carriage with all its gay appointments, and the Countess of Bloomfield and Mrs. Smythe, precisely answering the description of persons who then had the *entree*, they readily obtained admission. And while they are being conducted to his important presence, it may be as well to state who and what he really was. Lord Lionfield, then, was one of those very long-headed members of the peerage, who had managed so dexterously to steer himself over the ocean of party interests, as to have acquired the distinguished reputation of belonging to no party in particular, and yet to be courted by them all when the opportunity served. From his early youth upwards, he had been a *roué*; and, if the truth must be told, a clever blackguard. At forty, he found himself a titled beggar, with a little army of illegitimate children to support; and the first thing he did, was to get rid of the whole lot, by pushing the boys who were old enough into the army and navy, getting the younger ones admitted into Christ's Hospital; and disposing of the girls as well as he could, chiefly by marrying off the mothers with small portions, or packing them off to the colonies, where women were scarce, and the men, consequently, covetous of anything that wore petticoats. He was thus, in the prime of life, with nothing much ailing him, except an occasional twinge of the gout, to begin life anew. And that he certainly did upon more economical principles. He placed his estates out at nurse, and turned active political intriguer. A sinecure office enabled him to maintain his accustomed style of living; and instead of paying, as of yore, for his voluptuous enjoyments, he levied tolls on the pastures of the married; and, in a very short time, not only secured for himself any number of personal favours, but those equally pleasant pecuniary ones, which merry wives are in the habit of levying on the resources of their husbands, for the attainment of certain objects upon which they have resolutely set their hearts. He cultivated his private influence with the court and successive cabinets to such an extent, that he became the most successful procurer of government appointments in the House of Lords; and this was so well known in the circles of the initiated, that it was currently whispered that, for a *consideration*, he could do anything with a minister. From the peculiar nature of his organisation, he preferred transacting such business with ladies, because, not only were they more liberal in cash compliments, but, upon emergencies—as when either pressingly solicitous, or naturally inclined—would not hesitate to bestow upon him more delicate and tender acknowledgments of their gratitude—or, it might, in the majority of instances, more truthfully be said, *payment*—for the services they required at his hands. Mrs. Smythe and the countess were well acquainted with these peculiarities in his character; and the former was resolved, come what would, that his lordship should exert his interest in favour of Captain Morris. The countess, less chivalrous, but infused with some of her friend's sanguineness, carried her cheque-book with her, in the hope that the purport of one of its slips would be a sort of Aladdin's lamp to the cashiered friend of her childhood and discarded lover.

Lord Lionfield had attained the age of fifty-five, but he was still a portly and erect gentleman, with a smooth, florid face, and dark hair, only slightly tinged with grey. He was a pleasant enough man to look upon—quite a dandy in his dress—oily in speech—and gallant in demeanour. In short, he was what a certain class of women call a clean old man. As he made it a point to know and be known to everybody worth knowing, it is not surprising that he well knew both the ladies who now waited upon him, and behaved towards them with the cordial familiarity he knew so well how to assume. Wherever he went—and in his own house remarkably so—he had the rare faculty of making people in his company feel themselves quite emancipated from restraint—in short, as the phrase goes, at home; and, in a few minutes after the introduction, the countess and Mrs. Smythe were chatting with him quite at their ease. And in these glib encounters of the tongue, how soon gossipping about mutual acquaintances brings about the very subject that lurks behind the prattle of the moment.

"And how fares our old friend, the lady-killing Colonel Stanley?" inquired his lordship.

The countess and Mrs. Smythe both blushed; the latter, not quite so deeply as her friend, as she archly replied:

"His wounds, I presume, are not yet healed."

"I rather suspect, if that be the only motive for his retirement, we shall have to sigh a long time for his gallant presence," said his lordship, glancing boldly at the heightened colour of his visitors; "indeed it is whispered that he is about to retire altogether from the army, and travel for the benefit of his health. The East, it would appear, is the modern Coventry for gentlemen who have committed mistakes."

"Do you think there is any truth in the rumour?" inquired the countess."

"I have every reason to believe that he will retire," said his lordship, significantly.

"In that event," said the countess, eagerly, "all obstacles to the restoration of Captain Morris's commission would be removed?"

"I am not so sure of that," replied Lord Lionfield, instantly divining the object of their visit, and falling back upon his habitual cunning and aptitude for secret negotiations. "The authorities are determined to suppress duelling in the army; and although it's a pity the service should lose such a fine young fellow as Captain Morris, I'm afraid they will not make any exception in his case."

"Can nothing be done in the matter?" inquired the countess, anxiously.

"You are all-powerful, my lord," said Mrs. Smythe, as she discharged the full power of her eyes upon his face; "and a word from you in a certain quarter—only a word—would get the poor young man his commission back again."

Lord Lionfield felt the effect of that warm glance in a certain tickling sensation that pervaded his whole frame, and he hastily said:

"May I inquire whether you are interested in the affair?"

The countess replied:

"Walter—I mean Captain Morris—was one of my earliest friends; his family and ours are distantly related."

"And he is my friend, too," echoed Mrs. Smythe; "and he ought to be esteemed as the friend of every woman, for he perilled all his prospects in the defence—the gallant, manly, and chivalrous defence—of a helpless young lady."

"Ah! you are acquainted with the particulars of the quarrel between him and Stanley!" cried his lordship.

"We are," replied the countess, promptly; "but, for family reasons, we wish them to remain undivulged. Colonel Stanley has been severely punished for his cruel audacity, and while he remains silent, the family of the lady do not see that any exposure of him is necessary. They reserve that for chastisement at a future day, should he provoke it."

The countess spoke warmly, for her indignation was always roused when she reflected on the indignity which her gentle sister Lucy had received from Colonel Stanley.

His lordship was too polite to press his inquiry any further, but his face glowed not a little as he regarded the ravishing beauty of the countess; and his dark, meaning eyes actually sparkled again as they perused the bolder *ensemble* presented by the luxurious features and figure of Mrs. Smythe.

The latter encouraged him by her rather significant glances; and, as she observed him moving uneasily in his chair, she more pressingly resumed the subject of her visit to him.

"Come, my lord," said she, "you must interfere and obtain Walter's commission for him. You can do it if you like."

The latter was spoken so archly, and with such a peculiar tone of voice and expression of feature, that the old lord sprang from his chair, and paced the room uneasily.

"I'll see what can be done," said he; "the Duke's terribly severe; but—but—upon my word, I shall be promising more than I can perform."

"Oh, don't say that!" said Mrs. Smythe, laughingly; "or I shall begin to fancy the world has given you credit for more than it ought to have done."

"I am aware," said the countess, hesitatingly, "that these sort of things are not done without considerable expense; and as I should not wish you to be a loser for doing an act of kindness, I must beg of you to take this, and do the best you can with it for our friend Captain Morris."

His lordship mechanically took the cheque offered for his acceptance, and not without surprise saw that it was drawn for a thousand pounds.

"Lady Bloomfield!" he stammered; "what—what is this for?"

"Don't say a word," said Mrs. Smythe, placing her long, white hand on his lips; "you can do it, and you must do it."

Carried by storm, as it were, he promised to see several official personages in the course of the afternoon, and report progress. The countess and Mrs. Smythe tendered him their warmest thanks, and,

amid a profusion of compliments and adieus, he bowed the pair to the door. Mrs. Smythe was the last, and, apparently, purposely lingered a little behind her companion. This gave his lordship, under cover of the half-open door, an opportunity to whisper softly in her ear:

"To-night, at ten, I shall have news, and will be alone."

Mrs. Smythe returned him a look of intelligence in reply; and, upon the door being closed, his lordship pirouetted through the room, heedless of gout or rheumatism, and joyously snapped his fingers in token of triumph—or at all events in glowing anticipation of realising the very daring conceptions he had formed during the *tête-à-tête*.

Mrs. Smythe no sooner gained the carriage than she burst out into a fit of merry laughter, in which, upon due explanation being given, the countess heartily joined.

"What an old fool," said the countess, "to think of such a thing!"

"The old men are worse than the young ones," replied Mrs. Smythe; "and they have such terrible assurance."

"I hate them," said the countess; "they stare at one so."

"If their performances only equalled the ardour of their looks what a populous world this would be! Why, we women then would be afraid of going near a man!" said Mrs. Smythe, her face radiant with mirth, and the excitement peculiar to her organisation.

"Oh, fie!" exclaimed the countess, her own face brightening up under the influence of kindred sensual suggestions; "but of course you won't keep the appointment."

"Oh, won't I!" said Mrs. Smythe; "why I wouldn't on any account lose such a bit of rich fun. If I don't drive him stark staring mad, I'll—I'll go down on my knees to my brute of a husband, and beg of him to sleep with me!"

"What a rattle-pate you are!" said the countess. "Am I to understand that you are going?"

"Certainly."

"I have been told that these wicked old men are vicious."

"They bark, but can't bite."

"Don't be too sure."

"I know it. My Lord Lionfield will not be the first amorous old man to whom I have taught a lesson. Besides, for Walter's sake, I ought to go. Don't you be alarmed, Violet. This naughty old lord shall hang a calf-skin on his recreant limbs before I have done with him. I'll lead him a dance he little expects."

The countess reluctantly assented to the proposed assignation; and, after many cautions from her, and the usual exchange of the cordial kisses of affection, the two friends separated until late in the evening, when they agreed to meet at a party to which they had both received invitations. Mrs. Smythe paid a few more visits, and then, as her conjugal duties were now very light indeed—ranging over no greater extent of matrimonial ground than being a very handsome wife, with all her time at her own disposal, and her free use of it, only burthened with the slight restriction, that she herself thought it prudent to sleep at home, and preside over any festivities which her extremely convenient spouse thought proper to indulge in—she had herself driven to the residence of Horace Singleton, where, finding him at home, she remained a few hours, enjoying all the sweets of love, and the flow of a conversation, at one moment intellectual, and the next as delicately amorous as

Aspasia herself could have desired. After this entertaining *reunion*, she adjourned to her residence to dress, and prepare herself for her engagement with Lord Lionfield. Her costume was the most elaborate conceivable. Her beautifully-developed and most voluptuously-defined figure was displayed in all its splendid perfection of proportion. The bust, in its delicate amplitude of detail, was so arrayed that its witcheries were to be seen, or rather guessed at, without its manifold attractions being undisguisedly subjected to the vulgar eye of scrutiny, in its lowest forms of appreciation. The glowing neck and bosom rose grandly from the tapering waist and full, flowing robe that spread out beneath, and were crowned by a face, in every feature of which the loves—the Paphian loves, that madden men and melt women—seemed to have nestled themselves, and made a home in every play of the muscles and vibration of the nerves. The hair, sparkling and wavy in its raven glossiness, was redolent of the rarest perfume—that which comes in gushes, and seems to be breathed out of the fibres of Nature's regal ornament, and, mingling with the rosy-tinted vapour of the incense that hallows the precincts of the mouth, when burnt upon its altar, makes burning summer when its comes; and, when gone, a memory gilded with the hues of a rainbow, to brighten many an after-coming winter. She was, in sooth, a dazzling creature; and as her trusty footman held open the door of her carriage for her to step into, he stood, for a minute or so, agape with wonder, and mounted to his seat behind, like one in a dream. Lord Lionfield had dressed himself with studied elegance; and as he stood in his noble drawing-room—an apartment pasted over, it might be said, with the "trifles" he had received for the peculiar services which he had rendered to applicants for offices—he appeared very much like a gentleman rather nervous, on the score of ability, to complete the engagement to which he had pledged all the powers, physical and mental, he possessed.

Mrs. Smythe arrived punctually at the hour named; and animated, no doubt, by a desire to revenge the numerous exactions from her sex on similar occasions, greeted the enraptured peer with such a soul-killing glance, as he kissed her hand and conducted her to a seat, that it was some minutes before he could utter anything but the most incoherent compliments and undisguised expressions of admiration. Mrs. Smythe allowed him to place her on a couch, and take a seat by her side, while he dwelt on the immense efforts he had made to promote her suit.

"You cannot conceive the difficulties I had to encounter, even in broaching such a subject!" said he.

"Yet I suspect you have broached, as you call it, more difficult things in your life," replied Mrs. Smythe, with a silvery laugh.

His lordship could only respond to this sally by a fit of pleasantry, to which, however, the lady strongly demurred, by moving away from him.

"Don't tax my patience," at length uttered Mrs. Smythe. "You know my sex are not proverbial for endurance in that respect."

"O you queen of the coaxers, I suppose I must tell you," said he. "Well, then, I saw his lordship, the minister for ——, and at first he gave me not the slightest hope—in fact, repulsed me; and I was obliged to make use of strong arguments to induce him to listen to me. After a good deal of beating about the bush he did so, and promised to speak to his grace on the subject. Not satisfied with even his assurance, I saw the minister for ——, and upon an exchange of interests, in the shape of my sacrificing my opposition to a certain measure, I received his support; and

now all that remains to do is to win over the Horse-Guards."

Lord Lionfield, upon this, thought he had said enough to entitle him to some reward in anticipation; and as a preliminary, began to squeeze Mrs. Smythe's hand, and to look some unutterable things in her face.

"When will you see his grace?" inquired she, quite composedly, and slightly — very slightly—returning the pressure of her hand.

"To-morrow morning," replied he, insinuating his left arm round her waist; "but upon one condition —not a hard one."

"Name it?"

"Give me a kiss?"

Mrs. Smythe promptly held forth her lips, but just as he was about to fasten on them she drew her head quickly aside, and the salute was expended on the air. Too old a courtier to be so repulsed, he caught her in his still very nervous arms, and strained her convulsively to his bosom. She at that moment breathed hotly in his face, and just touching his mouth with hers, suddenly sprang from his embrace, and with the momentum brought him headlong to the floor, to the great damage of certain members of his lower extremities. When he arose he perceived her standing at some distance from him, displaying such a dazzling array of pearly teeth, amid wreaths of smiles, that he felt like one enchanted. He moved towards her, but, placing a table between him and her, she kept him at bay. Lord Lionfield's mettle was up, and he essayed a race—but it was a cart-horse pursuing a thorough-bred filly. Determined to give him enough of it, Mrs. Smythe now and then approached near enough to give him a poke in the ribs and other regions, and to pinch him in divers tender parts. This only rendered his control of himself the more ungovernable, and he pursued her with such a lustful expression of countenance, that Mrs. Smythe began to feel apprehensive for her ultimate safety. His eyes protruded from his head, and the foam gathered on his lips before, from sheer fatigue, he was obliged to desist, by sinking, parched and panting, into a chair.

"Adorable woman!" he gasped, "drive me not frantic!"

"Wait; you are unnerved—too excited!" cried Mrs. Smythe.

"One kiss—only one?" he implored.

"When you have seen his grace."

"Now—now—or I shall go mad?"

"Would you insult me?"

"Divine perfection of a woman! peri of my everlasting dreams of thy sex, teach me how to love thee?"

"To-morrow."

"Command me — my house — my fortune — my name—my influence. Take all I possess!"

"And disorder my apparel? No, no, my lord—procure for me the commission, signed, sealed, and delivered, and then perhaps I may be merciful. Until then take this as earnest."

And thus saying she sprang behind him, and suddenly imprinted so warm a kiss on his glowing cheek, that my Lord Lionfield fancied the chair under him had dissolved, and he was sinking, blind and stunned, into the realms of red-hot space. When he recovered from his swoon Mrs. Smythe had vanished; and, in answer to his furious ringing of the bell, he was told that she had just departed in her carriage. With a cry, something between the neighing of a stallion and the bellowing of a bull, he rushed to the apartments of his young and buxom housekeeper, and sank into her arms, completely exhausted by his own excess of the wildest of animal emotions when thoroughly aroused.

The scene had certainly imparted to Mrs. Smythe's complexion a deep carnation; but its extravagance had diverted her attention from its real object, and she felt more inclined to be merry than excited. Nevertheless, when late in the evening she encountered some extremely handsome men, it was only the memory of Horace Singleton that calmed the tumult of her truant thoughts.

"Have you succeeded without being insulted?" inquired the countess, as she advanced towards her, with a visible anxiety.

"I left the poor old fellow in such a state of fidgets, that he will never let the matter sleep until he obtains what he imagines will induce me to yield to him out of pure gratitude," was the saucy reply.

"Which will be when——"

"There's not a young fellow worthy of a woman left in all broad England."

The pair laughed over the whimsicalities, as they termed them, of the adventure; and, then to make sure that everything possible for Walter was done that could be effected, they arranged to wait upon the high authority to which Lord Lionfield had alluded.

Accordingly, on the second day after the infliction on the latter of the retributive torture he had richly merited by his lust and avarice, the merry wives waited upon the illustrious personage who held the fate of Walter, as a soldier, in his hands. He received them with his accustomed affability, for, like every brave warrior, he was extremely partial to the society of the ministering angels of human society. Iron to his own sex, he was as ductile as virgin gold to the other, and for sixty years had ever greeted a woman, whether old or young, with a smile and a cordial welcome.

"Walter Morris!" exclaimed he, as soon as the purport of their mission had been explained to him. "I'm plagued to death by the fellow: half the ministry have written to me about him, and I do believe Lord Lionfield will never let me rest until I break through all the regulations of the service, and eat my own words into the bargain!"

There was a little petulance about the manner in which this was spoken, but not the slightest particle of anger or ill-nature.

"Besides," continued he, "I'm determined to put down duelling in the army; it's against all discipline, and the service generally loses the best men by it. If the rogues only fell, or were crippled, it would not much matter; but our best officers get all the pepper, and the survivors invariably becomes bullies and nuisances. It won't do, my dear ladies—it's a bad system, and we must put it down."

Both the countess and Mrs. Smythe hinted that his immortal self had never hesitated to expose his valuable person to the bullet of the duellist, when the provocation was such as no gentleman could endure.

"Very true—very true," he replied; "but times are altered; public opinion is against the practice; and, I am bound to say, public opinion is right. That great commander, Napoleon, disapproved of duelling."

"But," argued Mrs. Smythe, "how are we poor weak women to be protected, if every ruffian is to be allowed to insult us with impunity?"

"The law, my dear madam—the British law—and, I trust, British honour, is an ample shield for the most helpless."

"Law!" urged Mrs. Smythe, passionately; "there are cases, like this one in which poor Captain Morris was compromised, which the law can never reach; for few women, however grossly or vilely wronged, would like to be dragged before the eye of public curiosity."

"True, true," answered the great man, as he looked at the agitated ladies good-humouredly.

"It was in defence of my sister—my only one, your grace—that Captain Morris became compromised," said the countess, regarding the veteran with moistened eyes.

"Your sister—sister—sister? I never heard a word of it. Pray explain?" was the quick demand.

The countess, feeling unable to do so, appealed to Mrs. Smythe with an imploring glance, and the latter promptly answered:

"Miss Villiers was on her way to the family residence, in Montgomeryshire, when, by some jugglery or another—chiefly through an artful woman who travelled by the same train—her servants were inveigled from her side, and, in a lonely part of the country, quite out of her proper road, she was induced to alight from the post-chaise, to partake of some refreshment at this creature's house, as she called it—but, as it was afterwards proved, it was Stanley's. There some drug was administered to her, and when she recovered from its effects, she found herself a prisoner. Her absence soon became known to her family: the London detective police were set to work, and Captain Morris and one of them went down into the country, and were lucky enough to discover the horrible place just in time to save poor Lucy; for she was discovered struggling with the colonel. Morris, I presume, was so exasperated—as any man of proper feeling would be—at the villany of this Colonel Stanley, that he challenged and chastised him on the spot. The duel was fought at midnight, and even the colonel admits it was perfectly fair!"

The animation of the fair speaker rivetted the stern yet kind old warrior's attention, and, when she had concluded, he smiled approvingly, and said:

"A brave fellow, that Captain Morris—very brave—noble! quite right in him, as a man, but da—I mean shockingly bad, as a soldier."

"Would not your grace have done the same, under the circumstances?" inquired the countess.

"Perhaps I should, forty years ago; but now I should have given the scoundrel into the custody of a policeman. Captain Morris lowered himself by fighting with such a poltroon!"

"Will you forgive him?" said the countess, pathetically; "he is young!"

"And as brave as steel!" added Mrs. Smythe.

"He led three forlorn hopes in India!" said the countess.

"And fought all through the Sikh war!" continued Mrs. Smythe.

"His name was mentioned with every honour in every despatch!" pursued the countess.

"And he won every step of promotion he gained without purchase!" concluded Mrs. Smythe, in a tone of triumph, as she observed a twitching about the corners of the ——'s mouth.

Both the ladies, in their excitement, had advanced so close to his person that one stood on each side of him.

"Will the young lady for whom Captain Morris risked so much, marry him?" he inquired, turning, and locking archly at the countess.

"Aye, that she will!" exclaimed Mrs. Smythe; "and all her friends approve of the match."

The —— dwelt for a few seconds with pleasure on the beaming, beautiful countenances that looked so pleadingly upon his own; and as he did so thought, n all his long life, he had never beheld two more fascinating creatures before. How could he resist the spell they threw around him? he whose conquests, both in war and love, rivalled those of Cæsar, Marc Antony, and Napoleon! He could not, and least of all in a virtuous cause. After stroking his chin for awhile, he said, gaily:

"Will you be answerable for his future behaviour?"

"Oh, yes!" exclaimed both the ladies, simultaneously.

"And have him married right off, to prevent his falling into any other scrape of the kind?"

"We will do our best."

"Then I think we can manage it for him. Stanley has sold out, and, as he was wrong, I don't think there will be any impropriety in giving Morris his commission back."

Both the countess and Mrs. Smythe seized one of his hands, and carried it respectfully to their lips. They could only murmur their gratitude, but he silenced them by gallantly insisting upon being rewarded with a kiss from each. Neither offered the smallest scruple of an objection, but modestly proffered their cheeks. The game old warrior, though, preferred the lips, and, after a brace of salutes, given with a right good will, the two ladies, blushing like summer roses, were conducted to their carriage.

"Now to find out Walter!" exclaimed they, when they had reached Bloomfield House. Mrs. Wriggles was summoned, and undertook that kind office, but suggested that it would be preferable to wait until the commission had arrived, and then summon Lucy from the country, and have her present it to him. The truth was, Mrs. Wriggles wished Walter to complete the affair he had undertaken with Bloomfield before he was apprised of his good fortune. The ladies, ignorant of this, joyfully assented to the proposal, and, after entering into sundry festive arrangements, separated. Mrs. Smythe, however, had to learn that Lord Lionfield was not at all disposed to let her escape him so easily. He was dreadfully enraged when he found out that the commission had been restored entirely independent of his intercession; and, to add to his mortification, he received a polite intimation to the effect that the less he interfered with a certain distinguished person's duties, the higher would that person hold him in his estimation. In addition to the feeling of resentment thus created in his breast, his carnal nature had become inflamed with the beauteous Mrs. Smythe, and he was resolved, by fair means or foul, to extort from her a fulfilment of her promise, or at least what he considered to be equivalent to one.

He sought for a ninterview with Mrs. Smythe, and, finding her deaf to his gentle remonstrances, roundly taxed her with ingratitude and duplicity.

"Ingratitude!" she scornfully retorted; "your puling and whining did the cause more harm than good. You did nothing beyond pocketing a thousand pounds—his grace may know of that yet, if you are impudent—and attempting the honour of the wife of a man to whom you are largely indebted."

Livid with rage, his lordship advanced a step towards her, and menacingly said:

"Do you remember the scandal of Lady Mary —— ?"

"Yes, wretch, you circulated a falsehood, and nobody believed it."

"A falsehood, eh?" sneered he; "the joke of the affair was that it was not a falsehood. She defied me as you have done, and the little bird I have for such errands went singing all over the town."

"Why Lady Mary told me all about it," said Mrs. Smythe, jeeringly; "you were unable to take advantage of your good fortune. You were like a keen sportsman returning home after a long day's sport, who, seeing a pheasant in view, levelled his piece, but, to his chagrin, found that he had not a single charge left."

"This is too much!" cried his lordship, stung to the quick by her rather plain-spoken inuendo; "and we shall see whether you escape as cheaply as her nimble ladyship. I give you three days to reflect; and if, at the end of that time, you do not re-consider your determination, consider me your enemy; and, trust me, you will find me no trifling one!"

So saying, his lordship swept away, and was soon lost in the throng of the gay salons where they met. Mrs. Smythe, although so bold of speech, did not feel altogether at ease. She knew the deep malignity of his lordship's nature, and that he would not hesitate to propagate the grossest slanders against her. She feared, too, that, with his numerous band of spies, he might become acquainted with some truths; and she was slightly unnerved when she remembered the incident about the Lady Mary. His lordship, it appeared, had done her ladyship some favours at court, and had confidently anticipated that she would have been kind to him in return; but her sense of duty was too strong for her appreciation of his favours, and she repulsed him with scorn. To be revenged, he circulated the rumour that she had yielded to his passion for her. The immediate consequences were dreadful to the poor lady. She was excluded from the court, cut by all her acquaintances—even by those who were really frail—and regarded with suspicion in her own family circle. Her husband fortunately happened to be a man of feeling and sound sense; and to him, as her best friend, she confided the whole particulars. Exasperated beyond endurance, he first of all inflicted an ignominious chastisement on Lord Lionfield, then wounded him in a duel, and finally brought an action against him for false and malicious defamation of character. His lordship, goaded by these energetic proceedings, compromised the matter by denying the libel, or that there was the slightest foundation for it, and prudently consented to a verdict for 5000l., not to be enforced, but to be suspended over him in terrorem. His usefulness as a politician—he had half a dozen boroughs under his thumb—and his skill as an intriguer soon regained him his lost caste, and he pursued his career more daringly than ever.

Mrs. Smythe communicated her apprehensions to the countess, but all that the latter could advise, was that Captain Morris should charge himself with her protection.

"No," argued Mrs. Smythe, "he is a stranger—at least no relative, only a friend—and would compromise me more by his interference. My husband is the proper party, but he would maliciously treat the affair as a capital joke. Besides, he is too great a coward to face a man like Lord Lionfield. I must sleep upon it."

The next day—so great was her dread of this terrible ogre of a peer—she felt half inclined to indulge him in his whim.

"He is only an old man," thought she, "and can't hurt me. Pah! the idea disgusts me; and, as he has threatened, I must endeavour to cause his threat to recoil on his own head. If I asked him, I know Walter would shoot the wretch immediately; but that must be my last resource. Horace has a long head, so I think I had better consult him first."

Horace Singleton, now installed in expensive lodgings, under the thin disguise of being her brother and a gentleman of fortune, was furious, and instantly volunteered to cut his lordship's throat or blow out his brains.

Mrs. Smythe wisely declined such rash preventives, and bade Horace think of some more notable scheme.

"I have it!" he exclaimed, after scratching his head for half an hour. "Do you remember the scene in *Measure for Measure*, where Lord Angelo enjoys Mariani, his discarded sweetheart, instead of Isabella, who appointed to meet him in the dark?"

"Yes."

"Well then, suppose we have something of the kind?"

"How?"

"You shall agree to meet him at a certain place, and we'll get some girl to personate you. In the morning he will discover his mistake; and then, with a number of witnesses present to overwhelm him with confusion, he will be nicely disposed to come to terms. Besides, the fear of ridicule will deter him from put-ting his threat against you into execution. There is no weapon so powerful against such a scoundrel as ridicule. Why, if the circumstance came to be generally known, he would be quizzed to death. And if he should be rash enough to provoke your vengeance, you can retort upon him by exposing all the facts of the case, and thus bring down the public upon him, and so alarm the ministry and the people in office, that his influence will vanish in smoke; and, with the fact of the notoriety of the deception practised upon him, nobody will believe a word of what he may say respecting you."

Horace received a hundred kisses, and something more substantial for his suggestion, and Mrs. Smythe and he agreed to set about its immediate execution. Horace undertook to procure the substitute: indeed he caused Mrs. Smythe a few jealous pangs, when he declared that he knew a pale young person remarkably resembling her; but upon his positive assertion that the said accommodating spinster was not more indifferent to him than he was to her, the anger of Mrs. Smythe abated, and she entered heartily into the scheme. A highly-perfumed note was dispatched to his lordship, apologising for her warmth on the previous day, and requesting him to name an hotel where they could meet as husband and wife, under assumed names. The prompt reply specified a second-rate West-End one, and suggested the use of the incognito "Stroker." The acknowledging mission was as prompt, but insisted on the lady's retiring to rest an hour before his lordship; and that, to conceal her blushes, he should extinguish the light in the bed-room as soon as he had undressed himself, and before getting into bed. He readily agreed to the terms, and night rapidly approached. The girl proved an apt pupil, and was so fallen as to entertain a degree of pride at the idea of sleeping a whole night in the arms of a genuine English lord. Precisely at half-past nine she alighted in a cab at the door of the hotel, with some mock luggage, as if she had but just alighted from a railway carriage; and, after supping heartily, she retired to the chamber assigned her, leaving behind her the intimation that her husband had promised to come to town by the next train, and she momentarily expected him. Precisely at half-past ten o'clock his lordship arrived; and, after consuming a bottle of port, to refresh his agitated nerves, required to be shown to the chamber of his wife—Mrs. Stroker. The requests insisted upon by his supposed victim's modesty were obeyed to the letter, and the amorous peer, almost frenzied with the idea of lying in the arms of such a deliciously-fine woman as the banker's wife, flung himself into the capacious bed, utterly oblivious of damp sheets, or anything else a gouty gentleman should dread. In the morning, when daylight had entered the room, his lordship awoke, and, turning softly to his slumbering *chere amie* to steal a kiss, he started when he beheld features which were totally strange to him. He rubbed his eyes, and looked again. No—the face was certainly a handsome one, but rather old and disfigured by the lines of dissipation, he thought; but most unquestionably not the one he had anticipated seeing on the pillow beside him. He shook her energetically.

"Go to ——!" was the elegant, half-awake, half-asleep response.

His lordship redoubled his efforts, and at length succeeded.

"Who are you?"

"Fanny Thompson."

"Fanny Thompson! My God! what a mistake! I'm afraid I have been too free—in fact, unconsciously taken too great a liberty with you."

"Oh, don't mention it: I'm satisfied if you are, Mr. Stroker!"

"Mr. Stroker!"

"Yes; have you forgotten your own name?"

His lordship, stunned and amazed, crept like a kicked hound out of the bed, and proceeded to put on his apparel as hastily as he could. The girl, as instructed, informed him of the cheat, and completed his consternation by addressing him by his real name—Lord Lionfield! Horror! the gay, the fascinating, the invincible Lord Lionfield, pass the night with a common drab! He was annihilated—in one of the common, but expressive idioms of the day, done brown! He had just discretion enough left to liberally reward the girl, discharge the bill of the house, and then he panted to get safely and unseen out of the to him detestable place. As he emerged into the street, preparatory to slipping into a cab, which had been called, the heavy hand of a tall, gentlemanly-looking young man was laid on his shou'der, and a voice whispered in his ear:

"You were coward enough, my Lord Lionfield, to threaten a woman with a lie; now remember her resentment of the affront, and tremble!"

The speaker was Horace Singleton. His lordship tottered into the cab, and the next day took to his bed, where he lay for six weeks, a martyr to one of the most acute attacks of gout he had ever experienced. He took care, however, as soon as possible, to enter into a solemn league of peace and amity with Mrs. Smythe, and never afterwards felt the slightest inclination to break the engagement.

CHAPTER XXV.

TAMING A RAKISH HUSBAND.

LORD BLOOMFIELD, after the disappearance of Laura Bell, fell into the dark despair, the hideous leprosy of his accumulated desires. Drink maddened him on to the commission of every description of outrage against decorum, and the conventional proprieties that even the lowest of the human species respect. Wholly absenting himself from home, he gave the rein to his perverted habits, and added to his degradation by taking the man-fiend Jasper Sampson into still closer boon companionship. Together, in the language of the old comedies, they scoured the town in quest of novelty and adventure; and nearly the whole of Jasper's time was occupied either in the society of his lordship, or acting as a scout to his propensities. His lordship had fallen so low that he frequented a vulgar tavern in the Haymarket, and, owing to his liberality and profuse expenditure of money, became quite a lion among the sharpers, sots, and prostitutes who frequented the house. When he wished to be alone he had a room up stairs at his disposal, and there he would sit chatting with, and abusing his crony, Mr. Sampson, as he was designated by the people who frequented the place, and arranging his night's or morrow's adventures. It was three o'clock in the afternoon, and the pair were alone, drinking brandy-and-water. His lordship smoked a cigar, and Jasper a German silver-mounted pipe, of formidable dimensions.

"Anything up for to-day?" inquired lordship, who, not yet quite recovered from the "fit of blues" into which the previous night's debauch had thrown him, was not in a very pleasant humour.

"Plenty, my lord."

"D——n you! I'm not 'my lord' here. I'll shy this glass at your head if you don't mind."

Thus corrected, Jasper addressed his lordship as Mr. Johnson.

"There's the card party at Waterford's," said Jasper.

"I'm tired of playing cards," replied his lordship, snappishly.

"There's the pic-nic with Towler's and Wilson's girls, in Richmond Park."

"I hate the whole lot: Sally's as fusty as an old mare, and Polly has grown as common as any Regent Street drab!"

"There's the dancing at White-headed Bob's, both gals and men stripped!"

"Won't do! Lost my purse and watch the last time I was there."

"There's a ball at Mother Carey's, and some new pieces will be there."

THE MERRY WIVES OF LONDON.

187

"Ah, that might do, if you can't invent anything else."

"Would you like to see a bull-bait, or a badger drawn, or a fight? Black Jack and Devil's Own are going to set-to in earnest to-night."

"I may look in. Put Mother Carey's ball and the fight down on the list."

Jasper drew a tiny set of tablets from his waistcoat pocket, and made the required memoranda.

"Anything else? Curse you! take some brandy, and sharpen your wits up," cried his lordship.

Jasper, nothing loth, instantly obeyed the command; and then, suddenly tapping his forehead as if smitten with a recollection, exclaimed:

"There's that girl!"

"What girl?"

"Why that modest piece you picked up at the Casino, the other night."

"Oh, I remember something about it, but I was too moony to follow the game up. What of her?"

"I have found out all about her, and, s'elp my tatur, my—I mean Mr. Johnson—she's as clean looking, fresh, and virgin a bit of flesh as ever I looked upon. She's horridly handsome!"

"I know that: her touch made my pulse beat a hundred and twenty to a minute. But I missed her all at once!"

"She was frightened, and cut home!"

"How did you find her out? Fill your glass again, and tell me all about it."

His lordship set the example by draining his glass to the bottom, and replenishing; a precedent which the iron-headed Jasper was not slow to copy.

"Why, you see, my lord—I beg pardon—Mr Johnson," said he, "I saw you were sweet on the girl, and not quite *compos mentis* enough to carry on the war yourself, so I set my wits to work, and, after talking with a few of the reg'lar gals about her, I found out that she had a mother and brother living at Islington, and that she was an artificial flower maker, of rather a gay turn, but quite innocent-like, always going to tea-gardens, casinos, and such-like, with her beau—a silly chap wot madly doats on her. I got her address—No. 18, —— Street, Islington; and after a little trouble I got to speak with her, and gammoned her that a great lord was in love with her, and would make her a lady if she'd only be kind to him and be a good girl, and all that sort of thing. She said she wouldn't tell anybody; and, upon my soul, from the flash of her eye, I think she's ripe for the game you want to play with her. I promised to see her again to-night, and if your lordship—I mean if you like, I'll take you to her."

"With all my heart," yawned his lordship; "I am tired of the things that I pick up without any trouble."

At this moment the door was unceremoniously opened, and Walter Morris, scattering a little army of waiters right and left, burst into the room.

"Ah, Walter, my boy," exclaimed Bloomfield, "glad to see you! Do as we do. Here, Jasper, order in some more brandy, hot water, and cigars, and then cut—vanish—mizzle!"

Jasper, not daring to disobey, had the command executed, and then left the room, casting upon Walter, as he did so, a look of intense and savage hatred.

"Thank heaven!" thought Walter, "that I never fell so low as to be obliged to resort to such a place as this in search of excitement. Faugh! it smells as rank as a camp hospital. However, Bloomfield can

only be won over by gentle means, and the plan proposed by old Mother Wriggles is about the best I can think of."

Bloomfield's reflections partook somewhat of the same character with reference to Walter, whom he fancied had flown to dissipation to relieve the tedium engendered by his misfortune, and want of profitable occupation. All serious emotions with the peer were, however, very slight; a glassful of brandy-and-water was sufficient to wash the deepest away; and, after a few remarks of a common-place description, he ventured upon a remark which introduced the topic of his own domestic affairs.

"Pray how is the countess?" inquired Walter; "it is long since I saw her."

Bloomfield shrugged his shoulders very expressively, as he replied:

"The world wags dolefully with me in that quarter. I don't think I have exchanged half a dozen words with Violet this month past. Indeed she insisted upon my entering into a compact—a solemn signed, sealed, and delivered agreement—that if I would keep away from her, she would not molest me; and so, perforce, for the sake of peace, I have submitted to her terms, and, as the coal-heaver would say, been on the 'jolly drunk' ever since. Never mind, here's her health, God bless her. I do believe things would go on squarer if I were a better husband; and, taking everything into consideration, she is a wife in a thousand. Provocation, Walter—you understand me—makes women do scores of things they would never have dreamed of. Not that I say Violet has done anything—not a bit of it—she's too proud to do wrong—but she might have done it, so no thanks to me—and here's reformation to all of us!"

With this rather incoherent and lax sentiment, Bloomfield took a long pull at his glass, and then, indulging in a vigorous puff from his cigar, looked at Walter with that hideous, half-tipsy stare, which, in slang interpretation, unequivocally means, "What do you think of it, my boy?"

Walter thought a good deal about it, but contented himself with the prudent remark, that no man could be compulsorily manufactured into a saint; and that "let well alone" was sage counsel to a husband in a state of "tiff" with his wife. With a few such wholesome reflections as these, he shook a few reefs out of the sails of his conscience, and proposed a spree, or something which should wile away a few of the hours they were both too prone to abstract from the treasury of their lives.

"What do you say to a woman?" suggested Bloomfield.

"I never refuse fresh meat when it can be procured," wickedly responded Walter.

"I have found out a nice piece."

"The devil you have!"

"Fact! And as the girls now-a-days go abroad in pairs, why there is a chance for each of us."

"I'm your man, if you can promise me an adventure."

"Promise!" cried Bloomfield; "I am sure of it. Why, my boy, she is a virgin, and has got a sentimental sweetheart—a young fellow, who is working himself to death in the blessed hope that he will soon be able to marry her."

"Who beat up the game for you?"

"Jasper."

"Phew!" Walter would have said, but the ejaculation died away on his lips, and he merely remarked:

"Extraordinary man, that, Bloomfield!"

"Very!" rejoined the latter, chuckling.

"Where did you pick him up?" inquired Walter.

"Stanley recommended him to me," was the reply; "and, between you and me, Walter, I have found him deucedly useful ever since I had him. His morals are queer—if I were quite sober I should not hesitate to term them shockingly bad, and prognosticate a rather public termination to his eventful career; but as I am not sober, all I can say is, that he is a d——d clever fellow!"

"Is he not a cripple in certain abdominal regions?" asked Walter, looking as innocently as if he had not the slightest knowledge of the matter.

"Hush!" said Bloomfield, attempting an expression of profound facial wisdom. "A wife's revenge—a woman's awful retaliation; but whoever she may be, I'll wager a round sum against a five-pound note he'll be one with her, before long, for it."

"Then it's understood that we undertake the conquest of the girls you alluded to?" said Walter, as he summarily waived the subject of Jasper's infirmities.

"Certainly; and to-night, my boy!" replied Bloomfield, applying himself to the bell-rope suspended close to his shoulders.

Jasper himself obeyed the summons; and, after casting upon Walter another of his looks of ferocious hatred, silently awaited his master's orders.

"That girl—that Louisa Thornton" — hiccupped Bloomfield—"where does she live?"

"—— Street, Islington. A cab would take you there in ten minutes."

"What is the arrangement? are you to see her first, and bring her to the Casino? or how?"

"Why, my lord, just as you please; but I think it would be better for me to see her first, and then you could meet her at the same place as last time."

"Very well, let it be so; and you may as well go about it at once. I will be at the rooms about nine."

Jasper, thus instructed to prosecute his errand of mischief, departed at once, but not without bestowing upon Walter another of his peculiarly-unpleasant glances.

"What does that scoundrel mean?" inquired the soldier, of himself. "I don't remember ever having given him a kicking; but it strikes me very forcibly that he is striving hard to deserve one."

However, the door had scarcely closed upon Jasper, when Walter dismissed both him and his insolent demeanour from his consideration, and turned his attention to the difficult task of inducing Bloomfield to drink without his becoming thoroughly intoxicated. He wished him to be in such a state of mental and moral incompetency, that he would be ripe for any experiment to which he might think proper to subject him. In fact, Walter had resolved to lead him, step by step, into a state of blind, helpless insanity—the utter prostration of body and soul that precedes that awful affliction, delirium tremens. Being fully aware that to bring this about his patient should be indulged in every whim, and not in the slightest degree contradicted, he had resolved to accompany him in his expedition against the virtue of the girl whom Jasper had marked out for a victim; and to enable Walter to accomplish that, and his ulterior purposes, he saw the necessity for husbanding as much as practicable Bloomfield's power of endurance. He therefore proposed, as some hours intervened before the appointment had to be kept, that they should amuse themselves with a game at cards

Bloomfield agreed to the proposal, and the pair played uninterruptedly, until Walter suggested some ablutionary preparations, with the addition of soda-water, to enable them to be in time to fulfil the assignation. While they are thus engaged, it will be as well to ascertain how Jasper fared on his evil mission.

Chafing sorely at being obliged to leave his employer in the society of such a man as Captain Morris —for he both feared and detested that individual—he bent his footsteps to the nearest cab-stand, and, plunging moodily into the first that shot from the rank, bade the driver take him to the Angel at Islington.

"I have served *her* out," growled he, to himself; "and as this Captain Morris is the only one I knew for certain had to do with her, I don't see why I shouldn't make him smart a bit. Besides, he not only crept between my sheets, but jeered at me whenever I met him; and once—oh, hell! shall I ever forget that once—he gave me the best milling ever I had in my life; and what for? why, because I was going to pitch into my wife—wife! oh! ah! he, he, he! I think I did that trick nicely—turned the tables on her neatly. Oh! how she's a blessing of me on the salt seas at this identical moment!"

Jasper, as he dwelt with the gusto of a fiend over the recollection of the monstrous revenge he had inflicted on his wife—the once gay and merry Alice Burton—grinned hideously, snapped his fingers, then clenched his fists and drew his legs under him, as if he would retain the thought of the horrible retribution in his memory for ever.

The never-ceasing, burning thirst that tormented him both night and day, obliged him to stop the cab at divers public-houses on his short journey, and "wet his whistle," as he termed it, and, in these libations the driver of course participating, by the time the vehicle had arrived at its destination, that functionary was in such a state of bewilderment, that he pocketed the fare tendered him without a murmur; and then, scrambling up to the roof, with his legs dangling behind, and his back to his ancient and faithful steed, commenced such an onslaught with his whip on the innocent atmosphere, that a policeman flew to the horse's head, and ingloriously led both steed and driver to a place of security.

This little bit of amusement served to restore to Jasper some portion of his self-possession and habitual cynicism; and, stalking through the crowd with the air of a man who sadly deplored such exhibitions of human weakness, he walked gently along the High Street until he came to a respectable-looking milliner's shop.

And now this veracious narrative must halt, to tell of a naughty girl and a negligent mistress.

The girl was the Louisa Thornton referred to so flippantly by Jasper; and to state that she was beautiful, would be merely averring an undoubted fact: she was more—she was lovely—and she knew it, and so did her fair-complexioned and bright-ringleted mistress. Louisa was a favourable specimen of your true Cockney girl. Arch, lively, and *piquante,* she could boast of a skin of unimpeachable snow, features glowing with radiant health, and faultless in symmetry; and, above them, in endless waves of luxuriance, a mass of rich brown hair, which, when unconfined by comb or pin, stretched thickly and shiningly far below a waist just emancipated from the thraldom of sylphism, and yet bordering on that fanciful idea of quantity with which the eye ever associates the proportions of a finely-formed woman. In stature she was superior to the majority of her sex, and in gait and gesture proud and defiant, yet withal coaxingly loving; as if the virgin, with all her youthful pulses warmly playing, was in a perpetual struggle with busy promptings on the one hand, and feminine timidity, dashed with sensual coquetry, on the other. The dress of this pretty creature heightened her charms, and she was placed in the shop as an attraction—one of her duties being to sit behind the broad glass case called a window, so as to be seen by every passer-by, and criticised with all the acumen of vulgar admiration. Her mistress derived considerable business from this exposure, and the girl's vanity was so flattered, that the compliments profusely showered upon her, were received into thirsty ears, and, in the course of a few months, were regarded as nothing else but her due. Gentlemen, it is generally thought, have no taste for visiting these costly ladies' establishments; but this is a mistake, for they are the most liberal customers milliners have, when the latter happen to be surrounded by a bevy of assistants, in all the glory of youth, health, and beauty. And so the poor vain things are used as baits to catch the roving eyes of sensuality; and should any one fall a victim to her credulity and easily-excited passions, why her place can easily be supplied from out of the ranks of the needy preponderant female population of the metropolis; and so the system is considered an easily-worked and profitable one.

The proprietors of these places are fully aware of the danger to which they subject the young things committed to their charge; but, being generally themselves of the genus scrago, have little sympathy with any other feeling than that of insatiable avarice.

Mrs. Skimpton was one of this class of milliners, and Louisa Thornton had been her apprentice for about a year, when the superlative charms of the girl—not her proficiency—were the sole cause of her being transferred from the parlour behind to the shop in front, with the nominal office of principal assistant—nominal, because she was not benefited to the extent of a shilling by her promotion.

Jasper, whose peregrinations extended to all quarters of the town, discovered this peri one day, and immediately marked her out as a tit-bit for his lordship, or "any nobleman or gentleman who would feel disposed to come down handsomely with the vilely-earned remuneration." To step into the shop and make a trifling purchase was his first act; and, as he made many inquiries, he soon artfully engaged the girl in a conversation which enabled him quickly to form a pretty shrewd estimate of her natural character. He saw that her leading sentiment was vanity, and that her love of applause, acting upon her maturing propensities and instincts, had generated within her desires which only required skilful management to lead to gratification.

"A woman from top to toe," he reasoned, "whom a little more flattery would render as amorous as a cat. I see it in the sparkle of her eye, the flush of her brow, the wagging of her bustle, and the swimming, gliding action of her limbs! By heavens! if I were a perfect man, I would not wish to cross a better blooded filly; but as I am not a man—only a worm, a wretch, an abortion, as my master says—why I must leave such steeple-chase riding to those who are able for it. Louisa Thornton—not an ugly name, and now to find out all about her."

This information was soon obtained, for it only amounted to the fact that she lived with her mother, a widow in straitened circumstances, and that she had a beau who toiled as a mechanic from the sun's rising to its setting; and from the hours he devoted to additional labour at home, managed to snatch a few, which he expended in her society. This was quite sufficient for Jasper; and he laid himself out accordingly, for the conquest. Mrs. Skimpton was not remarkable for anything but a vinegar aspect; so Jasper discarded the notion of purchasing her goodwill, and applied himself to watching the girl's habits and pursuits when out of the shop. A love of gaiety, he soon found out, was her present ruling propensity; and he traced her through the whole series of dancing-rooms she frequented, until he placed himself one morning before her in a celebrated casino. The recognition was mutual; and the silly girl, proud of the honour of waltzing with one of her mistress's rich customers, resigned herself to the bold embrace of the sternest woman-hater that ever breathed. An introduction to Bloomfield next took place; and the handsome peer soon made a sensible impression on the susceptible heart of the sempstress. In disposition she was far from vicious; but, after her clandestine acceptance of several articles of jewellery and a gay dress or two, it is not doing her any injustice to say that she entirely owed the preservation of her chastity to the sustained inebriety of Bloomfield. Had he been perfectly sober she would have fallen long ago; but, satiated with amours and weakened by drink, he had dallied with his conquest, and would perhaps have forgotten it, had it not been for the frequent hints he received from the iniquitous Jasper; who, having set his heart on the girl's ruin, had malignantly resolved that either Bloomfield or some one equally prodigal of cash should have the honour (?) of being the man that should effect his purpose. A previous arrangement had been made to meet at the Casino; but, to prevent any disappointment, Jasper had determined to see the girl, and, if possible, bring her along with him. It was about six o'clock as Jasper reached the shop, into which he walked with the demeanour of one to whom the place was no stranger. Louisa, who was sitting beside the advertising glass case, sewing, received him with a deep blush; for, ignorant as she was of the grossness of the evil of the temptation that surrounded her, she was not insensible to the indelicacy of the acquaintance, or the disquietude caused by the concealment she instinctively practised. Like most girls of her age and class, Louisa had long penetrated all the sexual secrets, but was extremely ill-informed on the subject of their abuse, and misapplication to improper purposes. Her physical training had been left entirely to chance and nature. And is it to be wondered that she was more liable to worship at the shrine of pleasure than of moral rectitude? But (yet, however active her inclination was, her sense of propriety was not wholly blunted: perhaps a lurking sympathy, a yearning towards the pure affection of her humble lover, mellowed and softened her more ardent aspirations, and thus kept her in subjection to the restraints imposed by custom and habit. Whatever it was, the seeds of a saving power were not absent from the virgin soil of her nature. But deceit, fraud, seduction, or any adverse circumstance, might trample them down far below the sunshine, and bury them in the darkness of a whole life of vice. The tempter was before her. Jasper, under cover of a purchase of some artificial flowers, addressed her in his usual unabashed strain of familiarity.

"I cannot go to-night—indeed I cannot," she objected.

"Tut! tut! you mustn't break your word. This is one of the grand nights; and you know you are engaged to dance with my friend. He has got such a nice present for you—a pair of bracelets, I think."

Louisa shook her head, as she opened another box of flowers; but Jasper was a wily rascal in such an affair: he knew she envied a young friend the possession of a pair of sparkling ornaments for the wrists; and that the prospect of gratifying her wish in that respect, would do much to sap the foundation of almost any prudent resolution she had formed.

"They are such a handsome pair," continued Jasper. "He must have given at least twenty pounds for them; and I am sure they would become you admirably—make you the belle of the room."

"Poor girls like me, don't want such fine things," said she.

"You mean that rich, ugly women don't want them," replied Jasper, persuasively; "it is only beauty that should wear gold and diamonds. But you will come—you are only saying you won't to plague me; besides, if you don't, my friend will break his heart. He is rich and honourable—I might tell you more if I dared—and who knows what he might do for you; rich men like pretty wives, and, as he is smitten, you might keep the best of company, instead of hiding your beauty behind this counter, which, to me, is pretty much like a rose in full bloom wasting its fragrance on a barren island."

With wily talk like this, he beguiled the vain, credulous girl of a promise to meet him soon after she had left the shop; and, he, to be assured, did not quit the vicinity until he had watched her to her humble home, and then saw her emerge from it smartly attired, with a small parcel in her hand, which he well knew contained a pair of ball-room slippers. To accost her, hail a cab, and place her in it, was the work of a few minutes; and the poor milliner's assistant, with a heated cheek and fluttering heart, seemed likely to realise the destiny which the scoundrel of a pander by her side had chalked out for her. But during his absence from Bloomfield, several things had concurred to render his success problematical. Walter, in his free and easy manner, had extracted sufficient out of Bloomfield to assure him that some piece of villany was being meditated; and, being seized with an uncontrollable desire to thwart it, whatever it might be, succeeded in obtaining the address of the shop from which Bloomfield's intended paramour was to be procured, and, having left him at the Casino, in the society of one of its fair and frail *habitués*, hastened to Islington, where, by frightening Mrs. Skimpton into the belief that she had, wittingly and willingly, lent herself, and reputation for unblemished chastity, to a case of cruel seduction—if not something approaching cruel violation—she furnished him with information which enabled him easily to find out the abode of the mother of the infatuated Louisa. She was a plain, homely-looking woman, who kept a small shop, in which she dispensed groceries, butter, and bread, to her humble neighbours. Walter introduced himself as gently as he could; but he soon perceived that the mother was one of those weak persons, who fly into rages when offered advice on the subject of their domestic economy.

"My daughter has got sense enough to take care of herself; she's been well edicated," said she, smartly.

"But, my dear woman," persisted Walter, "your daughter has fallen into bad company, and, unless she is more strictly guarded, she will be ruined."

The mother paled at this, and, moderating her tone said :

"She has only gone to see a friend: she told me where she was going to."

"I am grieved to say you are deceived," said Walter, really compassionating the weak being before him; "she is now, or will be soon, in the company of a profligate nobleman—a married man; one who is not bad himself, but is made bad by evil associates, and particularly a wretch who is continually laying snares to catch young girls."

"My God!" exclaimed the woman, sinking into a crazy chair, and wringing her hands.

After an hysterical gasp or two, she slid to the floor; as Walter stooped to raise her up, he detected the fumes of gin in her breath, and in that state he correctly judged that it would be hopeless to expect any assistance from her. A more sensible neighbour happening to step in, the dilemma was explained to her, and she promptly suggested the wisdom of calling upon the girl's sweetheart, and requesting his assistance. Walter went to the house indicated, but the young man was not at home—he had not returned from his daily toil; so Walter was fain obliged to content himself with leaving a hurried but significant note, warning him of his supposed true-hearted love's danger, and of her being at the Casino, which he designated by name.

Being satisfied that he had done his utmost to prevent the flighty girl from plunging her family into misery, he hastened to the scene of profligacy, under the mask of relaxation and amusement, to attend to Bloomfield, and, if possible, frustrate the schemes of Jasper. That ignoble worthy, having succeeded in placing Louisa in the custody of Bloomfield, left her to the latter's blandishments, and betook himself to his customary amusement of tickling a girl while dancing with her, and drinking whenever his horrible thirst compelled him. Walter saw through the manœuvre, and, having obtained a promise from Bloomfield not to leave the rooms without first speaking to him, resolved to watch the proceedings of Mr. Jasper Sampson, and bring him to condign punishment the moment a pretext was afforded. None, however, came, for Jasper studiously avoided him; and Walter saw, with some concern, that Bloomfield was making rapid progress with the heart of Miss Louisa Thornton. The young girl's eyes sparkled intensely, and she indulged in such vivacity that he felt convinced she had received the last proposal a modest woman should tolerate. He was beginning to despair, when his attention was attracted from the girl he was gossiping with by a young man, decently dressed, but evidently not of the gent. species, who was wandering about the rooms in a hurried manner, as if in search of some person.

"The lover, by St. George!" muttered he. "There is hope now!"

The young man rapidly approached Louisa, and, as he drew near, he could distinctly hear him implore her to return home; and to his entreaties added the information that her mother was alarmingly ill. The girl's pride was touched, and, believing the story to have been concocted for the purpose of inducing her to leave the place, she haughtily repulsed him, and, thrusting her arm through Bloomfield's, swept away from the spot, with a disdainful toss of the head. Enraged at such a contemptuous rebuff, the young mechanic commenced a furious assault on Bloomfield, and immediately there was the confusion incidental to a row. The keepers of the rooms, used to all kinds of disturbances, rushed to the spot, and the champion of virtue was ignominiously expelled, and handed over to the police, who, despite his desperate struggles, conveyed him to the lock-up, on the grave charge of indiscriminate assault and battery. This incident determined Walter to act promptly and resolutely. Bloomfield had received several severe contusions on the face—among them being those which unmistakingly betokened the approach of a pair of black eyes; and, while he was being administered to by Jasper, who was *au fait* at such accidents, Walter availed himself of the opportunity to address the now trembling and agitated cause of the *fracas*.

"Your friend," said he, "told you the truth—your mother is dangerously ill! I left her insensible."

"You!" exclaimed she, in surprise.

"Even so," replied Walter, drawing her arm through his own, and leading her out of the throng which had gathered around her: "she is acquainted with your being here—a most dangerous place for a young girl—and the discovery was more than she could bear. Go to her at once, or the most fatal consequences might ensue!"

Louisa, feeling faint, leaned rather heavily on Walter, for support; and he, having prevailed on her to partake of a glass of iced water, renewed his entreaties to depart.

"This is frightful company for an innocent girl like you!" said he, earnestly; "the men here are all leagued against the honour and happiness of young girls; and the women—I cannot, although they are young, call them girls—are —— !"

Observing him hesitate, the abashed girl timidly said:

"What?"

"Prostitutes!"

At the mention of that horrid word, a cold shiver ran through the young woman's frame; and then, as if conscious that she was menaced by some terrible hidden calamity, she sprang towards the door.

Walter maintained his place by her side until he had seen her bonneted and shawled; and then, having had a cab called, placed her inside; and, after taking down the number, and thrusting his card into Louisa's hand, imperatively bade the driver conduct her home safely, and as speedily as possible.

"And now to settle accounts with you, Mr. Jasper!" muttered Walter, between his teeth, as he strode back into the now extremely-crowded ball-room. Bloomfield was there, staring about him rather wildly, in search of Louisa, while Jasper was busied in threading the lines of promenaders, on the same errand.

"Caught a stinger on the nose," said Bloomfield, laughingly, as he essayed to walk steadily; "but I fancy I gave the fellow as much as he sent. But where the deuce has the girl gone to?"

"Bolted, by G—d!" cried Jasper, who, having ascertained the fact of Louisa's disappearance through the instrumentality of Walter, unceremoniously approached and interrupted their conference.

"Bolted!" repeated he, glancing menacingly at Walter.

"Bolted!" echoed Bloomfield; "well, that is cruel, for she was just in the humour to let me have a bit of fun with her! Never mind, another time will do quite as well—perhaps better. Who was that fellow that assaulted me?"

"The mechanic I told you about," answered Jasper.

"He was the girl's lover," interposed Walter; "and as you know the old text, 'O, beware of jealousy,

my lord,' &c., you will find an excuse for his unceremonious conduct."

"Jealousy!" growled Jasper, losing his temper. "Who set the fool on? who made him fly to the fake we had on?"

Without heeding either his words or passionate gestures, Walter led Bloomfield away, and ultimately induced him to leave the place altogether; but could not prevail upon him to forbear visiting a well-known sporting house in Holborn. After a stay there for about two hours, he became insensibly drunk; and Walter, after seeing Jasper carefully convey him to a bed in the tavern in which he was, lighted his cigar, and strolled gently homewards. A light shone in his bachelor drawing-room; and, as he opened the door, the beaming face of Laura Bell met his view. The truth is that Walter, charmed with the Socialist girl's beauty of person and originality of character, had taken her into keeping; so that the occupation afforded him by her society may partly account for his visitor's zeal on behalf of Louisa Thornton. It must be admitted, though, to the credit of his latent appreciation of chastity, that he had never, throughout the whole of his commerce with the sex, resorted to any deceptive or disgraceful expedients to gain a favour. Frank, bold, and prepossessing, he commanded success without a superfluity of words, where there was a corresponding inclination. This was especially the case with Laura, a woman of a high sensual temperament; and the amour cost neither of them a single twinge of conscience: for both believed that, by their alliance, they were obeying, instead of outraging and defiling, one of the sacred laws of nature. However, Walter, with his military habits, and an engagement before him, never lingered in the arms of a woman. The next morning he was up betimes, and, after an early breakfast, proceeded to the police-office, in which the young mechanic was to appear after his night's incarceration. The disorderlies are generally the first cases called on; and in due turn James Leigh appeared at the bar of summary justice to answer for his misdeeds. No prosecutor appeared; but the police trumped up two charges of assault on their valuable persons; and the poor fellow was mulcted in penalties, which, with costs, amounted to twelve pounds. Walter, although he could ill spare the money, stepped forward and paid the fines; and then, upon handing his card to the bench, explained the whole affair, taking care to omit all mention of, or allusion to, Lord Bloomfield. The bench, upon receiving this statement, instantly remitted the penalties; but Walter, not to be outdone in generosity, paid five pounds into the poor box, and triumphantly left the court, with the liberated James Leigh, whom he accompanied to his humble, but neat and tidy home.

"Do you love this young woman?" inquired Walter, after he had eased the poor fellow's troubled mind by a candid account of all that had occurred regarding her; taking care to soften, as much as possible, every point that told most strongly in favour of her indiscretion.

"Love her!" exclaimed James Leigh, who, by the way, was a very comely, manly kind of young fellow; "I am ashamed to say that I do, dearly. She and I have been acquainted since we were children, and if anything wrong was to happen to her, it would break my heart."

"Would you marry her if you had the chance?" inquired Walter.

"Aye, that I would!" was the animated reply; "and as you have been so kind to me, I don't mind telling you that we were as good as engaged; and I have been working hard and saving up these two years, to enable us to start in the world fairly."

"I have no doubt what has happened will be a lesson of prudence to her," said Walter; "but I tell you what, my friend, you must take her from that cursed shop, and marry her at once."

The young man shook his head, and intimated that the mother, Mrs. Thornton, being a tradesman's widow, objected to the marriage of her daughter to a mechanic; and that he had promised to remove her scruples by saving up two hundred pounds, which sum he could not possibly complete in less than another year.

"Don't let that be an obstacle," said Walter, gaily; "you shall have the money, if I advance it out of my own pocket; so, as the Scotch say, don't fash yourself about it any more. Besides, the parties who have been the cause of all this pain, will, upon explanation, make handsome compensation for the annoyance, and you will be a gainer instead of a loser by the adventure."

The overjoyed James Leigh blushingly stammered forth his thanks; but Walter stopped his utterance, by bidding him set about regaining the affections of his sweetheart, and inform him when the courtship was likely to be happily consummated.

"Take her from that shop!" was Walter's parting salutation; and, having received the lover's permission, he proposed waiting upon and expostulating with the girl herself.

The mother was at home, but, upon hearing the name of Captain Morris, became so flurried that she was unable to speak rationally; and Walter, determined to conclude a mission he had undertaken with such good intentions, and so far prospered in, adjourned to Mrs. Skimpton's, where the first object he saw was the fair Louisa, doing her duty as usual as an advertisement, by the exposed glass case. She looked pale and languid, and appeared excessively agitated when Walter addressed her.

"Your mother and James wish to see you," said he.

"James?" replied she, in an incredulous tone.

"Yes, even James, my dear girl. He knows all, and all's forgiven. You were not much to blame, but if you will take my advice, you will not stay another minute in this shop. You are too pretty to be stuck in a window like a wax doll, for every puppy to stare at. Had you have never sat here to show the crowds outside your lovely countenance, you would never have fallen into the snare that was laid for your destruction."

This was such unusual language for the pretty and coaxed Louisa to hear, that her vanity was wounded, and she burst into tears.

Mrs. Skimpton, ensconced behind the glass door of the little room at the end of the counter, seeing her apprentice in distress, deemed it her duty to rush to the rescue.

"What's all this about, Louisa?" exclaimed she, tartly; "who is this gentleman?"—person she would have said—but Walter's fine bearing and handsome face overawed her.

Louisa was unable to reply, and Walter took the office on himself.

"I should be sorry to say anything unpolite to one of your sex," said he, severely; "but I must candidly tell you that you have nearly been the cause of the ruin of this poor girl."

"Me, sir?" said Mrs. Skimpton, her withered chastity taking the alarm.

"Yes, you, madam!" was the rather warm reply. "You get a pretty girl into your hands, under the pretence of teaching her your business; but, instead of doing that, you make a public show of her, dress her out to attract custom to your shop—in fact, make a sign-board of her, to catch the eye of lecherous old age and amorous youth; and can it be wondered at that a young girl placed in such a position should have her head turned with admiration, and be ready to fall a prey to the first clever scoundrel who crept into her confidence. Madam, your system of doing business is bad—it's immoral; and you must be cautious, or before long you will have the parents of some ruined child pulling the place down about your ears. Come, Louisa, put on your things, and leave this infamous place. I will conduct you to your anxious parent."

Louisa silently complied with the request; and no wonder, for his manner and tone were peremptory, and much of what he said came upon her, for the first time, with such forcible truth, that a feeling of shame and degradation came over her, and banished any reluctance she might have entertained at leaving so abruptly. Mrs. Skimpton was speechless at this, as she deemed it, unparalleled piece of assurance; and beheld her apprentice carried off by a total stranger, without her being able to offer the slightest resistance, or utter the feeblest cries for assistance. As soon as Walter had gained the residence of the girl he took her aside, and painted to her, in its true colours, the risk she ran in receiving the attentions of strangers, and, above all, in frequenting such demoralising places as the casinos. The girl's eyes were opened very wide indeed; and, as Mr. James Leigh happened at that moment to step into the room, she regarded him through her tears more graciously than ever she had done in her life before. Walter having good-naturedly bid them adieu, and left them together, there can be no doubt they kissed each other and were very good friends again. It may as well be mentioned here, that Walter completed the good work he had so energetically commenced; for he saw the pair happily married, and more comfortably settled in life than ever they had anticipated in their most sanguine moments. Bloomfield, when restored to his senses, contributed largely to this felicity; for, although, for obvious reasons, he chose to remain in the back-ground, Walter was a faithful almoner; and both, in after years, when reflection became more consistent and poignant, had reason to be grateful, when they beheld in Louisa a blooming wife and deliciously-happy mother, instead of the abandoned strumpet she would inevitably have become, had she submitted to the false and meretricious caresses of the professed rake.

However, to return to the current of events. Elate with the joy he had been the instrument of conveying to two young unpolluted hearts, Walter, when he left the Thorntons' house, was too much engaged with his own pleasant meditations to notice that close upon his heels followed Jasper, with an awful scowl on his blanched face. His aspect was so menacing that a pedestrian touched Walter on the shoulder, and warned him of the enemy being in his rear. Quick as lightning he turned round and confronted the now ungovernable Jasper.

"Scoundrel!" he exclaimed, "have you been dogging my steps?"

"I have," was the impudent reply.

"By whose orders, pray?" inquired Walter, who, suspecting Bloomfield, was too brave to quarrel with a menial for performing services ordered by his master.

"My own," hissed Jasper; "and a pretty kettle-of-fish I find your meddling has made with his lordship's

affairs! He'll shoot you for it as dead as a her-ring!"

Walter lifted the cane he carried, with the intention of applying it to Jasper's shoulders; but the latter prevented it by crying out:

"Not here, mighty captain! I have an old score to settle with you, and it may as well be done to-day as another time! If you have any pluck, I can take you to a place where we can settle our differences, and have fair play!"

Almost laughing at what he deemed the fellow's impudent audacity, he turned upon his heel, and with a "pish!" stalked leisurely away.

"Coward!" shouted Jasper. "You can insult a poor man, seduce his wife, and then refuse him justice because he is poor!"

"What do you mean?" inquired Walter, bewildered by such an accusation.

"Follow me, and I will tell you. The streets ain't exactly the place to have a grudge out in!"

"Lead on, vile parody on human nature! and if I find you trifle with me, I'll break every bone in your accursed and filthy carcase! Proceed in advance, at least ten yards: such company as yours does no suit my reputation in the day-time!"

Walter spoke so sternly that Jasper had no appre-hension that he would follow; and, with his low, hor-rible, dry laugh, did as requested.

Clerkenwell has many strange nooks and corners—some dark ones, too, where strange orgies are held, and fearful deeds perpetrated; but perbaps the most mysterious of them all was the place to which Jasper conducted Walter. Outside it had the appearance of a marine-store dealer's shop; but the privileged well knew that the interior presented other features. It was, in fact, a thieves' den. A score of vaults for the reception of stolen goods and concealment of felons pursued by justice, extended under the neighbouring houses and streets; and one of them communicated with the immense sewer that intersects the parish. The opening was convenient, for the dead thrown into it were washed into the Thames; and thus all traces of the murder were effectually removed. The apart-ments in this dwelling of crime were variously fur-nished—some meanly, some neat, and some luxu-riously. The one to which Jasper led Walter was of the latter class; and on a sideboard there was a profuse display of decanters, filled with wines and spirits. Jasper coolly helped himself to some brandy out of a decanter, and then, seating himself, pushed it over the table to where Walter was standing, wondering at the surprising difference of appearance the house had inside and out. Suspecting some foul play, he sternly demanded to know why he had been brought thither.

"I'll tell you," said Jasper; "did you know one Alice Burton?"

"Alice Burton!" repeated Walter, surprised; "why ask me such as a question?"

"Because I knew you did know Alice Burton."

"Did know? Why Alice Burton is still Lady Bloomfield's attendant?"

"Oho! I thought you knew her; but you are mistaken if you think she is still at Bloomfield House. She's gone to India—married—bolted with a green young hofficer."

"Did you bring me here to tell me such a bagatelle as that?" said Walter, angrily, and feeling inclined to put his threat against Jasper into execution.

"No, valiant captain, I did not," replied Jasper. "And p'rhaps, as beating about the bush aint very agreeable, you will tell me whether you didn't go with Alice Burton many a time?"

"Scoundrel! this impertinence ——"

"Hold, valiant captain! Don't get into a passion. You went with her scores of times in Bloomfield House."

"Liar!"

"Not so fast. You slept with her at Charlton, the night you gammoned Smythe that you hadn't been pawing and feeling his wife all the afternoon."

Walter gazed upon Jasper as if he had been the arch-fiend. Such a revelation, because true, came upon him with the force of a thunderbolt.

"You are flabbergasted, are you?" sneered Jasper. "Here's to tell you more. You slept with her at a coffee-house in the Strand not long ago; and after that she went many times to your lodgings, and staid for hours. Am I telling lies or not—eh, most valiant and amorous town-bull?"

"Insulting vagabond! I'll pound you to a jelly!" cried Walter, springing forward.

"Wait a bit," said Jasper, keeping the table between him and the enraged Walter; "do you ever remember to have seen me before I went to Bloomfield House?"

"No, villain! Where should I encounter such ugly monsters?"

"I'll sharpen your memory, captain, then. Perhaps you remember seeing a man following a young woman one fine morning, and she, to get out of his way, going right into the arms of another man—her lawful husband—who hadn't seen her for ever so long? The man that was a following of her was you, the young woman was Alice Burton, and the man you whopped was me—Harry Burton—her true and lawful husband. Now do you remember?"

Walter had a distinct recollection of the incident; but as to there being any identity between the ruffian he beat on that occasion and the hideous-looking being before him, he laughed the idea to scorn.

"You laugh; p'rhaps you'll laugh on the other side of your face before we part!" said Jasper, savagely; "but as true as you stand there my name's Harry Burton, and I'm the cove you pitched into that identical morning."

"You? Impossible!"

"I tell you I am; and partly owing to you I am changed from what I was. The thrashing you gave me incensed my bitch of a wife to do worse than kill me. She coaxed me to a place, got me drunk, and, while I was strapped down and beaten by fifty she-devils, she got a surgeon to make me—a—?—a thingumy—a eunuch—ah! ah! ah!"

The fellow laughed so horribly, that Walter started in some trepidation.

"Will you believe it now?" shouted Jasper, writhing with passion. "I was a stout chap before, but the next day I was grey; and day after day I dried up until I am what I am in look, but still Harry Burton, who has sworn to be revenged on all the female sex, and never to forgive an injury."

"Why do you tell me this shocking story?" inquired Walter, composedly.

"Why!" ejaculated Jasper, as if surprised at the other's obtuseness; "why! only hear him—only hear him! Why, indeed! Why, didn't you disgrace me before my blasted bitch of a wife, and then lie with her, go with her, paddle in her titties, feel her smooth thighs, &c. &c.?"

"Well!" said Walter, calmly, for he began to suspect a more serious termination to the adventure than he had anticipated, and so nerved himself to meet the worst results.

"Well!" echoed Jasper; "why do everything to her she at first wouldn't let me, and then made me that I couldn't."

"Well, and what then?"

"And what then? Why you must give me satisfaction—fight me, or never leave this place alive!"

As Jasper uttered this he jumped to his feet, and, facing Walter, placed himself in an attitude for boxing. Walter's composure did not desert him, for he eyed his antagonist with the glittering eye of a man prepared to meet any danger, and promptly answered:

"I will fight you: I cannot refuse your challenge; but this is neither the time nor place. Besides, we shall need seconds."

"They are here!" shouted Jasper; and, clutching at a bell-rope, he pulled it lustily. A middle-aged man, in a faded yellow livery, made his appearance.

"Is the court ready?" demanded Jasper.

"It is, and the men, too. Joe Sykes has whacked Bill Stiggins, and so you can have the ring at once," was the somewhat professional reply.

"Show the way, and see that there's plenty of sawdust down, for we shall have hard knocks," cried Jasper, with an effort at gaiety that was very forced indeed. Walter followed, prepared for the most trying emergency, for he felt convinced that going on was better than retreating. Ruffians have always a sympathy with valour, in whatever shape it presents itself—no matter to them whether under the fur coat of the gentleman, or the fustian of the labourer. The metal in both cases has the same sterling sound.

The court was a square-roofed building, with a regular ring for pugilistic encounters, formed of ropes, in the centre. The company present comprised about half a dozen well-known athletæ of the day, and some score of ill-looking blackguards as an audience. As Walter stepped into the ring, one of the prize-fighters, a young Hercules in figure, with a good-natured expression of countenance, whispered in his ear:

"Polish the fellow off as quick as you can, captain. There's treachery intended to you."

Walter looked at the man, and recognised in him a young fellow whom, with some military friends, he had backed in a fight a few months before. He gave him a smile of recognition, and, upon the choice of seconds being made, selected him, and another whom he pointed out as being trustworthy. And then the preparations began. Walter refused to strip to the buff, but persisted in doing battle in his shirt. His figure and scientific attitude in taking his place were the theme of admiration among the professionals.

Jasper stripped to the skin, and contrasted rather disadvantageously with the fleshy and elastic-looking ex-guardsman. The fight began; and, after the first round, the issue could not for a moment be doubted. Jasper, neither in height, weight, length of reach, nor knowledge of the art, was any match for Walter. The latter played with him as easily as if he had been but a boy. Jasper, seeing this, lost his temper, and indulged in several foul practices, to the great disgust of the professionals, who, to a man, sided with Walter.

"Go in and win," whispered Walter's second; "finish him off at once: them fellows there are a smugging together about something, and we shall have to rush before long, or my name's Walker."

This was too sensible advice to be rejected, for Walter himself had observed the suspicious signs pointed out by his second; and, although he did not wish to injure Jasper at all, he felt that, in self-defence—perhaps not only of liberty but his life—it was necessary that he should bring the combat to a close. This he effected in prime style, for he punished Jasper terribly about the head and chest; and, finally closing with him, threw him so heavily, that he gave vent to a deep groan, and sank into a state of complete insensibility.

"Hoora!" cried the boxers, making a rush towards the door, and carrying the victor along with them.

"Stop them"—"Down with them"—"That's the cove we're to slate!" vociferated the mob. But they were too late. The pugilists knocked them down as if they had only been nine-pins; and, after a desperate struggle, fought their way out of the house, before which they gave three stentorian cheers, and then bore off Walter in triumph to a neighbouring tavern.

"You have had a narrow escape for your life!" said Walter's second; "it was touch and go. If we hadn't been there, you'd a' been murdered! We heard of it a day or two ago; but, not knowing who the cove was, we didn't care. But when we saw it was you—a friend that stuck to us in need—why, it was quite another thing."

Walter, assured that he owed his life to the men around him, becomingly acknowledged the obligation, by presenting them with all his loose money, and promising them a larger reward if they would send one of their number to him in the morning.

"D—n the ready!" said the young Hercules; "will you back me for a cool fifty against Slashing Jack?"

Walter readily promised to do so; and, after a shake of the hand all round, he jumped into a cab, minus his hat, coat, and waistcoat. Proceeding to his lodgings, he rearrayed himself, and, without a mark—not even a scratch—to show the nature of his morning's amusement and danger, went in search of Bloomfield.

Bloomfield arose in the morning, with the brawler's deep mourning rings encircling his eyes: the mechanic had amply avenged the outrageous attempt on the chastity of the girl whom he had selected to be his wife; and, as the peer viewed his disfigured countenance in the glass, a feeling of disgust mingled with his fevered assurance. He was ashamed of himself; and the appearance of his early friend, Walter Morris, looking the very picture of health, cheerfulness, and sobriety, although he was pleased with such a display of attention, made the degradation smart more keenly.

"Bad work this, Walter?" said he, with a melancholy attempt at a smile.

"Not the thing at all; but we must expect a few knocks now and then," was the hearty reply; "so let us set about repairing the catastrophe."

"How did it all happen? I must have drunk more than I ought to have done," said Bloomfield, with a rueful expression of countenance.

"Woman—lovely woman!" replied Walter; "you have much to answer for! Your beauty first leads us into danger, and then leaves us to shift for ourselves. However, never risk never win; and I have always found that a scrimmage now and then freshens one up amazingly."

"But how the deuce did it all happen?" again asked Bloomfield, regarding his discoloured visage with increasing apprehension.

"Why, you would have that girl—what did you call her?—Louisa Thornton; her sweetheart caught you and her together, and as his blood was up, and you were jolly, there was a set-to, and the young fellow was dragged to the station-house."

"My God! there will be be an exposure! my name will be gibbeted in the papers!" exclaimed Bloomfield, who, with all his irregularities, had a nervous dread of their obtaining publicity.

"Not a bit of it," was the assuring reply. "I have arranged it all: pacified the man by telling him you wouldn't mind a cool hundred or two when he got married."

"I am so obliged, my dear fellow," said the gratified peer, shaking Walter by the hand; "I shan't forget your kindness in a hurry, I can assure you; but what the devil's that you mentioned about marrying? You don't surely mean to say that I am to be bilked out of a fine girl by a common mechanic?"

"Fact—upon my honour it is; the game's up, for the girl has taken the alarm, and won't see you again," was Walter's somewhat solemn assurance.

"She is too fine a girl to lose altogether," said the erratic peer; "and if I can't enjoy her when a maid, I'll see what I can do when she is married. A merry wife makes a merrier bedfellow than a timid girl."

With this consoling reflection my Lord Bloomfield applied himself to the business of his toilet, which when he had concluded, he endeavoured to partake of a little breakfast; but he found that his appetite was completely vitiated, and he was fain obliged to have recourse to his usual stimulant, brandy. Walter encouraged him in this propensity by following his example, and the pair, by mutual agreement, resolved to have a long gossip until dinner-time—for Bloomfield, with his dreadful face, would not venture out of doors; then a game of cards, brandy-and-water ad libitum, and any other excitement the house could afford, even to the addition to their society of half a score of the plastic beauties whom five minutes' trouble would suffice to pick up at almost any hour in Holborn and its vicinity. The latter, though, were not needed, for Walter plied Bloomfield with drink until he had reduced him to a state of insensibility, and then had him put to bed in the same house; to rise on the following day, and repeat the same scene of gambling and intoxication, for the mere love of the drink and its accompanying frenzy. On the third day, Walter, whose well-disciplined brain had begun to reel and evince signs of insubordination, fancied that the task assigned him was nearly accomplished, for Bloomfield had fallen into one of the last stages of maudlin and helpless intoxication.

The prostration of mind and body was completed, and, as Walter rightly judged, any further persistence in the course they were pursuing might be attended with fatal consequences. He therefore exerted himself to have Bloomfield conveyed home, whither the pair arrived at about ten o'clock at night. Bloomfield was placed on a sofa until his medical attendant should have seen him; and Walter, after delivering himself of a hasty message to the countess, to the effect that he would see her early in the morning, hastened away. The truth was, that although he had skilfully concealed his own condition from the servants, he was well convinced that he could not as effectually do so with the countess; and, as he thought the explanation had better be deferred until he was unmistakeably *compos-mentis*, he took a rather precipitate departure. And there lay my Lord Bloomfield, the last male descendant of an illustrious house, gasping, foaming, and stuttering, like some human monster at his midnight devotions in the kennel. It was a pitiable sight, from which even his menials shrank with a sensation of loathing. His hair hung in thick, sloppy masses over his deadly-white brows and sunken eyes, round which the tokens of his Casino quarrel had now deepened into the livid hue that marks the brawler and blackguard, and imparted to his appearance something repelling and disgusting. He was perfectly helpless, and the faculty of speech was rapidly deserting him altogether. The countess, who had been made acquainted with the fact of his arrival, stepped into the room where he was, but hurried out of it again, after casting one look at him, as if some poisonous reptile had met her view. A powerful loathing, mingled with scorn, crept over her, as she recollected that she had once lain in his besom—his, the *drunkard's*—the *thing* so enervated and detestable, that, in her agitation, she could not find a more expressive term by which to designate him. So intense were her emotions, that her frame quivered again; and, in her passion, she was about to invoke the imprecations of Providence upon his head; but a visit from her husband's medical attendant seemed to devote all her attention to the announcement of his being in imminent danger.

"Die!" she ejaculated, more surprised at the moment than shocked; "do men in—in that state die?"

"Frequently. But do not be alarmed; although there is danger—and great danger, too—in this case, I don't see that anything dreadfully serious is to be apprehended. Nevertheless, he will have a long fit of sickness, and, as the crisis draws near, you must be prepared for the most distressing symptoms. Let him now slumber as long as he can; and, above all, should he wake, only let him have what I have prescribed —no spirits or wines—he will crave for them."

"Die!" said the countess to herself, after the departure of the man of bodily science; "and in his prime; and such a death—oh, no—no! there's madness in the thought—and I was about to curse—to invoke the most fearful maledictions on his head! God must be good, for he has spared me that crime."

The idea of losing the man to whom she had, in halcyon days, not very remote, surrendered her virgin person, was too oppressive for her sustaining indignation at the profligacy of his conduct, and she burst into tears. Love—all divine, immortal love—sprang like bright streams of unpolluted light from the recesses of her heart, and, in the radiance diffused throughout her soul, she saw not the shadow of her husband. The bridegroom of her youth leapt into her presence, and such a gush of sweet, warm sensations stole upon her troubled senses, that all anger, all resentment—every sentiment hostile to her affection for him, vanished—they fell from her eyes in a long-continued chrystal shower. In that sweet mood she knelt and prayed—offered up such a prayer as only a loving woman can, for the man to whom she has yielded up the sovereignty of her affections.

Bloomfield, meanwhile, was carefully put in bed, with instructions to be watched during the whole of the night. He did not, however, awake until the morning; and the countess, restrained by the advice of the physician, did not venture into his presence.

"It would only irritate him; and, as the worst is to come, it would be cruelty to aggravate the symptoms."

The countess did not comprehend the exact meaning of all this—for the reports brought to her of the condition of her husband were that he was quiet and rational; but she construed it into a command, and obeyed. Bloomfield himself was so calm and collected, that he had not the remotest suspicion that he was unwell, or, indeed, beyond a slight headache, had anything the matter with him. He was soon to be undeceived. The flames of the hell he had so industriously fed were soon to break forth, and temporarily overwhelm him in their fury.

He felt much refreshed—even vivacious; but there was a languor in his movements, and a dead fire in his eye, which did not support his sanguine pretensions. Strange to say, the desire for drink had vanished—he had exhausted his appetite. Towards noon, feeling depressed, he tried to sleep, but could not. He then endeavoured to read, but the words appeared an unintelligible mass of letters, and he laid the book down, attributing the visual weakness to the pugilistic reminiscences on his face. A cigar then tempted him; but, after two or three whiffs, he threw it away in disgust. He afterwards applied himself to the arrangement of his books and papers, and a strange feeling of suspicion came over him. He placed everything he fancied belonged exclusively to himself under lock; and, having put the keys carefully aside, forgot them, and began to conceal the money he had in his possession in different parts of the sitting-room. After he had disarranged almost everything in the apartment, he seemed more satisfied; and, throwing himself into a seat, gazed intently into the fire. Presently he turned quickly round, and, looking towards the door, said, rather angrily:

"What do you want?"

There was no one there, nor could he hear the slightest sound; for a profound silence reigned throughout the establishment.

"Go away!" he exclaimed, peevishly; and, rising from his seat, he fancied the action had driven the unwelcome visitor away. After he had been seated for a few minutes, he thought he saw a multitude of the most horrid faces grinning at him out of the fire; and, exasperated at what he considered such insolence, he stirred it with a vigour which sent the red-hot cinders flying all over the room. Then he cooled down a little, and shaded his eyes with his hands, but quickly removed the obstruction in horror, for he fancied that rats and mice were crawling over them, and the sleeves of his coat. This startling incident caused him to gaze around with terror-stricken looks; and, upon directing his glance to a remote corner of the room, he thought he saw the glaring eye-balls and frothy mouth of a mad dog! Hydrophobia, when in health, was one of his greatest dreads; and he uttered a cry, which quickly brought his alarmed attendant into his presence.

"Don't go near it!" he exclaimed, as he half pushed the amazed man into the opposite corner of the room; "it's mad! Bring me my pistols—a gun—a knife—anything."

He could say no more; for, with a shiver, he sank exhausted into the chair beside him. The man directed a frightened look at his pale, distorted countenance and inflamed eye-balls, and, with a shudder, thought him insane. However, not wishing to alarm the house, and subduing his fears, he pencilled a note to the doctor, and, ringing the bell for another servant, requested it to be delivered immediately. The interval was a dreadful one, for his lordship grew worse; for as his mental prostration increased, so did his terrors. He swore the room was swarming with rats and mice, and that they nibbled at his toes, and crept up his clothes to fasten their teeth in his throat. Then he saw the horrible vision of the mad dog scattering the vermin right and left; and he clung to the man for protection with a ringing cry, which, to his excited sense of hearing, sounded very much like the barking of the animal to which his lordship so shockingly referred. A remark, *en passant*.

It has been observed, when the mind is reduced to this deplorable state of delirium, that the prejudices and weaknesses of the individual when in a state of health became stronger and more vivid. The dread of hydrophobia is one of the most powerful entertained by the human mind, and, when exasperated, becomes hideously tormenting. The idea of madness—horrible madness! and the figure of an enraged, ugly dog are continually before the mind's eye, and the sufferer, trembling and perspiring at every pore, is unable to drive it away! Lord Bloomfield detested rats and mice, and it has been seen that the idea that he was infested by them had assumed a strong and ineradicable shape. Thus did his antipathies become the punishers of his excesses; and it would appear to have been wisely ordained, that for every self-inflicted injury to the mind, it, by its own power of exacting vengeance, subjects the individual to that species of punishment of which he had formed a morbid conception when in health.

When the medical gentleman arrived he found all his previous anticipations completely fulfilled. His lordship was labouring under the early symptoms of delirium tremens; having prescribed opiates, he directed that two able-bodied men should watch by his bed-side during the whole night. The countess, screened from his view by the bed-curtains, insisted upon remaining; and, as she listened for an hour or so to his incoherent remarks and wild cries, the scene contrasted so darkly with those that brightened her early wedded life, that she gave vent to copious floods of tears. The night wore on, and at last the wretched man fell into a deep, groaning slumber, and dreamed a dream, the memory of which he ever afterwards recalled with a shudder.

THE DRUNKARD'S DREAM.

He thought he was once more in the pure, unstained element of his boyhood, and that the stars crowded on his sight thick as daisies; but that one stood by his side with a chalice in his hand, from which he was bidden to drink to the Queen of Heaven.

"Drink, and so wash away the scales that hide beauty from thy eyes."

The youth drank, and a thrill, like that of some divine ecstacy, shot through his frame. His vision became keener, and over the plain he saw dancing towards him a lightly-clad nymph. Her eyes had a strange light in them, and, as she wreathed her arms round his enchanted body, her warm breath mingled with his, and created such a delicious fury in his mind, that he returned her embrace, and together they wantoned it all a summer's day on the soft carpet, that heaved like a couch to their wild boundings and delirious transports. Presently stars and daisies vanished, a virgin moon peeped out for a moment, and then, quenched in a wilderness of flying clouds, left a darkness which sealed up the lovers' eyes in slumber, as they reclined side by side, with an arm about each other, thrown on a couch of springing mossiness. In the morning the vision of his wife-love had gone, and the daisies around him were crushed or drooping, as if in grief; and wherever he turned his gaze, a faint mist rose up before him.

"Drink," cried the form, "for it is only the merry heart that maketh itself and all things near it beautiful."

The youth obeyed, and lo! he found himself a man, and another, but more stately female form, stood before him, and enthralled his senses. The measure they trod was more stately, but the fire of their caresses burned more brightly, as, with lip glued to lip, they drank in from each other's flaming orbs the passion that gratifies its mad promptings only to create fiercer longings, and more insatiable cravings. Darker grew the face of nature to him after that night, for the cup was clutched day by day with greater relish; and more voluptuous forms dazzled and bewildered his blood-red imagination. The bacchanal song, and the wanton caress, hounded him on to wilder deeds; and his days and nights became blended into one. The daisies and the stars were drowned in the dull, red sea of desire, in which he laved like a strong swimmer in his glory; and the only friend he acknowledged, was the form by his side, with the gemmed cup of pleasure ever in its ready-proffered hand.

"Drink!" and he obeyed the high behest until lurid flames scorched his heart and brain; and he went through the darkness in which he moved like one in a dream. Fairy forms and bright eyes were ever at his command; but, as the darkness deepened, and the flames shot up more madly in his system, one by one they left him, and by-and-bye he was alone—alone on a wide, wide sea of horrible darkness!"

"Drink!" cried the form; but, lo! the chalice was empty, and he found himself seized by a hundred grim demons and mocking forms, with angel faces, but liquid harlot glances; and they hurried him to the judgment seat, to the vain, damning chorus of "Drink! drink! drink!"

"Behold thyself and thy doom!"

He looked, and beheld a hideous pit, in which struggled and shrieked millions of beings fashioned like himself, but fierce and savage with their gnawing, unappeased, and unappeasable habits. On the borders of this dreadful hole he saw himself in the grasp of a woman-fiend — Semiramis' self — who opened to him the temple of his body: it was empty—the fire-cup had withered and destroyed the ark of his earthly covenant.

"Burnt heart!" cried a dreadful voice,—"the drunkard's doom is the never-ceasing hell of his own desires and abused propensities. Hurl him into the pestilential lake of his living kindred, and there let him bide until his passions rave themselves hoarse for carnal food. Away with him! The stars and the daisies are to him extinguished for evermore. Such is the final doom of the burnt heart!"

A shout of savage laughter, mingled with the frightful songs of the mad, smote upon his ear, as he felt himself hurled over that horrid gulf; and he awoke to consciousness of his dream, but insensible to aught real around him,—for he was insane. Brain fever had now completed his prostration; and there he lay before his agonised wife, the wreck of all that she had esteemed as manly, noble, and pure.

Weeks rolled over before he returned to life, and the first word he uttered after the recovery of his faculties was—

"Violet!"

She was by his side, and impressed a sweet kiss on his wasted cheek.

"My wife—my darling wife!" "My husband!" and they fell into each other's embrace, and wept. From that hallowed moment the errors of the past became to them a sealed book of iniquity: all was forgiven—all was forgotten; they bathed themselves in the waters of charity and forbearance, and afterwards, when Bloomfield's health was perfectly re-established, he found, to his inexpressible rapture, that Violet—his own beautiful Violet! was the only really merry wife he had ever strained to his beating heart.

While this physical and moral convalescence was thus satisfactorily progressing, several events occurred to give it tone and stability; and not the least of these was the total severance of the vicious alliance between Jasper Sampson and Lord Bloomfield. His lordship was reclining in his easy chair, reading, an occupation he now much indulged in when the countess was not present, when Jasper entered unannounced. At the sight of that wicked man, an angry flush rose to his lordship's face, succeeded by one of pallor, as he recollected the dreadful scenes in which they had mingled, and the iniquities they together had practised.

"I thought I had given orders you were not to be admitted?" said his lordship, regarding Jasper with a look of horror and disgust."

"So you did; but where there's a will there's a way," was the saucy reply, as the fellow deliberately took a seat.

"What do you want?" inquired Bloomfield, applying his hand to the bell-rope.

"What do I want! Come, that's a pretty question to an old crony!" sneered Jasper. "What do I want! Come that's good—very!"

"Scoundrel!" exclaimed his lordship, his indignation mastering all his abhorrence.

"Fine names are for fine birds," said Jasper; "but they aint no manner of use to me. So, let's go to business at once."

"What in the name of heaven do you want?"

"Money."

"I have given you all I ever intended."

"You have been a good master—very; but I wants more for what I did. You aint a-going to suppose for what I did I am a-going to take the wages of a walley!"

"Horrible wretch! your hideous countenance makes me blush for my depravity. Begone, before I have you kicked out of the house!"

"Suppose I peaches on you," grinned Jasper,—"tells the countess and the aristocracy, and the shopmen and the people, what an uncommon nice lord you have been among the girls!"

Bloomfield, in his present nervous state, felt alarmed at this threat; but, after a moment's consideration, he determined on his mode of action. Ringing the bell, he requested Captain Morris—whom he had a shrewd guess was in the house—to wait upon him. The captain promptly answered the summons; and, as he was acquainted with the particulars of the odious connection between his lordship and Jasper, a few words explained the cause of the latter's presence with a bullying, menacing aspect. Walter's blood—never any of the coolest upon provocation—turned fiercely upon Jasper, and said to him:

"In this matter you will deal with me; so state what you want, and be brief."

Jasper bestowed upon him one of his looks of ferocious hatred, and became speechless with passion.

"We don't want a second hand in the business between me and his lordship," said he, at length; "I won't have it,—and, if I did, it shouldn't be you."

"My friend Morris, and none other, shall deal with you," exclaimed his lordship, excitedly.

"Speak villain, or leave the room!" cried Walter, his anger rising at the remembrance of the plot laid for his destruction.

"Well, if it must be, it must," said Jasper; "and, as you—the curses and the spit of hell be upon you all your life!—I say, as you seem to understand it all, don't you think I am entitled to five thousand pounds?"

"Five thousand pounds!" ejaculated Walter, amazed at the man's audacity.

"Five thousand," coolly repeated Jasper; "and I won't take a farthing less."

"Monstrous! Five thousand pounds for being a discarded pimp!" said Walter.

"Pimp in your teeth, Master Captain!" growled Jasper; "and keep your tongue in your teeth, or I'll split on you one of these fine days!"

"Paltry, contemptible wretch!" exclaimed Walter, "it is only my contempt that restrains me from calling in a police officer, and giving you into custody for attempting to murder me."

"Murder!" said Jasper, paling; for that word, uttered publicly, always appalled him. In his days of robust manhood he perpetrated a deed, the naming of which clung even to his seared and gnarled conscience.

"Yes, murder, ruffian!" said Walter, following up his advantage; "and not the first you have attempted, and by no means the only one you succeeded in!"

"Only once!" stammered Jasper.

"Hold!" thundered Walter; "we are no father confessors, neither do we wish to be instruments in the punishment of so detestable a thing! You bear the marks of a woman's just vengeance, and you cannot be plunged into a worse hell than the one you are in! So begone in peace."

"Give me four thousand, and I'll never say a word about any of his lordship's doings?" said Jasper, quailing before the steady demeanour of the gallant soldier.

"Not a penny," was the firm refusal.

"Three thousand?"

"Leave the room."

"Two thousand?"

"Not to save you from the gallows!"

"Gallows! What do you mean? A thousand, then—well five hundred—four—"

"Begone!" roared Walter, exasperated by the fellow's pertinacity.

"I'll tell all about Mrs. Bond, Alice Lumley, Agnes Rathbone, Amy Jackson, Ellen ——"

His further enunciation was summarily suspended by Walter seizing him by the collar, and forcing him from the room, then along the hall, and finally into the street, where he left him, after a parting salute with a boot, which made every bone in the rascal's body shake and rattle. These little demonstrations invariably create a crowd; and as Jasper, stunned and overpowered by the unexpected result of the interview, stood in the midst of one, he raised his clenched hand, and, shaking it at the residence from which he had been so ignominiously expelled, accompanied the action with some muttered denunciations of his crushed and broken, but not half-destroyed wrath. His countenance at this moment was so hideously ugly and revolting, that the mob on all sides fell away from him, alarmed at the spectacle, and he stole away like one smitten by a curse.

"A good riddance," said his lordship, much relieved by Walter's prompt mode of dealing with such a character.

"I don't think he will ever trouble you again," was Walter's assuring remark; "for I rather think I have alarmed him on the score of the safety of his wretched carcase. Hush—here comes the countess!"

It was that now incomparable lady, as glowing and radiant as a rosy summer's morn. Her reconciliation with her husband, and his reformation, had considerably enhanced the beauty of her charms. The smiles and gaiety of her happy early wifehood had returned to her, and Walter, as he gazed at her, thought he had never seen a lovelier creature. When the heart of a woman beats to noble music, the face never clouds or wrinkles.

"Walter, my friend," said his lordship, extending his hand; "my earliest and truest friend, there is only one thing I fancy necessary to render the felicity of Violet and myself complete."

"Name it: if possible, you can surely command it," was the somewhat agitated answer.

"Lucy—have you forgotten her, Walter?" inquired the countess, with silvery accents.

Now, although Captain Walter Morris was as erratic, wild, heedless, assuring, and reckless as a confirmed rake ought to be, or rather is, necessarily, he could blush—and excessively, too—when the occasion suited; and, on this, he did so very deeply, to the no small amusement of the countess, who was tolerably well acquainted with the nature of his late habits.

"Walter, why don't you speak?" said his lordship, as he fondly pressed his wife's hand within his own.

"I have not forgotten Miss Villiers," said Walter, recovering from his confusion; "I never shall; but since I lost my commission, I never presumed to think of her, but as a friend. I have been guilty of many follies, but never of an act so base and criminal, as to wish to take a lovely young girl from her quiet home, her delicious virgin repose and purity, and expose her to the chances of fortune, with a remarkably good prospect of falling into the dreary company of her foster-child—poverty."

"A sermon! and from a soldier, too!" cried her ladyship. But tears trembled on her eye-lashes; for she well knew the noble heart of the man who had given her his first and purest love.

Bloomfield shook Walter warmly by the hand; at a sign from him, the countess left the room, and, in a few seconds, reappeared, leading her trembling sister by the hand.

"Lucy!" exclaimed Walter, blushing and paling alternately.

"Never be afraid, sis.," said the countess, gaily, as she led the agitated girl up to where the soldier

stood. "Restore to your deliverer what he never should have lost."

Lucy timidly presented an unsealed packet to Walter, which he opened in nervous haste, and then, in glad surprise, pressed its contents to his lips.

"My commission!" he exclaimed; "and brought to my thankful heart by an angel!"

He sank down gracefully on his knee, and raised the long, white hand of the beautiful Lucy to his lips. She did not withdraw it; and when he arose, and their eyes met, the expression in each was so full of love and trusting confidence, that Walter drew her towards him, and folded her in a long and passionate embrace. Abashed at such boldness, they both started from each other's arms, and looked around them; but Bloomfield and his weeping countess had disappeared.

"Lucy—my own sweet Lucy!" murmured Walter.

"Walter!" she faintly uttered; their glad eyes met once more, and he led her to a seat; and they talked and looked, as only true lovers can, until they had exchanged the primal vows of eternal fidelity, which bind woman to man in the golden link which connects earth with heaven.

CHAPTER XXVI.
THE CONCLUSION.

THE world we live in requires to be looked fairly in the face before we can estimate it at its real value. We may study its partial contributions to the stock of character in its moral and useful efforts to make itself distinguished for valuable exertions in the cause of human progress; but for the real prompting features we must dive far beneath the surface, and, like miners, deal with the strata as we are instructed or desired, to render their products valuable to the inquirer. During the progress of this narrative, the compiler has had to deal with the vulgarities and perversions of passions; he has had to fulfil the difficult duty of showing virtue to be more brilliant by its contrast with vice, and at the same time to make the narrative so acceptable to popular taste as to be readable. In all this he has been actuated by an undiluted desire to contribute something towards the stock of physical knowledge; and, without any beating about the bush, he congratulates himself that he has partially succeeded in his design. He has shown that female virtue, to be pure and intact in its purity, must be trained to be so; that moral training is useless without physical training; and that, however laudable may be our exertions in the propagation of either religious convictions, or moral sentiment, they are absurd expenditures of industry, unless the functions and innate partialities of the material portion of the human constitution be taken into consideration. The human being is but a brute animal without cultivation; and why, in this respect, should affectation, and a fierce and implacable sensual worship, endeavour to place woman without the pale of the axiom? Moved, and being moved, by the same physical and spiritual causes as man, her individual responsibility is as great, her summary of conduct as justly open to criticism, and the whole machinery of her character as liable to be deranged and put out of order. This, in plain language, has been the philosophy by which the writer has been imbued; and if he has not rendered a just and equitable account of his lucubrations, blame the theme and not the compiler—author he never has presumed to call himself.

The "Merry Wives of London" has been his text,

their frailties and virtues his subject-matter, and sundry adventures of the high-born and low-born, the honest and dishonest, his embellishing features. May the shadow of the truth-teller or traducer, however he may be esteemed, never grow less. He has taken a portion of the female world as he found it, and, in the endeavour to do ample justice to both good and bad, satisfied his own conscience that he has not inflicted even the tail of the shadow of an injury upon a single individual or class. The *denouement* of his narrative will unquestionably substantiate his assertion, and prove that, in discarding a gross, familiar hypocrisy, he has done justice to the roses that distribute liberal showers of their perfume over the face of creation. So, without further circumlocution he proceeds to his duty.

The separate fortunes of the merry wife Mrs. Smythe, the queen of voluptuaries, Mrs. Wriggles, her sworn foe, Dr. Wriggles, the surgeon and the Jesuit, and the remaining characters of this veracious and unobtrusively intituled narrative, have, therefore, to be strictly dealt with. So, with the reader's most gracious permission, the context of the narrative will be resumed in the singular apartment of that most mysterious of sexagenarian mortals, Dr. Wriggles.

He was alone—unless the society of the bear, Leoline, may be taken in contradiction of the assertion—and engaged in his usual and, apparently, everlasting devotion to chemical science. A retort, with glowing and bubbling contents was held in his hands, and he was employed in a nicely-critical examination of its contents, when a summons at the door withdrew his attention. The slide was opened with the usual caution, and the brightly-blooming face of Mrs. Smythe appeared in the aperture. To admit her and provide her with a seat was the work of an instant; and, after the doctor had placed himself contiguous to her, he announced that he was prepared to listen to what she had to say.

"You remember your promise?" was the opening remark of the lady.

"I do," responded Wriggles; "the child."

"Have you discovered it?" inquired Mrs. Smythe, labouring under an agitation which, despite all her assurance, she was unable to subdue.

"I have," was the laconic response.

"And I shall see it, press it to my bosom, kiss it, and hear it call me mother?"

"You shall."

"Oh, joy, as great as the yielding action that called it into being!" was the softly-murmured exclamation of the proud woman of the world, the lady of fashion, and the merry wife of a husband who stultified his conjugal dignity by his own beastly, accommodating connivance at his own dishonour.

"Madam," said the stoical doctor, "do not give way to transports which may be premature. Are you ready to fulfil the conditions I shall propose?"

"Conditions—reward you mean?" promptly answered Mrs. Smythe.

"No, madam, conditions," replied Dr. Wriggles, in calm, measured tones; "and they are such, that unless you subscribe to them you will never embrace your child."

"Name them?" requested Mrs. Smythe, impatiently.

"The first is, that you pay me down five thousand pounds."

"What for, in the name of goodness?"

"For the education, careful training, attention to the development of every faculty, and complete extension of the moral, mental, and physical faculties of your child."

Mrs. Smythe looked her amazement at this erudite particularisation of a pecuniary demand; and the doctor, to relieve her, said, with less appearance of levity:

"My dear madam, I am entitled to something for the preservation of the secret. I knew whom you were all along."

"Indeed?"

"Yes. Ever since the moment the poor girl came into the world, I knew who was the mother; so that I am entitled to compensation for the manner in which I preserved my trust; and, in the next place, having kept my word in that respect, I have a claim for a careful, affectionate nurture of the poor thing—for bringing her up tenderly, and imparting to her mind faculties, which will enable her, when plunged into the vortex of society, to avoid the quicksands and slightly-covered pitfalls which swallow up such numbers of your sex."

The mother, half subdued, murmured her thanks, and, in the next breath, admitted her willingness to submit to the demand.

"What is your next claim?" she asked.

"That on the day you succeed to the strictly-entailed estates of your uncle, you pay me or my heirs five-and-twenty thousand pounds," replied the doctor, in solemn, serious accents.

Mrs. Smythe started from her seat, as much amazed at the amount of the claim as the revelation.

"Madam," said the doctor, observing her amazement, "I know all—I am acquainted with your uncle—I knew him well—he is a loyal gentleman, and a true Catholic. I know you well—your early school adventures, your loves, your marriage, your amusements, your everything, but one, that belongs to you; but rest assured—in my keeping all your secrets are safe. I am a true *authorised* son of the true Son!"

These asseverations, coupled with the peculiar meaning of the latter, which she well understood, overwhelmed her with mingled astonishment and disquietude; and she was prepared to subscribe to any terms the Jesuit might propose for her acceptance.

"Do you," she inquired, "belong to our—our——" she hesitated.

"I am a son of the only true Church," said the doctor, proudly; "one of its ministers—to you I may say a propagandist—and you must know, that in my keeping, all its daughters are as safe as if they were in heaven!"

Utterly vanquished by this announcement, Mrs. Smythe made a low obeisance to the Father, and placed herself entirely at his disposal.

"Sign this document," said he; "it is a mortgage on your real estates, to which the trustees, being Catholics—one of them a priest in orders—will undoubtedly consent; and, upon payment of the five thousand pounds in cash, your child shall be delivered to you."

Mrs. Smythe looked at him for a few seconds fixedly, as if endeavouring to ascertain whether he was deceiving her; but his eye was as firm and cold as marble; and, as if guessing the meaning of her scrutiny, he said:

"Doubt me not: true daughters of our faith never mistrust their pastors. But, to relieve your maternal anxiety, I swear to you on the Evangelists that the money you place at my disposal is intended for, and will inevitably be devoted to, the service of our persecuted church in Britain. She needs it much, and

your name shall not be forgotten in the holy recognition of the gift."

Mrs. Smythe was a true Roman Catholic—the leaven of superstition was heavy within her: and, upon hearing this explanation from the doctor, she unhesitatingly subscribed her signature to the documents which the wily priest placed before her.

"My child!" she exclaimed; "let me see my child, and I shall be satisfied! And believe me, father, I think for so great a boon the sacrifice is slight, slight indeed! For what is wealth to love? divine, superhuman love! Oh, give me my child!"

"Daughter," said the surgeon-priest, "you have done well, and shall be rewarded. Remain here for a few minutes, and, as strangers are apt to intrude, and be dangerous, accept the guardianship of the most faithful friend I have yet found on this side of the grave. Here, Leoline, Leoline!" he shouted, and the huge bear crawled out, and placed herself, in obedience to his command, in a crouching attitude, at the feet of Mrs. Smythe.

"Fear nothing," said the doctor, as he noticed her perturbed look; "but, should you be molested, call out the name Laurentine Valois, and Leoline here will spring to your assistance."

With these rather ominous instructions the doctor disappeared through one of the doors of his singular study, leaving Mrs. Smythe in no very enviable or placid state of mind, although sustained by the hope of a speedy reunion with her long-lost and long-neglected child!

The suspense of the mother was not procrastinated beyond the few minutes which the doctor required for tutoring and preparing the child for her new duties and position. Nervous with anxiety, she listened for the creak of the doctor's boots; and perhaps in that brief interval felt more acute apprehension than ever she had done at the most critical periods of her life. There was a powerful struggle in her bosom between maternal love and the dread of discovery, and its consequent exposure and shame. There was also an oppressive sense of parental neglect, which made her almost fear to look her child in the face. Presently all these contending emotions were hushed, as the door through which the doctor had vanished silently opened, and he again stood before her, leading by the hand the young clairvoyante—the Fanny introduced to the reader in the early portion of this work. She was well and tastefully attired; and as she earnestly regarded Mrs. Smythe, the striking resemblance between the features of the mother and child was unmistakeably apparent. There was the same large dark eye, the same red lips, and ardent, handsome nose, the same luxuriant, raven hair; and, to make the likeness stronger, the same firm, gliding, and, withal, queenly gait. Both regarded each other without speaking, so agitated were they by the powerful magnetic sympathy that drew them together. At length Mrs. Smythe broke the silence, by turning an imploring glance upon Dr. Wriggles.

"This is your child," said he; "and may she prove as dutiful to you as she has been to me!"

"What proofs have you?" inquired Mrs. Smythe. "My heart tells me she is mine; but a mother's fondness pleads for other sureties of the fact."

"Do you not read a copy of yourself in every lineament of her face?" said the doctor.

"I do—I do. The sight of her makes me go back to the time when I was as young as she is," replied Mrs. Smythe. "Eighteen years seem to have fallen from my head in her presence. But can you not fully satisfy me?"

"I can," was the calm reply. "Do you remember the last words I addressed to you in this very room, fourteen years ago?"

"I have a faint impression that you said something about a mark—a—a—but I have forgotten the precise words," said Mrs. Smythe.

"Then I will refresh your memory," replied the doctor; "and what I said was this: the day will come when your heart will yearn for the child you commit to my care; and in order that you may be assured of the identity, I will imprint the symbol of your faith on its bosom, and call it, as you desire, Fanny."

At the mention of her name the young girl started, and made a movement towards where her mother sat; the latter at the same instant rose, and, starting up to her child, tremblingly removed her dress a little: on the breast was disclosed to her the blue sign of the cross. Mrs. Smythe's first action was to kiss this token of her creed, and then to fold her child to her heart in one long and passionate embrace. Tears of mingled joy and grief at the same time burst from her eyes, and the girl, yielding to an uncontrollable emotion, returned her caresses, and murmured the holy name of mother.

"Mother!" sobbed the frail woman—"mother! I never knew, until this moment, what magic there is in the word. Mother!" she repeated, as she raised the young girl's head from her bosom, and gazed long and earnestly into the large jet eyes, that looked into her own with an expression of unutterable fondness.

"Mother! bless you for the word, my child! Yes, I am your mother, but have yet to prove that I deserve the honour. This long absence will make you dearer to me than all the pleasures and treasures in the world. Will you forgive me for being away from you all this time? Will you love me?"

Fanny's only reply was a warm embrace, and a kiss, the first the mother had ever received from her abandoned offspring, and one which thrilled through her to the remotest nerve. The doctor witnessed this reunion of mother and child with his habitual stoicism; and, when Mrs. Smythe had become more collected, suggested the propriety of their immediate departure.

"Mrs. Wriggles," said he, significantly, "is indisposed to part with the child."

"What for?" inquired Mrs. Smythe.

"Because she hates you."

"Hates me!"

"Even so; and you would do well to avoid her. She is as powerful as she is vindictive."

"I never gave her any cause. Besides, I do not know Mrs. Wriggles."

The doctor indulged in one of his peculiar smiles; and, for the safety and promotion of some plans he had in view with reference to Mrs. Smythe, proceeded to astound her by a terrible revelation.

"Are you ignorant of the fact, that Mrs. Wriggles is the person who brought you to me?"

Mrs. Smythe blushed, and was silent.

"The gipsy who waylaid you, and the incomparable Mrs. Wriggles, are one and the same; and, as I perceive you know it, I have only to tell you that she had a deep and settled object in introducing you to me."

"Indeed!" said Mrs. Smythe, surprised. "May I inquire what it was?"

"Revenge!" replied the doctor, coolly. "She bears to you and all your race an invincible hatred."

At this announcement Mrs. Smythe, who was by no means a timid woman, drew her child closer to her side, and requested an explanation of such an incomprehensible circumstance.

"Your maiden name was Fitzherbert, I believe."

"It was."

"Can you recal to your memory any of the reminiscences of your family?"

"Not many. All but myself and uncle died when I was young."

"Did you never hear any stories concerning them?"

"O yes. Ours is one of the most ancient families in the country; and our traditions are very numerous."

"And dark and gloomy?" added the doctor.

"Some of them," replied Mrs. Smythe, crossing herself, as in infancy she had been taught to, when any of the misdeeds of her ancestors were referred to in her presence.

There was a pause, which the doctor broke by saying:

"You have heard, probably, the tale about one Harriet Fitzherbert, the daughter of one of your uncles?"

"I have, but only from gossips; the name was never allowed to be mentioned when I was a young girl at home. I can well recollect my father's gloomy look when I asked him who she was, and what she had done to make her a bogie to us children."

"Do you recollect any of the particulars of what was communicated to you?" inquired the doctor.

Mrs. Smythe hesitated, as well she might, for the story was one she had, in some respects, faithfully copied in her conduct.

"She brought scandal and disgrace into the family, I believe," said she, at length.

"She fell in love, and had a little child; is not that the truth of the affair?" said the doctor, laughingly.

"I heard it was something of the kind," stammered Mrs. Smythe.

"And for that very natural but perhaps naughty act, she was driven forth to ignominy, poverty, exile and infamy?" said the doctor, severely.

Mrs. Smythe was silent.

"Yes; but for yielding to the natural promptings of a warm, and imperfectly-trained organisation, she was thrust forth to the mercy of the pitiless world, with curses on her head, and the ban of her kith, to hound her on to pollution and death!" continued the doctor, who had a motive for fastening himself as firmly as possible in her sympathy; and this he knew he could do effectually by affecting commiseration for the fate of an unfortunate ancestress, whose errors had been of a description kindred to some of her own. The subject was too painful for the lady to be disposed to be communicative, so the doctor proceeded: "You probably never heard what became of that Harriet Fitzherbert?"

"Never. It was reported that she died by her own hand, and that in the long winter nights her spirit used to be seen in the park, near the old hall."

"She did not die: the story is the mere invention of the superstitious peasantry; and, moreover, she is not dead yet!" said the doctor.

Mrs. Smythe shuddered at this announcement; and, with an ashy countenance, asked what grounds there were for such an extraordinary statement.

"The very best in the world," replied the doctor; "for they are neither more nor less than the presence of the party herself, alive and well in body!"

"Impossible! why the affair occurred more than half a century ago," exclaimed Mrs. Smythe.

"Not so much," replied the doctor; "only forty-seven years ago; and at that time Harriet Fitzherbert was only seventeen years of age, so that now she would only be sixty, which is no very great age."

Mrs. Smythe regarded the doctor with some awe, and tremulously desired to know how he had learned so much about her family. The doctor evaded the question, and asked her to endeavour to recollect whether she had not heard that Harriet Fitzherbert had sworn a mortal hatred to her family, at the time they banished her.

"Yes," answered Mrs. Smythe; "my old nurse once told me that, as Harriet was being thrust from the hall-door for the last time, she turned round and cursed her brothers, and uttered a fearful vow to involve them all, from the eldest to the youngest, wives and children, in one common and terrible destruction. It is also said she appeared at the hall some few years afterwards, and uttered a still more terrible malediction."

"Do you think her curses were ever realised?" said the doctor, regarding her steadfastly.

"I don't know," answered Mrs. Smythe, a solemn dread creeping over her, as she listened to such sinister interrogatories.

"You and your bed-ridden uncle are the last of your race, are you not?" inquired the doctor.

"Yes."

"Did not the majority of your family die suddenly? Wives in their husbands' arms—children in the playground—fathers in the prime of life, over the wine-cup, or at the festive board?"

"They did: the end of all my family has been sudden, and the circumstance has passed into a proverb in our neighbourhood. 'Die young, like the Fitzes,' is the common saying among the peasantry."

"Exactly so. But were no suspicions of foul play ever entertained?"

"Never that I know. But it was said that the bogie Harriet always appeared about the hall, the day any one of the family died."

"Exactly so. And is it not also said that the brother now alive was the only member of the family who pitied her?"

"It was."

"And wherefore did he not die like the rest?"

Amazed at such a question, Mrs. Smythe looked up wonderingly in the doctor's face.

"Why," continued the doctor, "because he was exempted from the curse. He spoke words of comfort to the stricken girl, and she blessed instead of cursing him. All the others, root and branch, she devoted to the sacrifice. And now let me ask you—was not the curse of the blighted heart fulfilled?"

"Terribly!" shuddered Mrs. Smythe.

"You and your child yet live," resumed the doctor.

"Whom and what have we to fear?" said Mrs. Smythe, an awful oppression weighing on her spirits.

"The vengeance of the abused Harriet Fitzherbert!" was the solemn reply. "You are destined to be her last victim. The child's life has only been preserved by her to render your pangs more bitter!"

"And this horrible woman yet lives, say you?" exclaimed Mrs. Smythe, starting to her feet, and uttering a scream of terror.

"She does," replied the doctor; "and in this house."

"This house?"

"Aye, this house; for know that Harriet Fitzherbert and the so-called Mrs. Wriggles are one," said the doctor, slowly.

This ominous announcement made Mrs. Smythe's flesh creep with horror; cold drops of perspiration stood on her brow, and, after gasping for a second or two, she fainted. Her newly-recovered daughter, with a wild scream, flung herself on the insensible form, and it was with some difficulty the doctor could tear her away, so as to enable him to administer restoratives.

It was nearly an hour before she recovered, and when she did, Mrs. Smythe frantically implored the doctor to allow her to leave the house forthwith.

"Your danger is greater out of this house than in it, for your enemy uses a subtle, active, unseen agent, in her work of death!" said the doctor.

"Explain your meaning, I implore you, by this hallowed relic?" entreated Mrs. Smythe.

"Poison!" whispered the doctor.

Mrs. Smythe started, as if stung by an asp, and, throwing her arms around her daughter, strained her in a convulsive embrace.

"Listen to me," said the doctor. "Take your child with you, and leave England at once—this night. Have you a male friend upon whom you can depend?"

Mrs. Smythe thought of her paramour, Horace Singleton, of whom she had begun to be doatingly fond, and promptly answered in the affirmative.

"Lover or friend," said the doctor, laughingly, "it's all the same—the church is indulgent; but away with you at once. Go to Paris, and remain, where I will instruct you, in concealment, until you hear from me. This is necessary, because my amiable spouse has agents all over Europe."

Mrs. Smythe murmured her thanks; and, from her manner, the doctor, to his immense satisfaction, saw that he had gained a complete ascendancy over her mind.

The adieus of Fanny and the old man were brief, but sincere, for he had always entertained a partiality for her; the stronger, perhaps, because he had reserved her for this little bit of retaliation on the death-dealing Mrs. Wriggles. The farewell between the young girl and the bear was more affecting, for the child parted from her rough companion with bitter tears and deep sobs. Indeed her mother had to appeal to her newly-awakened love, before she could be induced to leave the side of her old play-mate.

Mrs. Smythe received her final instructions as to her concealment in Paris, together with an epistle from the doctor, written in a mysterious cypher; after giving him a solemn promise to follow his advice to the letter, he gave her his blessing, and, glad to escape from that dread abode, she hurried away. A cab soon carried her home, where she packed up all her jewellery and valuables, provided herself with the cash at her banker's and in her own possession, which altogether was upwards of ten thousand pounds, the fruits of her savings, and then hastened to the lodgings of Horace Singleton. A few words were sufficient to explain to that energetic individual the reason and the necessity for instant departure; and, as it did not much matter to him what part of the world he lived in, he was prepared to accompany her anywhere she liked.

"All explanations can be given on the road," said he, gaily, as he packed up his luggage, and, in an incredibly short space of time, had the mother and child conveyed to the London Bridge Station, where a special train was soon procured, and the trio were speedily on their way to Folkestone, at the dashing rate of forty miles an hour.

"Mine—mine!" chuckled Doctor Wriggles, as he rubbed his hands, and quickly paced his apartment; "and now my only difficulty is to pacify Jackina, *alias* Mrs. Wriggles, *alias* Harriet Fitzherbert, the most spiteful, vindictive, cruel, clever, useful old woman ever I met with, or heard of! Ah! a knock! Who are you, I wonder!"

It was Jasper Sampson, upon whose countenance there sat a more than ordinary gloom and repulsiveness; the traces of several scars tended in no slight degree to heighten the horror of his visage. The doctor regarded him askance, in much the same manner as a superior fiend would regard a lesser one. He spoke roughly to him, and seemed to intimate that the period had arrived when their connection should cease. To be candid, the doctor was one of those prudent men who never like to have near them any one whom they have injured. He knew that if Jasper dared he would amply avenge the mutilation he had received at his hands; and that conviction had induced him to wish that the temptation should be lessened by a total separation. Besides, the doctor, with the funds he now had at his disposal, had resolved upon playing a higher game in the world, and selecting more appropriate agents than those he had hitherto been in the habit of employing. Jasper was too vulgar to be of use to him, and his horrible lust presented an insurmountable barrier to his being intrusted with missions of a delicate character. Every way it appeared desirable that the connection should cease; but, as the doctor was only potent in superior knowledge and cunning, he thought it necessary for his personal safety not to provoke his aversion too far by any violent exhibitions of repugnance. However, in the presence of Leoline, whom he had studiously trained to be his protector, he allowed himself a license in which in her absence he did not indulge.

"What do you want?" said he, gruffly.

Jasper looked at him in some surprise, and quite as surlily answered:

"Revenge!"

"On whom?"

"Everybody."

"Tush! are you going to turn mad bull, and dash your brains out against some wall?"

"I have left Bloomfield House. I was kicked out by a man I hate!"

"Captain Morris, was it not? I have heard all about it, so don't tease me with a long story! What do you want? Speak, for I have two or three important affairs to attend to."

Jasper felt inclined to strangle him, but the presence of the bear nipped his very amiable intention in the bud.

"Being out of berth, what am I to do?" said he, moderating his tone.

"Do, de?" exclaimed the doctor; "'pon my soul I don't know, unless you turn Methodist preacher!"

"D——n! Besides, I abominate the snivelling ——s."

"Can't you tease the women? there are plenty of opportunities, for your religious ladies, as they are called, are horridly randy; and you, with your devilish tricks, might punish their amorousness a little?"

"Not a bad idea; but how can I do it, when the very sight of a woman makes me as wild as a caged beast?"

"That may be avoided. I will give you a recipe for the cooler you have been taking, so that when you want it you may purchase it at any chemist's shop."

"Will you though?" exclaimed Jasper, brightening up at the proposal; "then I'm d—d if I don't turn 'spounder of the word, and gammon the men, and send the women stark staring mad! My eye, won't I make a lot of w——s out of my congregation! Curse the whole breed! anything to sarve 'em out!"

The doctor handed him the promised recipe, and, as he did so, said:

"Have you made up the money you were talking about yet?"

"I have," replied Jasper; "and it's all in the funds for my kinchin when I'm gone, and I shall have the interest while I live."

"Ten thousand?" said the doctor.

Jasper nodded an affirmative, and, after an interchange of a few parting civilities, and the present of a few shrewd instructions from the doctor as to the best mode of getting a pious congregation together, Jasper took his leave.

"There goes lust on worse than crutches," thought the doctor; "miserable devil! if he had only a grain of sense he would be grateful for his misfortune instead of being savage at it, for it has been the means of his acquiring an independence. Had he continued to be a burly ruffian, he would never have thought of scraping even a shilling together. But some people don't know when they are happy; and few—precious few—how to take advantage of, and turn a calamity to a good account."

The doctor then resumed the chemical pursuits in which he had been interrupted by the entrance of his visitors; and, while thus engaged, his busy mind was revolving scheme after scheme for the advancement of his cherished objects. The vision of the anger of Mrs. Wriggles did now and then obtrude itself upon him; but, having no fear of the result, he did not permit it seriously to disturb his musings. Although far beyond the age at which men die, he had the indomitable courage of youth. He had cultivated his intellect until it was so fairly balanced, that scarcely anything disturbed its majestic serenity; and when the head of a man is iron, his heart rarely gives way to any species of youthful impulse. Dr. Wriggles had long ago resolved to live far above the ordinary period of human longevity, and, devoted to the accomplishment of a cherished purpose, his bodily functions seemed in this respect to be in complete subjection to his adamantine will.

"Those are fools who die, when, by studying how to live, they might live!" was his daring reflection; but the doctor had early sought out the most effectual means of preserving his life. He was habitually temperate, and restrained all his appetites—in fact, he husbanded his bodily powers with the care of a miser for his treasure, and for upwards of forty years had never allowed himself an injurious indulgence. Still he was no anchorite: choosing good food and pure, harmless drinks, with the occasional use of a stimulant of his own preparation, and his mental and business occupations—he did not experience any of that sense of loneliness which is apt to oppress men when they have passed the meridian of life by a score or so of years.

"The mind makes the man," was another of the doctor's axioms; and in his own surprising person he seemed to fully realise its truthfulness. Money seemed to be the object of his affection, but in reality it was only the agent he employed for the promotion of his higher purposes. As a confidential agent of the Jesuits in London, he could do nothing without money, and hence his devotion to its acquisition. In furtherance of his plans, he had ever found in Mrs. Wriggles an invaluable assistant; and as that venerable lady had affairs of her own to manage in which he never, until this one of Mrs. Smythe's, interfered, they had been enabled to live together in harmony. This auspicious state was fated to be rudely disturbed, but the doctor never imagined the possibility of its being altogether destroyed.

He was, as stated, busy with his chemical apparatus when Mrs. Wriggles entered his apartment. Her countenance wore a settled gloom, her manner was troubled, and a rather menacing fire slumbered in her eyes.

"Ah, Jackina!" said the doctor; "how is the dove to-night?"

Mrs. Wriggles made no reply; but, throwing herself into a chair, remained for some minutes in an attitude of thought. The doctor continued his operations without attempting to disturb her meditations, and when at length she spoke, he bestowed upon her a most gracious attention.

"The Bloomfields are happy now," said she, with some bitterness; "and my room is better liked now than my company."

"Does not the favourable change in that pet family of yours afford you intense gratification?" said the doctor, with a slight sneer in his tone.

"No; by heaven, no!" exclaimed Mrs. Wriggles; "at one time I thought it would, but now I find out that my proper vocation is a dark one. I am too old to be loved, so I ought to strive to make myself feared."

"Nay, nay, be not so sombre—all that you have done may be undone?" suggested the doctor.

"No," was the resolute reply; "for good or evil I keep my word; and for the good I have done to Violet Villiers, now the happy Countess of Bloomfield, I will heap tenfold disgrace and misery on the head of that abandoned strumpet Caroline Fitzherbert, or, as the silly world calls her, Mrs. Smythe. I have already fired the train, for this very night her shame will be blazoned throughout all fashionable London, and the newspapers to-morrow will cram the greedy mob with the prurient intelligence. Once let her be

sent to Coventry, and then I'll wring her heart through her child, and make her a beggar; for, after such an exposure, neither husband nor uncle will give her a penny, and then what resource will she have but the streets—the pawings of drunken lechers, and the morning horror of a pollution to be repeated at night, and for bread—for bread—or she will starve! She will become a harlot, and, with her love of life and strong sensuality, will rather die on the dunghill of her shame, than take the bold leap that carries shame, misery, disease—all into the bottomless pit of profound and welcome eternity. Yes, the streets shall be her doom, and then there will only be her brat's neck to twist; after that my vow will have been fulfilled, and the revenge of Harriet Fitzherbert nobly consummated, and I shall die thankful that not one of the hated brood survives me."

"Calm your fury, Jackina," said the doctor, mildly; "for I rather fancy Mrs. Smythe is far beyond your reach."

"How?" exclaimed the old woman, her eyes flashing fire.

"If my intelligence be correct, she is by this time on the continent, where, I am informed, she purposes taking up her permanent residence," replied the doctor, with unruffled calmness.

Mrs. Wriggles greedily fastened her eyes on his countenance, as if to read his inmost thoughts; but the scrutiny did not avail her anything.

"How did you learn this?" inquired she.

"From a very good source, being no less than from her own ripe lips," said the doctor."

"Has she been here?"

"She has."

"And informed you of her going, and you took no steps to prevent her?"

"Exactly so."

"Fiends and furies! Dotard! But, stay, you are only teasing me! Say so, and I will be calm."

"I never lie unless it suits my purpose," was the cold reply. "I have told you the truth. The woman—I mean Mrs. Smythe—come here about her child."

"Her child!" screamed Mrs. Wriggles.

"Her child, Jackina—our little Fanny—and begged so piteously that I could not refuse her request," said the doctor."

Stupified at this overwhelming intelligence, Mrs. Wriggles could only gaze at him in ashy amazement: her utterance was suspended.

"I am never cruel, unless upon compulsion," continued he; "and in this case we had everything to gain, and nothing to lose, by yielding to the mother's claim."

"Yield!" cried Mrs. Wriggles, the real facts bursting slowly upon her mind.

"Certainly; she pleaded so piteously that I could not resist."

"And you gave her the—the ——"

"I gave her the child."

"Traitor! villain!"

"The terms were good. I had gold, bright, beautiful gold, for the image of clay,—five thousand sovereigns, and no less. Think of that, Jackina! and the child was of no use to us."

"And the mother took the child by the hand, and, with your permission, took it away with her?" said Mrs. Wriggles, with preternatural calmness.

"Even so."

"And for a few paltry pieces of dross, you have betrayed me—sold me to my arch-enemy—and defeated the only wish of my heart?"

"Pshaw!" said the doctor. "You would have

killed them. I did better—I made a concession and a good bargain. This money, besides other you do not dream of, will bring us influence, station, authority, command; and is not that better than gratifying the vulgar passion of taking life? Give me gold before murder any day, Jackina!"

Mrs. Wriggles was slowly recovering from the stupor into which she had been thrown by the communication; and the pale, concentrated look of rage she bestowed upon her partner in iniquity was dreadful. Even the doctor, imperturbable as he generally was, slightly quailed before it, and instantly bethought him of some means of self-defence.

"Judas!" hissed she, as she spat on him. "Revenge is dearer than gold—it is the honey on which I have fed for forty years; and to be juggled out of it at last by a false priest—a fellow with one foot in the grave and the other in the devil's mouth, is more than I can endure. So, mark me! 'I'll follow the w——e and her brat to the uttermost ends of the earth, before I will be cheated. If gone to hell, I will drag her from thence, to torture her once more with a glimpse of the only heaven she yearned after—this sensual world—and then plunge her into a horror which even Satan himself never contrived. As for you, false, juggling fiend—detestable, hoary Judas! prepare yourself for the scaffold, for the hangman's touch, the mob's derision, and the writhing and black choking of a hideous death! I will denounce you and all your schemes; drag the Jesuit, the spy, and the *poisoner*, before the bar of justice! I have proofs — proofs, Judas, that will hang thee; and I will be one to see thy white hairs flutter in the breeze before a savage throng! Fool, to come between me and my revenge! Poor, drivelling wretch! like the devil's apothecary, you have been too diligent, and shall be rewarded!"

She then gave way to a burst of uncontrollable fury, intermingled with the most dreadful imprecations; when the doctor, rendered rigid as marble by her threats, instantly comprehended his danger, and, as she was about to move away, darted towards her, and hounded on the bear to prevent her escape. The animal, accustomed to obey only its master's commands, at once threw its huge paws around her, bore her to the floor, and there held her. While in that position, the doctor, by means of a handkerchief, applied chloroform to her nostrils and mouth, and in a few seconds she became insensible. The bear then, at his command, released her form from its grasp, and the doctor, standing over her, leisurely contemplated her death-like features.

"She must die!" muttered he; "a woman never forgives a treacherous act! I would rather place myself at the mercy of a hungry tiger in its lonely jungle, than of a woman whose relentless malevolence has been excited!"

He then sat down, and, with horrid calmness, said:

"How shall I kill her, and escape detection? I have poisons as subtle as the foetid air of a churchyard! but I should like to invent a new manner of death—one that will baffle all inquiry, all research!"

After dwelling on his murderous intent for some time, he suddenly exclaimed:

"I have it! the region of her body that caused her fall when a girl, shall be the receiver of her death-potion when a woman!"

He then procured a leaden syringe and a small phial, out of which he charged his instrument of destruction, and, kneeling over the insensible partner of his deceptions and crimes, inserted his arm up her clothes, and in a second the deed was done. His victim neither moved, sighed, nor gave the slightest sign of suffering. A kind of shadowy film came over her countenance, and in a few minutes afterwards her limbs began gradually to get cold and stiffen, and then the murderer knew that his fell task had been completed. With the assistance of Leoline, he conveyed her to her chamber, and placed her on the bed. He then double-locked the door, and left the room by a secret entrance, known only to himself and his late but now lifeless companion. Returning to his own room, he threw the syringe and the phial into the crucible; and, when all traces of them had disappeared in the white-hot metal, sat down, and remained for hours in an attitude of profound thought.

"The end sanctifies the means," muttered he, at length. "Had she lived she would have been a burthen and a curse to herself; for her days have been lengthened solely by her morbid desire for revenge! To me she could only have proved a bitter enemy, a mar-plot of my schemes, and a spy on my actions. In her end, therefore, I have sought security, and given her peace!"

After a few more moments' reflection the old sinner murmured:

"*Requiescat in pace!*" and, devoutly crossing himself, appeared to have dismissed the atrocity from his consideration as an inevitable necessity.

In the morning Mrs. Wriggles—or, as she was known by the people of the house in which her body lay, Madame Robertina—not making her appearance at the usual hour, excited surprise among the people who had about her, to enable her to carry on her clairvoyante and graphiologist deceptions. Upon receiving no answer to their repeated summonses at her chamber the utmost alarm was excited, and, upon her door being forced open, she was found, as she had been carefully deposited by the doctor on the previous evening, dead! The majority present at the discovery were too callous for grief, but manifested much surprise when they found their mistress so differently attired from what she was usually. Instead of the black satin of Madame Robertina, there was the brown stuff dress of Mrs. Wriggles. After various comments on the strange circumstances, for their own protection the police were called in by the servants, and, as a matter of course, subsequently the usual official inquiry took place. Nothing, however, was elicited to throw any light on the transaction; the medical gentleman examined attributed the death to natural causes, and detailed such particulars of the general state of the health, including mention of a frightful ulcer in the womb, that the court were satisfied, and the jury, at the recommendation of the coroner, returned an open verdict of "Found Dead!" Her effects, consisting of handsome household furniture, plate, and some three hundred pounds in cash, were taken possession of by the proper authorities, and in a very short time the clairvoyante, graphiologist, and matrimonial adventuress, was entirely forgotten. In about six months after her decease Dr. Wriggles became the purchaser of the whole range of premises, which he beautified and embellished, and completed the garniture of the outside by affixing on the stately hall-door an enormous brass plate, which bore the following inscription:—

DR. WRIGGLES,
CONSULTING SURGEON, ETC, ETC.

The house and the plate are in the same position to this day, for aught the compiler of this book knows to the contrary; for, never having had the misfortune to consult any one of the mercurial pill-making, swindling tribe of Israel, he has not troubled himself to inquire whether the veritable Dr. Wriggles be still in existence. *Any Jesuit, lay or clerical, if willing, could supply the information.*

The fate of the remaining *dramatis personæ* shall be taken in the order of their introduction to the reader. And first and foremost, there is that inimitable fellow, Jasper. As advised by Dr. Wriggles, he took upon his dreadfully-wicked shoulders the character of a minister of the gospel. At first he had to encounter the wrath of the congregation from whom poor Mrs. Bond had been so feloniously abstracted; but this, instead of doing him an injury, served as a kind of advertisement, and his chapel, in time, came to be better attended than those of his rivals. He preached with such fervour, and with such an air of originality, especially upon carnal subjects, that the women flocked to him in droves; and perhaps no father confessor, either in Paris or Madrid, ever had such a number of holy daughters under his ghostly care. In the outset Jasper practised all manner of beastialities upon his flock—especially the pretty married women; but gradually, as he began to dive deeper into the mysteries of the book he so shockingly profaned, his propensities took another direction, until, in about a year, they had become enlisted in the cause of religious fanaticism. His ardent temperament, denied the pleasures of physical enjoyments, betook itself to an enthusiasm which operated as a vent-hole to his evil passions, and in time, from being a scoffing doubter, he became a fiery believer. His deranged functions contributed largely to endow his mind with the wild frenzy which, in preaching, is mistaken for eloquence and piety; and no sooner had this more spiritual type taken deep root in his organisation, than he strove to forget the past in a new sphere of unceasing activity. He abandoned his chapel, and, having allowed his beard to grow, took to the highways and bye-ways of this metropolis of sin, as an itinerant expounder of the gospel. His first essays were among his old associates—the ruffians who live upon prize-fighting, badger-drawing, bear-baiting, and other brutal amusements, besides, in extremity, flicking a purse, or knocking down and robbing drunken pedestrians in the suburbs. But all his endeavours failed to penetrate their hardened hearts: they met his exhortations by ribald jokes, proffers of pots of beer, and the society of a "blowen." Growing desperate at this failure, he next tried his hand on the hordes who exist, somehow or another, on the banks of the muddy Thames; but here again his failure was complete; and, in sheer despair of being able to make an impression upon the benighted multitude, he hied his sacred carcase to Smithfield, and there, on a Sunday morning, he was to some extent successful, for he had a numerous, and, taken altogether, a patient audience. It is true he was occasionally interrupted by a dirty, unshaven Socialist, or a drunken drover; but his low, ready wit soon silenced them, and he would pour out his fevered and disjointed sentences, until St. Bartholomew's clock struck one, when his congregation would silently betake themselves to the neighbouring taverns, to slake their thirst. After this Jasper diversified his performances by trips into the country, and actually traversed Britain, from the Land's End to John o'Groat's. What were the fruits of his labours is not actually known; but it is positive that at certain seasons of the year he would retire to a little cottage he had purchased in Epping Forest, far from any other human habitation, where he would amuse

himself with the cultivation of a large plot of land, and sedulously attend to the education, after his own fashion, of a remarkably fine boy, whom he had had christened Henry Burton Sampson. The only other inhabitant of the cottage was an old woman of rather repulsive aspect, but kind heart; for the boy loved her, and, had she been as ugly in disposition as feature, that would have been impossible.

When Jasper did not labour or read his Bible or Testament—the only book he ever took into his hands—he would employ himself in giving lessons to his boy, or dreamily listening to his prattle. On several of these occasions the lad had made mention of an old woman—Bogie, he termed her—who had frequently waylaid him in his rambles, and begged him to kiss her. Jasper did not much heed this, as he well knew the forest was infested by gipsies and old women, who frequented it to gather wild herbs. Jasper had but a few days before returned from one of his discursive pilgrimages, and was digging in the flower garden before his cottage, when his attention was suddenly attracted by piercing screams from his boy; and, on looking in the direction from which the sounds came, he perceived him struggling in the arms of a meanly-clad woman.

On the approach of Jasper, she released her hold and fled, and Jasper, whose limbs trembled and eyes rolled fearfully, did not pursue. After this incident the boy was forbidden to stray beyond the open space in the forest before the door, and Jasper gradually sank into a state of profound gloom, and rarely uttered a word.

Towards the close of autumn, the woman once more appeared, hovering about the cottage as if endeavouring to catch a glimpse of the boy; and when this was told to Jasper, he became dreadfully agitated, and applied himself with more assiduity than ever to his Bible. Repeated visits of the kind unnerved him so much, that his reason tottered, and at last wholly fell. He was walking through the forest about noon one day, holding his child by the hand, when the woman who was the boy's terror suddenly confronted him.

She was homely but decently clad, and wore a thick veil that completely concealed her features. At the sight of Jasper, she uttered a piercing shriek; and the wind at the same time blowing aside her veil, disclosed to his view a countenance of such horror—it was more a fleshless death's head than a human figure, and was rendered more ghastly by two rows of dazzling white teeth—that he, too, shrieked, and, taking up his boy in his arms, fled like a deer from the spot. That same night he lay on his bed a moping idiot—the lamp of reason had for ever gone out. The old woman took upon herself the administration of his affairs; and, being a shrewd woman of the world, applied to the clergyman of the parish for advice. That worthy referred her to his solicitor, who promptly had Jasper found to be a lunatic, and the boy made a ward in Chancery, under the guardianship of his old nurse and the good clergyman. Jasper, whose madness had been attributed to his devotion to religious teaching, and who was remarkably quiet, was allowed to remain in the cottage attended by the old woman; but the clergyman judiciously insisted upon sending the boy to a foundation school, where he would be respectably educated and trained, so that, when he attained manhood, he would be in a condition to enjoy and appreciate the ten thousand pounds his father had accumulated and invested for his benefit. As for Jasper, he would wander through the forest, and, fancying groups of dwarfed trees his audiences, would pull out his Bible, and deliver himself of a most elaborate discourse. Sometimes he would have a tribe of gipsies for a congregation; and their natural superstition always protected him from insult. Believing him to be inspired, they listened to his ravings with a feeling approaching to reverence, and brought their children to receive his blessing. Jasper took them to a running brook, and solemnly went through the rite of baptism; but it was remarked that he called all the boys Harry, and all the girls Alice. Every other Christian patronymic had been banished from his memory. He encountered the same veiled figure but once again—it was in the depth of winter, and the snow lay deep on the ground; but her presence did not seem to alarm him, for he commenced pelting her with snow, and invited her to join him in some winter's boy-sports. She appeared to have guessed his condition, for she rapidly disappeared, and was never seen in the forest again. Jasper, after her departure, commenced a very lively game of snow-balling; as he had only the trees for opponents, he had all the fun to himself, but he persevered in it for a long time—now chasing an imaginary companion in the sport, now laughing at his discomfiture, and then retreating himself, as if from a coming snowy salute. As darkness set in, he commenced singing, as he had done in his boyhood's days, when returning homewards from such genial sport, and wandered on into the depths of the wooded country around him, totally insensible to the cold, or that he was travelling in a direction which led him still further away from his home, or, indeed, any human habitations. In the morning, when search was made for him, he was found a corpse at the foot of a tree, in one of his favourite haunts, with his arms under his head, just as he used to place them when, a bold, light-hearted boy, he slept in the fields under hedge-rows after a long day's play, under a bright-blue summer sky.

The next claimants upon the reader's attention are the banker and his wife, the volatile, and, with all her sexual faults, fascinating and voluptuous Mrs. Smythe. The former, goaded on by his own sense of self-importance and desire to be distinguished in the fashionable world for independence in marital matters, no sooner had ascertained the fact of his spouse's undisguised frailty, than he forthwith called into active requisition the talents of his solicitor; together they concocted such a strong case against the delinquent wife, that a verdict, coupled with enormous damages, was obtained against the defendant; and the plaintiff, exulting in his success, went into the house of Lords with such clean hands, that even my Lord B—— had not a single sarcastic remark to make against the bill for divorce, and it passed without a single dissentient voice; so, perforce, and as a matter of direct consequence, Mr. Smythe, the banker, was freely and entirely privileged to wed again, and destroy as many women's happiness as his physical ability and moral incompetency would allow him.

The lady, being freed from her legal contact—not contract—with such a ruffian of a husband, led a gay life for several months in the society of her paramour, Mr. Horace Singleton; but, in obedience to a secret and not to be disobeyed summons, a change came over the volatility of their amatory experience; and she hastened forthwith to London, where, meeting with her father confessor—a hoary gentleman of sixty—she was induced to place her daughter in a nunnery, and to become herself a lay sister, or rather out-pensioner or supporter of one lying in the vicinity of Clapham. As for Horace, being classically educated, his introduction into the only true and apostolic church was a matter of little difficulty; and, after a separation of a few weeks, he found himself installed as a spiritual adviser to a primitive community of nuns, and father confessor to the patroness of the charitable institution that had them in care—the late Mrs. Smythe.

It only remains to be mentioned, that the experiences of Laura Bell, the Socialist girl, have yet to be written and published.

THE END.